BOLITAR'S GAME

A Mystery Guild Lost Classics Omnibus

Books by Harlan Coben

DEAL BREAKER
DROP SHOT
FADE AWAY
BACK SPIN
ONE FALSE MOVE
THE FINAL DETAIL
DARKEST FEAR
TELL NO ONE
GONE FOR GOOD

BOLITAR'S GAME:

BACK SPIN
THE FINAL DETAIL
DARKEST FEAR

by
Harlan Coben

Mystery Guild
Garden City, New York

Contents

BACK SPIN

For the Armstrongs,
The World's Greatest In-Laws,
Jack and Nancy
Molly, Jane, Eliza, Sara, John and Kate
Thank you all for Anne

1

Myron Bolitar used a cardboard periscope to look over the suffocating throngs of ridiculously clad spectators. He tried to recall the last time he'd actually used a toy periscope, and an image of sending in proof-of-purchase seals from a box of Cap'n Crunch cereal flickered in front of him like headache-inducing sunspots.

Through the mirrored reflection, Myron watched a man dressed in knickers—knickers, for crying out loud—stand over a tiny white sphere. The ridiculously clad spectators mumbled excitedly. Myron stifled a yawn. The knickered man crouched. The ridiculously clad spectators jostled and then settled into an eerie silence. Sheer stillness followed, as if even the trees and shrubs and well-coiffed blades of grass were holding their collective breath.

Then the knickered man whacked the white sphere with a stick.

The crowd began to murmur in the indistinguishable syllables of backstage banter. As the ball ascended, so did the volume of the murmurs. Words could be made out. Then phrases. "Lovely golf stroke." "Super golf shot." "Beautiful golf shot." "Truly fine golf stroke." They always said *golf* stroke, like someone might mistake it for a *swim* stroke, or—as Myron was currently contemplating in this blazing heat—a *sun*stroke.

"Mr. Bolitar?"

Myron took the periscope away from his eyes. He was tempted to yell "Up periscope," but feared some at stately, snooty Merion Golf Club would view the act as immature. Especially during the U.S. Open. He looked down at a ruddy-faced man of about seventy.

"Your pants," Myron said.

"Pardon me?"

"You're afraid of getting hit by a golf cart, right?"

They were orange and yellow in a hue slightly more luminous than a bursting supernova. To be fair, the man's clothing hardly stood out. Most in the crowd seemed to have woken up wondering what apparel they possessed that would clash with, say, the free world. Orange and green tints found exclusively in several of your tackiest neon signs adorned many. Yellow and some strange shades of purple were also quite big—usually together—like a color scheme rejected by a Midwest high school cheerleading squad. It was as if being surrounded by all this God-given natural beauty made one want to do all in his power to offset it. Or maybe there was something else at work here. Maybe the ugly clothes had a more functional origin. Maybe in the old days, when animals roamed free, golfers dressed this way to ward off dangerous wildlife.

Good theory.

"I need to speak with you," the elderly man whispered. "It's urgent."

The rounded, jovial cheeks belied his pleading eyes. He suddenly gripped Myron's forearm. "Please," he added.

"What's this about?" Myron asked.

The man made a movement with his neck, like his collar was on too tight. "You're a sports agent, right?"

"Yes."

"You're here to find clients?"

Myron narrowed his eyes. "How do you know I'm not here to witness the enthralling spectacle of grown men taking a walk?"

The old man did not smile, but then again, golfers were not known for their sense of humor. He craned his neck again and moved closer. His whisper was hoarse. "Do you know the name Jack Coldren?" he asked.

"Sure," Myron said.

If the old man had asked the same question yesterday, Myron wouldn't have had a clue. He didn't follow golf that closely (or at all), and Jack Coldren had been little more than a journeyman over the past twenty years or so. But Coldren had been the surprise leader after the U.S. Open's first day, and now, with just a few holes remaining in the second round, Coldren was up by a commanding eight strokes. "What about him?"

"And Linda Coldren?" the man asked. "Do you know who she is?"

This one was easier. Linda Coldren was Jack's wife and far and away the top female golfer of the past decade. "Yeah, I know who she is," Myron said.

The man leaned in closer and did the neck thing again. Seriously annoying—not to mention contagious. Myron found himself fighting off the desire to mimic the movement. "They're in deep trouble," the old man whispered. "If you help them, you'll have two new clients."

"What sort of trouble?"

The old man looked around. "Please," he said. "There are too many people. Come with me."

Myron shrugged. No reason not to go. The old man was the only lead he'd unearthed since his friend and business associate Windsor Horne Lockwood III—Win, for short—had dragged his sorry butt down here. Being that the U.S. Open was at Merion—home course of the Lockwood family for something like a billion years—Win had felt it would be a great opportunity for Myron to land a few choice clients. Myron wasn't quite so sure. As near as he could tell, the major component separating him from the hordes of other locust-like agents swarming the green meadows of Merion Golf Club was his naked aversion for golf. Probably not a key selling point to the faithful.

Myron Bolitar ran MB SportsReps, a sports representation firm located on Park Avenue in New York City. He rented the space from his former college roommate, Win, a Waspy, old-money, big-time investment banker whose family owned Lock-Horne Securities on the same Park Avenue in New York. Myron handled the negotiations while Win, one of the country's most respected brokers, handled the investments and finances. The other member of the MB team, Esperanza Diaz, handled everything else. Three branches with checks and balances. Just like the American government. Very patriotic.

Slogan: *MB SportsReps—the other guys are commie pinkos.*

As the old man ushered Myron through the crowd, several men in green blazers—another look sported mostly at golf courses, perhaps to camouflage oneself against the grass—greeted him with whispered, "How do, Bucky," or "Looking good, Buckster," or "Fine day for golf, Buckaroo." They all had the accent of the rich and preppy, the kind of inflection where *mommy* is pronounced "mummy" and summer and winter are verbs. Myron was about to comment on a grown man being called Bucky, but when your name is Myron, well, glass houses and stones and all that.

Like every other sporting event in the free world, the actual playing area looked more like a giant billboard than a field of competition. The leader board was sponsored by IBM. Canon handed out the periscopes. American Airlines employees worked the food stands (an airline handling food—what think tank came up with that one?). Corporate Row was jam-packed with companies who shelled out over one hundred grand a pop to set up a tent for a few days, mostly so that company executives had an excuse to go. Travelers Group, Mass Mutual, Aetna (golfers must like insurance), Canon, Heublein. Heublein. What the hell was a Heublein?

They looked like a nice company. Myron would probably buy a Heublein if he knew what one was.

The funny thing was, the U.S. Open was actually less commercialized than most tourneys. At least they hadn't sold their name yet. Other tournaments were named for sponsors and the names had gotten a little silly. Who could get up for winning the JC Penney Open or the Michelob Open or even the Wendy's Three-Tour Challenge?

The old man led him to a primo parking lot. Mercedeses, Caddies, limos. Myron spotted Win's Jaguar. The USGA had recently put up a sign that read MEMBERS PARKING ONLY.

Myron said, "You're a member of Merion." Dr. Deduction.

The old man twisted the neck thing into something approaching a nod. "My family dates back to Merion's inception," he said, the snooty accent now more pronounced. "Just like your friend Win."

Myron stopped and looked at the man. "You know Win?"

The old man sort of smiled and shrugged. No commitment.

"You haven't told me your name yet," Myron said.

"Stone Buckwell," he said, hand extended. "Everyone calls me Bucky."

Myron shook the hand.

"I'm also Linda Coldren's father," he added.

Bucky unlocked a sky-blue Cadillac and they slid inside. He put the key in the ignition. The radio played Muzak—worse, the Muzak version of "Raindrops Keep Falling on My Head." Myron quickly opened the window for air, not to mention noise.

Only members were allowed to park on the Merion grounds, so it wasn't too much of a hassle getting out. They made a right at the end of the driveway and then another right. Bucky mercifully flipped off the radio. Myron stuck his head back in the car.

"What do you know about my daughter and her husband?" Bucky asked.

"Not much."

"You are not a golf fan, are you, Mr. Bolitar?"

"Not really."

"Golf is truly a magnificent sport," he said. Then he added, "Though the word *sport* does not begin to do it justice."

"Uh-huh," Myron said.

"It's the game of princes." Buckwell's ruddy face glowed a bit now, the eyes wide with the same type of rapture one saw in the very religious. His voice was low and awed. "There is nothing quite like it, you know. You alone against the course. No excuses. No teammate. No bad calls. It's the purest of activities."

"Uh-huh," Myron said again. "Look, I don't want to appear rude, Mr. Buckwell, but what's this all about?"

"Please call me Bucky."

"Okay. Bucky."

He nodded his approval. "I understand that you and Windsor Lockwood are more than business associates," he said.

"Meaning?"

"I understand you two go back a long way. College roommates, am I correct?"

"Why do you keep asking about Win?"

"I actually came to the club to find him," Bucky said. "But I think it's better this way."

"What way?"

"Talking to you first. Maybe after . . . well, we'll see. Shouldn't hope for too much."

Myron nodded. "I have no idea what you're talking about."

Bucky turned onto a road adjacent to the course called Golf House Road. Golfers were so creative.

The course was on the right, imposing mansions on the left. A minute later, Bucky pulled into a circular driveway. The house was fairly big and made of something called river rock. River rock was big in this area, though Win always referred to it as "Mainline Stone." There was a white fence and lots of tulips and two maple trees, one on each side of the front walk. A large porch was enclosed on the right side. The car came to a stop, and for a moment neither of them moved.

"What's this all about, Mr. Buckwell?"

"We have a situation here," he said.

"What kind of situation?"

"I'd rather let my daughter explain it to you." He grabbed the key out of the ignition and reached for the door.

"Why come to me?" Myron asked.

"We were told you could possibly help."

"Who told you that?"

Buckwell started rolling his neck with greater fervor. His head looked like it'd been attached by a loose ball socket. When he finally got it under control, he managed to look Myron in the eyes.

"Win's mother," he said.

Myron stiffened. His heart plummeted down a dark shaft. He opened his mouth, closed it, waited. Buckwell got out of the car and headed for the door. Ten seconds later, Myron followed.

"Win won't help," Myron said.

Buckwell nodded. "That's why I came to you first."

They followed a brick path to a door slightly ajar. Buckwell pushed it open. "Linda?"

Linda Coldren stood before a television in the den. Her white shorts and sleeveless yellow blouse revealed the lithe, toned limbs of an athlete. She was tall with short spunky black hair and a tan that accentuated the smooth, long muscles. The lines around her eyes and mouth placed her in her late thirties, and he could see instantly why she was a commercial darling. There was a fierce splendor to this woman, a beauty derived from a sense of strength rather than delicacy.

She was watching the tournament on the television. On top of the set were framed family photographs. Big, pillowy couches formed a V in one, corner. Tactfully furnished, for a golfer. No putting green, AstroTurf carpet. None of that golf artwork that seemed a step or two below the aesthetic class of, say, paintings of dogs playing poker. No cap with a tee and ball on the brim hanging from a moose head.

Linda Coldren suddenly swung her line of vision toward them, firing a glare past Myron before settling on her father. "I thought you were going to get Jack," she snapped.

"He hasn't finished the round yet."

She motioned to the television. "He's on eighteen now. I thought you were going to wait for him."

"I got Mr. Bolitar instead."

"Who?"

Myron stepped forward and smiled. "I'm Myron Bolitar."

Linda Coldren flicked her eyes at him, then back to her father. "Who the hell is he?"

"He's the man Cissy told me about," Buckwell said.

"Who's Cissy?" Myron asked.

"Win's mother."

"Oh," Myron said. "Right."

Linda Coldren said, "I don't want him here. Get rid of him."

"Linda, listen to me. We need help."

"Not from him."

"He and Win have experience with this type of thing."

"Win," she said slowly, "is psychotic."

"Ah," Myron said. "Then you know him well?"

Linda Coldren finally turned her attention to Myron. Her eyes, deep and brown, met his. "I haven't spoken to Win since he was eight years old," she said. "But you don't have to leap into a pit of flames to know it's hot."

Myron nodded. "Nice analogy."

She shook her head and looked back at her father. "I told you before: no police. We do what they say."

"But he's not police," her father said.

"And you shouldn't be telling anyone."

"I only told my sister," Bucky protested. "She'd never say anything."

Myron felt his body stiffen again. "Wait a second," he said to Bucky. "Your sister is Win's mother?"

"Yes."

"You're Win's uncle." He looked at Linda Coldren. "And you're Win's first cousin."

Linda Coldren looked at him like he'd just peed on the floor. "With smarts like that," she said, "I'm glad you're on our side."

Everyone's a wiseass.

"If it's still unclear, Mr. Bolitar, I could break out some poster board and sketch a family tree for you."

"Could you use lots of pretty colors?" Myron said. "I like pretty colors."

She made a face and turned away. On the television, Jack Coldren lined up a twelve-foot putt. Linda stopped and watched. He tapped it; the ball took off and arched right into the hole. The gallery applauded with modest enthusiasm. Jack picked up the ball with two fingers and then tipped his hat. The IBM leader board flashed on the screen. Jack Coldren was up by a whopping nine strokes.

Linda Coldren shook her head. "Poor bastard."

Myron kept still. So did Bucky.

"He's waited twenty-three years for this moment," she continued. "And he picks now."

Myron glanced at Bucky. Bucky glanced back, shaking his head.

Linda Coldren stared at the television until her husband exited to the clubhouse. Then she took a deep breath and looked at Myron. "You see, Mr. Bolitar, Jack has never won a professional tournament. The closest he ever came was in his rookie year twenty-three years ago, when he was only nineteen. It was the last time the U.S. Open was held at Merion. You may remember the headlines."

They were not altogether unfamiliar. This morning's papers had re-hashed it a bit. "He lost a lead, right?"

Linda Coldren made a scoffing sound. "That's a bit of an understate-ment, but yes. Since then, his career has been completely unspectacular. There were years he didn't even make the tour."

"He picked a hell of a time to snap his streak," Myron said. "The U.S. Open."

She gave him a funny look and folded her arms under her chest. "Your name rings a bell," she said. "You used to play basketball, right?"

"Right."

"In the ACC. North Carolina?"

"Duke," he corrected.

"Right, Duke. I remember now. You blew out your knee after the draft."

Myron nodded slowly.

"That was the end of your career, right?"

Myron nodded again.

"It must have been tough," she said.

Myron said nothing.

She made a waving motion with her hand. "What happened to you is nothing compared to what happened to Jack."

"Why do you say that?"

"You had an injury. It may have been tough, but at least you weren't at fault. Jack had a six-stroke lead at the U.S. Open with only eight holes left. Do you know what that's like? That's like having a ten-point lead with a minute left in the seventh game of the NBA finals. It's like missing a wide-open slam dunk in the final seconds to lose the championship. Jack was never the same man after that. He never recovered. He has spent his whole life since, just waiting for the chance of redemption." She turned back to the television. The leader board was back up. Jack Coldren was still up by nine strokes.

"If he loses again . . ."

She did not bother finishing the thought. They all stood in silence. Linda staring at the television. Bucky craning his neck, his eyes moist, his face quivering near tears.

"So what's wrong, Linda?" Myron asked.

"Our son," she said. "Somebody has kidnapped our son."

2

I shouldn't be telling you this," Linda Coldren said. "He said he'd kill him."

"Who said?"

Linda Coldren took several deep breaths, like a child atop the high board. Myron waited. It took some time, but she finally took the plunge.

"I got a call this morning," she said. Her large indigo eyes were wide and everywhere now, settling down on no one spot for more than a second. "A man said he had my son. He said if I called the police, he would kill him."

"Did he say anything else?"

"Just that he'd call back with instructions."

"That's it?"

She nodded.

"What time was this?" Myron asked.

"Nine, nine-thirty."

Myron walked over to the television and picked up one of the framed photographs. "Is this a recent photograph of your son?"

"Yes."

"How old is he?"

"Sixteen. His name is Chad."

Myron studied the photograph. The smiling adolescent had the fleshy features of his father. He wore a baseball cap with the brim curled the way kids like to nowadays. A golf club rested proudly on his shoulder like a minuteman with a bayonet. His eyes were squinted as though he were looking into the sun. Myron looked over Chad's face, as if it might give him a clue or some rare insight. It didn't.

"When did you first notice that your son was missing?"

Linda Coldren gave her father a quick glance, then straightened up, holding her head high as if she were readying himself for a blow. Her words came slow. "Chad had been gone for two days."

"Gone?" Myron Bolitar, Grand Inquisitor.

"Yes."

"When you say gone—"

"I mean just that," she interrupted. "I haven't seen him since Wednesday."

"But the kidnapper just called today?"

"Yes."

Myron started to speak, stopped himself, softened his voice. Tread gently, fair Myron. Ever gently. "Did you have any idea where he was?"

"I assumed he was staying with his friend Matthew," Linda Coldren replied.

Myron nodded, as if this statement showed brilliant insight. Then nodded again. "Chad told you that?"

"No."

"So," he said, aiming for casual, "for the past two days, you didn't know where your son was."

"I just told you: I thought he was staying with Matthew."

"You didn't call the police."

"Of course not."

Myron was about to ask another follow-up question, but her posture made him rethink his words. Linda took advantage of his indecisiveness. She walked to the kitchen with an upright, fluid grace. Myron followed. Bucky seemed to snap out of a trance and trailed.

"Let me make sure I'm following you," Myron said, approaching from a different angle now. "Chad vanished before the tournament?"

"Correct," she said. "The Open started Thursday." Linda Coldren pulled the refrigerator handle. The door opened with a sucking pop. "Why? Is that important?"

"It eliminates a motive," Myron said.

"What motive?"

"Tampering with the tournament," Myron said. "If Chad had vanished today—with your husband holding such a big lead—I might think that someone was out to sabotage his chances of winning the Open. But two days ago, before the tournament had begun . . ."

"No one would have given Jack a snowball's chance in hell," she finished for him. "Oddsmakers would have put him at one in five thousand. At best." She nodded as she spoke, seeing the logic. "Would you like some lemonade?" she asked.

"No, thanks."

"Dad?"

Bucky shook his head. Linda Coldren bent down into the refrigerator.

"Okay," Myron said, clapping his hand together, trying his best to sound casual. "We've ruled out one possibility. Let's try another."

Linda Coldren stopped and watched him. A gallon glass pitcher was gripped in her hand, her forearm bunching easily with the weight. Myron debated how to approach this. There was no easy way.

"Could your son be behind this?" Myron asked.

"What?"

"It's an obvious question," Myron said, "under the circumstances."

She put the pitcher down on a wooden center block. "What the hell are you talking about? You think Chad faked his own kidnapping?"

"I didn't say that. I said I wanted to check out the possibility."

"Get out."

"He was gone two days, and you didn't call the police," Myron said. "One possible conclusion is that there was some sort of tension here. That Chad had run away before."

"Or," Linda Coldren countered, her hands tightening into fists, "you could conclude that we trusted our son. That we gave him a level of freedom compatible with his level of maturity and responsibility."

Myron looked over at Bucky. Bucky's head was lowered. "If that's the case—"

"That's the case."

"But don't responsible kids tell their parents where they're going? I mean, just to make sure they don't worry."

Linda Coldren took out a glass with too much care. She set it on the counter and slowly poured herself some lemonade. "Chad has learned to be very independent," she said as the glass filled. "His father and I are both professional golfers. That means, quite frankly, that neither one of us is home very often."

"Your being away so much," Myron said. "Has it led to tension?"

Linda Coldren shook her head. "This is useless."

"I'm just trying—"

"Look, Mr. Bolitar, Chad did not fake this. Yes, he's a teenager. No, he's not perfect, and neither are his parents. But he did not fake his own kidnapping. And if he did—I know he didn't, but let's just pretend for the sake of argument that he did—then he is safe and we do not need you. If this is some kind of cruel deception, we'll learn it soon enough. But if my son is in danger, then following this line of thought is a waste of time I can ill afford."

Myron nodded. She had a point. "I understand," he said.

"Good."

"Have you called his friend since you heard from the kidnapper? The one you thought he might've been staying with?"

"Matthew Squires, yes."

"Did Matthew have any idea where he was?"

"None."

"They're close friends, right?"

"Yes."

"Very close?"

She frowned. "Yes, very."

"Does Matthew call here a lot?"

"Yes. Or they talk by E-mail."

"I'll need Matthew's phone number," Myron said.

"But I just told you I spoke to him already."

"Humor me," Myron said. "Okay, now let's back up a second. When was the last time you saw Chad?"

"The day he disappeared."

"What happened?"

She frowned again. "What do you mean, what happened? He left for summer school. I haven't seen him since."

Myron studied her. She stopped and looked back at him a little too steadily. Something here was not adding up. "Have you called the school," he asked, "to see if he was there that day?"

"I didn't think of it."

Myron checked his watch. Friday. Five P.M. "I doubt anyone will still be there, but give it a shot. Do you have more than one phone line?"

"Yes."

"Don't call on the line the kidnapper called in on. I don't want the line tied up in case he calls back."

She nodded. "Okay."

"Does your son have any credit cards or ATM cards or anything like that?"

"Yes."

"I'll need a list. And the numbers, if you have them."

She nodded again.

Myron said, "I'm going to call a friend, see if I can get an override Caller ID put in on this line. For when he calls back. I assume Chad has a computer?"

"Yes," she said.

"Where is it?"

"Up in his room."

"I'm going to download everything on it to my office via his modem.

I have an assistant named Esperanza. She'll comb through it and see what she can find."

"Like what?"

"Frankly I have no idea. E-mails. Correspondence. Bulletin boards he participates in. Anything that might give us a clue. It's not a very scientific process. You check out enough stuff and maybe something will click."

Linda thought about it for a moment. "Okay," she said.

"How about you, Mrs. Coldren? Do you have any enemies?"

She sort of smiled. "I'm the number one–rated woman golfer in the world," she said. "That gives me a lot of enemies."

"Anyone you can imagine doing this?"

"No," she said. "No one."

"How about your husband? Anybody who hates your husband enough?"

"Jack?" She forced out a chuckle. "Everyone loves Jack."

"What's that supposed to mean?"

She just shook her head and waved him off.

Myron asked a few more questions, but there was little left for him to excavate. He asked if he could go up to Chad's room and she led him up the stairs.

The first thing Myron saw when he opened Chad's door were the trophies. Lots of them. All golf trophies. The bronze figure on the top was always a man coiled in postswing position, the golf club over his shoulder, his head held high. Sometimes the little man wore a golf cap. Other times he had short, wavy hair like Paul Hornung in old football reels. There were two leather golf bags in the right corner, both jammed past capacity with clubs. Photographs of Jack Nicklaus, Arnold Palmer, Sam Snead, Tom Watson blanketed the walls. Issues of *Golf Digest* littered the floor.

"Does Chad play golf?" Myron asked.

Linda Coldren just looked at him. Myron met her gaze and nodded sagely.

"My powers of deduction," he said. "They intimidate some people."

She almost smiled. Myron the Alleviator, Master Tension-Easer. "I'll try to still treat you the same," she said.

Myron stepped toward the trophies. "Is he any good?"

"Very good." She turned away suddenly and stood with her back to the room. "Do you need anything else?"

"Not right now."

"I'll be downstairs."

She didn't wait for his blessing.

Myron walked in. He checked the answering machine on Chad's phone. Three messages. Two from a girl named Becky. From the sound of it, she was a pretty good friend. Just calling to say, like, hi, see if he wanted to, like, do anything this weekend, you know? She and Millie and Suze were going to, like, hang out at the Heritage, okay, and if he wanted to come, well, you know, whatever. Myron smiled. Times they might be a-changin', but her words could have come from a girl Myron had gone to high school with or his father or his father's father. Generations cycle in. The music, the movies, the language, the fashion—they change. But that's just outside stimuli. Beneath the baggy pants or the message-cropped hair, the same adolescent fears and needs and feelings of inadequacy remained frighteningly constant.

The last call was from a guy named Glen. He wanted to know if Chad wanted to play golf at "the Pine" this weekend, being that Merion was off-limits because of the Open. "Daddy," Glen's preppy taped voice assured Chad, "can get us a tee time, no prob."

No messages from Chad's close buddy Matthew Squires.

He snapped on the computer. Windows 95. Cool. Myron used it too. Chad Coldren, Myron immediately saw, used America Online to get his E-mail. Perfect. Myron hit FLASHSESSION. The modem hooked on and screeched for a few seconds. A voice said, "Welcome. You have mail." Dozens of messages were automatically downloaded. The same voice said, "Good-bye." Myron checked Chad's E-mail address book and found Matthew Squires's E-mail address. He skimmed the downloaded messages. None were from Matthew.

Interesting.

It was, of course, entirely possible that Matthew and Chad were not as close as Linda Coldren thought. It was also entirely possible that even if they were, Matthew had not contacted his friend since Wednesday—even though his friend had supposedly vanished without warning. It happens.

Still, it was interesting.

Myron picked up Chad's phone and hit the redial button. Four rings later a taped voice came on. "You've reached Matthew. Leave a message or don't. Up to you."

Myron hung up without leaving a message (it was, after all, "up to him"). Hmm. Chad's last call was to Matthew. That could be significant. Or it could have nothing to do with anything. Either way, Myron was quickly getting nowhere.

He picked up Chad's phone and dialed his office. Esperanza answered on the second ring.

"MB SportsReps."

"It's me." He filled her in. She listened without interrupting.

Esperanza Diaz had worked for MB SportReps since its inception. Ten years ago, when Esperanza was only eighteen years old, she was the Queen of Sunday Morning Cable TV. No, she wasn't on any infomercial, though her show ran opposite plenty of them, especially that one with the abdominal exerciser that bore a striking resemblance to a medieval instrument of torture; rather, Esperanza had been a professional wrestler named Little Pocahontas, the Sensual Indian Princess. With her petite, lithe figure bedecked in only a suede bikini, Esperanza had been voted FLOW's (Fabulous Ladies Of Wrestling) most popular wrestler three years running—or, as the award was officially known, the Babe You'd Most Like to Get in a Full Nelson. Despite this, Esperanza remained humble.

When he finished telling her about the kidnapping, Esperanza's first words were an incredulous, "Win has a mother?"

"Yep."

Pause. "There goes my spawned-from-a-satanic-egg theory."

"Ha-ha."

"Or my hatched-in-an-experiment-gone-very-wrong theory."

"You're not helping."

"What's to help?" Esperanza replied. "I like Win, you know that. But the boy is—what's the official psychiatric term again?—cuckoo."

"That cuckoo saved your life once," Myron said.

"Yeah, but you remember how," she countered.

Myron did. A dark alley. Win's doctored bullets. Brain matter tossed about like parade confetti. Classic Win. Effective but excessive. Like squashing a bug with a wrecking ball.

Esperanza broke the long silence. "Like I said before," she began softly, "cuckoo."

Myron wanted to change the subject. "Any messages?"

"About a million. Nothing that can't wait, though." Then she asked, "Have you ever met her?"

"Who?"

"Madonna," she snapped. "Who do you think? Win's mother."

"Once," Myron said, remembering. More than ten years ago. He and Win had been having dinner at Merion, in fact. Win hadn't spoken to her on that occasion. But she had spoken to him. The memory made Myron cringe anew.

"Have you told Win about this yet?" she asked.

"Nope. Any advice?"

Esperanza thought a moment. "Do it over the phone," she said. "At a very safe distance."

3

They got a quick break.

Myron was still sitting in the Coldrens' den with Linda when Esperanza called back. Bucky had gone back to Merion to get Jack.

"The kid's ATM card was accessed yesterday at 6:18 P.M.," Esperanza said. "He took out $180. A First Philadelphia branch on Porter Street in South Philly."

"Thanks."

Information like that was not difficult to obtain. Anybody with an account number could pretty much do it with a phone by pretending they were the account holder. Even without one, any semi-human who had ever worked in law enforcement had the contacts or the access numbers or at least the wherewithal to pay off the right person. It didn't take much anymore, not with today's overabundance of user-friendly technology. Technology did more than depersonalize; it ripped your life wide open, gutted you, stripped away any pretense of privacy.

A few keystrokes revealed all.

"What is it?" Linda Coldren asked.

He told her.

"It doesn't necessarily mean what you think," she said. "The kidnapper could have gotten the PIN number from Chad."

"Could have," Myron said.

"But you don't believe it, do you?"

He shrugged. "Let's just say I'm more than a little skeptical."

"Why?"

"The amount, for one thing. What was Chad's max?"

"Five hundred dollars a day."

"So why would a kidnapper only take $180?"

Linda Coldren thought a moment. "If he took too much, someone might get suspicious."

Myron sort of frowned. "But if the kidnapper was that careful," he began, "why risk so much for $180? Everyone knows that ATMs are equipped with security cameras. Everyone also knows that even the simplest computer check can yield a location."

She looked at him evenly. "You don't think my son is in danger."

"I didn't say that. This whole thing may look like one thing and be another. You were right before. It's safest to assume that the kidnapping is real."

"So what's your next step?"

"I'm not sure. The ATM machine was on Porter Street in South Philadelphia. Is that someplace Chad likes to hang out?"

"No," Linda Coldren said slowly. "In fact, it's a place I would never imagine him going."

"Why do you say that?"

"It's a dive. One of the sleaziest parts of the city."

Myron stood. "You got a street map?"

"In my glove compartment."

"Good. I'll need to borrow your car for a little while."

"Where are you going?"

"I'm going to drive around this ATM."

She frowned. "What for?"

"I don't know," Myron admitted. "Like I said before, investigating is not very scientific. You do some legwork and you push some buttons and you hope something happens."

Linda Coldren reached into a pocket for her keys. "Maybe the kidnappers grabbed him there," she said. "Maybe you'll see his car or something."

Myron almost slapped himself in the head. A car. He had forgotten something so basic. In his mind, a kid disappearing on his way to or from school conjured up images of yellow buses or strolling sprightly with a book bag. How could he have missed something as obvious as a car trace?

He asked her the make and model. Gray Honda Accord. Hardly a car that stands out in a crowd. Pennsylvania license plate 567-AHJ. He called it in to Esperanza. Then he gave Linda Coldren his cellular phone number.

"Call me if anything happens."

"Okay."

"I'll be back soon," he said.

The ride wasn't far. He traveled, it seemed, from green splendor to concrete crap instantaneously—like on *Star Trek* where they step through one of those time portals.

The ATM was a drive-through located in what would generously be labeled a business district. Tons of cameras. No human tellers. Would a kidnapper really risk this? Very doubtful. Myron wondered where he could get a copy of the bank's videotape without alerting the police. Win might know somebody. Financial institutions were usually anxious to cooperate with the Lockwood family. The question was, would Win be willing to cooperate?

Abandoned warehouses—or at least, they looked abandoned—lined the road. Eighteen-wheelers hurried by like something out of an old convoy movie. They reminded Myron of the CB craze from his childhood. Like everyone else, his dad had bought one—a man born in the Flatbush section of Brooklyn who grew up to own an undergarment factory in Newark, barking "breaker one nine" with an accent he had picked up watching the movie *Deliverance*. Dad would be driving on Hobart Gap Road between their house and the Livingston Mall—maybe a one-mile drive—asking his "good buddies" if there was any sign of "smokeys." Myron smiled at the memory. Ah, CBs. He was sure that his father still had his someplace. Probably next to the eight-track player.

On one side of the ATM was a gas station so generic that it didn't even bother having a name. Rusted cars stood upon crumbling cinder blocks. On the other side, a dirt-bag, no-tell motel called the Court Manor Inn greeted customers with green lettering that read: $19.99 PER HOUR.

Myron Bolitar Traveling Tip #83: You may not be dealing with a five-star deluxe property when they prominently advertise hourly rates.

Under the price, in smaller black print, the sign read, MIRRORED CEILINGS AND THEME ROOMS SLIGHTLY EXTRA. Theme rooms. Myron didn't even want to know. The last line, back in the green big print: ASK ABOUT OUR FREQUENT VISITORS CLUB. Jesus.

Myron wondered if it was worth a shot and decided, why not? It probably wouldn't lead to anything, but if Chad was hiding out—or even if he'd been kidnapped—a no-tell was as good a place as any to disappear.

He parked in the lot. The Court Manor was a textbook two-level dump. The outer stairs and walkway terraces were made of rotting wood. The cement walls had that unfinished, swirling look that could cut your hand if you leaned against it wrong. Small chunks of concrete lay on the ground. An unplugged Pepsi machine guarded the door like one of the Queen's guards. Myron passed it and entered.

He'd expected to find the standard no-tell lobby interior—that is, an unshaven Neanderthal in a sleeveless, too-short undershirt chewing on a toothpick while sitting behind bullet-proof glass burping up a beer. Or something like that. But that was not the case. The Court Manor Inn had a high wooden desk with a bronze sign reading CONCIERGE on top of it. Myron tried not to snicker. Behind the desk, a well-groomed, baby-faced man in his late twenties stood at attention. He wore a pressed shirt, starched collar, dark tie tied in a perfect Windsor knot. He smiled at Myron.

"Good afternoon, sir!" he exclaimed. He looked and sounded like a John Tesh substitute on *Entertainment Weekly*. "Welcome to the Court Manor Inn!"

"Yeah," Myron said. "Hi."

"May I be of some service to you today, sir?"

"I hope so."

"Great! My name is Stuart Lipwitz. I'm the new manager of the Court Manor Inn." He looked at Myron expectantly.

Myron said, "Congrats."

"Well, thank you, sir, that's very kind. If there are any problems—if anything at the Court Manor does not meet your expectations—please let me know immediately. I will handle it personally." Big smile, puffed-out chest. "At the Court Manor, we guarantee your satisfaction."

Myron just looked at him for a minute, waiting for the full-wattage smile to dim a bit. It didn't. Myron took out the photograph of Chad Coldren.

"Have you seen this young man?"

Stuart Lipwitz did not even look down. Still smiling, he said, "I'm sorry, sir. But are you with the police?"

"No."

"Then I'm afraid I can't help you. I'm very sorry."

"Pardon me?"

"I'm sorry, sir, but here at the Court Manor Inn we pride ourselves on our discretion."

"He's not in any trouble," Myron said. "I'm not a private eye trying to catch a cheating husband or anything like that."

The smile did not falter or sway. "I'm sorry, sir, but this is the Court Manor Inn. Our clientele use our services for a variety of activities and often crave anonymity. We at the Court Manor Inn must respect that."

Myron studied the man's face, searching for some signal that this was a put-on. Nothing. His whole persona glowed like a performer in an *Up with People* halftime show. Myron leaned over the desk and checked out the shoes. Polished like twin mirrors. The hair was slicked back. The sparkle in the eye looked real.

It took Myron some time, but he finally saw where this was leading. He took out his wallet and plucked a twenty from the billfold. He slid it across the counter. Stuart Lipwitz looked at it but made no move.

"What's this for, sir?"

"It's a present," Myron said.

Stuart Lipwitz did not touch it.

"It's for one piece of information," Myron continued. He plucked out another and held it in the air. "I have another, if you'd like."

"Sir, we have a credo here at the Court Manor Inn: The guest must come first."

"Isn't that a prostitute's credo?"

"Pardon me, sir?"

"Never mind," Myron said.

"I am the new manager of the Court Manor Inn, sir."

"So I've heard."

"I also own ten percent."

"Your mom must be the envy of her mah-jongg group."

Still the smile. "In other words, sir, I am in it for the long term. That's how I look at this business. Long term. Not just today. Not just tomorrow. But into the future. For the long term. You see?"

"Oh," Myron said flatly. "You mean long term?"

Stuart Lipwitz snapped his fingers. "Precisely. And our motto is this: There are many places you can spend your adultery dollar. We want it to be here."

Myron waited a moment. Then he said, "Noble."

"We at the Court Manor Inn are working hard to earn your trust, and trust has no price. When I wake up in the morning, I have to look at myself in the mirror."

"Would that mirror be on the ceiling?"

Still smiling. "Let me explain it another way," he said. "If the client knows that the Court Manor Inn is a place he can feel safe to commit an indiscretion, he or she will be more likely to return." He leaned forward, his eyes wet with excitement. "Do you see?"

Myron nodded. "Repeat business."

"Precisely."

"Referrals too," Myron added. "Like, 'Hey, Bob, I know a great place to get some ass on the side.' "

A nod added to the smile. "So you understand."

"That's all very nice, Stuart, but this kid is fifteen years old. Fifteen." Actually, Chad was sixteen, but what the hey. "That's against the law."

The smile stayed, but now it signaled disappointment in the favorite pupil. "I hate to disagree with you, sir, but the statutory rape law in this state is fourteen. And secondly, there is no law against a fifteen-year-old renting a motel room."

The guy was dancing too much, Myron thought. No reason to go through this rigmarole if the kid had never been here. Then again, let's face facts. Stuart Lipwitz was probably enjoying this. The guy was several french fries short of a Happy Meal. Either way, Myron thought, it was time to shake the tree a bit.

"It is when he is assaulted in your motel," Myron said. "It is when he claims that someone got an extra key from the front desk and used it to break into the room." Mr. Bluff Goes to Philadelphia.

"We don't have extra keys," Lipwitz said.

"Well, he got in somehow."

Still the smile. Still the polite tone. "If that were the case, sir, the police would be here."

"That's my next stop," Myron said, "if you don't cooperate."

"And you want to know if this young man"—Lipwitz gestured to the photograph of Chad—"stayed here?"

"Yes."

The smile actually brightened a bit. Myron almost shaded his eyes. "But, sir, if you are telling the truth, then this young man would be able to tell if he was here. You wouldn't need me for that, correct?"

Myron's face remained neutral. Mr. Bluff had just been outsmarted by the new manager of the Court Manor Inn. "That's right," he said, changing tactics on the fly. "I already know he was here. It was just an opening question. Like when the police ask you to state your name even though they already know it. Just to get the ball rolling." Mr. Improvision Takes Over for Mr. Bluff.

Stuart Lipwitz took out a piece of paper and began to scribble. "This is the name and telephone number of the Court Manor Inn's attorney. He will be able to help you with any problems you may have."

"But what about that handling it personally stuff? What about the satisfaction guarantee?"

"Sir." He leaned forward, maintaining eye contact. Not a hint of impatience had crept into his voice or face. "May I be bold?"

"Go for it."

"I don't believe a word you're saying."

"Thanks for the boldness," Myron said.

"No, thank you, sir. And do come again."

"Another prostitution credo."

"Pardon me?"

"Nothing," Myron said. "May I too be bold?"

"Yes."

"I may punch you in the face very hard if you don't tell me if you've seen this kid." Mr. Improvisation Loses His Cool.

The door swung open hard. A couple entwined about one another stumbled in. The woman was openly rubbing the man's crotch. "We need a room pronto," the man said.

Myron turned to them and said, "Do you have your frequent visitor card?"

"What?"

Still the smile from Stuart Lipwitz. "Good-bye, sir. And have a nice day." Then he rejuvenated the smile and moved toward the writhing mound. "Welcome to the Court Manor Inn. My name is Stuart Lipwitz. I'm the new manager."

Myron headed out to his car. He took a deep breath in the parking lot and looked back behind him. The whole visit already had an unreal feeling, like one of those descriptions of alien abductions *sans* the anal probe. He got in the car and dialed Win's cellular. He just wanted to leave him a message on the machine. But to Myron's surprise, Win answered.

"Articulate," he drolled.

Myron was momentarily taken aback. "It's me," he said.

Silence. Win hated the obvious. "It's me," was both questionable grammar (at best) and a complete waste. Win would know who it was by the voice. If he didn't, hearing "It's me" would undeniably not help.

"I thought you didn't answer the phone on the course," Myron said.

"I'm driving home to change," Win said. "Then I'm dining at Merion." Mainliners never ate; they dined. "Care to join me?"

"Sounds good," Myron said.

"Wait a second."

"What?"

"Are you properly attired?"

"I don't clash," Myron said. "Will they still let me in?"

"My, my, that was very funny, Myron. I must write that one down. As soon as I stop laughing, I plan on locating a pen. However, I am so filled with mirth that I may wrap my precious Jag around an upcoming telephone pole. Alas, at least I will die with jocularity in my heart."

Win.

"We have a case," Myron said.

Silence. Win made this so easy.

"I'll tell you about it at dinner."

"Until then," Win said, "it'll be all I can do to douse my mounting excitement and anticipation with a snifter of cognac."

Click. Gotta love that Win.

Myron hadn't driven a mile when the cellular phone rang. Myron switched it on.

It was Bucky. "The kidnapper called again."

4

"W hat did he say?" Myron asked.

"They want money," Bucky said.

"How much?"

"I don't know."

Myron was confused. "What do you mean, you don't know? Didn't they say?"

"I don't think so," the old man said.

There was noise in the background. "Where are you?" Myron asked.

"I'm at Merion. Look, Jack answered the phone. He's still in shock."

"Jack answered?"

"Yes."

Doubly confused. "The kidnapper called Jack at Merion?"

"Yes. Please, Myron, can you get back over here? It'll be easier to explain."

"On my way."

He drove from the seedy motel to a highway and then into green. Lots of green. The Philadelphia suburbs were lush lawns and high bushes and shady trees. Amazing how close it was—at least in a geographic sense—to the meaner streets of Philly. Like most cities, there was tremendous segregation in Philadelphia. Myron remembered driving with Win to Veterans Stadium for an Eagles game a couple of years back. They'd gone through an Italian block, a Polish block, an African American block; it was as if some powerful, invisible force field—again, like on *Star Trek*—isolated each ethnicity. The City of Brotherly Love could almost be called Little Yugoslavia.

Myron turned down Ardmore Avenue. Merion was about a mile away.

His thoughts turned to Win. How, he wondered, would his old friend react to the maternal connection in this case?

Probably not well.

In all the years they had been friends, Myron had heard Win mention his mother on only one occasion.

It had been during their junior year at Duke. They were college roommates, just back from a wild frat party. The beer had flowed. Myron was not what you'd call a good drinker. Two drinks and he'd usually end up trying to French-kiss a toaster. He blamed this on his ancestry—his people had never handled spirits well.

Win, on the other hand, seemed to have been weaned on schnapps. Liquor never really affected him much. But at this particular party, the grain alcohol–laced punch made even his steps wobble a bit. It took Win three tries to unlock their dorm room door.

Myron quickly collapsed on his bed. The ceiling spun counterclockwise at a seemingly death-defying speed. He closed his eyes. His hands gripped the bed and held on in terror. His face had no color. Nausea clamped down painfully on his stomach. Myron wondered when he would vomit and prayed it would be soon.

Ah, the glamour of college drinking.

For a while neither of them said anything. Myron wondered if Win had fallen asleep. Or maybe Win was gone. Vanished into the night. Maybe he hadn't held on to his spinning bed tightly enough and the centrifugal force had hurled him out the window and into the great beyond.

Then Win's voice cut through the darkness. "Take a look at this."

A hand reached out and dropped something on Myron's chest. Myron risked letting go of the bed with one hand. So far, so good. He fumbled for whatever it was, found it, lifted it into view. A streetlight from outside—campuses are lit up like Christmas trees—cast enough illumination to make out a photograph. The color was grainy and faded, but Myron could still make out what looked to be an expensive car.

"Is that a Rolls-Royce?" Myron asked. He knew nothing about cars.

"A Bentley S Three Continental Flying Spur," Win corrected, "1962. A classic."

"Is it yours?"

"Yes."

The bed spun silently.

"How did you get it?" Myron asked.

"A man who was fucking my mother gave it to me."

The end. Win had shut down after that. The wall he put up was not only impenetrable but unapproachable, filled with land mines and a moat and lots of high-voltage electric wires. Over the ensuing decade and a half, Win had never again mentioned his mother. Not when the packages came to the dorm room every semester. Not when the packages came to Win's office on his birthday even now. Not even when they saw her in person ten years ago.

The plain dark wood sign merely read MERION GOLF CLUB. Nothing else. No "For Members Only." No "We're Elitist and We Don't Want You." No "Ethnics Use Service Entrance." No need. It was just a given.

The last U.S. Open threesome had finished a while back and the crowd was mostly gone now. Merion could hold only seventeen thousand for a tournament—less than half the capacity of most courses—but parking was still a chore. Most spectators were forced to park at nearby Haverford College. Shuttle buses ran constantly.

At the top of the driveway a guard signaled him to stop.

"I'm here to meet Windsor Lockwood," Myron said.

Instant recognition. Instant wave-through.

Bucky ran over to him before he had the car in park. The rounded face was more jowly now, as if he were packing wet sand in his cheeks.

"Where is Jack?" Myron asked.

"The western course."

"The what?"

"Merion has two courses," the older man explained, stretching his neck again. "The east, which is the more famous one, and the west. During the Open, the western course is used as a driving range."

"And your son-in-law is there?"

"Yes."

"Driving balls?"

"Of course." Bucky looked at him, surprised. "You always do that after a round. Every golfer on the tour knows that. You played basketball. Didn't you used to practice your shot after a game?"

"No."

"Well, as I told you earlier, golf is very special. Players need to review their play immediately after a round. Even if they've played well. They focus in on their good strokes, see if they can figure out what went wrong with the bad strokes. They recap the day."

"Uh-huh," Myron said. "So tell me about the kidnapper's call."

"I'll take you to Jack," he said. "This way."

They walked across the eighteen fairway and then down sixteen. The air smelled of freshly cut grass and pollen. It'd been a big year for pollen on the East Coast; nearby allergists swooned with greedy delight.

Bucky shook his head. "Look at these roughs," he said. "Impossible."

He pointed to long grass. Myron had no idea what he was talking about so he nodded and kept walking.

"Damn USGA wants this course to bring the golfers to their knees," Bucky ranted on. "So they grow the rough way out. Like playing in a rice paddy, for chrissake. Then they cut the greens so close, the golfers might as well be putting on a hockey rink."

Myron remained silent. The two men kept walking.

"This is one of the famed stone-quarry holes," Bucky said, calmer now.

"Uh-huh." The man was babbling. People do that when they're nervous.

"When the original builders reached sixteen, seventeen, and eighteen," Bucky continued, sounding not unlike a tour guide in the Sistine Chapel, "they ran across a stone quarry. Rather than giving up then and there, they plowed ahead, incorporating the quarry into the hole."

"Gosh," Myron said softly, "they were so brave back then."

Some babble when nervous. Some grow sarcastic.

They reached the tee and made a right, walking along Golf House Road. Though the last group had finished playing more than an hour ago, there were still at least a dozen golfers hitting balls. The driving range. Yes, professional golfers hit balls here—practicing with a wide array of woods and irons and big clubs, nay, warheads, they called Bertha and Cathy and the like—but that was only part of what went on. Most touring pros used the range to work out strategies with their caddies, check on equipment with their sponsors, network, socialize with fellow golfers, smoke a cigarette (a surprising amount of pros chain-smoke), even talk to agents.

In golf circles, the driving range was called the office.

Myron recognized Greg Norman and Nick Faldo. He also spotted Tad Crispin, the new kid on the block, the latest next Jack Nicklaus—in a phrase, the dream client. The kid was twenty-three, good-looking, quiet, engaged to an equally attractive, happy-just-to-be-here woman. He also did not yet have an agent. Myron tried not to salivate. Hey, he was as human as the next guy. He was, after all, a sports agent. Cut him some slack.

"Where is Jack?" Myron asked.

"Down this way," Bucky said. "He wanted to hit alone."

"How did the kidnapper reach him?"

"He called the Merion switchboard and said it was an emergency."

"And that worked?"

"Yes," Bucky said slowly. "Actually, it was Chad on the phone. He identified himself as Jack's son."

Curious. "What time did the call come in?"

"Maybe ten minutes before I called you." Bucky stopped, gestured with his chin. "There."

Jack Coldren was a touch pudgy and soft in the middle, but he had forearms like Popeye's. His flyaway hair did just that in the breeze, revealing bald spots that had started off the day better covered. He whacked the ball with a wood club and an uncommon fury. To some this might all seem very strange. You have just learned your son is missing and you go out and hit golf balls. But Myron understood. Hitting balls was comfort food. The more stress Myron was under, the more he wanted to go in his driveway and shoot baskets. We all have something. Some drink. Some do drugs. Some like to take a long drive or play a computer game. When Win needed to unwind, he often watched videotapes of his own sexual exploits. But that was Win.

"Who's that with him?" Myron asked.

"Diane Hoffman," Bucky said. "Jack's caddie."

Myron knew that female caddies were not uncommon on the men's pro tour. Some players even hired their wives. Saves money. "Does she know what's going on?"

"Yes. Diane was there when the call came in. They're pretty close."

"Have you told Linda?"

Bucky nodded. "I called her right away. Do you mind introducing yourself? I'd like to go back to the house and check up on her."

"No problem."

"How will I reach you if something comes up?"

"Call my cellular."

Bucky nearly gasped. "Cellular phones are forbidden at Merion." Like it was a papal command.

"I walk on the wild side," Myron said. "Just call."

Myron approached them. Diane Hoffman stood with her feet shoulder-width apart, her arms folded, her face intent on Coldren's backswing. A cigarette dangled from her lips almost vertically. She didn't even glance at Myron. Jack Coldren coiled his body and then let go, snapping like a released spring. The ball rocketed over the distant hills.

Jack Coldren turned, looked at Myron, smiled tightly, nodded a hello. "You're Myron Bolitar, right?"

"Right."

He shook Myron's hand. Diane Hoffman continued to study her player's every move, frowning as if she'd spotted a flaw in his hand-shaking technique. "I appreciate your helping us out," he said.

Face-to-face now—no more than a few feet away—Myron could see the devastation on the man's face. The jubilant glow after nailing the putt on eighteen had been snuffed out by something more pasty and sickly.

His eyes had the surprised, uncomprehending look of a man who'd just been sucker punched in the stomach.

"You tried making a comeback recently," Jack said. "With New Jersey."

Myron nodded.

"I saw you on the news. Gutsy move, after all these years."

Stalling. Not sure how to begin. Myron decided to help. "Tell me about the call."

Jack Coldren's eyes swerved over the expanse of green. "Are you sure it's safe?" he asked. "The guy on the phone told me no police. To just act normal."

"I'm an agent seeking clients," Myron said. "Talking to me is about as normal as it gets."

Coldren thought about that for a moment then nodded. He still hadn't introduced Diane Hoffman. Hoffman didn't seem to mind. She remained about ten feet away, rock-still. Her eyes remained narrow and suspicious, her face weathered and pinched. The cigarette ash was incredibly long now, almost defying gravity. She wore a cap and one of those caddie vests that looked like a jogger's night reflector.

"The club president came up to me and whispered that there was an emergency call from my son. So I went inside the clubhouse and picked it up."

He stopped suddenly and blinked several times. His breathing became heavier. He was wearing a tad-too-tight, yellow V-necked golf shirt. You could see his body expand against the cotton blend with each inhale. Myron waited.

"It was Chad," he finally spat out. "All he could say was 'Dad,' before someone grabbed the phone away from him. Then a man with a deep voice came on the line."

"How deep?" Myron asked.

"Pardon?"

"How deep was the voice?"

"Very."

"Did it sound funny to you? A little robotic?"

"Now that you mention it, yes, it did."

Electronic altering, Myron guessed. Those machines could make Barry White sound like a four-year-old girl. Or vice versa. They weren't hard to get. Even Radio Shack sold them now. The kidnapper or kidnappers could be any sex. Linda and Jack Coldren's description of a "male voice" was irrelevant. "What did he say?"

"That he had my son. He told me that if I called the police or anybody like that, Chad would pay. He told me that someone would be watching me all the time." Jack Coldren accentuated the point by looking around again. No one suspicious lurked about, though Greg Norman waved and gave them a smiling thumbs-up. G'day, mate.

"What else?" Myron asked.

"He said he wanted money," Coldren said.

"How much?"

"He just said a lot. He wasn't sure yet how much, but he wanted me to get it ready. He said he'd call back."

Myron made a face. "But he didn't tell you how much?"

"No. Just that it would be a lot."

"And that you should get it ready."

"Right."

This made no sense. A kidnapper who wasn't sure how much ransom to extort? "May I be blunt, Jack?"

Coldren stood a little taller, tucked in his shirt. He was what some would call boyishly and disarmingly handsome. His face was big and un-threatening with cottony, malleable features. "Don't sugarcoat anything for me," he said. "I want the truth."

"Could this be a hoax?"

Jack shot a quick glance at Diane Hoffman. She moved slightly. Might have been a nod. He turned back to Myron. "What do you mean?"

"Could Chad be behind this?"

The longer flyaway hairs got caught up in a cross-breeze and fell down into his eyes. He pushed them away with his fingers. Something came across his face. Rumination, maybe? Unlike Linda Coldren, the idea had not snapped him into a defensive stance. He was pondering the possibil-ity, or perhaps merely grasping at an option that meant safety for his son.

"There were two different voices," Coldren said. "On the phone."

"It could be a voice changer." Myron explained what that was.

More rumination. Coldren's face scrunched up. "I really don't know."

"Is it something you can imagine Chad doing?"

"No," Coldren replied. "But who can imagine anyone's kid doing something like this? I'm trying to remain objective here, hard as that is. Do I think my boy could do something like this? Of course not. But then again, I wouldn't be the first parent to be wrong about my kid; now, would I?"

Fair enough, Myron thought. "Has Chad ever run away?"

"No."

"Any trouble in the family? Anything that might make him want to do something like this?"

"Something like fake his own kidnapping?"

"It doesn't have to be that extreme," Myron said. "Maybe something you or your wife did that got him upset."

"No," he said, his voice suddenly faraway. "I can't think of anything." He looked up. The sun was low and not very strong anymore, but he still sort of squinted up at Myron, the side of his hand resting on his forehead in an eye-shading salute. The posture reminded Myron of the photograph of Chad he'd seen at the house.

Jack said, "You have a thought, Myron, don't you?"

"Barely."

"I'd still like to hear it," Coldren said.

"How badly do you want to win this tournament, Jack?"

Coldren gave a half-smile. "You were an athlete, Myron. You know how badly."

"Yes," Myron said, "I do."

"So what's your point?"

"Your son is an athlete. He probably knows too."

"Yes," Coldren said. Then: "I'm still waiting for the point."

"If someone wanted to hurt you," Myron said, "what better way than to mess up your chance of winning the Open?"

Jack Coldren's eyes had that sucker punched look again. He took a step back.

"I'm only theorizing," Myron added quickly. "I'm not saying your son is doing that. . . ."

"But you need to explore every avenue," Jack Coldren finished for him.

"Yes."

Coldren recovered, but it took him a little time. "Even if what you're saying is true, it doesn't have to be Chad. Someone else could have done this to get at me." Again he glanced over at his caddie. Still looking at her, he said, "Wouldn't be the first time."

"What do you mean?"

Jack Coldren didn't answer right away. He turned away from both of them and squinted out toward where he'd been hitting balls. There was nothing to see. His back was to Myron. "You probably know I lost the Open a long time ago."

"Yes."

He didn't elaborate.

"Did something happen back then?" Myron asked.

"Maybe," Jack Coldren said slowly. "I don't know anymore. The point is, someone else might be out to get me. It doesn't have to be my son."

"Maybe," Myron agreed. He didn't go into the fact that he'd pretty much dismissed this possibility because Chad had vanished before Coldren had his lead. No reason to go into it now.

Coldren turned back to Myron. "Bucky mentioned something about an ATM card," he said.

"Your son's ATM card was accessed last night. At Porter Street."

Something crossed his face. Not for long. Not for more than a second. A flash and then it was gone. "On Porter Street?" he repeated.

"Yep. A First Philadelphia Bank on Porter Street in South Philadelphia."

Silence.

"Are you familiar with that part of town?"

"No," Coldren said. He looked over at his caddie. Diane Hoffman remained the statue. Arms still folded. Feet still shoulder-width apart. Ash finally gone.

"Are you sure?"

"Of course I am."

"I visited there today," Myron said.

His face remained steady. "Did you learn anything?"

"No."

Silence.

Jack Coldren gestured behind him. "You mind if I take a few more swings while we talk?"

"Not at all."

He put on his glove. "Do you think I should play tomorrow?"

"That's up to you," Myron said. "The kidnapper said to act normal. Your not playing would certainly draw suspicion."

Coldren bent down to put a ball on the tee. "Can I ask you something, Myron?"

"Sure."

"When you played basketball, how important was winning to you?"

Odd question. "Very."

Jack nodded like he'd been expecting that. "You won the NCAA championship one year, right?"

"Yes."

Coldren shook his head. "Must have been something."

Myron did not reply.

Jack Coldren picked up a club and flexed his fingers around the grip. He lined up next to the ball. Again the smooth coil-and-release movement. Myron watched the ball sail away. For a moment no one spoke. They just looked off into the distance and watched the final streaks of sun color the sky purple.

When Coldren finally spoke, his voice was thick. "You want to hear something awful?"

Myron moved closer to him. Coldren's eyes were wet.

"I still care about winning this thing," Coldren said. He looked at Myron. The pain on his face was so naked, Myron almost reached out and hugged him. He imagined that he could see the reflection of the man's past in his eyes, the years of torment, of thinking of what might have been, of finally having the chance at redemption, of having that chance suddenly snatched away.

"What kind of man still thinks about winning at a time like this?" Coldren asked.

Myron didn't say anything. He didn't know the answer. Or maybe he feared that he did.

5

Merion's clubhouse was an expanded white farmhouse with black shutters. The only splash of color came from the green awnings shading the famed back porch and even that was muted by the surrounding green of the golf course. You expected something more awe-inspiring or intimidating at one of the country's most exclusive clubs, and yet the simplicity seemed to say, "We're Merion. We don't need more."

Myron walked past the pro shop. Golf bags were lined up on a metal stand. The men's locker room door was on his right. A bronze sign read that Merion had been designated a historic landmark. A bulletin board listed members' handicaps. Myron skimmed the names for Win's. Three handicap. Myron didn't know much about golfing, but he knew that was pretty damn good.

The outside porch had a stone floor and about two dozen tables. The legendary dining area did more than overlook the first tee—it actually seemed perched right over it. From here, members watched golfers tee off with the practiced glares of Roman senators at the Colosseum. Powerful businessmen and community leaders often crumbled under such century-old scrutiny. Even professionals were not immune—the porch's dining facility was kept open during the Open. Jack Nicklaus and Arnold Palmer and Ben Hogan and Bobby Jones and Sam Snead had all been subjected to the small restaurant noises, the grating tinkling of glass and silverware blending most disharmoniously with golf's hushed crowds and distant cheers.

The porch was packed with members. Most were men—elderly and red-faced and well fed. They wore blue or green blazers with different crests on them. Their ties were loud and usually striped. Many had floppy white or yellow hats on their heads. Floppy hats. And Win had been worried about Myron's "attire."

Myron spotted Win at a corner table with six chairs. He sat alone. His expression was both glacial and serene, his body completely at ease. A mountain lion patiently waiting for prey. One would think that the blond hair and patrician good looks would be life assets for Win. In many ways, they were; in many more ways, they branded him. His entire appearance reeked of arrogance, old money, and elitism. Most people did not respond well to that. A specific, seething hostility frothed and boiled over when people looked at Win. To look at such a person was to hate him. Win was used to it. People who judged purely on looks did not concern him. People who judged purely on looks were oft surprised.

Myron greeted his old friend and sat down.

"Would you care for a drink?" Win said.

"Sure."

"If you ask for a Yoo-Hoo," Win said, "I'll shoot you in the right eye."

"Right eye," Myron repeated with a nod. "Very specific."

A waiter who must have been a hundred years old materialized. He wore a green jacket and pants—green, Myron surmised, so that even the help would blend into the famed milieu. Didn't work, though. The old waiter looked like the Riddler's grandfather. "Henry," Win said, "I'll have an iced tea."

Myron was tempted to ask for a "Colt 45, like Billy Dee," but decided against it. "I'll have the same."

"Very good, Mr. Lockwood."

Henry left. Win looked over at Myron. "So tell me."

"It's a kidnapping," Myron said.

Win arched an eyebrow.

"One of the players' sons is missing. The parents have gotten two calls." Myron quickly told him about them. Win listened in silence.

When Myron finished, Win said, "You left something out."

"What?"

"The name of the player."

Myron kept his voice steady. "Jack Coldren."

Win's face betrayed nothing, but Myron still felt a cold gust blow across his heart.

Win said, "And you've met Linda."

"Yes."

"And you know that she is related to me."

"Yes."

"Then you must have realized that I will not help."

"No."

Win sat back, steepled his fingers. "Then you realize it now."

"A boy might be in real danger," Myron said. "We have to help."

"No," Win said. "I do not."

"You want me to drop it?"

"What you do is your affair," Win said.

"Do you want me to drop it?" Myron repeated.

The iced teas came. Win took a gentle sip. He looked off and tapped his chin with his index finger. His signal to end the topic. Myron knew better than to push it.

"So who are the other seats for?" Myron asked.

"I am mining a major lead."

"A new client?"

"For me, almost definitely. For you, a barely remote possibility."

"Who?"

"Tad Crispin."

Myron's chin dropped. "We're having dinner with Tad Crispin?"

"As well as our old friend Norman Zuckerman and his latest rather attractive ingenue."

Norm Zuckerman was the owner of Zoom, one of the largest sneaker and sporting apparel companies in the country. He was also one of Myron's favorite people. "How did you get to Crispin? I heard he was agenting himself."

"He is," Win said, "but he still wants a financial adviser." Barely in his mid-thirties, Win was already something of a Wall Street legend. Reaching out to Win made sense. "Crispin is quite a shrewd young man, actually," he went on. "Unfortunately, he believes that all agents are thieves. That they have the morals of a prostitute practicing politics."

"He said that? A prostitute practicing politics?"

"No, I came up with that one myself." Win smiled. "Pretty good, no?"

Myron nodded. "No."

"Anyway, the Zoom folks here are tailing him like a lapdog. They're introducing a whole new line of men's clubs and clothing on the back of young Mr. Crispin."

Tad Crispin was in second place, a goodly distance behind Jack Coldren. Myron wondered how happy Zoom was about Coldren possibly stealing their thunder. Not very, he supposed.

"So what do you make of Jack Coldren's good showing?" Myron asked. "You surprised?"

Win shrugged. "Winning was always very important to Jack."

"Have you known him long?"

Flat eyes. "Yes."

"Did you know him when he lost here as a rookie?"

"Yes."

Myron calculated the years. Win would have been in elementary school. "Jack Coldren hinted that he thought someone tried to sabotage his chances back then."

Win made a noise. "Guff," he said.

"Guff?"

"You don't recall what happened?"

"No."

"Coldren claims his caddie gave him the wrong club on sixteen," Win said. "He asked for a six iron and supposedly his caddie handed him an eight. His shot landed short. More specifically, in one of the rock quarry bunkers. He never recovered."

"Did the caddie admit the error?"

"He never commented, as far as I know."

"What did Jack do?"

"He fired him."

Myron chewed on that tidbit. "Where is the caddie now?"

"I do not have the slightest idea," Win said. "He wasn't a young man at the time and this was more than twenty years ago."

"Do you remember his name?"

"No. And this conversation is officially terminated."

Before Myron could ask why, a pair of hands covered his eyes. "Guess who?" came a familiar sing-song. "I'll give you a couple of hints: I'm smart, good-looking, and loaded with talent."

"Gee," Myron said, "before that hint, I would have thought you were Norm Zuckerman."

"And with the hint?"

Myron shrugged. "If you add 'adored by women of all ages,' I'd think it was me."

Norman Zuckerman laughed heartily. He bent down and gave Myron a big, loud smack on the cheek. "How are you, meshuggener?"

"Good, Norm. You?"

"I'm cooler than Superfly in a new Coupe de Ville."

Zuckerman greeted Win with a loud hello and an enthusiastic handshake. Diners stared in distaste. The stares did not quiet Norman Zuckerman. An elephant gun could not quiet Norman Zuckerman. Myron liked the man. Sure, a lot of it was an act. But it was a genuine act. Norm's zest for everything around him was contagious. He was pure energy; the kind of person who made you examine yourself and left you feeling just a little wanting.

Norm brought forward a young woman who'd been standing behind him. "Let me introduce you to Esme Fong," he said. "She's one of my marketing vee-pees. In charge of the new golf line. Brilliant. The woman is absolutely brilliant."

The attractive ingenue. Early-to-mid twenties, Myron guessed. Esme Fong was Asian with perhaps a hint of Caucasian. She was petite with almond eyes. Her hair was long and silky, a black fan with an earthy auburn tinge. She wore a beige business suit and white stockings. Esme nodded a hello and stepped closer. She wore the serious face of an attractive young woman who was afraid of not being taken seriously because she was an attractive young woman.

She stuck out her hand. "A pleasure to meet you, Mr. Bolitar," she said crisply. "Mr. Lockwood."

"Doesn't she have a firm handshake?" Zuckerman asked. Then turning to her: "What's with all the *misters*? This is Myron and Win. They're practically family, for crying out loud. Okay, Win's a little goyish to be in my family. I mean, his people came over on the *Mayflower,* while most of mine fled a czar pogrom in a cargo ship. But we're still family, right, Win?"

"As rain," Win said.

"Sit down already, Esme. You're making me nervous with all the seriousness. Try a smile, okay?" Zuckerman demonstrated, pointing at his teeth. Then he turned to Myron, spread his hands. "The truth, Myron. How do I look?"

Norman was over sixty. His customary loud clothing, matching the man's personality, hardly stood out after what Myron had seen today. His skin was dark and rough; his eyes dropped inside black circles; his features jutted out in classical Semitism; his beard and hair were too long and somewhat unkempt.

"You look like Jerry Rubin at the Chicago Seven trial," Myron said.

"Just the look I wanted," Norm said. "Retro. Hip. Attitude. That's what's in nowadays."

"Hardly Tad Crispin's look," Myron said.

"I'm talking about the real world, not golf. Golfers don't know from hip or attitude. Hasidim are more open to change than golfers, you know what I'm saying? I'll give you an example: Dennis Rodman is not a golfer. You know what golfers want? The same thing they've wanted since the dawn of sports marketing: Arnold Palmer. That's what they want. They wanted Palmer, then Nicklaus, then Watson—always good ol' boys." He pointed a thumb at Esme Fong. "Esme is the one who signed Crispin. He's her boy."

Myron looked at her. "Quite a coup," he said.

"Thank you," she said.

"We'll see how big a coup it is," Zuckerman said. "Zoom is moving into golf in a very big way. Huge. Humongous. Gigantic."

"Enormous," Myron said.

"Mammoth," Win added.

"Colossal."

"Titantic."

"Bunyanesque."

Win smiled. "Brobdingnagian," he said.

"Oooo," Myron said. "Good one."

Zuckerman shook his head. "You guys are funnier than the Three Stooges without Curly. Anyway, it's a helluva campaign. Esme is running it for me. Male and female lines. Not only have we got Crispin, but Esme's landed the numero uno female golfer in the world."

"Linda Coldren?" Myron asked.

"Whoa!" Norm clapped his hands once. "The Hebrew hoopster knows his golf! By the way, Myron, what kind of name is *Bolitar* for a member of the tribe?"

"It's a long story," Myron said.

"Good, I wasn't interested anyway. I was just being polite. Where was I?" Zuckerman threw one leg over the other, leaned back, smiled, looked about. A ruddy-faced man at a neighboring table glared. "Hi, there," Norm said with a little wave. "Looking good."

The man made a huffing noise and looked away.

Norm shrugged. "You'd think he never saw a Jew before."

"He probably hasn't," Win said.

Norm looked back over at the ruddy-faced man. "Look!" Zuckerman said, pointing to his head. "No horns!"

Even Win smiled.

Zuckerman turned his attention back to Myron. "So tell me, you trying to sign Crispin?"

"I haven't even met him yet," Myron said.

Zuckerman put his hand to his chest, feigning surprise. "Well then, Myron, this is some eerie coincidence. You being here when we're about to break bread with him—what are the odds? Wait." Norm stopped, put his hand to his ear. "I think I hear *Twilight Zone* music."

"Ha-ha," Myron said.

"Oh, relax, Myron. I'm teasing you. Lighten up, for crying out loud. But let me be honest for a second, okay? I don't think Crispin needs you, Myron. Nothing personal, but the kid signed the deal with me himself. No agent. No lawyer. Handled it all on his own."

"And got robbed," Win added.

Zuckerman put a hand to his chest. "You wound me, Win."

"Crispin told me the numbers," Win said. "Myron would have gotten him a far better deal."

"With all due respect to your centuries of upper-crust inbreeding, you don't know what the hell you're talking about. The kid left a little money in the till for me, that's all. Is that a crime nowadays—for a man to make a profit? Myron's a shark, for crying out loud. He rips off my clothes when we talk. He leaves my office, I don't even have undies left. I don't even have furniture. I don't even have an office. I start out with this beautiful office and Myron comes in and I end up naked in some soup kitchen someplace."

Myron looked at Win. "Touching."

"He's breaking my heart," Win said.

Myron turned his attention to Esme Fong. "Are you happy with how Crispin's been playing?"

"Of course," she said quickly. "This is his first major, and he's in second place."

Norm Zuckerman put a hand on her arm. "Save the spinning for those morons in the media. These two guys are family."

Esme Fong shifted in her seat. She cleared her throat. "Linda Coldren won the U.S. Open a few weeks ago," she said. "We're running dual television, radio, and print ads—they'll both be in every spot. It's a new line, completely unknown to golf enthusiasts. Naturally, if we could introduce Zoom's new line with two U.S. Open winners, it would be helpful."

Norm pointed his thumb again. "Ain't she something? *Helpful.* Nice word. Vague. Look, Myron, you read the sports section, am I right?"

"As rain."

"How many articles did you see on Crispin before the tournament began?"

"A lot."

"How much coverage has he gotten in the past two days?"

"Not much."

"Try none. All anybody is talking about is Jack Coldren. In two days that poor son of a bitch is either going to be a miracle man of messianic proportions or the most pitiful loser in the history of the world. Think about it for a second. A man's entire life—both his past and his future—will be shaped by a few swings of a stick. Nuts, when you think about it. And you know what the worst part is?"

Myron shook his head.

"I hope like hell he messes up! I feel like a major son of a bitch, but that's the truth. My guy comes back and wins, you wait and see the way Esme spins it. The brilliant play of newcomer Tad Crispin forces a veteran to crack. The new kid stares down the pressure like Palmer and

Nicklaus combined. You know what it'll mean to the launch of the new line?" Zuckerman looked over at Win and pointed. "God, I wish I looked like you. Look at him, for crying out loud. He's beautiful."

Win, in spite of himself, laughed. Several ruddy-faced men turned and stared. Norman waved at them, friendly-like. "Next time I come," Norm said to Win, "I'm wearing a yarmulke."

Win laughed harder. Myron tried to remember the last time he'd seen his friend laugh so openly. It'd been a while. Norm had that effect on people.

Esme Fong glanced at her watch and rose. "I only stopped by to say hello," she explained. "I really must be going."

All three men stood. Norm bussed her cheek. "Take care, Esme, okay? I'll see you tomorrow morning."

"Yes, Norm." She gave Myron and Win demure smiles accompanied by a shy lowering of the head. "Nice meeting you, Myron. Win."

She left. The three men sat. Win steepled his fingers. "How old is she?" Win asked.

"Twenty-five. Phi Beta Kappa from Yale."

"Impressive."

Norm said, "Don't even think it, Win."

Win shook his head. He wouldn't. She was in the business. Harder to disentangle. When it came to the opposite sex, Win liked quick and absolute closure.

"I stole her from those sons of bitches at Nike," Norm said. "She was a bigwig in their basketball department. Don't get me wrong. She was making a ton of dough, but she smartened up. Hey, it's like I told her: There's more to life than money. You know what I'm saying?"

Myron refrained from rolling his eyes.

"Anyway, she works like a dog. Always checking and rechecking. In fact, she's on her way to Linda Coldren's right now. They're going to have a late-night tea party or something girly-girl."

Myron and Win exchanged a glance. "She's going to Linda Coldren's house?"

"Yeah, why?"

"When did she call her?"

"What do you mean?"

"Was this appointment made a long time ago?"

"What, now, I look like a receptionist?"

"Forget it."

"Forgotten."

"Excuse me a second," Myron said. "Do you mind if I go make a call?"

"Am I your mother?" Zuckerman made a shooing motion. "Go already."

Myron debated using his cellular phone but decided not to piss off the Merion gods. He found a phone booth in the men's locker room foyer and dialed the Coldrens' house. He used Chad's line. Linda Coldren answered.

"Hello?"

"Just checking in," Myron said. "Anything new?"

"No," Linda said.

"Are you aware that Esme Fong is coming over?"

"I didn't want to cancel," Linda Coldren explained. "I didn't want to do anything that would draw attention."

"You'll be okay, then?"

"Yes," she said.

Myron watched Tad Crispin walk by in the direction of Win's table. "Were you able to reach the school?"

"No; nobody was there," she said. "So what do we do next?"

"I don't know," Myron said. "I have the override Caller ID on your phone. If he calls again, we should be able to get the number."

"What else?"

"I'll try to speak to Matthew Squires. See what he can tell me."

"I already spoke to Matthew," Linda said impatiently. "He doesn't know anything. What else?"

"I could get the police involved. Discreetly. There's not much else I can do on my own."

"No," she said firmly. "No police. Jack and I are both adamant on that point."

"I have friends in the FBI—"

"No."

He thought about his conversation with Win. "When Jack lost at Merion, who was his caddie?"

She hesitated. "Why would you want to know that?"

"I understand Jack blamed his caddie for the loss."

"In part, yes."

"And that he fired him."

"So?"

"So I asked about enemies. How did the caddie feel about what happened?"

"You're talking about something that happened over twenty years ago," Linda Coldren said. "Even if he did harbor a deep hatred for Jack, why would he wait so long?"

"This is the first time the Open has been at Merion since then. Maybe that's reawakened dormant anger. I don't know. Chances are there's nothing to this, but it might be worth checking out."

He could hear talking on the other end of the line. Jack's voice. She asked Myron to hold on a moment.

A few moments later, Jack Coldren came on the line. Without preamble, he said, "You think there's a connection between what happened to me twenty-three years ago and Chad's disappearance?"

"I don't know," Myron said.

His tone was insistent. "But you think—"

"I don't know what I think," he interrupted. "I'm just checking out every angle."

There was a stony silence. Then: "His name was Lloyd Rennart," Jack Coldren said.

"Do you know where he lives?"

"No. I haven't seen him since the day the Open ended."

"The day you fired him."

"Yes."

"You never bumped into him again? At the club or a tournament or something?"

"No," Jack Coldren said slowly. "Never."

"Where did Rennart live back then?"

"In Wayne. It's the neighboring town."

"How old would he be now?"

"Sixty-eight." No hesitation.

"Before this happened, were you two close?"

Jack Coldren's voice, when he finally spoke, was very soft. "I thought so," he said. "Not on a personal level. We didn't socialize. I never met his family or visited his home or anything like that. But on the golf course"—he paused—"I thought we were very close."

Silence.

"Why would he do it?" Myron asked. "Why would he purposely ruin your chances of winning?"

Myron could hear him breathing. When he spoke again, his voice was hoarse and scratchy. "I've wanted to know the answer to that for twenty-three years."

6

Myron called in Lloyd Rennart's name to Esperanza. It probably wouldn't take much. Again modern technology would simplify the feat. Anyone with a modem could type in the address www.switchboard.com—a Web site that was virtually a telephone directory of the entire country. If that site didn't work, there were others. It probably wouldn't take long, if Lloyd Rennart was still among the living. If not, well, there were sites for that too.

"Did you tell Win?" Esperanza asked.

"Yes."

"How did he react?"

"He won't help."

"Not surprising," she said.

"No," he agreed.

Esperanza said, "You don't work well alone, Myron."

"I'll be fine," he said. "You looking forward to graduation?"

Esperanza had been going to NYU Law School at night for the past six years. She graduated on Monday.

"I probably won't go."

"Why not?"

"I'm not big on ceremony," she said.

Esperanza's only close relative, her mother, had died a few months back. Myron suspected that her death had more to do with Esperanza's decision than not being big on ceremony.

"Well, I'm going," Myron said. "Sitting front row center. I want to see it all."

Silence.

Esperanza broke it. "Is this the part where I choke back tears because someone cares?"

Myron shook his head. "Forget I said anything."

"No, really, I want to get it right. Should I break down in loud sobs or just sniffle a little? Or better yet, I could get a little teary, like Michael Landon on *Little House on the Prairie*."

"You're such a wiseass."

"Only when you're being patronizing."

"I'm not being patronizing. I care. Sue me."

"Whatever," she said.

"Any messages?"

"About a million, but nothing that I can't handle until Monday," she said. "Oh, one thing."

"What?"

"The bitch asked me out to lunch."

"The bitch" was Jessica, the love of Myron's life. Putting it kindly, Esperanza did not like Jessica. Many assumed that this had something to do with jealousy, with some sort of latent attraction between Esperanza and Myron. Nope. For one thing, Esperanza liked, er, flexibility in her love life. For a while she had dated a guy named Max, then a woman named Lucy, and now another woman named Hester. "How many times have I asked you not to call her that?" Myron said.

"About a million."

"So are you going?"

"Probably," she said. "I mean, it's a free meal. Even if I do have to look at her face."

They hung up. Myron smiled. He was a bit surprised. While Jessica did not reciprocate Esperanza's animosity, a lunch date to thaw out their personal cold war was not something Myron would have anticipated. Perhaps now that they were living together, Jess figured it was time to offer an olive branch. What the hell. Myron dialed Jessica.

The machine picked up. He heard her voice. When the beep came on, he said, "Jess? Pick up."

She did. "God, I wish you were here right now." Jessica had a way with openings.

"Oh?" He could see her lying on the couch, the phone cord twisted in her fingers. "Why's that?"

"I'm about to take a ten-minute break."

"A full ten minutes?"

"Yup."

"Then you'd be expecting extended foreplay?"

She laughed. "Up for it, big guy?"

"I will be," he said, "if you don't stop talking about it."

"Maybe we should change the subject," she said.

Myron had moved into Jessica's Soho loft a few months ago. For most people, this would be a somewhat dramatic change—moving from a suburb in New Jersey to a trendy section of New York, moving in with a woman you love, etc.—but for Myron, the change rivaled puberty. He had spent his entire life living with his mom and dad in the classic suburban town of Livingston, New Jersey. Entire life. Age zero to six in the upstairs bedroom on the right. Age six to thirteen in the upstairs bedroom on the left. Age thirteen to thirty-something in the basement.

After that long, the apron strings become steel bands.

"I hear you're taking Esperanza out for lunch," he said.

"Yup."

"How come?"

"No reason."

"No reason?"

"I think she's cool. I want to go to lunch. Stop being so nosy."

"You realize, of course, that she hates you."

"I can handle it," Jessica said. "So how's the golf tournament?"

"Very strange," he said.

"How so?"

"Too long a story to tell now, sweetcakes. Can I call you later?"

"Sure." Then: "Did you say 'sweetcakes'?"

When they hung up, Myron frowned. Something was amiss. He and Jessica had never been closer, their relationship never stronger. Moving in together had been the right move, and a lot of their past demons had been exorcised away of late. They were loving toward each other, considerate of each other's feelings and needs, and almost never fought.

So why did Myron feel like they were standing on the cusp of some deep abyss?

He shook it off. All of this was just the by-product of an overstimulated imagination. Just because a ship is sailing upon smooth waters, he surmised, does not mean it is heading for an iceberg.

Wow, that was deep.

By the time he got back to the table, Tad Crispin was sipping an iced tea too. Win made the introductions. Crispin was dressed in yellows, lots of yellows, kind of like the man with the yellow hat from the Curious George books. Everything was yellow. Even his golf shoes. Myron tried not to make a face.

As if reading his mind, Norm Zuckerman said, "This isn't our line."

"Good to hear," Myron said.

Tad Crispin stood. "Nice to meet you, sir."

Myron offered up a great big smile. "It's a true honor to meet you, Tad." His voice reeked with the sincerity of, say, a chain-store appliance salesman. The two men shook hands. Myron kept on smiling. Crispin began to look wary.

Zuckerman pointed a thumb at Myron and leaned toward Win. "Is he always this smooth?"

Win nodded. "You should see him with the ladies."

Everyone sat.

"I can't stay long," Crispin said.

"We understand, Tad," Zuckerman said, doing the shooing thing again with both hands. "You're tired, you need to concentrate on tomorrow. Go already, get some sleep."

Crispin sort of smiled a little and looked at Win. "I want you to have my account," he said.

"I don't 'have' accounts," Win corrected. "I advise on them."

"There's a difference?"

"Most definitely," Win said. "You are in control of your money at all times. I will make recommendations. I will make them to you directly. No one else. We will discuss them. You will then make a final decision. I will not buy or sell or trade anything without you being fully aware of what is going on."

Crispin nodded. "That sounds good."

"I thought it might," Win said. "From what I see, you plan on watching your money carefully."

"Yes."

"Savvy," Win said with a nod. "You've read about too many athletes retiring broke. Of being taken advantage of by unscrupulous money managers and the like."

"Yes."

"And it will be my job to help you maximize your return, correct?"

Crispin leaned forward a bit. "Correct."

"Very well, then. It will be my task to help maximize your investment opportunities *after* you earn it. But I would not be serving your best interests if I did not also tell you how to make more."

Crispin's eyes narrowed. "I'm not sure I follow."

Zuckerman said, "Win."

Win ignored him. "As your financial consultant, I would be remiss if I did not make the following recommendation: You need a good agent."

Crispin's line of vision slid toward Myron. Myron remained still, looking back at him steadily. He turned back to Win. "I know you work with Mr. Bolitar," Crispin said.

"Yes and no," Win said. "If you decide to use his services I do not make one penny more. Well, that's not exactly true. If you choose to use Myron's services, you will make more money and subsequently I will have more of your money to invest. So in that way, I will make more."

"Thanks," Crispin said, "but I'm not interested."

"That's up to you," Win said, "but let me just explain a little further what I meant by yes and no. I manage assets worth approximately four hundred million dollars. Myron's clients represent less than three percent of that total. I am not employed by MB SportsReps. Myron Bolitar is not employed by Lock-Horne Securities. We do not have a partnership. I have not invested in his enterprise and he is not invested in mine. Myron has never looked at, asked about, or in any way discussed the financial situation of any of my clients. We are totally separate. Except for one thing."

All eyes were on Win. Myron, not famous for knowing when to keep his mouth shut, knew now.

"I am the financial consultant for every one of his clients," Win said. "Do you know why?"

Crispin shook his head.

"Because Myron insists upon it."

Crispin looked confused. "I don't understand. If he gets nothing out of it—"

"I didn't say that. He gets plenty out of it."

"But you said—"

"He, too, was an athlete; did you know that?"

"I heard something about it."

"He knows what happens to athletes. How they get cheated. How they squander their earnings, never fully accepting the fact that their careers can be over in a heartbeat. So he insists—insists, mind you—that he does not handle their finances. I've seen him refuse clients because of this. He further insists that I handle them. Why? For the same reason you sought me out. He knows I am the best. Immodest but true. Myron further insists that they see me in person at least once every quarter. Not just phone calls. Not just faxes or E-mails or letters. He insists that I go over every item in the account personally with them."

Win leaned farther back and steepled his fingers. The man loved to steeple his fingers. It looked good on him. Gave him an air of wisdom. "Myron Bolitar is my best friend. I know he'd give his life for me and I for him. But if he ever thought that I was not doing what was in a client's best interest, he would take away their portfolios without a second thought."

Norm said, "Beautiful speech, Win. Got me right there." He pointed to his stomach.

Win gave him the look. Norm stopped smiling.

"I made the deal with Mr. Zuckerman on my own," Crispin said. "I could make others."

"I won't comment on the Zoom deal," Win said. "But I will tell you this. You are a bright young man. A bright man knows not only his strengths but equally important, he knows his weaknesses. I do not, for example, know how to negotiate an endorsement contract. I may know the basics, but it is not my business. I'm not a plumber. If a pipe in my house broke, I would not be able to fix it. You are a golfer. You are one of the greatest talents I have ever seen. You should concentrate on that."

Tad Crispin took a sip of iced tea. He crossed his ankle on his knee. Even his socks were yellow. "You are making a hard sale for your friend," he said.

"Wrong," Win said. "I would kill for my friend, but financially I owe him nothing. You, on the other hand, are my client, and thus I have a very serious fiscal responsibility with regard to you. Stripping it bare, you have asked me to increase your portfolio. I will suggest several investment sources to you. But this is the best recommendation I can make."

Crispin turned to Myron. He looked him up and down, studying him hard. Myron almost brayed so he could examine his teeth. "He makes you sound awfully good," Crispin said to Myron.

"I am good," Myron said. "But I don't want him to give you the wrong impression. I'm not quite as altruistic as Win might have made me sound. I don't insist clients use him because I'm a swell guy. I know that having him handle my clients is a major plus. He improves the value of my services. He helps keep my clients happy. That's what I get out of it. Yes, I insist on having clients heavily involved in the decision-making on money matters, but that's as much to protect me as them."

"How so?"

"Obviously you know something about managers or agents robbing athletes."

"Yes."

"Do you know why so much of that occurs?"

Crispin shrugged. "Greed, I suppose."

Myron tilted his head in a yes-and-no gesture. "The main culprit is apathy. An athlete's lack of involvement. They get lazy. They decide it's easier to fully trust their agent, and that's bad. Let the agent pay the bills, they say. Let the agent invest the money. That kind of thing. But that won't ever happen at MB SportsReps. Not because I'm watching. Not because Win's watching. But because you are watching."

"I'm watching now," Crispin said.

"You're watching your money, true. I doubt you're watching everything else."

Crispin considered that for a moment. "I appreciate the talk," he said, "but I think I'm okay on my own."

Myron pointed at Tad Crispin's head. "How much are you getting for that hat?" he asked.

"Excuse me?"

"You're wearing a hat with no company logo on it," Myron explained. "For a player of your ilk, that's a loss of at least a quarter of a million dollars."

Silence.

"But I'm going to be working with Zoom," Crispin said.

"Did they purchase hat rights from you?"

He thought about it. "I don't think so."

"The front of the hat is a quarter million. We can also sell the sides if you want. They'll go for less. Maybe we'll total four hundred grand. Your shirt is another matter."

"Now just wait one minute here," Zuckerman interjected. "He's going to be wearing Zoom shirts."

"Fine, Norm," Myron said. "But he's allowed to wear logos. One on the chest, one on either sleeve."

"Logos?"

"Anything. Coca-Cola maybe. IBM. Even Home Depot."

"Logos on my shirt?"

"Yep. And what do you drink out there?"

"Drink? When I play?"

"Sure. I can probably get you a deal with Powerade or one of the soda companies. How about Poland Spring water? They might be good. And your golf bag. You have to negotiate a deal for your golf bag."

"I don't understand."

"You're a billboard, Tad. You're on television. Lots of fans see you. Your hat, your shirt, your golf bag—those are all places to post ads."

Zuckerman said, "Now hold on a second. He can't just—"

A cell phone began to sound, but it never made it past the first ring. Myron's finger reached the ringer and turned it off with a speed that would have made Wyatt Earp retire. Fast reflexes. They came in handy every once in a while.

Still, the brief sound had drawn the ire of nearby club members. Myron looked around. He was on the receiving end of several dagger-glares, including one from Win.

"Hurry around behind the clubhouse," Win said pointedly. "Let no one see you."

Myron gave a flippant salute and rushed out like a man with a suddenly collapsing bladder. When he reached a safe area near the parking lot, he answered the call.

"Hello."

"Oh, God . . ." It was Linda Coldren. Her tone struck the marrow of his bone.

"What's wrong?"

"He called again," she said.

"Do you have it on tape?"

"Yes."

"I'll be right ov—"

"No!" she shouted. "He's watching the house."

"You saw him?"

"No. But . . . Don't come here. Please."

"Where are you calling from?"

"The fax line in the basement. Oh God, Myron, you should have heard him."

"Did the number come up on the Caller ID?"

"Yes."

"Give it to me."

She did. Myron took out a pen from his wallet and wrote the number down on an old Visa receipt.

"Are you alone?"

"Jack is right here with me."

"Anybody else? What about Esme Fong?"

"She's upstairs in the living room."

"Okay," Myron said. "I'll need to hear the call."

"Hold on. Jack is plugging the machine in now. I'll put you on the speaker so you can hear."

7

The tape player was snapped on. Myron heard the phone ringing first. The sound was surprisingly clear. Then he heard Jack Coldren: "Hello?"

"Who's the chink bitch?"

The voice was very deep, very menacing, and definitely machine-altered. Male or female, young or old, it was anyone's guess.

"I don't know what—"

"You trying to fuck with me, you dumb son of a bitch? I'll start sending you the fucking brat in little pieces."

Jack Coldren said, "Please—"

"I told you not to contact anyone."

"We haven't."

"Then tell me who that chink bitch is who just walked into your house."

Silence.

"You think we're stupid, Jack?"

"Of course not."

"So who the fuck is she?"

"Her name is Esme Fong," Coldren said quickly. "She works for a clothing company. She's just here to set up an endorsement deal with my wife, that's all."

"Bullshit."

"It's the truth, I swear."

"I don't know, Jack. . . ."

"I wouldn't lie to you."

"Well, Jack, we'll just see about that. This is gonna cost you."

"What do you mean?"
"One hundred grand. Call it a penalty price."
"For what?"
"Never you fucking mind. You want the kid alive? It's gonna cost you one hundred grand now. That's in—"
"Now hold on a second." Coldren cleared his throat. Trying to gain some footing, some degree of control.
"Jack?"
"Yes?"
"You interrupt me again and I'm going to stick your kid's dick in a vise."
Silence.
"You get the money ready, Jack. One hundred grand. I'll call you back and let you know what to do. Do you understand?"
"Yes."
"Don't fuck up, Jack. I enjoy hurting people."
The brief silence was shattered by a sharp, sudden scream, a scream that jangled nerve endings and raised hackles. Myron's hand tightened on the receiver.
The phone disconnected. Then a dial tone. Then nothing.
Linda Coldren took him off the speaker. "What are we going to do?"
"Call the FBI," Myron said.
"Are you out of your mind?"
"I think it's your best move."
Jack Coldren said something in the background. Linda came back on the line. "Absolutely not. We just want to pay the ransom and get our son back."
No point in arguing with them. "Sit tight. I'll call you back as soon as I can."
Myron disconnected the call and dialed another number. Lisa at New York Bell. She'd been a contact of theirs since the days he and Win had worked for the government.
"A Caller ID came up with a number in Philadelphia," he said. "Can you find an address for me?"
"No problem," Lisa said.
He gave her the number. People who watch too much television think this sort of thing takes a long time. Not anymore. Traces are instantaneous now. No "keep him on a little longer" or any of that stuff. The same is true when it comes to finding the location of a phone number. Any operator almost anywhere can plug the number into her computer or use one of those reverse directories, and whammo. Heck, you don't even need an

operator. Computer programs on CD-ROM and Web sites did the same thing.

"It's a pay phone," she said.

Not good news, but not unexpected either. "Do you know where?"

"The Grand Mercado Mall in Bala-Cynwyd."

"A mall?"

"Yes."

"You're sure?"

"That's what it says."

"Where in the mall?"

"I have no idea. You think they list it 'between Sears and Victoria's Secret'?"

This made no sense. A mall? The kidnapper had dragged Chad Coldren to a mall and made him scream into a phone?

"Thanks, Lisa."

He hung up and turned back toward the porch. Win was standing directly behind him. His arms were folded, his body, as always, completely relaxed.

"The kidnapper called," Myron said.

"So I overheard."

"I could use your help tracking this down."

"No," Win said.

"This isn't about your mother, Win."

Win's face did not change, but something happened to his eyes. "Careful," was all he said.

Myron shook his head. "I have to go. Please make my excuses."

"You came here to recruit clients," Win said. "You claimed earlier that you agreed to help the Coldrens in the hopes of representing them."

"So?"

"So you are excruciatingly close to landing the world's top golf protégé. Reason dictates that you stay."

"I can't."

Win unfolded his arms, shook his head.

"Will you do one thing for me? To let me know if I'm wasting time or not?"

Win remained still.

"You know how I told you about Chad using his ATM card?"

"Yes."

"Get me the security videotape of the transaction," he said. "It may tell me if this whole thing is just a hoax on Chad's part."

Win turned back to the porch. "I'll see you at the house tonight."

8

Myron parked at the mall and checked his watch. Seven forty-five. It had been a very long day and it was still relatively early. He entered through a Macy's and immediately located one of those big table blueprints of the mall. Public telephones were marked with blue locators. Eleven altogether. Two at the south entrance downstairs. Two at the north entrance upstairs. Seven at the food court.

Malls were the great American geographical equalizer. Between shiny anchor stores and beneath excessively floodlit ceilings, Kansas equaled California, New Jersey equaled Nevada. No place was truly more Americana. Some of the stores inside might be different, but not by much. Athlete's Foot or Foot Locker, Rite Aid or CVS, Williams-Sonoma or Pottery Barn, the Gap or Banana Republic or Old Navy (all, coincidentally, owned by the same people), Waldenbooks or B. Dalton, several anonymous shoe stores, a Radio Shack, a Victoria's Secret, an art gallery with Gorman, McKnight, and Behrens, a museum store of some kind, two record stores—all wrapped up in some Orwellian, sleek-chrome neo-Roman Forum with chintzy fountains and overstated marble and dentist-office sculptures and unmanned information booths and fake ferns.

In front of a store selling electric organs and pianos sat an employee dressed in an ill-fitting navy suit and a sailor's cap. He played "Muskrat Love" on an organ. Myron was tempted to ask him where Tenille was, but he refrained. Too obvious. Organ stores in malls. Who goes to the mall to buy an organ?

He hurried past the Limited or the Unlimited or the Severely Challenged or something like that. Then Jeans Plus or Jeans Minus or Shirts Only or Pants Only or Tank Top City or something like that. They all looked pretty much the same. They all employed lots of skinny, bored teenagers who stocked shelves with the enthusiasm of a eunuch at an orgy.

There were lots of high school kids draped about—just hanging, man—and looking very, er, rad. At the risk of sounding like a reverse racist, all the white boys looked the same to him. Baggie shorts. White T-shirts. Unlaced black hundred-dollar high-top sneakers. Baseball cap pulled low with the brim worked into a nifty curve, covering a summer buzzcut. Thin. Lanky. Long-limbed. Pale as a Goya portrait, even in the summer. Poor posture. Eyes that never looked directly at another human being. Uncomfortable eyes. Slightly scared eyes.

He passed a hair salon called Snip Away, which sounded more like a vasectomy clinic than a beauty parlor. The Snip Away beauticians were either reformed mall girls or guys named Mario whose fathers were named Sal. Two patrons sat in a window—one getting a perm, the other a bleach job. Who wanted that? Who wanted to sit in a window and have the whole world watch you get your hair done?

He took an escalator up past a plastic garden complete with plastic vines to the crowned jewel of the mall: the food court. It was fairly empty now, the dinner crowd long since gone. Food courts were the final outpost of the great American melting pot. Italian, Chinese, Japanese, Mexican, Middle Eastern (or Greek), a deli, a chicken place, one fast food chain like McDonald's (which had the biggest crowd), a frozen yogurt place, and then a few strange offshoots—the ones started by people who dream of franchising themselves into becoming the next Ray Kroc. Ethiopian Ecstasy. Sven's Swedish Meatballs. Curry Up and Eat.

Myron checked for numbers on the seven phones. All had been whited out. Not surprising, the way people abused them nowadays. No problemo either. He took out his cellular phone and punched in the number from the Caller ID. A phone starting ringing immediately.

Bingo.

The one on the far right. Myron picked it up to make sure. "Hello?" he said. He heard the hello in his cellular phone. Then he said to himself through the cellular, "Hello, Myron, nice to hear from you." He decided to stop talking to himself. Too early in the evening to be this goofy.

He hung up the phone and looked around. A group of mall girls inhabited a table not far away. They sat in a closed circle with the protectiveness of coyotes during mating season.

Of the food stands, Sven's Swedish Meatballs had the best view of the phone. Myron approached. Two men worked the booth. They both had dark hair and dark skin and Saddam Hussein mustaches. One's name tag read Mustafa. The other Achmed.

"Which one of you is Sven?" he asked.

No smiles.

Myron asked about the phone. Mustafa and Achmed were less than helpful. Mustafa snapped that he worked for a living, and didn't watch phones. Achmed gestured and cursed him in a foreign tongue.

"I'm not much of a linguist," Myron said, "but that didn't sound like Swedish."

Death glares.

"Bye now. I'll be sure to tell all my friends."

Myron turned toward the table of mall girls. They all quickly looked down, like rats scurrying in the glare of a flashlight. He stepped toward them. Their eyes darted to and fro with what they must have thought were surreptitious glances. He heard a low cacophony of "ohmygod!ohmygod!ohmygod!he'scomingover!"

Myron stopped directly at their table. There were four girls. Or maybe five or even six. Hard to say. They all seemed to blend into one another, into one hazy, indistinct mesh of hair and black lipstick and Fu Manchu–length fingernails and earrings and nose rings and cigarette smoke and too-tight halter tops and bare midriffs and popping gum.

The one sitting in the middle looked up first. She had hair like Elsa Lancaster in *The Bride of Frankenstein* and what looked like a studded dog collar around her neck. The other faces followed suit.

"Like, hi," Elsa said.

Myron tried his most gentle, crooked smile. Harrison Ford in *Regarding Henry*. "Do you mind if I ask you a few questions?"

The girls all looked at one another. A few giggles escaped. Myron felt his face redden, though he wasn't sure why. They elbowed one another. No one answered. Myron proceeded.

"How long have you been sitting here?" he asked.

"Is this, like, one of those mall surveys?"

"No," Myron said.

"Good. Those are, like, so lame, you know?"

"Uh-huh."

"It's like, get away from me already, Mr. Polyester Pants, you know?"

Myron said "uh-huh" again. "Do you remember how long you've been sitting here?"

"Nah. Amber, you know?"

"Like, we went to the Gap at four."

"Right, the Gap. Fab sale."

"Ultra sale. Love that blouse you bought, Trish."

"Isn't it, like, the total package, Mindy?"

"Totally. Ultra."

Myron said, "It's almost eight now. Have you been here for the past hour?"

"Like, hello, anybody home? At least."

"This is, like, our spot, you know?"

"No one else, like, sits here."

"Except that one time when those gross lame-os tried to move in."

"But, like, whoa, don't even go there, 'kay?"

They stopped and looked at Myron. He figured the answer to his prior question was yes, so he plowed ahead. "Have you seen anybody use that pay phone?"

"Are you, like, a cop or something?"

"As if."

"No way."

"Way."

"He's too cute to be a cop."

"Oh, right, like Jimmy Smits isn't cute."

"That's, like, TV, dumb wad. This is real life. Cops aren't cute in real life."

"Oh, right, like Brad isn't totally cute? You, like, love him, remember?"

"As if. And he's not a cop. He's, like, some rent-a-uniform at Florsheim."

"But he's so hot."

"Totally."

"Ultra buff."

"He likes Shari."

"Eeeuw. Shari?"

"I, like, hate her, you know?"

"Me too. Like, does she only shop at Sluts 'R' Us, or what?"

"Totally."

"It's, like, 'Hello, Dial-a-Disease, this is Shari speaking.' "

Giggles.

Myron looked for an interpreter. "I'm not a cop," he said.

"Told you."

"As if."

"But," Myron said, "I am dealing with something very important. Life-and-death. I need to know if you remember anyone using that phone—the one on the far right—forty-five minutes ago."

"Whoa!" The one called Amber pushed her chair back. "Clear out, because I'm, like, gonna barf for days, you know?"

"Like, Crusty the Clown."

"He was, like, so gross!"

"Totally gross."

"Totally."

"He, like, winked at Amber!"

"As if!"

"Totally eeeuw!"

"Gag city."

"Bet that slut Shari would have Frenched him."

"At least."

Giggles.

Myron said, "You saw somebody?"

"Serious groatie."

"Totally crusty."

"He was, like, hello, ever wash your hair?"

"Like, hello, buy your cologne at the local Gas-N-Go?"

More giggles.

Myron said, "Can you describe him to me?"

"Blue jeans from, like, 'Attention, Kmart shoppers.' "

"Work boots. Definitely not Timberland."

"He was, like, so skinhead wanna-be, you know?"

Myron said, "Skinhead wanna-be?"

"Like, a shaved head. Skanky beard. Tattoo of that thing on his arm."

"That thing?" Myron tried.

"You know, that tattoo." She kind of drew something in the air with her finger. "It kinda looks like a funny cross from, like, the old days."

Myron said, "You mean a swastika?"

"Like, whatever. Do I look like a history major?"

"Like, how old was he?" Like. He'd said *like*. If he stayed here much longer, he'd end up getting some part of him pierced. Way.

"Old."

"Grampa-ville."

"Like, at least twenty."

"Height?" Myron asked. "Weight?"

"Six feet."

"Yeah, like six feet."

"Bony."

"Very."

"Like, no ass at all."

"None."

"Was anybody with him?" Myron asked.

"As if."

"Him?"

"No way."

"Who would be with a skank like that?"

"Just him by that phone for like half an hour."

"He wanted Mindy."

"Did not!"

"Wait a second," Myron said. "He was there for half an hour?"

"Not that long."

"Seemed a long time."

"Maybe like fifteen minutes. Amber, like, always exaggerates."

"Like, fuck you, Trish, all right? Just fuck you."

"Anything else?" Myron asked.

"Beeper."

"Right, beeper. Like anybody would ever call that skank."

"Held it right up to the phone, too."

Probably not a beeper. Probably a microcassette player. That would explain the scream. Or a voice changer. They also came in a small box.

He thanked the girls and handed out business cards that listed his cellular phone number. One of the girls actually read it. She made a face.

"Like, your name is really Myron?"

"Yes."

They all just stopped and looked at him.

"I know," Myron said. "Like, ultra lame-o."

He was heading back to his car when a nagging thought suddenly resurfaced. The kidnapper on the phone had mentioned a "chink bitch." Somehow he had known about Esme Fong arriving at the house. The question was, how?

There were two possibilities. One, they had a bug in the house.

Not likely. If the Coldren residence was bugged or under some kind of electronic surveillance, the kidnapper would also have known about Myron's involvement.

Two, one of them was watching the house.

That seemed most logical. Myron thought a moment. If someone had been watching the house only an hour or so ago, it was fair to assume that they were still there, still hiding behind a bush or up a tree or something. If Myron could locate the person surreptitiously, he might be able to follow them back to Chad Coldren.

Was it worth the risk?

Like, totally.

9

Ten o'clock.

Myron used Win's name again and parked in Merion's lot. He checked for Win's Jaguar, but it was nowhere to be seen. He parked and checked for guards. No one. They'd all been stationed at the front entrance. Made things easier.

He quickly stepped over the white rope used to hold back the galley and started crossing the golf course. It was dark now, but the lights from the houses across the way provided enough illumination to cross. For all its fame, Merion was a tiny course. From the parking lot to Golf House Road, across two fairways, was less than a hundred yards.

Myron trudged forward. Humidity hung in the air in a heavy blanket of beads. Myron's shirt began to feel sticky. The crickets were incessant and plenteous, their swarming tune as monotonous as a Mariah Carey CD, though not quite as grating. The grass tickled Myron's sockless ankles.

Despite his natural aversion to golf, Myron still felt the appropriate sense of awe, as if he were trespassing over sacred ground. Ghosts breathed in the night, the same way they breathed at any sight that had borne legends. Myron remembered once standing on the parquet floor at Boston Garden when no one else was there. It was a week after he had been picked by the Celtics in the first round of the NBA draft. Clip Arnstein, the Celtics' fabled general manager, had introduced him to the press earlier that day. It had been enormous fun. Everybody had been laughing and smiling and calling Myron the next Larry Bird. That night, as he stood alone in the famed halls of the Garden, the championship flags hanging from the rafters actually seemed to sway in the still air, beckoning him forward and whispering tales of the past and promises of what was to come.

Myron never played a game on that parquet floor.

He slowed as he reached Golf House Road and stepped over the white rope. Then he ducked behind a tree. This would not be easy. Then again, it would not be easy for his quarry either. Neighborhoods like this noted anything suspicious. Like a parked car where it didn't belong. That had been why Myron had parked in the Merion lot. Had the kidnapper done likewise? Or was his car out on the street? Or had someone dropped him off?

He kept low and darted to another tree. He looked, he assumed, rather doofy—a guy six-feet four inches tall and comfortably over two hundred pounds darting between bushes like something left on the cutting room floor of *The Dirty Dozen*.

But what choice did he have?

He couldn't just casually walk down the street. The kidnapper might spot him. His whole plan relied on the fact that he could spot the kidnapper before the kidnapper spotted him. How to do this? He really did not have a clue. The best he could come up with was to keep circling closer and closer to the Coldren house, looking out for, er, uh, something.

He scanned the surroundings—for what, he wasn't sure. Someplace for a kidnapper to use as a lookout spot, he guessed. A safe place to hide, maybe, or a perch where a man with binoculars could survey the scene. Nothing. The night was absolutely windless and still.

He circled the block, dashing haphazardly from one bush to another, feeling now very much like John Belushi breaking into Dean Wormer's office in *Animal House*.

Animal House and *The Dirty Dozen*. Myron watched too many movies.

As he continued to spiral closer to the Coldrens' residence, Myron realized that there was probably a good chance that he'd be the "spottee" rather than the "spotter." He tried to hide himself better, to concentrate on making himself become part of the night, to blend in to the background and become invisible.

Myron Bolitar, Mutant Ninja Warrior.

Lights twinkled from spacious homes of stone and black shutters. They were all imposing and rather beautiful with a tutelary, stay-away coziness about them. Solid homes. The third-little-piggie homes. Settled and staying and proud homes.

He was getting very close to the Coldren house now. Still nothing— not even a single car parked on the roads. Sweat coated him like syrup on a stack of pancakes. God, he wanted to take a shower. He hunched down and watched the house.

Now what?

Wait. Be on the lookout for movement of some kind. Surveillance and the like was not Myron's forte. Win usually handled that kind of stuff. He had the body control and the patience. Myron was already getting fidgety. He wished he'd brought a magazine or something to read.

The three minutes of monotony was broken when the front door opened. Myron sat up. Esme Fong and Linda Coldren appeared in the door frame. They said their good-byes. Esme gave Linda the firm handshake and headed to her çar. Linda Coldren shut the front door. Esme Fong started her car and left.

A thrill a second, this surveillance stuff.

Myron settled back behind a shrub. There were lots of shrubs around here. Everywhere one looked, there were shrubs of various sizes and shapes and purposes. Rich blue bloods must really like shrubs, Myron decided. He wondered if they had had any on the *Mayflower*.

His legs were beginning to cramp from all this crouching. He straightened them out one at a time. His bad knee, the one that ended his basketball career, began to throb. Enough. He was hot and sticky and in pain. Time to get out of here.

Then he heard a sound.

It seemed to be coming from the back door. He sighed, creaked to his feet, and circled. He found yet another comfy shrub and hid behind it. He peered out.

Jack Coldren was in the backyard with his caddie, Diane Hoffman. Jack held a golf club in his hands, but he wasn't hitting. He was talking with Diane Hoffman. Animatedly. Diane Hoffman was talking back. Equally animated. Neither one of them seemed very pleased. Myron could not hear them, but they were both gesturing like mad.

An argument. A rather heated argument.

Hmm.

Of course, there probably was an innocent explanation. Caddies and players argue all the time, Myron guessed. He remembered reading how Seve Ballesteros, the Spanish former wunderkind, was always fighting with his caddie. Bound to happen. Routine stuff, a caddie and a pro having a little tiff, especially during such a pressure-filled tournament as the U.S. Open.

But the timing was curious.

Think about it a second. A man gets a terrifying call from a kidnapper. He hears his son scream in apparent fright or pain. Then, a couple of hours later, he is in his backyard arguing about his backswing with his caddie.

Did that make sense?

Myron decided to move closer, but there was no straight path. Shrubs again, like tackle dummies at a football practice. He'd have to move to the side of the house and circle in behind them. He made a quick bolt to his left and risked another glance. The heated argument continued. Diane Hoffman took a step closer to Jack.

Then she slapped him in the face.

The sound sliced through the night like a scythe. Myron froze. Diane Hoffman shouted something. Myron heard the word *bastard,* but nothing else. Diane flicked her cigarette at Jack's feet and stormed off. Jack looked down, shook his head slowly, and went back inside.

Well, well, Myron thought. Must have been some trouble with that backswing.

Myron stayed behind the shrub. He heard a car start in the driveway. Diane Hoffman's, he assumed. For a moment, he wondered if she had a role in this. Obviously she had been in the house. Could she be the mysterious lookout? He leaned back and considered the possibility. The idea was just starting to soak in and settle when Myron spotted the man.

Or at least he assumed it was a man. It was hard to tell from where he was crouched. Myron could not believe what he was seeing. He had been wrong. Dead wrong. The perpetrator hadn't been hiding in the bushes or anything like that. Myron watched now in silence as someone dressed completely in black climbed out an upper-floor window. More specifically—if memory didn't fail him—Chad Coldren's bedroom window.

Hello there.

Myron ducked down. Now what? He needed a plan. Yes, a plan. Good thinking. But what plan? Did he grab the perp now? No. Better to follow him. Maybe he'd lead him back to Chad Coldren. That would be nice.

He took another peek out. The black-clad figure had scaled down a white lattice fence with entwined ivy. He jumped the last few feet. As soon as he hit the ground, he sprinted away.

Great.

Myron followed, trying to stay as far behind the figure as possible. The figure, however, was running. This made following silently rather difficult. But Myron kept back. Didn't want to risk being seen. Besides, chances were good that the perpetrator had brought a car or was getting picked up by someone. These streets barely had any traffic. Myron would be bound to hear an engine.

But then what?

What would Myron do when the perp got to the car? Run back to get his own? No, that wouldn't work. Follow a car on foot? Er, not likely. So what exactly was he going to do?

Good question.

He wished Win were here.

The perp kept running. And running. Myron was starting to suck air. Jesus, who the hell was he chasing anyway, Frank Shorter? Another quarter mile passed before the perp abruptly veered to the right and out of view. The turn was so sudden that for a moment Myron wondered if he'd been spotted. Impossible. He was too far back and his quarry had not so much as glanced over his shoulder.

Myron tried to hurry a bit, but the road was gravelly. Running silently would be impossible. Still, he had to make up ground. He ran high atop his tiptoes, looking not unlike Baryshnikov with dysentery. He prayed nobody would see him.

He reached the turn. The name of the street was Green Acres Road. Green Acres. The old TV show theme song started in his head, like someone had pressed buttons on a jukebox. He couldn't stop it. Eddie Albert rode a tractor. Eva Gabor opened boxes in a Manhattan penthouse. Sam Drucker waved from behind the counter of his general store. Mr. Haney pulled his suspenders with both thumbs. Arnold the pig snorted.

Man, the humidity was definitely getting to him.

Myron wheeled to the right and looked ahead.

Nothing.

Green Acres was a short cul-de-sac with maybe five homes. Fabulous homes, or so Myron assumed. Towering shrub walls—again with the shrubs—lined either side of the street. Locked gates were on the driveways, the kind that worked by remote control or by pushing a combination in a keypad. Myron stopped and looked down the road.

So where was our boy?

He felt his pulse quicken. No sign of him. The only escape route was through the woods between two houses in the cul-de-sac. He must have gone in there, Myron surmised—if, that is, he was trying to escape and not, say, hide in the bushes. He might, after all, have spotted Myron. He might have decided to duck down somewhere and hide. Hide and then pounce when Myron walked by.

These were not comforting thoughts.

Now what?

He licked the sweat off his upper lip. His mouth felt terribly dry. He could almost hear himself sweat.

Suck it up, Myron, he told himself. He was six-four and two hundred and twenty pounds. A big guy. He was also a black belt in tae kwon do and a well-trained fighter. He could fend off any attack.

Unless the guy was armed.

True. Let's face it. Fight training and experience were helpful, but they did not make one bullet-proof. Not even Win. Of course, Win wouldn't have been stupid enough to get himself into this mess. Myron carried a weapon only when he thought it was absolutely necessary. Win, on the other hand, carried at least two guns and one bladed instrument at all times. Third world countries should be as well armed as Win.

So what to do?

He looked left and right, but there was no place much for anybody to hide. The shrub walls were thick and fully impenetrable. That left only the woods at the end of the road. But there were no lights down that way and the woods looked dense and forbidding.

Should he go in?

No. That would be pointless at best. He had no idea how big the woods were, what direction to head in, nothing. The odds of finding the perpetrator were frighteningly remote. Myron's best hope was that the perp was just hiding for a while, waiting for Myron to clear out.

Clear out. That sounded like a plan.

Myron moved back to the end of Green Acres. He turned left, traveled a couple of hundred yards, and settled behind yet another shrub. He and shrubs were on a first-name basis by now. This one he named Frank.

He waited an hour. No one appeared.

Great.

He finally stood up, said good-bye to Frank, and headed back to the car. The perpetrator must have escaped through the woods. That meant that he had planned an escape route or, more probably, he knew the area well. Could mean that it was Chad Coldren. Or it could mean that the kidnappers knew what they were doing. And if that was so, it meant there was a good chance that they now knew about Myron's involvement and the fact that the Coldrens had disobeyed them.

Myron hoped like hell it was just a hoax. But if it wasn't, if this was indeed a real kidnapping, he wondered about repercussions. He wondered how the kidnappers would react to what he had done. And as he continued on his way, Myron remembered their previous phone call and the harrowing, flesh-creeping sound of Chad Coldren's scream.

10

"M eanwhile, back at stately Wayne Manor . . ."

That voice-over from the TV *Batman* always came to Myron when he reached the steely gates of the Lockwood estate. In reality, Win's family home looked very little like Bruce Wayne's house, though it did offer up the same aura. A tremendous serpentine driveway wound to an imposing stone mansion on the hill. There was grass, lots of it, all the blades kept at a consistently ideal length, like a politician's hair in an election year. There were also lush gardens and hills and a swimming pool, a pond, a tennis court, horse stables, and a horse obstacle course of some kind.

All in all, the Lockwood estate was very "stately" and worthy of the term "manor," whatever that meant.

Myron and Win were staying at the guest house—or as Win's father liked to call it, "the cottage." Exposed beams, hardwood floors, fireplace, new kitchen with a big island in the middle, pool room—not to mention five bedrooms, four and half baths. Some cottage.

Myron tried to sort through what was happening, but all he came up with was a series of paradoxes, a whole lot of "which came first, the chicken or the egg?" Motive, for example. On the one hand, it might make sense to kidnap Chad Coldren to throw off Jack Coldren. But Chad had been missing since *before* the tournament, which meant the kidnapper was either very cautious or very prophetic. On the other hand, the kidnapper had asked for one hundred grand, which pointed to a simple case of kidnapping for money. A hundred grand was a nice, tidy sum—a little low for a kidnapping, but not bad for a few days' work.

But if this was merely a kidnapping to extort mucho dinero, the timing was curious. Why now? Why during the one time a year the U.S. Open was played? More than that, why kidnap Chad during the one time in the last twenty-three years the Open was being played at Merion—the one time in almost a quarter of a century that Jack Coldren had a chance to revisit and redeem his greatest failing?

Seemed like a hell of a coincidence.

That brought it back to a hoax and a scenario that went something like this: Chad Coldren disappears before the tournament to screw around with his dad's mind. When that doesn't work—when, to the contrary, Dad starts winning—he ups the ante and fakes his own kidnapping. Taking it a step further, one could assume that it had been Chad Coldren who had been climbing out of his own window. Who better? Chad Coldren knew the area. Chad Coldren probably knew how to go through those woods. Or maybe he was hiding out at a friend's house who lived on Green Acres Road. Whatever.

It added up. It made sense.

All of this assumed, of course, that Chad truly disliked his father. Was there evidence of that? Myron thought so. Start off with the fact that Chad was sixteen years old. Not an easy age. Weak evidence for sure, but worth keeping in mind. Second—and far, far more important—Jack Coldren was an absent father. No athlete is away from home as much as a golfer. Not basketball players or football players or baseball players or hockey players. The only ones who come close are tennis players. In both tennis and golf, tournaments are taking place almost all year—there is little so-called off season—and there is no such thing as a home game. If you were lucky, you hit your home course once a year.

Lastly—and perhaps most crucial of all—Chad had been gone for *two* days without raising eyebrows. Forget Linda Coldren's discourse on responsible children and open child-raising. The only rational explanation for their nonchalance was that this had happened before, or at the very least, was not unexpected.

But there were problems with the hoax scenario too.

For example, how did Mr. Total Grunge from the mall fit in?

There was indeed the rub. What role was the Crusty Nazi playing in all this? Did Chad Coldren have an accomplice? Possibly, but that really didn't fit in well with a revenge scenario. If Chad was indeed behind all this, Myron doubted that the preppy golfer would join forces with a "skinhead wanna-be," complete with a swastika tattoo.

So where did that leave Myron?

Baffled.

As Myron pulled up to the guest house, he felt his heart constrict. Win's Jag was there. But so was a green Chevy Nova.

Oh, Christ.

Myron got out of the car slowly. He checked the license plate on the Nova. Unfamiliar. As he expected. He swallowed and moved away.

He opened the cottage's front door and welcomed the sudden on-slaught of air-conditioning. The lights were out. For a moment he just stood in the foyer, eyes closed, the cool air tingling his skin. An enormous grandfather clock ticked.

Myron opened his eyes and flicked on a light.

"Good evening."

He pivoted to his right. Win was seated in a high-back leather chair by the fireplace. He cupped a brandy snifter in his hand.

"You were sitting in the dark?" Myron asked.

"Yes."

Myron frowned. "A bit theatrical, don't you think?"

Win switched on a nearby lamp. His face was a tad rosy from the brandy. "Care to join me?"

"Sure. I'll be right back."

Myron grabbed a cold Yoo-Hoo from the refrigerator and sat on the couch across from his friend. He shook the can and popped it open. They drank in silence for several minutes. The clock ticked. Long shadows snaked across the floor in thin, almost smoky tendrils. Too bad it was summertime. This was the kind of setting that begged for a roaring fire and maybe some howling wind. An air conditioner just didn't cut it.

Myron was just getting comfortable when he heard a toilet flush. He looked a question at Win.

"I am not alone," Win said.

"Oh." Myron adjusted himself on the couch. "A woman?"

"Your gifts," Win said. "They never cease to amaze."

"Anybody I know?" Myron asked.

Win shook his head. "Not even somebody I know."

The norm. Myron looked steadily at his friend. "You want to talk about this?"

"No."

"I'm here if you do."

"Yes, I see that." Win swished around the drink in the snifter. He fin-ished it in one gulp and reached for the crystal decanter. There was a slight slur in his speech. Myron tried to remember the last time he had seen Win the vegetarian, the master of several martial arts, the transcen-dental meditator, the man so at ease and in focus with his surroundings, have too much to drink.

It had been a very long time.

"I have a golf question for you," Myron said.

Win nodded for him to proceed.

"Do you think Jack Coldren can hang on to this lead?"

Win poured the brandy. "Jack will win," he said.

"You sound pretty sure."

"I am sure."

"Why?"

Win raised the glass to his mouth and looked over the rim. "I saw his eyes."

Myron made a face. "What's that supposed to mean?"

"He has it back. The look in the eyes."

"You're kidding, right?"

"Perhaps I am. But let me ask you something."

"Go ahead."

"What separates the great athletes from the very good? The legend from the journeyman? Simply put, what makes winners?"

"Talent," Myron said. "Practice. Skill."

Win gave a slight shake of the head. "You know better than that."

"I do?"

"Yes. Many have talent. Many practice. There is more to the art of creating a true winner."

"This look-in-the-eye thing?"

"Yes."

Myron winced. "You're not going to start singing 'Eye of the Tiger,' are you?"

Win cocked his head. "Who sang that song?"

The continuing trivia game. Win knew the answer, of course. "It was in *Rocky II*, right?"

"*Rocky III*," Win corrected.

"That the one with Mr. T?"

Win nodded. "Who played . . . ?" he prompted.

"Clubber Lange."

"Very good. Now who sang the song?"

"I don't remember."

"The name of the group was Survivor," Win said. "Ironic name when you think of how quickly they vanished, no?"

"Uh-huh," Myron said. "So what is this great divider, Win? What makes a winner?"

Win took another swish and sip. "Wanting," he said.

"Wanting?"

"Hunger."

"Uh-huh."

"The answer isn't surprising," Win said. "Look in Joe DiMaggio's eyes. Or Larry Bird's. Or Michael Jordan's. Look at pictures of John McEnroe in his prime, or Chris Evert. Look at Linda Coldren." He stopped. "Look in the mirror."

"The mirror? I have this?"

"When you were on the court," Win said slowly, "your eyes were barely sane."

They fell into silence. Myron took a swig of Yoo-Hoo. The cold aluminum felt good in his hand. "You make the whole 'wanting' thing sound like it's all foreign to you," Myron said.

"It is."

"Bull."

"I am a good golfer," Win said. "Correction: I am a very good golfer. I practiced quite a bit in my youth. I have even won my share of tournaments. But I never wanted it bad enough to move up to that next level."

"I've seen you in the ring," Myron countered. "In martial arts tournaments. You seemed plenty 'wanting' to me."

"That is very different," Win said.

"How so?"

"I do not view a martial arts tournament as a sporting contest, whereby the winner brings home a chintzy trophy and brags to colleagues and friends—nor do I view it as a competition that will lead to some sort of empty emotion that the insecure among us perceive as glory. Fighting is not a sport to me. It's about survival. If I could lose in there"—he motioned to an imaginary ring—"I could lose in the real world." Win looked up in the air. "But . . ." His voice drifted off.

"But?" Myron repeated.

"But you may be on to something."

"Oh?"

Win steepled his fingers. "You see, fighting is life-and-death to me. That's how I treat it. But the athletes we've been talking about take it a step further. Every competition, even the most banal, is viewed by them as life-and-death—and losing is death."

Myron nodded. He didn't buy it, but what the hell. Keep him talking. "I don't get something," he said. "If Jack has this special 'wanting,' why hasn't he ever won a professional tournament?"

"He lost it."

"The wanting?"

"Yes."

"When?"

"Twenty-three years ago."

"During the Open?"

"Yes," Win said again. "Most athletes lose it in a slow burnout. They grow weary or they win enough to quench whatever inferno rages in their bellies. But that was not the case with Jack. His fire was extinguished in one crisp, cold gust. You could almost see it. Twenty-three years ago. The sixteenth hole. The ball landing in the stone quarry. His eyes have never been the same."

"Until now," Myron added.

"Until now," Win agreed. "It took him twenty-three years, but he stoked the flames back to life."

They both drank. Win sipped. Myron guzzled. The chocolaty coldness felt wonderful sliding down his throat. "How long have you known Jack?" Myron asked.

"I met him when I was six years old. He was fifteen."

"Did he have the 'wanting' back then?"

Win smiled at the ceiling. "He would sooner carve out his own kidney with a grapefruit spoon than lose to someone on the golf course." He lowered his gaze to Myron. "Did Jack Coldren have the 'wanting'? He was the pure definition."

"Sounds like you admired him."

"I did."

"You don't anymore?"

"No."

"What made you change?"

"I grew up."

"Wow." Myron took another swig of Yoo-Hoo. "That's heavy."

Win chuckled. "You wouldn't understand."

"Try me."

Win put down the brandy snifter. He leaned forward very slowly. "What is so great about winning?"

"Pardon?"

"People love a winner. They look up to him. They admire—nay, revere—him. They use terms like *hero* and *courage* and *perseverance* to describe him. They want to be near him and touch him. They want to be like him."

Win spread his hands. "But why? What about the winner do we want to emulate? His ability to blind himself to anything but the pursuit of empty aggrandizement? His ego-inflating obsession with wearing a hunk of metal around his neck? His willingness to sacrifice anything, including people, in order to best another human being on a lump of AstroTurf for a cheesy statuette?" He looked up at Myron, his always serene face suddenly lost. "Why do we applaud this selfishness, this self-love?"

"Competitive drive isn't a bad thing, Win. You're talking about extremes."

"But it is the extremists we admire most. By its nature, what you call 'competitive drive' leads to extremism and destroys all in its path."

"You're being simplistic, Win."

"It is simple, my friend."

They both settled back. Myron stared up at the exposed beams. After some time, he said, "You have it wrong."

"How so?"

Myron wondered how to explain it. "When I played basketball," he began, "I mean, when I really got into it and reached these levels you're talking about—I barely thought about the score. I barely thought about my opponent or about beating somebody. I was alone. I was in the zone. This is going to sound stupid, but playing at the top of my game was almost Zen-like."

Win nodded. "And when did you feel this way?"

"Pardon?"

"When did you feel your most—to use your word—*Zen*?"

"I don't follow."

"Was it at practice? No. Was it during an unimportant game or when your team was up by thirty points? No. What brought you to this sweat-drenched state of Nirvana, my friend, was competition. The desire—the naked need—to defeat a top-level opponent."

Myron opened his mouth to counter. Then he stopped. Exhaustion was starting to take over. "I'm not sure I have an answer to that," he said. "At the end of the day, I like to win. I don't know why. I like ice cream too. I don't know why either."

Win frowned. "Impressive simile," he said flatly.

"Hey, it's late."

Myron heard a car pull up front. A young blond entered the room and smiled. Win smiled back. She bent down and kissed him. Win had no problem with that. Win was never outwardly rude to his dates. He was not the type to rush them out. He had no problem with them staying the night, if it made them happier. Some might mistake this for kindness or a tender spot in the soul. They'd be wrong. Win let them stay because they meant so little to him. They could never reach him. They could never touch him. So why not let them stay?

"That's my taxi," the blonde said.

Win's smile was blank.

"I had fun," she said.

Not even a blink.

"You can reach me through Amanda if you want"—she looked at Myron, then back at Win—"well, you know."

"Yes," Win said. "I know."

The young woman offered up an uncomfortable smile and left.

Myron watched, trying to keep his face from registering shock. A prostitute! Christ, she was a prostitute! He knew that Win had used them in the past—in the mid-eighties, he used to order in Chinese food from Hunan Grill and Asian prostitutes from the Noble House bordello for what he called "Chinese Night"—but to still partake, in this day and age?

Then Myron remembered the Chevy Nova and his whole body went cold.

He turned to his friend. They looked at each other. Neither one of them said anything.

"Moralizing," Win said. "How nice."

"I didn't say anything."

"Indeed." Win stood.

"Where are you going?"

"Out."

Myron felt his heart pound. "Mind if I go with you?"

"Yes."

"What car are you taking?"

Win did not bother responding. "Good night, Myron."

Myron's mind raced for solutions, but he knew it was hopeless. Win was going. There was no way to stop him.

Win stopped at the door and turned back to him. "One question, if I may."

Myron nodded, unable to speak.

"Was Linda Coldren the one who first contacted you?" Win asked.

"No," Myron said.

"Then who?"

"Your uncle Bucky."

Win arched an eyebrow. "And who suggested us to Bucky?"

Myron looked back at Win steadily, but he couldn't stop shaking. Win nodded and turned back to the door.

"Win?"

"Go to sleep, Myron."

11

yron did not go to sleep. He didn't even bother trying.

He sat in Win's chair and tried to read, but the words never registered. He was exhausted. He leaned back against the rich leather and waited. Hours passed. Disjointed images of Win's potential handiwork wrested free in a heavy spray of dark crimson. Myron closed his eyes and tried to ride it out.

At 3:30 A.M., Myron heard a car pull up. The ignition died. A key clicked in the door and then it swung open. Win stepped inside and looked at Myron with nary a trace of emotion.

"Good night," Win said.

He walked away. Myron heard the bedroom door close and let loose a held breath. Fine, he thought. He lifted himself into a standing position and made his way to his bedroom. He crawled under the sheets, but sleep still would not come. Black, opaque fear fluttered in his stomach. He had just begun to slide into true REM sleep when the bedroom door flew open.

"You're still asleep?" a familiar voice asked.

Myron managed to tear his eyes open. He was used to Esperanza Diaz barging into his office without knocking; he wasn't used to her doing it where he slept.

"What time is it?" he croaked.

"Six-thirty."

"In the morning?"

Esperanza gave him one of her patented glares, the one road crews tried to hire out to raze large rock formations. With one finger she tucked a few spare strands of her raven locks behind her ear. Her shimmering dark skin made you think of a Mediterranean cruise by moonlight, of clear waters and puffy-sleeved peasant blouses and olive groves.

"How did you get here?" he asked.

"Amtrak red-eye," she said.

Myron was still groggy. "Then what did you do? Catch a cab?"

"What are you, a travel agent? Yes, I took a cab."

"Just asking."

"The idiot driver asked me for the address three times. Guess he's not used to taking Hispanics into this neighborhood."

Myron shrugged. "Probably thought you were a domestic," he said.

"In *these* shoes?" She lifted her foot so he could see.

"Very nice." Myron adjusted himself in the bed, his body still craving sleep. "Not to belabor the point, but what exactly are you doing here?"

"I got some information on the old caddie."

"Lloyd Rennart?"

Esperanza nodded. "He's dead."

"Oh." Dead. As in dead end. Not that it had been much of a beginning. "You could have just called."

"There's more."

"Oh?"

"The circumstances surrounding his death are"—she stopped, bit her lower lip—"fuzzy."

Myron sat up a bit. "Fuzzy?"

"Lloyd Rennart apparently committed suicide eight months ago."

"How?"

"That's the fuzzy part. He and his wife were on vacation in a mountain range in Peru. He woke up one morning, wrote a brief note, then he jumped off a cliff of some kind."

"You're kidding."

"Nope. I haven't been able to get too many details yet. The *Philadelphia Daily News* just had a brief story on it." There was a hint of a smile. "But according to the article, the body had not yet been located."

Myron was starting to wake up in a big hurry. "What?"

"Apparently Lloyd Rennart took the plunge in a remote crevasse with no access. They may have located the body by now, but I couldn't find a follow-up article. None of the local papers carried an obituary."

Myron shook his head. No body. The questions that sprang to mind were obvious: could Lloyd Rennart still be alive? Did he fake his own death in order to plot out his revenge? Seemed a tad out there, but you never know. If he had, why would he have waited twenty-three years? True, the U.S. Open was back at Merion. True, that could make old wounds resurface. But still. "Weird," he said. He looked up at her. "You could have told me all this on the phone. You didn't have to come all the way down here."

"What the hell is the big deal?" Esperanza snapped. "I wanted to get out of the city for the weekend. I thought seeing the Open would be fun. You mind?"

"I was just asking."

"You're so nosy sometimes."

"Okay, okay." He held up his hands in mock surrender. "Forget I asked."

"Forgotten," she said. "You want to fill me in on what's going on?"

He told her about the Crusty Nazi at the mall and about losing the black-clad perpetrator.

When he finished, Esperanza shook her head. "Jesus," she said. "Without Win, you're hopeless."

Ms. Morale Booster.

"Speaking of Win," Myron said, "don't talk to him about the case."

"Why?"

"He's reacting badly."

She watched him closely. "How badly?"

"He went night visiting."

Silence.

"I thought he stopped doing that," she said.

"I thought so too."

"Are you sure?"

"There was a Chevy parked in the driveway," Myron said. "He took it out of here last night and didn't get back till three-thirty."

Silence. Win stored a bunch of old, unregistered Chevys. Disposable cars, he called them. Completely untraceable.

Esperanza's voice was soft. "You can't have it both ways, Myron."

"What are you talking about?"

"You can't ask Win to do it when it suits you, then get pissed off when he does it on his own."

"I never ask him to play vigilante."

"Yeah, you do. You involve him in violence. When it suits your needs, you unleash him. Like he's a weapon of some kind."

"It's not like that."

"It is like that," she said. "It is exactly like that. When Win goes out on these night errands, he doesn't hurt the innocent, does he?"

Myron considered the question. "No," he said.

"So what's the problem? He is just attacking a different type of guilty. He picks out the guilty instead of you."

Myron shook his head. "It's not the same thing."

"Because you judge?"

"I don't send him out to hurt people. I send him out to watch people or to back me up."

"I'm not sure I see the difference."

"Do you know what he does when he night visits, Esperanza? He walks through the worst neighborhoods he can find in the middle of the night. Old FBI buddies tell him where drug dealers or child pornographers or street gangs hang out—alleyways, abandoned buildings, whatever—and he goes strolling through those hellholes no cop would dare tread."

"Sounds like Batman," Esperanza countered.

"You don't think it's wrong?"

"Oh, I think it's wrong," she replied steadily. "But I'm not sure you do."

"What the hell is that supposed to mean?"

"Think about it," she said. "About why you're really upset."

Footsteps approached. Win stuck his head in the doorway. He was smiling like a guest star on the opening credits of the *Love Boat*. "Good morning, all," he said with far too much cheer. He bussed Esperanza's cheek. He was decked out in classic, though fairly understated, golf clothes. Ashworth shirt. Plain golf cap. Sky-blue pants with pleats.

"Will you be staying with us, Esperanza?" he asked in his most solicitous tone.

Esperanza looked at him, looked at Myron. Nodded.

"Wonderful. You can use the bedroom down the hall on the left." Win turned to Myron. "Guess what?"

"I'm all ears, Mr. Happy Face," Myron said.

"Crispin still wants to meet with you. It appears that your walking out last night actually made something of an impression on him." Big smile, spread hands. "The reluctant suitor approach. I must try it sometime."

Esperanza said, "Tad Crispin? *The* Tad Crispin?"

"The very," Win replied.

She gave Myron an approving look. "Wow."

"Indeed," Win said. "Well, I must be going. I'll see you at Merion. I'll be at the Lock-Horne tent most of the day." Renewing the smile. "Ta-ta."

Win started to leave, stopped, snapped his fingers. "I almost forgot." He tossed Myron a videotape. "Maybe this will save you some time."

The videotape landed on the bed. "Is this . . . ?"

"The bank security tape from First Philadelphia," Win said. "Six-eighteen on Thursday afternoon. As per your request." One more smile, one more wave. "Have a great day."

Esperanza watched him go. " 'Have a great day'?" she repeated.

Myron shrugged.

"Who the hell was that guy?" she asked.

"Wink Martindale," Myron said. "Come on. Let's go downstairs and watch this."

12

Linda Coldren opened the door before Myron knocked.

"What is it?" she asked.

Linda's face was drawn, accentuating the already high cheekbones. Her eyes had a lost and hollow look. She hadn't slept. The pressure was growing unbearable. The worrying. The not knowing. She was strong. She was trying to stand up to it. But her son's disappearance was beginning to gnaw away at her core.

Myron held up the videotape. "Do you have a VCR?" he asked.

In something of a daze, Linda Coldren led him to the same television he had seen her watching yesterday when they first met. Jack Coldren appeared from a back room, his golf bag on his shoulder. He, too, looked worn. There were sacks under his eyes, fleshy pouches like soft cocoons. Jack tried to toss up a welcoming smile, but it sputtered up like a lighter low on fluid.

"Hey, Myron."

"Hey, Jack."

"What's going on?"

Myron slid the tape into the opening. "Do you know anybody who lives on Green Acres Road?" he asked.

Jack and Linda looked at each other.

"Why do you want to know that?" Linda asked.

"Because last night I watched your house. I saw somebody crawl out a window."

"A window?" It was Jack. He lowered his eyebrows. "What window?"

"Your son's."

Silence.

Then Linda asked, "What does that have to do with Green Acres Road?"

"I followed whoever it was. He turned down Green Acres Road and disappeared—either into a house or into the woods."

Linda lowered her head. Jack stepped forward and spoke. "The Squires live on Green Acres Road," he said. "Chad's best friend Matthew."

Myron nodded. He was not surprised. He flicked on the television. "This is a bank security tape from First Philadelphia."

"How did you get it?" Jack asked.

"It's not important."

The front door opened and Bucky entered. The older man, dressed today in checked pants with a yellow-and-green top, stepped into the den doing his customary neck craning bit. "What's going on here?" he demanded.

Nobody replied.

"I said—"

"Just watch the screen, Dad," Linda interrupted.

"Oh," Bucky said softly, moving in closer.

Myron turned the channel to Three and hit the PLAY button. All eyes were on the screen. Myron had already seen the tape. He studied their faces instead, watching for reactions.

On the television, a black-and-white image appeared. The bank's driveway. The view was from up high and a bit distorted, a concave fish-eye effect to capture as much space as possible. There was no sound. Myron had the tape all cued up on the right spot. Almost immediately a car pulled into view. The camera was on the driver's side.

"It's Chad's car," Jack Coldren announced.

They watched in rapt silence as the car window lowered. The angle was a bit odd—above the car and from the machine's point of view—but there was no doubt. Chad Coldren was the driver. He leaned out the window and put his card in the ATM machine slot. His fingers tripped across the buttons like an experienced stenographer's.

Young Chad Coldren's smile was bright and happy.

When his fingers finished their little rumba, Chad settled back into the car to wait. He turned away from the camera for a moment. To the passenger seat. Someone was sitting next to Chad. Again Myron watched for a reaction. Linda, Jack, and Bucky all squinted, all trying to make out a face, but it was impossible. When Chad finally turned back to the camera, he was laughing. He pulled the money out, grabbed his card, leaned back into the car, closed the window, and drove off.

Myron switched off the VCR and waited. Silence flooded the room. Linda Coldren slowly lifted her head. She kept her expression steady, but her jaw trembled from being so set.

"There was another person in the car," Linda offered. "He could have had a gun on Chad or—"

"Stop it!" Jack shouted. "Look at his face, Linda! For crying out loud, just look at his goddamn smirking face!"

"I know my son. He wouldn't do this."

"You don't know him," Jack countered. "Face it, Linda. Neither one of us knows him."

"It's not what it looks like," Linda insisted, speaking more to herself than anyone in the room.

"No?" Jack gestured at the television, his face reddening. "Then how the hell do you explain what we just saw? Huh? He was laughing, Linda. He's having the time of his life at our expense." He stopped, struggled with something. "At my expense," he corrected himself.

Linda gave him a long look. "Go play, Jack."

"That's exactly what I am going to do."

He lifted his bag. His eyes met Bucky's. Bucky remained silent. A tear slid down the older man's cheek. Jack tore his gaze away and started for the door.

Myron called out, "Jack?"

Coldren stopped.

"It still might not be what it looks like," Myron said.

Again with the eyebrows. "What do you mean?"

"I traced the call you got last night," Myron explained. "It was made from a mall pay phone." He briefly filled them in on his visit to the Grand Mercado Mall and the Crusty Nazi. Linda's face kept slipping from hope to heartbreak and mostly confusion. Myron understood. She wanted her son to be safe. But at the same time, she did not want this to be some cruel joke. Tough mix.

"He is in trouble," Linda said as soon as he'd finished. "That proves it."

"That proves nothing," Jack replied in tired exasperation. "Rich kids hang out at malls and dress like punks too. He's probably a friend of Chad's."

Again Linda looked at her husband hard. Again she said in a measured tone, "Go play, Jack."

Jack opened his mouth to say something, then stopped. He shook his head, adjusted the bag on his shoulder, and left. Bucky crossed the room. He tried to hold his daughter, but she stiffened at his touch. She moved away, studying Myron's face.

"You think he's faking too," she said.

"Jack's explanation makes sense."

"So you're going to stop looking?"

"I don't know," Myron said.

She straightened her back. "Stay with it," she began, "and I promise to sign with you."

"Linda . . ."

"That's why you're here in the first place, right? You want my business. Well, here's the deal. You stay with me and I'll sign whatever you want. Hoax or no hoax. It'll be quite a coup, no? Signing the number one–ranked female golfer in the world?"

"Yes," Myron admitted. "It would be."

"So there you go." She stuck out her hand. "Do we have a deal?"

Myron kept his hands by his side. "Let me ask you something."

"What?"

"Why are you so sure it's not a hoax, Linda?"

"You think I'm being naive?"

"Not really," he said. "I just want to know what makes you so certain."

She lowered her hand and turned away from him. "Dad?"

Bucky seemed to snap out of a daze. "Hmm?"

"Would you mind leaving us alone for a minute?"

"Oh," Bucky said. Neck crane. Then another. Two of them back-to-back. Good thing he wasn't a giraffe. "Yes, well, I wanted to get to Merion anyway."

"You go ahead, Dad. I'll meet you there."

When they were alone, Linda Coldren began to pace the room. Myron was again awed by her looks—the paradoxical combination of beauty, strength and now delicacy. The strong, toned arms, yet the long, slender neck. The harsh, pointed features, yet the soft indigo eyes. Myron had heard beauty described as "seamless"; hers was quite the opposite.

"I'm not big on"—Linda Coldren made quote marks in the air with her fingers—"woman's intuition or any of that mother-knows-her-boy-best crap. But I know that my son is in danger. He wouldn't just disappear like this. No matter how it looks, that's not what happened."

Myron remained silent.

"I don't like asking for help. It's not my way—to depend on someone else. But this is a situation. . . . I'm scared. I've never felt fear like this in all of my life. It's all-consuming. It's suffocating. My son is in trouble and I can't do anything to help him. You want proof that this is not a hoax. I can't provide that. I just know. And I'm asking you to please help me."

Myron wasn't sure how to respond. Her argument came straight from the heart, *sans* facts or evidence. But that didn't make her suffering any less real. "I'll check out Matthew's house," he said finally. "Let's see what happens after that."

13

In the light of day, Green Acres Road was even more imposing. Both sides of the street were lined with ten-foot-high shrubs so thick that Myron couldn't tell how thick. He parked his car outside a wrought iron gate and approached an intercom. He pressed a button and waited. There were several surveillance cameras. Some remained steady. Some whirred slowly from side to side. Myron spotted motion detectors, barbed wire, Dobermans.

A rather elaborate fortress, he thought.

A voice as impenetrable as the shrubs came through the speaker. "May I help you?"

"Good morning," Myron said, offering up a friendly-but-not-a-salesman smile to the nearest camera. Talking to a camera. He felt like he was on *Nightline*. "I'm looking for Matthew Squires."

Pause. "Your name, sir?"

"Myron Bolitar."

"Is Master Squires expecting you?"

"No." *Master* Squires?

"Then you do not have an appointment?"

An appointment to see a sixteen-year-old? Who is this kid, Doogie Howser? "No, I'm afraid I don't."

"May I ask the purpose of your visit?"

"To speak to Matthew Squires." Mr. Vague.

"I am afraid that will not be possible at this time," the voice said.

"Will you tell him it involves Chad Coldren?"

Another pause. Cameras pirouetted. Myron looked around. All the lenses were aiming down from up high, glaring at him like hostile space aliens or lunchroom monitors.

"In what way does it involve Master Coldren?" the voice asked.

Myron squinted into a camera. "May I ask with whom I am speaking?" No reply.

Myron waited a beat, then said, "You're supposed to say, 'I am the great and powerful Oz.'"

"I am sorry, sir. No one is admitted without an appointment. Please have a nice day."

"Wait a second. Hello? Hello?" Myron pressed the button again. No reply. He leaned on it for several seconds. Still nothing. He looked up into the camera and gave his best caring-homespun-family-guy smile. Very Tom Brokaw. He tried a small wave. Nothing. He took a small step backward and gave a great big Jack Kemp fake-throwing-a-football wave. Nada.

He stood there for another minute. This was indeed odd. A sixteen-year-old with this kind of security? Something was not quite kosher. He pressed the button one more time. When no one responded he looked into the camera, put a thumb in either ear, wiggled his fingers and stuck out his tongue.

When in doubt, be mature.

Back at his car, Myron picked up the car phone and dialed his friend Sheriff Jake Courter.

"Sheriff's office."

"Hey, Jake. It's Myron."

"Fuck. I knew I shouldn't have come in on Saturday."

"Ooo, I'm wounded. Seriously, Jake, do they still call you the Henny Youngman of law enforcement?"

Heavy sigh. "What the fuck do you want, Myron? I just came in to get a little paperwork done."

"No rest for those vigilantly pursuing peace and justice for the common man."

"Right," Jake said. "This week, I went out on a whole twelve calls. Guess how many of them were for false burglar alarms?"

"Thirteen."

"Pretty close."

For more than twenty years, Jake Courter had been a cop in several of the country's meanest cities. He'd hated it and craved a quieter life. So Jake, a rather large black man, resigned from the force and moved to the picturesque (read: lily-white) town of Reston, New Jersey. Looking for a cushy job, he ran for sheriff. Reston was a college (read: liberal) town, and thus Jake played up his—as he put it—"blackness" and won easily.

The white man's guilt, Jake had told Myron. The best vote-getter this side of Willie Horton.

"Miss the excitement of the big city?" Myron asked.

"Like a case of herpes," Jake countered. "Okay, Myron, you've done the charm thing on me. I'm like Play-Doh in your paws now. What do you want?"

"I'm in Philly for the U.S. Open."

"That's golf, right?"

"Yeah, golf. And I wanted to know if you've heard of a guy name Squires."

Pause. Then: "Oh, shit."

"What?"

"What the fuck are you involved in now?"

"Nothing. It's just that he's got all this weird security around his house—"

"What the fuck are you doing by his house?"

"Nothing."

"Right," Jake said. "Guess you were just strolling by."

"Something like that."

"Nothing like that." Jake sighed. Then: "Ah what the hell, it ain't on my beat anymore. Squires. Reginald Squires aka Big Blue."

Myron made a face. "Big Blue?"

"Hey, all gangsters need a nickname. Squires is known as Big Blue. Blue, as in blue blood."

"Those gangsters," Myron said. "Pity they don't channel their creativity into honest marketing."

" 'Honest marketing,' " Jake repeated. "Talk about your basic oxymoron. Anyway Squires got a kiloton of family dough and all this blue-blood breeding and schooling and shit."

"So what's he doing keeping such bad company?"

"You want the simple answer? The son of a bitch is a serious wacko. Gets his jollies hurting people. Kinda like Win."

"Win doesn't get his jollies hurting people."

"If you say so."

"If Win hurts someone, there's a reason. To prevent them from doing it again or to punish or something."

"Sure, whatever," Jake said. "Kinda touchy though, aren't we, Myron?"

"It's been a long day."

"It's only nine in the morning."

Myron said, "For what breeds time but two hands on a clock?"

"Who said that?"

"No one. I just made it up."

"You should consider writing greeting cards."

"So what is Squires into, Jake?"

"Want to hear something funny? I'm not sure. Nobody is. Drugs and prostitution. Shit like that. But very upscale. Nothing very well organized or anything. It's more like he plays at it, you know? Like he gets involved in whatever he thinks will give him a thrill, then dumps it."

"How about kidnapping?"

Brief pause. "Oh shit, you are involved in something again, aren't you?"

"I just asked you if Squires was into kidnapping."

"Oh. Right. Like it's a hypothetical question. Kinda like, 'If a bear shits in the forest and no one is around, does it still reek'?"

"Precisely. Does kidnapping reek like his kind of thing?"

"Hell if I know. The guy is a major league loon, no question. He blends right into all that snobbish bullshit—the boring parties, the shitty food, the laughing at jokes that aren't remotely funny, the talking with the same boring people about the same boring worthless bullshit—"

"It sounds like you really admire them."

"Just my point, my friend. They got it all, right? On the outside. Money, big homes, fancy clubs. But they're all so fucking boring—shit, I'd kill myself. Makes me wonder if maybe Squires feels that way too, you know?"

"Uh-huh," Myron said. "And Win is the scary one here, right?"

Jake laughed. "Touché. But to answer your question, I don't know if Squires would be into kidnapping. Wouldn't surprise me though."

Myron thanked him and hung up. He looked up. At least a dozen security cameras lined the top of the shrubs like tiny sentinels.

What now?

For all he knew, Chad Coldren was laughing his ass off, watching him on one of those security cameras. This whole thing could be an exercise in pure futility. Of course, Linda Coldren had promised to be a client. Much as he didn't want to admit it to himself, the idea was not wholly unpleasant. He considered the possibility and started to smile. If he could also somehow land Tad Crispin . . .

Yo, Myron, a kid may be in serious trouble.

Or, more likely, a spoiled brat or neglected adolescent—take your pick—is playing hooky and having some fun at his parents' expense.

So the question remained: What now?

He thought again about the videotape of Chad at the ATM machine. He didn't go into details with the Coldrens, but it bothered him. Why there? Why that particular ATM machine? If the kid was running away or hiding out, he might have to pick up money. Fine and dandy, that made sense.

But why would he do it at Porter Street?

Why not do it at a bank closer to home? And equally important, what was Chad Coldren doing in that area in the first place? There was nothing there. It wasn't a stop between highways or anything like that. The only thing in that neighborhood that would require cash was the Court Manor Inn. Myron again remembered *motelier extraordinaire* Stuart Lipwitz's attitude and wondered.

He started the car. It might be something. Worth looking into, at any rate.

Of course, Stuart Lipwitz had made it abundantly clear that he would not talk. But Myron thought he had just the tool to make him change his mind.

14

Smile!"

The man did not smile. He quickly shifted the car in reverse and backed out. Myron shrugged and lowered the camera. It was on a neck strap and bounced lightly against his chest. Another car approached. Myron lifted the camera again.

"Smile!" Myron repeated.

Another man. Another no smile. This guy managed to duck down before shifting his car into reverse.

"Camera shy," Myron called out to him. "Nice to see in this age of paparazzi overkill."

It didn't take long. Myron had been on the sidewalk in front of the Court Manor Inn for less than five minutes when he spotted Stuart Lipwitz sprinting toward him. Big Stu was in full custom—gray tails, wide tie, a concierge key pin in the suit's lapel. Gray tails at a no-tell motel. Like a maître d' at Burger King. Watching Stu move closer, a Pink Floyd song came to mind: *Hello, hello, hello, is there anybody out there?* David Bowie joined in: *Ground control to Major Tom.*

Ah, the seventies.

"You there," he called out.

"Hi, Stu."

No smile this time. "This is private property," Stuart Lipwitz said, a little out of breath. "I must ask you to remove yourself immediately."

"I hate to disagree with you, Stu, but I am on a public sidewalk. I got every right to be here."

Stuart Lipwitz stammered, then flapped his arms in frustration. With the tails, the movement kind of reminded Myron of a bat. "But you can't just stand there and take pictures of my clientele," he semi-whined.

" 'Clientele,' " Myron repeated. "Is that a new euphemism for *john*?"

"I'll call the police."

"Ooooo. Stop scaring me like that."

"You are interfering with my business."

"And you are interfering with mine."

Stuart Lipwitz put his hands on his hips and tried to look threatening. "This is the last time I'll ask you nicely. Leave the premises."

"That wasn't nice."

"Excuse me?"

"You said it was the last time you'd ask me nicely," Myron explained. "Then you said, 'Leave the premises.' You didn't say *please*. You didn't say, 'Kindly leave the premises.' Where's the nice in that?"

"I see," Lipwitz said. Beads of sweat dotted his face. It was hot and the man was, after all, in tails. "Please kindly leave the premises."

"Nope. But now, at least, you're a man of your word."

Stuart Lipwitz took several deep breaths. "You want to know about the boy, don't you? The one in the picture."

"You bet."

"And if I tell you if he was here, will you leave?"

"Much as it would pain me to leave this quaint locale, I would somehow tear myself away."

"That, sir, is blackmail."

Myron looked at him. "I would say '*blackmail* is such an ugly word,' but that would be too cliché. So instead I'll just say 'Yup.' "

"But"—Lipwitz started stammering—"that's against the law!"

"As opposed to, say, prostitution and drug dealing and whatever other sleazy activity goes on in this fleabag?"

Stuart Lipwitz's eyes widened. "Fleabag? This is the Court Manor Inn, sir. We are a respectable—"

"Stuff it, Stu. I got pictures to take." Another car pulled up. Gray Volvo station wagon. Nice family car. A man about fifty years old was neatly attired in a business suit. The young girl in the passenger seat must have shopped—as the mall girls had recently taught him—at Sluts "R" Us.

Myron smiled and leaned toward the window. "Whoa, sir, vacationing with your daughter?"

The man splashed on a classic deer-caught-in-the-headlights look. The young prostitute whooped with laughter. "Hey, Mel, he thinks I'm your daughter!" She whooped again.

Myron raised the camera. Stuart Lipwitz tried to step in his way, but Myron swept him away with his free hand. "It's Souvenir Day at the

Court Manor," Myron said. "I can put the picture on a coffee mug if you'd like. Or maybe a decorative plate?"

The man in the business suit reversed the car. They were gone several seconds later.

Stuart Lipwitz's face reddened. He made two fists. Myron looked at him. "Now Stuart . . ."

"I have powerful friends," he said.

"Ooooo. I'm getting scared again."

"Fine. Be that way." Stuart turned away and stormed up the drive. Myron smiled. The kid was a tougher nut to crack than he'd anticipated, and he really didn't want to do this all day. But let's face it: There were no other leads and besides, playing with Big Stu was fun.

Myron waited for more customers. He wondered what Stu was up to. Something frantic, no doubt. Ten minutes later, a canary yellow Audi pulled up and a large black man slid out. The black man was maybe an inch shorter than Myron, but he was built. His chest could double as a jai alai wall and his legs resembled the trunks of redwoods. He glided when he moved—not the bulky moves one usually associated with the over-muscled.

Myron did not like that.

The black man had sunglasses on and wore a red Hawaiian shirt with blue jean shorts. His most noticeable feature was his hair. The kinks had been slicked straight and parted on the side, like old photographs of Nat King Cole.

Myron pointed at the top of the man's head. "Is that hard to do?" he asked.

"What?" the black man said. "You mean the hair?"

Myron nodded. "Keeping it straight like that."

"Nah, not really. Once a week I go to a guy named Ray. In an old-fashioned barbershop, as a matter of fact. The kind with the pole in front and everything." His smile was almost wistful. "Ray takes care of it for me. Also gives me a great shave. With hot towels and everything." The man stroked his face for emphasis.

"Looks smooth," Myron said.

"Hey, thanks. Nice of you to say. I find it relaxing, you know? Doing something just for me. I think it's important. To relieve the stress."

Myron nodded. "I hear you."

"Maybe I'll give you Ray's number. You could stop by and check it out."

"Ray," Myron repeated. "I'd like that."

The black man stepped closer. "Seems we have a little situation here, Mr. Bolitar."

"How did you know my name?"

He shrugged. Behind the sunglasses, Myron sensed that he was being sized up. Myron was doing the same. Both were trying to be subtle. Both knew exactly what the other was doing.

"I'd really appreciate it if you would leave," he said very politely.

"I'm afraid I can't do that," Myron said. "Even though you did ask nicely."

The black man nodded. He kept his distance. "Let's see if we can work something out here, okay?"

"Okeydokey."

"I got a job to do here, Myron. You can appreciate that, can't you?"

"Sure can," Myron said.

"And so do you."

"That's right."

The black man took off his sunglasses and put them in his shirt pocket. "Look, I know you won't be easy. And you know I won't be easy. If push comes to shove, I don't know which one of us will win."

"I will," Myron said. "Good always triumphs over evil."

The man smiled. "Not in this neighborhood."

"Good point."

"I'm also not sure it's worth it to either one of us to find out. I think we're both probably past the proving-himself, macho-bullshit stage."

Myron nodded. "We're too mature."

"Right."

"It seems then," Myron continued, "that we've hit an impasse."

"Guess so," the black man agreed. "Of course, I could always take out a gun and shoot you."

Myron shook his head. "Not over something this small. Too many repercussions involved."

"Yeah. I didn't think you'd go for it, but I had to give it a whirl. You never know."

"You're a pro," Myron agreed. "You'd feel remiss if you didn't at least try. Hell, I'd have felt cheated."

"Glad you understand."

"Speaking of which," Myron said, "aren't you a tad high-level to be dealing with this situation?"

"Can't say I disagree." The black man walked closer to Myron. Myron felt his muscles tighten; a not-unpleasant anticipatory chill steeled him.

"You look like a guy who can keep his mouth shut," the man said.

Myron said nothing. Proving the point.

"The kid you had in that picture, the one that got Leona Helmsley's panties in a bunch? He was here."

"When?"

The black man shook his head. "That's all you get. I'm being very generous. You wanted to know if the kid was here. The answer is yes."

"Nice of you," Myron said.

"I'm just trying to make it simple. Look, we both know that Lipwitz is a dumb kid. Acts like this urinal is the Beverly Wilshire. But the people who come here, they don't want that. They want to be invisible. They don't even want to look at themselves, you know what I'm saying?"

Myron nodded.

"So I gave you a freebie. The kid in the picture was here."

"Is he still here?"

"You're pushing me, Myron."

"Just tell me that."

"No. He only stayed that one night." He spread his hands. "Now you tell me, Myron. Am I being fair with you?"

"Very."

He nodded. "Your turn."

"I guess there's no way you'll tell me who you're working for."

The black man made a face. "Nice meeting you, Myron."

"Same here."

They shook hands. Myron got into his car and drove away.

He had almost reached Merion when the cellular rang. He picked up and said hello.

"Is this, like, Myron?"

Mall girl. "Hi, yes. Actually this is Myron, not just like him."

"Huh?"

"Never mind. What's up?"

"That skank you were, like, looking for last night?"

"Right."

"He's, like, back at the mall."

"Where at the mall?"

"The food court. He's on line at the McDonald's."

Myron spun the car around and hit the gas pedal.

15

The Crusty Nazi was still there.

He sat at a corner table by himself, downing a burger of some sort like it had personally offended him. The girls were right. *Skank* was the only word to describe him, even though Myron didn't know what the word meant or if it even existed. The punk's face was aiming for tough-guy-unshaven, but a lack of testosterone made it land far closer to upkempt-adolescent-Hasid. He wore a black baseball cap with a skull and crossbones decal. His ripped white T-shirt was rolled all the way up to reveal milky, reedy arms, one with a swastika tattoo. Myron shook his head. Swastika. The kid was too old to be so utterly clueless.

The Crusty Nazi took another vicious bite, clearly furious with his burger now. The mall girls were there, pointing toward Crusty like Myron might not know which guy they'd been talking about. Myron signaled them to stop with a shushing finger at his lips. They obeyed, overcompensating by engaging in a too-loud, too-casual conversation, sliding furtive-to-the-point-of-totally-obvious glances in his direction. Myron looked away.

The Crusty Nazi finished his burger and stood. Good timing. As advertised, Crusty was very skinny. The girls were right—the boy had no ass. None at all. Myron couldn't tell if the kid was going for that too-big-jeans look or if it was because he lacked a true backside, but every few steps, Crusty paused to hitch up the pants. Myron suspected a bit of both.

He followed him outside into the blazing sun. Hot. Damn hot. Myron felt almost a nostalgic longing for the omnipresent mall air-conditioning. Crusty strutted cool-like into the lot. Going to his car, no doubt. Myron veered to the right so as to get ready to follow. He slid into his Ford Taurus (read: Chick Trawler) and started up the engine.

He slowly cruised the lot and spotted Crusty heading way out to the last row of cars. Only two vehicles were parked out there. One was a silver Cadillac Seville. The other was a pickup truck with those semi-monster wheels, a Confederate flag decal, and the words BAD TO THE BONE painted on the side. Using his years of investigative know-how, Myron deduced that the pickup truck was probably Crusty's vehicle. Sure enough, Crusty opened the door and hopped up and in. Amazing. Sometimes Myron's powers of deduction bordered on the psychic. Maybe he should get a 900 line like Jackie Stallone.

Tailing the pickup truck was hardly a challenge. The vehicle stuck out like a golfer's clothing in a monastery, and El Crust-ola wasn't heavy on the gas pedal. They drove for about half an hour. Myron had no idea where they were going, but up ahead he recognized Veterans Stadium. He'd gone with Win to several Eagles games there. Win always had seats on the fifty-yard line, lower tier. Being an old stadium, the "luxury" skyboxes at the Vet were too high up; Win did not care for them. So he chose instead to sit with the masses. Big of him.

About three blocks before the stadium, Crusty pulled down a side road. He threw his pickup into park and got out running. Myron once again debated calling Win for backup, but it was pointless. Win was at Merion. His phone would be off. He wondered again about last night and about Esperanza's accusations this morning. Maybe she was right. Maybe he was, at least partially, responsible for what Win did. But that wasn't the point. He knew that now. The truth, the one that scared Esperanza too, was far clearer:

Maybe Myron didn't care so much.

You read the papers and you watch the news and you see what Myron has seen and your humanity, your basic faith in human beings, begins to look frighteningly Pollyanna. That was what was really eating away at him—not that he was repulsed by what Win did, but that it really didn't bother him that much.

Win had an eerie way of seeing the world in black and white; lately, Myron had found his own gray areas blackening. He didn't like that. He did not like the change that experience—seeing the cruelty man inflicts on man—was forcing upon him. He tried to hold on to his old values, but the rope was getting awfully slick. And why was he holding on, anyway? Was it because he truly believed in these values, or because he liked himself more as a person who believed?

He didn't know anymore.

He should have brought a gun. Stupid. Still he was only following some grunge-ball. Of course, even a grunge-ball could fire a gun and kill him. But what choice did he have? Should he call the police? Well, that would appear a bit extreme based on what he had. Come back later with a firearm of some sort? By that time, Crusty could be gone—along with Chad Coldren maybe.

Nope, he had to follow. He'd just be careful.

Myron was not sure what to do. He stopped the car at the end of the block and got out. The street was crowded with low-rise brick dwellings that all looked the same. At one time, this might have been a nice area, but now the neighborhood looked like a man who'd lost his job and stopped bathing. There was an overgrown, faded quality to it, like a garden that no one bothered to tend anymore.

Crusty turned down an alleyway. Myron followed. Lots of plastic garbage bags. Lots of rusted fire escapes. Four legs stuck out of a refrigerator box. Myron heard snoring. At the end of the alley, Crusty turned right. Myron trailed slowly. Crusty had gone into what looked like an abandoned building through a fire door. There was no knob or anything, but the door was slightly ajar. Myron reached in with his fingers and pried it open.

As soon as he crossed the musty threshold, Myron heard a primal scream. Crusty. Right in front of him. Something swung toward Myron's face. Fast reflexes paid off. Myron managed to duck enough so that the iron bar only clipped his shoulder blade. A quick flash of pain bolted down his arm. Myron dropped to the ground. He rolled across the cement floor and stood back up.

There were three of them now. All armed with crowbars or tire irons. All with shaved heads and tattooed swastikas. They were like sequels to the same awful movie. The Crusty Nazi was the original. Beneath the Planet of Crusty Nazi—the one on his left—was smiling with idiotic glee. The one on his right—Escape from the Planet of Crusty Nazi—looked a bit more frightened. The weak link, Myron thought.

"Changing a tire?" Myron asked.

The Crusty Nazi slapped the tire iron against his palm for emphasis. "Gonna flatten yours."

Myron raised his hand in front of him with the palm facing down. He shook it back and forth and said, "Eh."

"Why the fuck you following me, asshole?"

"Me?"

"Yeah, you. Why the fuck you following me?"

"Who says I'm following you?"

There was momentary confusion on Crusty's face. Then: "You think I'm fucking stupid or something?"

"No, I think you're Mr. Mensa."

"Mister what?"

Beneath the Planet of Crusty Nazi said, "He's just fucking with you, man."

"Yeah," Escape chimed in. "Fucking with you."

Crusty's wet eyes bulged out. "Yeah? Is that what you're doing, asshole? You fucking with me, huh? Is that what you're doing? Fucking with me?"

Myron looked at him. "Can we move on please?"

Beneath said, "Let's fuck him up a little. Soften his ass up."

Myron knew that three of them were probably not experienced fighters, but he also knew that three armed men beat one good man on almost any given day. They were also a bit too jittery, their eyes as glazed as morning doughnuts. They were constantly sniffing and rubbing their noses.

Two words: Coked up. Or Nose Candy. Or Toot Sweet. Take your pick.

Myron's best chance was to confuse and strike. Risky. You wanted to piss them off, to upset their already-tipsy equilibrium. But at the same time, you wanted to control it, to know when to back off a bit. A delicate balance requiring Myron Bolitar, darling of the high wire, to perform high above the crowd without the benefit of a safety net.

Once again Crusty asked, "Why the fuck you following me, asshole?"

"Maybe I'm just attracted to you," Myron said. "Even if you don't have an ass."

Beneath started cackling. "Oh man, oh man, let's fuck him up. Let's fuck him up good."

Myron tried to give them the tough-guy look. Some mistook this for constipation, but he was getting better at it. Practice. "I wouldn't do that if I were you."

"Oh no?" It was Crusty. "Give me one good reason why we don't just fuck you up. Give me one good reason why I don't break every fucking rib in your body with this." He raised the tire iron. In case Myron thought he was being too subtle.

"You asked before if I thought you were stupid," Myron said.

"Yeah, so?"

"So do you think I'm stupid? Do you think somebody who meant you harm would be dumb enough to follow you in here—knowing what was about to go down?"

That made all three of them pause.

"I followed you," Myron continued, "as a test."

"What the fuck you talking about?"

"I work for certain people. We won't mention names." Mostly, Myron thought, because he didn't know what the hell he was talking about. "Let's just say they are in a business you guys frequent."

"Frequent?" More nose rubbing. Toot, sweet, toot, sweet.

"Frequent," Myron repeated. "As in occurring or appearing quite often or at close intervals. Frequent."

"What?"

Jesus. "My employer," Myron said, "he needs someone to handle certain territory. Somebody new. Somebody who wants to make ten percent on sales and get all the free blow they can."

Eyes went buggy.

Beneath turned to Crusty. "You hear that, man?"

"Yeah, I hear him."

"Shit, we don't get no commission from Eddie," Beneath went on. "The fucker is so small-time." He gestured at Myron with the tire iron. "This guy, man, look how fucking old he is. He's gotta be working for somebody with juice."

"Got to be," Escape added.

The Crusty One hesitated, squinted suspicion. "How did you find out about us?"

Myron shrugged. "Word gets around." Shovel, shovel.

"So you was just following me for some kinda fucking test?"

"Right."

"Just came to the mall and decided to follow me?"

"Something like that."

Crusty smiled. He looked at Escape and at Beneath. His grip on the tire iron tightened. Uh-oh. "Then how the fuck come you were asking about me last night, huh? How come you want to know about a call I made?"

Uh-oh.

Crusty stepped closer, eyes aglow.

Myron raised his hand. "The answer is simple." They all hesitated. Myron took advantage. His foot moved like a piston, shooting out and landing squarely on the knee of the unprepared Escape. Escape fell. Myron was already running.

"Get the fucker!"

They chased, but Myron had already slammed his shoulder into the fire door. The "macho-bullshit" part of him, as his friend at the Court Manor Inn had described it, wanted to try to take them on, but he knew that would be foolhardy. They were armed. He wasn't.

By the time Myron reached the end of the alley, his lead was only about ten yards. He wondered if he'd have enough time to open his car door and get in. No choice. He'd have to try.

He grabbed the handle and swung the door open. He was sliding in when a tire iron whacked his shoulder. Pain erupted. He kept rolling, closing the door. A hand grabbed it, offered resistance. Myron used his weight and leaned into the pull.

His window exploded.

Glass tinkled down into his face. Myron kicked his heel through the open window and hit face. The grip on the door released. He already had the key out and in the ignition. He turned it as the other car window exploded. Crusty leaned into the car, his eyes blazing with fury.

"Motherfucker, you're gonna die!"

The tire iron was heading toward his face again. Myron blocked it. From behind him, he felt a sharp blow connect with his lower neck. Numbness ensued. Myron shifted into reverse and flew out of the spot, tires squealing. Crusty tried to leap into the car through the broken window. Myron elbowed him in the nose and Crusty's grip eased. He fell hard to the pavement, but then he jumped right back up. That was the problem with fighting cokeheads. Pain often does not register.

All three men ran for the pickup, but Myron already had too big a lead. The battle was over. For now.

16

Myron called in the pickup truck's license plate number, but that was a dead end. The plate had expired four years ago. Crusty must have taken it off a car in a dump or something. Not uncommon. Even petty crooks knew enough not to use their real plates when committing a traceable crime.

He circled back and checked the inside of the building for clues. Bent syringes and broken vials and empty bags of Doritos lay scattered about the cement. There was also an empty garbage can. Myron shook his head. Bad enough being a drug dealer. But a litterbug?

He looked around a bit more. The building was abandoned and half–burned out. There was no one inside. And no clues.

Okay, so what did this all mean? Were the three cokeheads the kidnappers? Myron had a hard time picturing it. Cokeheads break into houses. Cokeheads jump people in alleyways. Cokeheads attack with tire irons. Cokeheads, by and large, do not plan elaborate kidnappings.

But on the other hand, how elaborate was this kidnapping? The first two times the kidnapper called, he didn't even know how much money to extort. Wasn't that a little odd? Could it be that all this was merely the work of some out-of-their-league crusty cokeheads?

Myron got into his car and headed toward Win's house. Win had plenty of vehicles. He'd switch for a car without smashed windows. The residual damage to his body seemed to be clearing up. A bruise or two but nothing broken. None of the blows had landed flush, except the ones to his car windows.

He ran several possibilities through his head and eventually managed to come up with a pretty decent scenario. Let's say that for some reason

Chad Coldren decided to check into the Court Manor Inn. Maybe to spend some time with a girl. Maybe to buy some drugs. Maybe because he enjoyed the friendly service. Whatever. As per the bank surveillance camera, Chad grabbed some dough at a local ATM. Then he checked in for the night. Or the hour. Or whatever.

Once at the Court Manor Inn, something went awry. Stu Lipwitz's denials notwithstanding, the Court Manor is a sleazy joint patronized by sleazy people. It wouldn't be hard to get in trouble there. Maybe Chad Coldren tried to buy drugs from Crusty. Maybe he witnessed a crime. Maybe the kid just talked too much and some nasty people realized that he came from money. Whatever. The life orbits of Chad Coldren and the Crusty Nazi's crew dovetailed. The end result was a kidnapping.

It kinda fit.

The key word here: *kinda*.

On the road toward Merion, Myron helped deflate his own scenario with several well-placed puncture holes. First of all, the timing. Myron had been convinced that the kidnapping had something to do with Jack's return to playing the U.S. Open at Merion. But in his Crusty-orbit scenario, the nagging timing question had to be written off as mere coincidence. Okay, maybe Myron could live with that. But then how, for example, had the Crusty Nazi—stationed at a mall pay phone—known that Esme Fong was in the Coldren house? How did the man who climbed out the window and disappeared on Green Acres Road—a person Myron had been sure was either Matthew Squires or Chad Coldren—fit into all this? Was the well-shielded Matthew Squires in cahoots with the Crusties? Or was it just a coincidence that the window man disappeared down Green Acres Road?

The scenario balloon was going *ssssss* in a very big way.

By the time Myron got to Merion, Jack Coldren was on the fourteenth hole. His partner for today's round was none other than Tad Crispin. No surprise there. First place and second place were normally the final twosome of the day.

Jack was still playing well, though not spectacularly. He'd lost only one stroke off his lead, remaining a very comfortable eight strokes ahead of Tad Crispin. Myron trudged toward the fourteenth green. Green—that word again. Everything was so dang green. The grass and trees, naturally, but also tents, overhangs, scoreboards, the many television towers and scaffolds—everything was lush green to blend in with the picturesque natural surroundings, except, of course, for the sponsors' boards, which drew the eye with all the subtlety of Vegas hotel signs. But hey, the sponsors paid Myron's salary. Be kinda hypocritical to complain.

"Myron, sweetheart, get your wiggly ass over here."

Norm Zuckerman beckoned Myron forward with a big wave. Esme Fong stood next to him. "Over here," he said.

"Hey, Norm," Myron said. "Hi, Esme."

"Hi, Myron," Esme said. She was dressed a bit more casual today, but she still clutched at her briefcase like it was a favorite stuffed animal.

Norm threw his arm around Myron's back, draping the hand over the sore shoulder. "Myron, tell me the truth here. The absolute truth. I want the truth, okay?"

"The truth?"

"Very funny. Just tell me this. Nothing more, just this. Am I not a fair man? The truth, now. Am I a fair man?"

"Fair," Myron said.

"Very fair, am I right? I am a very fair man."

"Let's not push it, Norm."

Norm put up both hands, palms out. "Fine, be that way. I'm fair. Good enough, I'll take it." He looked over toward Esme Fong. "Keep in mind, Myron is my adversary. My worst enemy. We're always on opposite sides. Yet he is willing to admit that I'm a fair man. We straight on that?"

Esme rolled her eyes. "Yes, Norm, but you're preaching to the converted. I already told you that I agreed with you on this—"

"Whoa," Norm said, as though reining in a frisky pony. "Just hold the phone a sec, because I want Myron's opinion too. Myron, here's the deal. I bought a golf bag. Just one. I wanted to test it out. Cost me fifteen grand for the year."

Buying a golf bag meant pretty much what it said. Norm Zuckerman had bought the rights to advertise on a golf bag. In other words, he put a Zoom logo on it. Most of the golf bags were bought by the big golf companies—Ping, Titleist, Golden Bear, that kind of thing. But more and more often, companies that had nothing to do with golf advertised on the bags. McDonald's, for example. Spring-Air mattresses. Even Pennzoil oil. Pennzoil. Like someone goes to a golf tournament, sees the Pennzoil logo, and buys a can of oil.

"So?" Myron said.

"So, look at it!" Norm pointed at a caddie. "I mean, just look at it!"

"Okay, I'm looking."

"Tell me, Myron, do you see a Zoom logo?"

The caddie held the golf bag. Like on every golf bag, there were towels draped over the top in order to clean off the clubs.

Norm Zuckerman spoke in a first-grade–teacher singsong. "You can answer orally, Myron, by uttering the syllable 'no.' Or if that's too taxing on your limited vocabulary, you can merely shake your head from side to side like this." Norm demonstrated.

"It's under the towel," Myron said.

Norm dramatically put his hand to his ear. "Pardon?"

"The logo is under the towel."

"No shit it's under the towel!" Norm railed. Spectators turned and glared at the crazy man with the long hair and heavy beard. "What good does that do me, huh? When I film an advertisement for TV, what good would it do me if they stick a towel in front of the camera? When I pay all those schmucks a zillion dollars to wear my sneakers, what good would it do me if they wrapped their feet in towels? If every billboard I had was covered with a great big towel—"

"I get the picture, Norm."

"Good. I'm not paying fifteen grand for some idiot caddie to cover my logo. So I go over to the idiot caddie and I kindly tell him to move the towel away from my logo and the son of a bitch gives me this look. This look, Myron. Like I'm some brown stain he couldn't rinse out of the toilet. Like I'm this little ghetto Jew who's gonna take his goy crap."

Myron looked over at Esme. Esme smiled and shrugged.

"Nice talking to you, Norm," Myron said.

"What? You don't think I'm right?"

"I see your point."

"So if it was your client, what would you do?"

"Make sure the caddie kept the logo in plain view."

"Exactamundo." He swung his arm back around Myron's shoulder and lowered his head conspiratorially. "So what's going on with you and golf, Myron?" he whispered.

"What do you mean?"

"You're not a golfer. You don't have any golf clients. All of a sudden I see you with my very own eyes closing in on Tad Crispin—and now I hear you're hanging out with the Coldrens."

"Who told you that?"

"Word gets around. I'm a man with tremendous sources. So what's the deal? Why the sudden interest in golf?"

"I'm a sports agent, Norm. I try to represent athletes. Golfers are athletes. Sort of."

"Okay, but what's up with the Coldrens?"

"What do you mean?"

"Look, Jack and Linda are lovely people. Connected, if you know what I mean."

"I don't know what you mean."

"LBA represents Linda Coldren. Nobody leaves LBA. You know that. They're too big. Jack, well, Jack hasn't done anything in so long, he hasn't even bothered with an agent. So what I'm trying to figure out is, why are the Coldrens suddenly hot to trot with you?"

"Why do you want to figure that out?"

Norm put his hand on his chest. "Why?"

"Yeah, why would you care?"

"Why?" Norm repeated, incredulous now. "I'll tell you why. Because of you, Myron. I love you, you know that. We're brothers. Tribe members. I want nothing but the best for you. Hand to God, I mean that. You ever need a recommendation, I'll give it to you, you know that."

"Uh-huh." Myron was less than convinced. "So what's the problem?"

Norm threw up both hands. "Who said there's a problem? Did I say there was a problem? Did I even use the word *problem*? I'm just curious, that's all. It's part of my nature. I'm a curious guy. A modern-day *yenta*. I ask a lot of questions. I stick my nose in where it doesn't belong. It's part of my makeup."

"Uh-huh," Myron said again. He looked over at Esme Fong, who was now comfortably out of earshot. She shrugged at him. Working for Norm Zuckerman probably meant you did a lot of shrugging. But that was part of Norm's technique, his own version of good-cop, bad-cop. He came across as erratic, if not totally irrational, while his assistant—always young, bright, attractive—was the calming influence you grabbed on to like a life preserver.

Norm elbowed him and nodded toward Esme. "She's a looker, huh? Especially for a broad from Yale. You ever see what that school matriculates? No wonder they're known as the Bulldogs."

"You're so progressive, Norm."

"Ah, screw progressive. I'm an old man, Myron. I'm allowed to be insensitive. On an old man, insensitive is cute. A cute curmudgeon, that's what they call it. By the way, I think Esme is only half."

"Half?"

"Chinese," Norm said. "Or Japanese. Or whatever. I think she's half white too. What do you think?"

"Good-bye, Norm."

"Fine, be that way. See if I care. So tell me, Myron, how did you hook up with the Coldrens? Win introduce you?"

"Good-bye, Norm."

Myron walked off a bit, stopping for a moment to watch a golfer hit a drive. He tried to follow the ball's route. No go. He lost sight of it almost immediately. This shouldn't be a surprise really—it is, after all, a tiny white sphere traveling at a rate of over one hundred miles per hour for a distance of several hundred yards—except that Myron was the only person in attendance who couldn't achieve this ophthalmic feat of hawklike proportions. Golfers. Most of them can't read an exit sign on an interstate, but they can follow the trajectory of a golf ball through several solar systems.

No question about it. Golf is a weird sport.

The course was packed with silent fans, though *fan* didn't exactly feel like the right word to Myron. *Parishioners* was a hell of a lot closer. There was a constant reverie on a golf course, a hushed, wide-eyed respect. Every time the ball was hit, the crowd release was nearly orgasmic. People cried sweet bliss and urged the ball with the ardor of *Price Is Right* contestants: Run! Sit! Bite! Grab! Grow teeth! Roll! Hurry! Get down! Get up!—almost like an aggressive mambo instructor. They lamented over a snap hook and a wicked slice and a babied putt and goofy greens and soft greens and waxed greens and the rub of the green and the pursuit of a snowman and being stymied and when the ball traveled off the fairway and on the fringe and in the rough and deep lies and rough lies and bad lies and good lies. They showed admiration when a player got all of that one or ripped a drive or banged it home and gave dirty looks when someone loudly suggested that a certain tee-shot made a certain player "da man." They accused a putter who did not reach the hole of hitting the ball "with your purse, Alice." Players were constantly playing shots that were "unplayable."

Myron shook his head. All sports have their own lexicons, but speaking golfese was tantamount to mastering Swahili. It was like rich people's rap.

But on a day like today—the sun shining, the blue sky unblemished, the summer air smelling like a lover's hair—Myron felt closer to the chalice of golf. He could imagine the course free of spectators, the peace and tranquillity, the same aura that drew Buddhist monks to mountaintop retreats, the double-cut grass so rich and green that God Himself would want to run barefoot. This did not mean Myron got it—he was still a nonbeliever of heretic proportions—but for a brief moment he could at least envision what it was about this game that ensnared and swallowed so many whole.

When he reached the fourteenth green, Jack Coldren was lining up for a fifteen-foot putt. Diane Hoffman took the pin out of the hole. At almost every course in the world, the "pin" had a flag on the top. But that would just not do at Merion. Instead, the pole was topped with a wicker basket. No one seemed to know why. Win came up with this story about how the old Scots who invented golf used to carry their lunch in baskets on sticks, which could then double as hole markers, but Myron smelled the pungent odor of lore in Win's rationale rather than fact. Either way, Merion's members made a big fuss over these wicker baskets on the end of a big stick. Golfers.

Myron tried to move in closer to Jack Coldren, looking for Win's "eye of the tiger." Despite his protestations, Myron knew very well what Win had meant the previous night, the intangibles that separated raw talent from on-field greatness. Desire. Heart. Perseverance. Win spoke about these things as though they were evil. They were not. Quite the opposite, in fact. Win, of all people, should know better. To paraphrase and completely abuse a famous political quote: Extremism in the pursuit of excellence is no vice.

Jack Coldren's expression was smooth and unworried and distant. Only one explanation for that: the zone. Jack had managed to squeeze his way into the hallowed zone, that tranquil room in which no crowd or big payday or famous course or next hole or knee-bending pressure or hostile opponent or successful wife or kidnapped son may reside. Jack's zone was a small place, comprising only his club, a small dimpled ball, and a hole. All else faded away now like the dream sequence in a movie.

This, Myron knew, was Jack Coldren stripped to his purest state. He was a golfer. A man who wanted to win. Needed to. Myron understood. He had been there—his zone consisting of a large orange ball and a metallic cylinder—and a part of him would always be enmeshed in that world. It was a fine place to be—in many ways, the best place to be. Win was wrong. Winning was not a worthless goal. It was noble. Jack had taken life's hits. He had striven and battled. He had been battered and bloodied. Yet here he stood, head high, on the road to redemption. How many people are awarded this opportunity? How many people truly get the chance to feel this vibrant, to reside for even a short time on such a plateau, to have their hearts and dreams stirred with such unquenchable inner passion?

Jack Coldren stroked the putt. Myron found himself watching the ball slowly arc toward the hole, lost in that vicarious rush that so fiercely drew spectators to sports. He held his breath and felt something like a tear well up in his eye when the ball dropped in. A birdie. Diane Hoffman made a fist and pumped it. The lead was back up to nine strokes.

Jack looked up at the applauding galley. He acknowledged them with a tip of his hat, but he saw nothing. Still in the zone. Fighting to stay there. For a moment, his eyes locked on Myron's. Myron nodded back, not wanting to nudge him back to reality. Stay in that zone, Myron thought. In that zone, a man can win a tournament. In that zone, a son does not purposely sabotage a father's lifelong dream.

Myron walked past the many portable toilets—they'd been provided by a company with the semiaccurate name Royal Flush—and headed toward Corporate Row. Golf matches had an unprecedented hierarchy for ticket holders. True, at most sporting arenas there was a grading of one sort or another—some had better seats, obviously, while some had access to skyboxes or even courtside seats. But in those cases, you handed a ticket to an usher or ticket collector and took your place. In golf, you displayed your entrance pass all day. The general-admission folk (read: serfs) usually had a sticker plastered on their shirt, not unlike, say, a scarlet letter. Others wore a plastic card that dangled from a metal chain wrapped around their neck. Sponsors (read: feudal lords) wore either red, silver, or gold cards, depending on how much money they spent. There were also different passes for players' family and friends, Merion club members, Merion club officers, even steady sports agents. And the different cards gave you different access to different places. For example, you had to have a colored card to enter Corporate Row. Or you needed a gold card if you wanted to enter one of those exclusive tents—the ones strategically perched on hills like generals' quarters in an old war movie.

Corporate Row was merely a row of tents, each sponsored by one enormous company or another. The theoretical intention of spending at least one hundred grand for a four-day tent rental was to impress corporate clients and gain exposure. The truth, however, was that the tents were a way for the corporate bigwigs to go to the tournament for free. Yes, a few important clients were invited, but Myron also noticed that the company's major officers always managed to show too. And the hundred grand rental fee was just a start. It didn't include the food, the drinks, the employees—not to mention the first-class flights, the deluxe hotel suites, the stretch limos, et cetera, for the bigwigs and their guests.

Boys and girls, can you say, "Chu-ching goes the cash register"? I thought you could.

Myron gave his name to the pretty young woman at the Lock-Horne tent. Win was not there yet, but Esperanza was sitting at a table in the corner.

"You look like shit," Esperanza said.

"Maybe. But at least I feel awful."

"So what happened?"

"Three crackheads adorned with Nazi memorabilia and crowbars jumped me."

She arched an eyebrow. "Only three?"

The woman was constant chuckles. He told her about his run-in and narrow escape. When he was finished, Esperanza shook her head and said, "Hopeless. Absolutely hopeless."

"Don't get all dewy-eyed on me. I'll be fine."

"I found Lloyd Rennart's wife. She's an artist of some kind, lives on the Jersey shore."

"Any word on Lloyd Rennart's body?"

Esperanza shook her head. "I checked the NVI and Treemaker Web sites. No death certificate has been issued."

Myron looked at her. "You're kidding."

"Nope. But it might not be on the Web yet. The other offices are closed until Monday. And even if one hasn't been issued, it might not mean anything."

"Why not?" he asked.

"A body is supposed to be missing for a certain amount of time before the person can be declared dead," Esperanza explained. "I don't know— five years or something. But what often happens is that the next of kin files a motion in order to settle insurance claims and the estate. But Lloyd Rennart committed suicide."

"So there'd be no insurance," Myron said.

"Right. And assuming everything was held jointly between Rennart and his wife, then there would be no need for her to press it."

Myron nodded. It made sense. Still it was yet another nagging hangnail that needed to be clipped. "You want something to drink?" he asked.

She shook her head.

"I'll be right back." Myron grabbed a Yoo-Hoo. Win had made sure the Lock-Horne tent stocked them. What a pal. A television monitor in the upper corner had a scoreboard. Jack had just finished the fifteenth hole. Both he and Crispin had parred it. Barring a sudden collapse, Jack was going to take a huge lead into tomorrow's final round.

When Myron got settled again, Esperanza said, "I want to talk to you about something."

"Shoot."

"It's about my graduating law school."

"Okay," Myron said, dragging out the word.

"You've been avoiding the subject," she said.

"What are you talking about? I'm the one who wants to go to your graduation, remember?"

"That's not what I mean." Her fingers found and began to fiddle with a straw wrapper. "I'm talking about what happens *after* I graduate. I'm going to be a full-fledged attorney soon. My role in the company should change."

Myron nodded. "Agreed."

"For one thing, I'd like an office."

"We don't have the space."

"The conference room is too large," she countered. "You can slice a little out of there and a little out of the waiting room. It won't be a huge office, but it'll be good enough."

Myron nodded slowly. "We can look into that."

"It's important to me, Myron."

"Okay, it sounds possible."

"Second, I don't want a raise."

"Don't?"

"That's right."

"Odd negotiating technique, Esperanza, but you convinced me. Much as I might like to give you a raise, you will not receive one penny more. I surrender."

"You're doing it again."

"Doing what?"

"Joking around when I'm serious. You don't like change, Myron. I know that. It's why you lived with your parents until a few months ago. It's why you still keep Jessica around when you should have forgotten about her years ago."

"Do me a favor," he said wearily. "Spare me the amateur analysis, okay?"

"Just stating the facts. You don't like change."

"Who does? And I love Jessica. You know that."

"Fine, you love her," Esperanza said dismissively. "You're right, I shouldn't have brought it up."

"Good. Are we done?"

"No." Esperanza stopped playing with the straw wrapper. She crossed her legs and folded her hands in her lap. "This isn't easy for me to talk about," she said.

"Do you want to do it another time?"

She rolled her eyes. "No, I don't want to do it another time. I want you to listen to me. Really listen."

Myron stayed silent, leaned forward a little.

"The reason I don't want a raise is because I don't want to work for someone. My father worked his whole life doing menial jobs for a variety of assholes. My mother spent hers cleaning other people's houses." Esperanza stopped, swallowed, took a breath. "I don't want to do that. I don't want to spend my life working for anyone."

"Including me?"

"I said *anyone,* didn't I?" She shook her head. "Jesus, you just don't listen sometimes."

Myron opened his mouth, closed it. "Then I don't see where you're going with this."

"I want to be a part owner," she said.

He made a face. "Of MB SportsReps?"

"No, of AT&T. Of course MB."

"But the name is MB," Myron said "The M is for Myron. B for Bolitar. Your name is Esperanza Diaz. I can't make it MBED. What kind of name is that?"

She just looked at him. "You're doing it again. I'm trying to have a serious conversation."

"Now? You pick now when I just got hit over the head with a tire iron—"

"Shoulder."

"Whatever. Look, you know how much you mean to me—"

"This isn't about our friendship," she interrupted. "I don't care what I mean to you right now. I care about what I mean to MB SportsReps."

"You mean a lot to MB. A hell of a lot." He stopped.

"But?"

"But nothing. You just caught me a little off balance, that's all. I was just jumped by a group of neo-Nazis. That does funny things to the psyche of people of my persuasion. I'm also trying to solve a possible kidnapping. I know things have to change. I planned on giving you more to do, letting you handle more negotiations, hiring someone new. But a partnership . . . that's a different kettle of gefilte."

Her voice was unyielding. "Meaning?"

"Meaning I'd like to think about it, okay? How do you plan on becoming a partner? What percentage do you want? Do you want to buy in or work your way in or what? These are things we'll have to go over, and I don't think now is the time."

"Fine." She stood up. "I'm going to hang around the players' lounge. See if I can strike up a conversation with one of the wives."

"Good idea."

"I'll see you later." She turned to leave.

"Esperanza?"

She looked at him.

"You're not mad, right?"

"Not mad," she repeated.

"We'll work something out," he said.

She nodded. "Right."

"Don't forget. We're meeting with Tad Crispin an hour after they finish. By the pro shop."

"You want me there?"

"Yes."

She shrugged. "Okay." Then she left.

Myron leaned back and watched her go. Great. Just what he needed.

His best friend in the world as a business partner. It never worked. Money screwed up relationships; it was simply one of life's givens. His father and his uncle—two closer brothers you never saw—had tried it. The outcome had been disastrous. Dad finally bought Uncle Morris out, but the two men didn't speak to each other for four years. Myron and Win had labored painstakingly to keep their businesses separate while maintaining the same interests and goals. It worked because there was no cross-interference or money to divide up. With Esperanza things had been great, but that was because the relationship had always been boss and employee. Their roles were well defined. But at the same time, he understood. Esperanza deserved this chance. She had earned it. She was more than an important employee to MB. She was a part of it.

So what to do?

He sat back and chugged the Yoo-Hoo, waiting for an idea. Fortunately, his thoughts were waylaid when someone tapped his shoulder.

17

Hello."

Myron turned around. It was Linda Coldren. Her head was wrapped in a semi-babushka and she wore dark sunglasses. Greta Garbo circa 1984. She opened her purse. "I forwarded the home phone here," she whispered, pointing to a cellular phone in the purse. "Mind if I sit down?"

"Please do," Myron said.

She sat facing him. The sunglasses were big, but Myron could still see a hint of redness around the rims of her eyes. Her nose, too, looked like it had been rubbed raw by a Kleenex overdose. "Anything new?" she asked.

He told her about the Crusty Nazis jumping him. Linda asked several follow-up questions. Again the internal paradox tore at her: she wanted her son to be safe, yet she did not want it all to be a hoax. Myron finished by saying, "I still think we should get in touch with the feds. I can do it quietly."

She shook her head. "Too risky."

"So is going on like this."

Linda Coldren shook her head again and leaned back. For several moments they sat in silence. Her gaze was cast somewhere over his shoulder. Then she said, "When Chad was born, I took off nearly two years. Did you know that?"

"No," Myron said.

"Women's golf," she muttered. "I was at the height of my game, the top female golfer in the world, and yet you never read about it."

"I don't follow golf much," Myron said.

"Yeah, right," she snorted. "If Jack Nicklaus took two years off, you would have heard about it."

Myron nodded. She had a point. "Was it tough coming back?" he asked.

"You mean in terms of playing or leaving my son?"

"Both."

She took a breath and considered the question. "I missed playing," she said. "You have no idea how much. I regained the number one spot in a couple of months. As for Chad, well, he was still an infant. I hired a nanny to travel with us."

"How long did that last?"

"Until Chad was three. That's when I realized that I couldn't drag him around anymore. It wasn't fair to him. A child needs some sort of stability. So I had to make a choice."

They fell into silence.

"Don't get me wrong," she said. "I'm not into the self-pity thing and I'm glad women are given choices. But what they don't tell you is that when you have choices, you have guilt."

"What kind of guilt?"

"A mother's guilt, the worst kind there is. The pangs are constant and ceaseless. They haunt your sleep. They point accusatory fingers. Every joyous swing of the golf club made me feel like I was forsaking my own child. I flew home as often as I could. I missed some tournaments that I really wanted to play in. I tried damn hard to balance career and motherhood. And every step of the way, I felt like a selfish louse." She looked at him. "Do you understand that?"

"Yes, I think so."

"But you don't really sympathize," she added.

"Of course I do."

Linda Coldren gave him a skeptical glance. "If I had been a stay-at-home mother, would you have been so quick to suspect that Chad was behind this? Didn't the fact that I was an absent mother sway your thinking?"

"Not an absent mother," Myron corrected. "Absent parents."

"Same thing."

"No. You were making more money. You were by far the more successful parent business-wise. If anyone should have stayed home, it was Jack."

She smiled. "Aren't we politically correct?"

"Nope. Just practical."

"But it's not that simple, Myron. Jack loves his son. And during the years he didn't qualify for the tour, he did stay home with him. But let's face facts: Like it or not, it's the mother who bears that burden."

"Doesn't make it right."

"Nor does it let me off the hook. Like I said, I made my choices. If I had to do it all over again, I still would have toured."

"And you still would have felt guilty."

She nodded. "With choice comes guilt. No escaping it."

Myron took a sip of his Yoo-Hoo. "You said that Jack stayed home some of the time."

"Yes," she said. "When he failed Q school."

"Q school?"

"Qualifying school," she said. "Every year the top 125 moneymakers get their PGA Tour card automatically. A couple of other players get sponsor exemptions. The rest are forced to go to Q school. Qualifying school. If you don't do well there, you don't play for the year."

"One tournament decides all that?"

She tilted the glass at him as though making a toast. "That's right."

Talk about pressure. "So when Jack failed Q school, he'd stay home for the year?"

She nodded.

"How did Jack and Chad get along?"

"Chad used to worship his father," Linda said.

"And now?"

She looked off, her face vaguely pained. "Now Chad is old enough to wonder why his father keeps losing. I don't know what he thinks anymore. But Jack is a good man. He tries very hard. You have to understand what happened to him. Losing the Open that way—it might sound overly melodramatic, but it killed something inside him. Not even having a son could make him whole."

"It shouldn't matter so much," Myron said, hearing the echo of Win in his words. "It was just one tournament."

"You were involved in a lot of big games," she said. "Ever choke away a victory like Jack did?"

"No."

"Neither have I."

Two gray-haired men sporting matching green ascots made their way down the buffet table. They leaned over each food selection and frowned like it had ants. Their plates were still piled high enough to cause the occasional avalanche.

"There's something else," Linda said.

Myron waited.

She adjusted the sunglasses and put her hands on the table palms down. "Jack and I are not close. We haven't been close in many years."

When she didn't continue, Myron said, "But you've stayed married."

"Yes."

He wanted to ask why, but the question was so obvious, just hanging out there within easy view, that to voice it would be redundant.

"I am a constant reminder of his failures," she continued. "It's not easy for a man to live with that. We're supposed to be life partners, but I have what Jack longs for most." Linda tilted her head. "It's funny."

"What?"

"I never allow mediocrity on the golf course. Yet I allowed it to dominate my personal life. Don't you find that odd?"

Myron made a noncommittal motion with his head. He could feel Linda's unhappiness radiating off her like a breaking fever. She looked up now and smiled at him. The smile was intoxicating, nearly breaking his heart. He found himself wanting to lean over and hold Linda Coldren. He felt this almost uncontrollable urge to press her against him and feel the sheen of her hair in his face. He tried to remember the last time he had held such thought for any woman but Jessica; no answer came to him.

"Tell me about you," Linda suddenly said.

The change of subject caught him off guard. He sort of shook his head. "Boring stuff."

"Oh, I doubt that," she said, almost playfully. "Come on now. It'll distract me."

Myron shook his head again.

"I know you almost played pro basketball. I know you hurt your knee. I know you went to law school at Harvard. And I know you tried to make a comeback a few months ago. Want to fill in the blanks?"

"That's pretty much it."

"No, I don't think so, Myron. Aunt Cissy didn't say that you could help us because you were good at basketball."

"I worked a bit for the government."

"With Win?"

"Yes."

"Doing what?"

Again he shook his head.

"Top secret, huh?"

"Something like that."

"And you date Jessica Culver?"

"Yes."

"I like her books."

He nodded.

"Do you love her?"

"Very much."

"So what do you want?"

"Want?"

"Out of life. What are your dreams?"

He smiled. "You're kidding, right?"

"Just getting to the heart of the matter," Linda said. "Humor me. What do you want, Myron?" She looked at him with keen interest. Myron felt flushed.

"I want to marry Jessica. I want to move to the suburbs. I want to raise a family."

She leaned back as though satisfied. "For real?"

"Yes."

"Like your parents?"

"Yes."

She smiled. "I think that's nice."

"It's simple," he said.

"Not all of us are built for the simple life," she said, "even if it's what we want."

Myron nodded. "Deep, Linda. I don't know what it means, but it sounded deep."

"Me neither." She laughed. It was deep and throaty and Myron liked the sound of it. "Tell me where you met Win."

"At college," Myron said. "Freshman year."

"I haven't seen him since he was eight years old." Linda Coldren took a swallow of her seltzer. "I was fifteen then. Jack and I had already been dating a year, believe it or not. Win loved Jack, by the way. Did you know that?"

"No," Myron said.

"It's true. He followed Jack everywhere. And Jack could be such a prick back then. He bullied other kids. He was mischievous as all hell. At times he was downright cruel."

"But you fell for him?"

"I was fifteen," she said, as if that explained everything. And maybe it did.

"What was Win like as a kid?" Myron asked.

She smiled again, the lines in the corners of her eyes and lips deepening. "Trying to figure him out, eh?"

"Just curious," Myron said, but the truth in her words stung. He suddenly wanted to withdraw the question, but it was too late.

"Win was never a happy kid. He was always"—Linda stopped, searching for the word—"off. I don't know how else to put it. He wasn't crazy or flaky or aggressive or anything like that. But something was not right with him. Always. Even as a child, he had this strange ability to detach."

Myron nodded. He knew what she meant.

"Aunt Cissy is like that too."

"Win's mother?"

Linda nodded. "The woman can be pure ice when she wants to be. Even when it comes to Win. She acts as though he doesn't exist."

"She must talk about him," Myron said. "To your father, at least."

Linda shook her head. "When Aunt Cissy told my father to contact Win, it was the first time she'd mentioned his name to him in years."

Myron said nothing. Again the obvious question hung in the air unasked: What had happened between Win and his mother? But Myron would never voice it. This conversation had already gone too far. Asking would be an unforgivable betrayal; if Win wanted him to know, he'd tell him.

Time passed, but neither one of them noticed. They talked, mostly about Chad and the kind of son he was. Jack had held on and still led by eight strokes. A gigantic lead. If he blew it this time, it would be worse than twenty-three years ago.

The tent began to empty out, but Myron and Linda stayed and talked some more. A feeling of intimacy began to warm him; he found it hard to breathe when he looked at her. For a moment he closed his eyes. Nothing, he realized, was really going on here. If there was an attraction of some sort, it was simply a classic case of damsel-in-distress syndrome— and there was nothing less politically correct (not to mention Neanderthal) than that.

The crowd was gone now. For a long time nobody came into view. At one point, Win stuck his head into the tent. Seeing them together, he arched an eyebrow and then slipped back out.

Myron checked his watch. "I have to go. I have an appointment."

"With whom?"

"Tad Crispin."

"Here at Merion?"

"Yes."

"Do you think you'll be long?"

"No."

She started fiddling with her engagement ring, studying it as though making an appraisal. "Do you mind if I wait?" she asked. "We can catch dinner together." She took off her glasses. The eyes were puffy, but they were also strong and focused.

"Okay."

He met up with Esperanza at the clubhouse. She made a face at him. "What?" he said.

"You thinking about Jessica?" Esperanza asked suspiciously.

"No, why?"

"Because you're making your nauseating, lovesick-puppy face. You know. The one that makes me want to throw up on your shoes."

"Come on," he said. "Tad Crispin is waiting."

The meeting ended with no deal. But they were getting close.

"That contract he signed with Zoom," Esperanza said. "A major turkey."

"I know."

"Crispin likes you."

"We'll see what happens," Myron said.

He excused himself and walked quickly back to the tent. Linda Coldren was in the same seat, her back to him, her posture still queenlike.

"Linda?"

"It's dark now," she said softly. "Chad doesn't like the dark. I know he's sixteen, but I still leave the hall light on. Just in case."

Myron remained still. When she turned toward him—when he first saw her smile—it was like something corkscrewed into his heart. "When Chad was little," she began, "he always carried around this red plastic golf club and Wiffle ball. It's funny. When I think about him now, that's how I see him. With that little red club. For a long time I hadn't been able to picture him like that. He's so much like a man now. But since he's been gone, all I see is that little, happy kid in the backyard hitting golf balls."

Myron nodded. He stretched out his hand toward hers. "Let's go, Linda," he said gently.

She stood. They walked together in silence. The night sky was so bright it looked wet. Myron wanted to reach out and hold her hand. But he didn't. When they got to her car, Linda unlocked it with a remote control. Then she opened the door as Myron began circling for the passenger side. He stopped suddenly.

The envelope was on her seat.

For several seconds, neither of them moved. The envelope was manila, big enough for an eight-by-ten photograph. It was flat except for an area in the middle that puffed up a bit.

Linda Coldren looked up at Myron. Myron reached down, and using his palms, he picked up the envelope by the edges. There was writing on the back. Block letters:

I WARNED YOU NOT SEEK HELP
NOW CHAD PAYS THE PRICE
CROSS US AGAIN AND IT WILL GET MUCH WORSE.

Dread wrapped Myron's chest in tight steel bands. He slowly reached out and tentatively touched the puffy part with just a knuckle. It felt clay-like. Carefully, Myron slit the seal open. He turned the envelope upside down and let the contents fall to the car seat.

The severed finger bounced once and then settled onto the leather.

18

Myron stared, unable to speak.

Ohmygodohmygodohmygodohmygod . . .

Raw terror engulfed him. He started shivering, and his body went numb. He looked down at the note in his hand. A voice inside his head said, *Your fault, Myron. Your fault.*

He turned to Linda Coldren. Her hand fluttered near her mouth, her eyes wide.

Myron tried to step toward her, but he staggered like a boxer who didn't take advantage of a standing eight count. "We have to call someone," he managed, his voice sounding distant even to him. "The FBI. I have friends—"

"No." Her tone was strong.

"Linda, listen to me. . . ."

"Read the note," she said.

"But—"

"Read the note," she repeated. She lowered her head grimly. "You're out of this now, Myron."

"You don't know what you're dealing with."

"Oh no?" Her head snapped up. Her hands tightened into fists. "I'm dealing with a sick monster," she said. "The kind of monster who maims at the slightest provocation." She stepped closer to the car. "He cut off my son's finger just because I talked to you. What do you think he'd do if I went directly against his orders?"

Myron's head swirled. "Linda, paying off the ransom doesn't guarantee—"

"I know that," she interrupted.

"But . . ." His mind flailed about helplessly and then said something exceedingly dumb. "You don't even know if it's his finger."

She looked down now. With one hand, she held back a sob. With the other, she caressed the finger lovingly, without a trace of repulsion on her face. "Yes," Linda said softly. "I do."

"He may already be dead."

"Then it makes no difference what I do, does it?"

Myron stopped himself from saying any more. He had sounded asinine enough. He just needed a moment or two to gather himself, to figure out what the next step should be.

Your fault, Myron. Your fault.

He shook it off. He had, after all, been in worse scrapes. He had seen dead bodies, taken on some very bad people, caught and brought killers to justice. He just needed—

All with Win's help, Myron. Never on your own.

Linda Coldren lifted the finger into view. Tears streamed down her cheeks, but her face remained a placid pool.

"Good-bye, Myron."

"Linda . . ."

"I'm not going to disobey him again."

"We have to think this through—"

She shook her head. "We should never have contacted you."

Cupping her son's severed finger like a baby chick, Linda Coldren slid into the car. She put the finger down carefully and started the car. Then she shifted it into gear and drove away.

Myron made his way to his car. For several minutes he sat and took deep breaths, willing himself to calm down. He had studied martial arts since Win had first introduced him to tae kwon do when they were college freshmen. Meditation was a big part of what they'd learned, yet Myron never quite grasped the critical nuances. His mind had a habit of drifting. Now he tried to practice the simple rules. He closed his eyes. He breathed in through the nose slowly, forcing it down low, letting only his stomach, not his chest, expand. He released it through the mouth, even slower, draining his lungs fully.

Okay, he thought, what is your next step?

The first answer to float to the surface was the most basic: Give up. Cut your losses. Realize that you are very much out of your element. You never really worked for the feds. You only accompanied Win. You were way out of your league on this and it cost a sixteen-year-old boy his finger and maybe more. As Esperanza had said, "Without Win, you're hopeless." Learn your lesson and walk away.

And then what? Let the Coldrens face this crisis alone?

If he had, maybe Chad Coldren would still have ten fingers.

The thought made something inside of him crumble. He opened his eyes. His heart started trip-hammering again. He couldn't call the Coldrens. He couldn't call the feds. If he pursued this on his own, he would be risking Chad Coldren's life.

He started up the car, still trying to regain his balance. It was time to be analytical. It was time to be cold. He had to look at this latest development as a clue for a moment. Forget the horror. Forget the fact that he might have screwed up. The finger was just a clue.

One: The placement of the envelope was curious—inside Linda Coldren's locked (yes, it had been locked—Linda had used the remote control to open it) car. How had it gotten there? Had the kidnapper simply broken into the vehicle? Good possibility, but would he have had time in Merion's parking lot? Wouldn't someone have reported it? Probably. Did Chad Coldren have a key that the kidnapper could have used? Hmm. Very good possibility, but one he couldn't confirm unless he spoke to Linda, which was out of the question.

Dead end. For now.

Two: More than one person was involved in this kidnapping. This hardly took brilliant detective work. First off, you have the Crusty Nazi. The phone call at the mall proved that he had something to do with this—not to mention his subsequent behavior. But there was no way a guy like Crusty could sneak into Merion and plant the envelope in Linda Coldren's car. Not without drawing suspicion. Not during the U.S. Open. And the note had warned the Coldrens not to "cross" them again. Cross. Did that sound like a Crusty word?

Okay, good. What else?

Three: The kidnappers were both vicious and dumb. Vicious was again obvious—the dumb part maybe less so. But look at the facts. For example, making a large ransom demand over a weekend when you know that the banks won't be open until Monday—was that bright? Not knowing how much to ask for the first two times they called—didn't that say ding-a-ling? And lastly, was it really prudent to cut off a kid's finger just because his parents happened to talk to a sports agent? Did that even make sense?

No.

Unless, of course, the kidnappers knew that Myron was more than a sports agent.

But how?

Myron pulled into Win's long driveway. Unfamiliar people were taking horses out of the stable. As he approached the guest house, Win appeared in the doorway. Myron pulled into a spot and got out.

"How did your meeting with Tad Crispin go?" Win asked.

Myron hurried over to him. "They chopped off his finger," he managed, breathy to the point of almost hyperventilating. "The kidnappers. They cut off Chad's finger. Left it in Linda's car."

Win's expression did not change. "Did you discover this before or after your meeting with Tad Crispin?"

Myron was puzzled by the question. "After."

Win nodded slowly. "Then my original question remains: How did your meeting go with Tad Crispin?"

Myron stepped back as though slapped. "Jesus Christ," he said in an almost reverent tone. "You can't be serious."

"What happens to that family does not concern me. What happens to your business dealings with Tad Crispin does."

Myron shook his head, stunned. "Not even you could be that cold."

"Oh please."

"Please what?"

"There are far greater tragedies in this world than a sixteen-year-old boy losing his finger. People die, Myron. Floods wipe out entire villages. Men do horrible things to children every day." He paused. "Did you, for example, read this afternoon's paper?"

"What are you rambling about?"

"I'm just trying to make you understand," Win continued in too slow, too measured a voice. "The Coldrens mean nothing to me—no more than any other stranger and perhaps less. The newspaper is filled with tragedies that hit me on a more personal level. For example . . ."

Win stopped and looked at Myron very steadily.

"For example what?" Myron asked.

"There was a new development in the Kevin Morris case," Win replied. "Are you familiar with that one?"

Myron shook his head.

"Two seven-year-old boys—Billy Waters and Tyrone Duffy—have been missing for nearly three weeks. They disappeared while riding their bikes home from school. The police questioned one Kevin Morris, a man with a long record of perversion, including molestation, who had been hanging around the school. But Mr. Morris had a very sharp attorney. There was no physical evidence and despite a fairly convincing circumstantial case—they found the boys' bikes in a Dumpster not far from his home—Mr. Morris was set free."

Myron felt something cold press against his heart. "So what was the new development, Win?"

"The police received a tip late last night."

"How late?"

Again Win looked at him steadily. "Very late."

Silence.

"It seems," Win went on, "that someone had witnessed Kevin Morris burying the bodies off a road in the woods near Lancaster. The police dug them up last night. Do you know what they found?"

Myron shook his head again, afraid to even open his mouth.

"Billy Waters and Tyrone Duffy were both dead. They'd been sexually molested and mutilated in ways that even the media couldn't report. The police also found enough evidence at the burial site to arrest Kevin Morris. Fingerprints on a medical scalpel. Plastic bags that matched ones in his kitchen. Semen samples that offer a preliminary match in both boys."

Myron flinched.

"Everyone seems quite confident that Mr. Morris will be convicted," Win finished.

"What about the person who called in the tip? Will he be a witness?"

"Funny thing," Win said. "The man called from a pay phone and never gave his name. No one, it seems, knows who he was."

"But the police captured Kevin Morris?"

"Yes."

The two men stared at each other.

"I'm surprised you didn't kill him," Myron said.

"Then you really don't know me."

A horse whinnied. Win turned and looked at the magnificent animal. Something strange came across his face, a look of loss.

"What did she do to you, Win?"

Win kept staring. They both knew whom Myron was talking about.

"What did she do to make you hate so much?"

"Don't engage in too much hyperbole, Myron. I am not that simple. My mother is not solely responsible for shaping me. A man is not made up of one incident, and I am a far cry from crazy, as you suggested earlier. Like any other human being, I choose my battles. I battle quite a bit—more than most—and usually on the right side. I battled for Billy Waters and Tyrone Duffy. But I do not wish to battle for the Coldrens. That is my choice. You, as my closest friend, should respect that. You should not try to prod or guilt me into a battle I do not wish to fight."

Myron was not sure what to say. It was scary when he could understand Win's cold logic. "Win?"

Win wrested his gaze from the horse. He looked at Myron.

"I'm in trouble," Myron said, hearing the desperation in his tone. "I need your help."

Win's voice was suddenly soft, his face almost pained. "If that were true, I'd be there. You know that. But you are not in any trouble from which you cannot easily disentangle. Just back away, Myron. You have the option of ending your involvement. To draw me into this against my will—using our friendship in that way—is wrong. Walk away this time."

"You know I can't do that."

Win nodded and headed toward his car. "Like I said, we all choose our battles."

When he entered the guest house, Esperanza was screaming, "Bankrupt! Lose a turn! Bankrupt!"

Myron came up behind her. She was watching *Wheel of Fortune*.

"This woman is so greedy," Esperanza said, gesturing at the screen. "She's got over six thousand dollars and she keeps spinning. I hate that."

The wheel stopped, landing on the glittery $1,000. The woman asked for a *B*. There were two of them. Esperanza groaned. "You're back early," she said. "I thought you were going out to dinner with Linda Coldren."

"It didn't work out."

Esperanza finally turned around and looked at his face. "What happened?"

He told her. Her dark complexion lost a bit of color along the way. When he finished, Esperanza said, "You need Win."

"He won't help."

"Time to swallow your macho pride and ask him. Beg him if you have to."

"Been there, done that. He's out." On the television, the greedy woman bought a vowel. This always baffled Myron. Why do contestants who clearly know the puzzle's solution still buy vowels? To waste money? To make sure their opponents know the answer too?

"But," he said, "you're here."

Esperanza looked at him. "So?"

It was, he knew, the real reason she had come down in the first place. On the phone she had told him that he didn't work well alone. The words spoke volumes about her true motivation for fleeing the Big Apple.

"Do you want to help?" he asked.

The greedy woman leaned forward, spun the wheel, and then started clapping and shouting, "Come on, a thousand!" Her opponents clapped too. Like they wanted her to do well. Right.

"What do you want me to do?" Esperanza asked.

"I'll explain on the way. If you want to come."

They both watched the wheel decelerate. The camera moved in for a close-up. The arrow slowed and slowed before settling on the word BANK-RUPT. The audience groaned. The greedy woman kept the smile, but now she looked like someone had just punched her hard in the stomach.

"That's an omen," Esperanza said.

"Good or bad?" Myron asked.

"Yes."

19

The girls were still at the mall. Still at the food court. Still at the same table. It was amazing, when you thought about it. The long summer days beckoned with sunny skies and chirping birds. School was out, and yet so many teenagers spent all their time inside a glorified school cafeteria, probably lamenting the day they would have to return to school.

Myron shook his head. He was complaining about teenagers. A sure sign of lost youth. Soon he'd be screaming at someone for turning up the thermostat.

As soon as he entered the food court, the girls all turned in his direction. It was like they had people-we-know detectors at every entrance. Myron did not hesitate. Making his expression as stern as possible, he rushed toward them. He studied each face as he approached. These were, after all, just teenagers. The guilty one, Myron was sure, would show it.

And she did. Almost instantly.

She was the one that had been teased yesterday, the one they taunted for being the recipient of a Crusty smile. Missy or Messy or something. It all made sense now. Crusty hadn't spotted Myron's tail. He'd been tipped off. In fact, the whole thing had been arranged. That was how Crusty had known that Myron had been asking questions about him. That explained the seemingly fortuitous timing—that is, Crusty hanging around the food court just long enough for Myron to arrive.

It had all been a big setup.

The one with Elsa Lancaster hair screwed up her face and said, "Like, what's the matter?"

"That guy tried to kill me," Myron said.

Lots of gasps. Faces lit up with excitement. To most of them, this was like a television show come to life. Only Missy or Messy or some name with an *M* remained rock-still.

"Not to worry though," Myron continued. "We've just about got him. In an hour or two, he'll be under arrest. The police are on their way to find him right now. I just wanted to thank you all for your cooperation."

The *M* girl spoke: "I thought you weren't a cop."

A sentence without the word *like*. Hmm. "I'm undercover," Myron said.

"Oh. My. God."

"Get out!"

"Whoa!"

"You mean like on *New York Undercover?*"

Myron, no stranger to TV, had no idea what she was talking about. "Exactly," he said.

"This is *so* cool."

"Are we, like, going to be on TV?"

"The six o'clock news?"

"That guy on Channel Four is *so* cute, you know?"

"My hair totally sucks."

"No way, Amber. But mine is like a total rat nest."

Myron cleared his throat. "We have this pretty much all wrapped up. Except for one thing. The accomplice."

Myron waited for one of them to say, "Accomplice?" No one did. Myron elaborated. "Someone in this very mall helped that creep set me up."

"In, like, here?"

"In *our* mall?"

"Not *our* mall. No way."

They said the word *mall* like some people said the word *synagogue.*

"Someone helped that skank?"

"*Our* mall?"

"Eeeuw."

"I can't, like, believe it."

"Believe it," Myron said. "In fact, he or she is probably here right now. Watching us."

Heads swirled about. Even *M* managed to get into the act, though it was an uninspired display.

Myron had shown the stick. Now the carrot. "Look, I want you ladies to keep your eyes and ears open. We'll catch the accomplice. No question about it. Guys like that always talk. But if the accomplice was just a hapless dupe . . ."

Blank faces.

"If she, like, didn't really know the score"—not exactly hip-hop lingo, but they nodded now—"and she came to me right away, before the cops nail her, well, then I'd probably be able to help her out. Otherwise, she could be charged with attempted murder."

Nothing. Myron had expected that. *M* would never admit this in front of her friends. Jail was a great fear-inducer, but it was little more than a wet match next to the bonfire that was teenage peer pressure.

"Good-bye, ladies."

Myron moved to the other side of the food court. He leaned against a pillar, putting himself in the path between the girls' table and the bathroom. He waited, hoping she'd make an excuse and come over. After about five minutes, *M* stood up and began walking toward Myron. Just as he planned. Myron almost smiled. Maybe he should have been a high school guidance counselor. Mold young minds, change lives for the better.

The *M* girl veered away from him and toward the exit.

Damn.

Myron quickly trotted over, the smile on full blast. "Mindy?" He had suddenly remembered her name.

She turned to him but said nothing.

He put on the soft voice and the understanding eyes. A male Oprah. A kinder, gentler Regis. "Whatever you say to me is confidential," he said. "If you're involved in this—"

"Just stay away from me, okay? I'm not, like, involved in anything."

She pushed past him and hurried past Foot Locker and the Athlete's Foot—two stores Myron had always assumed were the same, alter egos if you will, like you never saw Batman and Bruce Wayne in the same room.

Myron watched her go. She hadn't cracked, which was a bit of a surprise. He nodded and his backup plan went into action. Mindy kept hurrying away, glancing behind her every few steps to make sure Myron wasn't following her. He wasn't.

Mindy, however, did not notice the attractive, jean-clad Hispanic woman just a few feet to her left.

Mindy found a pay phone by the record store that looked exactly like every other mall record store. She glanced about, put a quarter into the slot, and dialed a number. Her finger had just pressed the seventh digit when a small hand reached over her shoulder and hung up the phone.

She spun toward Esperanza. "Hey!"

Esperanza said, "Put down the phone."

"Hey!"

"Right, hey. Now put down the phone."

"Like, who the fuck are you?"

"Put down the phone," Esperanza repeated, "or I'll shove it up a nostril."

Wide-eyed with confusion, Mindy obeyed. Several seconds later, Myron appeared. He looked at Esperanza. "Up a nostril?"

She shrugged.

Mindy shouted, "You can't, like, do that."

"Do what?" Myron said.

"Like"—Mindy stopped, struggled with the thought—"like, make me hang up a phone?"

"No law against that," Myron said. He turned to Esperanza. "You know any law against that?"

"Against hanging up a phone?" Esperanza emphatically shook her head. "No, señor."

"See, no law against it. On the other hand, there is a law against aiding and abetting a criminal. It's called a felony. It means jail time."

"I didn't aid nothing. And I don't bet."

Myron turned to Esperanza. "You get the number?"

She nodded and gave it to him.

"Let's trace it."

Again, the cyber-age made this task frightening easy. Anybody can buy a computer program at their local software store or hop on certain Web sites like Biz, type in the number, and voilà, you have a name and address.

Esperanza used a cellular phone to dial the home number of MB SportsReps' new receptionist. Her name was, fittingly, Big Cyndi. Six-five and over three hundred pounds, Big Cyndi had wrestled professionally under the moniker Big Chief Mama, tag-team partner of Esperanza "Little Pocahontas" Diaz. In the ring, Big Cyndi wore makeup like Tammy Faye on steroids; spiked hair that would have been the envy of Sid and Nancy; ripped muscle-displaying T-shirts; and an awful, sneering glare complete with a ready growl. In real life, well, she was exactly the same.

Speaking Spanish, Esperanza gave Cyndi the number.

Mindy said, "Hey, I'm, like, outta here."

Myron grabbed her arm. " 'Fraid not."

"Hey! You can't, like, hold me here."

Myron maintained his grip.

"I'll scream rape."

Myron rolled his eyes. "At a mall pay phone. In broad fluorescent light. When I'm standing here with my girlfriend."

Mindy looked at Esperanza. "She's your girlfriend?"

"Yes."

Esperanza began whistling "Dream Weaver."

"But you can't, like, make me stay with you."

"I don't get it, Mindy. You look like a nice girl." Actually, she was wearing black leggings, too-high pumps, a red halter top, and what looked like a dog choker around her neck. "Are you trying to tell me that this guy is worth going to jail over? He deals drugs, Mindy. He tried to kill me."

Esperanza hung up. "It's a bar called the Parker Inn."

"You know where it is?" he asked Mindy.

"Yeah."

"Come on."

Mindy pulled away. "Let go," she said, stretching out the last word.

"Mindy, this isn't fun and games here. You helped someone try to kill me."

"So you say."

"What?"

Mindy put her hands on her hips, chewed gum. "So, like, how do I know that you're not the bad one, huh?"

"Excuse me?"

"You, like, come up to us yesterday, right, all mysterious and stuff, right? You don't, like, have a badge or nothing. How do I know that you aren't, like, after Tito? How do I know that you aren't another drug dealer trying to take over his turf?"

" 'Tito?' " Myron repeated, looking at Esperanza. "A neo-Nazi named Tito?"

Esperanza shrugged.

"None of his friends, like, call him Tito," Mindy went on. "It's way too long, you know? So they call him Tit."

Myron and Esperanza exchanged a glance, shook their heads. Too easy.

"Mindy," Myron said slowly, "I wasn't kidding back there. Tito is not a nice fellow. He may, in fact, be involved in kidnapping and maiming a boy about your age. Somebody cut off the boy's finger and sent it to his mother."

Her face pinched up. "Oh, that's, like, so gross."

"Help me, Mindy."

"You a cop?"

"No," Myron said. "I'm just trying to save a boy."

She waved her hands dismissively. "Then, like, go. You don't need me."

"I'd like you to come with us."

"Why?"

"So you don't try to warn Tito."

"I won't."

Myron shook his head. "You also know how to get to Parker Inn. It'll save us time."

"Uh-uh, no way. I'm not going with you."

"If you don't," Myron said, "I'll tell Amber and Trish and the gang all about your new boyfriend."

That snared her attention. "He's not my boyfriend," she insisted. "We just, like, hung out a couple of times."

Myron smiled. "So I'll lie," he said. "I'll tell them you slept with him."

"I did not!" she screamed. "That's, like, so unfair."

Myron shrugged helplessly.

She crossed her arms and chewed her gum. Her version of defiance. It didn't last long. "Okay, okay, I'll go." She pointed a finger at Myron. "But I don't want Tit to see me, okay? I stay in the car."

"Deal," Myron said. He shook his head. Now they were after a man named Tit. What next?

The Parker Inn was a total redneck, biker, skeezer bar. The parking lot was packed with pickup trucks and motorcycles. Country music blared from the constantly opening door. Several men in John Deere baseball caps were using the side of the building as a urinal. Every once in a while one would turn and piss on another. Curses and laughter spewed forward. Fun city.

From his car parked across the street, Myron looked at Mindy and said, "You used to hang out here?"

She shrugged. "I, like, came here a couple of times," she said. "For excitement, you know?"

Myron nodded. "Why didn't you just douse yourself with gasoline and light matches?"

"Fuck you, all right? You my father now?"

He held his hands up. She was right. None of his business. "Do you see Tito's truck?" Myron just couldn't call him Tit. Maybe if he got to know him better.

Mindy scanned the lot. "No."

Neither did Myron. "Do you know where he lives?"

"No."

Myron shook his head. "He deals drugs. He wears a swastika tattoo. And he has no ass. But don't tell me . . . underneath all that, Tito is really sweet."

Mindy shouted, "Fuck you, all right? Just fuck you."

"Myron," Esperanza said by way of warning.

Again Myron put his hands up. They all sat back and watched. Nothing happened.

Mindy sighed as audibly as possible. "So, like, can I go home now?"

Esperanza said, "I have a thought."

"What?" Myron asked.

Esperanza pulled the tail of her blouse out of her jeans. She tied it up, making a knot under her rib cage and revealing plenty of flat, dark stomach. Then she unbuttoned her top to a daring low. A black bra was now visible, Myron noticed, trained detective that he was. She pulled down the visor mirror and began to apply makeup. Lots of makeup. Far too much makeup. She mussed up her hair a bit and rolled up her jeans cuffs. When she finished she smiled at Myron.

"How do I look?" she asked.

Even Myron felt a little weak at the knees. "You're going to walk in there looking like that?"

"That's how everyone in there dresses."

"But everyone doesn't look like you," he said.

"Oh, my, my," Esperanza said. "A compliment."

"I meant, like a chorus dancer in *West Side Story*."

" 'A boy like that,' " Esperanza sang, " 'he keel your brother, forget that boy, go find another—' "

"If I do make you a partner," Myron said, "don't dress like this at board meetings."

"Deal," Esperanza said. "Can I go now?"

"First call me on the cellular now. I want to make sure I can hear everything that goes on."

She nodded, dialed the phone. He picked it up. They tested the connection.

"Don't go playing hero," he said. "Just find out if he's there. Something gets out of hand, you get out of there pronto."

"Okay."

"And we should have a code word. Something you say if you need me."

Esperanza nodded, feigning seriousness. "If I say the words premature ejaculation, it means I want you to come."

"So to speak."

Esperanza and even Mindy groaned.

Myron reached into his glove compartment. He snapped it open and pulled out a gun. He was not going to be caught unprepared again. "Go," he said.

Esperanza hopped out of the car and crossed the street. A black Corvette with flame decals on the hood and an extra-*vrooming* engine pulled up. A gold-chain–enmeshed primate raced the engine and leaned his head out the window. He smiled greasily at Esperanza. He hit the gas again, giving off a few more deep *vroom*s. Esperanza looked at the car, then at the driver. "Sorry to hear about your penis," she deadpanned.

The car drove off. Esperanza shrugged and waved at Myron. It wasn't an original line, but it never failed her.

"God, I love that woman," Myron said.

"She's, like, totally hot," Mindy agreed. "I wish I looked like her."

"You should wish to be like her," he corrected.

"What's the difference? She must, like, really work out, right?"

Esperanza entered the Parker Inn. The first thing that hit her was the smell—a pungent combination of dried vomit and body odor, only less olfactorily pleasing. She wrinkled her nose and continued inside. The floor was hardwood with lots of sawdust. The light was dingy, coming off the pool table ceiling fixtures that were supposed to look like imitation Tiffany lamps. The crowd was probably two-to-one men over women. Everyone was dressed—in a word—cheesy.

Esperanza looked around the room. Then she spoke out loud so that Myron would hear her through the phone. "About a hundred guys in here fit your description," she said. "It's like asking me to find an implant in a strip club."

Myron's phone was on mute, but she'd bet he was laughing. An implant at a strip club. Not bad, she thought. Not bad at all.

So now what?

People were staring at her, but she was used to that. Three seconds passed before a man approached her. He had a long, kinky beard; bits of coagulated food were lodged in it. He smiled toothlessly, looked her up and down unapologetically.

"I've got a great tongue," he said to her.

"Now all you need is some teeth."

She pushed past him and made her way to the bar. Two seconds later, a guy jumped toward her. He wore a cowboy hat. Cowboy hat. Philadelphia. What's wrong with this picture?

"Hey, sweetheart, don't I know you?"

Esperanza nodded. "Another line that smooth," she said, "and I may start to undress."

The cowboy whooped it up like it was the funniest thing he had ever heard. "No, little darling, I'm not handing you a line. I'm serious here. . . ." His voice sort of drifted off. "Holy shit!" the man cried. "It's Little Pocahontas! The Indian Princess! You're Little Pocahontas, right? Don't deny it now, darling. It's you! I can't believe it!"

Myron was probably laughing his ass off right now.

"Nice to see you," Esperanza said. "Thank you very much for remembering."

"Shit, Bobby, take a lookie here. It's Little Pocahontas! Remember? That hot little vixen on FLOW?"

FLOW, of course, stood for the "Fabulous Ladies Of Wrestling." The organization's original name had been the "Beautiful Ladies Of Wrestling," but once they became popular enough for television, the networks insisted on a new acronym.

"Where?" Another man approached, eyes wide and drunk and happy. "Holy shit, you're right! It's her! It's really her!"

"Hey, thanks for the memories, fellas, but—"

"I remember this one time, you were fighting Tatiana the Siberian Husky? Remember that one? Shit, my hard-on nearly poked a hole clean through my bedroom window."

Esperanza hoped to file that little tidbit under Too Much Information.

An enormous bartender came over. He looked like the pullout centerfold for *Leather Biker Monthly*. Extra big and extra scary. He had long hair, a long scar, and tattoos of snakes slithering up both arms. He shot the two men a glare and—poof—they were gone. Like the glare had evaporated them. Then he turned his eyes toward Esperanza. She met the glare and gave him one back. Neither backed down.

"Lady, what the fuck are you?" he asked.

"Is that a new way of asking what I'm drinking?"

"No." The mutual glaring continued. He leaned two massive snake-arms on the bar. "You're too good-looking to be a cop," he said. "And you're too good-looking to be hanging out in this toilet."

"Thanks, I guess," Esperanza said. "And you are?"

"Hal," he said. "I own this toilet."

"Hi, Hal."

"Hi back. Now what the fuck do you want?"

"I'm trying to score some blow," she said.

"Nah," Hal said with a shake of his head. "You'd go to Spic City for that. Buy it from one of your own kind, no offense." He leaned even closer now. Esperanza couldn't help but wonder if Hal would be a good match for Big Cyndi. She liked big biker guys. "Let's cut the crap, sweetheart. What do you want?"

Esperanza decided to try the direct approach. "I'm looking for a sliver of scum named Tito. People call him Tit. Skinny, shaved head—"

"Yeah, yeah, I *might* know him. How much?"

"Fifty bucks."

Hal made a scoffing sound. "You want me to sell out a customer for fifty bucks?"

"A hundred."

"Hundred and fifty. The deadbeat sack of shit owes me money."

"Deal," she said.

"Show me the money."

Esperanza took the bills out of her wallet. Hal reached for it, but she pulled back. "You first," she said.

"I don't know where he lives," Hal said. "He and his goose-stepping faggots come in every night except Wednesdays and Saturdays."

"Why not Wednesdays and Saturdays?" she asked.

"How the fuck am I supposed to know? Bingo night and Saturday night mass maybe. Or maybe they all do a circle jerk crying 'Heil, Hitler' when they shoot off. How the fuck do I know?"

"What's his real name?"

"I don't know."

She looked around the bar. "Any of the boys here know?"

"Nah," Hal said. "Tit always comes in with the same limp-dicked crew and they leave together. They don't talk to no one else. It's *verboten.*"

"Sounds like you don't like him."

"He's a stupid punk. They all are. Assholes who blame the fact that they're genetic mutations on other people."

"So why do you let them hang out here?"

"Because unlike them, I know that this is the U.S. of A. You can do what you want. Anyone is welcome here. Black, white, Spic, Jap, whatever. Even stupid punks."

Esperanza almost smiled. Sometimes you find tolerance in the strangest places. "What else?"

"That's all I know. It's Saturday night. They'll be here tomorrow."

"Fine," Esperanza said. She ripped the bills in half. "I'll give you the other half of the bills tomorrow."

Hal reached out his big hand and closed it over her forearm. His glare grew a little meaner. "Don't be too smart, hot legs," he said slowly. "I can yell *gang bang* and have you on your back on a pool table in five seconds. You give the hundred and fifty now. Then you rip another hundred in half to keep my mouth shut. You got it?"

Her heart was beating wildly in her chest. "Got it," she said. She handed him the other half of the bills. Then she took out another hundred, ripped it, and handed it to him.

"Get out, sweet buns. Like now."

He didn't have to tell her twice.

20

There was nothing else they could do tonight. To approach the Squires estate would be foolhardy, at best. He couldn't call or contact the Coldrens. It was too late to try to reach Lloyd Rennart's widow. And lastly—and perhaps most important—Myron was bone-tired.

So he spent the evening at the guest house with his two best friends in the world. Myron, Win, and Esperanza lay sprawled on separate couches like Dalí clocks. They wore T-shirts and shorts and buried themselves deep within puffy pillows. Myron drank too much Yoo-Hoo; Esperanza drank too much diet Coke; Win drank almost enough Brooklyn Lager (Win drank only lager, never beer). There were pretzels and Fritos and Ruffles and freshly delivered pizza. The lights were out. The big-screen television was on. Win had recently taped a whole bunch of *Odd Couple* episodes. They were on the fourth in a row. The best thing about the *Odd Couple*, Myron surmised, was the consistency. They never had a weak episode—how many shows could say that?

Myron bit into a slice of pizza. He needed this. He had barely slept in the millennium since he'd first encountered the Coldrens (in reality, it only had been yesterday). His brain was fried; his nerves were fraying like overused floss. Sitting with Win and Esperanza, their faces blue-lit by the picture tube, Myron felt true contentment.

"It's simply not true," Win insisted.

"No way," Esperanza agreed, tossing down a Ring-Ding.

"I'm telling you," Myron said. "Jack Klugman is wearing a hairpiece."

Win's voice was firm. "Oscar Madison would never wear a rug. Never, I say. Felix, maybe. But Oscar? It simply cannot be."

"It is," Myron said. "That's a hairpiece."

"You're still thinking of the last episode," Esperanza said. "The one with Howard Cosell."

"Yes, that's it," Win agreed with a snap of his fingers. "Howard Cosell. He wore a hairpiece."

Myron looked up at the ceiling, exasperated. "I'm not thinking of Howard Cosell. I know the difference between Howard Cosell and Jack Klugman. I'm telling you. Klugman is sporting a rug."

"Where's the line?" Win challenged, pointing at the screen. "I cannot see a break or a line or a discoloration. And I'm usually quite good at spotting lines."

"I don't see it either," Esperanza added, squinting.

"That's two against one," Win said.

"Fine," Myron said. "Don't believe me."

"He had his own hair on *Quincy*," Esperanza said.

"No," Myron said, "he didn't."

"Two against one," Win repeated. "Majority rules."

"Fine," Myron repeated. "Wallow in ignorance."

On the screen, Felix fronted for a band called Felix Unger and the So-phisticatos. They rambled through an up-tempo number with the repeated phrase "Stumbling all around." Kinda catchy.

"What makes you so sure it's a rug?" Esperanza asked.

"*The Twilight Zone*," Myron said.

"Come again?"

"*The Twilight Zone*. Jack Klugman was in at least two episodes."

"Ah, yes," Win said. "Now, don't tell me, let me see if I remember." He paused, tapping his lip with his index finger. "The one with the little boy Pip. Played by . . . ?" Win knew the answer. Life with his friends was an ever-continuing game of Useless Trivia.

"Bill Mumy." It was Esperanza.

Win nodded. "Whose most famous role was . . . ?"

"Will Robinson," Esperanza said. "*Lost in Space.*"

"Remember Judy Robinson?" Win sighed. "Quite the Earth babe, no?"

"Except," Esperanza interjected, "what was up with her clothes? Kmart velour sweaters for space travel? Who came up with that one?"

"And we cannot forget the effervescent Dr. Zachery Smith," Win added. "The first gay character on series TV."

"Scheming, conniving, gutless—with a hint of pedophilia," Esperanza said with a shake of her head. "He set back the movement twenty years."

Win grabbed another slice of pizza. The pizza box was white with red-and-green lettering and had the classic caricature of a heavy-set chef twirling a thin mustache with his finger. The box read—and this is absolutely true:

Whether it's a pizza or submarine,
We buy the best,
To prepare the best,
And leave it to you for the rest.

Wordsworth.

"I don't recall Mr. Klugman's second *Twilight Zone*," Win said.

"The one with the pool player," Myron answered. "Jonathan Winters was in it too."

"Ah, yes," Win said with a serious nod. "Now I remember. Jonathan Winters's ghost shoots pool against Mr. Klugman's character. For bragging rights or some such thing."

"Correct answer."

"So what do those two *Twilight Zone* episodes have to do with Mr. Klugman's hair?"

"You got them on tape?"

Win paused. "I believe that I do. I taped the last *Twilight Zone* marathon. One of those episodes is bound to be on it."

"Let's find it," Myron said.

It took the three of them almost twenty minutes of sifting through his vast video collection before they finally found the episode with Bill Mumy. Win put it in the VCR and reclaimed his couch. They watched in silence.

Several minutes later, Esperanza said, "I'll be damned."

A black-and-white Jack Klugman was calling out "Pip," the name of his dead son, his tormented cries chasing a tender apparition from his past. The scene was quite moving, but also very much beside the point. The key factor, of course, was that even though this episode predated the *Odd Couple* by some ten years, Jack Klugman's hairline was in a serious state of retreat.

Win shook his head. "You are good," he said in a hushed voice. "So very good." He looked at Myron. "I am truly humbled to be in your presence."

"Don't feel bad," Myron said. "You're special in your own way."

This was about as heavy as the conversation got.

They laughed. They joked. They made fun of one another. No one talked about a kidnapping or the Coldrens or business or money matters or landing Tad Crispin or the severed finger of a sixteen-year-old boy.

Win dozed off first. Then Esperanza. Myron tried to call Jessica again, but there was no answer. No surprise. Jessica often didn't sleep well. Taking walks, she claimed, inspired her. He heard her voice on the machine and felt something inside him plunge. When the beep came on, he left a message:

"I love you," he said. "I will always love you."

He hung up. He crawled back onto the couch and pulled the cover up to his neck.

21

When Myron arrived at Merion Golf Club the next morning, he wondered briefly if Linda Coldren had told Jack about the severed finger. She had. By the third hole, Jack had already dropped three strokes off his lead. His complexion was cartoon Casper. His eyes were as vacant as the Bates Motel, his shoulders slumped like bags of wet peat moss.

Win frowned. "Guess that finger thing is bothering him."

Mr. Insight.

"That sensitivity workshop," Myron said, "it's really starting to pay off."

"I did not expect Jack's collapse to be so total."

"Win, his son's finger was chopped off by a kidnapper. That's the kind of thing that could distract someone."

"I guess." Win didn't sound convinced. He turned away and started heading up the fairway. "Did Crispin show you the numbers in his Zoom deal?"

"Yes," Myron said.

"And?"

"And he got robbed."

Win nodded. "Not much you can do about it now."

"Plenty I can do about it," Myron said. "It's called renegotiate."

"Crispin signed a deal," Win said.

"So?"

"Please do not tell me that you want him to back out of it."

"I didn't say I wanted him to back out. I said I wanted to renegotiate."

" 'Renegotiate,' " Win repeated as though the word tasted vinegary. He continued trudging up the fairway. "How come an athlete who performs poorly never renegotiates? How come you never see a player who has a terrible season restructure his deal downward?"

"Good point," Myron said. "But, you see, I have this job description. It reads something like this: Get the most money I can for a client."

"And ethics be damned."

"Whoa, where did that come from? I may search for legal loopholes, but I always play by the rules."

"You sound like a criminal defense attorney," Win said.

"Ooo, now that's a low blow," Myron said.

The crowd was getting caught up in the unfolding drama in an almost disturbing way. The whole experience was like watching a car crash in super slow motion. You were horrified; you stared; and part of you almost cheered the misfortune of a fellow human being. You gaped, wondering about the outcome, almost hoping the crash would be fatal. Jack Coldren was slowly dying. His heart was crumbling like brown leaves caught in a closed fist. You saw it all happening. And you wanted it to continue.

On the fifth hole Myron and Win met up with Norm Zuckerman and Esme Fong. They were both on edge, especially Esme, but then again she had a hell of a lot riding on this round. On the eighth hole they watched Jack miss an easy putt. Stroke by stroke, the lead shrank from insurmountable to comfortable to nail-biting.

On the back nine Jack managed to control the hemorrhaging a bit. He continued to play poorly, but with only three holes left to play, Jack was still hanging on to a two-stroke lead. Tad Crispin was applying pressure, but it would still take a fairly major gaffe on Jack Coldren's part for Tad to win.

Then it happened.

The sixteenth hole. The same hazard that had laid waste to Jack's dream twenty-three years ago. Both men started off fine. They hit good tee-shots to what Win called "a slightly offset fairway." Uh-huh. But on Jack's second shot, disaster struck. He came over the top and left the sucker short. Way short.

The ball landed in the stone quarry.

The crowd gasped. Myron watched in horror. Jack had done the unthinkable. Again.

Norm Zuckerman nudged Myron. "I'm moist," he said giddily. "Swear to God, I'm moist in my nether regions. Go ahead, feel for yourself."

"I'll take your word for it, Norm."

Myron turned to Esme Fong. Her face lit up. "Me too," she said.

A more intriguing proposal but still no sale.

Jack Coldren barely reacted, as if some internal wiring had shorted out. He was not waving a white flag, but it looked like he should have been.

Tad Crispin took advantage. He hit a fine approach shot and was left with an eight-foot putt that would give him the lead. As young Tad stood over the ball, the silence in the gallery was overwhelming—not just the crowd, but it was as if the nearby traffic and overhead planes and even the grass, the trees, the very course had all aligned themselves against Jack Coldren.

This was big-time pressure. And Tad Crispin responded in a big way.

When the putt dropped into the cup, there was no polite golf clap. The crowd erupted like Vesuvius in the last days. The sound spilled forward in a powerful wave, warming the young newcomer and sweeping aside the dying warhorse. Everyone seemed to want this. Everyone wanted to crown Tad Crispin and behead Jack Coldren. The young handsome man against the ruffled veteran—it was like the golf equivalent of the Nixon-Kennedy debates.

"What a yip master," someone said.

"A major case of the yips," another agreed.

Myron looked a question at Win.

"Yip," Win said. "The latest euphemism for *choke*."

Myron nodded. There was nothing worse you could call an athlete. It was okay to be untalented or to screw up or to have an off day—but not to choke. Never to choke. Chokers were gutless. Chokers had their very manhood questioned. Being called a choker was tantamount to standing naked in front of a beautiful woman while she pointed and laughed.

Er, or so Myron imagined.

He spotted Linda Coldren in a private grandstand tent overlooking the eighteenth hole. She wore sunglasses and a baseball cap pulled low. Myron looked up at her. She did not look back. Her expression was one of mild confusion, like she was working on a math word problem or trying to recall the name behind a familiar face. For some reason, the expression troubled Myron. He stayed in her line of vision, hoping she'd signal to him. She didn't.

Tad Crispin took a one-stroke lead into the final hole. The other golfers were finished for the day, many coming out and standing around the eighteenth green to watch the final act of golf's greatest collapse.

Win started playing Mr. Merion. "The eighteenth hole is a four hundred and sixty-five yard, par four," he began. "The tee is in the stone quarry. You need to hit it up the hill—a two-hundred yard carry."

"I see," Myron said. Huh?

Tad was up first. He hit what looked like a good, solid drive. The gallery did that polite golf-clap thing. Jack Coldren took his turn. His shot climbed higher, seemingly pulling itself against the elements.

"Very nice golf shot," Win said. "Super."

Myron turned to Esme Fong. "What happens if it ends in a tie? Sudden death?"

Esme shook her head. "Other tournaments, yes. But not at the Open. They make both players come back tomorrow and play a whole round."

"All eighteen holes?"

"Yes."

Tad's second shot left him just short of the green.

"A solid golf shot," Win informed him. "Sets him up nicely for the par."

Jack took out an iron and approached the ball.

Win smiled at Myron. "Recognize this?"

Myron squinted. Déjà vu swarmed in. He was no golf fan, but from this angle even he recognized the spot. Win kept the picture on his credenza at the office. Almost every golf book or golf pub or golf whatever had the photograph. Ben Hogan had stood exactly where Jack Coldren now stood. In 1950 or thereabouts. Hogan had stroked the famous one-iron that had made him the U.S. Open champion. It was the golf equivalent of "Havlicek stole the ball!"

As Jack took his practice swing, Myron could not help but wonder about old ghosts and strange possibilities.

"He has an almost impossible task," Win said.

"Why's that?"

"The pin placement is brutal today. Behind that yawning bunker."

A yawning bunker? Myron did not bother asking.

Jack fired a long iron at the green. He reached it, but as Win had predicted, he still left himself a good twenty-plus feet away. Tad Crispin took his third shot, a beautiful little chip that came to rest within six inches of the hole. Tad tapped it in for par. That meant that Jack had no chance of winning in regulation. The best he could do was force a tie. If he made this putt.

"A twenty-two-foot putt," Win said with a grim shake of the head. "No chance."

He had said twenty-two feet—not twenty-one feet or twenty-three feet. Twenty-two feet. Win could tell from a quick glance from over fifty yards away. Golfers. Go figure.

Jack Coldren strolled to the green. He bent down, picked up his ball, put down a marker, picked up the marker, put down the ball again in the exact same spot. Myron shook his head. Golfers.

Jack looked very far away, like he was putting from New Jersey. Think about it. He was twenty-two feet away from a hole four-and-a-quarter inches in diameter. Break out a calculator. Do the math.

Myron, Win, Esme, and Norm waited. This was it. The coup de grâce. The part where the matador finally drives the long, thin blade home.

But as Jack studied the break in the green, some sort of transformation seemed to take place. The fleshy features hardened. The eyes became focused and steely and—though it was probably Myron's imagination—a hint of yesterday's "eye" seemed to flint up in them. Myron looked behind him. Linda Coldren had spotted the change too. For a brief moment she let her attention slip and her eyes sought out Myron's, as if for confirmation. Before Myron could do more than meet her gaze, she looked away.

Jack Coldren took his time. He read the green from several angles. He squatted down, his club pointing in front of him the way golfers do. He talked to Diane Hoffman at some length. But once he addressed the ball, there was no hesitation. The club went back like a metronome and kissed the ball hard on the way down.

The tiny white sphere carrying all of Jack Coldren's dreams circled toward the hole like an eagle seeking its prey. There was no question in Myron's mind. The pull was almost magnetic. Several seemingly infinite seconds later, the tiny white sphere dropped to the bottom of the hole with an audible clink. For a moment there was silence and then another eruption, this one more from surprise than exhilaration. Myron found himself applauding wildly.

Jack had done it. He'd tied the score.

Over the crowd's cacophony, Norm Zuckerman said, "This is beautiful, Esme. The whole world will be watching tomorrow. The exposure will be incredible."

Esme looked stunned. "Only if Tad wins."

"What do you mean?"

"What if Tad loses?"

"Hey, second place at the U.S. Open?" Norm said, palms up to the sky. "Not bad, Esme. Not bad at all. That's where we were this morning. Before all this happened. Nothing lost, nothing gained."

Esme Fong shook her head. "If Tad loses now, he doesn't come in second place. He's just a loser. He would have gone one-on-one with a famed choke-artist and lost. Outchoked the ultimate choker. It'll be worse than the Buffalo Bills."

Norm made a scoffing noise. "You worry too much, Esme," he said, but his usual bluster had tapered off.

The crowd began to dissipate, but Jack Coldren just stood in the same position, still holding his putter. He did not celebrate. He did not move, even when Diane Hoffman began to pound his back. His features seemed to lose their tone again, his eyes suddenly more glazed than ever. It was as if the effort of that one stroke had drained every ounce of energy, karma, strength, life force right out of him.

Or maybe, Myron wondered, there was something else at work here. Something deeper. Maybe that last moment of magic had given Jack some new insight—some new life clarity—as to the relative, long-term importance of this tournament. Everyone else saw a man who had just sunk the most important putt of his life. But maybe Jack Coldren saw a man standing alone wondering what the big deal was and if his only son was still alive.

Linda Coldren appeared on the fringe of the green. She tried to look enthusiastic as she approached her husband and dutifully kissed him. A television crew followed her. Long-lensed cameras clicked and their flashes strobed. A sportscaster came up to them, microphone at the ready. Linda and Jack both managed to smile.

But behind the smiles, Linda looked almost wary. And Jack looked positively terrified.

22

Esperanza had come up with a plan. "Lloyd Rennart's widow's name is Francine. She's an artist."

"What kind?"

"I don't know. Painting, sculpture—what's the difference?"

"Just curious. Go ahead."

"I called her up and said that you were a reporter for the *Coastal Star*. It's a local paper in the Spring Lake area. You are doing a lifestyle piece on several local artists."

Myron nodded. It was a good plan. People rarely refuse the chance to be interviewed for self-promoting puff pieces.

Win had already gotten Myron's car windows fixed. How, Myron had no idea. The rich. They're different.

The ride took about two hours. It was eight o'clock Sunday night. Tomorrow Linda and Jack Coldren would drop off the ransom money. How would it be done? A meeting in a public place? A go-between? For the umpteenth time, he wondered how Linda and Jack and Chad were faring. He took out the photograph of Chad. He imagined what Chad's young, carefree face must have looked like when his finger was being severed off. He wondered if the kidnapper had used a sharp knife or a cleaver or an axe or a saw or what.

He wondered what it felt like.

Francine Rennart lived in Spring Lake Heights, not Spring Lake. There was a big difference. Spring Lake was on the Atlantic Ocean and about as beautiful a shore town as you could hope to find. There was plenty of sun, very little crime, and almost no ethnics. It was a problem, actually. The wealthy town was nicknamed the Irish Riviera. That meant no good restaurants. None. The town's idea of *haute cuisine* was food served on a plate rather than in a basket. If you craved exotic, you drove to a Chinese take-out place whose eclectic menu included such rare delicacies as chicken chow mein, and for the especially adventurous, chicken *lo* mein. This was the problem with some of these towns. They needed some Jews or gays or something to spice things up, to add a bit of theater and a couple of interesting bistros.

One man's opinion.

If Spring Lake was an old movie, then Spring Lake Heights would be the other side of the tracks. There weren't slums or anything like that. The area where the Rennarts lived was a sort of tract-house suburbia—the middle ground between a trailer park and circa 1967 split-level colonials. Solid Americana.

Myron knocked on the door. A woman he guessed was Francine Rennart pushed open the screen. Her ready smile was shadowed by a daunting beak of a nose. Her burnt-auburn hair was wavy and undisciplined, like she'd just taken out her curlers but hadn't had time to comb it out.

"Hi," Myron said.

"You must be from the *Coastal Star*."

"That's right." Myron stuck out his hand. "I'm Bernie Worley." Scoop Bolitar uses a disguise.

"Your timing is perfect," Francine said. "I've just started a new exhibit."

The living room furniture didn't have plastic on it, but it should have. The couch was off-green. The BarcaLounger—a real, live Barca-Lounger—was maroon with duct tape mending rips. The console television had rabbit ears on top. Collectors plates Myron had seen advertised in *Parade* were neatly hung on a wall.

"My studio's in the back," she said.

Francine Rennart led him to a big addition off the kitchen. It was a sparsely furnished room with white walls. A couch with a spring sticking out of it sat in the middle of the room. A kitchen chair leaned against it. So did a rolled-up carpet. There was something that looked like a blanket draped over the top in a triangular pattern. Four bathroom wastepaper baskets lined the back wall. Myron guessed that she must have a leak.

Myron waited for Francine Rennart to ask him to sit down. She didn't. She stood with him in the entranceway and said, "Well?"

He smiled, his brain stuck in a cusp where he was not dumb enough to say, "Well what?" but not smart enough to know what the hell she was talking about. So Myron froze there with his anchorman-waiting-to-go-to-commercial grin.

"You like it?" Francine Rennart asked.

Still the grin. "Uh-huh."

"I know it's not for everybody."

"Hmm." Scoop Bolitar engages in sparkling repartee.

She watched his face for a moment. He kept up the idiot grin. "You don't know anything about installation art, do you?"

He shrugged. "Got me." Myron shifted gears on the fly. "Thing is, I don't do features normally. I'm a sports writer. That's my beat." Beat. Note the authentic reporter lingo. "But Tanya—she's my boss—she needed somebody to handle a lifestyle piece. And when Jennifer called in sick, well, the job fell to me. It's a story on a variety of local artists— painters, sculptors . . ." He couldn't think of any other kind of artist, so he stopped. "Anyway, maybe you could explain a little bit about what it is you do."

"My art is about space and concepts. It's about creating a mood."

Myron nodded. "I see."

"It's not art, per se, in the classic sense. It goes beyond that. It's the next step in the artistic evolutionary process."

More nods. "I see."

"Everything in this exhibit has a purpose. Where I place the couch. The texture of the carpeting. The color of the walls. The way the sunlight shines in through the windows. The blend creates a specific ambience."

Oh, boy.

Myron motioned at the, uh, art. "So how do you sell something like this?"

She frowned. "You don't sell it."

"Pardon?"

"Art is not about money, Mr. Worley. True artists do not put a monetary value on their work. Only hacks do that."

Yeah, like Michelangelo and Da Vinci, those hacks. "But what do you do with this?" he asked. "I mean, do you just keep the room like this?"

"No. I change it around. I bring in other pieces. I create something new."

"And what happens to this?"

She shook her head. "Art is not about permanence. Life is temporary. Why shouldn't art be the same?"

Oooookay.

"Is there a name for this art?"

"Installation art. But we do not like labels."

"How long have you been an, uh, installation artist?"

"I've been working on my masters at the New York Art Institute for two years."

He tried not to look shocked. "You go to school for this?"

"Yes. It's a very competitive program."

Yeah, Myron thought, like a TV/VCR repair course advertised by Sally Struthers.

They finally moved back into the living room. Myron sat on the couch. Gently. Might be art. He waited to be offered a cookie. Might be art too.

"You still don't get it, do you?"

Myron shrugged. "Maybe if you threw in a poker table and some dogs."

She laughed. Mr. Self-Deprecation strikes again. "Fair enough," she said.

"Let me shift gears for a moment, if I may," Myron said. "How about a little something on Francine Rennart, the person?" Scoop Bolitar mines the personal angle.

She looked a bit wary, but she said, "Okay, ask away."

"Are you married?"

"No." Her voice was like a slamming door.

"Divorced?"

"No."

Scoop Bolitar loves an garrulous interviewee. "I see," he said. "Then I guess you have no children."

"I have a son."

"How old is he?"

"Seventeen. His name is Larry."

A year older than Chad Coldren. Interesting. "Larry Rennart?"

"Yes."

"Where does he go to school?"

"Right here at Manasquan High. He's going to be a senior."

"How nice." Myron risked it, nibbled on a cookie. "Maybe I could interview him too."

"My son?"

"Sure. I'd love a quote from the prodigal son on how proud he is of his mom, of how he supports what she's doing, that kinda thing." Scoop Bolitar grows pathetic.

"He's not home."

"Oh?"

He waited for her to elaborate. Nothing.

"Where is Larry?" Myron tried. "Is he staying with his father?"

"His father is dead."

Finally. Myron put on the big act. "Oh, sheesh, I'm sorry. I didn't . . . I mean, you being so young and all. I just didn't consider the possibility that . . ." Scoop Bolitar as Robert DeNiro.

"It's okay," Francine Rennart said.

"I feel awful."

"No need to."

"Have you been widowed long?"

She tilted her head. "Why do you ask?"

"Background," he said.

"Background?"

"Yes. I think it's crucial to understanding Francine Rennart the artist. I want to explore how being widowed affected you and your art." Scoop Bolitar shovels it good.

"I've only been a widow a short time."

Myron motioned toward the, uh, studio. "So when you created this work, did your husband's death have any bearing on the outcome? On the color of the wastebaskets maybe. Or the way you rolled up that rug."

"No, not really."

"How did your husband die?"

"Why would you—"

"Again, I think it's important for digesting the entire artistic statement. Was it an accident, for example? The kind of death that makes you ponder fickle fate. Was it a long illness? Seeing a loved one suffer—"

"He committed suicide."

Myron feigned aghast. "I'm so sorry," he said.

Her breathing was funny now, her chest giving off short hitches. As Myron watched her, an awful pang struck him deep in the chest. Slow down, he told himself. Stop focusing solely on Chad Coldren and remember that this woman, too, has suffered. She had been married to this man. She had loved him and lived with him and built a life with him and had a child with him.

And after all that, he had chosen to end his life rather than spend it with her.

Myron swallowed. Fiddling with her pathos like this was, at best, unfair. Belittling her artistic expression because he did not understand it was cruel. Myron did not like himself much right now. For a moment he debated just going away—the odds that any of this had anything to do with the case were so remote—but then again, he couldn't simply forget a sixteen-year-old boy with a missing finger, either.

"Were you married long?"

"Almost twenty years," she said softly.

"I don't mean to intrude, but may I ask you his name?"

"Lloyd," she said. "Lloyd Rennart."

Myron narrowed his eyes as though scanning for a memory. "Why does that name ring a bell?"

Francine Rennart shrugged. "He co-owned a tavern in Neptune City. The Rusty Nail."

"Of course," Myron said. "Now I remember. He hung out there a lot, right?"

"Yes."

"My God, I met the man. Lloyd Rennart. Now I remember. He used to teach golf, right? Was in the big time for a while."

Francine Rennart's face slid closed like a car window. "How do you know that?"

"The Rusty Nail. And I'm a huge golf fan. A real duffer, but I follow it like some people follow the Bible." He was flailing, but maybe he was getting somewhere. "Your husband caddied Jack Coldren, right? A long time ago. We talked about it a bit."

She swallowed hard. "What did he say?"

"Say?"

"About being a caddie."

"Oh, not much. We mostly talked about some of our favorite golfers. Nicklaus, Trevino, Palmer. Some great courses. Merion mostly."

"No," she said.

"Ma'am?"

Her voice was firm. "Lloyd never talked about golf."

Scoop Bolitar steps in it in a big way.

Francine Rennart skewered him with her eyes. "You can't be from the insurance company. I didn't even try to make a claim." She pondered that for a moment. Then: "Wait a second. You said you're a sports writer. That's why you're here. Jack Coldren is making a comeback, so you want to do a where-are-they-now story."

Myron shook his head. Shame flushed his face. Enough, he thought. He took a few deep breaths and said, "No."

"Then who are you?"

"My name is Myron Bolitar. I'm a sports agent."

She was confused now. "What do you want with me?"

He searched for the words, but they all sounded lame. "I'm not sure. It's probably nothing, a complete waste of time. You're right. Jack Coldren is making a comeback. But it's like . . . it's like the past is haunting him. Terrible things are happening to him and his family. And I just thought—"

"Thought what?" she snapped. "That Lloyd came back from the dead to claim vengeance?"

"Did he want vengeance?"

"What happened at Merion," she said. "It was a long time ago. Before I met him."

"Was he over it?"

Francine Rennart thought about that for a while. "It took a long time," she said at last. "Lloyd couldn't get any golf work after what happened. Jack Coldren was still the fair-haired boy and no one wanted to cross him. Lloyd lost all his friends. He started drinking too much." She hesitated. "There was an accident."

Myron stayed still, watching Francine Rennart draw breaths.

"He lost control of his car." Her voice was robot-like now. "It slammed into another car. In Narberth. Near where he used to live." She stopped and then looked at him. "His first wife died on impact."

Myron felt a chill rush through him. "I didn't know," he said softly.

"It was a long time ago, Mr. Bolitar. We met not long after that. We fell in love. He stopped drinking. He bought the tavern right away—I know, I know, it sounds weird. An alcoholic owning a bar. But for him, it worked. We bought this house too. I—I thought everything was okay."

Myron waited a beat. Then he asked, "Did your husband give Jack Coldren the wrong club on purpose?"

The question did not seem to surprise her. She plucked at the buttons on her blouse and took her time before answering. "The truth is, I don't know. He never talked about this incident. Not even with me. But there was something there. It may have been guilt, I don't know." She smoothed her skirt with both hands. "But all of this is irrelevant, Mr. Bolitar. Even if Lloyd did harbor ill feelings toward Jack, he's dead."

Myron tried to think of a tactful way of asking, but none came to him. "Did they find his body, Mrs. Rennart?"

His words landed like a heavyweight's hook. "It-it was a deep crevasse," Francine Rennart stammered. "There was no way . . . the police said they couldn't send anyone down there. It was too dangerous. But Lloyd couldn't have survived. He wrote a note. He left his clothes there. I still have his passport. . . ." Her voice faded away.

Myron nodded. "Of course," he said. "I understand."

But as he showed himself out, he was pretty sure that he understood nothing.

23

Tito the Crusty Nazi never showed at the Parker Inn.

Myron sat in a car across the street. As usual, he hated surveillance. Boredom didn't set in this time, but the devastated face of Francine Rennart kept haunting him. He wondered about the long-term effects of his visit. The woman had been privately dealing with her grief, locking her private demons in a back closet, and then Myron had gone and blown the hinges off the door. He had tried to comfort her. But in the end what could he say?

Closing time. Still no sign of Tito. His two buddies—Beneath and Escape—were another matter. They'd arrived at ten-thirty. At one A.M. they both exited. Escape was on crutches—the aftertaste, Myron was sure, of the nasty side kick to the knee. Myron smiled. It was a small victory, but you take them where you can.

Beneath had his arm slung around a woman's neck. She had a dye job from the planet Bad Bottle and basically looked like the type of woman who might go for a tattoo-infested skinhead—or to say the same thing in a slightly different way, she looked like a regular on the *Jerry Springer* show.

Both men stopped to urinate on the outside wall. Beneath actually kept his arm around the girl while emptying his bladder. Jesus. So many men peed on that wall that Myron wondered if there was a bathroom inside. The two men broke off. Beneath got into the passenger side of a Ford Mustang. Bad Bleach drove. Escape hobbled onto his own chariot, a motorcycle of some kind. He strapped the crutches onto the side. The two vehicles drove off in separate directions.

Myron decided to follow Escape. When in doubt, tail the one that's lame.

He kept far back and remained extra careful. Better to lose him than risk in the slightest way the possibility of being spotted. But the tail didn't last long. Three blocks down the road, Escape parked and headed into a shabby excuse for a house. The paint was peeling off in flakes the size of manhole covers. One of the support columns on the front porch had completely given way, so the front lip of the roof looked like it'd been ripped in half by some giant. The two upstairs windows were shattered like a drunk's eyes. The only possible reason that this dump hadn't been condemned was that the building inspector had not been able to stop laughing long enough to write up a summons.

Okay, so now what?

He waited an hour for something to happen. Nothing did. He had seen a bedroom light go on and off. That was it. The whole night was fast turning into a complete waste of time.

So what should he do?

He had no answer. So he changed the question around a bit.

What would Win do?

Win would weigh the risks. Win would realize that the situation was desperate, that a sixteen-year-old boy's finger had been chopped off like a bothersome thread. Rescuing him imminently was paramount.

Myron nodded to himself. Time to play Win.

He got out of the car. Making sure he kept out of sight, Myron circled around to the back of the dump. The yard was bathed in darkness. He trampled through grass long enough to hide Viet Cong, occasionally stumbling across a cement block or rake or a garbage can top. His shin got whacked twice; Myron had to bite down expletives.

The back door was boarded up with plywood. The window to its left, however, was open. Myron looked inside. Dark. He carefully climbed into the kitchen.

The smell of spoilage assaulted his nostrils. Flies buzzed about. For a moment, Myron feared that he might find a dead body, but this stink was different, more like the odor of a Dumpster at a 7-Eleven than anything in the rotting flesh family. He checked the other rooms, walking on tiptoes, avoiding the several spots on the floor where there was no floor. No sign of a kidnap victim. No sixteen-year-old boy tied up. No one at all. Myron followed the snoring to the room he had seen the light in earlier. Escape was on his back. Asleep. Without a care.

That was about to change.

Myron leapt into the air and landed hard on Escape's bad knee. Escape's eyes widened. His mouth opened in a scream that Myron cut off with a snap punch in the mouth. He moved quickly, straddling Escape's chest with his knees. He put his gun against the punk's cheek.

"Scream and die," Myron said.

Escape's eyes stayed wide. Blood trickled out of his mouth. He did not scream. Still, Myron was disappointed in himself. Scream and die? He couldn't come up with anything better than scream and die?

"Where is Chad Coldren?"

"Who?"

Myron jammed the gun barrel into the bleeding mouth. It hit teeth and nearly gagged the man. "Wrong answer."

Escape stayed silent. The punk was brave. Or maybe, just maybe, he couldn't talk because Myron had stuck a gun in his mouth. Smooth move, Bolitar. Keeping his face firm, Myron slowly slid the barrel out.

"Where is Chad Coldren?"

Escape gasped, caught his breath. "I swear to God, I don't know what you're talking about."

"Give me your hand."

"What?"

"Give me your hand."

Escape lifted his hand into view. Myron grabbed the wrist, turned it, and plucked out the middle finger. He curled it inward and flattened the folded digit against the palm. The kid bucked in pain. "I don't need a knife," Myron said. "I can just grind it into splinters."

"I don't know what you're talking about," the kid managed. "I swear!"

Myron squeezed a little harder. He did not want the bone to snap. Escape bucked some more. Smile a little, Myron thought. That's how Win does it. He has just a hint of a smile. Not much. You want your victim to think you are capable of anything, that you are completely cold, that you might even enjoy it. But you don't want him thinking you are a complete lunatic, out of control, a nut who would hurt you no matter what. Mine that middle ground.

"Please . . ."

"Where is Chad Coldren?"

"Look, I was there, okay? When he jumped you. Tit said he'd give me a hundred bucks. But I don't know no Chad Coldren."

"Where is Tit?" That name again.

"At his crib, I guess. I don't know."

Crib? The neo-Nazi was using dated urban street lingo. Life's ironies. "Doesn't Tito usually hang out with you guys at the Parker Inn?"

"Yeah, but he never showed."

"Was he supposed to?"

"I guess. It's not like we talk about it."

Myron nodded. "Where does he live?"

"Mountainside Drive. Right down the street. Third house on the left after you make the turn."

"If you're lying to me, I will come back here and slice your eyes out."

"I ain't lying. Mountainside Drive."

Myron pointed at the swastika tattoo with the barrel of the gun. "Why do you have this?"

"What?"

"The swastika, moron."

"I'm proud of my race, that's why."

"You want to put all the 'kikes' in gas chambers? Kill all the 'niggers'?"

"That ain't what we're about," he said. More confidence in his voice now that he was on well-rehearsed ground. "We're for the white man. We're tired of being overrun by niggers. We're sick of being trampled on by the Jews."

Myron nodded. "Well, by this Jew anyway," he said. In life, you take satisfaction where you can. "You know what duct tape is."

"Yeah."

"Gee, and I thought all neo-Nazis were dumb. Where is yours?"

Escape's eyes kinda narrowed. Like he was actually thinking. You could almost hear rusty gears churning. Then: "I don't have none."

"Too bad. I was going to use it to tie you up, so you couldn't warn Tito. But if you don't have any, I'll just have to shoot both your kneecaps."

"Wait!"

Myron used up almost the entire roll.

Tito was in the driver's seat of his pickup truck with the monster wheels.

He was also dead.

Two shots in the head, probably from very close range. Very bloody. There wasn't much of a head left anymore. Poor Tito. No head to match his no ass. Myron didn't laugh. Then again, gallows humor was not his forte.

Myron remained calm, probably because he was still in Win mode. No lights were on in the house. Tito's keys were still in the ignition. Myron took them and unlocked the front door. His search confirmed what he'd already guessed: no one was there.

Now what?

Ignoring the blood and brain matter, Myron went back to the truck and did a thorough search. Talk about not his forte. Myron reclicked the Win icon. Just protoplasm, he told himself. Just hemoglobin and platelets and enzymes and other stuff he'd forgotten since ninth-grade biology. The blocking worked enough to allow him to dig his hands under the seats and into the cushion crevices. His fingers located lots of crud. Old sandwiches. Wrappers from Wendy's. Crumbs of various shapes and sizes.

Fingernail clippings.

Myron looked at the dead body and shook his head. A little late for a scolding, but what the hell.

Then he hit pay dirt.

It was gold. It had a golf insignia on it. The initials *C.B.C.* were engraved lightly on the inside—Chad Buckwell Coldren.

It was a ring.

Myron's first thought was that Chad Coldren had cleverly taken it off and left it behind as a clue. Like in a movie. The young man was sending a message. If Myron was playing his part correctly, he would shake his head, toss the ring in the air, and mutter admiringly, "Smart kid."

Myron's second thought, however, was far more sobering.

The severed finger in Linda Coldren's car had been the ring finger.

24

What to do?

Should he contact the police? Just leave? Make an anonymous call? What?

Myron had no idea. He had to think first and foremost of Chad Coldren. What risk would calling the police put the kid in?

No idea.

Christ, what a mess. He wasn't even supposed to be involved in this anymore. He was supposed to have—should have—stayed out. But now the proverbial doo-doo was hitting a plethora of proverbial fans. What should he do about finding a dead body? And what about Escape? Myron couldn't just leave him tied and gagged indefinitely. Suppose he vomited into the duct tape, for chrissake?

Okay, Myron, think. First, you should not—repeat, not—call the police. Someone else will discover the body. Or maybe he should make an anonymous call from a pay phone. That might work. But don't the police tape all incoming calls nowadays? They'd have his voice on tape. He could change it maybe. The rhythm and tempo. Make the tone a little deeper. Add an accent or something. Oh, right, like Meryl Streep. Tell the dispatcher to hurry because "the dingo's got ma baby."

Wait, hold the phone.

Think about what had just happened. Rewind to about an hour ago and see how it looks. Without provocation, Myron had broken into a man's house. He had physically assaulted the man, threatened him in terrible ways, left him tied and gagged—all in the pursuit of Tito. Not long after this incident, the police get an anonymous call. They find Tito dead in his pickup.

Who is going to be the obvious suspect?

Myron Bolitar, sports agent of the terminally troubled.

Damn.

So now what? No matter what Myron did at this stage—call or not call—he was going to be a suspect. Escape would be questioned. He would tell about Myron, and then Myron would look like the killer. Very simple equation when you thought about it.

So the question remained: What to do?

He couldn't worry about what conclusions the police might leap upon. He also couldn't worry about himself. The focus must be on Chad Coldren. What would be best for him? Hard to say. The safest bet, of course, would be to upset the apple cart as little as possible. Try not to make his presence in all this known.

Okay, good, that made sense.

So the answer was: Don't report it. Let the body lay where it was. Put the ring back in the seat cushion in case the police need it as evidence later. Good, this looked like a plan—a plan that seemed the best way of keeping the kid safe and also obeying the Coldrens' wishes.

Now, what about Escape?

Myron drove back to Escape's shack. He found Escape right where he left him—on his bed, hog-tied and gagged with gray duct tape. He looked half dead. Myron shook him. The punk started to, his face the green of seaweed. Myron ripped off the gag.

Escape retched and did a few dry heaves.

"I have a man outside," Myron said, removing more duct tape. "If he sees you move from this window, you will experience an agony very few have been forced to endure. Do you understand?"

Escape nodded quickly.

Experience an agony very few have been forced to endure. Jesus.

There was no phone in the house, so he didn't have to worry about that. With a few more harsh warnings lightly sprinkled with torture clichés—including Myron's personal favorite, "Before I'm finished, you'll beg me to kill you"—he left the neo-Nazi alone to quake in his goose-stepping black boots.

No one was outside. The proverbial coast was clear. Myron got in the car, wondering yet again about the Coldrens. What was going on with them right now? Had the kidnapper already called? Had he given them instructions? How did Tito's death affect what was happening? Had Chad suffered more bloodshed or had he escaped? Maybe he'd gotten hold of the gun and shot someone.

Maybe. But doubtful. More likely, something had gone awry. Someone had lost control. Someone had gone nuts.

He stopped the car. He had to warn the Coldrens.

Yes, Linda Coldren had clearly instructed him to stay away. But that was before he'd found a dead body. How could he sit back now and leave them blind? Someone had chopped off their son's finger. Someone had murdered one of the kidnappers. A "simple" kidnapping—if there is such a thing—had spun off its axis. Blood had been splattered about freely.

He had to warn them. He had to contact the Coldrens and let them know what he had learned.

But how?

He pulled onto Golf House Road. It was very late now, almost two in the morning. Nobody would be up. Myron flicked off his lights and cruised silently. He glided the car into a spot on the property line between two houses—if by some chance one of the occupants was awake and looked out the window, he or she might believe the car belonged to someone visiting a neighbor. He stepped out and slowly made his way on foot toward the Coldren house.

Keeping out of sight, Myron moved closer. He knew, of course, that there was no chance the Coldrens would be asleep. Jack might give it a token effort; Linda wouldn't even sit down. But right now, that didn't much matter.

How was he going to contact them?

He couldn't call on the phone. He couldn't walk up and knock on the door. And he couldn't throw pebbles at the window, like some clumsy suitor in a bad romantic comedy. So where did that leave him?

Lost.

He moved from shrub to shrub. Some of the shrubs were familiar from his last sojourn into these parts. He said hello to them, chatted, offered up his best cocktail-party banter. One shrub gave him a stock tip. Myron ignored it. He circled closer to the Coldren house, slowly, still careful not to be seen. He had no idea what he was going to do, but when he got close enough to see a light on in the den, an idea came to him.

A note.

He would write a note, telling them of his discovery, warning them to be extra careful, offering up his services. How to get the note close to the house? Hmm. He could fold the note into a paper airplane and fly it in. Oh, sure, with Myron's mechanical skills, that would work. Myron Bolitar, the Jewish Wright Brother. What else? Tie the note to a rock maybe? And then what? Smash a window?

As it happened, he didn't have to do any of that.

He heard a noise to his right. Footsteps. On the street. At two in the morning.

Myron quickly dove back down behind a shrub. The footsteps were moving closer. Faster. Someone approaching. Running.

He kept down, his heart beating wildly in his chest. The footsteps grew louder and then suddenly stopped. Myron peeked around the side of the shrub. His view was blocked by still more hedges.

He held his breath. And waited.

The footsteps started up again. Slower this time. Unhurried. Casual. Taking a walk now. Myron craned his neck around the other side of the shrub. Nothing. He moved into a crouch now. Slowly he raised himself, inch by inch, his bad knee protesting. He fought through the pain. His eyes reached the top of the shrub. Myron looked out and finally saw who it was.

Linda Coldren.

She was dressed in a blue sweat suit with running sneakers. Out for a jog? Seemed like a very strange time for it. But you never know. Jack drove golf balls. Myron shot baskets. Maybe Linda was into late-night jogging.

He didn't think so.

She neared the top of the driveway. Myron had to reach her. He clawed a rock out of the dirt and skimmed it toward her. Linda stopped and looked up sharply, like a deer interrupted while drinking. Myron threw another rock. She looked toward the bush. Myron waved a hand. Christ, this was subtle. But if she had felt safe enough to leave the house—if the kidnapper had not minded her taking a little night stroll—then walking toward a bush shouldn't cause a panic either. Bad rationale, but it was getting late.

If not out for a jog, why was Linda out so late?

Unless . . .

Unless she was paying off the ransom.

But no, it was still Sunday night. The banks wouldn't be open. She couldn't raise one hundred grand without going to a bank. She had made that clear, hadn't she?

Linda Coldren slowly approached the bush. Myron was almost tempted to light the bush on fire, deepen his voice, and say, "Come forward, Moses." More gallows humor. More not-funny.

When she was about ten feet away, Myron raised his head into view. Linda's eyes nearly leaped out of their sockets.

"Get out of here!" Linda whispered.

Myron wasted no time. Whispering back, he said, "I found the guy from the pay phone dead. Shot twice in the head. Chad's ring was in his car. But no sign of Chad."

"Get out!"

"I just wanted to warn you. Be careful. They're playing for keeps."

Her eyes darted about the yard. She nodded and turned away.

"When's the drop-off?" Myron tried. "And where's Jack? Make sure you see Chad with your own eyes before you hand over anything."

But if Linda heard him, she gave no indication. She hurried down the driveway, opened the door, and disappeared from sight.

25

Win opened the bedroom door. "You have visitors."

Myron kept his head on the pillow. Friends not knocking hardly fazed him anymore. "Who is it?"

"Law enforcement officials," Win said.

"Cops?"

"Yes."

"Uniformed?"

"Yes."

"Any idea what it's about?"

"Oooo, sorry. That would be a no. Let's move on to Kitty Carlisle."

Myron picked the sleep out of his eyes and threw on some clothes. He slipped into a pair of Top-Siders without socks. Very Win-like. A quick brush of the teeth, for the sake of breath rather than long-term dental health. He opted for a baseball cap rather than taking the time to wet his hair. The baseball cap was red and said TRIX CEREAL in the front and SILLY RABBIT on the back. Jessica had bought it for him. Myron loved her for it.

The two uniforms waited with cop-patience in the living room. They were young and healthy-looking. The taller one said, "Mr. Bolitar?"

"Yes."

"We'd appreciate it if you would accompany us."

"Where?"

"Detective Corbett will explain when we arrive."

"How about a hint?"

Two faces of stone. "We'd rather not, sir."

Myron shrugged. "Let's go then."

Myron sat in the back of the squad car. The two uniforms sat in the front. They drove at a pretty good clip but kept their siren off. Myron's cell phone rang.

"Do you guys mind if I take a call?"

Taller said, "Of course not, sir."

"Polite of you." Myron hit the *on* switch. "Hello."

"Are you alone?" It was Linda Coldren.

"Nope."

"Don't tell anyone I'm calling. Can you please get here as soon as possible? It's urgent."

"What do you mean you can't deliver it until Thursday?" Mr. Throw Them Off Track.

"I can't talk right now either. Just get here as soon as you can. And don't say anything until you do. Please. Trust me on this."

She hung up.

"Fine, but then I better get free bagels. You hear me?"

Myron turned off the cell phone. He looked out the window. The route the cops were taking was overly familiar. Myron had taken the same one to Merion. When they reached the club entranceway on Ardmore Avenue, Myron saw a plethora of media vans and cop cars.

"Dang," the taller cop said.

"You knew it wouldn't stay quiet for long," Shorter added.

"Too big a story," Taller agreed.

"You fellas want to clue me in?"

The shorter cop twisted his head toward Myron. "No, sir." He turned back around.

"Okeydokey," Myron said. But he didn't have a good feeling about this.

The squad car drove steadily through the press gauntlet. Reporters pushed against the windows, peering in. Flashes popped in Myron's face. A policeman waved them through. The reporters slowly peeled off the car like dandruff flakes. They parked in the club lot. There were at least a dozen other police cars, both marked and unmarked, nearby.

"Please come along," Taller said.

Myron did so. They walked across the eighteenth fairway. Lots of uniformed officers were walking with their heads down, picking up pieces of lord-knows-what and putting them in evidence bags.

This was definitely not good.

When they reached the top of the hill, Myron could see dozens of officers making a perfect circle in the famed stone quarry. Some were taking photos. Crime scene photos. Others were bent down. When one stood up, Myron saw him.

He felt his knees buckle. "Oh no . . ."

In the middle of the quarry—sprawled in the famed hazard that had cost him the tournament twenty-three years ago—lay the still, lifeless body of Jack Coldren.

The uniforms watched him, gauging his reaction. Myron showed them nothing. "What happened?" he managed.

"Please wait here, sir."

The taller cop walked down the hill; the shorter stayed with Myron. Taller spoke briefly to a man in plainclothes Myron suspected was Detective Corbett. Corbett glanced up at Myron as the man spoke. He nodded to the shorter cop.

"Please follow me, sir."

Still dazed, Myron trudged down the hill into the stone quarry. He kept his eye on the corpse. Coagulated blood coated Jack's head like one of those spray-on toupees. The body was twisted into a position it was never supposed to achieve. Oh, Christ. Poor, sad bastard.

The plainclothes detective greeted him with an enthusiastic handshake. "Mr. Bolitar, thank you so much for coming. I'm Detective Corbett."

Myron nodded numbly. "What happened?"

"A groundskeeper found him this morning at six."

"Was he shot?"

Corbett smiled crookedly. He was around Myron's age and petite for a cop. Not just short. Plenty of cops were on the short side. But this guy was small-boned to the point of being almost sickly. Corbett covered up the small physique with a trench coat. Not a great summer look. Too many episodes of *Columbo,* Myron guessed.

"I don't want to be rude or anything," Corbett said, "but do you mind if I ask the questions?"

Myron glanced at the still body. He felt light-headed. Jack dead. Why? How did it happen? And why had the police decided to question him? "Where is Mrs. Coldren?" Myron asked.

Corbett glanced at the two officers, then at Myron. "Why would you want to know that?"

"I want to make sure she's safe."

"Well then," Corbett began, folding his arms under his chest, "if that's the case, you should have asked, 'How is Mrs. Coldren?' or 'Is Mrs. Coldren all right?'—not 'Where is Mrs. Coldren?' I mean, if you're really interested in how she is."

Myron looked at Corbett for several seconds. "God. You. Are. Good."

"No reason for sarcasm, Mr. Bolitar. You just seem very concerned about her."

"I am."

"You a friend?"

"Yes."

"A close friend?"

"Pardon me?"

"Again, I don't want to appear rude or anything," Corbett said, spreading his hands, "but have you been—you know—porking her?"

"Are you out of your mind?"

"Is that a yes?"

Calm down, Myron. Corbett was trying to keep him off balance. Myron knew the game. Dumb to let it get to him. "The answer is no. We've had no sexual contact whatsoever."

"Really? That's odd."

He wanted Myron to bite with a "What's odd?" Myron did not oblige him.

"You see, a couple of witnesses saw you two together several times over the past few days. At a tent in Corporate Row, mostly. You sat alone for several hours. Very snuggly. Are you sure you weren't playing a little kissy-face?"

Myron said, "No."

"No, you weren't playing a little kissy-face, or no—"

"No, we weren't playing kissy-face or anything like that."

"Uh-huh, I see." Corbett feigned chewing over this little tidbit. "Where were you last night, Mr. Bolitar?"

"Am I a suspect, Detective?"

"We're just chatting amicably, Mr. Bolitar. That's all."

"Do you have an estimated time of death?" Myron asked.

Corbett offered up another cop-polite smile. "Once again, far be it from me to be obtuse or rude, but I would rather concentrate on you right now." His voice gathered a little more muster. "Where were you last night?"

Myron remembered Linda's call on the cell phone. Undeniably the police had already questioned her. Had she told them about the kidnapping? Probably not. Either way, it was not his place to mention it. He didn't know where things stood. Speaking out of turn could jeopardize Chad's safety. Best to get out of here pronto.

"I'd like to see Mrs. Coldren."

"Why?"

"To make sure she's okay."

"That's sweet, Mr. Bolitar. And very noble. But I'd like you to answer my question."

"I'd like to see Mrs. Coldren first."

Corbett gave him the narrow cop-eyes. "Are you refusing to answer my questions?"

"No. But right now my priority is my potential client's welfare."

"Client?"

"Mrs. Coldren and I have been discussing the possibility of her signing on with MB SportsReps."

"I see," Corbett said, rubbing his chin. "So that explains your sitting together in the tent."

"I'll answer your questions later, Detective. Right now I'd like to check up on Mrs. Coldren."

"She's fine, Mr. Bolitar."

"I'd like to see for myself."

"You don't trust me?"

"It's not that. But if I am going to be her agent, then I must be at her disposal first and foremost."

Corbett shook his head and raised his eyebrows. "That's some crock of shit you're peddling, Bolitar."

"May I go now?"

Corbett gave the big hand spread again. "You're not under arrest. In fact"—he turned to the two officers—"please escort Mr. Bolitar to the Coldren residence. Make sure nobody bothers him on the way."

Myron smiled. "Thank you, Detective."

"Think nothing of it." As Myron began to walk away, Corbett called out, "Oh, one more thing." The man had definitely watched too much *Columbo*. "That call you got in the squad car just now. Was that from Mrs. Coldren?"

Myron said nothing.

"No matter. We can check the phone records." He gave the Columbo wave. "Have a special day."

26

There were four more cop cars outside the Coldren house. Myron walked to the door on his own and knocked. A black woman Myron did not recognize opened it.

Her eyes flicked at the top of his head. "Nice hat," she said without inflection. "Come on in."

The woman was about fifty years old and wore a nicely tailored suit. Her coffee skin looked leathery and worn. Her face was kind of sleepy, her eyes half-closed, her expression perpetually bored. "I'm Victoria Wilson," she said.

"Myron Bolitar."

"Yes, I know." Bored voice too.

"Is anybody else here?"

"Just Linda."

"Can I see her?"

Victoria Wilson nodded slowly; Myron half expected her to stifle a yawn. "Maybe we should talk first."

"Are you with the police?" Myron asked.

"The opposite," she said. "I'm Mrs. Coldren's attorney."

"That was fast."

"Let me put this plainly," she ho-hummed, sounding like a diner waitress reading off the specials in the last hour of a double shift. "The police believe that Mrs. Coldren killed her husband. They also think that you're involved in some way."

Myron looked at her. "You're kidding, right?"

The same sleepy expression. "Do I look like a prankster, Mr. Bolitar?"

Rhetorical question.

"Linda does not have a solid alibi for late last night," she went on, still with the flat tone. "Do you?"

"Not really."

"Well, let me tell you what the police already know." The woman took blasé and raised it to an art form. "First"—raising a finger in the air seemed to take great effort—"they have a witness, a groundskeeper, who saw Jack Coldren enter Merion at approximately one in the morning. The same witness also saw Linda Coldren do likewise thirty minutes later. He also saw Linda Coldren leave the grounds not long after that. He never saw Jack Coldren leave."

"That doesn't mean—"

"Second"—another finger in the air, making a peace sign—"the police received a report last night at approximately two in the morning that your car, Mr. Bolitar, was parked on Golf House Road. The police will want to know what you were doing parking in such a strange spot at such a strange time."

"How do you know all this?" Myron asked.

"I have good connections with the police," she said. Again bored. "May I continue?"

"Please."

"Third"—yep, another finger—"Jack Coldren had been seeing a divorce attorney. He had, in fact, begun the process of filing papers."

"Did Linda know this?"

"No. But one of the allegations Mr. Coldren made concerned his wife's recent infidelity."

Myron put both hands to his chest. "Don't look at me."

"Mr. Bolitar?"

"What?"

"I am just stating facts. And I'd appreciate it if you didn't interrupt. Fourth"—final finger—"on Saturday, at the U.S. Open golf tournament, several witnesses described you and Mrs. Coldren as being a bit more than chummy."

Myron waited. Victoria Wilson lowered the hand, never showing the thumb.

"Is that it?" Myron asked.

"No. But that's all we'll discuss for now."

"I met Linda for the first time on Friday."

"And you can prove that?"

"Bucky can testify to it. He introduced us."

Another big sigh. "Linda Coldren's father. What a perfect, unbiased witness."

"I live in New York."

"Which is less than two hours by Amtrak from Philadelphia. Go on."

"I have a girlfriend. Jessica Culver. I live with her."

"And no man has ever cheated on his girlfriend before. Stunning testimony."

Myron shook his head. "So you're suggesting—"

"Nothing," Victoria Wilson interrupted him with the monotone. "I am suggesting absolutely nothing. I am telling you what the police believe—that Linda killed Jack. The reason why there are so many police officers surrounding this house is because they want to make sure that we do not remove anything before a search warrant is issued. They have made it crystal clear that they want no Kardashians on this one."

Kardashian. As in O.J. The man had changed law lexicon forever. "But . . ." Myron stopped. "This is ridiculous. Where is Linda?"

"Upstairs. I've informed the police that she is too grief-stricken to speak to them at this time."

"You don't understand. Linda shouldn't even be a suspect. Once she tells you the whole story, you'll see what I mean."

Another near yawn. "She has told me the whole story."

"Even about . . . ?"

"The kidnapping," Victoria Wilson finished for him. "Yes."

"Well, don't you think that kind of exonerates her?"

"No."

Myron was confused. "Do the police know about the kidnapping?"

"Of course not. We are saying nothing at this time."

Myron made a face. "But once they hear about the kidnapping, they'll focus on that. They'll know Linda couldn't be involved."

Victoria Wilson turned away. "Let's go upstairs."

"You don't agree?"

She didn't respond. They began to climb the staircase. Victoria said, "You are an attorney."

It didn't sound like a question, but Myron still said, "I don't practice."

"But you passed the bar."

"In New York."

"Good enough. I want you to be co-counsel in this case. I can get you an immediate dispensation."

"I don't do criminal law," Myron said.

"You don't have to. I just want you to be an attorney of record for Mrs. Coldren."

Myron nodded. "So I can't testify," he said. "So everything I hear falls under privilege."

Still bored. "You are a smart one." She stopped next to a bedroom door and leaned against a wall. "Go in. I'm going to wait out here."

Myron knocked. Linda Coldren told him to come in. He opened the door. Linda stood by the far window looking out onto her backyard.

"Linda?"

Her back still faced him. "I'm having a bad week, Myron." She laughed. It was not a happy sound.

"Are you okay?" he asked.

"Me? Never better. Thanks for asking."

He stepped toward her, unsure what to say. "Did the kidnappers call about the ransom?"

"Last night," Linda said. "Jack spoke to them."

"What did they say?"

"I don't know. He stormed out after the call. He never told me."

Myron tried to picture this scene. A call comes in. Jack answers it. He runs out without saying anything. It didn't exactly mesh.

"Have you heard from them again?" he tried.

"No, not yet."

Myron nodded, even though she wasn't facing him. "So what did you do?"

"Do?"

"Last night. After Jack stormed out."

Linda Coldren folded her arms across her chest. "I waited a few minutes for him to calm down," she said. "When he didn't come back, I went out looking for him."

"You went to Merion," Myron said.

"Yes. Jack likes to stroll the grounds. To think and be alone."

"Did you see him there?"

"No. I looked around for a while. Then I came back here. That's when I ran into you."

"And Jack never came back," Myron said.

With her back still to him, Linda Coldren shook her head. "What tipped you off, Myron? The dead body in the stone quarry?"

"Just trying to help."

She turned to him. Her eyes were red. Her face was drawn. She was still incredibly beautiful. "I just need someone to take it out on." She shrugged, tried a smile. "You're here."

Myron wanted to step closer. He refrained. "You've been up all night?"

She nodded. "I've been standing right here, waiting for Jack to come home. When the police knocked on the door, I thought it was about Chad. This is going to sound awful, but when they told me about Jack, I was almost relieved."

The phone rang.

Linda spun around with enough speed to start up a wind tunnel. She looked at Myron. He looked at her.

"It's probably the media," he said.

Linda shook her head. "Not on that line." She reached for the phone, pressed the lit-up button, picked up the receiver.

"Hello," she said.

A voice replied. Linda gasped and bit down in mid-scream. Her hand flew to her mouth. Tears pushed their way out of her eyes. The door flew open. Victoria Wilson stepped into the room, looking like a bear stirred from a power nap.

Linda looked up at them both. "It's Chad," she said. "He's free."

27

Victoria Wilson took control. "We'll go pick him up," she said. "You stay on the line with him."

Linda started shaking her head. "But I want—"

"Trust me on this, honey. If you go, every cop and news reporter will follow. Myron and I can lose them if we have to. I don't want the police talking to your son until I have. You just stay here. You say nothing. If the police come in with a warrant, you let them in. You don't say a word. No matter what. Do you understand?"

Linda nodded.

"So where is he?"

"On Porter Street."

"Okay, tell him Aunt Victoria is on the way. We'll take care of him."

Linda grabbed her arm, her face pleading. "Will you bring him back here?"

"Not right away, hon." The voice was still matter-of-fact. "The police will see. I can't have that. It'll raise too many questions. You'll see him soon enough."

Victoria Wilson turned away. There was no debate with this woman.

In the car, Myron asked, "How do you know Linda?"

"My mother and father were servants for the Buckwells and Lockwoods," she replied. "I grew up on their estates."

"But somewhere along the line you went to law school?"

She frowned. "You writing my biography?"

"I'm just asking."

"Why? You surprised that a middle-aged black woman is the attorney for rich WASPs?"

"Frankly," Myron said, "yes."

"Don't blame you. But we don't have time for that now. You got any important questions?"

"Yes," Myron said. He was doing the driving. "What aren't you telling me?"

"Nothing that you need to know."

"I'm an attorney of record on the case. I need to know everything."

"Later. Let's concentrate on the boy first."

Again the no-argument monotone.

"Are you sure we're doing the right thing?" Myron continued. "Not telling the police about the kidnapping?"

"We can always tell them later," Victoria Wilson replied. "That's the mistake most defendants make. They think they have to talk their way out of it right away. But that's dangerous. There is always time to talk later."

"I'm not sure I agree."

"Tell you what, Myron. If we need some expertise on negotiating a sneaker deal, I'll put you in charge. But while this thing is still a criminal case, let me take the lead, okay?"

"The police want to question me."

"You say nothing. That is your right. You don't have to say a word to the police."

"Unless they subpoena me."

"Even then. You are Linda Coldren's attorney. You don't say anything."

Myron shook his head. "That only works for what was said *after* you asked me to be co-counsel. They can ask me about anything that happened before."

"Wrong." Victoria Wilson gave a distracted sigh. "When Linda Coldren first asked you to help, she knew you were a bar-appointed attorney. Therefore everything she told you fell under attorney-client."

Myron had to smile. "That's reaching."

"But that's the way it is." He could feel her eyes on him now. "No matter what you might want to do, morally and legally you are not allowed to talk to anyone."

She was good.

Myron drove a bit faster. No one was tailing them; the police and the reporters had stuck to the house. The story was all over the radio. The anchorman kept repeating a one-line statement issued by Linda Coldren: "We are all saddened by this tragedy. Please allow us to grieve in peace."

"You issue that statement?" Myron asked.

"No. Linda did it before I got there."

"Why?"

"She thought it would keep the media off her back. She knows better now."

They pulled up on Porter Street. Myron scanned the sidewalks.

"Up there," Victoria Wilson said.

Myron saw him. Chad Coldren was huddled on the ground. The telephone receiver was still gripped in one hand, but he wasn't talking. The other hand was heavily bandaged. Myron felt a little queasy. He hit the gas pedal. The car jerked forward. They pulled up to the boy. Chad stared straight ahead.

Victoria Wilson's indifferent expression finally melted a bit. "Let me handle this," she said.

She got out of the car and walked over to the boy. She bent down and cradled him. She took the receiver away from him, talked into it, hung up. She helped Chad to his feet, stroking his hair, whispering comforts. They both got into the backseat. Chad leaned his head against her. She made soothing shushing noises. She nodded at Myron. Myron put the car in drive.

Chad did not speak during the drive. Nobody asked him to. Victoria gave Myron directions to her office building in Bryn Mawr. The Coldren family doctor—a gray-haired, old family friend named Henry Lane—had his office there too. He unwrapped Chad's bandage and examined the boy while Myron and Victoria waited in another room. Myron paced. Victoria read a magazine.

"We should take him to a hospital," Myron said.

"Dr. Lane will decide if that's necessary." Victoria yawned and flipped a page.

Myron tried to take it all in. With all the activity surrounding the police accusation and Chad's safe recovery, he had almost forgotten about Jack Coldren. Jack was dead. It was almost impossible for Myron to comprehend. The irony did not escape him: the man finally has the chance at redemption and he ends up dead in the same hazard that altered his life twenty-three years ago.

Dr. Lane appeared in the doorway. He was everything you wanted a doctor to look like—Marcus Welby without the receding hairline. "Chad is better now. He's talking. He's alert."

"How's his hand?" Myron asked.

"It'll need to be looked at by a specialist. But there's no infection or anything like that."

Victoria Wilson stood. "I'd like to talk to him."

Lane nodded. "I would warn you to go easy on him, Victoria, but I know you never listen."

Her mouth almost twitched. Not a smile. Not even close. But there was

a sign of life. "You'll have to stay out here, Henry. The police may ask
you what you heard."

The doctor nodded again. "I understand."

Victoria looked at Myron. "I'll do the talking."

"Okay."

When Myron and Victoria entered the room, Chad was staring down
at his bandaged hand like he expected the missing finger to grow back.

"Chad?"

He slowly looked up. There were tears in his eyes. Myron remembered
what Linda had said about the kid's love of golf. Another dream lay in
ashes. The kid did not know it, but right now he and Myron were kindred
spirits.

"Who are you?" Chad asked Myron.

"He's a friend," Victoria Wilson replied. Even with the boy, the tone
was completely detached. "His name is Myron Bolitar."

"I want to see my parents, Aunt Vee."

Victoria sat across from him. "A lot has happened, Chad. I don't want
to go into it all now. You'll have to trust me, okay?"

Chad nodded.

"I need to know what happened to you. Everything. From the beginning."

"A man car-jacked me," Chad said.

"Just one man?"

"Yeah."

"Go on. Tell me what happened."

"I was at a traffic light, and this guy just opens the passenger door and
gets in. He's wearing a ski mask and sticks this gun in my face. He told
me to keep driving."

"Okay. What day was this?"

"Thursday."

"Where were you Wednesday night?"

"At my friend Matt's house."

"Matthew Squires?"

"Yes."

"Okay, fine." Victoria Wilson's eyes did not wander from the boy's
face. "Now where were you when this man got into your car?"

"A couple of blocks from school."

"Did this happen before or after summer school?"

"After. I was on my way home."

Myron kept quiet. He wondered why the boy was lying.

"Where did the man take you?"

"He told me to drive around the block. We pulled into this parking lot.

Then he put something over my head. A burlap bag or something. He made me lie down in the back. Then he started driving. I don't know where we went. I never saw anything. Next thing I knew I was in a room someplace. I had to keep the bag on my head all the time so I didn't see anything."

"You never saw the man's face?"

"Never."

"Are you sure it was a man? Could it have been a woman?"

"I heard his voice a few times. It was a man. At least, one of them was."

"There was more than one?"

Chad nodded. "The day he did this . . ." He lifted his bandaged hand into view. His face went totally blank. He looked straight ahead, his eyes unfocused. "I had that burlap bag over my head. My hands were hand-cuffed behind my back." His voice was as detached as Victoria's now. "That bag was so itchy. I used to rub my chin against my shoulder. Just for relief. Anyway, the man came in and unlocked the handcuffs. Then he grabbed my hand and put it flat on the table. He didn't say anything. He didn't warn me. The whole thing took less than ten seconds. He just put my hand on the table. I never saw a thing. I just heard a whack. Then I felt this weird sensation. Not even pain at first. I didn't know what it was. Then I felt a warm wetness. From the blood, I guess. The pain came a few seconds later. I passed out. When I woke up, my hand was wrapped. The throbbing was awful. The burlap bag was back over my head. Someone came in. Gave me some pills. It dulled the pain a little. Then I heard voices. Two of them. It sounded like they were arguing."

Chad Coldren stopped as though out of breath. Myron watched Victoria Wilson. She did not go over and comfort him.

"Were the voices both male?"

"Actually, one sounded like a female. But I was pretty out of it. I can't say for sure."

Chad looked back down at his bandages. He moved his fingers a bit. Testing them out.

"What happened next, Chad?"

He kept his eyes on the bandages. "There's not a lot to tell, Aunt Vee. They kept me that way for a few days. I don't know how many. They fed me mostly pizza and soda. They brought a phone in one day. Made me call Merion and ask for my dad."

The ransom call at Merion, Myron thought. The kidnapper's second call.

"They also made me scream."

"Made you scream?"

"The guy came in. He told me to scream and to make it scary. Otherwise, he would make me scream for real. So I tried different screams for, like, ten minutes. Until he was satisfied."

The scream from the call at the mall, Myron thought. The one where Tito demanded a hundred grand.

"That's about it, Aunt Vee."

"How did you escape?" Victoria asked.

"I didn't. They let me go. A little while ago someone led me to a car. I still had the burlap bag on my head. We drove a little. Then the car stopped. Someone opened the door and pulled me out. Next thing I knew, I was free."

Victoria looked over at Myron. Myron looked back. Then she nodded slowly. Myron took that as his cue.

"He's lying."

Chad said, "What?"

Myron turned his attention to him. "You're lying, Chad. And worse, the police will know you're lying."

"What are you talking about?" His eyes sought Victoria's. "Who is this guy?"

"You used your ATM card at 6:18 P.M. on Thursday on Porter Street," Myron said.

Chad's eyes widened. "That wasn't me. It was the asshole who grabbed me. He took my wallet—"

"It's on videotape, Chad."

He opened his mouth, but nothing came out. Then: "They made me." But his voice was weak.

"I saw the tape, Chad. You were smiling. You were happy. You were not alone. You also spent an evening at the sleazy motel next door."

Chad lowered his head.

"Chad?" It was Victoria. She did not sound pleased. "Look at me, boy."

Chad slowly raised his eyes.

"Why are you lying to me?"

"It has nothing to do with what happened, Aunt Vee."

Her face was unyielding. "Start talking, Chad. And now."

He looked down again, studying the bandaged hand. "It's just like I said—except the man didn't grab me in my car. He knocked on my door at that motel. He came in with a gun. Everything else I told you is the truth."

"When was this?"

"Friday morning."

"So why did you lie to me?"

"I promised," he said. "I just wanted to keep her out of this."

"Who?" she asked.

Chad looked surprised. "You don't know?"

"I have the tape," Myron said, giving a little bluff here. "I haven't shown it to her yet."

"Aunt Vee, you have to keep her out of it. This could really hurt her."

"Honey, listen to me now. I think it's sweet that you're trying to protect your girlfriend. But I don't have time for that."

Chad looked from Myron to Victoria. "I want to see my mom please."

"You will, honey. Soon. But first you have to tell me about this girl."

"I promised that I would keep her out of it."

"If I can keep her name out of this, I will."

"I can't, Aunt Vee."

"Forget it, Victoria," Myron said. "If he won't tell, we can all just watch the tape together. Then we can call the girl on her own. Or maybe the police will find her first. They'll have a copy of the tape too. They won't be so worried about her feelings."

"You don't understand," Chad said, looking from Victoria Wilson to Myron, then back at Victoria again. "I promised her. She can get in serious trouble."

"We'll talk to her parents, if need be," Victoria said. "We'll do what we can."

"Her parents?" Chad looked confused. "I'm not worried about her parents. She's old enough. . . ." His voice died away.

"Who were you with, Chad?"

"I swore I'd never say anything, Aunt Vee."

"Fine," Myron said. "We can't waste time on this, Victoria. Let the police track her down."

"No!" Chad looked down. "She had nothing to do with it, okay? We were together. She went out for a little while and that's when they grabbed me. It wasn't her fault."

Victoria shifted in her seat. "Who, Chad?"

His words came out slow and grudging. But they were also quite clear. "Her name is Esme Fong. She works for a company called Zoom."

28

I t was all starting to make awful, horrible sense.

Myron did not wait for permission. He stormed out of the office and down the corridor. It was time to confront Esme.

A scenario was fast taking shape in Myron's mind. Esme Fong meets Chad Coldren while negotiating the Zoom deal with his mother. She seduces him. Why? Hard to say. For kicks maybe. Not important.

Anyway, Chad spends Wednesday night with his buddy Matthew. Then on Thursday he meets up with Esme for a romantic tryst at the Court Manor Inn. They pick up some cash at an ATM. They have their fun. And then things get interesting.

Esme Fong has not only signed Linda Coldren, but she has managed to land wunderkind Tad Crispin. Tad is playing wonderfully well in his first U.S. Open. After one round, he is in second place. Amazing. Great publicity. But if Tad could somehow win—if he could catch the veteran with a gigantic lead—it would give Zoom's launch into the golf business a nuclear boost. It would be worth millions.

Millions.

And Esme had the leader's son right in front of her.

So what does the ambitious Esme Fong do? She hires Tito to grab the boy. Nothing complicated. She wants to distract Jack big-time. Make him lose that edge. What better way than kidnapping his kid?

It all kinda fit together.

Myron turned his attention to some of case's more bothersome aspects. First of all, the not demanding the ransom for so long suddenly made sense. Esme Fong is no expert at this and she doesn't want a payoff—that would just complicate manners—so the first few calls are awkward. She forgets to demand a ransom. Second, Myron remembered Tito's "chink bitch" call. How had he known Esme was there? Simple. Esme had told him when she would be there—to scare the hell out of the Coldrens and make them think they were being watched.

Yep. It fit. Everything had been going according to Esme Fong's plan. Except for one thing.

Jack continued to play well.

He maintained his insurmountable lead through the next round. The kidnapping may have stunned him a bit, but he had regained his footing. His lead was still huge. Drastic action was necessary.

Myron got into the elevator and headed down to the ground-floor lobby. He wondered how it had happened. Maybe it had been Tito's idea. Maybe that was why Chad had heard two voices arguing. Either way, someone decided to do something that was guaranteed to throw Jack off his game.

Cut off Chad's finger.

Like it or not—Tito's idea or hers—Esme Fong took advantage. She had Linda's car keys. She knew what her car looked like. It wouldn't take much. Just a turn of the key, a quick drop on the car seat. Easy for her. Nothing suspicious. Who would notice an attractive, well-dressed woman unlocking a car with a key?

The severed finger did the trick, too. Jack's game was left in shambles. Tad Crispin stormed back. It was everything she wanted. But, alas, Jack had one more trick up his sleeve. He managed to land a big putt on the eighteenth hole, forcing a tie. This was a nightmare for Esme. She could not take the risk of Tad Crispin losing to Jack, the ultimate choker, in a one-on-one situation.

A loss would be disastrous.

A loss would cost them millions. Maybe destroy her entire campaign.

Man, did it fit.

When Myron thought about it, hadn't he heard Esme voice that very viewpoint with Norm Zuckerman? Her Buffalo Bill analogy—hadn't he been standing right there when she said it? Now that she was trapped, was it so hard to believe that she'd go the extra mile? That she would call Jack on the phone last night? That she would set up a rendezvous at the course? That she would insist he come alone—right now—if he wanted to see his son alive?

Ka-bang.

And once Jack was dead, there was no reason to hold on to the kid anymore. She let him go.

The elevator slid open. Myron stepped out. Okay, there were holes. But maybe after confronting Esme, he would be able to plug a few of them up. Myron pushed open the glass door. He headed into the parking lot. There were taxis waiting near the street. He was midway through the lot when a voice reached out and pulled him to a stop.

"Myron?"

An icy nerve-jangle punctured a hole through his heart. He had heard the voice only once before. Ten years ago. At Merion.

29

Myron froze.

"I see you've met Victoria," Cissy Lockwood said.

He tried a nod, but it wouldn't happen.

"I called her as soon as Bucky told me about the murder. I knew she'd be able to help. Victoria is the best lawyer I know. Ask Win about her."

He tried the nod again. Got a little motion going this time.

Win's mother stepped closer. "I'd like a word with you in private, Myron."

He found his voice. "It's not a good time, Ms. Lockwood."

"No, I imagine not. Still, this won't take long."

"Really, I should go."

She was a beautiful woman. Her ash-blond hair was streaked with gray, and she had the same regal bearing as her blood niece Linda. The porcelain face, however, she had given almost verbatim to Win. The resemblance was uncanny.

She took one more step forward, her eyes never off him. Her clothes were a bit odd. She wore a man's oversize shirt, untucked, and stretch pants. Annie Hall goes maternity shopping. It was not what he'd have expected, but then again, he had bigger worries than fashion right now.

"It's about Win," she said.

Myron shook his head. "Then it's none of my business."

"True enough. But that does not make you immune to responsibility, does it? Win is your friend. I count myself lucky that my son has a friend who cares like you do."

Myron said nothing.

"I know quite a bit about you, Myron. I've had private investigators keep tabs on Win for years now. It was my way of staying close. Of course, Win knew about it. He never said anything, but you can't keep something like that from Win, now can you?"

"No," Myron said. "You can't."

"You're staying at the Lockwood estate," she said. "In the guest cottage."

He nodded.

"You've been there before."

Another nod.

"Have you ever seen the horse stables?"

"Only from a distance," Myron said.

She smiled Win's smile. "You've never been inside?"

"No."

"I'm not surprised. Win doesn't ride anymore. He used to love horses. More than golf even."

"Ms. Lockwood—"

"Please call me Cissy."

"I really don't feel comfortable hearing this."

Her eyes hardened a bit. "And I do not feel comfortable telling you this. But it must be done."

"Win wouldn't want me to hear it," Myron said.

"That's too bad, but Win cannot always have what he wants. I should have learned that long ago. He did not want to see me as a child. I never forced it. I listened to the experts, who told me that my son would come around, that compelling him to see me would be counterproductive. But they did not know Win. By the time I stopped listening to them it was too late. Not that it mattered. I don't think ignoring them would have changed anything."

Silence.

She stood proud and tall, her slender neck high. But something was going on. Her fingers kept flexing, as if she were fighting off the desire to make fists. Myron's stomach knotted up. He knew what was coming next. He just didn't know what to do about it.

"The story is simple," she began, her voice almost wistful. She was no longer looking at Myron. Her gaze rose above his shoulder, but he had no idea what she was actually seeing. "Win was eight years old. I was twenty-seven at the time. I married young. I never went to college. It was not as though I had a choice. My father told me what to do. I had only one friend—one person I could confide in. That was Victoria. She is still my dearest friend, not unlike what you are to Win."

Cissy Lockwood winced. Her eyes closed.

"Ms. Lockwood?"

She shook her head. The eyes slowly opened. "I am getting off track," she said, catching her breath. "I apologize. I'm not here to tell you my life story. Just one incident in it. So let me just state it plainly."

A deep breath. Then another.

"Jack Coldren told me that he was taking Win out for a golf lesson. But it never happened. Or perhaps they had finished far earlier than expected. Either way, Jack was not with Win. His father was. Somehow Win and his father ended up going into the stables. I was there when they entered. I was not alone. More specifically, I was with Win's riding instructor."

She stopped. Myron waited.

"Do I need to spell this out for you?"

Myron shook his head.

"No child should see what Win saw that day," she said. "And worse, no child should ever see his father's face under those circumstances."

Myron felt tears sting his eyes.

"There is more to it, of course. I won't go into it now. But Win has never spoken to me since that moment. He also never forgave his father. Yes, his father. You think he hates only me and loves Windsor the Second. But it is not so. He blames his father, too. He thinks that his father is weak. That he allowed it to happen. Utter nonsense, but that is the way it is."

Myron shook his head. He didn't want to hear any more. He wanted to run and find Win. He wanted to hug his friend and shake him and somehow make him forget. He thought of the lost expression on Win's face as he watched the horse stables yesterday morning.

My God. Win.

When Myron spoke, his voice was sharper than he'd expected. "Why are you telling me this?"

"Because I am dying," she replied.

Myron slumped against a car. His heart ripped anew.

"Again, let me put this simply," she said in too calm a voice. "It has reached the liver. It is eleven centimeters long. My abdomen is swelling from liver and kidney failure." That explained the wardrobe—the un-tucked, oversize shirt and the stretch pants. "We are not talking months. We are talking perhaps weeks. Probably less."

"There are treatments," Myron tried lamely. "Procedures."

She simply dismissed this with a shake of her head. "I am not a fool-ish woman. I do not have delusions of engaging in a moving reunion with my son. I know Win. That will not happen. But there is still unfinished business here. Once I am dead, there will be no chance for him to disen-tangle himself again. It will be over. I do not know what he will do with this opportunity. Probably nothing. But I want him to know. So that he can decide. It is his last chance, Myron. I do not believe he will take it. But he should."

With that, she turned away and left. Myron watched her walk away. When she was out of sight, Myron hailed a taxi. He got in the back.

"Where to, bud?"

He gave the man the address where Esme Fong was staying. Then he settled back in the seat. His eyes stared blankly out the window. The city passed by in a misty, silent blur.

30

When he thought that his voice would not betray him, Myron called Win on the cell phone.

After a quick hello, Win said, "Bummer about Jack."

"From what I hear, he used to be your friend."

Win cleared his throat. "Myron?"

"What?"

"You know nothing. Remember that."

True enough. "Can we have dinner tonight?"

Win hesitated. "Of course."

"At the cottage. Six-thirty."

"Fine."

Win hung up. Myron tried to put it out of his mind. He had other things to worry about.

Esme Fong paced the sidewalk outside the entrance to the Omni Hotel on the corner of Chestnut Street and Fourth. She wore a white suit and white stockings. Killer legs. She kept wringing her hands.

Myron got out of the taxi. "Why are you waiting out here?" he asked.

"You insisted on talking privately," Esme answered. "Norm is upstairs."

"You two live in the same room?"

"No, we have adjoining suites."

Myron nodded. The no-tell motel was making more sense now. "Not much privacy, huh?"

"No, not really." She gave him a tentative smile. "But it's okay. I like Norm."

"I'm sure you do."

"What's this about, Myron?"

"You heard about Jack Coldren?"

"Of course. Norm and I were shocked. Absolutely shocked."

Myron nodded. "Come on," he said. "Let's walk."

They headed up Fourth Street. Myron was tempted to stay on Chestnut Street, but that would have meant strolling past Independence Hall and that would have been a tad too cliché for his liking. Still, Fourth Street was in the colonial section. Lots of brick. Brick sidewalk, brick walls and fence, brick buildings of tremendous historical significance that all looked the same. White ash trees lined the walk. They turned right into a park that held the Second Bank of the United States. There was a plaque with a portrait of the bank's first president. One of Win's ancestors. Myron looked for a resemblance but could not find one.

"I've tried to reach Linda," Esme said. "But the phone is busy."

"Did you try Chad's line?"

Something hit her face, then fled. "Chad's line?"

"He has his own phone in the house," he said. "You must have known that."

"Why would I know that?"

Myron shrugged. "I thought you knew Chad."

"I do," she said, but her voice was slow, careful. "I mean, I've been over to the house a number of times."

"Uh-huh. And when was the last time you saw Chad?"

She put her hand to her chin. "I don't think he was there when I went over Friday night," she said, the voice still slow. "I don't really know. I guess a few weeks ago."

Myron made a buzzing noise. "Incorrect answer."

"Excuse me?"

"I don't get it, Esme."

"What?"

Myron continued walking, Esme stayed in step. "You're what," he said, "twenty-four years old?"

"Twenty-five."

"You're smart. You're successful. You're attractive. But a teenage boy—what's up with that?"

She stopped. "What are you talking about?"

"You really don't know?"

"I don't have the slightest idea."

His eyes bore into hers. "You. Chad Coldren. The Court Manor Inn. That help?"

"No."

Myron gave her skeptical. "Please."

"Did Chad tell you that?"

"Esme . . ."

"He's lying, Myron. My God, you know how teenage boys are. How could you believe something like that?"

"Pictures, Esme."

Her face went slack. "What?"

"You two stopped at an ATM machine next door to the motel, remember? They have cameras. Your face was clear as day." It was a bluff. But it was a damn good one. She caved a little piece at a time. She looked around and then collapsed on a bench. She turned and faced a colonial building with a lot of scaffolding. Scaffolding, Myron thought, ruined the effect—like armpit hair on a beautiful woman. It shouldn't really matter, but it did.

"Please don't tell Norm," she said in a faraway voice. "Please don't."

Myron said nothing.

"It was dumb. I know that. But it shouldn't cost me my job."

Myron sat next to her. "Tell me what happened."

She looked back at him. "Why? What business is this of yours?"

"There are reasons."

"What reasons?" Her voice was a little sharper now. "Look, I'm not proud of myself. But who appointed you my conscience?"

"Fine. I'll go ask Norm then. Maybe he can help me."

Her mouth dropped. "Help you with what? I don't understand. Why are you doing this to me?"

"I need some answers. I don't have time to explain."

"What do you want me to say? That I was dumb? I was. I could tell you that I was lonely being in a nice place. That he seemed like a sweet, handsome kid and that at his age, I figured there'd be no fear of disease or attachments. But at the end of the day, that does not change much. I was wrong. I'm sorry, okay?"

"When was the last time you saw Chad?"

"Why do you keep asking me that?" Esme insisted.

"Just answer my questions or I'll go to Norm, I swear it."

She studied his face. He put on his most impermeable face, the one he'd learned from really tough cops and toll collectors on the New Jersey Turnpike. After a few seconds she said, "At that motel."

"The Court Manor Inn?"

"Whatever it was called. I don't remember the name."

"What day was that?" Myron asked.

She thought a moment. "Friday morning. Chad was still sleeping."

"You haven't seen or spoken to him since?"

"No."

"You didn't have any plans to rendezvous for another tryst?"

She made an unhappy face. "No, not really. I thought he was just out for some fun, but once we were there, I could see he was developing a crush. I didn't count on that. Frankly I was worried."

"Of what exactly?"

"That he'd tell his mother. Chad swore he wouldn't, but who knew what he'd do if I hurt him? When I didn't hear from him again, I was relieved."

Myron searched her face and her story for lies. He couldn't find one. Didn't mean they weren't there.

Esme shifted on the bench, crossing her legs. "I still don't understand why you're asking me all this." She thought about it a moment and then something seemed to spark in her eyes. She squared her shoulders toward Myron. "Does this have something to do with Jack's murder?"

Myron said nothing.

"My God." Her voice quaked. "You can't possibly think that Chad has something to do with it."

Myron waited a beat. All-or-nothing time. "No," he said. "But I'm not so sure about you."

Confusion set camp on her face. "What?"

"I think you kidnapped Chad."

She raised both hands. "Are you out of your mind? Kidnapped? It was completely consensual. Chad was more than willing, believe me. Okay, he was young. But do you think I took him to that motel at gunpoint?"

"That's not what I mean," Myron said.

Confusion again. "Then what the hell do you mean?"

"After you left the motel on Friday. Where did you go?"

"To Merion. I met you there that night, remember?"

"How about last night? Where were you?"

"Here."

"In your suite?"

"Yes."

"What time?"

"From eight o'clock on."

"Anybody who can verify that?"

"Why would I need someone to verify that?" she snapped. Myron put on the impermeable face again—not even gases could get through. Esme sighed. "I was with Norm until midnight. We were working."

"And after that?"

"I went to bed."

"Would the hotel's nightman be able to verify that you never left your suite after midnight?"

"I think so, yes. His name is Miguel. He's very nice."

Miguel. He'd have Esperanza track down that one. If her alibi stuck, his neat little scenario went down the toilet. "Who else knew about you and Chad Coldren?"

"No one," she said. "At least, I told no one."

"How about Chad? Did he tell anyone?"

"It sounds to me like he told you," she said pointedly. "He might have told someone else, I don't know."

Myron thought about it. The black-clad man crawling out Chad's bedroom window. Matthew Squires. Myron remembered his own teenage years. If he had somehow managed to bed an older woman who looked like Esme Fong, he would have been busting to tell someone—especially if he'd been staying at his best friend's house the night before.

Once again, things circled back to the Squires kid.

Myron asked, "Where will you be if I need to reach you?"

She reached into her pocket and pulled out a card. "My cell phone number is on the bottom."

"Good-bye, Esme."

"Myron?"

He turned to her.

"Are you going to tell Norm?"

She seemed only worried about her reputation and her job, not a murder rap. Or was this just a clever diversion? No way of knowing for sure.

"No," he said. "I won't tell."

At least, not yet.

31

E piscopal Academy. Win's high school alma mater.
Esperanza had picked him up in front of Esme Fong's and
driven him here. She parked across the street. She turned off the
ignition and faced him.

"Now what?" she asked.

"I don't know. Matthew Squires is in there. We can wait for a lunch
break. Try to get in then."

"Sounds like a plan," Esperanza said with a nod. "A really bad one."

"You have a better idea?"

"We can go in now. Pretend we're touring parents."

Myron thought about it. "You think that'll work?"

"Better than hanging out here doing nothing."

"Oh, before I forget. I want you to check out Esme's alibi. The hotel
nightman named Miguel."

"Miguel," she repeated. "It's because I'm Hispanic, right?"

"Pretty much, yeah."

She had no problem with that. "I put a call in to Peru this morning."

"And?"

"I spoke to some local sheriff. He says Lloyd Rennart committed suicide."

"What about the body?"

"The cliff is called *El Garganta del Diablo*—in English, Throat of the
Devil. No bodies are ever located. It's actually a fairly common suicide
plunge."

"Great. Think you can do a little more background stuff on Rennart?"

"Like what?"

"How did he buy the bar in Neptune? How did he buy the house in Spring Lake Heights? Stuff like that."

"Why would you want to know that?"

"Lloyd Rennart was a caddie for a rookie golfer. That isn't exactly loads of dough."

"So?"

"So maybe he had a windfall after Jack blew the U.S. Open."

Esperanza saw where he was going. "You think somebody paid Rennart off to throw the Open?"

"No," Myron said. "But I think it's a possibility."

"It's going to be hard to trace after all this time."

"Just give it a shot. Also, Rennart got into a serious car accident twenty years ago in Narberth. It's a small town right around here. His first wife was killed in the crash. See what you can find out about it."

Esperanza frowned. "Like what?"

"Like was he drunk. Was he charged with anything. Were there other fatalities."

"Why?"

"Maybe he pissed off someone. Maybe his first wife's family wants vengeance."

Esperanza kept the frown. "So they—what?—waited twenty years, followed Lloyd Rennart to Peru, pushed him off a cliff, came back, kidnapped Chad Coldren, killed Jack Coldren. . . . Are you getting my point?"

Myron nodded. "And you're right. But I still want you to run down everything you can on Lloyd Rennart. I think there's a connection somewhere. We just have to find what it is."

"I don't see it," Esperanza said. She tucked a curl of black hair behind her ear. "Seems to me that Esme Fong is still a much better suspect."

"Agreed. But I'd still like you to look into it. Find out what you can. There's also a son. Larry Rennart. Seventeen years old. See if we can find out what he's been up to."

She shrugged. "A waste of time, but okay." She gestured toward the school. "You want to go in now?"

"Sure."

Before they moved, a giant set of knuckles gently tapped on Myron's window. The sound startled him. Myron looked out his window. The large black man with the Nat King Cole hair—the one from the Court Manor Inn—was smiling at him. "Nat" made a cranking motion with his hand, signaling Myron to lower the window. Myron complied.

"Hey, I'm glad we ran into you," Myron said. "I never got the number of your barber."

The black man chuckled. He made a frame with his large hands—thumbs touching, arms outstretched—and tilted it back and forth the way a movie director does. "You with my doo," he said with a shake of his head. "Somehow I just don't see it."

He leaned into the car and stuck his hand across Myron toward Esperanza. "My name is Carl."

"Esperanza." She shook his hand.

"Yes, I know."

Esperanza squinted at him. "I know you."

"Indeed you do."

She snapped her fingers. "Mosambo, the Kenyan Killer, the Safari Slasher."

Carl smiled. "Nice to see Little Pocahontas remembers."

Myron said, "The Safari Slasher?"

"Carl used to be a professional wrestler," Esperanza explained. "We were in the ring together once. In Boston, right?"

Carl climbed into the backseat of the car. He leaned forward so his head was between Esperanza's right shoulder and Myron's left. "Hartford," he said. "At the Civic Center."

"Mixed tag-team," Esperanza said.

"That's right," Carl said with his easy smile. "Be a sweetheart, Esperanza, and start up the car. Head straight until the third traffic light."

Myron said, "You mind telling us what's going on?"

"Sure thing. See that car behind you?"

Myron used the passenger-side mirror. "The one with the two goons?"

"Yep. They're with me. And they are bad men, Myron. Young. Far too violent. You know how the kids are today. *Bam, bam,* no talk. The three of us are supposed to escort you to an unknown destination. In fact, I'm supposed to be holding a gun on you now. But hell, we're all friends here, right? No need, the way I see it. So just start heading straight. The goons will follow."

"Before we take off," Myron said, "do you mind if we let Esperanza go?"

Carl chuckled. "Kinda sexist, don't you think?"

"Excuse me?"

"If Esperanza were a man—like, say, your buddy Win—would you be making this gallant gesture?"

"I might," he said. But even Esperanza was shaking her head.

"Me thinks not, Myron. And trust me here: it would be the wrong move. The young goons back there, they'd want to know what's up. They'd see her get out of the car and they got those itchy fingers and those crazy eyes and they like hurting people. Especially women. And maybe, just maybe, Esperanza here is an insurance policy. Alone, you might try something dumb; with Esperanza right there, you might not be so inclined."

Esperanza glanced at Myron. Myron nodded. She started the car.

"Make a left at the third light," Carl said.

"Tell me something," Myron said. "Is Reginald Squires as big a nut-job as I hear?"

Still leaning forward, Carl turned to Esperanza. "Am I supposed to be wowed by his sharp deductive reasoning skills?"

"Yes," Esperanza replied. "He'll be terribly disappointed if you aren't."

"Figured that. And to answer your question, Squires is not that big a nut-job—when he stays on his medication."

"Very comforting," Myron said.

The young goons stayed right on their tail for the entire fifteen-minute drive. Myron was not surprised when Carl told Esperanza to turn down Green Acres Road. When they approached the ornate front entrance, the iron gates swung open like on the closing credits of *Get Smart*. They continued up a windy driveway through the heavily wooded property. After about a half mile, they hit a clearing with a building. The building was big and plain and rectangular, like a high school gym.

The only entrance Myron could see was a garage door. As if on cue, the door slid open. Carl told Esperanza to pull into it. Once far enough inside, he told her to park and kill the engine. The goon car came in behind them and did likewise.

The garage door came back down, slowly slicing out the sun. No lights were on inside; the room was submerged in total darkness.

"This is just like the haunted house at Six Flags," Myron said.

"Give me your gun, Myron."

Carl had his game face on. Myron handed him the gun.

"Step out of the car."

"But I'm afraid of the dark," Myron said.

"You too, Esperanza."

They all stepped out the car. So did the two goons behind them. Their movements echoed off the cement floor, hinting to Myron that they were in a very large room. The interior car lights provided a modicum of illumination, but that didn't last long. Myron made out nothing before the doors were closed.

Absolute blackness.

Myron made his way around the car and found Esperanza. She took his hand in hers. They remained still and waited.

A beacon, the kind used at a lighthouse or a movie premiere, snapped on in their faces. Myron's eyes slammed shut. He shaded them with his hand and slowly squinted them open. A man stepped in front of the bright light. His body cast a giant shadow on the wall behind Myron. The effect reminded Myron of the Bat Signal.

"No one will hear your screams," the man said.

"Isn't that a line from a movie?" Myron asked. "But I think the line was, 'No one will hear you scream,' I could be wrong about that."

"People have died in this room," the voice boomed. "My name is Reginald Squires. You will tell me everything I want to know. Or you and your friend will be next."

Oh, boy. Myron looked at Carl. Carl's face remained stoic. Myron turned back toward the light. "You're rich, right?"

"Very rich," Squires corrected.

"Then maybe you could afford a better scriptwriter."

Myron glanced back at Carl. Carl slowly shook his head no. One of the two young goons stepped forward. In the harsh light, Myron could see the man's psychotic, happy smile. Myron tensed, waited.

The goon cocked a fist and threw it at Myron's head. Myron ducked, and the punch missed. As the fist flew by him, Myron grabbed the goon's wrist. He put his forearm against the back of the man's elbow and pulled the joint back in a way it was never intended to bend. The goon had no choice. He dropped to the ground. Myron added a bit more pressure. The goon tried to squirm free. Myron snapped his knee straight into the goon's nose. Something splattered. Myron could actually feel the nose cartilage give way and fan out.

The second goon took out his gun and pointed it at Myron.

"Stop," Squires shouted.

Myron let the goon go. He slid to the floor like wet sand through a torn bag.

"You will pay for that, Mr. Bolitar." Squires liked to project his voice. "Robert?"

The goon with the gun said, "Yes, Mr. Squires."

"Hit the girl. Hard."

"Yes, Mr. Squires."

Myron said, "Hey, hit me. I'm the one who smarted off."

"And this is your punishment," Squires said calmly. "Hit the girl, Robert. Now."

Goon Robert moved toward Esperanza.

"Mr. Squires?" It was Carl.

"Yes, Carl."

Carl stepped into the light. "Allow me to do it."

"I did not think you were the type, Carl."

"I'm not, Mr. Squires. But Robert might do serious damage to her."

"But that's my intent."

"No, I mean, he'll leave bruising or break something. You want her to feel pain. That's my area of expertise."

"I realize that, Carl. It's why I pay you what I do."

"So then let me do my job. I can hit her without leaving a mark or permanent injury. I know control. I know the right spots."

The shadowy Mr. Squires considered this a moment. "Will you make it painful?" he asked. "Very painful?"

"If you insist." Carl sounded reluctant but resolved.

"I do. Right now. I want it to hurt her a great deal."

Carl walked up to Esperanza. Myron started to move toward him, but Robert placed the gun against his head. There was nothing he could do. He tried fire-throwing a warning glare at Carl.

"Don't," Myron said.

Carl ignored him. He stood in front of Esperanza now. She looked at him defiantly. Without preamble he punched her deep in the stomach.

The power of the blow lifted Esperanza off her feet. She made an oofing noise and folded at the waist like an old wallet. Her body landed on the floor. She curled up into a protective ball, her eyes wide, her chest heaving for air. Carl looked down at her without emotion. Then he looked at Myron.

"You son of a bitch," Myron said.

"It's your fault," Carl said.

Esperanza continued to roll on the ground in obvious agony. She still couldn't get any air into her lungs. Myron's whole body felt hot and red. He moved toward her, but Robert again stopped him by pressing the gun hard against his neck.

Reginald Squires did the big voice-projection again. "You will listen now, won't you, Mr. Bolitar?"

Myron took deep breaths. His muscles bunched. Every part of him fumed. Every part of him craved vengeance. He watched in silence as Esperanza writhed on the floor. After a while she managed to get to all fours. Her head was down. Her body heaved. A retching noise came out of her. Then another retching noise.

The sound made Myron pause.

Something about the sound . . . Myron searched his memory banks. Something about the whole scenario, the way she doubled up, the way she rolled on the floor—it was strangely familiar. As though he'd seen it before. But that was impossible. When would he . . . ? He stopped as the answer came to him.

In the wrestling ring.

My God, Myron thought. She was faking it!

Myron looked over at Carl. There was a hint of a smile on his face. Son of a bitch. It was an act!

Reginald Squires cleared his throat. "You have taken an unhealthy interest in my son, Mr. Bolitar," he continued, voice thundering. "Are you some sort of pervert?"

Myron almost flew off another wisecrack, but he bit it back. "No."

"Then tell me what you want with him."

Myron squinted into the light. He still couldn't see anything but the shadowy outline of Squires. What should he say? The guy was a major loony tune. No question about that. So how to play this . . . ?

"You've heard about Jack Coldren's murder," Myron said.

"Of course."

"I'm working on the case."

"You're trying to find out who murdered Jack Coldren?"

"Yes."

"But Jack was murdered last night," Squires countered. "You were asking about my son Saturday."

"It's a long story," Myron said.

The shadow's hands spread. "We have all the time in the world."

How did Myron know he was going to say that?

With nothing much to lose, Myron told Squires about the kidnapping. Most of it anyway. He emphasized several times that the actual abduction had happened at the Court Manor Inn. There was a reason for that. It had to do with the egocentricity. Reginald Squires—the ego in question—reacted in predictable fashion.

"Are you telling me," he shouted, "that Chad Coldren was kidnapped at *my* motel?"

His motel. Myron had figured that out by now. It was the only explanation for why Carl had run interference for Stuart Lipwitz.

"That's right," Myron said.

"Carl?"

"Yes, Mr. Squires?"

"Did you know anything about this kidnapping?"

"No, Mr. Squires."

"Well, something has to be done," Squires shouted. "No one does something like that on my turf. You hear me? No one."

This guy had seen waaaaaay too many gangster films.

"Whoever did this is dead," he ranted on. "Do you hear me? I want them dead. D-E-A-D. Do you understand what I'm saying, Mr. Bolitar?"

"Dead," Myron said with a nod.

The shadow pointed a long finger at Myron. "You find him for me. You find who did this and then you call me. You let me handle it. Do you understand, Mr. Bolitar?"

"Call you. You handle."

"Go then. Find the wretched bastard."

Myron said, "Sure thing, Mr. Squires. Sure thing." Hey, two can play the Bad Movie Dialogue game. "But the thing is, I need some help."

"What sort of help?"

"With your permission, I'd like to speak with your son Matthew. Find out what he knows about all this."

"What makes you think he knows anything?"

"He's Chad's best friend. He may have heard or seen something. I don't know, Mr. Squires, but I'd like to check it out."

There was a brief silence. Then Squires snapped, "Do it. Carl will take you back to the school. Matthew will speak freely to you."

"Thank you, Mr. Squires."

The light went off, bathing them again in thick darkness. Myron felt his way to the car door. The "recovering" Esperanza managed to do likewise. So did Carl. The three of them got in.

Myron turned around and looked at Carl. Carl shrugged his shoulders and said, "Guess he forgot to take his medication."

32

C had, like, told me he was hooking up with an older babe."

"Did he tell you her name?" Myron asked.

"Nah, man," Matthew Squires said. "Just that she was take-out."

"Take-out?"

"You know. Chinese."

Jesus.

Myron sat facing Matthew Squires. The kid was pure Yah Dude. His long, stringy hair was parted in the middle and hung past his shoulders. The coloring and texture reminded Myron of Cousin It from the *Addams Family*. He had acne, a fair amount of it. He was over six feet and weighed maybe one hundred twenty pounds. Myron wondered what it had been like for this kid growing up with Mr. Spotlight as a father.

Carl was on his right. Esperanza had taken a taxi to check out Esme Fong's alibi and look into Lloyd Rennart's past.

"Did Chad tell you where he was meeting her?"

"Sure, dude. That hot sheet is, like, my dad's haunt, you know."

"Did Chad know your father owned the Court Manor?"

"Nah. We don't, like, talk daddy's dinero or anything. Not righteous, you know what I'm saying?"

Myron and Carl exchanged a glance. The glance bemoaned today's youth.

"Did you go with him to the Court Manor?"

"Nah. I went later, you know. I figured the dude would want to party after getting a little, you know. Kinda celebrate and shit."

"So what time did you go to the Court Manor?"

"Ten-thirty, eleven, something like that."

"Did you see Chad?"

"Nah. Things got, like, so weird right away. Never got the chance."

"What do you mean, weird?"

Matthew Squires hesitated a bit. Carl leaned forward. "It's okay, Matthew. Your father wants you to tell him the whole story."

The kid nodded. When the chin went down, the stringy hair slid across the face. It was like a tasseled curtain opening and closing in rapid succession. "Okay, like, here's the deal: When I pulled my Benz into the parking lot, I saw Chad's old man."

Myron felt a queasy surge. "Jack Coldren? You saw Jack Coldren? At the Court Manor Inn?"

Squires nodded. "He was just, like, sitting in his car," he said. "Next to Chad's Honda. He looked really pissed off, man. I wanted no part of it, you know? So I took a hike."

Myron tried not to look too stunned. Jack Coldren at the Court Manor Inn. His son inside a room screwing Esme Fong. The next morning Chad Coldren would be kidnapped.

What the hell was going on?

"Friday night," Myron continued, "I saw someone climb out the window of Chad's room. Was that you?"

"Yeah."

"You want to tell me what you were doing?"

"Seeing if Chad was home. That's what we do. I climb through his window. Like Vinny used to do with Doogie Howser. Remember that show?"

Myron nodded. He did know. Kinda sad when you thought about it.

There was not much more to extract from young Matthew. When they finished up, Carl walked Myron to his car.

"Strange shit," Carl said.

"Yep."

"You'll call when you learn something?"

"Yep." Myron didn't bother telling him that Tito was already dead. No point. "Nice move, by the way. The fake punch with Esperanza."

Carl smiled. "We're professionals. I'm disappointed you spotted it."

"If I hadn't seen Esperanza in the ring, I wouldn't have. It was very nice work. You should be proud."

"Thanks." Carl stuck out his hand. Myron shook it. He got in the car and drove away. Now where?

Back to the Coldren house, he guessed.

His mind still reeled from this latest revelation: Jack Coldren had been at the Court Manor Inn. He had seen his son's car there. How the heck did that fit into this? Was Jack Coldren following Chad? Maybe. Was he just there by coincidence? Doubtful. So what other options were there? Why would Jack Coldren be following his own son? And where had he followed him from—Matthew Squires's house? Did that make sense? The man plays in the U.S. Open, has a great opening round, and then goes parking in front of the Squires estate waiting for his kid to pull out?

Nope.

Hold the phone.

Suppose Jack Coldren had not been following his son. Suppose he had been following Esme Fong.

Something in his brain went "click."

Maybe Jack Coldren had been having an affair with Esme Fong too. His marriage was on the rocks. Esme Fong was probably a bit of a kinkster. She had seduced a teenage boy—what would have stopped her from seducing his father? But did this make sense either? Was Jack stalking her? Had he somehow found out about the tryst? What?

And the larger question: What does any of this have to do with Chad Coldren's kidnapping and Jack Coldren's murder?

He pulled up to the Coldren house. The media had been kept back, but there were now at least a dozen cops on hand. They were hauling out cardboard boxes. As Victoria Wilson had feared, the police had gotten a search warrant.

Myron parked around the corner and walked toward the house. Jack's caddie, Diane Hoffman, sat alone on the curb across the street. He remembered the last time he had seen her at the Coldren house: in the backyard, fighting with Jack. He also realized that she had been one of the very few people who knew about the kidnapping—hadn't she been standing right there when Myron first talked about it with Jack at the driving range?

She was worth a conversation.

Diane Hoffman was smoking a cigarette. The several stubs by her feet indicated that she had been there for more than a few minutes. Myron approached.

"Hi," he said. "We met the other day."

Diane Hoffman looked up at him, took a deep drag of the cigarette, released it into the still air. "I remember." Her hoarse voice sounded like old tires on rough pavement.

"My condolences," Myron said. "You and Jack must have been very close."

Another deep drag. "Yeah."

"Caddy and golfer. Must be a tight relationship."

She looked up at him, squinting suspiciously. "Yeah."

"Almost like husband and wife. Or business partners."

"Uh-huh. Something like that."

"Did you two ever fight?"

She glared at him for a second, then she broke into a laugh that ended in a hacking cough. When she could talk again, she asked, "Why the hell do you want to know that?"

"Because I saw you two fighting."

"What?"

"Friday night. You two were in the backyard. You called him names. You threw down your cigarette in disgust."

Diane Hoffman crushed out the cigarette. There was the smallest smile on her face. "You some kinda Sherlock Holmes, Mr. Bolitar?"

"No. I'm just asking you a question."

"And I can tell you to go mind your own fucking business, right?"

"Right."

"Good. Then you go do that." The smile became fuller now. It was not a particularly pretty smile. "But first—to save you some time—I'll tell you who killed Jack. And also who kidnapped the kid, if you like."

"I'm all ears."

"The bitch in there." She pointed to the house behind her with a thumb. "The one you got the hots for."

"I don't have the hots for her."

Diane Hoffman sneered. "Right."

"What makes you so sure it was Linda Coldren?"

"Because I know the bitch."

"That's not much of an answer."

"Tough luck, cowpoke. Your girlfriend did it. You want to know why Jack and me was fighting? I'll tell you. I told him he was being an asshole for not calling the police about the kidnapping. He said he and Linda thought it best." She sneered. "He and Linda, my ass."

Myron watched her. Something wasn't meshing again.

"You think it was Linda's idea not to call the police?"

"Damn straight. She's the one who grabbed the kid. The whole thing was a big setup."

"Why would she do that?"

"Ask her." An awful smile. "Maybe she'll tell you."

"I'm asking you."

She shook her head. "Not that easy, cowpoke. I told you who did it. That's enough, don't you think?"

Time to approach from another angle. "How long have you been Jack's caddie?" he asked.

"A year."

"What's your qualifications, if I may ask? Why did Jack choose you?"

She snorted a chuckle. "Don't matter none. Jack didn't listen to caddies. Not since ol' Lloyd Rennart."

"Did you know Lloyd Rennart?"

"Nope."

"So why did Jack hire you?"

She did not answer.

"Were you two sleeping together?"

Diane Hoffman gave another cough-laugh. A big one. "Not likely." More hacking laughter. "Not likely with ol' Jack."

Somebody called his name. Myron turned around. It was Victoria Wilson. Her face was still sleepy, but she beckoned him with some urgency. Bucky stood next to her. The old man looked like a window draft would send him skittering.

"Better head on down there, cowpoke," she mocked. "I think your girlfriend is gonna need some help."

He gave her a last look and turned toward the house. Before he moved three steps, Detective Corbett was on him. "Need a word with you, Mr. Bolitar."

Myron brushed past him. "In a minute."

When he reached Victoria Wilson, she made herself very clear: "Do not talk to the cops," she said. "In fact, go to Win's and stay put."

"I'm not crazy about taking orders," Myron said.

"Sorry if I'm bruising your male ego," she said in a tone that made it clear she was anything but. "But I know what I'm doing."

"Have the police found the finger?"

Victoria Wilson crossed her arms. "Yes."

"And?"

"And nothing."

Myron looked at Bucky. Bucky looked away. He turned his attention back to Victoria Wilson. "They didn't ask you about it?"

"They asked. We refused to answer."

"But the finger could exonerate her."

Victoria Wilson sighed and turned away. "Go home, Myron. I'll call you if anything new turns up."

33

I t was time to face Win.

Myron rehearsed several possible approaches in the car. None felt right, but that really did not matter much. Win was his friend. When the time came, Myron would deliver the message and Win would adhere to it or not.

The trickier question was, of course, should the message be delivered at all? Myron knew that repression was unhealthy and all that—but did anybody really want to risk unbottling Win's suppressed rage?

The cell phone rang. Myron picked it up. It was Tad Crispin.

"I need your help," Tad said.

"What's up?"

"The media keep hounding me for a comment. I'm not sure what to say."

"Nothing," Myron told him. "Say nothing."

"Yeah, okay, but it's not that easy. Learner Shelton—he's the Commissioner of the USGA—called me twice. He wants to have a big trophy ceremony tomorrow. Name me U.S. Open champion. I'm not sure what to do."

Smart kid, Myron thought. He knows that if this is handled poorly, it could seriously wound him. "Tad?"

"Yes?"

"Are you hiring me?" Business was still business. Agenting was not charity work.

"Yeah, Myron, you're hired."

"Okay then, listen up. There'll be details to work out first. Percentages, that kinda thing. Most of it is fairly standard." Kidnapping, limb-severing, murder—nothing stopped the almighty agent from trying to turn a buck. "In the meantime, say nothing. I'll have a car come by to pick you up in a couple of hours. The driver will call up to your room before he gets there. Go straight to the car and say nothing. No matter what the press yells at you, keep silent. Do not smile or wave. Look grim. A man has just been murdered. The driver will bring you to Win's estate. We'll discuss strategy then."

"Thanks, Myron."

"No, Tad, thank you."

Profiting from a murder. Myron had never felt so much like a real agent in all his life.

The media had set up camp outside Win's estate.

"I've hired extra guards for the evening," Win explained, empty brandy snifter in hand. "If anybody approaches the gate, they've been instructed to shoot to kill."

"I appreciate that."

Win gave a quick head bow. He poured some Grand Marnier into the snifter. Myron grabbed a Yoo-Hoo from the fridge. The two men sat.

"Jessica called," Win said.

"Here?"

"Yes."

"Why didn't she call me on the cellular?"

"She wanted to speak with me," Win said.

"Oh." Myron shook his Yoo-Hoo, just like the side of the can said. SHAKE! IT'S GREAT! Life is poetry. "What about?"

"She was worried about you," Win said.

"Why?"

"For one thing, Jessica claimed that you left a cryptic message on the answering machine."

"Did she tell you what I said?"

"No. Just that your voice sounded strained."

"I told her that I loved her. That I'd always love her."

Win took a sip and nodded as though that explained everything.

"What?"

"Nothing," Win said.

"No, tell me. What?"

Win put down the snifter and steepled his fingers. "Who were you trying to convince?" he asked. "Her or you?"

"What the hell does that mean?"

Bouncing the fingers now instead of steepling. "Nothing."

"You know how much I love Jessica."

"Indeed I do," Win said.

"You know what I've gone through to get her back."

"Indeed I do."

"I still don't get it," Myron said. "That's why Jess called you? Because my voice sounded strained?"

"Not entirely, no. She'd heard about Jack Coldren's murder. Naturally, she was upset. She asked me to watch your back."

"What did you tell her?"

"No."

Silence.

Win lifted the snifter in the air. He swirled around the liquid and inhaled deeply. "So what did you wish to discuss with me?"

"I met your mother today."

Win took a slow sip. He let the liquid roll over his tongue, his eyes studying the bottom of the glass. After he swallowed, he said, "Pretend I just gasped in surprise."

"She wanted me to give you a message."

A small smile came to Win's lips. "I assume that dear ma-ma told you what happened."

"Yes."

A bigger smile now. "So now you know it all, eh, Myron?"

"No."

"Oh come, come, don't make it so easy. Give me some of that pop psychology you're so fond of expounding. An eight-year-old boy witnessing his grunting mother on all fours with another man—surely that scarred me emotionally. Can we not trace back everything I've become to that one dastardly moment? Isn't this episode the reason why I treat women the way I do, why I build an emotional fortress around myself, why I choose fists where others choose words? Come now, Myron. You must have considered all this. Tell me all. I am sure it will all be oh-so-insightful."

Myron waited a beat. "I'm not here to analyze you, Win."

"No?"

"No."

Win's eyes hardened. "Then wipe that pity off your face."

"It's not pity," Myron said. "It's concern."

"Oh please."

"It may have happened twenty-five years ago, but it had to hurt. Maybe it didn't shape you. Maybe you would have ended up the exact same person you are today. But that doesn't mean it didn't hurt."

Win relaxed his jaw. He picked up the snifter. It was empty. He poured himself more. "I no longer wish to discuss this," he said. "You know now why I want nothing to do with Jack Coldren or my mother. Let us move on."

"There's still the matter of her message."

"Ah, yes, the message," Win repeated. "You are aware, are you not, that dear ma-ma still sends me presents on my birthday and assorted holidays?"

Myron nodded. They had never discussed it. But he knew.

"I return them unopened," Win said. He took another sip. "I think I will do the same with this message."

"She's dying, Win. Cancer. She has maybe a week or two."

"I know."

Myron sat back. His throat felt dry.

"Is that the entire message?"

"She wanted you to know that it's your last chance to talk to her," Myron said.

"Well, yes, that's true. It would be very difficult for us to chat after she's dead."

Myron was flailing now. "She's not expecting any kind of big reconciliation. But if there are any issues you want to resolve . . ." Myron stopped. He was being redundant and obvious now. Win hated that.

"That's it?" Win asked. "That's your big message?"

Myron nodded.

"Fine, then. I'm going to order some Chinese. I hope that will be suitable with you."

Win rose from his seat and strolled toward the kitchen.

"You claim it didn't change you," Myron said. "But before that day, did you love her?"

Win's face was a stone. "Who says I don't love her now?"

34

The driver brought Tad Crispin in through the back entrance. Win and Myron had been watching television. A commercial came on for Scope. A married couple in bed woke up and turned their heads in disgust. Morning breath, the voice-over informed them. You need Scope. Scope cures morning breath.

Myron said, "So would, say, brushing your teeth?"

Win nodded.

Myron opened the door and led Tad into the living room. Tad sat on a couch across from Myron and Win. He glanced about, his eyes searching for a spot to settle on but not having any luck. He smiled weakly.

"Would you care for a beverage?" Win asked. "A croissant or a Pop Tart perhaps?" The Host with the Most.

"No, thank you." Another weak smile.

Myron leaned forward. "Tad, tell us about Learner Shelton's call."

The kid dove right in. "He said that he wanted to congratulate me on my victory. That the USGA had officially declared me the U.S. Open champion." For a moment, Tad stopped. His eyes hazed over, the words hitting him anew. Tad Crispin, U.S. Open champion. The stuff of dreams.

"What else did he say?"

Crispin's eyes slowly cleared. "He's holding a press conference tomorrow afternoon. At Merion. They'll give me the trophy and a check for $360,000."

Myron did not waste time. "First of all, we tell the media that you do not consider yourself the U.S. Open champion. If they want to call you that, fine. If the USGA wants to call you that, fine. You, however, believe that the tournament ended in a tie. Death should not rob Jack Coldren of his magnificent accomplishment or his claim to the title. A tie it ended. A tie it is. From your vantage point, you two are co-winners. Do you understand?"

Tad was hesitant. "I think so."

"Now, about that check." Myron strummed the end table with his fingers. "If they insist on giving you the full winner's purse, you'll have to donate Jack's portion to charity."

"Victims' rights," Win said.

Myron nodded. "That would be good. Something against violence—"

"Wait a second," Tad interrupted. He rubbed the palms of his hands on his thighs. "You want me to give away $180,000?"

"It'll be a tax write-off," Win said. "That knocks the value down to half that."

"And it'll be chicken feed compared to the positive press you'll get," Myron added.

"But I was charging back," Tad insisted. "I had the momentum. I would have won."

Myron leaned in a little closer. "You're an athlete, Tad. You're competitive and confident. That's good—heck, that's great. But not in this situation. This murder story is huge. It transcends sports. For most of the world's population, this will be their first look at Tad Crispin. We want them to see someone likable. Someone decent and trustworthy and modest. If we brag now about what a great golfer you are—if we dwell on your comeback rather than this tragedy—people are going to see you as cold, as another example of what's wrong with today's athletes. Do you see what I'm saying?"

Tad nodded. "I guess so."

"We have to present you in a certain light. We have to control the story as much as possible."

"So we do interviews?" Tad asked.

"Very few."

"But if we want publicity—"

"We want carefully orchestrated publicity," Myron corrected. "This story is so big, the last thing we need to do is create more interest. I want you to be reclusive, Tad. Thoughtful. You see, we have to maintain the right balance. If we toot our horn, it looks like we're grandstanding. If we do a lot of interviews, it looks like we're taking advantage of a man's murder."

"Disastrous," Win added.

"Right. What we want to do is control the flow of information. Feed the press a few tiny morsels. No more."

"Perhaps one interview," Win said. "One where you will be at your most contrite."

"With Bob Costas maybe."

"Or even Barbara Walters."

"And we don't announce your big donation."

"Correct, no press conference. You are far too magnanimous for such bravado."

That confused Tad. "How are we supposed to get good press if we don't announce it?"

"We leak it," Myron said. "We get someone at the charity to tell a nosy reporter, maybe. Something like that. The key is, Tad Crispin must remain far too modest a fellow to publicize his own good deeds. Do you see what we're aiming for here?"

Tad's nod was more enthusiastic now. He was warming up. Myron felt like a heel. Spin-doctoring—just another hat today's sports representative must wear. Being an agent was not always pretty. You had to get dirty sometimes. Myron did not necessarily like it, but he was willing. The media would portray events one way; he would present them another. Still he felt like a grinning political strategist after a debate, and you cannot get much lower than that.

They discussed details for a few more minutes. Tad started to look off again. He was rubbing the famed palms against the pants again. When Win left the room for a minute, Tad whispered, "I saw on the news that you're Linda Coldren's attorney."

"I'm one of them."

"Are you her agent?"

"I might be," Myron said. "Why?"

"Then you're a lawyer too, right? You went to law school and everything?"

Myron was not sure he liked where this was going. "Yes."

"So I can hire you to be my lawyer too, right? Not just my agent?"

Myron really didn't like where this was going. "Why would you need a lawyer, Tad?"

"I'm not saying I do. But if I did—"

"Whatever you tell me is confidential," Myron said.

Tad Crispin stood. He put his arms out straight and gripped an imaginary golf club. He took a swing. Air golf. Win played it all the time. All golfers do. Basketball players don't do that. It's not like Myron stops at every store window and checks the reflection of his shot in the mirror.

Golfers.

"I'm surprised you don't know about this already," Tad said slowly.

But the creeping feeling in the pit of Myron's stomach told him that maybe he did. "Don't know about what, Tad?"

Tad took another swing. He stopped his movement to check his backswing. Then his expression changed to one of panic. He dropped the imaginary club to the floor. "It was only a couple of times," he said, his words pouring out like silver beads. "It was no big deal really. I mean, we met while we were filming those ads for Zoom." He looked at Myron, his eyes pleading. "You've seen her, Myron. I mean, I know she's twenty years older than me, but she's so good-looking and she said her marriage was dead. . . ."

Myron did not hear the rest of his words; the ocean was crashing in his ears. Tad Crispin and Linda Coldren. He could not believe it, yet it made perfect sense. A young guy obviously charmed by a stunning older woman. The mature beauty trapped in a loveless marriage finding escape in young, handsome arms. Nothing really wrong with it.

Yet Myron felt his cheeks go scarlet. Something inside of him began to fume.

Tad was still droning on. Myron interrupted him.

"Did Jack find out?"

Tad stopped. "I don't know," he said. "But I think maybe he did."

"What makes you say that?"

"It was just the way he acted. We played two rounds together. I know we were competitors and that he was trying to intimidate me. But I kind of got the impression he knew."

Myron lowered his head into his hands. He felt sick to his stomach.

Tad asked, "Do you think it'll get out?"

Myron held back a chuckle. This would be one of the biggest news stories of the year. The media would attack like old women at a Loehmann's clearance sale. "I don't know, Tad."

"What do we do?"

"We hope it doesn't get out."

Tad was scared. "And if it does?"

Myron faced him. Tad Crispin looked so damn young—check that, he was young. Most kids his age are happily pulling fraternity pranks. And when you thought about it, what had Tad really done that was so bad? Slept with an older woman who for some odd reason remained in a dead marriage. Hardly unnatural. Myron tried to picture himself at Tad's age. If a beautiful older woman like Linda Coldren had come on to him, would he have stood a chance?

Like, duh. He probably did not stand a chance now.

But what about Linda Coldren? Why did she stay in this dead marriage? Religion? Doubtful. For the sake of her son? The kid was sixteen years old. It might not be easy, but he'd survive.

"Myron, what'll happen if the media find out?"

But Myron was suddenly no longer thinking about the media. He was thinking about the police. He was thinking about Victoria Wilson and reasonable doubt. Linda Coldren had probably told her ace attorney about her affair with Tad Crispin. Victoria would have seen it too.

Who is declared U.S. Open champion now that Jack Coldren is dead?

Who doesn't have to worry about out-choking the choker in front of a massive audience?

Who has all the same motives to kill Jack Coldren that Myron had earlier assigned to Esme Fong?

Whose squeaky-clean image might get soiled by a Coldren divorce, especially one where Jack Coldren would name his wife's indiscretion?

Who was having an affair with the deceased's wife?

The answer to all the above was sitting in front of him.

35

Tad Crispin left not long after that.

Myron and Win settled into the couch. They put on Woody Allen's *Broadway Danny Rose*, one of Woody's most under-rated masterpieces. What a flick. Rent it sometime.

During the scene where Mia drags Woody to the fortune-teller, Esperanza arrived.

She coughed into her fist. "I, ahem, don't want to sound didactic or fictitious in any manner," she began, doing a great Woody impression. She had his timing, the speech delay tactics. She had the hand mannerisms. She had the New York accent. It was her best work. "But I may have some important information."

Myron looked up. Win kept his eyes on the screen.

"I located the man Lloyd Rennart bought the bar from twenty years ago," Esperanza said, returning to her own voice. "Rennart paid him in cash. Seven grand. I also checked on the house in Spring Lake Heights. Bought at the same time for $21,000. No mortgage."

"Lots of expenses," Myron said, "for a washed-up caddie."

"Sí, señor. And to make matters more interesting, I also found no indication that he worked or paid taxes from the time he was fired by Jack Coldren until he purchased the Rusty Nail bar."

"Could be an inheritance."

"I would doubt it," Esperanza said. "I managed to go back to 1971 and found no record of him paying any inheritance tax."

Myron looked at Win. "What do you think?"

Win's eyes were still on the screen. "I'm not listening."

"Right, I forgot." He looked back at Esperanza. "Anything else?"

"Esme Fong's alibi checks out. I spoke to Miguel. She never left the hotel."

"Is he solid?"

"Yeah, I think so."

Strike one. "Anything else?"

"Not yet. But I found the office for the local paper in Narberth. They have the back editions in a storage room. I'll go through them tomorrow, see what I can dig up on the car accident."

Esperanza grabbed a take-out container and a pair of chopsticks from the kitchen and then she plopped down on the open couch. A mafioso hit man was calling Woody a cheesehead. Woody commented that he had no idea what that meant, but he was confident it wasn't a good thing. Ah, the Woodman.

Ten minutes into *Love and Death*, not long after Woody wondered how old Nahampkin could be younger than young Nahampkin, exhaustion overtook Myron. He fell asleep on the couch. A deep sleep. No dreams. No stirring. Nothing but the long fall down the deep well.

He woke up at eight-thirty. The television was off. A clock ticked and then chimed. Someone had laid a comforter over Myron while he'd been sleeping. Win probably. He checked the other bedrooms. Win and Esperanza were both gone.

He showered and dressed and put on some coffee. The phone rang. Myron picked it up and said, "Hello."

It was Victoria Wilson. She still sounded bored. "They arrested Linda."

Myron found Victoria Wilson in an attorney waiting area.

"How is she?"

"Fine," Victoria replied. "I brought Chad home last night. That made her happy."

"So where is Linda?"

"In a holding cell awaiting arraignment. We'll see her in a few minutes."

"What do they have?"

"Quite a bit, actually," Victoria said. She sounded almost impressed. "First, they have the guard who saw her entering and leaving an otherwise abandoned golf course at the time of the murder. With the exception of Jack, nobody else was seen going in or out all night."

"Doesn't mean nobody did. It's an awfully big area."

"Very true. But from their standpoint it gives Linda opportunity. Second, they found hairs and fibers on Jack's body and around the murder scene that preliminary tests link to Linda. Naturally, this one should be no problem to discredit. Jack is her husband; of course he'd have hair and fibers from her on his body. He could have spread them around the scene."

"Plus she told us she went to the course to look for Jack," Myron added.

"But we're not telling them that."

"Why not?"

"Because right now we are saying and admitting to nothing."

Myron shrugged. Not important. "What else?"

"Jack owned a twenty-two-caliber handgun. The police found it in a wooded area between the Coldren residence and Merion last night."

"It was just sitting out?"

"No. It was buried in fresh dirt. A metal detector picked it up."

"They're sure it's Jack's gun?"

She nodded. "The serial numbers match. The police ran an immediate ballistics test. It's the murder weapon."

Myron's veins iced up.

"Fingerprints?" he asked.

Victoria Wilson shook her head. "Wiped clean."

"Are they running a powder test on her?" The police run a test on the hands, see if there are any powder burns.

"It'll take a few days," Victoria said, "and it'll probably be negative."

"You had her scrub her hands?"

"And treat them, yes."

"Then you think she did it."

Her tone remained unruffled. "Please don't say that."

She was right. But it was starting to look bad. "Is there more?" he asked.

"The police found your tape machine still hooked up to the phone. They were obviously curious as to why the Coldrens found it necessary to tape all incoming calls."

"Did they find any tapes of the conversations with the kidnapper?"

"Just the one where the kidnapper refers to the Fong woman as a 'chink bitch' and demands one hundred grand. And to answer your next two questions, no, we did not elaborate on the kidnapping and yes, they are pissed off."

Myron pondered that for a moment. Something was not right. "That was the only tape they found?"

"That's it."

He frowned. "But if the machine was still hooked up, it should have taped the last call the kidnapper made to Jack. The one that got him to storm out of the house and head to Merion."

Victoria Wilson looked at him steadily. "The police found no other tapes. Not in the house. Not on Jack's body. Nowhere."

Again the ice in the veins. The implication was obvious: The most reasonable explanation for there being no tape was that there was no call. Linda Coldren had made it up. The lack of a tape would have been viewed as a major contradiction *if* she had said anything to the cops. Fortunately for Linda, Victoria Wilson had never let her tell her story in the first place.

The woman was good.

"Can you get me a copy of the tape the police found?" he asked.

Victoria Wilson nodded. "There is still more," she said.

Myron was almost afraid to hear it.

"Let's take the severed finger for a moment," she continued as though ordering it as an appetizer. "You found it in Linda's car in a manila envelope."

Myron nodded.

"The envelope is the type sold only at Staples—their brand, the number ten size. The writing was done by a red Flair pen, medium-point. Three weeks ago, Linda Coldren visited Staples. According to the receipt found at her house yesterday, she purchased numerous office supplies, including a box of Staples' number ten manila envelopes and a red Flair medium-point pen."

Myron could not believe what he was hearing.

"On the positive side, their handwriting analyst could not tell if the writing on the envelope came from Linda."

But something else was dawning on Myron. Linda had waited around for him at Merion. The two of them had gone to the car together. They had found the finger together. The district attorney would pounce upon that story. Why had she waited for Myron? The answer, the DA would claim, was obvious: she needed a witness. She had planted the finger in her own car—she could certainly do that without drawing suspicion—and she needed a hapless dupe to be with her when she found it.

Enter Myron Bolitar, the dupe du jour.

But of course, Victoria Wilson had neatly arranged it so that the DA would never hear that story. Myron was Linda's attorney. He could not tell. No one would ever know.

Yep, the woman was good—except for one thing.

"The severed finger," Myron said. "That has to be the kicker, Victoria. Who is going to believe that a mother would cut off her own son's finger?"

Victoria looked at her watch. "Let's go talk to Linda."

"No, hold up here. That's the second time you blew this off. What aren't you telling me?"

She slung her purse over her shoulder. "Come on."

"Hey, I'm getting a little tired of getting jerked around here."

Victoria Wilson nodded slowly, but she did not speak or stop walking. Myron followed her into a holding room. Linda Coldren was already there. She was decked out in a bright orange prison jumpsuit. Her hands were still manacled. She looked up at Myron through hollow eyes. There were no hellos or hugs or even pleasantries.

Without preamble, Victoria said, "Myron wants to know why I don't think the severed finger helps us."

Linda faced him. There was a sad smile on her face. "I guess that's understandable."

"What the hell is going on here?" Myron said. "I know you didn't cut off your own son's finger."

The sad smile remained. "I didn't do it," Linda said. "That part is true."

"What do you mean, that part?"

"You said I didn't cut off my son's finger," she continued. "But Chad is not my son."

36

Something in Myron's head clicked again.

"I'm infertile," Linda explained. She said the words with great ease, but the pain in her eyes was so raw and naked that Myron almost flinched. "I have this condition where my ovaries cannot produce eggs. But Jack still wanted a biological child."

Myron spoke softly. "You hired a surrogate?"

Linda looked toward Victoria. "Yes," she said. "Though it was not quite so aboveboard."

"It was all done to the letter of the law," Victoria interjected.

"You handled it for them?" Myron asked.

"I did the paperwork, yes. The adoption was completely legal."

"We wanted to keep it a secret," Linda said. "That's why I took off from the tour so early. I went into seclusion. The birth mother was never even supposed to know who we were."

Something else in his head went click. "But she found out."

"Yes."

Another click. "It's Diane Hoffman, isn't it?"

Linda was too exhausted to look surprised. "How did you know?"

"Just an educated guess." Why else would Jack hire Diane Hoffman as his caddie? Why else would she have gotten upset at the way they were handling the kidnapping? "How did she find you?"

Victoria answered that one. "As I said, it was all done legally. With all the new disclosure laws, it wasn't that hard to do."

Another click. "That's why you couldn't divorce Jack. He was the biological parent. He'd have the upper hand in a custody battle."

Linda slumped her shoulders and nodded.

"Does Chad know about all this?"

"No," Linda said.

"At least, not to your knowledge," Myron said.

"What?"

"You don't know for sure. Maybe he found out. Maybe Jack told him. Or Diane. Maybe that's how this whole thing got started."

Victoria crossed her arms. "I don't see it, Myron. Suppose Chad did find out. How would that have led to his own kidnapping and his father's murder?"

Myron shook his head. It was a good question. "I don't know yet. I need time to think it through. Do the police know all this?"

"About the adoption? Yes."

It was beginning to make sense now. "This gives the DA their motive. They'll say that Jack's suing for divorce worried Linda. That she killed him to keep her son."

Victoria Wilson nodded. "And the fact that Linda is not the biological mother could play one of two ways: either she loved her son so much that she killed Jack to keep him—or because Chad was not her own flesh and blood, she could indeed be driven to cut off his finger."

"Either way, finding the finger doesn't help us."

Victoria nodded. She did not say "I told you so," but she might as well have.

"Can I say something?" It was Linda. They turned and looked at her. "I didn't love Jack anymore. I told you that straight out, Myron. I doubt I would have, if I'd been planning on killing him."

Myron nodded. Made sense.

"But I do love my son—*my* son—more than life itself. The fact that it's more believable that I'd maim him because I'm an adoptive mother rather than a biological one is sick and grotesque in the extreme. I love Chad as much as any mother could love a child."

She stopped, her chest heaving. "I want you both to know that."

"We know," Victoria said. Then: "Let's all sit down."

When they were settled in their seats, Victoria continued to take charge. "I know it's early, but I want to start thinking about reasonable doubt. Their case will have holes. I'll be sure to exploit them. But I'd like to hear some alternative theories on what happened."

"In other words," Myron said, "some other suspects."

Victoria caught something in his tone. "That's exactly what I mean."

"Well, you already have one ace in the hole, don't you?"

Victoria nodded coolly. "I do."

"Tad Crispin, right?"

This time, Linda did indeed look surprised. Victoria remained unfazed. "Yes, he's a suspect."

"The kid hired me last night," Myron said. "Talking about him would be a conflict of interest."

"Then we won't talk about him."

"I'm not sure that's good enough."

"Then you'll have to dump him as a client," Victoria said. "Linda hired you first. Your obligation must be to her. If you feel that there is a conflict, then you'll have to call Mr. Crispin and tell him that you cannot represent him."

Trapped. And she knew it.

"Let's talk about other suspects," Myron said.

Victoria nodded. Battle won. "Go ahead."

"First off, Esme Fong." Myron filled them in on all the reasons that she made a good suspect. Again Victoria looked sleepy; Linda looked semi-homicidal.

"She seduced my son?" Linda shouted. "The bitch came into my house and seduced my son?"

"Apparently so."

"I can't believe it. That's why Chad was at that sleazy motel?"

"Yup—"

"Okay," Victoria interrupted. "I like it. This Esme Fong has motive. She has means. She was one of the few people who knew where Chad was."

"She also has an alibi for the killing," Myron added.

"But not a great one. There must be other ways in and out of that hotel. She could have worn a disguise. She could have sneaked out when Miguel took a bathroom break. I like her. Who else?"

"Lloyd Rennart."

"Who?"

"Jack's former caddie," Myron explained. "The one who helped throw the Open."

Victoria frowned. "Why him?"

"Look at the timing. Jack returns to the site of his greatest failure and suddenly all this happens. It can't be a coincidence. Firing Rennart ruined his life. He became a drunk. He killed his own wife in a car crash."

"What?" It was Linda.

"Not long after the Open, Lloyd totaled his car while DWI. His wife was killed."

Victoria asked, "Did you know her?"

Linda shook her head. "We never met his family. In fact, I don't think I ever saw Lloyd outside of our home or the golf course."

Victoria crossed her arms and leaned back. "I still do not see what makes him a viable suspect."

"Rennart wanted vengeance. He waited twenty-three years to get it."

Victoria frowned again.

"I admit that it's a bit of a stretch."

"A bit? It's ridiculous. Do you know where Lloyd Rennart is now?"

"That's a little complicated."

"Oh?"

"He may have committed suicide."

Victoria looked at Linda, then at Myron. "Would you please elaborate?"

"The body was never found," Myron said. "But everyone thinks he jumped off a cliff in Peru."

Linda groaned. "Oh, no . . ."

"What is it?" Victoria asked.

"We got a postcard from Peru."

"Who did?"

"It was addressed to Jack, but it was unsigned. It arrived last fall or winter."

Myron's pulse raced. Last fall or winter. About the time Lloyd allegedly jumped. "What did it say?"

"It only had two words on it," Linda said. " 'Forgive me.' "

Silence.

Victoria broke it. "That doesn't sound like the words of a man out for revenge."

"No," Myron agreed. He remembered what Esperanza had learned about the money Rennart had used to buy his house and bar. This postcard now confirmed what he had already suspected: Jack had been sabotaged. "But it also means that what happened twenty-three years ago was no accident."

"So what good does that do us?" Victoria asked.

"Someone paid Rennart off to throw the U.S. Open. Whoever did that would have motive."

"To kill Rennart maybe," Victoria countered. "But not Jack."

Good point. Or was it? Somebody had hated Jack enough twenty-three years ago to destroy his chances of winning the Open. Maybe that hatred had not died. Or maybe Jack had learned the truth and thus had to be quieted. Either way, it was worth looking into.

"I do not want to go digging into the past," Victoria said. "It could make things very messy."

"I thought you liked messy. Messy is fertile land for reasonable doubt."

"Reasonable doubt, I like," she said. "But the unknown, I don't. Look into Esme Fong. Look into the Squires family. Look into whatever. But stay away from the past, Myron. You never know what you might find back there."

37

On the car phone: "Mrs. Rennart? This is Myron Bolitar."

"Yes, Mr. Bolitar."

"I promised that I'd call you periodically. To keep you updated."

"Have you learned something new?"

How to proceed? "Not about your husband. So far, there is no evidence that suggests Lloyd's death was anything other than a suicide."

"I see."

Silence.

"So why are you calling me, Mr. Bolitar?"

"Have you heard about Jack Coldren's murder?"

"Of course," Francine Rennart said. "It's on every station." Then: "You don't suspect Lloyd—"

"No," Myron said quickly. "But according to Jack's wife, Lloyd sent Jack a postcard from Peru. Right before his death."

"I see," she said again. "What did it say?"

"It had only two words on it: 'Forgive me.' He didn't sign it."

There was a brief pause and then she said, "Lloyd is dead, Mr. Bolitar. So is Jack Coldren. Let it lie."

"I'm not out to damage your husband's reputation. But it is becoming clear that somebody either forced Lloyd to sabotage Jack or paid him to do it."

"And you want me to help you prove that?"

"Whoever it was may have murdered Jack and maimed his son. Your husband sent Jack a postcard asking for forgiveness. With all due respect, Mrs. Rennart, don't you think Lloyd would want you to help?"

More silence..

"What do you want from me, Mr. Bolitar? I don't know anything about what happened."

"I realize that. But do you have any old papers of Lloyd's? Did he keep a journal or a diary? Anything that might give us a clue?"

"He didn't keep a journal or a diary."

"But there might be something else." Gently, fair Myron. Tread gently. "If Lloyd did receive compensation"—a nice way of saying a bribe—"there may be bank receipts or letters or something."

"There are boxes in the basement," she said. "Old photos, some papers maybe. I don't think there are any bank statements." Francine Rennart stopped talking for a moment. Myron kept the receiver pushed against his ear. "Lloyd always did have a lot of cash," she said softly. "I never really asked where it came from."

Myron licked his lips. "Mrs. Rennart, can I look through those boxes?"

"Tonight," she said. "You can come by tonight."

Esperanza was not back at the cottage yet. But Myron had barely sat down when the intercom buzzed.

"Yes?"

The guard manning the front gate spoke with perfect diction. "Sir, a gentleman and a young lady are here to see you. They claim that they are not with the media."

"Did they give a name?"

"The gentleman said his name is Carl."

"Let them in."

Myron stepped outside and watched the canary-yellow Audi climb the drive. Carl pulled to a stop and got out. His flat hair looked freshly pressed, like he'd just gotten it "martinized," whatever that was. A young black woman who couldn't have been twenty years old came out of the passenger door. She looked around with eyes the size of satellite dishes.

Carl turned to the stables and cupped his big hand over his eyes. A female rider decked out in full gear was steering a horse through some sort of obstacle course.

"That what they call steeplechasing?" Carl asked.

"Got me," Myron said.

Carl continued to watch. The rider got off the horse. She unstrapped her black hat and patted the horse. Carl said, "You don't see a lot of brothers dressed like that."

"What about lawn jockeys?"

Carl laughed. "Not bad," he said. "Not great, but not bad."

Hard to argue. "You here to take riding lessons?"

"Not likely," Carl said. "This is Kiana. I think she may be of help to us."

"Us?"

"You and me together, bro." Carl smiled. "I get to play your likable black partner."

Myron shook his head. "No."

"Excuse me?"

"The likable black partner always ends up dead. Usually early on, too."

That stopped Carl a second. "Damn, I forgot about that."

Myron shrugged a what-can-you-do. "So who is she?"

"Kiana works as a maid at the Court Manor Inn."

Myron looked at her. She was still out of earshot. "How old is she?"

"Why?"

Myron shrugged. "Just asking. She looks young."

"She's sixteen. And guess what, Myron? She's not an unwed mother, she's not on welfare, and she's not a junkie."

"I never said she was."

"Uh-huh. Guess none of that racist shit ever seeps into your color-blind cranium."

"Hey, Carl, do me a favor. Save the racial-sensitivity seminar for a less active day. What does she know?"

Carl beckoned her forward with a tight nod. Kiana approached, all long limbs and big eyes. "I showed her this photo"—he handed Myron a snapshot of Jack Coldren—"and she remembered seeing him at the Court Manor."

Myron glanced at the photograph, and then at Kiana. "You saw this man at the motel?"

"Yes." Her voice was firm and strong and belied her years. Sixteen. She was the same age as Chad. Hard to imagine.

"Do you remember when?"

"Last week. I saw him there twice."

"Twice?"

"Yes."

"Would that have been Thursday or Friday?"

"No." Kiana kept up with the poise. No ringing hands or happy feet or darting eyes. "It was Monday or Tuesday. Wednesday at the latest."

Myron tried to process this tidbit. Jack had been at the Court Manor twice *before* his son. Why? The reason was fairly obvious: If the marriage was dead for Linda, it was probably dead for Jack. He, too, would be engaging in extramarital liaisons. Maybe that was what Matthew Squires witnessed. Maybe Jack had pulled in for his own affair and spotted his son's car. It kinda made sense. . . .

But it was also a hell of a coincidence. Father and son end up at the same hot sheets at the same time? Stranger things have happened, but what were the odds?

Myron gestured to Jack's photograph. "Was he alone?"

Kiana smiled. "The Court Manor doesn't rent out a lot of single rooms."

"Did you see who was with him?"

"Very briefly. The guy in the photograph checked them in. His partner stayed in the car."

"But you saw her? Briefly anyway."

Kiana glanced at Carl, then back at Myron. "It wasn't a her."

"Excuse me?"

"The guy in the photograph," she said. "He wasn't there with a woman."

A large boulder fell from the sky and landed on Myron's head. It was his turn now to glance at Carl. Carl nodded. Another click. A big click. The loveless marriage. He had known why Linda Coldren stayed in it—she was afraid of losing custody of her son. But what about Jack? Why hadn't he left? The answer was suddenly transparent: Being married to a beautiful, constantly traveling woman was the perfect cover. He remembered Diane Hoffman's reaction when he asked her if she'd been sleeping with Jack—the way she laughed and said, "Not likely with ol' Jack."

Because ol' Jack was gay.

Myron turned his focus back to Kiana. "Could you describe the man he was with?"

"Older—maybe fifty or sixty. White. He had this long dark hair and a bushy beard. That's about all I can tell you."

But Myron did not need more.

It was starting to come together now. It wasn't there. Not yet anyway. But he was suddenly a quantum leap closer.

38

s Carl drove out, Esperanza drove in.

"Find anything?" Myron asked her.

Esperanza handed him a photocopy of an old newspaper clipping. "Read this."

The headline read: CRASH FATALITY

Economy of words. He read on:

Mr. Lloyd Rennart of 27 Darby Place crashed his automobile into a parked car on South Dean Street near the intersection of Coddington Terrace. Mr. Rennart was taken into police custody under suspicion of driving while intoxicated. The injured were rushed to St. Elizabeth's Medical Center, where Lucille Rennart, Mr. Lloyd Rennart's wife, was pronounced dead. Funeral services are to be arranged.

Myron reread the paragraph twice. " 'The injured were rushed,' " he read out loud. "As in more than one."

Esperanza nodded.

"So who else was hurt?"

"I don't know. There was no follow-up article."

"Nothing on the arrest or the arraignment or the court case?"

"Nothing. At least, nothing I could find. There was no further mention of any Rennarts. I also tried to get something from St. Elizabeth's, but they wouldn't help. Hospital-patient confidentiality, they claimed. I doubt their computers go back to the seventies anyway."

Myron shook his head. "This is too weird," he said.

"I saw Carl heading out," Esperanza said. "What did he want?"

"He came by with a maid from the Court Manor. Guess who Jack Coldren was linking up with for a little afternoon delight?"

"Tonya Harding?"

"Close. Norm Zuckerman."

Esperanza tilted her head back and forth, as though sizing up an abstract work at the Met. "I'm not surprised. About Norm anyway. Think about it. Never married. No family. In public, he always surrounds himself with young, beautiful women."

"For show," Myron said.

"Right. They're beards. Camouflage. Norm is the front man for a major sports fashion business. Being a known gay could destroy him."

"So," Myron said, "if it got out that he was gay . . ."

"It would hurt a lot," Esperanza said.

"Is that a motive for murder?"

"Sure," she said. "It's millions of dollars and a man's reputation. People kill for a lot less."

Myron thought about it. "But how did it happen? Let's say Chad and Jack meet up at the Court Manor by accident. Suppose Chad figures out what Daddy and Norm are up to. Maybe he mentions it to Esme, who works for Norm. Maybe she and Norm . . ."

"They what?" Esperanza finished. "They kidnap the kid, cut off his finger, and then let him go?"

"Yeah, it doesn't mesh," Myron agreed. "Not yet anyway. But we're getting close."

"Oh sure, we're really narrowing down the field. Let's see. It could be Esme Fong. It could be Norm Zuckerman. It could be Tad Crispin. It could be a still-alive Lloyd Rennart. It could be his wife or his kid. It could be Matthew Squires or his father or both. Or it could be a combination plan of any of the above—the Rennart family perhaps, or Norm and Esme. And it could be Linda Coldren. How does she explain the gun from her house being the murder weapon? Or the envelopes and the pen she bought?"

"I don't know," Myron said slowly. Then: "But you may be on to something here."

"What?"

"Access. Whoever killed Jack and cut off Chad's finger had access to the Coldren house. Barring a break-in, who could have gotten hold of the gun and the stationery supplies?"

Esperanza barely hesitated. "Linda Coldren, Jack Coldren, maybe the Squires kid, since he liked to crawl in through the window." She paused. "I guess that's it."

"Okay, good. Now let's move on a little. Who knew that Chad Coldren was at the Court Manor Inn? I mean, whoever kidnapped him had to know where he was, right?"

"Right. Okay, Jack again, Esme Fong, Norm Zuckerman, Matthew Squires again. Boy, Myron, this is really helpful."

"So what names show up on both lists?"

"Jack and Matthew Squires. And I think we can leave Jack's name off—his being the victim and all."

But Myron stopped for a moment. He thought about his conversation with Win. About the naked desire to win. How far would Jack go to guarantee victory? Win had said that he would stop at nothing. Was he right?

Esperanza snapped her fingers in his face. "Yo, Myron?"

"What?"

"I said, we can eliminate Jack Coldren. Dead people rarely bury murder weapons in nearby woods."

That made sense. "So that leaves Matthew Squires," Myron said, "and I don't think he's our boy."

"Neither do I," Esperanza said. "But we're forgetting someone— someone who knew where Chad Coldren was and had complete access to the gun and stationery supplies."

"Who?"

"Chad Coldren."

"You think he cut off his own finger?"

Esperanza shrugged. "What about your old theory? The one where the kidnapping was a hoax that went out of control. Think about it. Maybe he and Tito had a falling-out. Maybe it was Chad who killed Tito."

Myron considered the possibility. He thought about Jack. He thought about Esme. He thought about Lloyd Rennart. Then he shook his head. "This is getting us nowhere. Sherlock Holmes warned that you should never theorize without all the facts because then you twist facts to suit theories rather than theories to suit facts."

"That never stopped us before," Esperanza said.

"Good point." Myron checked his watch. "I gotta go see Francine Rennart."

"The caddie's wife."

"Yup."

Esperanza went sniff, sniff.

"What?" Myron asked.

One more big sniff. "I smell a complete waste of time," she said.

She smelled wrong.

39

Victoria Wilson called on the car phone. What, Myron wondered, did people do before the car phone, before the cell phone, before the beeper?

Probably had a lot more fun.

"The police found the body of your neo-Nazi friend," she said. "His last name is Marshall."

"Tito Marshall?" Myron frowned. "Please tell me you're joking."

"I don't joke, Myron."

Of that he had little doubt. "Do the police have any idea he's tied into this?" Myron asked.

"None whatsoever."

"And I assume he died of a gunshot wound."

"That's the preliminary finding, yes. Mr. Marshall was shot twice in the head at close range with a thirty-eight."

"A thirty-eight? But Jack was killed with a twenty-two."

"Yes, Myron, I know."

"So different guns killed Jack Coldren and Tito Marshall."

Victoria did the bored thing again. "Hard to believe you're not a professional ballistics expert."

Everyone's a smart-ass. But this new development threw a whole bunch of scenarios out of whack. If two different guns had killed Jack Coldren and Tito Marshall, did that mean there were two different killers? Or was the killer smart enough to use different weapons? Or had the killer disposed of the thirty-eight after killing Tito and was thus forced to use the twenty-two on Jack? And what kind of warped mind names a kid Tito Marshall? Bad enough to go through life with a moniker like Myron.

But Tito Marshall? No wonder the kid had turned out as a neo-Nazi. Probably started out as a virulent anti-Communist.

Victoria interrupted his thoughts. "I called for another reason, Myron."

"Oh?"

"Did you pass on the message to Win?"

"You set that up, didn't you? You told her I'd be there."

"Please answer the question."

"Yes, I delivered the message."

"What did Win say?"

"I delivered the message," Myron said. "But that doesn't mean I'm giving out reports on my friend's reaction."

"She's getting worse, Myron."

"I'm sorry."

Silence.

"Where are you right now?" she asked.

"I just hit the New Jersey Turnpike. I'm on my way to Lloyd Rennart's house."

"I thought I told you to leave that path alone."

"So you did."

More silence.

"Good-bye, Myron."

She hung up. Myron sighed. He suddenly longed for the days before the car phone, the cell phone, the beeper. Reaching out and touching someone was getting to be a real pain in the ass.

An hour later, Myron parked again in front of the Rennarts' modest home. He knocked on the door. Mrs. Rennart opened it immediately. She studied his face for a few long seconds. Neither of them spoke. Not even a greeting or salutation.

"You look tired," she said at last.

"I am."

"Did Lloyd really send that postcard?"

"Yes."

The answer had been automatic. But now he wondered—had Lloyd Rennart sent a postcard? For all he knew, Linda was simply sizing him for the title role in *Big Sap: The Musical.* Take the missing taped phone call, for example. If indeed the kidnapper had called Jack before his death, where was the tape of the call? Maybe the call had never occurred. Maybe Linda had lied about it. Maybe she was lying about the postcard too. Maybe she was lying about everything. Maybe Myron was simply being semi-seduced, like the hormone-driven male in one of those cheesy, unrated, direct-to-video, *Body Heat* rip-offs co-starring women with names like Shannon or Tawny.

Not a pleasant thought.

Francine Rennart silently led him into a dark basement. When they hit bottom, she reached up and switched on one of those swinging lightbulbs like something out of *Psycho*. The room was pure cement. There was a water heater, a gas heater, a washer and dryer, and storage containers of various sizes, shapes, and material. Four boxes lay on the floor in front of him.

"That's his old stuff," Francine Rennart said without looking down.

"Thank you."

She tried, but she could not make herself look at the boxes. "I'll be upstairs," she said. Myron watched her feet disappear from view. Then he turned to the boxes and squatted down. The boxes were taped shut. He took out his key-chain penknife and slit the packing tape.

The first box had golf memorabilia. There were certificates and trophies and old tees. A golf ball was mounted to a wooden base with a rusty plaque that read:

HOLE IN ONE—15TH HOLE AT HICKORY PARK
JANUARY 17, 1972

Myron wondered what life had been like for Lloyd on that clear, crisp golf afternoon. He wondered how often Lloyd had replayed the shot in his mind, how many times he'd sat alone in that BarcaLounger and tried to recapture that pure, cold rush. Had he remembered the feel of the club's grip, the tightness in his shoulders as he began the backswing, the clean, solid stroke of the ball, the floating follow-through.

In the second box, Myron found Lloyd's high school diploma. He found a yearbook from Penn State. There was a picture of the golf team. Lloyd Rennart had been captain. Myron's finger touched upon a large, felt *P.* Lloyd's varsity letter. There was a recommendation letter from his golf coach at Penn State. The words *bright future* jumped out at Myron. Bright future. The coach may have been a great motivator, but he made a lousy soothsayer.

The third box started off with a photograph of Lloyd in Korea. It was a casual group photo, a dozen or so boys/men in unbuttoned fatigues, arms dangling loosely around neighboring necks. Lots of smiles, seemingly happy smiles. Lloyd was thinner there, but he saw nothing gaunt or drawn in the eyes.

Myron put the picture down. In the background, Betty Buckley was not singing "Memory," but maybe she should have been. These boxes were a life—a life that in spite of these experiences and dreams and wants and hopes had chosen to terminate itself.

From the bottom of the box Myron pulled out a wedding album. The faded gold leaf read: *Lloyd and Lucille, November 17, 1968, Now and Forever*. More irony. The fake-leather cover was crusted with what looked like drink ringlets. Lloyd's first marriage, neatly wrapped and packed away in the bottom of a box.

Myron was about to put the album to the side when his curiosity got the better of him. He sat all the way down, his legs splayed like a kid with a new pack of baseball cards. He placed the photo album on the cement floor and began to open it. The binding made a cracking noise from the years of disuse.

The first photograph almost made Myron scream out loud.

40

Myron's accelerator foot never eased.

Chestnut Street near Fourth is a no-parking zone, but that did not even make Myron pause. He was out of the car before it had come to a complete stop, ignoring the chorus of honking horns. He hurried through the Omni's lobby and into an open elevator. When he got off on the top floor, he found the right room number and knocked hard.

Norm Zuckerman opened the door. "*Bubbe*," he said with a big smile. "What a nice surprise."

"Can I come in?"

"You? Of course, sweetheart, anytime."

But Myron had already pushed by him. The suite's outer room was— to use hotel brochure lingo—spacious and elegantly appointed. Esme Fong sat on a couch. She looked up at him with the cornered-rabbit face. Posters and blueprints and advertisements and similar paraphernalia carpeted the floor and cascaded off the coffee table. Myron spotted blown-up images of Tad Crispin and Linda Coldren. Zoom logos were everywhere, inescapable, like vengeful ghosts or telemarketers.

"We were just doing a little strategizing," Norm said. "But hey, we can always take a break, right, Esme?"

Esme nodded.

Norm made his way behind a wet bar. "You want something, Myron? I don't think they have any Yoo-Hoo in here, but I'm sure—"

"Nothing," Myron interrupted.

Norm did the mock surrender thing with his hands. "Sheesh, Myron, relax," he said. "What's twisting your nipple?"

"I wanted to warn you, Norm."

"Warn me about what?"

"I don't want to do this. As far as I'm concerned, your love life should be personal. But it's not that easy. Not anymore. It's going to get out, Norm. I'm sorry."

Norm Zuckerman did not move. He opened his mouth as though readying to protest. Then he stopped. "How did you find out?"

"You were with Jack. At the Court Manor Inn. A maid saw you."

Norm looked at Esme, who kept her head high. He turned back to Myron. "Do you know what will happen if words gets out that I'm a *faygeleh*?"

"I can't help that, Norm."

"I am the company, Myron. Zoom is about fashion and image and sports—which just so happens to be the most blatantly homophobic entity on this planet. Perception is everything in this business. If they find out I'm an old queen, you know what happens? Zoom goes plop down the septic tank."

"I'm not sure I agree," Myron said, "but either way, it can't be helped."

"Do the police know?" Norm asked.

"No, not yet."

Norm threw up his hands. "So why does it have to come out? It was just a fling, for crying out loud. Okay, so I met Jack. So we were attracted to each other. So we both had a ton to lose if either of us opened our traps. No big whup. It's got nothing to do with his murder."

Myron stole a glance at Esme. She looked back at him with eyes that urged him to keep silent. "Unfortunately," Myron said, "I think it does."

"You think? You're going to destroy me on an 'I think'?"

"I'm sorry."

"I can't talk you out of it?"

"I'm afraid not."

Norm moved away from the bar and half-collapsed into a chair. He put his face in the palms of his hands, his fingers sliding toward the back, meeting up in the hair, interweaving. "I've spent my entire life with lies, Myron," he began. "I spent my childhood in Poland pretending I wasn't a Jew. Can you believe that? Me, Norm Zuckerman, pretending I was some slack-jawed *goy*. But I survived. I came here. And then I spent my adult life pretending I was a real man, a Casanova, a guy who always had a beautiful girl on his arm. You get used to lying, Myron. It gets easier, you know what I mean? The lies become a sort of second reality."

"I'm sorry, Norm."

He breathed deeply and forced up a tired smile. "Maybe it's for the best," Norm said. "Look at Dennis Rodman. He cross-dresses, for crying out loud. Hasn't hurt him any, has it?"

"No. It hasn't."

Norm Zuckerman lifted his eyes toward Myron. "Hey, once I got to this country, I became the most in-your-face Jew you ever saw. Didn't I? Tell me the truth. Am I not the most in-your-face Jew you've ever met, or what?"

"In my face," Myron said.

"Bet your skinny *melinka* of a butt I am. And when I first started out, everyone told me to tone it down. Stop being so Jewish, they said. So ethnic. You'll never be accepted." His face had true hope now. "Maybe I can do the same for us closet *faygelehs*, Myron. Be in the world's face again, you know what I'm saying?"

"Yes, I do," Myron said softly. Then he asked, "Who else knew about you and Jack?"

"Knew?"

"Did you tell anybody?"

"No, of course not."

Myron gestured toward Esme. "How about one of those beautiful girlfriends on your arm? How about someone who practically lived with you? Wouldn't it have been easy for her to find out?"

Norm shrugged. "I suppose so. You get this close to someone, you trust them. You drop your guard. So maybe she knew. So what?"

Myron looked at Esme. "You want to tell him?"

Esme's voice was cool. "I don't know what you're talking about."

"Tell me what?"

Myron kept his eyes on hers. "I wondered why you'd seduce a sixteen-year-old boy. Don't get me wrong. You gave a bravo performance—all that talk about being lonely and Chad being sweet and disease-free. You waxed quite eloquent. But it still rang hollow."

Norm said, "What the hell are you talking about, Myron?"

Myron ignored him. "And then there was the matter of the bizarre coincidence—you and Chad showing up at the same motel at the same time as Jack and Norm. Too weird. I just couldn't buy it. But of course, we both know that it wasn't a coincidence. You planned it that way, Esme."

"What plan?" Norm interjected. "Myron, will you tell me what the hell is going on?"

"Norm, you mentioned that Esme used to work on Nike's basketball campaign. That she quit that job to come to you."

"So?"

"Did she take a cut in salary?"

"A little." Norm shrugged. "Not much."

"When exactly did she hook up with you?"

"I don't know."

"Within the past eight months?"

Norm thought a moment. "Yeah, so?"

"Esme seduced Chad Coldren. She set up a liaison with him at the Court Manor Inn. But she wasn't bringing him there for sex or because she was lonely. She brought him there as part of a setup."

"What kind of setup?"

"She wanted Chad to see his father with another man."

"Huh?"

"She wanted to destroy Jack. It was no coincidence. Esme knew your routine. She learned about your affair with Jack. So she tried to set it up so Chad would see what his father was really about."

Esme remained silent.

"Tell me something, Norm. Were you and Jack supposed to meet Thursday night?"

"Yeah," Norm said.

"What happened?"

"Jack called it off. He pulled into the lot and got spooked. He said he saw a familiar car."

"Not just familiar," Myron said. "His son's. That's where Esme screwed up. Jack spotted the car. He left before Chad had a chance to see him."

Myron stood and walked toward Esme. She remained still. "I almost had it right from the beginning," he told her. "Jack took the lead at the Open. His son was there, right in front of you. So you kidnapped Chad to throw Jack's game off. It was just like I thought. Except I missed your real motive. Why would you kidnap Chad? Why would you crave such vengeance against Jack Coldren? Yes, money was part of the motive. Yes, you wanted Zoom's new campaign to succeed. Yes, you knew that if Tad Crispin won the Open, you'd be heralded as the marketing genius of the world. All that played into it. But, of course, that never explained why you brought Chad to the Court Manor Inn in the first place—*before* Jack had the lead."

Norm sighed. "So tell us, Myron. What possible reason could she have for wanting to hurt Jack?"

Myron reached into his pocket and pulled out a grainy photograph. The first page of the wedding album. Lloyd and Lucille Rennart. Smiling. Happy. Standing side by side. Lloyd in a tux. Lucille holding a bouquet of flowers. Lucille looking stunning in a long white gown. But that wasn't what had shocked Myron to the core. What shocked him had nothing to do with what Lucille wore or held; rather, it was what she was.

Lucille Rennart was Asian.

"Lloyd Rennart was your father," Myron said. "You were in the car that day when he crashed into a tree. Your mother died. You were rushed to the hospital too."

Esme's back was rod-straight, but her breathing was coming out in hitches.

"I'm not sure what happened next," he continued. "My guess would be that your father had hit rock bottom. He was a drunk. He had just killed his own wife. He felt washed-up, useless. So maybe he realized that he couldn't raise you. Or he didn't deserve to raise you. Or maybe an arrangement was reached with your mother's family. In return for not pressing charges, Lloyd would give Lucille's family custody of you. I don't know what happened. But you ended up being raised by your mother's family. By the time Lloyd straightened himself out, he probably felt it would be wrong to tear you out by the roots. Or maybe he was afraid that his daughter wouldn't take back the father who'd been responsible for killing her mother. Whatever, Lloyd kept quiet. He never even told his second wife about you."

Tears were streaming down Esme's cheeks now. Myron felt like crying too.

"How close am I, Esme?"

"I don't even know what you're talking about."

"There'll be records," Myron said. "Birth certificates, for certain. Probably adoption papers. It won't take the police long to trace." He held up the photograph, his voice soft.

"The resemblance between you and your mother is almost enough."

Tears continued to flow, but she was not crying. No sobs. No hitching. No quivering facial muscles. Just tears. "Maybe Lloyd Rennart was my father," Esme said. "But you still have nothing. The rest is pure conjecture."

"No, Esme. Once the police confirm your parentage, the rest will be easy. Chad will tell them that it was you who suggested you go to the Court Manor Inn. They'll look closely into Tito's death. There'll be a connection there. Fibers. Hairs. It'll all come together. But I have one question for you."

She remained still.

"Why did you cut off Chad's finger?"

Without warning, Esme broke into a run. Myron was caught off guard. He jumped over the couch to block her path. But he had misjudged her. She had not been heading for an exit; she was going into a bedroom. Her bedroom. Myron hurdled back over the couch. He reached her room, but he was a little late.

Esme Fong had a gun. She pointed it at Myron's chest. He could see in her eyes that there'd be no confession, no explanations, no talk. She was ready to shoot.

"Don't bother," Myron said.

"What?"

He pulled out his cell phone and handed it to her. "This is for you."

Esme did not move for a moment. Then, with her hand still on the gun, she reached out and took the phone. She pressed it against her ear, but Myron could hear just fine.

A voice said, "This is Detective Alan Corbett from the Philadelphia Police Department. We are standing outside your door listening to every word that has been said. Put down the gun."

Esme looked back at Myron. She still had the gun aimed at his chest. Myron felt a bead of sweat run down his back. Looking into the barrel of a gun was like staring into the cavern of death. Your eyes saw the barrel, only the barrel, as though it were growing impossibly larger, preparing to swallow you whole.

"It would be dumb," he said.

She nodded then and lowered the gun. "And pointless."

The weapon dropped to the floor. Doors burst open. Police swarmed in.

Myron looked down at the gun. "A thirty-eight," he said to Esme. "That the gun you killed Tito with?"

Her expression gave him the answer. The ballistics tests would be conclusive. She would be prosecutorial toast.

"Tito was a lunatic," Esme said. "He chopped off the boy's finger. He started making money demands. You have to believe that."

Myron gave a noncommittal nod. She was testing out her defense, but it sort of sounded like the truth to Myron.

Corbett snapped handcuffs onto her wrists.

Her words were spilling out fast now. "Jack Coldren destroyed my entire family. He ruined my father and killed my mother. And for what? My father did nothing wrong."

"Yes," Myron said, "he did."

"He pulled the wrong club out of a golf bag, if you believe Jack Coldren. He made a mistake. An accident. Should it have cost him so much?"

Myron said nothing. It was no mistake, no accident. And Myron had no idea what it should have cost.

41

The police cleaned up. Corbett had questions, but Myron was not in the mood. He left as soon as the detective was distracted. He sped to the police station where Linda Coldren was about to be released. He took the cement steps three or four at a clip, looking like a spastic Olympian timing the triple jump.

Victoria Wilson almost—the key word being *almost*—smiled at him. "Linda will be out in a few minutes."

"Do you have that tape I asked you to get?"

"The phone call between Jack and the kidnapper?"

"Yes."

"I have it," she said. "But why—"

"Please give it to me," Myron said.

She heard something in his tone. Without argument, she reached into her handbag and pulled it out. Myron took it. "Do you mind if I drive Linda home?" he said.

Victoria Wilson regarded him. "I think maybe that would be a good idea."

A policeman came out. "She's ready to leave," he said.

Victoria was about to turn away, when Myron said, "I guess you were wrong about digging into the past. The past ended up saving our client."

Victoria held his eye. "It's like I said before," she began. "You never know what you will find."

They both waited for the other to break the eye contact. Neither did until the door behind them opened.

Linda was back in civilian clothes. She stepped out tentatively, like she'd been in a dark room and wasn't sure her eyes could handle the sudden light. Her face broke into a wide smile when she saw Victoria. They hugged. Linda dug her face into Victoria's shoulder and rocked in her arms. When they released, Linda turned and hugged Myron. Myron closed his eyes and felt his muscles unbunch. He smelled her hair and felt the wondrous skin of her cheek against his neck. They embraced for a long time, almost like a slow dance, neither wanting to let go, both perhaps a little bit afraid.

Victoria coughed into her fist and made her excuses. With the police leading the way, Myron and Linda made it to the car with a minimum of press fuss. They strapped on their seat belts in silence.

"Thank you," she said.

Myron said nothing. He started the car. For a while neither of them spoke. Myron switched on the air-conditioning.

"We have something here, don't we?"

"I don't know," Myron said. "You were worried about your son. Maybe that's all it was."

Her face said that she was not buying. "How about you?" Linda asked. "Did you feel anything?"

"I think so," he said. "But part of that might be fear, too."

"Fear of what?"

"Of Jessica."

She gave a weary grin. "Don't tell me you're one of those guys who fears commitment."

"Just the opposite. I fear how much I love her. I fear how much I want to commit."

"So what's the problem?"

"Jessica left me once before. I don't want to be exposed like that again."

Linda nodded. "So you think that's what it was? Fear of abandonment?"

"I don't know."

"I felt something," she said. "For the first time in a very long time. Don't get me wrong. I've had affairs. Like with Tad. But that's not the same thing." She looked at him. "It felt nice."

Myron said nothing.

"You're not making this very easy," Linda said.

"We have other things to talk about."

"Like what?"

"Victoria filled you in on Esme Fong?"

"Yes."

"If you remember, she had a solid alibi for Jack's murder."

"A night clerk at a big hotel like the Omni? I doubt that will hold up on scrutiny."

"Don't be so sure," Myron said.

"Why do you say that?"

Myron did not answer. He turned right and said, "You know what always bothered me, Linda?"

"No, what?"

"The ransom calls."

"What about them?" she asked.

"The first one was made on the morning of the kidnapping. You answered. The kidnappers told you that they had your son. But they made no demands. I always found that odd, didn't you?"

She thought about it. "I guess so."

"Now I understand why they did that. But back then, we didn't know what the real motive for the kidnapping was."

"I don't understand."

"Esme Fong kidnapped Chad because she wanted revenge on Jack. She wanted to make him lose the tournament. How? Well, I'd thought that she'd kidnapped Chad to fluster Jack. Make him lose his focus. But that was too abstract. She wanted to make sure Jack lost. That was her ransom demand right from the beginning. But you see, the ransom call came in a little late. Jack was already at the course. You answered the phone."

Linda nodded. "I think I see what you're saying. She had to reach Jack directly."

"She or Tito, but you're right. That's why she called Jack at Merion. Remember the second call, the one Jack got after he finished the round?"

"Of course."

"That was when the ransom demand was made," Myron said. "The kidnapper told Jack plain and simple—you start losing or your son dies."

"Hold up a second," Linda said. "Jack said they didn't make any demands. They told him to get some money ready and they'd call back."

"Jack lied."

"But . . . ?" She stopped, and then said, "Why?"

"He didn't want us—or more specifically, you—to know the truth."

Linda shook her head. "I don't understand."

Myron took out the cassette Victoria had given him. "Maybe this will help explain." He pushed the tape into the cassette player. There were several seconds of silence and then he heard Jack's voice like something from beyond the grave:

"Hello?"

"Who's the chink bitch?"

"I don't know what—"

"You trying to fuck with me, you dumb son of a bitch? I'll start send-ing you the fucking brat in little pieces."

"Please—"

"What's the point of this, Myron?" Linda sounded a little annoyed.

"Just hold on another second. The part I'm interested in is coming up."

"Her name is Esme Fong. She works for a clothing company. She's just here to set up an endorsement deal with my wife, that's all."

"Bullshit."

"It's the truth, I swear."

"I don't know, Jack. . . ."

"I wouldn't lie to you."

"Well, Jack, we'll just see about that. This is gonna cost you."

"What do you mean?"

"One hundred grand. Call it a penalty price."

"For what?"

Myron hit the STOP button. "Did you hear that?"

"What?"

" 'Call it a penalty price.' Clear as day."

"So?"

"It wasn't a ransom demand. It was a penalty."

"This is a kidnapper, Myron. He's probably not all that caught up in semantics."

" 'One hundred grand,' " Myron repeated. " 'Call it a penalty price.' As if a ransom demand had already been made. As if the hundred grand was something he'd just decided to tack on. And what about Jack's reac-tion? The kidnapper asks for one hundred grand. You would figure he would just tell him fine. But instead he says, 'For what?' Again, because it's in addition to what he's already been told. Now listen to this." Myron pushed the PLAY button.

"Never you fucking mind. You want the kid alive? It's gonna cost you one hundred grand now. That's in—"

"Now hold on a second."

Myron hit the STOP button again. " 'It's gonna cost you one hundred grand *now.*' " Myron repeated. "*Now.* That's the key word. *Now.* Again as if it's something new. As if before this call there was another price. And then Jack interrupts him. The kidnapper says, 'That's in—' when Jack jumps in. Why? Because Jack doesn't want him to finish the thought. He knew that we were listening. 'That's in addition.' I'd bet any-thing that was the next word he was about to say. 'That's in addition to our original demand.' Or, 'that's in addition to losing the tournament.' "

Linda looked at him. "But I still don't get it. Why wouldn't Jack just tell us what they wanted?"

"Because Jack had no intention of complying with their demand."

That stopped her. "What?"

"He wanted to win too badly. More than that—he needed to win. Had to. But if you learned the truth—you who had won so often and so easily—you would never understand. This was his chance at redemption, Linda. His chance of going back twenty-three years and making his life worth living. How badly did he want to win, Linda? You tell me. What would he have sacrificed?"

"Not his own son," Linda countered. "Yes, Jack needed to win. But not badly enough to forfeit his own son's life."

"But Jack didn't see it that way. He was looking through his own rose-tinted prism of desire. A man sees what he wants to, Linda. What he has to. When I showed you and Jack the bank videotape, you both saw something different. You didn't want to believe your son could do something so hurtful. So you looked for explanations that would counter that evidence. Jack did just the opposite. He wanted to believe that his son was behind it. That it was only a big hoax. That way he could continue to try his hardest to win. And if by some chance he was wrong—if Chad had indeed been kidnapped—well, the kidnappers were probably bluffing anyway. They'd never really go through with it. In other words, Jack did what he had to do: he rationalized the danger away."

"You think his desire to win clouded his thinking that much?"

"How much clouding did he need? We all had doubts after watching that bank tape. Even you. So how hard would it be for him to go the extra step?"

Linda sat back. "Okay," she said. "Maybe I buy it. But I still don't see what this has to do with anything."

"Bear with me a little while longer, okay? Let's go back to when I showed you the bank videotape. We're at your house. I show the tape. Jack storms out. He is upset, of course, but he still plays well enough to keep the big lead. This angers Esme. He's ignoring her threat. She realizes that she has to up the ante."

"By cutting off Chad's finger."

"It was probably Tito, but that's not really relevant right now anyway. The key thing is, the finger is severed, and Esme wants to use it to show Jack she's serious."

"So she plants it in my car and we find it."

"No," Myron said.

"What?"

"Jack finds it first."

"In my car?"

Myron shook his head. "Remember that Chad's key chain has Jack's car keys on it as well as yours. Esme wants to warn Jack, not you. So she puts the finger in Jack's car. He finds it. He's shocked, of course, but he's in the lie too deep now. If the truth came out, you'd never forgive him. Chad would never forgive him. And the tournament would be over for him. He has to get rid of the finger. So he puts the finger in an envelope and writes that note. Remember it? 'I warned you not to seek help.' Don't you see? It's the perfect distraction. It not only draws attention away from him, but it also gets rid of me."

Linda chewed on her lower lip. "That would explain the envelope and pen," she said. "I bought all the office supplies. Jack would have had some in his briefcase."

"Exactly. But here is where things get really interesting."

She arched an eyebrow. "They're not interesting now?"

"Just hold on. It's Sunday morning. Jack is about to head into the final round with an insurmountable lead. Bigger than he had twenty-three years ago. If he loses now, it would be the greatest golf collapse in history. His name would forever be synonymous with choking—the one thing Jack hated more than anything else. But on the other hand, Jack was not a complete ogre. He loved his son. He knew now that the kidnapping was not a hoax. He was probably torn, not sure what to do. But in the end he made a decision. He was going to lose the tournament."

Linda said nothing.

"Stroke by stroke, we watched him die. Win understands the destructive side of wanting to win far better than I. He also saw that Jack had the fire back, that old need to win. But despite all that, Jack still tried to lose. He didn't completely collapse. That would have looked too suspicious. But he started dropping strokes. He made it close. And then he purposely fumbled big-time in the stone quarry and lost his lead.

"But imagine what was going on in his head. Jack was fighting against everything that he was. They say a man can't drown himself. Even if it means saving his own child's life, a man cannot keep himself under water until his lungs burst. I'm not so sure that's any different than what Jack was trying to do. He was literally killing himself. His sanity was probably ripping away like divots on the course. On the eighteenth green, the survival instinct took over. Maybe he started rationalizing again—or more likely, he just couldn't help himself. But we both saw the transformation, Linda. We saw his face suddenly crystallize on eighteen. Jack stroked that putt home and tied the score."

Linda's voice was barely audible. "Yes," she said. "I saw him change."

She sat up in her seat and let loose a long breath. "Esme Fong must have been in a panic by then."

"Yes."

"Jack had left her no choice. She had to kill him."

Myron shook his head. "No."

She looked confused again. "But it adds up. Esme was desperate. You said so yourself. She wanted vengeance for her father, and on top of that she was now worried about what would happen if Tad Crispin lost. She had to kill him."

"One problem," Myron said.

"What?"

"She called your house that night."

"Right," Linda said. "To set up the meeting at the course. She probably told Jack to come alone. To not tell me anything."

"No," Myron said. "That's not what happened."

"What?"

"If that was what happened," Myron continued, "we'd have the call on tape."

Linda shook her head. "What are you talking about?"

"Esme Fong did call your house. That part is true. My bet is that she just threatened him some more. Let him know that she meant business. Jack probably begged forgiveness. I don't know. I'll probably never know. But I'd bet he ended the call by promising to lose the next day."

"So?" Linda said. "What does that have to do with the call being taped?"

"Jack was going through hell," Myron went on. "The pressure was too much. He was probably close to a breakdown. So he ran out of the house—just as you said—and ended up at his favorite place in the world. Merion. The golf course. Did he go out there just to think? I don't know. Did he bring the gun with him, maybe even contemplating suicide? Again, I don't know. But I do know that the tape machine was still hooked up to your phone. The police confirmed that. So where did the tape of that last conversation go?"

Linda's tone was suddenly more measured. "I don't know."

"Yes, Linda, you do."

She gave him a look.

"Jack might have forgotten the call was recorded," Myron continued. "But you didn't. When he ran out of the house, you went down to the basement. You played the tape. And you heard everything. What I'm telling you in this car is not new to you. You knew why the kidnappers had taken your child. You knew what Jack had done. You knew where he liked to go when he took his walks. And you knew you had to stop him."

Myron waited. He missed the turnoff, took the next one, U-turned back onto the highway. He found the right exit and put on his blinker.

"Jack did bring the gun," Linda said too calmly. "I didn't even know where he kept it."

Myron gave a slight nod, silently trying to encourage.

"You're right," she continued. "When I played back the tape, I realized that Jack couldn't be trusted. He knew it too. Even with the threat of his own son's death, he had nailed that putt on eighteen. I followed him out to the course. I confronted him. He started to cry. He said he would try to lose. But"—she hesitated, weighed her words—"that drowning man example you gave. That was Jack."

Myron tried to swallow, but his throat was too dry.

"Jack wanted to kill himself. And I knew he had to. I'd listened to the tape. I'd heard the threats. And I had no doubts: If Jack won, Chad was dead. I also knew something else."

She stopped and looked at Myron.

"What?" he said.

"I knew Jack would win. Win was right—the fire was back in Jack's eyes. But it was a raging inferno now. One that even he couldn't control anymore."

"So you shot him," Myron said.

"I struggled to get the gun from him. I wanted to injure him. Seriously injure him. If there was the possibility he could play again, I was afraid the kidnapper might just hold on to Chad indefinitely. The voice on the phone sounded that desperate. But Jack wouldn't surrender the gun—nor would he pull it away from me. It was weird. He just held on and looked at me. Almost like he was waiting. So I curled my finger around the trigger and pulled." Her voice was very clear now. "It didn't go off accidentally. I had hoped to wound him seriously, not kill him. But I fired. I fired to save my son. And Jack ended up dead."

More silence.

"Then you headed back to the house," Myron said. "You buried the gun. You saw me in the bushes. When you got inside, you erased the tape."

"Yes."

"And that was why you released that press announcement so early. The police wanted to keep it quiet, but you needed the story to go public. You wanted the kidnappers to know that Jack was dead, so they'd let Chad go."

"It was my son or my husband," Linda said. She turned her body to face him. "What would you have done?"

"I don't know. But I don't think I would have shot him."

" 'Don't think'?" she repeated with a laugh. "You talk about Jack being under pressure, but what about me? I hadn't slept. I was stressed and I was confused and I was more scared than I had ever been in my entire life—and yes, I was enraged that Jack had sacrificed our son's chance of playing the game we all so loved. I didn't have the luxury of an I-don't-know, Myron. My son's life was hanging in the balance. I only had time to react."

They turned up Ardmore Avenue and drove in silence past the Merion Golf Club. They both looked out the window at the course's gently sloping sea of green broken up only by the clean, white faces of sand. It was, Myron had to admit, a magnificent sight.

"Are you going to tell?" she asked.

She already knew the answer. "I'm your attorney," Myron said. "I can't tell."

"And if you weren't my attorney?"

"It wouldn't matter. Victoria would still be able to offer up enough reasonable doubt to win the case."

"That's not what I meant."

"I know," Myron said. He left it at that. She waited, but no answer was coming.

"I know you don't care," Linda continued, "but I meant what I said before. My feelings for you were real."

Neither of them spoke again. Myron pulled into the driveway. The police kept the media back. Chad was outside, waiting. He smiled at his mother and ran toward her. Linda opened the car door and got out. They might have embraced, but Myron did not see it. He was already backing out the drive.

42

Victoria opened the door.

"In the bedroom. Follow me."

"How is she?" Myron asked.

"She's been sleeping a lot. But I don't think the pain is that bad yet. We have a nurse and a morphine drip ready if she needs it."

The decor was far simpler and less opulent than Myron had expected. Solid-colored furniture and pillows. Uncluttered white walls. Pine bookcases with artifacts gathered from vacations to Asia and Africa. Victoria had told him that Cissy Lockwood loved to travel.

They stopped in front of a doorway. Myron looked inside. Win's mother lay in bed. Exhaustion emanated from her. Her head was back on the pillow as though it were too heavy to lift. An IV bag was attached to her arm. She looked at Myron and mustered a gentle smile. Myron smiled back. With his peripheral vision, he saw Victoria signal to the nurse. The nurse stood and moved past him. Myron stepped inside. The door closed behind him.

Myron moved closer to the bed. Her breathing was labored and constricted, as though she was being slowly strangled from inside. Myron did not know what to say. He had seen people die before, but those had been quick, violent deaths, the life force snuffed out in one big, powerful gust. This was different. He was actually watching a human being die, her vitality dripping out of her like the liquid in her IV bag, the light in her eyes almost imperceptibly dimming, the grinding whir of tissues and sinews and organs eroding under the onslaught of whatever manic beast had lain claim to her.

She lifted a hand and put it on his. Her grip was surprisingly strong.

She was not bony or pale. Her muscles were still toned, her summer tan only slightly faded.

"You know," she said.

Myron nodded.

She smiled. "How?"

"A lot of little things," he said. "Victoria not wanting me to dig into the past. Jack's mischievous past. Your too-casual comment about how Win was supposed to be playing golf with Jack that day. But mostly it was Win. When I told him about our conversation, he said that I now knew why he wanted nothing to do with you and Jack. You, I could understand. But why Jack?"

Her chest heaved a bit. She closed her eyes for a moment. "Jack destroyed my life," she said. "I realize that he was only a teenager pulling a prank. He apologized profusely. He told me that he had not realized that my husband was on the premises. He said that he was certain I would hear Win coming and hide. It was all a joke, he said. Nothing more. But none of that made him less liable. I lost my son forever because of what he did. He had to face the consequences."

Myron nodded. "So you paid off Lloyd Rennart to sabotage Jack at the Open."

"Yes. It was an inadequate punishment for what he had done to my family, but it was the best I could do."

The bedroom door opened, and Win stepped into the room. Myron felt the hand release his. A sob came out of Cissy Lockwood. Myron did not hesitate or say good-bye. He turned away and walked out the door.

She died three days later. Win never left her side. When the last pitiful breath was drawn, when the chest mercifully stopped rising and falling and her face froze in a final, bloodless death mask, Win appeared in the corridor.

Myron stood and waited. Win looked at him. His face was serene, untroubled.

"I did not want her to die alone," he said.

Myron nodded. He tried to stop shaking.

"I am going to take a walk."

"Is there anything I can do?" Myron asked.

Win stopped. "Actually," he said, "there is."

"Name it."

They played thirty-six holes at Merion that day. And thirty-six more the next. And by the third day, Myron was starting to get it.

THE FINAL DETAIL

For Aunt Evelyn in Revere,
with lots and lots of love

And in memory of Larry Gerson
1962–1998
Close your eyes and you can still see the smile

1

Myron lay sprawled next to a knee-knockingly gorgeous brunette clad only in a Class-B-felony bikini, a tropical drink sans umbrella in one hand, the aqua clear Caribbean water lapping at his feet, the sand a dazzling white powder, the sky a pure blue that could only be God's blank canvas, the sun as soothing and rich as a Swedish masseur with a snifter of cognac, and he was intensely miserable.

The two of them had been on this island paradise for, he guessed, three weeks. Myron had not bothered counting the days. Neither, he imagined, had Terese. The island seemed as remote as Gilligan's—no phone, some lights, no motorcar, plenty of luxury, not much like Robinson Crusoe, and well, not as primitive as can be either. Myron shook his head. You can take the boy out of the television, but you can't take the television out of the boy.

At the horizon's midway point, slicing toward them and ripping a seam of white in the aqua-blue fabric, came the yacht. Myron saw it, and his stomach clenched.

He did not know where they were exactly, though the island did indeed have a name: St. Bacchanals. Yes, for real. It was a small patch of planet, owned by one of those mega-cruise lines that used one side of the island for passengers to swim and barbecue and enjoy a day on their "own personal island paradise." Personal. Just them and the other twenty-five hundred *turistas* squeezed onto a short stretch of beach. Yep, personal, bacchanallike.

This side of the island, however, was quite different. There was only this one home, owned by the cruise line's CEO, a hybrid between a thatched hut and a plantation manor. The only person within a mile was a servant. Total island population: maybe thirty, all of whom worked as caretakers hired by the cruise line.

The yacht shut off its engine and drifted closer.

Terese Collins lowered her Bolle sunglasses and frowned. In three weeks no vessel except the mammoth cruise liners—they had subtle names like the *Sensation* or the *Ecstasy* or the *G Spot*—had ambled past their stretch of sand.

"Did you tell anybody where we were?" she asked.

"No."

"Maybe it's John."

John was the aforementioned CEO of said cruise line, a friend of Terese's.

"I don't think so," Myron said.

Myron had first met Terese Collins, well, a little more than three weeks ago. Terese was "on leave" from her high-profile job as prime-time anchorwoman for CNN. They both had been bullied into going to some charity function by well-meaning friends and had been immediately drawn to each other as though their mutual misery and pain were magnetic. It started as little more than a dare: Drop everything and flee. Just disappear with someone you found attractive and barely knew. Neither backed down, and twelve hours later they were in St. Maarten. Twenty-four hours after that they were here.

For Myron, a man who had slept with a total of four women in his entire life, who had never really experienced one-night stands even in the days when they were fashionable or ostensibly disease-free, who had never had sex purely for the physical sensation and without the anchors of love or commitment, the decision to flee felt surprisingly right.

He had told no one where he was going or for how long—mostly because he didn't have a clue himself. He'd called Mom and Dad and told them not to worry, a move tantamount to telling them to grow gills and breathe underwater. He'd sent Esperanza a fax and gave her power of attorney over MB SportsReps, the sports agency they now partnered. He had not even called Win.

Terese was watching him. "You know who it is."

Myron said nothing. His heartbeat sped up.

The yacht came closer. A cabin door in the front opened, and as Myron feared, Win stepped out on deck. Panic squeezed the air out of him. Win was not one for casual drop-bys. If he was here, it meant something was very wrong.

Myron stood. He was still too far to yell, so he settled for a wave. Win gave a small nod.

"Wait a second," Terese said. "Isn't that the guy whose family owns Lock-Horne Securities?"

"Yes."

"I interviewed him once. When the market plunged. He has some long, pompous name."

"Windsor Horne Lockwood the third," Myron said.

"Right. Weird guy."

She should only know.

"Good-looking as all hell," Terese continued, "in that old-money, country-club, born-with-a-silver-golf-club-in-his-hands kinda way."

As though on cue, Win put a hand through the blond locks and smiled.

"You two have something in common," Myron said.

"What's that?"

"You both think he's good-looking as all hell."

Terese studied Myron's face. "You're going back." There was a hint of apprehension in her voice.

Myron nodded. "Win wouldn't have come otherwise."

She took his hand. It was the first tender moment between them in the three weeks since the charity ball. That might sound strange—lovers alone on an island, the sex constant, who had never shared a gentle kiss or a light stroke or soft words—but their relationship had been about forgetting and surviving: two desperate souls standing in the rubble with no interest in trying to rebuild a damn thing.

Terese had spent most days taking long walks by herself; he'd spent them sitting on the beach and exercising and sometimes reading. They met up for food, sleep, and sex. Other than that, they left each other alone to—if not heal—at least stave off the blood flow. He could see that she too had been shattered, that some recent tragedy had struck her deep and hard and to the bone. But he never asked her what had happened. And she never asked him either.

An unspoken rule of their little folly.

The yacht stopped and dropped anchor. Win stepped down onto a motorized dinghy. Myron waited. He shifted his feet, bracing himself. When the dinghy was close enough to the shore, Win snapped off the motor.

"My parents?" Myron called out.

Win shook his head. "They're fine."

"Esperanza?"

Slight hesitation. "She needs your help."

Win stepped gingerly into the water, almost as though he expected it to hold his weight. He was dressed in a white button-down oxford and Lilly Pulitzer shorts with colors loud enough to repel sharks. The Yacht

Yuppie. His build was on the slight side, but his forearms looked like steel snakes coiling beneath the skin.

Terese stood as Win approached. Win admired the view without ogling. He was one of the few men Myron knew who could get away with that. Breeding. He took Terese's hand and smiled. They exchanged pleasantries. Fake smiles and pointless bandies followed. Myron stood frozen, not listening. Terese excused herself and headed to the house.

Win carefully watched her saunter away. Then he said, "Quality derrière."

"Would you be referring to me?" Myron asked.

Win kept his eyes keenly focused on the, er, target. "On television she's always sitting behind that anchor desk," he noted. "One would never guess that she had such a high-quality derrière." He shook his head. "It's a shame really."

"Right," Myron said. "Maybe she should stand a couple times during each broadcast. Twirl around a few times, bend over, something like that."

"There you go." Win risked a quick glance at Myron. "Take any action snapshots, perhaps a videotape?"

"No, that would be you," Myron said, "or maybe an extra-perverse rock star."

"Shame."

"Yeah, shame, I got that." Quality derrière? "So what's wrong with Esperanza?"

Terese finally disappeared through the front door. Win sighed softly and turned toward Myron. "The yacht will take half an hour to refuel. We'll leave then. Mind if I sit?"

"What happened, Win?"

He did not answer, choosing instead to sit on a chaise longue and ease back. He put his hands behind his head and crossed his ankles. "I'll say this for you. When you decide to wig out, you do it in style."

"I didn't wig out. I just needed a break."

"Uh-hmm." Win looked off, and a realization smacked Myron in the head: He had hurt Win's feelings. Strange but probably true. Win might be a blue-blooded, aristocratic sociopath, but hey, he was still human, sort of. The two men had been inseparable since college, yet Myron had run off without even calling. In many ways Win had no one else.

"I meant to call you," Myron said weakly.

Win kept still.

"But I knew if there was a problem, you'd be able to find me." That was true. Win could find a Hoffa needle in a Judge Crater haystack.

Win waved a hand. "Whatever."

"So what's wrong with Esperanza?"

"Clu Haid."

Myron's first client, a right-handed relief pitcher in the twilight of his career. "What about him?"

"He's dead," Win said.

Myron felt his legs buckle a bit. He let himself land on the chaise.

"Shot three times in his own abode."

Myron lowered his head. "I thought he'd straightened himself out."

Win said nothing.

"So what does Esperanza have to do with this?"

Win looked at his watch. "Right about now," he said, "she is in all likelihood being arrested for his murder."

"What?"

Win said nothing again. He hated to repeat himself.

"They think Esperanza killed him?"

"Good to see your vacation hasn't dulled your sharp powers of deduction." Win tilted his face toward the sun.

"What sort of evidence do they have?"

"The murder weapon, for one. Bloodstains. Fibers. Do you have any sunblock?"

"But how . . . ?" Myron studied his friend's face. As usual, it gave away nothing. "Did she do it?"

"I have no idea."

"Did you ask her?"

"Esperanza does not wish to speak with me."

"What?"

"She does not wish to speak with you either."

"I don't understand," Myron said. "Esperanza wouldn't kill anyone."

"You're quite sure about that, are you?"

Myron swallowed. He had thought that his recent experience would help him understand Win better. Win had killed too. Often, in fact. Now that Myron had done likewise, he thought that there would be a fresh bond. But there wasn't. Just the opposite, in fact. Their shared experience was opening a whole new chasm.

Win checked his watch. "Why don't you go get packed?"

"There's nothing I need to bring."

Win motioned to the house. Terese stood there, watching them silently. "Then say good-bye to La Derrière and let's be on our way."

2

Terese had put on a robe. She leaned against the doorway and waited.

Myron was not sure what to say. He settled for "Thank you." She nodded.

"Do you want to come along?" he asked.

"No."

"You can't stay here forever."

"Why not?"

Myron thought about it for a moment. "You know anything about boxing?"

Terese sniffed the air. "Do I detect the distinct odor of an upcoming sports metaphor?"

"I'm afraid so," he said.

"Ugh. Go on."

"This whole thing is sort of like a boxing match," Myron began. "We've been ducking and diving and weaving and trying to keep away from our opponent. But we can only do that for so long. Eventually we have to throw a punch."

She made a face. "Christ, that was lame."

"Spur of the moment."

"And inaccurate," she added. "Try this. We've tasted our opponent's power. It dropped us to the canvas. Somehow we managed to get back to our feet. But our legs are still rubbery, and our eyes are still hazed over. Another big blow and the fight will be over. Better to keep dancing. Better to avoid getting hit and hope to go the distance."

Hard to argue.

They fell into silence.

Myron said, "If you come up to New York, give me a call and—"

"Right."

Silence.

"We know what would happen," Terese said. "We'd meet up for drinks, maybe hop back in the sack, but it won't be the same. We'll both be uncomfortable as all hell. We'll pretend that we'll get together again, and we won't even exchange Christmas cards. We're not lovers, Myron. We're not even friends. I don't know what the hell we are, but I'm grateful."

A bird cawed. The small waves hummed their soft song. Win stood by the shore, his arms crossed, his body frighteningly patient.

"Have a good life, Myron."

"You too," he replied.

He and Win took the dinghy to the yacht. A crew member offered Myron his hand. Myron grabbed it and hoisted himself on board. The yacht took off. Myron stood on the deck and watched the shore grow smaller. He was leaning on a teakwood rail. Teakwood. Everything on this vessel was dark and rich and teak.

"Here," Win said.

Myron turned. Win tossed him a Yoo-Hoo, Myron's favorite drink, kind of a cross between a soda pop and chocolate milk. Myron smiled. "I haven't had one of these in three weeks."

"The withdrawal pains," Win said. "They must have been agony."

"No TV and no Yoo-Hoo. It's a wonder I survived."

"Yes, you practically lived like a monk," Win said. Then, looking back at the island, he added, "Well, like a monk who gets laid a lot."

They were both stalling.

"How long until we get back?" Myron asked.

"Eight hours on the boat," Win said. "A chartered jet is waiting at St. Bart's. The flight should take about four hours."

Myron nodded. He shook the can and popped it. He took a deep swig and turned back toward the water.

"I'm sorry," he said.

Win ignored the statement. Or maybe it was enough for him. The yacht picked up speed. Myron closed his eyes and let the water and gentle spray caress his face. He thought a moment about Clu Haid. Clu hadn't trusted agents—"a small step below pedophile" was how he put it—so he asked Myron to negotiate his contract, even though Myron was merely a first-year student at Harvard Law. Myron did it. He liked it. And MB SportsReps soon followed.

Clu was a lovable screw up. He unapologetically pursued wine, women, and song—not to mention any high he could get his hands/ nose/veins on. Clu never met a party he didn't like. He was a redheaded big guy with a teddy bear gut, handsome in a boyish way, an almost old-fashioned cad, and immensely charming. Everyone loved Clu. Even Bonnie, his long-suffering wife. Their marriage was a boomerang. She'd throw him out, he'd spin in the air for a while, and then she'd catch him on the return.

Clu had seemed to be slowing down a bit. After all the times Myron had gotten him out of trouble—drug suspensions, drunk driving charges, whatever—Clu had gone puffy, reached the end of his charm reign. The Yankees had traded for him, putting him on strict probation, giving him one last chance at redemption. Clu had stayed in rehab for the first time. He'd been attending the AA meetings. His fastball was back up in the nineties.

Win interrupted his thoughts. "Do you want to hear what happened?"

"I'm not sure," Myron said.

"Oh?"

"I screwed up last time. You warned me, but I didn't listen. A lot of people died because of me." Myron felt the tears come to his eyes. He pushed them back down. "You have no idea how bad it ended."

"Myron?"

He turned to his friend. Their eyes met.

"Get over yourself," Win said.

Myron made a noise—one part sob, two parts chuckle. "I hate when you coddle me."

"Perhaps you would prefer it if I served up some useless platitudes," Win said. He swirled his liquor and tasted a bit. "Please select one of the following and then we'll move on: Life is hard; life is cruel; life is random; sometimes good people are forced to do bad things; sometimes innocent people die; yes, Myron, you screwed up, but you'll do better this time; no, Myron, you didn't screw up, it wasn't your fault; everyone has a breaking point and now you know yours. Can I stop now?"

"Please."

"Then let us begin with Clu Haid."

Myron nodded, took another swig of Yoo-Hoo, emptied the can.

"Everything seemed to be going swimmingly for our old college chum," Win said. "He was pitching well. Domestic bliss seemed to reign. He was passing his drug tests. He was making curfew with hours to spare. That all changed two weeks ago when a surprise drug test produced a positive result."

"For what?"

"Heroin."

Myron shook his head.

"Clu kept his mouth shut to the media," Win said, "but privately he claimed the test was fixed. That someone had tampered with his food or some such nonsense."

"How do you know that?"

"Esperanza told me."

"He went to Esperanza?"

"Yes, Myron. When Clu failed the test, he naturally looked to his agent for help."

Silence.

"Oh," Myron said.

"I don't want go into the fiasco that is MB SportsReps right now. Suffice to say that Esperanza and Big Cyndi did the best they could. But it's your agency. Clients hired you. Many have been more than unhappy by your sudden disappearance."

Myron shrugged. He would probably care one day. "So Clu failed the test."

"And he was immediately suspended. The media moved in for the kill. He lost all his endorsement deals. Bonnie threw him out. The Yankees disowned him. With nowhere else to turn, Clu repeatedly visited your office. Esperanza told him that you were unavailable. His temper rose with each visit."

Myron closed his eyes.

"Four days ago Clu confronted Esperanza outside the office. At the Kinney parking lot, to be more exact. They had words. Harsh and rather loud words. According to witnesses, Clu punched her in the mouth."

"What?"

"I saw Esperanza the next day. Her jaw was swollen. She could barely talk, though she still managed to tell me to mind my own business. My understanding is more damage would have been inflicted had Mario and several other parking attendants not pulled them apart. Supposedly Esperanza made threats of the I'll-get-you-for-this-you-limp-dick-son-of-a-bitch variety as they were being held back."

Myron shook his head. This made no sense.

"The next afternoon Clu was found dead in the apartment he rented in Fort Lee," Win continued. "The police learned about the earlier altercation. They were then issued a slew of search warrants and found the murder weapon, a nine millimeter, in your office."

"My office?"

"MB's office, yes."

Myron shook his head again. "It had to be a plant."

"Yes, perhaps. There were also fibers that matched the carpeting in Clu's apartment."

"The fibers are meaningless. Clu was in the office. He probably dragged them there."

"Yes, perhaps," Win said again. "But the specks of blood in the trunk of the company car might be harder to explain."

Myron almost fell over. "Blood in the Taurus?"

"Yes."

"And the police confirmed the blood as Clu's?"

"Same blood type. The DNA test will take several weeks."

Myron could not believe what he was hearing. "Had Esperanza been using the car?"

"That very day. According to the E-Z Pass records, the car crossed the Washington Bridge back into New York within an hour of the murder. And as I said, he was killed in Fort Lee. The apartment is maybe two miles from the bridge."

"This is crazy."

Win said nothing.

"What's her motive?" Myron asked.

"The police don't have a solid one yet. But several are being offered."

"Such as?"

"Esperanza was a new partner at MB SportsReps. She'd been left in charge. The company's inaugural client was about to walk out the door."

Myron frowned. "Pretty flimsy motive."

"He had also recently assaulted her. Perhaps Clu blamed her for all the bad things that were happening to him. Perhaps she wanted vengeance. Who knows?"

"You said something before about her not talking to you."

"Yes."

"So you asked Esperanza about the charges?"

"Yes."

"And?"

"And she told me that she had the matter under control," Win said. "And she told me not to contact you. That she did not wish to speak with you."

Myron looked puzzled. "Why not?"

"I haven't a clue."

He pictured Esperanza, the Hispanic beauty he had met in the days when she wrestled professionally under the moniker Little Pocahontas. A lifetime ago. She had been with MB SportsReps since its inception—first as a secretary and now that she'd graduated law school, as a full-fledged partner.

"But I'm her best friend," Myron said.

"As I am well aware."

"So why would she say something like that?"

Win guessed the question was rhetorical. He kept silent.

The island was out of sight now. In every direction there was nothing but the churning warm blue of the Atlantic.

"If I hadn't run away," Myron began.

"Myron?"

"What?"

"You're whining again. I cannot handle whining."

Myron nodded and leaned against the teakwood.

"Any thoughts?" Win asked.

"She'll talk to me," Myron said. "Count on it."

"I just tried to call her."

"And?"

"No answer."

"Did you try Big Cyndi?"

"She now rooms with Esperanza."

No surprise. "What's today?" Myron asked.

"Tuesday."

"Big Cyndi still bounces at Leather-N-Lust. She might be there."

"During the day?"

Myron shrugged. "Sexual deviancy has no off hours."

"Thank God," Win said.

They fell into silence, the ship gently rocking them.

Win squinted into the sun. "Beautiful, no?"

Myron nodded.

"Must be sick of it after all this time."

"Very," Myron said.

"Come below deck. I think you'll be pleased."

3

Win had stocked the yacht with videos. They watched episodes of the old *Batman* show (the one with Julie Newmar as Cat Woman and Lesley Gore as Pussycat—double meow!), the *Odd Couple* (Oscar and Felix on *Password*), a *Twilight Zone* ("To Serve Man"), and for something more current, *Seinfeld* (Jerry and Elaine visit Jerry's parents in Florida). Forget pot roast. This was comfort food. But on the off chance that it wasn't substantial enough, there were also Doritos and Cheez Doodles and more Yoo-Hoos and even rewarmed pizza from Calabria's Pizzeria on Livingston Avenue.

Win. He might be a sociopath, but what a guy.

The effect of all this was beyond therapeutic, the time spent at sea and later in the air an emotional pressure chamber of sorts, a chance for Myron's soul to adjust to the bends, to the sudden reemergence into the real world.

The two friends barely spoke, except to sigh over Julie Newmar as Cat Woman (whenever she came on the screen in her tight black cat suit, Win said, "Puuuurrrrrfect"). They'd both been five or six years old when the show first aired, but something about Julie Newmar as Cat Woman completely blew away any Freudian notions of latency. Why, neither man could say. Her villainy perhaps. Or something more primal. Esperanza would no doubt have an interesting opinion. He tried not to think about her—useless and draining when he couldn't do anything about it—but the last time he had done something like this was in Philadelphia with both Win and Esperanza. He missed her. Watching the videos was not the same without her running commentary.

The boat docked and they headed for the private jet.

"We'll save her," Win said. "We are, after all, the good guys."

"Questionable."

"Have confidence, my friend."

"No, I mean us being the good guys."

"You should know better."

"Not anymore I don't," Myron said.

Win made his jutting jaw face, the one that had come over on the *Mayflower*. "This moral crisis of yours," he said. "It's *très* unbecoming."

A breathy blond bombshell like something out of an old burlesque skit greeted them in the cabin of the Lock-Horne company jet. She fetched them drinks between giggles and wiggles. Win smiled at her. She smiled back.

"Funny thing," Myron said.

"What's that?"

"You always hire curvaceous stewardesses."

Win frowned. "Please," he said. "She prefers to be called a flight attendant."

"Pardon my oafish insensitivity."

"Try a little harder to be tolerant," Win said. Then: "Guess what her name is."

"Tawny?"

"Close. Candi. With an *i*. And she doesn't dot it. She draws a heart over it."

Win could be a bigger pig, but it was hard to imagine how.

Myron sat back. The pilot came over the loudspeaker. He addressed them by name, and then they took off. Private jet. Yacht. Sometimes it was nice having wealthy friends.

When they reached cruising altitude, Win opened what looked like a cigar box and pulled out a telephone. "Call your parents," he said.

Myron stayed still for a moment. A fresh wave of guilt rolled over him, coloring his cheeks. He nodded, took the phone, dialed. He gripped the phone a bit too tightly. His mother answered.

Myron said, "Mom—"

Mom started bawling. She managed to yell for Dad. Dad picked up the downstairs extension.

"Dad—"

And then he started bawling too. Stereo bawling. Myron held the phone away from his ear for a moment.

"I was in the Caribbean," he said, "not Beirut."

An explosion of laughter from both. Then more crying. Myron looked at Win. Win sat impassively. Myron rolled his eyes, but of course he was also pleased. Complain all you want, but who didn't want to be loved like this?

His parents settled into a meaningless chatter—meaningless on purpose, Myron supposed. While they could undoubtedly be pests, Mom and Dad had a wonderful ability to know when to back off. He managed to explain where he'd been. They listened in silence. Then his mother asked, "So where are you calling us from?"

"Win's airplane."

Stereo gasps now. "What?"

"Win's company has a private jet. I just told you he picked me—"

"And you're calling on his phone?"

"Yes."

"Do you have any idea how much that costs?"

"Mom . . ."

But the meaningless chatter died down in a hurry then. When Myron hung up seconds later, he sat back. The guilt came again, bathing him in something ice cold. His parents were not young anymore. He hadn't thought about that before he ran. He hadn't thought about a lot of things.

"I shouldn't have done that to them," Myron said. "Or you."

Win shifted in his seat—major body language for him. Candi wiggled back into view. She lowered a screen and hit a switch. A Woody Allen film came on. *Love and Death*. Ambrosia of the mind. They watched without speaking. When it was over, Candi asked Myron if he wanted to take a shower before they landed.

"Excuse me?" Myron said.

Candi giggled, called him a "Big Silly," and wiggled away.

"A shower?"

"There's one in the back," Win said. "I also took the liberty of bringing you a change of clothes."

"You are a friend."

"I am indeed, Big Silly."

Myron showered and dressed, and then everyone buckled their seatbelts for approach. The plane descended without delay, the landing so smooth it could have been choreographed by the Temptations. A stretch limousine was waiting for them on the dark tarmac. When they got off the plane, the air felt strange and unfamiliar, as though he'd been visiting another planet rather than another country. It was also raining hard. They ran down the steps and into the already-open limo doors.

They shook off the wet. "I assume that you'll be staying with me," Win said.

Myron had been living in a loft down on Spring Street with Jessica. But that was before. "If it's okay."

"It's okay."

"I could move back in with my folks—"

"I said, it's okay."

"I'll find my own place."

"No rush," Win said.

The limousine started up. Win steepled his fingers. He always did that. It looked good on him. Still holding the steeple, he bounced his forefingers against his lips. "I'm not the best one to discuss these matters with," he said, "but if you want to talk about Jessica or Brenda or whatever . . ." He released the steeple, made a waving motion with his right hand. Win was trying. Matters of the heart were not his forte. His feelings on romantic entanglement could objectively be labeled "appalling."

"Don't worry about it," Myron said.

"Fine then."

"Thanks, though."

Quick nod.

After more than a decade struggling with Jessica—years of being in love with the same woman, having one major breakup, finding each other again, taking tentative steps, growing, finally moving in together again—it was over.

"I miss Jessica," Myron said.

"I thought we weren't going to talk about it."

"Sorry."

Win shifted in his seat again. "No, go on." Like he'd rather have an anal probe.

"It's just that . . . I guess part of me will always be enmeshed in Jessica."

Win nodded. "Like something in a machinery mishap."

Myron smiled. "Yeah. Like that."

"Then slice off the limb and leave it behind."

Myron looked at his friend.

Win shrugged. "I've been watching *Sally Jessy* on the side."

"It shows," Myron said.

"The episode entitled 'Mommy Took Away My Nipple Ring,' " Win said. "I'm not afraid to say it made me cry."

"Good to see you getting in touch with your sensitive side." As if Win had one. "So what next?"

Win checked his watch. "I have a contact at the Bergen County house of detention. He should be in by now." He hit the speaker phone and pressed in some numbers. They listened to the phone ring. After two rings a voice said, "Schwartz."

"Brian, this is Win Lockwood."

The usual reverent hush when you first hear that name. Then: "Hey, Win."

"I need a favor."

"Shoot."

"Esperanza Diaz. Is she there?"

Brief pause. "You didn't hear it from me," Schwartz said.

"Hear what?"

"Good, okay, long as we understand each other," he said. "Yeah, she's here. They dragged her through here in cuffs a coupla hours ago. Very hush-hush."

"Why hush-hush?"

"Don't know."

"When is she being arraigned?"

"Tomorrow morning, I guess."

Win looked at Myron. Myron nodded. Esperanza would be held overnight. This was not a good thing.

"Why did they arrest her so late?"

"Don't know."

"And you saw them drag her in cuffs?"

"Yep."

"Didn't they let her surrender on her own?"

"Nope."

Again the two friends looked at each other. The late arrest. The handcuffs. The overnight. Someone in the DA's office was pissed off and trying to make a point. Very not a good thing.

"What else can you tell me?" Win asked.

"Not much. Like I said, they're being quiet on this one. The DA hasn't even released it to the media yet. But he will. Probably before the eleven o'clock news. Quick statement, no time for questions, that kind of thing. Hell, I wouldn't know about it if I wasn't a big fan."

"A big fan?"

"Of professional wrestling. See, I recognized her from her old wrestling days. Did you know Esperanza Diaz used to be Little Pocahontas, the Indian Princess?"

Win glanced at Myron. "Yes, Brian, I know."

"Really?" Brian was big-time excited now. "Little Pocahontas was my absolute fave, bar none. An awesome wrestler. Top drawer. I mean, she used to enter the ring in this skimpy suede bikini, right, and then she'd start grappling with other chicks, bigger chicks really, writhing around on the floor and stuff—swear to God, she was so hot my fingernails would melt."

"Thank you for the visual," Win said. "Anything else, Brian?"

"No."

"Do you know who her attorney of record is?"

"No." Then: "Oh, one other thing. She's got someone, well, sort of with her."

"Sort of with her, Brian?"

"Outside. On the front steps of the courthouse."

"I'm not sure I'm following you," Win said.

"Out in the rain. Just sitting there. If I didn't know better, I'd swear it was Little Pocahontas's old tag team partner, Big Chief Mama. Did you know Big Chief Mama and Little Pocahontas were Intercontinental tag team champions three years running?"

Win sighed. "You don't say."

"Whatever Intercontinental means. I mean, what is that, Intercontinental? And I'm not talking about recently. Five, eight years ago, at least. But, man, they were awesome. Great wrestlers. Today, well, the league has no class anymore."

"Grappling bikini-clad women," Win said. "They just don't make them like they used to."

"Right, exactly. Too many fake, inflated breasts nowadays, at least that's how I see it. One of them is going to land on her stomach and bam, her boob is going to blow out like a worn tire. So I don't follow it much anymore. Oh, maybe if I'm flipping the channels and something catches my eye, I might watch a little—"

"You were talking about a woman out in the rain?"

"Right, Win, right, sorry. Anyway, she's out there, whoever she is. Just sitting there. The cops went by before and asked her what she was doing. She said she was going to wait for her friend."

"So she's there right now?"

"Yep."

"What does she look like, Brian?"

"Like the Incredible Hulk. Only scarier. And maybe greener."

Win and Myron exchanged glances. No doubt. Big Chief Mama aka Big Cyndi.

"Anything else, Brian?"

"No, not really." Then: "So you know Esperanza Diaz?"

"Yes."

"Personally?"

"Yes."

Silent awe. "Jesus, you lead some life, Win."

"Oh, indeed."

"Think you can get me her autograph?"

"I'll do my best, Brian."

"A picture autograph maybe? Of Little Pocahontas in costume? I'm a really big fan."

"So I gather, Brian. Good-bye."

Win hung up and sat back. He looked over at Myron. Myron nodded. Win picked up the intercom and gave the driver directions to the courthouse.

4

By the time they arrived at the courthouse in Hackensack, it was nearly 10:00 P.M. Big Cyndi sat in the rain, shoulders hunched; at least Myron thought it was Big Cyndi. From a distance, it looked like someone had parked a Volkswagen Bug on the courthouse steps.

Myron stepped out of the car and approached. "Big Cyndi?"

The dark heap let loose a low growl, a lioness warning off an inferior animal who'd wandered astray.

"It's Myron," he said.

The growl deepened. The rain had plastered Big Cyndi's hair spikes to her scalp, as if she were sporting an uneven Caesar coif. Today's color was hard to decipher—Big Cyndi liked diversity in her follicular tint—but it didn't look like any hue found in the state of nature. Big Cyndi sometimes liked to combine dyes randomly and see what happened. She also insisted on being called Big Cyndi. Not Cyndi. Big Cyndi. She had even had her name legally changed. Official documents read: Cyndi, Big.

"You can't stay here all night," Myron tried.

She finally spoke. "Go home."

"What happened?"

"You ran away." Big Cyndi's voice was childlike, lost.

"Yes."

"You left us alone."

"I'm sorry about that. But I'm back now."

He risked another step. If only he had something to placate her with. Like a half gallon of Häagen-Dazs. Or a sacrificial goat.

Big Cyndi started to cry. Myron approached slowly, semileading with his right hand in case she wanted to sniff it. But the growls were all gone now, replaced by sobs. Myron put his palm on a shoulder that felt like a bowling ball.

"What happened?" he asked again.

She sniffled. Loudly. The sound almost dented the limo's fender. "I can't tell you."

"Why can't you?"

"She said not to."

"Esperanza?"

Big Cyndi nodded.

"She's going to need help," Myron said.

"She doesn't want your help."

The words stung. The rain continued to fall. Myron sat on the step next to her. "Is she angry about my leaving?"

"I can't tell you, Mr. Bolitar. I'm sorry."

"Why not?"

"She told me not to."

"Esperanza can't bear the brunt of this on her own," Myron said. "She's going to need a lawyer."

"She has one."

"Who?"

"Hester Crimstein."

Big Cyndi gasped as though she realized she'd said too much, but Myron wondered if the slip had been intentional.

"How did she get Hester Crimstein?" Myron asked.

"I can't say any more, Mr. Bolitar. Please don't be mad at me."

"I'm not mad, Big Cyndi. I'm just concerned."

Big Cyndi smiled at him then. The sight made Myron bite back a scream. "It's nice to have you back," she said.

"Thank you."

She put her head on his shoulder. The weight made him teeter, but he remained relatively upright. "You know how I feel about Esperanza," Myron said.

"Yes," Big Cyndi said. "You love her. And she loves you."

"So let me help."

Big Cyndi lifted her head off his shoulder. Blood circulated again. "I think you should leave now."

Myron stood. "Come on. We'll give you a ride home."

"No, I'm staying."

"It's raining and it's late. Someone might try to attack you. It's not safe out here."

"I can take care of myself," Big Cyndi said.

He had meant that it wasn't safe for the attackers, but he let it pass. "You can't stay out here all night."

"I'm not leaving Esperanza alone."

"But she won't even know you're here."

Big Cyndi wiped the rain from her face with a hand the size of a truck tire. "She knows."

Myron looked back at the car. Win was leaning against the door now, arms crossed, umbrella resting on his shoulder. Very Gene Kelly. He nodded at Myron.

"You're sure?" Myron asked.

"Yes, Mr. Bolitar. Oh, and I'll be late for work tomorrow. I hope you understand."

Myron nodded. They stared at each other, the rain cascading down their faces. A howl of laughter made both of them turn to the right and look at the fortresslike structure that contained the holding cells. Esperanza, the person closest to them both, was incarcerated in there. Myron stepped toward the limousine. Then he turned back around.

"Esperanza wouldn't kill anyone," he said.

He waited for Big Cyndi to agree or at least nod her head. But she didn't. She hunched the shoulders back up and disappeared within herself.

Myron slid back into the car. Win followed, handing Myron a towel. The driver started up.

"Hester Crimstein is her attorney," Myron said.

"Ms. Court TV?"

"The same."

"Ah," Win said. "And what's the name of her show again?"

"Crimstein on Crime," Myron said.

Win frowned. "Cute."

"She had a book with the same title." Myron shook his head. "This is weird. Hester Crimstein doesn't take many cases anymore. So how did Esperanza land her?"

Win tapped his chin with his forefinger. "I'm not positive," he said, "but I believe Esperanza had a fling with her a couple of months back."

"You're kidding."

"Well, yes, I am such a mirthful fellow. And wasn't that just the funniest line?"

Wiseass. But it made sense. Esperanza was as perfect a bisexual as you could find—perfect because everyone, no matter what his or her sex or preference, found her immensely attractive. If you're going to go all ways, might as well have universal appeal, right?

Myron mulled this over a few moments. "Do you know where Hester Crimstein lives?" he asked.

"Two buildings up from me on Central Park West."

"So let's pay her a visit."

Win frowned. "Why?"

"Maybe she can fill us in."

"She won't talk to us."

"Maybe she will."

"What makes you say that?"

"For one thing," Myron said, "I'm feeling particularly charming."

"By God." Win leaned forward. "Driver, step on the gas."

5

Win lived at the Dakota, one of Manhattan's swankiest buildings. Hester Crimstein lived two blocks north at the San Remo, an equally swanky building. Occupants included Diane Keaton and Dustin Hoffman, but the San Remo was perhaps best known as the building that had rejected Madonna's application for residence.

There were two entranceways, both with doormen dressed like Brezhnev strolling Red Square. Brezhnev One announced in a clipped tone that Ms. Crimstein was "not present." He actually used the word *present* too; people don't often do that in real life. He smiled for Win and looked down his nose at Myron. This was no easy task—Myron was at least six inches taller—and required Brezhnev to tilt his head way back so that his nostrils looked like the westbound entrance to the Lincoln Tunnel. Why, Myron wondered, do servants of the rich and famous act snootier than their masters? Was it simple resentment? Was it because they were looked down upon all day and thus needed on occasion to be the one doing the looking down? Or—more simply—were people attracted to such jobs insecure asswipes?

Life's little mysteries.

"Are you expecting Ms. Crimstein back tonight?" Win asked.

Brezhnev opened his mouth, stopped, cast a wary eye as if he feared Myron might defecate on the Persian rug. Win read his face and led him to the side, away from the lowly member of the unwashed.

"She should be back soon, Mr. Lockwood." Ah, so Brezhnev had recognized Win. No wonder. "Ms. Crimstein's aerobics class concludes at eleven."

Exercising at eleven o'clock at night. Welcome to the nineties, where leisure time is sucked away like something undergoing liposuction.

There were no waiting or sitting areas at the San Remo—most of your finer buildings did not encourage even approved guests to loiter—so they moved outside to the street. Central Park was across the roadway. Myron could see, well, trees and a stone wall, and that was about it. Lots of taxis sped north. Win's stretch limousine had been dismissed—they both figured they could walk the two blocks to Win's place—but there were four other stretch limousines sitting in a no parking zone. A fifth pulled up. A silver stretch Mercedes. Brezhnev rushed to the car door like he really had to pee and there was a bathroom inside.

An old man, bald except for a white crown of hair, stumbled out, his mouth twisted poststroke. A woman resembling a prune followed. Both were expensively dressed and maybe a hundred years old. Something about them troubled Myron. They looked wizened, yes. Old, certainly. But there was more to it, Myron sensed. People talk about sweet little old people, but these two were so blatantly the opposite, their eyes beady, their movements shifty and angry and fearful. Life had sapped them, sucked out all the goodness and hope of youth, leaving them with a vitality based on something ugly and hateful. Bitterness was the only thing left. Whether the bitterness was directed at God or at their fellowman, Myron could not say.

Win nudged him. He looked to his right and saw a figure he recognized from TV as Hester Crimstein coming toward them. She was on the husky side, at least by today's warped Kate Mossian standards, and her face was fleshy and cherubic. She wore Reebok white sneakers, white socks, green stretch pants that would probably make Kate snicker, a sweatshirt, a knit hat with frosted blond hair sticking out the back. The old man stopped when he saw the attorney, grabbed the prune lady's hand, hurried inside.

"Bitch!" the old man managed through the good side of his face.

"Up yours too, Lou," Hester called out after him.

The old man stopped, looked like he wanted to say something more, limped off.

Myron and Win exchanged a glance and approached.

"Old adversary," she said in way of explanation. "You ever hear the old adage that only the good die young?"

"Uh, sure."

Hester Crimstein gestured with both hands at the old couple like Carol Merrill showing off a brand-new car. "There's your proof. Couple years back I helped his children sue the son of a bitch. You never saw anything like it." She tilted her head. "Ever notice how some people are like jackals?"

"Pardon?"

"They eat their young. That's Lou. And don't even get me started on that shriveled-up witch he lives with. Five-dollar whore who hit the jackpot. Hard to believe looking at her now."

"I see," Myron said, though he didn't. He tried to push ahead. "Ms. Crimstein, my name is—"

"Myron Bolitar," she interrupted. "By the way, that's a horrid name. Myron. What were your parents thinking?"

A very good question. "If you know who I am, then you know why I'm here."

"Yes and no," Hester said.

"Yes and no?"

"Well, I know who you are because I'm a sports nut. I used to watch you play. That NCAA championship game against Indiana was a frigging classic. I know the Celtics drafted you in the first round, what, eleven, twelve years ago?"

"Something like that."

"But frankly—and I mean no offense here—I'm not sure you had the speed to be a great pro, Myron. The shot, sure. You could always shoot. You could be physical. But what are you, six-five?"

"About that."

"You would have had a tough time in the NBA. One woman's opinion. But of course the fates took care of that by blowing out your knee. Only an alternate universe knows the truth." She smiled. "Nice chatting with you." She looked over at Win. "You too, gabby boy. Good night."

"Wait a second," Myron said. "I'm here about Esperanza Diaz."

She faked a gasp of surprise. "Really? And here I thought you just wanted to reminisce about your athletic career."

He looked at Win. "The charm," Win whispered.

Myron turned back toward Hester. "Esperanza is my friend," he said.

"So?"

"So I want to help."

"Great. I'll start sending you the bills. This case is going to cost a bundle. I'm very expensive, you know. You can't believe the upkeep of this building. And now the doormen want new uniforms. Something in mauve, I think."

"That's not what I meant."

"Oh?"

"I'd like to know what's going on with the case."

She scrunched up her face. "Where have you been the last few weeks?"

"Away."

"Where away?"

"The Caribbean."

She nodded. "Nice tan."

"Thanks."

"But you could have gotten it at a tanning booth. You look like the kind of guy who hangs out at tanning booths."

Myron looked at Win again. "The charm, Luke," Win whispered, doing his best Alec Guinness as Obi-Wan Kenobi. "Remember the charm."

"Ms. Crimstein—"

"Anyone who can verify your whereabouts in the Caribbean, Myron?"

"Pardon me?"

"Hearing problems? I asked if anyone can verify your whereabouts at the time of the alleged murder."

Alleged murder. The guy is shot three times in his home, but the murder is only "alleged." Lawyers. "Why do you want to know that?"

Hester Crimstein shrugged. "The alleged murder weapon was allegedly found at the offices of one MB SportsReps. That's your company, is it not?"

"It is."

"And you use the company car where the alleged blood and alleged fibers were allegedly found."

Win said, "The key word here is *alleged.*"

Hester Crimstein looked at Win. "It speaks."

Win smiled.

Myron said, "You think I'm a suspect?"

"Sure, why not? It's called reasonable doubt, sweet buns. I'm a defense attorney. We're big on reasonable doubt."

"Much as I'd like to help, there was a witness to my whereabouts."

"Who?"

"Don't worry about it."

Another shrug. "You're the one who said you wanted to help. Good night." She looked at Win. "By the way, you're the perfect man—good-looking and nearly mute."

"Careful," Win said to her.

"Why?"

Win pointed at Myron with his thumb. "Any minute now he's going to turn on the charm and reduce your willpower to rubble."

She looked at Myron and burst out laughing.

Myron tried again. "So what happened?" he asked.

"Excuse me?"

"I'm her friend."

"Yeah, I think you already said that."

"I'm her best friend. I care about her."

"Fine. Tomorrow I'll pass her a note during study hall, find out if she likes you too. Then you can meet at Pop's and share a soda."

"That's not what I—" Myron stopped, gave her the slow, slightly put-out-but-here-to-help smile. Smile 18: the Michael Landon model, except he couldn't crinkle the eyebrow. "I'd just like to know what happened. You can appreciate that."

Her face softened, and she nodded. "You went to law school, right?"

"Yes."

"At Harvard no less."

"Yes."

"So maybe you were absent the day they went over a little something we call attorney-client privilege. I can recommend some wonderful books on the subject, if you'd like. Or maybe you can watch any episode of *Law & Order.* They usually talk about it right before the old DA grouses to Sam Waterston that he's got no case and should cut a deal."

So much for charm. "You're just covering your ass," Myron said.

She looked behind her and down. Then she frowned. "No easy task, I assure you."

"I thought you were supposed to be a hotshot attorney."

She sighed, crossed her arms. "Okay, Myron, let's hear it. Why am I covering my ass? Why am I not the hotshot attorney you thought I was?"

"Because they didn't let Esperanza surrender. Because they dragged her in in cuffs. Because they're holding her overnight instead of getting her through the system in the same day. Why?"

She dropped her hands to her sides. "Good question, Myron. Why do you think?"

"Because someone there doesn't like her high-profile attorney. Someone in the DA's office probably has a hard-on for you and is taking it out on your client."

She nodded. "Good possibility. But I have another one."

"What?"

"Maybe they don't like her employer."

"Me?"

She started for the door. "Do us all a favor, Myron. Stay out of this. Just keep away. And maybe get yourself a lawyer."

Hester Crimstein spun around and disappeared inside then. Myron turned toward Win. Win was bent at the waist, squinting at Myron's crotch. "What the hell are you doing?"

Still squinting. "I wanted to see if she left you with even a sliver of a testicle."

"Very funny. What do you think she meant about them not liking her employer?"

"Not a clue," Win said. Then: "You mustn't blame yourself."

"What?"

"For your charm's seemingly lackluster performance. You forgot a crucial component in all this."

"That being?"

"Ms. Crimstein had an affair with Esperanza."

Myron saw where he was going with this. "Of course. She must be a lesbian."

"Precisely. It's the only rational explanation for her ability to resist you."

"That, or a really bizarre paranormal event."

Win nodded. They started walking down Central Park West.

"This is also further proof of a very frightening adage," Win said.

"What's that?"

"Most women you encounter are lesbians."

Myron nodded. "Almost every one."

6

They walked the two blocks to Win's place, watched a little television, went to bed. Myron lay in the dark exhausted, but sleep remained elusive. He thought about Jessica. Then he tried to think about Brenda, but the automatic defense mechanism deflected that one. Still too raw. And he thought about Terese. She was alone on that island tonight for the first time. During the day the island's solitude was peaceful and quiet and welcome; at night the solitude felt more like dark isolation, the island's black walls closing in, silent and cloying as a buried coffin. He and Terese had always slept wrapped in each other's arms. Now he pictured her lying in that deep blackness alone. And he worried about her.

He woke up the next morning at seven. Win was already gone, but he'd scribbled a note that he'd meet up with Myron at the courthouse at nine. Myron grabbed a bowl of Cap'n Crunch, discerned with a digging left hand that Win had already extracted the free toy inside, showered, dressed, checked his watch. Eight o'clock. Plenty of time to reach the courthouse in time.

He took the elevator down and crossed the famed Dakota courtyard. He had just reached the corner of Seventy-second Street and Central Park West when he spotted the three familiar figures. Myron felt his pulse quicken. FJ, short for Frank Junior, was bookended by two huge guys. The two huge guys looked like lab experiments gone very wrong, as if someone had potently mixed genetic glandular excess with anabolic steroids. They wore tank tops and those drawstring weightlifting pants that looked suspiciously like ugly pajama bottoms.

Young FJ silently smiled at Myron with thin lips. He sported a purple-blue suit so shiny it looked like someone had sprayed it with a sealant. FJ didn't move, didn't say anything, just smiled at Myron with unblinking eyes and those thin lips.

Today's word, boys and girls, is *reptilian.*

FJ finally took a step forward. "Heard you were back in town, Myron."

Myron bit back a rejoinder—it wasn't a very cutting one, something about the nice welcoming party—and kept his mouth shut.

"Remember our last conversation?" FJ continued.

"Vaguely."

"I mentioned something about killing you, right?"

"It might have come up," Myron said. "I don't remember. So many tough guys, so many threats."

The Bookends tried to scowl, but even their faces were overmuscled, and the movement took too much effort. They settled back into the steady frowns and lowered the eyebrows a bit.

"Actually, I was going to carry through with it," FJ continued. "About a month ago. I followed you out to some graveyard in New Jersey. I even sneaked up behind you with my gun out. Funny thing, no?"

Myron nodded. "Like Henny Youngman wrote it."

FJ tilted his head. "Don't you want to know why I didn't kill you?"

"Because of Win."

The sound of his name was like a cold glass of water in the faces of both Bookends. The two giants actually stepped back but recovered quickly with a few flexes. FJ remained unruffled. "Win doesn't scare me," he said.

"Even the dumbest animal," Myron said, "has an innate survival mechanism."

FJ's eyes met Myron's. Myron tried to maintain contact, but it was hard. There was nothing behind FJ's eyes but rot and decay; it was like staring into the broken windows of an abandoned building. "Sticks and stones, Myron. Sticks and stones. I didn't kill you because, well, you already looked so miserable. It was as though—how to put this?—as though killing you would have been an act of mercy. Like I said before, funny, right?"

"You should consider stand-up," Myron agreed.

FJ chuckled and waved a well-manicured hand at nothing in particular. "Anyway, bygones. My father and uncle like you, and yes, we see no reason to antagonize Win unnecessarily. They don't want you dead, so neither do I."

His father and uncle were Frank and Herman Ache, two of New York's legendary leading leg breakers. The elder Aches had grown up on the streets, slaughtered more people than the next guy, moved up the ladder.

Herman, the older brother and big cheese, was in his sixties now and liked to pretend he wasn't scum by surrounding himself with the finer things in life: restricted clubs that didn't want him, nouveau-riche art exhibits, well-coiffed charities, midtown French maître d's who treated anyone who tipped with less than a Jackson like something they couldn't scrape off the soles of their shoes. In other words, a higher-income scum. Herman's younger brother, Frank, the psycho who had produced the equally psycho offspring who now stood in front of Myron, remained what he had always been: an ugly hatchet man who considered K mart velour sweatsuits haute couture. Frank had calmed down over the last few years, but it never quite worked for him. Life, it seemed, had little meaning for Frank Senior without someone to torture or maim.

"What do you want, FJ?"

"I have a business proposition for you."

"Gee, I just know this is really going to interest me."

"I want to buy you out."

The Aches ran TruPro, a rather large sports representation firm. TruPro had always been devoid of any semblance of scruples, recruiting young athletes with as much moral restraint as a politician planning a fundraiser. But then their owner stacked up debts. Bad debts. The debts that attract the wrong kind of fungus. The appropriately named Ache brothers, the fungi in question, moved in and, like the parasitic entities they were, ate away all signs of life and were now gnawing on the carcass.

Still, being a sports agent was a legit way of making a living, sort of, and Frank Senior, wanting for his son what all fathers wanted, handed young FJ the reins straight out of business school. In theory FJ was supposed to run TruPro as legitimately as possible. His father had killed and maimed so that his son wouldn't have to—yep, the classic American dream with, granted, a rather deranged twist. But FJ seemed incapable of freeing himself from the old familial shackles. *Why* was a question that fascinated Myron. Was FJ's evil genetic, passed down from his father like a prominent nose, or was he, like so many other children, simply trying to gain his father's acceptance by proving the acorn could be as ferociously psychotic as the oak?

Nature or nurture. The argument rages on.

"MB SportsReps is not for sale," Myron said.

"I think you're being foolish."

Myron nodded. "I'll file that under 'One Day I Might Even Care.' "

The Bookends sort of grumbled, took a step forward, and cracked their necks in unison. Myron pointed to one, then the other. "Who does your choreography?"

They wanted to be insulted—you could just tell—except neither one of them knew what the word *choreography* meant.

FJ asked, "Do you know how many clients MB SportsReps lost in the last few weeks?"

"A lot?"

"I'd say a quarter of your list. A couple of them went with us."

Myron whistled, feigned nonchalant, but he was not happy to hear this. "I'll get them back."

"You think so?" FJ again smiled the reptilian smile; Myron almost expected a forked tongue to dart out between his lips. "Do you know how many more are going to leave when they hear about Esperanza's arrest?"

"A lot?"

"You'll be lucky to have one left."

"Hey, then I'll be like Jerry Maguire. Did you see that movie? Show me the money? I love black people?" Myron gave FJ his best Tom Cruise earnest. "You. Complete. Me."

FJ remained cool. "I'm willing to be generous, Myron."

"I'm sure you are, FJ, but the answer is still no."

"I don't care how clean your rep used to be. Nobody can survive the sort of money scandal you're about to go through."

It wasn't a money scandal, but Myron was not in the mood to issue corrections. "Are we finished, FJ?"

"Sure." FJ gave him one last scaly smile. The smile seemed to jump off his face, crawl toward Myron, and then slither its way up his back. "But why don't we get together and have lunch?"

"Any time," Myron said. "You have a cellular?"

"Of course."

"Call my partner right away and set it up."

"Isn't she in jail?"

Myron snapped his fingers. "Drat."

FJ found that amusing. "I mentioned that some of your old clients are now using my services."

"So you did."

"If you contact any of them"—he paused, thought it over—"I'd feel obliged to retaliate. Do I make myself clear?"

FJ was maybe twenty-five years old, less than a year out of Harvard Business School. He had gone undergrad to Princeton. Smart kid. Or powerful father. Either way, rumor had it that when a Princeton professor was about to accuse FJ of plagiarism, the professor disappeared and only his tongue was found—on the pillow of another professor who had considered leveling the same charges.

"Crystal, FJ."

"Great, Myron. Then we'll talk again."

If Myron still had his tongue.

The three men slid into their car and drove off without another word. Myron slowed his heart rate and checked his watch. Court time.

7

The courtroom in Hackensack looked very much like the ones you see on television. Shows like *The Practice* and *Law & Order* and even *Judge Judy* capture the physical appearance pretty well. They can't of course capture the essence emanating from the little things: the faint, underlying stench of fear-induced sweat, the overuse of disinfectant, the slightly sticky feel to all the benches and tables and handrails—what Myron liked to call the ooze factors.

Myron had his checkbook ready so bail could be posted immediately. He and Win had gone over it last night and figured the judge would come in around fifty to seventy-five grand. Esperanza had no record and a steady job. Those factors would play in her favor. If the money was higher, no problem. Myron's pockets might be only semideep, but Win's net worth was on par with the GNP of a small European country.

There were droves of reporters parked outside, tons of vans with wrapped cables and satellite dishes, and of course phallic antennas, stretching toward the heavens as though in search of the elusive god of higher ratings. Court TV was there. News 2 New York. ABC News. CNN. Eyewitness News. Every city in every region of the country had an Eyewitness News. Why? What was so appealing about that name? There were also the new sleazoid TV shows, like *Hard Copy, Access Hollywood, Current Affair,* though the distinction between them and the local news was becoming murky to the point of nonexistent. Hey, at least *Hard Copy* and the like were somewhat honest about the fact that they served no redeeming social value. And they didn't subject you to weathermen.

A couple of reporters recognized Myron and called out. Myron put on his game face—serious, unyielding, concerned, confident—and no-commented his way through them. When he entered the courtroom, he spotted Big Cyndi first—no surprise since she stuck out like Louis Farrakhan at B'nai B'rith. She was jammed into the aisle of a row empty except for Win. Not unusual. If you wanted to save seats, send Big Cyndi; people did not relish excusing themselves to squeeze past her. Most opted to stand. Or go home even.

Myron slid into Big Cyndi's row, actually high-stepping over two knees that looked like batting helmets, and sat between his friends.

Big Cyndi had not changed from last night or even washed up. The steady rain had rinsed out some of the hair dye; purple and yellow streaks had dried on the front and back of her neck. Her makeup, always applied in amounts thick enough to make a plaster bust, had also suffered under the rain's onslaught, her face now resembling multicolored menorah candles left too long in the sun.

In some major cities, murder arraignments were commonplace and handled in factory-line fashion. Not so here in Hackensack. This was big time—a murder case involving a celebrity. There would be no rush.

The bailiff started calling cases.

"I had a visitor this morning," Myron whispered to Win.

"Oh?"

"FJ and two goons."

"Ah," Win said. "Was the cover boy for *Modern Mobster* voicing his usual medley of colorful threats?"

"Yes."

Win almost smiled. "We should kill him."

"No."

"You're just putting off the inevitable."

"He's Frank Ache's son, Win. You just don't kill Frank Ache's son."

"I see. Then you'd rather kill somebody from a better family?"

Win logic. It made sense in the scariest way possible. "Let's just see how it plays out, okay?"

"Don't put off until tomorrow what must be exterminated today."

Myron nodded. "You should write one of those life-instruction books."

They fell into silence. Cases went by—a breaking and entering, a couple of assaults, too many car thefts. Every suspect looked young, guilty, and angry. Always scowling. Tough guys. Myron tried not to make a face, tried to remember innocent until proven guilty, tried to remember that Esperanza too was a suspect. But it didn't help much.

Finally Myron saw Hester Crimstein sweep into the courtroom, decked out in her best professional civvies: a sleek beige suit, cream blouse, and a tad overcoiffed, overfrosted hair. She took her spot at the defense table, and the room fell silent. Two guards led Esperanza through an open door. Myron saw her, and something akin to a mule kicked him in the chest.

Esperanza was dressed in a court-issued fluorescent orange jumpsuit. Forget gray or stripes—if a prisoner wanted to escape, he was going to stick out like a neon light in a monastery. Her hands were cuffed in front of her. Myron knew that Esperanza was petite—maybe five-two, a hundred pounds—but he had never seen her look so small. She kept her head high, defiant. Classic Esperanza. If she was afraid, she wasn't showing it.

Hester Crimstein put a comforting hand on her client's shoulder. Esperanza nodded at her. Myron tried desperately to catch her eye. It took a couple of moments, but eventually Esperanza turned his way, looking straight at him with a slight, resigned, I'm-okay smile. It made Myron feel better.

The bailiff called out, "The People versus Esperanza Diaz."

"What's the charge?" the judge asked.

The assistant district attorney, a fresh-faced kid who barely looked old enough to sport a pubic hair, stood by a pedestal. "Murder in the second degree, Your Honor."

"How do you plead?"

Esperanza's voice was strong. "Not guilty."

"Bail?"

The fresh-faced kid said, "Your Honor, the People request that Ms. Diaz be remanded without bail."

Hester Crimstein shouted, "What?" as if she had just heard the most irrational and dangerous words any human being had ever uttered under any circumstance.

Fresh Face was unfazed. "Miss Diaz is accused of killing a man by shooting him three times. We have strong evidence—"

"They have nothing, Your Honor. Circumstantial nothings."

"Miss Diaz has no family and no real roots in the community," Fresh Face continued. "We believe that she presents a substantial flight risk."

"That's nonsense, Your Honor. Miss Diaz is a partner in a major sports representation firm in Manhattan. She is a law school graduate who is currently studying for the bar. She has many friends and roots in the community. And she has no record whatsoever."

"But, Your Honor, she has no family—"

"So what?" Crimstein interrupted. "Her mother and father are dead. Is that now a reason to punish a woman? Dead parents? This is outrageous, Your Honor."

The judge, a woman in her early fifties, sat back. "Your request to deny bail does seem extreme," she said to Fresh Face.

"Your Honor, we believe that Miss Diaz has an unusual amount of resources at her disposal and very good reasons to flee the jurisdiction."

Crimstein kept up with the apoplectic. "What are you talking about?"

"The murder victim, Mr. Haid, has recently withdrawn cash funds in excess of two hundred thousand dollars. That money is missing from his apartment. It's logical to assume that the money was taken during the commission of the murder—"

"What logic?" Crimstein shouted. "Your Honor, this is nonsense."

"Counsel for the defense mentioned that Miss Diaz has friends in the community," Fresh Face continued. "Some of them are here, including her employer, Myron Bolitar." He pointed to Myron. All eyes turned. Myron stayed very still. "Our investigation shows that Mr. Bolitar has been missing for at least a week, perhaps in the Caribbean, even in the Cayman Islands."

"So what?" Crimstein shouted. "Arrest him if that's a crime."

But Fresh Face was not done. "And next to him is Miss Diaz's friend Windsor Lockwood of Lock-Horne Securities." When all eyes turned to Win, he nodded and gave a small regal wave. "Mr. Lockwood was the victim's financial adviser and held the account where the two hundred thousand dollars was withdrawn."

"So arrest him too," Crimstein ranted. "Your Honor, this has nothing to do with my client, except maybe to prove her innocence. Miss Diaz is a hardworking Hispanic woman who struggled her way through law school at night. She has no record and should be freed immediately. Short of that, she has a right to reasonable bail."

"Your Honor, there's just too much cash floating around," Fresh Face said. "The missing two hundred thousand dollars. Miss Diaz's possible connection with both Mr. Bolitar and, of course, Mr. Lockwood, who comes from one of the wealthiest families in the region—"

"Wait a second, Your Honor. First, the district attorney suggests that Miss Diaz has stolen and hidden away this alleged missing money and will use it to run. Then he suggests that she'll ask Mr. Lockwood, who is no more than a business associate, for the funds. Which is it? And while the district attorney's office is busy trying to manufacture some kind of money conspiracy, why would one of the already wealthiest men in the country deem it appropriate to conspire with a poor Hispanic woman to steal? The whole idea is ludicrous. The prosecution has no case, so they've come up with this money nonsense that sounds as plausible as an Elvis sighting—"

"Enough," the judge said. She leaned back and strummed her fingers on the big desk. She stared at Win for a second, then back at the defense table. "The missing money troubles me," she said.

"Your Honor, I assure you that my client knows nothing about any money."

"I'd be surprised if your position were different, Ms. Crimstein. But the facts presented by the district attorney are sufficiently troublesome. Bail denied."

Crimstein's eyes widened. "Your Honor, this is an outrage—"

"No need to shout, Counselor. I hear you just fine."

"I strenuously object—"

"Save it for the cameras, Ms. Crimstein." The judge hit the gavel. "Next case?"

Suppressed mumbles broke forth. Big Cyndi started wailing like a widow in a war newsreel. Hester Crimstein put her mouth to Esperanza's ear and whispered something. Esperanza nodded, but it didn't look like she was listening. The guards led Esperanza toward a door. Myron tried to catch her eyes again, but she didn't—or maybe wouldn't—face him.

Hester Crimstein turned and shot Myron a glare so nasty it almost made him duck. She approached him and fought to keep her face neutral. "Room seven," she said to Myron, not looking at him, barely moving her lips. "Down the hallway and to the left. Five minutes. Don't say anything to anyone."

Myron did not bother with a nod.

Crimstein hurried out, already starting with the no comments before she hit the door. Win sighed, took a piece of paper and a pen from his jacket pocket, began to scribble something down.

"What are you doing?" Myron asked.

"You'll see."

It did not take long. Two plainclothes cops accompanied by the stench of cheap cologne made their approach. Homicide division, no doubt. Before they could even introduce themselves, Win said, "Are we under arrest?"

The cops looked confused. Then one said, "No."

Win smiled and handed him the piece of paper.

"What the hell is this?"

"Our attorney's phone number," Win said. He rose and ushered Myron toward the door. "Have a special day."

They arrived in the defendant's conference room before the anointed five minutes. The room was empty.

"Clu withdrew cash?" Myron said.

"Yes," Win said.

"You knew about it?"

"Of course."

"How much?"

"The district attorney said two hundred thousand dollars. I have no reason to quibble with that estimate."

"And you just let him?"

"Pardon?"

"You just let Clu withdraw two hundred grand?"

"It's his money."

"But that much cash?"

"It was none of my business," Win said.

"You know Clu, Win. It could have been for drugs or gambling or—"

"Probably was," Win agreed. "But I am his financial adviser. I instruct him on investment strategies. Period. I am not his conscience or his mommy or his baby-sitter—or even his agent."

Ouch. But no time for that now. Once again Myron suppressed the guilt and mulled over the possibilities. "Clu okayed us receiving his financial statements, right?"

Win nodded. MB SportsReps insisted that all clients use Win's services and meet with him in person at least quarterly to go over their accounts. This was for their sake more than Myron's. Too many athletes get taken advantage of because of ignorance. But most of Myron's clients had copies of their statements sent to Myron so that he too could help keep track of the ins and outs, set up some automatic bill paying, that kind of thing.

"So a withdrawal that big would have come up on our screen," Myron said.

"Yes."

"Esperanza would have known about it."

"Yes again."

Myron frowned. "So that gives the DA another motive for the murder. She knew about the cash."

"Indeed."

Myron looked at Win. "So what did Clu do with the money?"

Win shrugged.

"Maybe Bonnie knows?"

"Doubtful," Win said. "They've separated."

"Big deal. They're always fighting, but she always takes him back."

"Perhaps. But this time she made the separation legal."

That surprised Myron. Bonnie had never gone that far before. Their turmoil cycle had always been consistent: Clu does something stupid, a big fight ensues, Bonnie throws him out for a couple of nights, maybe a week, Clu begs forgiveness, Bonnie takes him back, Clu behaves for a little while, Clu does something stupid, the cycle starts anew. "She got a lawyer and filed papers?"

"According to Clu."

"He told you that?"

"Yes, Myron. That's what 'According to Clu' means."

"When did he tell you all this?"

"Last week. When he took out the cash. He said that she had already begun divorce proceedings."

"How did he feel about it?"

"Badly. He craved yet another reconciliation."

"Did he say anything else when he withdrew the cash?"

"Nothing."

"And you have no idea—"

"None."

The conference room door flew open. Hester Crimstein came in, red-faced and fuming. "You dumb bastards. I told you to stay away."

"Don't put this on us," Myron said. "This is your screwup."

"What?"

"Getting her bail should have been a slam dunk."

"If you weren't in the courtroom, it would have been. You played right into the DA's hands. He wants to show the judge that the defendant has the resources to run away, and boom, he points to a famous ex-jock and one of the country's richest playboys sitting right in the front row."

She started stomping about as though the industrial gray carpet contained small brushfires. "This judge is a liberal schmuck," she said. "That's why I started with all that hardworking Hispanic crap. She hates rich people, probably because she is one. Having the *Preppy Handbook* here"—she gestured with her head at Win—"sit in the front row was like waving a Confederate flag at a black judge."

"You should drop the case," Myron said.

Her head jerked toward him. "Are you out of your mind?"

"Your fame is playing against you. The judge may not like rich people, but she doesn't much like celebrities either. You're the wrong attorney for this case."

"Bullshit. I've had three cases before this judge. I'm three and oh."

"Maybe she doesn't like that either."

Crimstein seemed to lose a little steam. She moved back and collapsed into a chair. "Bail denied," she said more to herself than anyone else. "I can't believe they even had the nerve to ask for no bail." She sat a bit straighter. "All right, here's how we play it. I'm going to press for answers. In the meantime you guys say nothing. No talking to the cops, the

DA, the press. Nobody. Not until we figure out what exactly they think the three of you did."

"The three of us?"

"Weren't you listening, Myron? They think it's a money scheme."

"Involving the three of us?"

"Yes."

"But how?"

"I don't know. They mentioned your going to the Caribbean, maybe the Cayman Islands. We all know what that means."

"Depositing cash in offshore accounts," Myron said. "But I left the country three weeks ago—before the money was even withdrawn. And I never went anywhere near the Caymans."

"They're probably still grasping at straws," Crimstein said. "But they're going to go after you in a big way. I hope your books are in order because I guarantee you they'll have them subpoenaed within the hour."

Money scandal, Myron thought. Hadn't FJ mentioned something about that?

Crimstein turned her attention to Win. "Is that stuff about a big cash withdrawal true?"

"Yes."

"Can they prove Esperanza knew about it?"

"Probably."

"Damn." She thought about this a moment.

Win moved into a corner. He took out his cell phone, dialed, started talking.

Myron said, "Make me co-counsel."

Crimstein looked up. "Excuse me?"

"As you pointed out last night, I'm a bar-appointed attorney. Make me her attorney, and anything she tells me falls under attorney-client."

She shook her head. "One, that'll never fly. The judge will see it for what it is, a loophole to make sure you can't testify. Two, it's moronic. Not only will it reek of a desperate defensive move, but it'll look like we're shutting you up because we have something to hide. Three, you may still be charged in all this."

"How? I already told you. I was in the Caribbean."

"Right. Where nobody but Preppy Boy could find you. How convenient."

"You think—"

"I don't think anything, Myron. I'm telling you what the DA *might* be thinking. For now we're just guessing. Go back to your office. Call your accountant. Make sure your books are in order."

"They're in order," Myron said. "I've never stolen a dime."

She turned to Win. "How about you?"

Win hung up the phone. "What about me?"

"They'll subpoena your books too."

Win arched the eyebrow. "They'll try."

"Are they clean?"

"You could eat off them," Win said.

"Fine, whatever. I'll let your lawyers handle it. I got enough to worry about."

Silence.

"So how do we get her out?" Myron asked.

"We don't get her out. I get her out. You stay away."

"I don't take orders from you."

"No? How about from Esperanza?"

"What about Esperanza?"

"This is her request as well as mine. Stay away from her."

"I don't believe she'd say that."

"Believe it."

"If she wants me out," Myron said, "she'll have to tell me to my face."

"Fine," Crimstein said with a heavy sigh. "Let's go take care of that now."

"What?"

"You want her to tell you herself? Give me five minutes."

8

Win said, "I have to get back to the office."

Myron was surprised. "You don't want to hear what Esperanza has to say?"

"No time."

His tone slammed the door on further discussion. Win reached for the knob.

"If you need my special talents," he said, "I'll have the cellular."

He hurried out as Hester Crimstein entered. She watched him disappear down the corridor. "Where's he going?"

"His office."

"Why's he in such a rush all of a sudden?"

"I didn't ask."

Hester Crimstein raised an eyebrow. "Hmm."

"Hmm what?"

"Win was the one in charge of the account with the missing money."

"So?"

"So maybe he had a reason to silence Clu Haid."

"That's ridiculous."

"Are you saying he's incapable of murder?"

Myron did not reply.

"If even half the stories I've heard about Windsor Lockwood are true—"

"You know better than to listen to rumors."

She looked at him. "So if I subpoena you to testify and if I ask if you've ever witnessed Windsor Horne Lockwood the Third kill someone, what would you say?"

"No."

"Uh-huh. Guess you also missed the class on perjury."

Myron did not bother with a comeback. "When can I see Esperanza?"

"Come on. She's waiting for you."

Esperanza sat at a long table. She still wore the orange prison suit, her now-uncuffed hands folded in front of her, her expression serene as a church statue's. Hester signaled to the trooper, and they both left the room.

When the door closed, Esperanza smiled at him. "Welcome back," she said.

"Thanks," Myron replied.

Her eyes took him in. "If your tan was any darker, you could pass for my brother."

"Thanks."

"Still got the smooth tongue with the ladies, eh?"

"Thanks."

She almost smiled. Even under these conditions, Esperanza still looked radiant. Her supple skin and ink black hair shimmered against the fluorescent orange backdrop. Her eyes still brought forth thoughts of Mediterranean moons and white peasant blouses.

"Are you feeling better now?" she asked him.

"Yes."

"Where were you anyway?"

"A private island in the Caribbean."

"For three weeks?"

"Yes."

"By yourself?"

"No."

When he didn't elaborate, Esperanza simply said, "Details."

"I ran off with a beautiful anchorwoman I barely knew."

Esperanza smiled. "Did she—how to put this delicately?—did she boff your brains out?"

"As it were."

"Glad to hear it. If any guy needed to have his brain boffed out—"

"Right, I'm the guy. Voted Most Boff Needy by the senior class."

She liked that one. She leaned back and crossed her legs cocktail-lounge casual. Odd in these surroundings, to put it mildly. "You didn't tell anybody where you were?"

"That's right."

"Yet Win still found you in a matter of hours," she said.

It surprised neither of them. They sat in silence for a moment or two. Then Myron asked, "You okay?"

"Fine."

"Do you need anything?"

"No."

Myron was not sure how to continue, what subject to broach or how to broach it. Once again Esperanza took the ball and started dribbling.

"So are you and Jessica through?" she asked.

"Yes." It was the first time he had said it out loud. It felt weird.

That made her smile, big time. "Ah, the silver lining," she said triumphantly. "So it's really over? Queen Bitch is gone for good?"

"Don't call her that."

"Is she gone for good?"

"I think so."

"Say yes, Myron. It'll make you feel better."

But he couldn't. "I'm not here to talk about me."

Esperanza crossed her arms, said nothing.

"We'll get you out of this," he said. "I promise."

She nodded, still playing casual; if she were a smoker, she'd be blowing rings. "You better get back to the office. We've already lost too many clients."

"I don't care about that."

"I do." Her voice had an edge now. "I'm a partner now."

"I know that."

"So I own part of MB SportsReps. If you want to self-destruct, fine. But don't drag my lusted-after ass down with you, okay?"

"I didn't mean it like that. I just meant we've got bigger worries right now."

"No."

"What?"

"*We* don't have bigger worries. I want you to stay out of this."

"I don't understand."

"I have one of the top criminal defense attorneys in the country working on my case. Let her handle it."

Myron tried to let her words settle in, but they were like unruly children after a sugar fix. He leaned forward a bit. "What's going on here?"

"I can't talk about it."

"What?"

"Hester told me I shouldn't talk about the case with anyone, even you. Our conversations are not protected."

"You think I'd tell?"

"You can be forced to testify."

"So I'd lie."

"You won't have to."

Myron opened his mouth, closed it, tried again. "Win and I can help here. We're good at this."

"No offense, Myron, but Win is psycho. I love him, but his kind of help I don't need. And you"—Esperanza stopped, looked up, unfolded her arms, lowered her gaze back to his—"you're damaged goods. I don't blame you for running away. It was probably the right thing to do. But let's not pretend you're back to normal."

"Not normal," he agreed. "But I'm ready for this."

She shook her head. "Concentrate on MB. It's going to take all your efforts to keep her afloat."

"You're not going to tell me what happened?"

"No."

"That doesn't make any sense."

"I just spelled out the reasons—"

"You're really afraid I'd testify against you?"

"I didn't say that."

"So what is it? If you think I'm not up for this, okay, maybe I buy it. But that wouldn't stop you from talking to me. In fact, you'd probably tell me just to keep me from poking around. So what's going on here?"

Her face slid closed. "Go to the office, Myron. You want to help? Save our business."

"Did you kill him?"

He regretted it the moment the words came out of his mouth. She looked at him as if he'd just reached across the table and slapped her face.

"I don't care if you did," he pressed on. "I'll stand by you no matter what. I want you to know that."

Esperanza regained her composure. She slid her chair back and stood. For a few moments she stared at him, studying his face as though searching for something that was normally there. Then she turned away, called for the guard, and left the room.

9

Big Cyndi was already manning the reception desk when Myron reached the offices of MB SportsReps. They had a prime location, right smack on Park Avenue in midtown. The Lock-Horne high-rise had been owned by Win's family since Great-Great-Et-Cetera Grandpa Horne (or was it Lockwood?) had torn down a tepee and started building it. Myron rented space at a premium discount from Win. In return Win handled all the finances for Myron's clients. This deal was a bargain for Myron. Between the *primo* address and the ability to guarantee his clients the financial services of the near-legendary Windsor Horne Lockwood III, MB SportsReps had an air of legitimacy few small firms could boast.

MB SportsReps was on the twelfth floor. An elevator opened directly into their reception room. *Muy* classy. The phones were beeping. Big Cyndi put people on hold and looked up at him. She looked even more ridiculous than usual. No easy task. In the first place, the furniture was too small for her, the desk legs actually teetering on her knees like something a father might experience when visiting his child's elementary school. In the second place, she still had not washed up or changed from last night. Normally Myron, the image-conscious entrepreneur, would comment on this, but now did not seem an appropriate (or safe) time.

"The press is pulling out all the tricks to get up here, Mr. Bolitar." Big Cyndi always called him Mr. Bolitar. She liked formalities. "Two of them even pretended to be prospective clients coming out of Division One schools."

Myron was hardly surprised. "I told the guard downstairs to be extra wary."

"A lot of clients are calling too. They're concerned."

"Patch them through. Get rid of everybody else."

"Yes, Mr. Bolitar." Like she wanted to salute. Big Cyndi handed him a pile of blue slips. "These are this morning's calls from clients."

He started thumbing through the stack.

"For your information," Big Cyndi continued, "we told everyone you were just gone for a day or two at first. Then a week or two. Then we started faking emergencies for you: family illnesses, helping a sick client, that sort of thing. But some clients got tired of the excuses."

He nodded. "You have a list of who left us?"

It was already in her hand. She handed it to him, and he started toward his office.

"Mr. Bolitar?"

He turned. "Yes?"

"Will Esperanza be okay?"

Again the tiny, distant voice belied her bulk, as though the looming form in front of him had swallowed a small child and the small child were now calling for help. "Yes, Big Cyndi. She'll be fine."

"You'll help her, won't you? Even though she doesn't want you to?"

Myron gave her a half nod. That didn't seem to satisfy her. So he said, "Yes."

"Good, Mr. Bolitar. That's the right thing to do."

He had nothing to add to that so he entered his inner office. Myron had not been to MB in six weeks. Strange. He had worked so hard and so long to build up MB SportsReps—M for Myron, B for Bolitar, snappy name, no?—and he had just abandoned her. Just like that. Abandoned his business. And his clients. And Esperanza.

The renovations had been completed—they'd sliced a bit of space out of the conference room and reception area so that Esperanza could have an office of her own—but the new room remained unfurnished. So Esperanza had been using his office. He sat at his desk and immediately the phone started ringing. He ignored it for a few seconds, his eyes latched on the client wall, the one with action photos of all the athletes MB represented. He zeroed in on Clu Haid's image. Clu was on the pitcher's mound, leaning forward, about to go into a stretch, his cheek bulging with tobacco chaw, his eyes squinting at a sign he would undoubtedly shake off.

"What did you do this time, Clu?" he said out loud.

The photo didn't reply, which was probably a good thing. But Myron continued to stare. He had pulled Clu out of so many jams over the years that he had to wonder: If he had not run off to the Caribbean, would he have been able to pull Clu out of this one too?

Useless introspection—one of Myron's many talents.

Big Cyndi buzzed him. "Mr. Bolitar?"

"Yes."

"I know you told me to only patch through clients, but Sophie Mayor is on the line."

Sophie Mayor was the new owner of the Yankees.

"Put her through." He heard a click and said hello.

"Myron, my God. What the hell is going on here?" Sophie Mayor wasn't big on chitchat.

"I'm still trying to sort it out myself."

"They think your secretary killed Clu."

"Esperanza is my partner," he corrected, though he was not sure why. "And she didn't kill anyone."

"I'm sitting here with Jared." Jared was her son and the "co-general manager" of the Yankees—*co* meaning *shares the title with someone who knows what he's doing because he got the job through nepotism. Jared* meaning *born after 1973.* "We need to tell the press something."

"I'm not sure how I can help, Ms. Mayor."

"You told me Clu was past all this, Myron."

He said nothing.

"The drugs, the drinking, the partying, the trouble," Sophie Mayor continued. "You said it was in the past."

He was about to defend himself but thought better of it. "I think it's better if we talk about all this in person," Myron said.

"Jared and I are on the road with the team. We're in Cleveland right now. We're flying home tonight."

"How about tomorrow morning then?"

"We'll be at the stadium," she said. "Eleven o'clock."

"I'll be there."

He hung up the phone. Big Cyndi immediately put through a client call.

"Myron here."

"Where the hell have you been?"

It was Marty Towey, a defensive tackle for the Vikings. Myron took a deep breath and let loose his semiprepared oration: he was back, things were great, don't worry, the financials are terrific, got the new contract right here, busy securing new endorsements, blah, blah, soothe, soothe.

Marty was a tough sell. "Dammit, Myron, I chose MB because I didn't want underlings handling me. I wanted to deal with the big boss. You know what I'm saying?"

"Sure, Marty."

"Esperanza's nice and all. But she ain't you. I hired you. Do you understand?"

"I'm back now, Marty. Everything is going to be fine, I promise. Look, you guys are in town in a couple of weeks, right?"

"We play the Jets in two weeks."

"Great. So I'll meet you at the game and we'll go out to dinner afterward."

When Myron hung up, it dawned on him that he'd been so uninvolved in his clients' affairs that he didn't even know if Marty was playing at an All-Pro level or nearly waived. Christ, he had a lot of catching up to do.

The calls went on in a similar vein for the next two hours. Most clients were assuaged. Some sat on the fence. No additional ones left him. He had not fixed anything, but he had managed to lessen the blood flow to a serious trickle.

Big Cyndi knocked and opened the office door. "Trouble, Mr. Bolitar."

An awful, though not unfamiliar, stench started emanating from the doorway.

"What the hell . . . ?" Myron began.

"Out of the way, hot stuff." The gruff voice came from behind Big Cyndi. Myron tried to see who it was, but Big Cyndi blocked his line of vision like a solar eclipse. Eventually she yielded, and the same two plainclothes officers from the courthouse hurried past her. The big one was fiftyish, bleary-eyed, world-weary and had the kind of face that looked unshaven even after a shave. He wore a trench coat with sleeves that barely reached his elbows and shoes that had more scuff marks than a Gaylord Perry baseball. The smaller guy was younger and really, well, ugly. His face reminded Myron of a magnified photo of head lice. He wore a light gray suit with vest—the Sears Casual Law Enforcer—and one of those *Looney Tunes* ties that screamed 1992.

The awful smell started permeating the walls.

"A warrant," the big guy groused. He wasn't chewing on a cigar, but he should have been. "And before you tell me we're out of our jurisdiction, we're still working with Michael Chapman, Manhattan North. Call him, you got a problem. Now get out of the chair, asshole, so we can search this place."

Myron crinkled his nose. "Jesus, which one of you is wearing the cologne?"

Head Lice gave a quick look toward his partner. The look said, Hey, I'll take a bullet for this guy, but I'm not taking the fall for that smell. Understandable.

"Listen up, dip shit," the big one said. "My name is Detective Winters—"

"Really? Your mother named you Detective?"

Barely a sigh. "—and this is Detective Martinez. Move out here now, dim wad."

The smell was getting to him. "Yo, Winters, you got to stop borrowing cologne from male flight attendants."

"Keep at it, funnyman."

"Seriously, does the label include the words *glaze liberally?*"

"You're a real comedian, Bolitar. So many bad asses are funny it's a pity they don't televise Sing Sing."

"I thought you already searched the place."

"We did. Now we're back for the financials."

Myron pointed to Head Lice. "Can't he do it alone?"

"What?"

"I'll never get the smell out of here."

Winters took out a pair of latex gloves, this so as not to mess up possible fingerprints. He snapped them on in dramatic fashion, including finger wiggling, and grinned.

Myron winked. "You want me to bend down and grab my ankles?"

"No."

"Dang, and me needing a date." Want to needle a cop? Use gay humor. Myron had yet to meet one who wasn't a complete homophobe.

Winters said, "We're going to trash this place, funnyman."

"Doubtful," Myron countered.

"Oh?"

Myron stood, reached into the file cabinet behind him.

"Hey, you can't touch anything in here."

Myron ignored him, pulled out a small videocamera. "Just keeping a record of your doings, officer. In today's climate of false police corruption charges, we wouldn't want any misunderstandings"—Myron snapped on the camera and aimed the lens at the big guy—"would we?"

"No," the big guy said, staring straight into the lens. "We wouldn't want any misunderstandings."

Myron kept his eye in the viewer. "The camera captures the real you, Detective. I bet if we played it back, we'd still smell your cologne."

Head Lice hid a smile.

"Please get out of our way, Mr. Bolitar," Winters said.

"Sure thing. Cooperation is my middle name."

They began the search, which basically consisted of packing every document they could lay their hands on in crates and carrying them out. The gloved hands touched everything, and it felt to Myron like they were touching him. He tried to look innocent—whatever that looked like—but he couldn't help being nervous. Guilt was a funny thing. He knew that there was nothing amiss in any of the files, but he still felt oddly defensive.

Myron gave the video camera to Big Cyndi and started making calls to clients who had left MB. Most didn't pick up. The few who did tried to defect. Myron played it soft, figuring that any overaggression would backfire. He merely told them that he was back and would like very much to speak with them at their earliest convenience. A lot of hemming and hawing from those who actually spoke to him. Not unexpected. If he were to regain their confidence, it would take time.

The cops finished up and left without so much as a good-bye. Manners. Big Cyndi and Myron watched the elevators close.

"This is going to be very difficult," Myron said.

"What?"

"Working without any files."

Big Cyndi opened her purse and showed him computer disks. "Everything is on these."

"Everything?"

"Yes."

"You backed up everything on these?"

"Yes."

"Letters and correspondences, okay, but I need the contracts—"

"Everything," she said. "I bought a scanner and ran every paper in the office through it. There's a backup set in a safety-deposit box at Citibank. I update the disks every week. In case of fire or other emergency."

When she smiled this time, Myron's cringe was barely perceptible.

"Big Cyndi, you are a surprising woman."

It was hard to tell under the melted Masque de Crayola, but it almost looked like she was blushing.

The intercom buzzed. Big Cyndi picked up the phone. "Yes?" Pause. Then her voice grew grave. "Yes, send her up." She replaced the receiver.

"Who is it?"

"Bonnie Haid is here to see you."

Big Cyndi showed the Widow Haid into his office. Myron stood behind his desk, not sure what to do. He waited for her to make the first move, but she didn't. Bonnie Haid had let her hair grow out, and for a moment he was back at Duke. Clu and Bonnie were sitting on the couch in the basement of the frat house, another major kegger behind them, his arm draped over her shoulder, she wearing a gray sweatshirt, her legs tucked under her.

He swallowed and moved toward her. She took a step back and closed her eyes. She put a hand up to stop him as though she could not bear the pain of his intimacy. Myron stayed where he was.

"I'm sorry," he said.

"Thank you."

They both stood there, two dancers waiting for the music to begin.

"Can I sit down?" Bonnie asked.

"Of course."

She sat. Myron hesitated and then chose to go back around his desk.

"When did you get back?" she asked.

"Last night," he said. "I didn't know about Clu before then. I'm sorry I wasn't here for you."

Bonnie cocked her head. "Why?"

"Pardon?"

"Why are you sorry you weren't here? What could you have done?"

Myron shrugged. "Help maybe."

"Help how?"

He shrugged again, spread his arms. "I don't know what to say, Bonnie. I'm flailing here."

She looked at him a moment, challenging, then dropped her eyes. "I'm just lashing out at whoever's in front of me," she said. "Don't pay any attention."

"I don't mind; lash away."

Bonnie almost managed a smile. "You're a good guy, Myron. You always were. Even at Duke there was something about you that was—I don't know—noble, I guess."

"Noble?"

"Sounds silly, doesn't it?"

"Very," he said. "How are the boys?"

She shrugged. "Timmy is only eighteen months old so he doesn't have a clue. Charlie is four so he's just pretty confused right now. My parents are taking care of them."

"I don't want to keep sounding like a bad cliché," Myron said, "but if there's anything at all I can do . . ."

"One thing."

"Name it."

"Tell me about the arrest."

Myron cleared his throat. "What about it?"

"I've met Esperanza a few times over the years. I guess I find it hard to believe she'd kill Clu."

"She didn't do it."

Bonnie squinted a bit. "What makes you so sure?"

"I know Esperanza."

"That's it?"

He nodded. "For now."

"Have you spoken to her?"

"Yes."

"And?"

"I can't talk about specifics"—mostly because he didn't know any; Myron was almost grateful that Esperanza had not told him anything— "but she didn't do it."

"What about all the evidence the police found?"

"I can't answer that yet, Bonnie. But Esperanza is innocent. We'll find the real killer."

"You sound so sure."

"I am."

They fell into silence. Myron waited, mapping out an approach. There were questions that needed to be asked, but this woman had just lost her husband. One had to tread gently lest one trip an emotional land mine.

"I'm going to look into the murder," Myron said.

She looked confused. "What do you mean, look into?"

"Investigate."

"But you're a sports agent."

"I have some background in this."

She studied his face. "Win too?"

"Yes."

She nodded as if something suddenly made sense. "Win always scared the crap out of me."

"That's only because you're sane."

"And now you're going to try to figure out who killed Clu?"

"Yes."

"I see," she said. She shifted in her chair. "Tell me something, Myron."

"Anything."

"What's your priority here: finding the murderer or getting Esperanza off?"

"One and the same."

"And if they're not? If you learn Esperanza killed him?"

Time to lie. "Then she'll be punished."

Bonnie started smiling as though she could see the truth. "Good luck," she said.

Myron put an ankle up on a knee. *Gentle now,* he thought. "Can I ask you something?"

She shrugged. "Sure."

Gently, gently. "I don't mean any disrespect, Bonnie. I'm not asking this to be nosy—"

"Subtlety is not your strong suit, Myron. Just ask your question."

"Were you and Clu having problems?"

A sad grin. "Weren't we always?"

"I hear this was something more serious."

Bonnie folded her arms below her chest. "My, my. Back less than a day and already you've learned so much. You work fast, Myron."

"Clu mentioned it to Win."

"So what do you want to know?"

"Were you suing him for divorce?"

"Yes." No hesitation.

"Can you tell me what happened?"

In the distance the fax machine started its primordial screech. The phone continued beeping. Myron had no fear that they'd be interrupted. Big Cyndi had worked for years as a bouncer at an S&M bar; when the situation called for it, she could be as nasty as a rabid rhino with a bad case of piles. Er, even when the situation didn't call for it.

"Why do you want to know?" Bonnie asked.

"Because Esperanza didn't kill him."

"That's becoming something of a mantra for you, Myron. Say it often enough and you start to believe it, right?"

"I believe it."

"So?"

"So if she didn't kill him, someone else did."

Bonnie looked up. "If she didn't kill him, someone else did," she repeated. Pause. "You weren't just bragging before. You really do have a background in this."

"I'm just trying to find out who killed him."

"By asking about our marriage?"

"By asking about anything turbulent in his life."

"Turbulent?" She let out a stab of a laugh. "This is Clu we're talking about here, Myron. Everything was turbulent. The hard thing to find would be patches of calm."

"How long were you two together?" Myron asked.

"You know the answer to that."

He did. Junior year at Duke. Bonnie had come bopping down to the frat house basement dressed in a monogram sweater and pearls and, yep, ponytail. Myron and Clu had been working the keg. Myron liked working the keg because it kept him so busy he didn't drink as much. Don't get the wrong idea here. Myron drank. It was pretty much a college requirement in those days. But he wasn't a very good drinker. He always seemed to miss that cusp of fun, that floaty buzz between sobriety and vomiting. It was almost nonexistent for him. Something in his ancestry, he assumed. It had actually helped him in recent months. Before running away with Terese, Myron had tried the old-fashioned approach of drowning one's sorrows. But, put bluntly, he usually threw up before reaching oblivion.

Nice way to prevent alcohol abuse.

Anyway, Clu and Bonnie's meeting was pretty simple. Bonnie walked in. Clu looked up from the keg and it was as if Captain Marvel had zapped him with a thunderbolt. "Wow," Clu muttered, the beer overflowing onto a floor so coated with beer that rodents often got stuck on it and died. Then Clu leaped over the bar, staggered toward Bonnie, dropped to one knee, and proposed. Three years later they tied the knot for real.

"So after all these years what happened?"

Bonnie looked down. "It had nothing to do with his murder," she said.

"That's probably true, but I need to get the full picture of his life, travel down any possible avenue—"

"Bullshit, Myron. I said it had nothing to do with the murder, okay? Leave it at that."

He licked his lips, folded his hands, put them on the desktop. "In the past you've thrown him out because of another woman."

"Not woman. Women. Plural."

"Is that what happened again this time?"

"He swore off women. He promised me that there'd be no more."

"And he broke that promise?"

Bonnie didn't answer.

"What was her name?"

Her voice was soft. "I never knew."

"But there was someone else?"

Again she didn't answer. No need. Myron tried to put on his attorney skin for a moment. Clu's having an affair was a very good thing for Esperanza's defense. The more motives you can find, the more reasonable doubt you can create. Did the girlfriend kill him because he still wanted to be with his wife? Did Bonnie do it out of jealousy? And then there was the missing money. Wouldn't the girlfriend and/or Bonnie have known about it? Couldn't that be an added motive for murder? Yep, Hester Crimstein would like this. Throw enough possibilities into a trial, muddy the waters enough, and an acquittal is almost inevitable. It was a simple equation: Confusion equals reasonable doubt equals a not-guilty verdict.

"He's had affairs before, Bonnie. What was different this time?"

"Give it a rest, Myron, okay? Clu isn't even in the ground yet."

He pulled back. "I'm sorry."

She looked away. Her chest rose and fell, her voice fighting to stay steady. "I know you're just trying to help," she said. "But the divorce stuff . . . it hurts too much right now."

"I understand."

"If you have other questions . . ."

"I heard Clu failed a drug test." So much for backing off.

"I only know what I read in the papers."

"Clu told Win it was a fix."

"What?"

"Clu claimed he was clean. What do you think?"

"I think Clu was a marvelous screwup. We both know that."

"So he was taking again?"

"I don't know." She swallowed and locked eyes with him. "I hadn't seen him in weeks."

"And before that?"

"He seemed clean, actually. But he was always good at hiding it. Remember that intervention we tried three years ago?"

Myron nodded.

"We all cried. We all begged him to stop. And finally Clu broke down too. He sobbed like a baby, said he was ready turn his life around. Two days later he paid off a guard and sneaked out of rehab."

"So you think he was just masking the symptoms?"

"He could have been. He was good at that." She hesitated. "But I don't think so."

"Why not?"

"I don't know. Wishful thinking, I guess, but I really thought he was clean this time. In the past you could almost see he was going through the motions. He was playing a part for me or the kids. But this time he seemed more determined. Like he knew this trade was his last chance to start fresh. He worked at it like I've never seen him work at anything. I thought he was beating it too. But something must have pushed him back off. . . ."

Bonnie's voice tailed off, and now her eyes filled. She was wondering, no doubt, if she had been that push, if Clu had indeed been clean and if she had thrown him out of their house and plunged him back into the world of his addictions. Myron almost told her not to blame herself, but good sense kept the grating cliché at bay.

"Clu always needed someone or something," she went on. "He was the most dependent person I ever knew."

Myron nodded, encouraging her.

"At first I found that attractive, that he needed me so much. But it got weary." Bonnie looked at him. "How many times did someone pull his ass out of the fire?"

"Too many," Myron admitted.

"I wonder, Myron." She sat up a bit, more clear-eyed now. "I wonder if we all did him a disservice. Maybe if we weren't always there to save him, he would have had to change. Maybe if I had dumped him years ago, he would have straightened himself out and survived all this."

Myron said nothing, not bothering to point out the inherent contradiction in her statement: She finally did dump him and he ended up dead.

"Did you know about the two hundred thousand dollars?" Myron asked.

"I heard about it from the police."

"Do you have any idea where it might be?"

"No."

"Or why he might have needed it?"

"No." Her voice was far away now, her gaze drifting over his shoulder.

"Do you think it was for drugs?"

"The papers said he tested positive for heroin," she said.

"That's my understanding."

"That would be a new one for Clu. I know it's an expensive addiction, but two hundred thousand seems extreme."

Myron agreed. "Was he in any trouble?"

She looked at him.

"I mean, besides the usual. Loan sharks or gambling or something like that?"

"It's possible, I guess."

"But you don't know."

Bonnie shook her head, still looking off at nothing. "You know what I was thinking about?"

"What?"

"Clu's first year as a pro. Class A with the New England Bisons. Right after he asked you to negotiate his contract. Do you remember that?"

Myron nodded.

"And again, I wonder."

"Wonder what?"

"That was the first time we all banded together to save his ass."

The late-night phone call. Myron swimming out of sleep and clutching the receiver. Clu crying, almost incoherent. He had been driving with Bonnie and his old Duke roommate, Billy Lee Palms, the Bisons' catcher. Drunk driving, to be more precise. He had smashed the car into a pole. Billy Lee's injuries were minor, but Bonnie had been rushed to the hospital. Clu, not a scratch on him, of course, had been arrested. Myron had hurried out to western Massachusetts, plenty of cash in hand.

"I remember," Myron said.

"You'd just signed Clu to that big chocolate milk endorsement. Drunk driving was bad enough, but with an injury to boot, well, it would have destroyed him. But we took care of him. The right people were bought off. Billy Lee and I made a statement about some pickup truck cutting us off. We saved him. And now I wonder if we did the right thing. Maybe if Clu had paid a price right then and there, maybe if he'd gone to jail instead of skating by . . ."

"He wouldn't have gone to jail, Bonnie. A suspended license maybe. Some community service."

"Whatever. Life is about ripples, Myron. There are some philosophers who think that everything we do changes the world forever. Even simple acts. Like if you left your house five minutes later, if you took a different route to work—it changes everything for the rest of your life. I don't necessarily buy that, but when it comes to the big things, yeah, sure, I think the ripples last. Or maybe it started before that. When he was a child. The first time he learned that because he could throw a white sphere with amazing velocity, people treated him special. Maybe we just continued the conditioning that day. Or brought it up to an adult level. Clu learned that someone would always save him. And we did. We got him off that night, and then there were the assault charges and the lewd behavior and the failed drug tests and whatever else."

"And you think his murder was the inevitable result?"

"Don't you?"

"No," Myron said. "I think the person who shot him three times is responsible. Period."

"Life is rarely that simple, Myron."

"But murder usually is. In the end someone shot him. That's how he died. He didn't die because we helped him through some self-destructive excesses. Someone murdered him. And that person—not you or me or those who cared about him—is to blame."

She thought about it. "Maybe you're right." But she didn't look convinced.

"Do you know why Clu would strike Esperanza?"

She shook her head. "The police asked me that too. I don't know. Maybe he was high."

"Did he get violent when he got high?"

"No. But it sounds like he was under a lot of pressure. Maybe he was just frustrated that she wouldn't tell him where you were."

Another wave of guilt. He waited for it to recede.

"Who else would he have gone to, Bonnie?"

"What do you mean?"

"You said he was needy. I wasn't around. You weren't talking to him. So where would Clu go next?"

She thought about it. "I'm not sure."

"Any friends, teammates?"

"I don't think so."

"How about Billy Lee Palms?"

She shrugged an I-don't-know.

Myron tossed out a few more questions, but nothing of consequence was batted back to him. After a while Bonnie feigned a check at the time. "I have to get back to the kids," she said.

He nodded, rose from his chair. This time she did not stop him. He hugged her and she hugged him back, gripping him fiercely.

"Do me one favor," she said.

"Name it."

"Clear your friend," she said. "I understand why you need to do that. And I wouldn't want her to go to jail for something she didn't do. But then let it be."

Myron pulled back a bit. "I don't understand."

"Like I said before, you're a noble guy."

He thought about the Slaughter family and how it all ended; something inside him was crushed anew. "College was a long time ago," he said softly.

"You haven't changed."

"You'd be surprised."

"You still need justice and neat endings and to do the right thing."

He said nothing.

"Clu can't give you that," Bonnie said. "He wasn't a noble man."

"He didn't deserve to be murdered."

She put a hand on his arm. "Save your friend, Myron. Then let Clu go."

10

Myron took the elevator up two floors to the nerve center of Lock-Horne Securities and Investments. Exhausted white men—there were women and minorities too, more and more each year, but the overall numbers were still woefully inadequate—darted about, particles under blaring heat, gray phones tethered to their ears like life-sustaining umbilical cords. The noise level and the open space reminded Myron of a Vegas casino, though the toupees were better. People cried out in joy and agony. Money was won and lost. Dice were rolled and wheels were spun and cards were dealt. The men constantly glanced up at an electronic ticker, awe in their faces, ardently watching the stock prices like gamblers waiting for the wheel to settle on a number or ancient Israelites peering up at Moses and his new stone tablets.

These were the trenches of finance, armed soldiers crowded together, each trying to survive in a world where earning low six figures meant cowardice and probably death. Computer terminals twinkled through an onslaught of yellow Post-It notes. The warriors drank coffee and buried framed family photos under a volcanic outpouring of stock analyses and financial statements and corporate reviews. They wore white button-down shirts and Windsor-knotted ties, their suit jackets neatly arrayed on the backs of chairs as though the chairs were a tad chilly or preparing for lunch at Le Cirque.

Win did not sit out here, of course. The generals in this war—the rainmakers, big producers, heavy hitters, what have you—were tented on the perimeter, their offices running along the windows, cutting off from the foot soldiers any hint of blue sky or fresh air or any element endemic to human beings.

Myron headed up a carpeted incline and toward the left corner suite. Win was usually alone in his office. Not today. Myron stuck his head in the door, and a bunch of suitheads swiveled toward him. Lots of suits. Myron couldn't say how many. Might have been six, maybe eight. They were a lumpy blur of gray and blue with streaks of tie-and-hankie red, like the aftermath of a Civil War reenactment. The older ones, distinguished white-haired guys with manicures and cuff links, sat in the burgundy leather chairs closest to Win's desk and nodded a lot. The younger ones were squeezed onto the couches against the wall, heads down, scratching notes on legal pads as though Win were divulging the secret of eternal life. Every once in a while the younger men would peer up at the older men, glimpsing their glorious future, which would basically consist of a more comfortable chair and less note taking.

The legal pads gave it away. These were attorneys. The older men probably over four hundred bucks an hour, the younger ones two-fifty. Myron didn't bother with the math, mostly because it would take too much effort to count how many suits were in the room. Didn't matter. Lock-Horne Securities could afford it. Redistributing wealth—that is, the act of moving money around without creation or production or making anything new—was incredibly profitable.

Myron Bolitar, Marxist Sports Agent.

Win clapped his hands and the men were dismissed. They rose as slowly as possible—attorneys billed by the minute, sort of like 900 sex lines minus the guaranteed, er, payoff—and filed out the office door. The older men departed first, the younger men trailing not unlike Japanese brides.

Myron stepped inside. "What's going on?"

Win signaled for Myron to sit. Then he leaned back and did the steeple thing with his hands. "This situation," he said, "has me troubled."

"You mean Clu's cash withdrawal?"

"In part, yes," Win said. He bounced the fingertips before resting the indexes on his lower lip. "I become very unhappy when I hear the words *subpoena* and *Lock-Horne* in the same sentence."

"So? You have nothing to hide."

Win smiled thinly. "Your point being?"

"Let them look at your records. You're a lot of things, Win. Honest being chief among them."

Win shook his head. "You are so naive."

"What?"

"My family runs a financial securities firm."

"So?"

"So even the whiff of innuendo can destroy said firm."

"I think you're overreacting," Myron said.

Win arched an eyebrow, put a hand to his ear. "Pardon *moi*?"

"Come on, Win. There's always some Wall Street scandal or other going on. People barely notice anymore."

"Those are insider trading scandals mostly."

"So?"

Win paused, looked at him. "Are you being purposely obtuse?"

"No."

"Insider trading is a completely different animal."

"How so?"

"Do you really need me to explain this to you?"

"Guess so."

"Fine then. Stripping it bare, insider trading is cheating or stealing. My clients do not care if I cheat or steal—as long it is done for their benefit. In fact, if a certain illegal act were to increase their portfolios, most clients would probably encourage it. But if their financial adviser is playing games with their personal accounts—or equally awful, if his banking institution is merely involved in something that will give the government the right to subpoena records—clients become understandably nervous."

Myron nodded. "I can see where there might be a problem."

Win strummed the top of his desk with his fingers. For him, this was major agitation. Hard to believe, but for the first time Win actually appeared a touch unnerved. "I have three law firms and two publicity firms working on the matter," he continued.

"Working on it how?"

"The usual," Win said. "Calling in political favors, preparing a lawsuit against the Bergen County DA's office for libel and slander, planting positive spins in the media, seeing what judges will be running for reelection."

"In other words," Myron said, "who can you pay off."

Win shrugged. "You say tomato, I say tomahto."

"The files haven't been subpoenaed yet?"

"No. I plan on quashing the possibility before any judge even thinks of issuing them."

"So maybe we should take the offensive."

Win resteepled. His big mahogany desk was polished to the point where his reflection was near-mirror clear, like something out of an old dish detergent commercial where a housewife gets waaaaay too excited about seeing herself in a dinner plate. "I'm listening."

He recounted his conversation with Bonnie Haid. The red phone on Win's credenza—his Batphone, so enamored with the old Adam West vehicle that he actually kept it under what looked like a glass cake cover—

interrupted him several times. Win had to take the calls. They were mostly from attorneys. Myron could hear the lawyerly panic travel through the earpiece and all the way across the desk. Understandable. Windsor Horne Lockwood III was not the kind of guy you wanted to disappoint.

Win remained calm. His end of the conversation could basically be broken down into two words: *How.* And *much.*

When Myron finished, Win said, "Let's make a list." He didn't reach for a pen. Neither did Myron. "One, we need Clu's phone records."

"He was staying at an apartment in Fort Lee," Myron said.

"The murder scene."

"Right. Clu and Bonnie rented the apartment when he first got traded in May." To the Yankees. A huge deal that gave Clu, an aging veteran, one last chance to squander. "They moved into the house in Tenafly in July, but the apartment's lease ran for another six months. So when Bonnie threw him out, that's where he ended up."

"You have the address?" Win asked.

"Yep."

"Fine then."

"Send the records down to Big Cyndi. I'll have her check through it."

Getting a phone record was frighteningly easy. Don't believe it? Open your local yellow pages. Choose a private investigator at random. Offer to pay him or her two grand for anyone's monthly phone bill. Some will simply say yes, but most will try to up you to three thousand, half the fee going to whatever phone company minion they bribe.

Myron said, "We also need to check out Clu's credit cards, his checkbook, ATM, whatever, see what he's been up to lately."

Win nodded. In Clu's case, this would be doubly easy. His entire financial portfolio was held by Lock-Horne Securities. Win had set up a separate management account for Clu so that he could manage his finances easier. It included a Visa debit card, electronic payments of monthly bills, and a checkbook.

"We also need to find this mystery girlfriend," Myron said.

"Shouldn't be too difficult," Win said.

"No."

"And as you suggested earlier, our old fraternity brother Billy Lee Palms might know something."

"We can track him down," Myron said.

Win raised a finger. "One thing."

"I'm listening."

"You will have to do the majority of the legwork on your own."

"Why's that?"

"I have a business to run."

"So do I," Myron said.

"You lose your business, you hurt two people."

"Three," Myron corrected. "You forgot Big Cyndi."

"No. I am speaking of Big Cyndi and Esperanza. I left you out for all the obvious reasons. Again if you require the prerequisite cliché, please choose one of the following: You made your bed, now lie in it—"

"I get the point," Myron interrupted. "But I still have a business to protect. For their sakes, if not my own."

"No question." Win motioned toward the trenches. "But at the risk of sounding melodramatic, I am responsible for those people out there. For their jobs and financial security. They have families and mortgages and tuition payments." He pierced Myron with the ice blues. "That's not something I take lightly."

"I know."

Win leaned back. "I'll stay involved, of course. And again if my particular talents are needed—"

"Let's hope they aren't," Myron interrupted.

Win shrugged again. Then he said, "Funny, isn't it?"

"What?"

"We haven't even mentioned Esperanza in all this. Why do you think that is?"

"I don't know."

"Perhaps," Win said, "we have some doubt about her innocence."

"No."

Win arched the eyebrow but said nothing.

"I'm not just being emotional," Myron said. "I've been thinking about it."

"And?"

"And it makes no sense. First off, why would Esperanza kill Clu? What's her motive?"

"The DA seems to think she killed him for the money."

"Right. And I think it's fair to say we both know better."

Win paused, nodded. "Esperanza would not kill for money, no."

"So we have no motive."

Win frowned. "I'd say that conclusion is at best premature."

"Okay, but now let's look at the evidence. The gun, for example."

"Go on," Win said.

"Think this through for a second. Esperanza has a major altercation with Clu in front of witnesses, right?"

"Yes."

Myron held up a finger. "One, would Esperanza be dumb enough to kill Clu so soon after a public fight?"

"Fair point," Win conceded. "But perhaps the battle in the garage just raised the stakes. Perhaps after that Esperanza realized that Clu was out of control."

"Fine, let's say that Esperanza was still dumb enough to kill him after the fight. She'd have to know she'd be a suspect, right? I mean, there were witnesses."

Win nodded slowly. "I'll go with that."

"So why was the murder weapon in the office? Esperanza isn't that stupid. She's worked with us before. She knows the ins and out. Hell, anybody with a television set would have known you're supposed to dump the gun."

Win hesitated. "I see what you're saying."

"So the gun had to be planted. And if the gun was planted, then it follows that the blood and the fibers were planted too."

"Logical." Win doing his best Mr. Spock. The Batphone rang again. Win picked up the receiver and dispatched the matter in seconds. They went back to thinking.

"On the other hand," Win said, "I have never encountered a perfectly logical murder."

"What do you mean?"

"Reality is messy and full of contradictions. Take the O.J. case."

"The what?"

"The O.J. case," Win repeated. "If all that blood was spilled and the Juice was drenched in it, why was so little found?"

"He changed clothes."

"So? Even if he did, you'd expect to find more than a few dashboard splatters, wouldn't you? If the Juice drove home and showered, why was no blood found on the tiles or in the pipes or what have you?"

"So you think O.J. was innocent?"

Win frowned again. "You are missing my point."

"Which is?"

"Murder investigations never make complete sense. There are always rips in the fabric of logic. Unexplainable flaws. Perhaps Esperanza made a mistake. Perhaps she did not believe the police would suspect her. Perhaps she thought the weapon would be safer in the office than, say, her house."

"She didn't kill him, Win."

Win spread his hands. "Who amongst us is incapable—given the right circumstances—of murder?"

Heavy silence.

Myron swallowed hard. "For the sake of argument, let's assume the weapon was planted."

Win nodded slowly, keeping his eyes on Myron's.

"The question is, who set her up?"

"And why," Win added.

"So we need to make a list of her enemies," Myron said.

"And ours."

"What?"

"This murder charge is seriously wounding both of us," Win said. "We thus have to look at several possibilities."

"For example?"

"First," Win said, "we may be reading too much into the frame-up."

"How so?"

"This may not be a personal vendetta at all. Perhaps the murderer heard about the garage altercation and concluded that Esperanza would make a convenient patsy."

"So then this is all just a way of deflecting attention from the real killer? Nothing personal?"

"It's a possibility," Win said. "No more or less."

"Okay," Myron agreed, "what else?"

"The murderer wants to do Esperanza great harm."

"The obvious choice."

"For whatever that's worth, yes," Win said. "And possibility number three: The murderer wants to do one of us great harm."

"Or," Myron said, "our businesses."

"Yes."

Something like a giant cartoon anvil landed on Myron's head. "Someone like FJ."

Win merely smiled.

"And," Myron went on, "if Clu was doing something illicit, something that needed large amounts of cash—"

"Then FJ and his family would be a prime possible recipient," Win finished for him. "And of course, if we forget the money for a moment, FJ would relish any opportunity to crush you. What better way than decimating your business and incarcerating your best friend?"

"Two birds, one stone."

"Precisely."

Myron sat back, suddenly exhausted. "I don't relish the idea of tangling with the Aches."

"Neither do I," Win said.

"You? Before, you wanted to kill FJ."

"That's just my point. I can't anymore. If young FJ is behind this, we have to keep him alive in order to prove it. Trapping vermin is chancy. Simple extermination is the preferred course of action."

"So we've now eliminated your favorite option."

Win nodded. "Sad, no?"

"Tragic."

"But it gets worse, old friend."

"How's that?"

"Innocent or guilty," Win said, "Esperanza is concealing something from us."

Silence.

"We have no choice," Win said. "We need to investigate her too. Delve into her personal life a bit."

"I don't relish the idea of tangling with the Aches," Myron said, "but I really don't relish the idea of invading Esperanza's privacy."

"Be afraid," Win agreed. "Be very afraid."

11

The first potential clue did two things to Myron: It scared the hell out of him, and it reminded him of *The Sound of Music.*

Myron liked the old Julie Andrews musical well enough—who didn't?—but he always found one song particularly dumb. One of the classics actually. "My Favorite Things." The song made no sense. Ask a zillion people to list their absolute favorite things, and how many of them are going to list doorbells, for crying out loud? You know what, Millie? I love doorbells! To hell with strolling on a quiet beach or reading a great book or making love or seeing a Broadway musical. Doorbells, Millie. Doorbells punch my ticket. Sometimes I just run up to people's houses and press their doorbells and well, I think I'm man enough to admit I shudder.

Another puzzling "favorite" was brown paper packages tied up with string, mostly because it sounded like something sent by a mail-order pornographer (er, not that Myron would know that from personal experience). But that was what Myron found in the large stack of mail. Plain brown packaging. Typed address label with the word *Personal* across the bottom. No return address. Postmarked New York City.

Myron slit open the brown paper package, shook it, and watched a floppy disk drop to his desktop.

Hello.

Myron picked it up, turned it over, turned it back. No label on it. No writing. Just a plain black square with the metal across the top. Myron studied it for a moment, shrugged, popped it into his computer, hit some keys. He was about to hit Windows Explorer and see what kind of file it was when something started to happen. Myron sat back and frowned. He hoped that the diskette didn't contain a computer virus of some sort. He should, after all, know better than to just stick a strange diskette into his computer. He didn't know where it had been, what sleazy computer drive it had been inserted into before, if it wore a condom or had a blood test. Nothing. His poor computer. Just "Wham, bam, thank you, RAM."

Groan.

The screen went black.

Myron tugged his ear. His finger stretched forward to strike the escape button—the escape button being the last refuge of a desperate computer-phobe—when an image appeared on the screen. Myron froze.

It was a girl.

She had long, semistringy hair with two flips in front and an awkward smile. He guessed her age at around sixteen, braces fresh off, the eyes looking to the side, the backdrop a fading swirl of school-portrait rain-bow. Yep, the picture belonged in a frame on Mommy and Daddy's man-tel or a suburban high school yearbook circa 1985, the kind of thing with a life-summing write-up underneath it, a life-defining quote from James Taylor or Bruce Springsteen followed by So-So enjoyed being secre-tary/treasurer of the Key Club, her fondest memories including hanging out with Jenny and Sharon T at the Big W, popcorn in Mrs. Kennilworth's class, band practice behind the parking lot, that kind of apple-pie stuff. Typical. Kind of an obituary to adolescence.

Myron knew the girl.

Or at least he'd seen her before. He couldn't put his finger on where or when or if he'd seen her in person or in a photograph or what. But there was no doubt. He stared hard, hoping to conjure up a name or even a fleeting memory. Nothing. He kept staring. And that was when it hap-pened.

The girl began to melt.

It was the only way to describe it. The girl's hair flips fell and blended into her flesh, her forehead sloped down, her nose dissolved, her eyes rolled back and then closed. Blood began to run down from the eye sock-ets, coating the face in crimson.

Myron bolted his chair back, nearly screaming.

The blood blanketed the image now, and for a moment Myron won-dered if it would actually start coming out of the screen. A laughing noise came from the computer speakers. Not a psycho laugh or cruel laugh but the healthy, happy laugh of a teenage girl, a normal sound that raised the hairs on the back of Myron's neck as no howl ever could.

Without warning, the screen went mercifully black. The laughter stopped. And then the Windows 98 main menu reappeared.

Myron gulped down a few breaths. His hands gripped the edge of the desk to the point of white knuckles.

What the hell?

His heart beat against his rib cage as though it wanted to break free. He reached back and grabbed the brown paper wrappings. The postmark was almost three weeks old. Three weeks. This awful diskette had been sitting in his pile of mail since he'd run away. Why? Who had sent this to him? And who was the girl?

Myron's hand was still shaking when he picked up the phone. He dialed. Even though Myron had call block on his phone, a man answered by saying, "What's up, Myron?"

"I need your help, PT."

"Jesus, you sound like hell. This about Esperanza?"

"No."

"So what have you got?"

"A computer diskette. Three-and-half-inch floppy. I need it analyzed."

"Go to John Jay. Ask for Dr. Czerski. But if you're looking for a trace, it's pretty unlikely. What's this about?"

"I got this diskette in the mail. It contains a graphic of a teenage girl. In an AVI file of some sort."

"Who's the girl?"

"I don't know."

"I'll call Czerski. You head over."

Dr. Kirstin Czerski sported a white lab coat and a frown as yielding as a former East German swimmer's. Myron tried Smile Patent 17—moist Alan Alda, post-*M*A*S*H*.

"Hi," Myron said. "My name is—"

"The diskette." She held out her hand. He handed it to her. She looked at it for a second and headed for a door. "Wait here."

The door opened. Myron got a brief view of a room that looked like the bridge on *Battlestar Galactica*. Lots of metal and wires and lights and monitors and reel-to-reel tapes. The door closed. Myron stood in a sparsely decorated waiting room. Linoleum floor, three molded plastic chairs, brochures on a wall.

Myron's cellular phone rang again. He stared at it for a second. Six weeks ago he had turned the phone off. Now that it was back on, the contraption seemed to be making up for lost time. He pressed a button and brought it to his ear.

"Hello?"

"Hi, Myron."

Pow. The voice walloped him like a palm blast to the sternum. A rushing noise filled his ears, as though the phone were a seashell clamped against him. Myron slid into a yellow plastic chair.

"Hello, Jessica," he managed.

"I saw you on the news," she said, her voice a tad too controlled. "So I figured you'd turn your phone back on."

"Right."

More silence.

"I'm in Los Angeles," Jessica continued.

"Uh-huh."

"But I needed to tell you a few things."

"Oh?" Myron's Smooth-Lines Fountain—he just couldn't turn it off.

"First off, I'll be gone for at least another month. I didn't change the locks or anything so you can stay at the loft—"

"I'm, uh, bunking at Win's."

"Yeah, I figured. But if you need anything or if you want to clear your stuff out—"

"Right."

"Don't forget the TV too. That's yours."

"You can keep it," he said.

"Fine."

More silence.

Jessica said, "We're being so adult about this, aren't we?"

"Jess—"

"Don't. I called for a reason."

Myron kept quiet.

"Clu called you several times. At the loft, I mean."

Myron had guessed that.

"He sounded pretty desperate. I told him I didn't know where you were. He said that he had to find you. That he was worried about you."

"About me?"

"Yes. He came by once, looking like absolute shit. He grilled me for twenty minutes."

"About what?"

"About where you were. He said that he had to reach you—for your sake more than his. When I insisted that I didn't know where you were, he started scaring me."

"Scaring you how?"

"He asked how I knew you weren't dead."

"Clu said those words? About my being dead?"

"Yes. I actually called Win when he left."

"What did Win say?"

"That you were safe and that I shouldn't worry."

"What else?"

"I'm talking about Win here, Myron. He said—and I quote—'he's safe, don't worry.' Then he hung up. I let it drop. I figured that Clu was engaging in a little hyperbole to get my attention."

"That was probably it," Myron said.

"Yeah."

More silence.

"How are you?" she asked.

"I'm good. And you?"

"I'm trying to get over you," she said.

He could barely breathe. "Jess, we should talk—"

"Don't," she said again. "I don't want to talk, okay? Let me put it simply: If you change your mind, call me. You know the number. If not, have a nice life."

Click.

Myron put down the phone. He took several deep breaths. He looked at the phone. So simple. He did indeed know the number. How easy it would be to dial it.

"Worthless."

He looked up at Dr. Czerski. "Pardon?"

She held up the diskette. "You said there was graphic on it?"

Myron quickly explained what he had seen.

"It's not there now," she said. "It must have deleted itself."

"How?"

"You say the program ran automatically?"

"Yes."

"It probably self-extracted, self-ran, and then self-deleted. Simple."

"Aren't there special programs so you can undelete a file?"

"Yes. But this file did more than that. It reformatted the whole diskette. Probably the final command in the chain."

"Meaning?"

"Whatever you saw is gone forever."

"Is there anything else on the diskette?"

"No."

"Nothing we can trace? No unique characteristics or anything?"

She shook her head. "Typical diskette. Sold in every software store in the country. Standard formatting."

"How about fingerprints?"

"That's not my department."

And, Myron knew, it would be a waste of time. If someone had gone to the trouble of destroying any computer evidence, chances were pretty good that all fingerprints had been wiped off too.

"I'm busy." Dr. Czerski handed him back the diskette and left without so much as a back glance. Myron stared at it and shook his head.

What the hell was going on here?

The cell phone rang again. Myron picked it up.

"Mr. Bolitar?" It was Big Cyndi.

"Yes."

"I am going through Mr. Clu Haid's phone records, as you requested."

"And?"

"Are you coming back to the office, Mr. Bolitar?"

"I'm on the way there now."

"There is something here you might find bizarre."

12

When the elevator opened, Big Cyndi was waiting for him. She'd finally scrubbed her face clean. All the makeup was gone. Must have used a sand blaster. Or a jackhammer.

She greeted him by saying, "Very bizarre, Mr. Bolitar."

"What's that?"

"Per your instructions, I was checking through Clu Haid's phone records," she said. Then she shook her head. "Very bizarre."

"What's bizarre?"

She handed him a sheet of paper. "I highlighted the number in yellow."

Myron looked at it while walking into this office. Big Cyndi followed, closing the door behind her. The number was in the 212 area code. That meant Manhattan. Other than that, it was totally unfamiliar. "What about it?"

"It's for a nightclub."

"Which one?"

"Take A Guess."

"Pardon?"

"That's the name of the place," Big Cyndi said. "Take A Guess. It's two blocks down from Leather-N-Lust." Leather-N-Lust was the S&M bar that employed Big Cyndi as a bouncer. Motto: Hurt The Ones You Love.

"You know this place?" he asked.

"A little."

"What kind of club is it?"

"Cross-dressers and transvestites, mostly. But they have a varied crowd."

Myron rubbed his temples. "When you say varied . . ."

"It's sort of an interesting concept really, Mr. Bolitar."

"I'm sure."

"When you go to Take A Guess, you never know for sure what you're getting. You know what I mean?"

Myron didn't have a clue. "Pardon my sexual naiveté, but could you explain?"

Big Cyndi scrunched her face in thought. It was not a pretty sight. "In part, it's what you might expect: men dress like women, women dress like men. But then sometimes a woman is just a woman and a man is just a man. Follow?"

Myron nodded. "Not even a little."

"That's why it's called Take A Guess. You never know for sure. For instance, you might see a beautiful woman who is unusually tall with a platinum wig. So you figure it's a he-she. But—and this is what makes Take A Guess special—maybe it's not."

"Not what?"

"A he-she. A transvestite or transsexual. Maybe it is indeed a beautiful woman who put on extra-high heels and a wig to confuse you."

"And the reason for this is?"

"That's the fun of the place. The doubt. There's a sign inside. TAKE A GUESS: IT'S ABOUT AMBIGUITY, NOT ANDROGYNY."

"Catchy."

"But that's the idea. It's a place of mystery. You bring someone home. You think it's a beautiful woman or a handsome man. But until the pants are all the way down, you're never sure. People come dressed to fool. You just never know until—well, you saw *The Crying Game*."

Myron made a face. "And this is a desirable thing?"

"If you're into that, sure."

"Into what?"

She smiled. "Exactly."

Myron rubbed the temples again. "So the patrons don't have a problem with"—he searched for the right word, but there wasn't one—"so a gay guy, for example, doesn't get pissed off when he finds out he brought home a woman?"

"It's why you go. The thrill. The uncertainty. The mystery."

"Sort of the sexual equivalent of a grab bag."

"Right."

"Except in this case, you can really be surprised by what you grab."

Big Cyndi considered that. "If you really think about it, Mr. Bolitar, there can be only one of two things."

He was no longer so sure.

"But I like your grab bag analogy," Big Cyndi continued. "You know what you're bringing to the party, but you have no idea what you're going to take home. One time a guy left with what he thought was an overweight woman. It turned out that it was a guy with a midget hiding under the dress."

"Please tell me you're joking."

Big Cyndi just looked at him.

"So," Myron continued, "you, uh, frequent this place?"

"I've been a couple of times. But not recently."

"Why not?"

"Two reasons. First, they compete with Leather-N-Lust. It's a different crowd, but we still draw from similar markets."

Myron nodded. "The pervert pool."

"They're not hurting anybody."

"At least nobody who doesn't want to be hurt."

She pouted, not a great look on a three-hundred-pound wrestler, especially without her mortarlike makeup. "Esperanza is right."

"About?"

"You can be very closed-minded."

"Yeah, I'm a regular Jerry Falwell. So what's the second reason?"

She hesitated. "I'm obviously for sexual freedom. I don't care what you're doing as long as it's consensual. And I've done some wild things myself, Mr. Bolitar." She looked straight at him. "*Very* wild."

Myron cringed, fearing she might share details.

"But Take A Guess started drawing the wrong kind of crowd," she said.

"Gee, that's surprising," Myron said. "You'd think a place like that would be a natural for vacationing families."

She shook her head. "You are so repressed, Mr. Bolitar."

"Because I like to know my partner's gender before getting naked?"

"Because of your attitude. People like you cause sexual hang-ups. Society becomes sexually repressed—so repressed, in fact, that they cross the line between sex and violence, between playacting and real danger. They reach a stage where they get off by hurting people who do not want to be hurt."

"And Take A Guess attracts that kind of crowd?"

"More than most."

Myron sat back and rubbed his face with both hands. He started hearing brain clicks. "This might explain a few things," he said.

"Like what?"

"Why Bonnie finally threw Clu out for good. It's one thing to have a string of girlfriends. But if Clu was frequenting a place like this, if he started leaning toward"—again, what would be the word?—"toward whatever. And if Bonnie found out, well, it would explain the legal separation." He nodded to himself as he heard more internal clicks. "And it would explain her odd behavior today."

"How so?"

"She made a point of asking me not to dig too deeply. She just wanted me to clear Esperanza and then drop the investigation."

Big Cyndi nodded. "She was afraid this would get out."

"Right. If something like this went public, what would it do to her kids?"

Another thought floating through Myron's brain got snagged on some jagged rock. He looked at Big Cyndi. "I assume that Take A Guess appeals mostly to bisexuals. I mean, if you're not sure what you're getting, who better than someone who wouldn't care?"

"More like ambisexuals," Big Cyndi said. "Or people who want some mystery. Who want something new."

"But bisexuals too."

"Yes, of course."

"How about Esperanza?"

Big Cyndi bristled. "What about her?"

"Did she frequent this place?"

"I wouldn't know, Mr. Bolitar. And I don't see the relevance."

"I'm not asking because it gives me jollies. You want me to help her, right? That means digging where we don't want to dig."

"I understand that, Mr. Bolitar. But you know her better than I do."

"Not this side of her," Myron said.

"Esperanza is a private person. I really don't know. She usually has a steady, but I don't know if she's gone there or not."

Myron nodded. Didn't matter much. If Clu had been hanging out in such a place, it would give Hester Crimstein more reasonable doubt. A rough trade place complete with a reputation for violence—it was a natural recipe for disaster. Clu could have brought home the wrong package. Or been the wrong package. And there was the cash to consider. Blackmail money? Did a customer recognize him? Threaten him? Videotape him?

Yep, lots of murky reasonable doubt.

And a good place to search for the elusive girlfriend. Or boyfriend. Or in-between friend. He shook his head. It was not a question of the ethics or moral dilemma for Myron; deviancy simply confused him. Repugnancy aside, he didn't get it. Lack of imagination, he supposed.

"I'll have to pay the Take A Guess a visit," he said.

"Not alone," Big Cyndi said. "I'll go with you."

Subtle surveillance was out. "Fine."

THE FINAL DETAIL **341**

"And not now. Take A Guess doesn't open until eleven."

"Okay. We'll go tonight then."

"I have just the outfit," she said. "What are you going to go as?"

"A repressed heterosexual man," he said. "All I'll have to do is slip on my Rockports." He looked at the phone record again. "You have another number highlighted in blue."

She nodded. "You mentioned an old friend named Billy Lee Palms."

"This his number?"

"No. Mr. Palms doesn't exist anywhere. No phone listing. And he hasn't paid taxes in four years."

"So whose number is this?"

"Mr. Palms's parents. Mr. Haid called them twice in the past month."

Myron checked the address. Westchester. He vaguely remembered meeting Billy Lee's parents during a Family Day at Duke. He looked at his watch. It would take an hour to get there. He grabbed his coat and headed for the elevator.

13

Myron's car, the business's Ford Taurus, had been confiscated by the police, so he rented a maroon Mercury Cougar. He hoped the women would be able to resist. When he started the car, the radio was tuned to Lite FM 106.7. Patti LaBelle and Michael McDonald were crooning a sad lite staple entitled "On My Own." This once blissfully happy couple were breaking up. Tragic. So tragic that, as Michael McDonald put it, "Now we're up to talking divorce . . . and we weren't even married."

Myron shook his head. For this Michael McDonald left the Doobie Brothers?

In college Billy Lee Palms had been the quintessential party boy. He had sneaky good looks, jet black hair, and a magnetic, albeit oily, combination of charisma and machismo, the kind of thing that played well with young coeds away from home for the first time. At Duke the frat brothers had dubbed him Otter, the pseudosuave character in the movie *Animal House*. It fitted. Billy Lee was also a great baseball player, a catcher who managed to reach the major leagues for a half season, riding the bench for the Baltimore Orioles the year they won the World Series.

But that was years ago.

Myron knocked on the door. Seconds later the door swung open fast and wide. No warning, nothing. Strange. In this day and age people looked through peepholes or cracks in chain-held doors or at the very least asked who it was.

A woman he vaguely recognized as Mrs. Palms said, "Yes?" She was small with a squirrel mouth and eyes that bulged like something behind them was pushing to get out. Her hair was tied back, but several strands escaped and drooped in front of her face. She pushed them back with splayed fingers.

"Are you Mrs. Palms?" he asked.

"Yes."

"My name is Myron Bolitar. I went to Duke with Billy Lee."

Her voice dropped an octave or two. "Do you know where he is?"

"No, ma'am. Is he missing?"

She frowned and stepped back. "Come in, please."

Myron moved into the foyer. Mrs. Palms was already heading down a corridor. She pointed to her right without turning around or breaking stride. "Just go into Sarah's wedding room. I'll be there in a second."

"Yes, ma'am."

Sarah's wedding room?

He followed where she had pointed. When he turned the corner, he heard himself give a little gasp. Sarah's wedding room. The decor was run-of-the-mill living room, something out of a furniture store circular. An off-white couch and matching love seat formed a broken L, probably the monthly special, $695 for both, the couch might fold out into a Serta sleeper, something like that. The coffee table was a semi oak square, a short stack of attractive, unread magazines on one end, silk flowers in the middle, a couple of coffee books on the other end. The wall-to-wall carpeting was light beige, and there were two torchère lamps à la the Pottery Barn.

But the walls were anything but ordinary.

Myron had seen plenty of houses with photographs on the walls. They were hardly uncommon. He had even been in a house or two where the photographs dominated rather than complemented the surroundings. That too would hardly give him reason to pause. But this was beyond surreal. Sarah's Wedding Room—heck, it should be capitalized—was a re-creation of that event. Literally. Color wedding photographs had been blown up to life size and pasted on as a wallpaper substitute. The bride and groom smiled at him invitingly from the right. On the left, Billy Lee in a tux, probably the best man or maybe just an usher, smiled at him. Mrs. Palms, dressed in a summer gown, danced with her husband. In front of him were the wedding tables, lots of them. Guests looked up and smiled at him—all life size. It was as though a panoramic wedding photo had been blown up to the size of Rembrandt's *Night Watch*. People slow-danced. A band played. There was a minister of sorts and floral arrangements and a wedding cake and fine china and white linen—again, all life size.

"Please sit down."

Myron turned to Mrs. Palms. Was it the real Mrs. Palms or one of the reproductions? No, she was casually dressed. The real McCoy. He almost reached out and touched her to make sure. "Thank you," he said.

"This is our daughter Sarah's wedding. She was married four years ago."

"I see."

"It was a very special day for us."

"I'm sure."

"We had it at the Manor in West Orange. You know it?"

"I was bar mitzvahed there," Myron said.

"Really? Your parents must have very fond memories of the day."

"Yes." But now he wondered. I mean, Mom and Dad kept most of the photos in an album.

Mrs. Palms smiled at him. "It's odd, I know, but . . . oh, I've explained this a thousand times. What's one more?" She sighed, signaled to a couch. Myron sat. She did likewise.

Mrs. Palms folded her hands and looked at him with the blank stare of a woman who sat too close to life's big screen. "People take pictures of their most special times," she began too earnestly. "They want to capture the important moments. They want to enjoy them and savor them and re-live them. But that's not what they do. They take the picture, they look at it once, and then they stick it in a box and forget about it. Not me. I re-member the good times. I wallow in them—re-create them, if I can. Af-ter all, we live for those moments, don't we, Myron?"

He nodded.

"So when I sit in this room, it warms me. I'm surrounded by one of the happiest moments in my life. I've created the most positive aura imagi-nable."

He nodded again.

"I'm not a big art fan," she continued. "I don't relish the idea of hang-ing impersonal lithographs on the walls. What's the point of looking at images of people and places I don't know? I don't care that much about interior design. And I don't like antiques or phony-baloney Martha Stew-art stuff. But do you know what I do find beautiful?" She stopped and looked at him expectantly.

Myron picked up his cue. "What?"

"My family," she replied. "My family is beautiful to me. My family is art. Does that make sense to you, Myron?"

"Yes." Oddly enough, it did.

"So I call this Sarah's Wedding Room. I know that's silly. Naming rooms. Blowing up old photographs and using them as wallpaper. But all the rooms are like this. Billy Lee's bedroom upstairs I call the Catcher's

Mitt. It's where he still stays when he's here. I think it comforts him." She raised her eyebrows. "Would you like to see it?"

"Sure."

She practically leaped off the couch. The stairwell was plastered with giant, seemingly old black and whites. A stern-faced couple in wedding gear. A soldier in full uniform. "This is the Generational Wall. That's my great-grandparents over there. And Hank's. My husband. He died three years ago."

"I'm sorry."

She shrugged. "This stairwell goes back three generations. I think it's a nice way of remembering our ancestors."

Myron didn't argue. He looked at the photograph of the young couple, just starting out their life together, probably a little scared. Now they were dead.

Deep Thoughts by Myron Bolitar.

"I know what you're thinking," she said. "But is it any stranger than hanging oils of dead relatives? Just more lifelike."

Hard to argue.

The walls in the upstairs corridor featured some sort of costume party from the seventies. Lots of leisure suits and bell-bottoms. Myron didn't ask, and Mrs. Palms didn't explain. Just as well. She turned left and Myron trailed her into the Catcher's Mitt. It lived up to its billing. Billy Lee's baseball life was laid out like a Hall of Fame display room. It started with Billy Lee in Little League, squatting in his catcher's stance, his smile huge and strangely confident for so young a child. The years flashed by. Little League to Babe Ruth League to high school to Duke, ending with his one glorious year with the Orioles, Billy Lee proudly showing off his World Series ring. Myron studied the Duke photographs. One had been taken out in front of Psi U, their frat house. A uniformed Billy Lee had his arm around Clu, plenty of frat brothers in the background, including, he saw now, him and Win. Myron remembered when the picture had been taken. The baseball team had just beaten Florida State to win the national championship. The party had lasted three days.

"Mrs. Palms, where is Billy Lee?"

"I don't know."

"When you say you don't know—"

"He ran off," she interrupted. "Again."

"He's done this before?"

She stared at the wall. Her eyes were glassy now. "Maybe Billy Lee doesn't find this room comforting," she said softly. "Maybe it reminds him of what could have been." She turned to him. "When was the last time you saw Billy Lee?"

Myron tried to remember. "It's been a long time."

"How come?"

"We were never that close."

She pointed to the wall. "That's you? In the background?"

"That's right."

"Billy Lee spoke about you."

"Really?"

"He said you were a sports agent. Clu's agent, if I'm not mistaken."

"Yes."

"You stayed friendly with Clu then?"

"Yes."

She nodded as though this explained everything. "Why are you looking for my son, Myron?"

He was not sure how to explain. "You've heard about Clu's death?"

"Yes, of course. That poor boy. A lost soul. Like Billy Lee in many ways. I think that's why they were drawn to each other."

"Have you seen Clu lately?"

"Why do you want to know?"

In for a penny and all that. "I'm trying to find out who killed him."

Her body stiffened as though his words held a small electric shock. "And you think Billy Lee had something to do with it?"

"No, of course not." But even as he said it, he began to wonder. Clu is murdered; maybe his killer runs away. More reasonable doubt. "It's just that I know how close they were. I thought maybe Billy Lee could help me out."

Mrs. Palms was staring at the image of the two ballplayers in front of Psi U. She reached out as though to stroke her son's face. But she pulled back. "Billy Lee was handsome, wasn't he?"

"Yes."

"The girls," she said. "They all loved my Billy Lee."

"I'd never seen anybody better with them," he said.

That made her smile. She kept staring at the image of her son. It was kinda creepy. Myron remembered the old episode of *The Twilight Zone* where the aging movie queen escapes reality by stepping into one of her old movies. It looked like Mrs. Palms craved doing likewise.

She finally tore her eyes away. "Clu came by a few weeks ago."

"Can you be more specific?"

"Funny."

"What?"

"That's just what the police asked."

"The police were here?"

"Sure."

They must have gone through the phone records too, Myron thought. Or found another link.

"I'll tell you the same thing I told them. I can't be more specific."

"Do you know what Clu wanted?"

"He came to see Billy Lee."

"Billy Lee was here?"

"Yes."

"He lives here then?"

"On and off. The past few years have not been very good to my son."

Silence.

"I don't mean to pry," Myron began, "but—"

"What happened to Billy Lee?" she finished. "Life caught up with him, Myron. The drinking, the drugs, the womanizing. He had stints in rehab. Are you familiar with Rockwell?"

"No, ma'am."

"It's a private clinic. He finished his fourth trip to Rockwell not two months ago. But he couldn't stay clean. When you're in college or even in your twenties, you can survive it. When you're a big star and people are looking out for you, you can get away with it. But Billy Lee wasn't good enough to reach that level. So he had no one to fall back upon. Except me. And I'm not that strong."

Myron swallowed. "Do you know why Clu came to see Billy Lee?"

"For old times' sake, I guess. They went out. Maybe they had a few beers and chased women. I really don't know."

"Did Clu visit Billy Lee a lot?"

"Well, Clu's been out of town," she said, a little too defensively. "He was only traded back to this area a few months ago. But of course, you know that."

"So this was just a casual visit?"

"I thought so at the time."

"And now?"

"Now my son is missing and Clu is dead."

Myron thought about it. "Where does he usually go when he runs off like this?"

"Wherever. Billy Lee is a bit of a nomad. He goes off, he does whatever horrible thing he does to himself, and when he hits rock bottom, he comes back here."

"So you don't know where he is?"

"That's right."

"Any idea at all?"

"No."

"No favorite haunts?"

"No."

"A girlfriend maybe?"

"No one I know about anyway."

"Any close friends he might stay with?"

"No," she said slowly. "He has no friends like that."

Myron took out his card and handed it to her. "If you hear from him, Mrs. Palms, could you please let me know?"

She studied the card as they moved out of the room and back down the stairs.

Before she opened the door, Mrs. Palms said, "You were the basketball player."

"Yes."

"The one who hurt his knee."

First preseason game as a pro. Myron had been the Boston Celtics' first-round draft pick. A terrible collision and his career was over. Just like that. Finished before it started. "Yes."

"You managed to put it behind you," she said. "You managed to get on with your life and be happy and productive." She cocked her head. "Why couldn't Billy Lee?"

Myron had no answer—in part because he was not sure her supposition was entirely accurate. He said his good-byes and left her alone with her ghosts.

14

Myron checked his watch. Dinnertime. Mom and Dad were expecting him. He'd hit the Garden State Parkway when the cell phone rang again.

"Are you in the car?" Win asked. Always with the pleasantries.

"Yes."

"Flip on 1010 WINS. I'll call back."

One of New York's all-news radio stations. Myron did as he was told. The guy in the helicopter was finishing up the traffic report. He handed it back to the woman at the news desk. She provided the teaser: "The latest bombshell in the murder of baseball superstar Clu Haid. In sixty seconds."

It was a long sixty seconds. Myron had to put up with a truly annoying Dunkin' Donuts commercial, and then some excited bozo had a way of turning five thousand dollars into twenty thousand dollars, though a softer, fast-speaking voice added that it didn't work all the time and in fact you could lose money too and probably would and you'd have to be a major moron to take investment advice from a radio ad. Finally the woman at the news desk came back on. She told the audience her name—like anyone cared—the name of her male counterpart, and the time. Then:

"ABC is reporting from an anonymous source in the Bergen County district attorney's office that hairs and quote other bodily materials unquote matching the murder suspect Esperanza Diaz have been found at the murder scene. According to the source, DNA tests are pending, but preliminary tests show a clear match with Ms. Diaz. The source also says that the hairs, some small, were found in various locations throughout the house."

Myron felt a flutter beneath his heart. Small hairs, he thought. Euphemism for pubic.

"No further details are available, but the district attorney's office clearly believes that Mr. Clu Haid and Ms. Esperanza Diaz were having a sexual relationship. Stay tuned to 1010 WINS for all the details."

The cell phone rang. Myron picked it up. "Jesus Christ."

"Not even close," Win said.

"I'll call you right back." Myron hung up. He called Hester Crimstein's office. The secretary said that Ms. Crimstein was unavailable. Myron stressed that this was urgent. Ms. Crimstein was still unavailable. But, Myron asked, doesn't Ms. Crimstein have a cell phone? The secretary disconnected the call. Myron hit the memory button. Win picked up.

"What's your take on this?" Myron asked.

"Esperanza was sleeping with him," Win said.

"Maybe not."

"Yes, of course," Win said. "Perhaps someone planted Esperanza's pubic hairs at the murder scene."

"It could be a false leak."

"Could be."

"Or maybe she visited his apartment. To talk business."

"And left stray pubic hairs behind?"

"Maybe she used the bathroom. Maybe she—"

"Myron?"

"What?"

"Please don't go into further detail, thank you. There is something else to consider."

"What?"

"The E-Z Pass records."

"Right," Myron said. "She crossed the Washington Bridge an hour after the murder. We know that. But maybe that fits now. Esperanza and Clu have a big argument at the parking garage. Esperanza wants to clear the air. So she drives out to his apartment."

"And when she gets there?"

"I don't know. Maybe she saw the body and panicked."

"Yes, of course," Win said. "So she ripped out a few pubic hairs and ran."

"I didn't say it was her first visit out there."

"Indeed not."

"What do you mean?"

"The E-Z Pass records for the Ford Taurus. According to the bill that arrived last week, the car crossed the bridge eighteen times in the past month."

Myron frowned. "You're kidding."

"Yes, I am a mirthful fellow. I also took the liberty of checking the month before. Sixteen crosses of the Washington Bridge."

"Maybe she had another reason for going out to North Jersey."

"Yes, of course. The malls in Paramus are quite an attraction."

"Okay," Myron said. "Let's assume they were having an affair."

"That would seem most prudent, especially since it offers a reasonable explanation for much that has happened."

"How's that?"

"It would explain Esperanza's silence."

"How?"

"Lovers always make wonderful suspects," Win said. "If, for example, Esperanza and Clu were dancing the sheet mambo, then we can assume that the altercation in the parking garage was something of a lovers' tiff. All in all, this development looks bad for her. She would want to hide it."

"But from us?" Myron countered.

"Yes."

"Why? She trusts us."

"Several reasons come to mind. Her attorney probably ordered her not to say anything."

"That wouldn't stop her."

"It might. But more important, Esperanza was probably embarrassed. You have recently promoted her to partner. She was in charge of the entire operation. I know that you believe Esperanza is too tough to care about such things, but I do not think she would relish your disapproval."

Myron mulled that one over. It made some sense, but he wasn't sure he bought it entirely. "I still think we're missing something."

"That's because we're ignoring the strongest motive for her keeping silent."

"That being?"

"She killed him."

Win hung up on that cheery note. Myron took Northfield Avenue toward Livingston. The familiar landmarks of his hometown popped into view. He thought about the news report and what Win had said. Could Esperanza be the mystery woman, the reason for Clu and Bonnie's breakup? If so, why wouldn't Bonnie say that? Maybe she didn't know. Or maybe—

Hold the phone.

Maybe Clu and Esperanza met up at Take A Guess. Did they go there together or just bump into each other? Is that how the affair started? Did they go there and participate in—in whatever? Maybe it was an accident.

Maybe they both arrived there in disguise and didn't realize who they were until, well, it was too late to stop? Did that make sense?

He made the right at Nero's Restaurant and onto Hobart Gap Road. Not far now. He was in the land of his childhood—check that, his entire life. He had lived here with his parents until a year or so ago, when he finally severed the apron strings and moved in with Jessica. Psychologists and psychiatrists and the like, he knew, would have a field day with the fact that he had lived with his parents into his thirties, theorizing all kinds of unnatural preoccupations that kept him so close to Mom and Dad. Maybe they'd be right. But for Myron, the answer had been far simpler. He liked them. Yes, they could be pests—what parents weren't?—and they liked to pry. But most of the pestering and prying were over the incidentals. They had given him privacy yet made him feel cared for and wanted. Was that unhealthy? Maybe. But it seemed a damn sight better than his friends who thrived on blaming their parents for any unhappiness in their lives.

He turned onto his street. The old neighborhood was wholly unspectacular. There were thousands like it in New Jersey, hundreds of thousands throughout the US of A. This was suburbia, the backbone of this country, the battleground of the fabled American Dream. Corny to say, but Myron loved it here. Sure, there was unhappiness and dissatisfaction and fights and all that, but he still thought that this was the "realest" place he had ever been. He loved the basketball court in the driveway and the training wheels on the new two-wheelers and the routine and the walking to school and the caring too much about the color of the grass. This was living. This was what it was all about.

In the end Myron guessed that he and Jessica had broken up for all the classic reasons, albeit with a gender twist. He wanted to settle down, buy a house in the 'burbs, raise a family; Jessica, fearing commitment, did not. He pulled into the driveway now, shaking his head. Too simple an explanation. Too pat. The commitment stuff had been an ongoing source of tension, no question, but there was more to it. There was the recent tragedy, for one thing.

There was Brenda.

Mom rushed out the door, sprinting toward him with her arms spread wide. She always greeted him like he was a recently released POW, but today was something extra special. She threw her arms around him, nearly knocking him over. Dad trailed behind, equally excited but playing it cool. Dad had always been about balance, the total love without the smothering, the caring without pushing. An amazing man, his father. When Dad reached him, there was no handshake. The two men hugged fiercely and without any hint of embarrassment. Myron kissed his father's

cheek. The familiar feel of Dad's rough skin made him understand a bit
what Mrs. Palms was trying to accomplish with the wallpapered images.

"Are you hungry?" Mom asked. Always her opening gambit.

"A little."

"You want me to fix something?"

Everyone froze. Dad made a face. "You're going to cook?"

"What's the big deal?"

"Let me make sure I have the number of poison control."

"Oh, Al, that's so funny. Ha-ha, I can't stop laughing. What a funny
man your father is, Myron."

"Actually, Ellen, go ahead and cook something. I need to drop a few
pounds."

"Wow, what a knee slapper, Al. You're killing me here."

"Better than a fat farm."

"Ho-ho."

"Just the thought is better than an appetite suppressor."

"It's like being married to Shecky Greene." But she was smiling.

They were in the house now. Dad took Mom's hand. "Let me show you
something, Ellen," Dad said. "See that big metal box over there? That's
called an oven. O-v-e-n. Oven. See that knob, the one with all the numbers on it? That's how you turn it on."

"You're funnier than a sober Foster Brooks, Al."

But they were all smiling now. Dad was speaking the truth. Mom
didn't cook. Almost never did. Her culinary skills could cause a prison
riot. When he was a kid, Myron's favorite home-cooked dinner was Dad's
scrambled eggs. Mom was an early career woman. The kitchen was a
place to read magazines.

"What do you want to eat, Myron?" Mom asked. "Chinese maybe.
From Fong's?"

"Sure."

"Al, call Fong's. Order something."

"Okay."

"Make sure you get shrimp with lobster sauce."

"I know."

"Myron loves Fong's shrimp with lobster sauce."

"I know, Ellen. I raised him too, remember?"

"You might forget."

"We've been ordering from Fong's for twenty-three years. We always
order shrimp with lobster sauce."

"You might forget, Al. You're getting old. Didn't you forget to pick up
my blouse at the laundry two days ago."

"It was closed."

"So you never picked up my blouse, am I right?"

"Of course not."

"I rest my case." She looked at her son. "Myron, sit. We need to talk. Al, call Fong's."

The men obeyed her orders. As always. Myron and Mom sat at the kitchen table.

"Listen to me closely," Mom said. "I know Esperanza is your friend. But Hester Crimstein is a fine lawyer. If she told Esperanza not to talk to you, it's the right thing."

"How do you know—"

"I've known Hester for years." Mom was a defense attorney, one of the best in the state. "We've worked cases together before. She called me. She said you're interfering."

"I'm not interfering."

"Actually she said you're bothering her and to butt out."

"She talked to you about this?"

"Of course. She wants you to leave her client alone."

"I can't."

"Why can't you?"

Myron squirmed a bit. "I have some information that might be important."

"Such as?"

"According to Clu's wife, he was having an affair."

"And you think Hester doesn't know that? The DA thinks he was having an affair with Esperanza."

"Wait a second." It was Dad. "I thought Esperanza was a lesbian."

"She's a bisexual, Al."

"A what?"

"Bisexual. It means she likes both boys and girls."

Dad thought about that. "I guess that's a good thing to be."

"What?"

"I mean, it gives you the double the options of everyone else."

"Great, Al, thanks for the insight." She rolled her eyes and turned back to Myron. "So Hester already knows that. What else?"

"Clu was desperate to find me before he was killed," Myron said.

"Most logically, *bubbe,* to say something incriminating about Esperanza."

"Not necessarily. Clu came to the loft. He told Jessica that I was in danger."

"And you think he meant it?"

"No, he was probably exaggerating. But shouldn't Hester Crimstein judge the significance?"

"She already has."

"What?"

"Clu came here too, darling." Her voice was suddenly soft. "He told your father and me the same thing he told Jessica."

Myron didn't push it. If Clu had told his parents the same thing he told Jessica, if he had used all that death talk when Mom and Dad didn't know where Myron was . . .

As though reading his mind, Dad said, "I called Win. He said you were safe."

"Did he tell you where I was?"

Mom took that one. "We didn't ask."

Silence.

She reached over and put a hand on his arm. "You've been through a lot, Myron. Your father and I know that."

They both looked at him with the deep-caring eyes. They knew part of what happened. About his breakup with Jessica. About Brenda. But they would never know it all.

"Hester Crimstein knows what's she doing," Mom went on. "You have to let her do her job."

More silence.

"Al?"

"What?"

"Hang up the phone," she said. "Maybe we should go out to eat."

Myron checked his watch. "It'll have to be quick. I have to get back to the city."

"Oh?" Mom raised an eyebrow. "You have a date already?"

He thought about Big Cyndi's description of Take A Guess.

"Not likely," he said. "But you never know."

15

From the outside Take A Guess looked pretty much like your standard Manhattan cantina-as-pickup-joint. The building was brick, the windows darkened to highlight the neon beer signs. Above the door, faded lettering spelled out *Take A Guess*. That was it. No "Bring Your Perversions." No "The Kinkier the Better." No "You Better Like Surprises." Nothing. A suit trudging home might happen by here, stop in, lay down his briefcase, spot something attractive, buy it a drink, make a few quasi-smooth moves warmed over from college mixers, take it home. Surprise, surprise.

Big Cyndi met him at the front door dressed like Earth, Wind, and Fire—not so much any one member as the entire group. "Ready?"

Myron hesitated, nodded.

When Big Cyndi pushed open the door, Myron held his breath and ducked in behind her. The interior too was not what he'd visualized. He had expected something . . . blatantly wacko, he guessed. Like the bar scene in *Star Wars* maybe. Instead Take A Guess just had the same neodesperate feel and stench of a zillion other singles' joints on a Friday night. A few patrons were colorfully dressed, but most wore khakis and business suits. There were also a handful of outrageously clad cross-dressers and leather devotees and one babe-a-rama packed into a vinyl catsuit, but nowadays you'd be hard pressed to find a Manhattan nightspot that didn't have any of that. Sure, some folks were in disguise, but when it came right down to it, who didn't wear a facade at a singles' bar?

Whoa, that was deep.

Heads and eyes swerved in their direction. For a moment Myron wondered why. But only for a moment. He was, after all, standing next to Big Cyndi, a six-six three-hundred-pound multihued mass blanketed with more sparkles than a Siegfried and Roy costume party. She drew the eye.

Big Cyndi seemed flattered by the attention. She lowered her eyes, playing demure, which was like Ed Asner playing coquettish. "I know the head bartender," she said. "His name is Pat."

"Male or female?"

She smiled, punched him on the arm. "Now you're getting the hang of it."

A jukebox played the Police's "Every Little Thing She Does Is Magic." Myron tried to count how many times Sting repeated the words *every little*. He lost count at a million.

They found two stools at the bar. Big Cyndi looked for Pat. Myron cased the joint, very detectivelike. He turned his back to the bar, eased his elbows against it, bobbed his head slightly to the music. Señor Slick. The babe-a-rama in the black catsuit caught his eye. She slithered to the seat next to him and curled into it. Myron flashed back to Julie Newmar as Cat Woman circa 1967, something he did far too often. This woman was dirty blond but otherwise frighteningly comparable.

Catsuit gave him a look that made him believe in telekinesis. "Hi," she said.

"Hi back." The Lady Slayer awakens.

She slowly reached for her neck and started toying with the catsuit's zipper. Myron managed to keep his tongue in the general vicinity of his mouth. He took a quick peek at Big Cyndi.

"Don't be too sure," Big Cyndi warned.

Myron frowned. There was cleavage here, for crying out loud. He stole another look—for the sake of science. Yep, cleavage. And plenty of it. He looked back at Big Cyndi and whispered, "Bosoms. Two of them."

Big Cyndi shrugged.

"My name is Thrill," Catsuit said.

"I'm Myron."

"Myron," she repeated, her tongue circling as though testing the word for taste. "I like that name. It's very manly."

"Er, thanks, I guess."

"You don't like your name?"

"Actually, I've always sort of hated it," he said. Then he gave her the big-guy look, cocking the eyebrow like Fabio going for deep thought. "But if you like it, maybe I'll reconsider."

Big Cyndi made a noise like a moose coughing up a turtle shell.

Thrill gave him another smoldering glance and picked up her drink. She did something that could roughly be called "taking a sip," but Myron doubted the Motion Picture Association would give it less than an R rating. "Tell me about yourself, Myron."

They started chatting. Pat, the bartender, was on break, so Myron and Thrill kept at it for a good fifteen minutes. He didn't want to admit it, but he was sort of having fun. Thrill turned toward him, full body. She slid a little closer. Myron again looked for telltale gender signs. He checked for the two Five O' clocks: Shadow and Charlie. Nothing. He checked the cleavage again. Still there. Damn if he wasn't a trained detective.

Thrill put her hand on his thigh. It felt hot through his jeans. Myron stared at the hand for a moment. Was the size odd? He tried to figure out if it was big for a woman or maybe small for a man. His head started spinning.

"I don't mean to be rude," Myron finally said, "but you're a woman, right?"

Thrill threw her head back and laughed. Myron looked for an Adam's apple. She had a black ribbon tied around the neck. Made it hard to tell. The laugh was a touch hoarse, but oh, come on now. This couldn't be a guy. Not with that cleavage. Not when the catsuit was so tight about the, er, nether region, if you catch the drift.

"What's the difference?" Thrill asked.

"Pardon?"

"You find me attractive, don't you?"

"What I see."

"So?"

Myron raised his hands. "So—and let me just state this plainly—if, during a moment of passion, there is a second penis in the room . . . well, it definitely kills the mood for me."

She laughed. "No other penises, eh?"

"That's right. Just mine. I'm funny that way."

"Are you familiar with Woody Allen?" she asked.

"Of course."

"Then let me quote him." Myron stayed still. Thrill was about to quote the Woodman. If she was a she, Myron was close to proposing." 'Sex is a beautiful thing between two people. Between five it's fantastic.' "

"Nice quote," Myron said.

"Do you know what it's from?"

"His old nightclub act. When Woody did stand-up comedy in the sixties."

Thrill nodded, pleased that the pupil had passed the test.

"But we're not talking group sex here," Myron said.

"Have you ever had group sex?" she asked.

"Well, uh, no."

"But if you did—if there were, say, five people—would it be a problem if one of them had a penis?"

"We're talking hypothetically here, right?"

"Unless you want me to call some friends."

"No, that's okay, really, thanks." Myron took a deep breath. "Yeah, okay, hypothetically, I guess it wouldn't be a huge problem, as long as the man kept his distance."

Thrill nodded. "But if I had a penis—"

"A major mood killer."

"I see." Thrill made small circles on Myron's thigh. "Admit you're curious."

"I am."

"So?"

"So I'm also curious about what goes through a person's mind when he jumps out of a skyscraper. Before he goes splat on the sidewalk."

She arched an eyebrow. "It's probably a hell of a rush."

"Yeah, but then there's that splat at the end."

"And in this case . . ."

"The splat would be a penis, yes."

"Interesting," Thrill said. "Suppose I'm a transsexual."

"Pardon?"

"Suppose I *had* a penis, but now it's gone. You'd be safe, right?"

"Wrong."

"Why?"

"Phantom penis," Myron said.

"Pardon?"

"Like in a war when a guy loses his limb and still thinks it's there. Phantom penis."

"But it's not your penis that would be missing."

"Still. Phantom penis."

"But that doesn't make any sense."

"Exactly."

Thrill showed him nice, even white teeth. Myron looked at them. Can't tell much about gender from teeth. Better to check the cleavage again. "You realize that you're massively insecure about your sexuality," she said.

"Because I like to know if a potential partner has a penis?"

"A real man wouldn't worry about being thought of as a fag."

"It's not what people think that bothers me."

"It's just the penis issue," she finished for him.

"Bingo."

"I still say you're sexually insecure."

Myron shrugged, palms raised. "Who isn't?"

"True." She shifted her rear. Vinyl on vinyl. Grrrr sound. "So why don't you ask me out on a date?"

"I think we just went over this."

"You find me attractive, right? What you see, I mean."

"Yes."

"And we're having a nice talk?"

"Yes."

"You find me interesting? Fun to be with?"

"Yes and yes."

"And you're single and unattached?"

He swallowed. "Two more yesses."

"So?"

"So—and again, don't take this personally—"

"But it's that penis thing again."

"Bingo."

Thrill leaned back, fiddled with the neckline zipper, pulled it up a bit. "Hey, it's a first date. We don't have to end up naked."

Myron thought about that. "Oh."

"You sound surprised."

"No . . . I mean—"

"Maybe I'm not that easy."

"My mistake for presuming . . . I mean, you're hanging out in this bar."

"So?"

"So I didn't think most of the patrons in here played hard to get. To quote Woody Allen, 'How did I misread those signs?' "

Thrill didn't hesitate. *"Play It Again, Sam."*

"If you are a woman," Myron said, "I may be falling in love."

"Thank you. And if we're reading signs from being in this bar, what are you doing here? You with your penis issue."

"Good point."

"So?"

"So what?"

"So why don't you ask me out?" Again with the smolder. "We could hold hands. Maybe kiss. You might even sneak a hand under my shirt, go for a little second base. The way you've been ogling, it's almost like you're there anyway."

"I'm not ogling," Myron said.

"No?"

"If I've been looking—and note I said *if*—it would be purely for the sake of gender clarification, I assure you."

"Thanks for straightening that out. But my point is, we can just go and have dinner. Or go to a movie. We don't have to have any genital contact."

Myron shook his head. "I'd still be wondering."

"Ah, but don't you like a little mystery?"

"I like mystery in lots of arenas. But when it comes to trouser content, well, I'm a pretty traditional guy."

Thrill shrugged. "I still don't understand why you're here."

"I'm looking for someone." He took out a photograph of Clu Haid and showed it to her. "Do you know him?"

Thrill looked at the photograph and frowned. "I thought you said you're a sports agent."

"I am. He was a client."

"Was?"

"He was murdered."

"He's the baseball player?"

Myron nodded. "Have you seen him here?"

Thrill grabbed a piece of paper and wrote something down. "Here's my phone number, Myron. Call me sometime."

"What about the guy in the photograph?"

Thrill handed him the scrap of paper, jumped off the stool, and undulated away. Myron watched her movements closely, looking for, umm, a concealed weapon. Big Cyndi elbowed him. He almost fell off the stool.

"This is Pat," Big Cyndi said.

Pat the bartender looked like someone Archie Bunker might have hired to work his place. He was mid-fifties, short, gray-haired, slouch-shouldered, world-weary. Even his mustache—one of those gray-turning-to-yellow models—drooped as though it'd seen it all. Pat's sleeves were rolled up, revealing Popeye-size forearms covered with hair. Myron hoped like hell Pat was a guy. This place was giving him a headache.

Behind Pat was a giant mirror. Next to that, a wall with the words *Customer Hall of Fame* painted in pink. The wall was covered with framed head shots of big-time right-wingers. Pat Buchanan. Jerry Falwell. Pat Robertson. Newt Gingrich. Jesse Helms.

Pat saw him looking at the photographs. "Ever notice that."

"Notice what?"

"How all the big antifags have sexually ambiguous first names? Pat, Chris, Jesse, Jerry. Could be a guy, could be a girl. See what I'm saying?"

Myron said, "Uh-huh."

"And what kind of name is Newt?" Pat added. "I mean, how the hell do you grow up with a healthy sexual attitude with a name like Newt?"

"I don't know."

"My theory?" Pat shrugged, wiped the bar with a dishrag. "These narrow assholes were all teased a lot as children. Makes them hostile on the whole gender issue."

"Interesting theory," Myron said. "But isn't your name Pat?"

"Yeah, well, I hate fags too," Pat said. "But they tip well."

Pat winked at Big Cyndi. Big Cyndi winked back. The jukebox changed songs. Lou Rawls crooned "Love Is in the Air." Timing.

The right-wing head shots were all "autographed." Jesse Helms's read: "I'm sore all over, Love and kisses, Jesse." Blunt. Several Xs and Os followed. There was also a big lipstick kiss impression as though Jesse himself had puckered up and laid down a wet one. Eeeuw.

Pat started cleaning out a beer mug with the dishrag. Casually. Myron half expected him to spit in it like in an old western. "So what can I get you?"

"Are you a sports fan?" Myron asked.

"You taking a poll?"

That line. It was always such a riot. Myron tried again.

"Does the name Clu Haid mean anything to you?"

Myron watched for a reaction but didn't get one. Meant nothing. The guy looked like a lifetime bartender. They show about as much range as a *Baywatch* regular. Hmm. Now why was that show on his mind?

"I asked you—"

"Name means nothing to me."

Big Cyndi said, "Please, Pat."

He shot her a look. "You heard me, Big C. I don't know him."

Myron pressed it. "Never heard of Clu Haid?"

"That's right."

"How about the New York Yankees?"

"I haven't followed them since the Mick retired."

Myron put the photograph of Clu Haid on the bar. "Ever seen him in here?"

Someone called out for a draft. Pat drew it. When he came back, he spoke to Big Cyndi. "This guy a cop?"

"No," Big Cyndi said.

"Then the answer is no."

"And if I was a cop?" Myron asked.

"Then the answer would be no . . . sir." Myron noticed that Pat had never so much as glanced at the photograph. "I might also add a little song and dance about how I'm too busy to notice faces in here. And how most people, especially celebrities, don't show their real faces in here anyway."

"I see," Myron said. He reached into his wallet, took out a fifty. "And if I showed you a photograph of Ulysses S. Grant?"

The jukebox changed songs. The Flying Machine started crooning for Rosemarie to "smile a little smile for me, Rosemarie." The Flying Machine. Myron had remembered the group's name. What did that say about a man?

"Keep your money," Pat said. "Keep your picture. Keep your questions. I don't like trouble."

"And this guy means trouble?"

"I haven't even looked at the picture, pal. And I don't plan to. Take a hike."

Big Cyndi stepped in. "Pat," she said, "please can't you help"—she batted her eyelashes; picture two crabs on their backs in the blazing sun—"for me?"

"Hey, Big C, I love you, you know that. But suppose I came into Leather-N-Lust with pictures? You gonna be anxious to help?"

Big Cyndi thought about that. "I guess not."

"There you go. I got customers."

"Fine," Myron said. He picked up the photograph. "Then maybe I'll stick around. Pass the picture around the room. Ask some questions. Maybe I'll stake this place out. Indiscreetly. Take photos of people entering and leaving this fine establishment."

Pat shook his head, smiled a bit. "You're one dumb son of a bitch, you know that."

"I'll do it," Myron said. "I don't want to, but I'll camp out on your doorstep with a camera."

Pat gave Myron a long look. Hard to read. Part hostile maybe. Mostly bored. "Big C, head out of here for a few minutes."

"No."

"Then I don't talk."

Myron turned to her, nodded. Big Cyndi shook her head. Myron pulled her aside. "What's the problem?"

"You shouldn't make threats in here, Mr. Bolitar."

"I know what I'm doing."

"I warned you about this place. I can't leave you alone."

"You'll be right outside. I can take care of myself."

When Big Cyndi frowned, her face resembled a freshly painted totem pole. "I don't like it."

"We have no choice."

She sighed. Picture Mount Vesuvius bubbling up a bit of lava. "Be careful."

"I will."

She lumbered toward the exit. The place was packed and Big Cyndi took up a wide berth. Still, people parted with a speed that would have made Moses jot notes. When she was all the way out the door, Myron turned back to Pat. "Well?"

"Well, you're a dumb asshole."

It happened without warning. Two hands snaked under Myron's arms, the fingers locking behind his neck. A classic full nelson. The hold was tightened, pushing back his arms like chicken wings. Myron felt something hot rip across his shoulder blades.

A voice near his ear whispered, "Care to dance, dreamboat?"

When it came to hand-to-hand combat, Myron was no Win, but he was no slouch either. He thus knew that if the perpetrator was good, there was no way to break a full nelson. That was why they were illegal in real wrestling matches. If you were standing, you could try to stomp on the person's instep. But only a moron fell for that, and a moron would not have had the speed or the strength to get this far. And Myron was not standing.

Myron's elbows were high up in the air, marionette fashion, his face helplessly exposed. The powerful arms locking him were covered in cardigan. Soft yellow cardigan, as a matter of fact. As in a soft yellow cardigan sweater. Jesus. Myron struggled. Nothing doing. The cardigan-clad arms pulled Myron's head back and then snapped it toward the bar, face first. Myron could do nothing but close his eyes. He tucked his chin just enough to keep his nose from taking the brunt of the blow. But his head bounced off the varnished teak in a way it was never intended to, jarring his skull. Something on his forehead split open. His head swam. He saw stars.

Another set of hands scooped up Myron's feet. He was in the air now and moving and very dizzy. Hands emptied his pockets. A door opened. Myron was carried through it into a dark room. The grip was released, and Myron fell like a potato sack onto his tailbone. The whole process, from the onset of the full nelson to the moment he was dumped on the floor, took all of eight seconds.

A light was snapped on. Myron touched his forehead and felt something sticky. Blood. He looked up at his attackers.

Two women.

No, cross-dressers. Both with blond wigs. One had gone with early-eighties Mall Girl hair—lots of height and teased more than a bed-wetter. The other one—the one with the soft yellow cardigan sweater (mono-grammed, for those who cared)—had hair like Veronica Lake on a particularly nasty bender.

Myron started to get to his feet. Veronica Lake let out a squeal and threw a side kick. The kick was fast and landed hard on his chest. Myron heard himself make a noise like "pluuu" and landed back on his rear. His hand automatically reached for his cellular. He'd hit the memory button and call Win. Then stall.

The phone was gone.

He looked up. Mall Girl had it. Damn. He took in his surroundings. There was a great view of the bar and Pat the bartender's back. He remembered the mirror. Of course. One-way glass. The patrons saw a mirror. The people back here saw, well, everything. Hard to steal from the till when you never knew who was watching.

The walls were corked and thus soundproof. The floor was cheap linoleum. Easier to clean, he guessed. Despite that, there were specks of blood on it. Not his. These specks were old and dried. But they were there. No mistaking them for something else. And Myron knew why. In a word: intimidation.

This was a classic pounding room. Lots of places have them. Especially sports arenas. Not so much now as in the old days. There was a time when an unruly fan was more than just escorted out of the stadium. The security guards took him into a back room and pounded on him a bit. It was fairly safe. What could the unruly fan claim after the fact? He was drunk off his rocker, had probably gotten into a fight in the stands, whatever. So the security boys added a few extra bruises for good measure. Who's to say where the bruises came from? And if the unruly fan threatened to press charges or make noise, stadium officials could whack him back with charges of public drunkenness and assault and whatever else they could dream up. They could also produce a dozen security guards to back their story and none to back the unruly fan's.

So the fan let it drop. And the pounding rooms remained. Probably still do in some places.

Veronica Lake giggled. It was not a pretty sound. "Care to dance, dreamboat?" he-she asked again.

"Let's wait for a slow song," Myron said.

A third cross-dresser stepped into the room. A redhead. He-she looked a lot like Bonnie Franklin, the plucky mother on the old sitcom *One Day at a Time*. The resemblance was, in fact, rather uncanny—the perfect mix of determination and cutes. Spunky. Scrappy.

"Where's Schneider?" Myron asked.

No reply.

Veronica Lake said, "Stand up, dreamboat."

"The blood on the floor," Myron said.

"What?"

"It's a nice touch, but it's overkill, don't you think?"

Veronica Lake lifted her right foot and pulled on her heel. It came off. Sort of. The heel was a covering actually. A sheath. For a steel blade.

Veronica showed it to Myron with an impressive display of martial art high kicks, the blade gleaming in the light.

Bonnie Franklin and Mall Girl started giggling.

Myron kept the fear at bay and looked steadily at Veronica Lake. "Are you new at cross-dressing?" he asked.

Veronica stopped kicking. "What?"

"I mean, aren't you taking the whole *stiletto* heel thing too far?"

Not his best joke, but anything to stall. Veronica looked at Mall Girl. Mall Girl looked at Bonnie Franklin. Then Veronica suddenly threw a sweep kick, leading with the blade heel. Myron saw the glint of steel shoot toward him. He rolled back, but the blade still sliced through his shirt and into his skin. He let out a little cry and looked down wide-eyed. The cut wasn't deep, but he was bleeding.

The three spread out, making fists. Bonnie Franklin had something in her hand. A black club maybe. Myron did not like this. He tried to spring to his feet, but again Veronica threw a kick. He leaped high, but the blade still hit his lower leg. He actually felt the blade get caught on the shin bone before scraping itself off.

Myron's heart was pounding now. More blood. Jesus Christ. Something about seeing your own blood. His breathing was too fast. *Keep cool,* he reminded himself. *Think.*

He faked left to the spot where Bonnie Franklin stood with the baton. Then he coiled right, his fist at the ready. Without hesitating, he threw a punch at the advancing Mall Girl. His knuckles landed flush below the eye and Mall Girl went down.

That was when Myron felt his heart stop.

There was a zapping sound and the back of his knee exploded. Myron spun in pure agony. His body jolted. Searing pain burst out of the nerve bundle behind the knee and traveled everywhere in an electric surge. He looked behind him. Bonnie Franklin had merely touched him with the baton. His legs seized up, lost power. He collapsed back to the floor and writhed fish-on-boat-deck fashion. His stomach clenched. Nausea consumed him.

"That was the lowest setting," Bonnie Franklin said, voice high-pitched little girl. "Just gets the cow's attention."

Myron looked up, trying to stop his body from quaking. Veronica lifted his leg and placed the heel blade near his face. One quick stomp and he was done. Bonnie showed him the cattle prod again. Myron felt a fresh shiver go through him. He looked through the one-way glass. No sign of Big Cyndi or any cavalry.

Now what?

Bonnie Franklin did the talking. "Why are you here?"

He focused on the cattle prod and how to avoid experiencing its wrath again. "I was asking about someone," he said.

Mall Girl had recovered. She-he stood up over him holding her-his face. "He hit me!" Her tone was a little deeper now, the shock and hurt dropping the feminine facade a bit.

Myron stayed still.

"You bitch!"

Mall Girl grimaced and threw a kick as though Myron's rib cage were a football. Myron saw the kick coming, saw the heel blade, saw the cattle prod, closed his eyes, and let it land.

He fell back.

Bonnie Franklin continued with the questions. "Who were you asking about?"

No secret. "Clu Haid."

"Why?"

"Because I wanted to know if he'd been here."

"Why?"

Telling them he was looking for his killer might not be the wisest course of action, especially if said killer was in the room. "He was a client of mine."

"So?"

"Bitch!" It was Mall Girl again. Another kick. It again landed on the bottom tip of the rib cage and hurt like hell. Myron swallowed away some bile that had worked its way up. He looked through the one-way glass again. Still no Big Cyndi. Blood flowed from the knife wounds to his chest and leg. His insides still trembled from the electric shock. He looked into the eyes of Veronica Lake. The calm eyes. Win had them too. The great ones always do.

"Who do you work for?" Bonnie asked.

"No one."

"Then why would you care if he came here?"

"I'm just trying to put some things together," he said.

"What things?"

"Just general stuff."

Bonnie Franklin looked at Veronica Lake. Both nodded. Then Bonnie Franklin made a show of turning up the cattle prod. " 'General stuff' is an unacceptable response."

Panic squeezed Myron's gut. "Wait—"

"No, I think not." Bonnie reached toward him with the cattle prod.

Myron's eyes widened. No choice really. He had to try it now. If the prod hit him again, he'd have nothing left. He just had to hope Veronica would not kill him.

He had been planning the move for the past ten seconds. Now he rolled all the way back over his neck and head. He landed on his feet and without warning shot himself forward as though from a cannon. The three cross-dressers backed off, prepared for the attack. But an attack would be suicide. Myron knew that. There were three of them, two armed, at least one very good. Myron could never beat them. He needed to surprise them. So he did. By *not* going for them.

He went instead for the one-way glass.

His legs had pushed off full throttle, propelling him rocket-ship fashion toward the glass. By the time his three captors realized what he was doing, it was too late. Myron squeezed his eyes shut, made two fists, and hit the glass with his full weight, Superman style. He held nothing back. If the glass did not give, he was a dead man.

The glass shattered on impact.

The sound was enormous, all-consuming. Myron flew through it, glass clattering to the floor around him. When he landed, he tucked himself into a tight ball. He hit the floor and rolled. Tiny shards of mirror bit into his skin. He ignored the pain, kept rolling, crashing hard into the bar. Bottles fell.

Big Cyndi had talked about the place's reputation. Myron was counting on that. And the Take A Guess clientele did not disappoint.

A pure New York melee ensued.

Tables were thrown. People screamed. Someone flew over the bar and landed on top of Myron. More glass shattered. Myron tried to get to his feet, but it wasn't happening. From his right, he saw a door open. Mall Girl emerged.

"Bitch!"

Mall Girl started toward him, carrying Bonnie's cattle prod. Myron tried to scramble away, but he couldn't get his bearings. Mall Girl kept coming, drawing closer.

And then Mall Girl disappeared.

It was like a scene from a cartoon, where the big dog punches Sylvester the Cat, and Sylvester flies across the room and the oversize fist stays there for a few seconds.

In this case the oversize fist belonged to Big Cyndi.

Bodies flew. Glasses flew. Chairs flew. Big Cyndi ignored it all. She scooped Myron up and threw him over her shoulder like a firefighter. They rushed outside as police sirens clawed through the milky night air.

16

B
ack at the Dakota, Win tsk-tsked and said, "You let a couple of girls beat you up?"

"They weren't girls."

Win took a sip of cognac. Myron gulped some Yoo-Hoo. "Tomorrow night," Win said, "we'll go back to this bar. Together."

It was not something Myron wanted to think about right now. Win called a doctor. It was after two in the morning, but the doctor, a gray-haired man straight from central casting, arrived in fifteen minutes. Nothing broken, he declared with a professional chuckle. Most of the medical treatment consisted of cleaning out the cuts from the heel blade and window bits. The two heel slices—the one on his stomach was shaped like a Z—required stitches. All in all, painful but relatively harmless.

The doctor tossed Myron some Tylenol with codeine, closed up his medical bag, tipped his hat, departed. Myron finished his Yoo-Hoo and stood slowly. He wanted to take a shower, but the doctor had told him to wait until the morning. He swallowed a couple of tablets and hit the sheets. When he fell asleep, he dreamed about Brenda.

In the morning he called Hester Crimstein at her apartment. The machine picked up. Myron said it was urgent. Midway through his message Hester took the call.

"I need to see Esperanza," he told the attorney. "Now."

Surprisingly, the attorney hesitated for only a moment before saying, "Okay."

*   *   *

"I killed someone," Myron said.

Esperanza sat across from him.

"I don't mean I actually fired a gun. But I might as well have. In many ways what I did was worse."

Esperanza kept her eyes on him. "This happened right before you ran away?"

"Within a couple of weeks, yes."

"But that's not why you left."

His mouth felt dry. "I guess not."

"You ran away because of Brenda."

Myron did not answer.

Esperanza crossed her arms. "So why are you sharing this little tidbit with me?"

"I'm not sure."

"I am," she said.

"Oh?"

"It's something of a ploy. You hoped that your big confession would help me open up."

"No," Myron said.

"Then?"

"You're the one I talk to about things like this."

She almost smiled. "Even now?"

"I don't understand why you're shutting me out," he said. "And okay, maybe I do hold out some hope that talking about this will help us return to—I don't know—some kind of sense of normalcy. Or maybe I just need to talk about this. Win wouldn't understand. The person I killed was evil incarnate. It would have presented him with a moral dilemma no more complex than choosing a tie."

"And this moral dilemma haunts you?"

"The problem is," Myron said, "it doesn't."

Esperanza nodded. "Ah."

"The person deserved it," he went on. "The courts had no evidence."

"So you played vigilante."

"In a sense."

"And that bothers you? No, wait, it doesn't bother you."

"Right."

"So you're losing sleep over the fact that you're not losing sleep."

He smiled, spread his hands. "See why I come to you?"

Esperanza crossed her legs and looked up in the air. "When I first met you and Win, I wondered about your friendship. About what first attracted you to each other. I thought maybe Win was a latent homosexual."

"Why does everyone say that? Can't two men just—"

"I was wrong," she interrupted. "And don't get all defensive, it'll make people wonder. You guys aren't gay. I realized that early on. Like I said, it was just a thought. Then I wondered if it was simply the old adage 'Opposites attract.' Maybe that's part of it." She stopped.

"And?" Myron prompted.

"And maybe you two are more alike than either one of you wants to believe. I don't want to get too deep here, but Win sees you as his humanity. If you like him, he reasons, how bad can he be? You, on the other hand, see him as a cold dose of reality. Win's logic is scary, but it's oddly appealing. There is a little part in all of us that likes what he does, the same side of us that thinks the Iranians might be on to something when they cut off a thief's hand. You grew up with all that suburban liberal crap about the disadvantaged. But now real-life experience is teaching you that some people are just plain evil. It shifts you a little closer to Win."

"So you're saying I'm becoming like Win? Gee, that's comforting."

"I'm saying your reaction is human. I don't like it. I don't think it's right. You may indeed be sinking into a quagmire. Bending the rules is getting easier and easier for you. Maybe the person you killed deserved it, but if you want to hear that, if you want absolution, go to Win."

Silence.

Esperanza's fingers fluttered near her mouth, debating between biting the nails and plucking her lower lip. "You've always been the finest person I know," she said. "Don't let anybody change that, okay?"

He swallowed, nodded.

"You're not bending the rules anymore," she continued. "You're decimating them. Just yesterday you told me you'd lie under oath to protect me."

"That's different."

Esperanza looked straight at him. "Are you sure about that?"

"Yes. I'll do whatever I have to to protect you."

"Including breaking laws? That's my point, Myron."

He shifted in his chair.

"And one other thing," she said. "You're using this whole moral dilemma thing to distract yourself from two truths you don't want to face."

"What truths?"

"One, Brenda."

"And two?"

Esperanza smiled. "Skipped over one pretty fast."

"And two?" he repeated.

Her smile was gentle, understanding. "Two, it gets your mind off why you're really here."

"And why's that?"

"You're starting to do more than wonder if I killed Clu. And you're trying to find a way to rationalize it away if I did. You killed once, ergo it may be justifiable if I killed too. You just want to hear a reason."

"He hit you," Myron said. "In the parking garage."

She said nothing.

"The radio said they found pubic hairs in his apartment—"

"Don't go there," she said.

"I have to."

"Just stay out."

"I can't."

"I don't need your help."

"There's more to it than that. I'm involved in this."

"Only because you want to be."

"Did Clu tell you I was in danger?"

She said nothing.

"He told my parents that. And Jessica. I thought at first it was hyperbole. But maybe it's not. I got this weird diskette in the mail. There was an image of a young girl."

"You're ranting," she said. "You think you're ready for this, but you're not. Learn something from your past mistakes. Keep away from this."

"But it won't keep away from me," Myron said. "Why did Clu say I was in danger? Why did he hit you? What happened at the Take A Guess bar?"

She shook her head. "Guard."

The guard opened the door. Esperanza kept her eyes down. She turned and left the room without looking back at Myron. Myron sat alone for a few seconds, gathered his thoughts. He checked his watch. Nine forty-five. Plenty of time to get to Yankee Stadium for his eleven o'clock meeting with Sophie and Jared Mayor. He had barely left the room when a man approached him.

"Mr. Bolitar?"

"Yes."

"This is for you."

The man handed him an envelope and disappeared. Myron opened it. A subpoena from the Bergen County district attorney's office. Case heading: "People of Bergen County v. Esperanza Diaz." Well, well. Esperanza and Hester had been right not to tell him anything.

He stuffed it into his pocket. At least now he wouldn't have to lie.

17

Myron did what every good boy should do when he gets into legal trouble: He called his mommy.

"Your aunt Clara will handle the subpoena," Mom said.

Aunt Clara wasn't really his aunt, just an old friend from the neighborhood. On the High Holy Days she still pinched Myron's cheek and cried out, "What a *punim*!" Myron sort of hoped she wouldn't do that in front of the judge: "Your Honor, I ask you to look at this face: Is that a *punim* or is that a *punim*?"

"Okay," Myron said.

"I'll call her, she'll call the DA. In the meantime you say nothing, understand?"

"Yes."

"See now, Mr. Smarty Pants? See what I was telling you now? About Hester Crimstein being right?"

"Yeah, Mom, whatever."

"Don't whatever me. They've subpoenaed you. But because Esperanza wouldn't tell you anything, you can't hurt her case."

"I see that, Mom."

"Good. Now let me go call Aunt Clara."

She hung up. And Mr. Smarty Pants did likewise.

Bluntly put, Yankee Stadium was located in a cesspool section of the ever-eroding Bronx. It didn't much matter. Whenever you first caught sight of the famed sports edifice, you still fell into an immediate church hush. Couldn't help it. Memories swarmed in and burrowed down. Images flashed in and out. His youth. A small child crammed standing on the 4 train, holding Dad's seemingly giant hand, looking up into his gentle face, the pregame anticipation tingling through every part of him. Dad had caught a fly ball when Myron was five years old. He could still see it sometimes—the arc of white rawhide, the crowd standing, his dad's arm stretching to an impossible height, the ball landing on the palm with a happy smack, the warm beam coming off Dad's face when he handed the prized possession to his son. Myron still had that ball, browning in the basement of his parents' house.

Basketball was Myron's sport of choice, and football was probably his favorite to watch on TV. Tennis was the game of princes, golf the game of kings. But baseball was magic. Early childhood memories are faint, but almost every boy can recall his first major-league baseball game. He can remember the score, who hit a home run, who pitched. But mostly he remembers his father. The smell of his after-shave is wrapped up in the smells of baseball—the freshly cut grass, the summer air, the hot dogs, the stale popcorn, the spilled beer, the overoiled glove complete with baseball breaking in the pocket. He remembers the visiting team, the way Yaz tossed grounders to warm up Petrocelli at short, the way the hecklers made gentle fun of Frank Howard's TV commercials for Nestlé's Quik, the way the game's greats rounded second and slid headfirst into third. You remember your sibling keeping stats, studying the lineups the way rabbinical scholars study the Talmud, baseball cards gripped in your hand, the ease and pace of a slow summer afternoon, Mom spending more time sunning herself than watching the action. You remember Dad buying you a pennant of the visiting team and later hanging it on your wall in a ceremony equal to the Celtics raising a banner in the old Boston Garden. You remember the way the players in the bullpen looked so relaxed, big wads of chew distorting their cheeks. You remember your healthy, respectful hate for the visiting team's superstars, the pure joy of going on Bat Day and treasuring that piece of wood as though it'd come straight from Honus Wagner's locker.

Show me a boy who didn't dream of being a big leaguer before age seven, before Training League or whatever slowly began to thin the herd in one of life's earliest lessons that the world can and will disappoint you. Show me a boy who doesn't remember wearing his Little League cap to school when the teachers would allow it, keeping it pitched high with a favorite baseball card tucked inside, wearing it to the dinner table, sleeping with it on the night table next to his bed. Show me a boy who doesn't remember playing catch with his father on the weekends or, better, on those precious summer nights when Dad would rush home from his job, shake off his work clothes, put on a T-shirt that was always a little too small, grab a mitt, and head into the backyard before the final rays faded away. Show me a boy who didn't stare in awe at how far his father could hit or throw a baseball—no matter how bad an athlete his father was, no matter how spastic or what have you—and for that shining moment Dad was transformed into a man of unimaginable ability and strength.

Only baseball had that magic.

The new majority owner of the New York Yankees was Sophie Mayor. She and her husband, Gary, had shocked the baseball world by buying the team from the longtime unpopular owner Vincent Riverton less than a year ago. Most fans had applauded. Vincent Riverton, a publishing mogul, had a love-hate relationship with the public (mostly hate) and the Mayors, a techno-nouveau-riche pair who had found their fortune through computer software, promised a more hands-off approach. Gary Mayor had grown up in the Bronx and promised a return to the days of the Mick and DiMaggio. The fans were thrilled.

But tragedy struck pretty fast. Two weeks before the deal to buy was finalized, Gary Mayor died of a sudden heart attack. Sophie Mayor, who had always been an equal, if not dominating, partner in the software business, insisted on going ahead with the transaction. She had public support and sympathy, but Gary and his roots had been the rope tethering her to the public. Sophie was a midwesterner, and with her love of hunting mixed with her background as a math genius, she hit the prenatally suspicious New Yorkers as being something of a kook.

Soon after taking over the helm, Sophie made her son Jared, a man with virtually no baseball experience, co-general manager. The public frowned. She made a quick trade, gutting the Yankee farm system on the chance that Clu Haid still had a good year or two left. The public cried. She had stood firm. She wanted a World Series in the Bronx immediately. Trading for Clu Haid was the way to get it. The public was skeptical.

But Clu pitched amazingly well during his first month with the team. His fastball was back over ninety, and his curves were breaking as if they were accepting signals from a remote control. He got better with each outing, and the Yankees grabbed first place. The public was appeased. For a little while anyway, Myron guessed. He had stopped paying attention, but he could imagine the backlash against the Mayor family when Clu tested positive for drugs.

Myron was led immediately into Sophie Mayor's office. She and Jared both stood to greet him. Sophie Mayor was probably mid-fifties, what was commonly called a handsome woman, her hair gray and neat, her back straight, her handshake firm, her arms tawny, her eyes twinkling with hints of mischief and cunning. Jared was twenty-fiveish. He wore his hair parted on the right with no hint of style, wire-rimmed glasses, a blue blazer, and a polka dot bow tie. Youths for George Will.

The office was sparsely decorated, or maybe it just appeared that way because the scene was dominated by a moose head hanging on a wall. A dead moose actually. A live moose is so hard to hang. Quite the decorating touch. Myron tried not to make a face. He almost said, "You must have hated this moose," à la Dudley Moore in *Arthur* but refrained. With age comes maturity.

Myron shook Jared's hand, then turned toward Sophie Mayor.

Sophie pounced. "Where the hell have you been, Myron?"

"Excuse me?"

She pointed to a chair. "Sit."

Like he was a dog. But he obeyed. Jared too. Sophie stayed on her feet and glowered down at him.

"In court yesterday they said something about your being in the Caribbean," she continued.

Myron made a noncommittal "uh-huh" sound.

"Where were you?"

"I was away."

"Away?"

"Yes."

She looked over at her son, then back at Myron. "For how long?"

"Three weeks."

"But Miss Diaz told me you were in town."

Myron said nothing.

Sophie Mayor made two fists and leaned toward him. "Why would she tell me that, Myron?"

"Because she didn't know where I was."

"In other words, she lied to me."

Myron did not bother replying.

"So where were you?" she pressed.

"Out of the country."

"The Caribbean?"

"Yes."

"And you never told anyone?"

Myron shifted in his chair, trying to find an opening or gain some sort of footing here. "I don't mean to sound rude," he said, "but I don't see how my whereabouts are any of your business."

"You don't?" A sharp chortle passed her lips. She looked at her son as if to say, *Do you believe this guy?,* then redirected her laser grays back toward Myron. "I relied on you," she said.

Myron said nothing.

"I bought this team and I decided to be hands-off. I know software. I know computers. I know business. I really don't know much about baseball. But I made one decision. I wanted Clu Haid. I had a feeling about him. I thought he still had something left. So I traded for him. People thought I was nuts—three good prospects for one has-been. I understood that concern. So I went to you, Myron, remember?"

"Yes."

"And you assured me he was going to stay clean."

"Wrong," Myron said. "I said he *wanted* to stay clean."

"Wanted, was going to . . . What is this, a lesson in semantics?"

"He was my client," Myron said. "It's my job to worry about his interests."

"And damn mine?"

"That's not what I said."

"Damn integrity and ethics too? Is that the way you work, Myron?"

"That's not it at all. Sure, we wanted this trade to happen—"

"You wanted it badly," she corrected him.

"Fine, we wanted it badly. But I never promised you he'd stay clean because it's not something I or anyone else can guarantee. I assured you we would try our hardest. I made it part of the deal. I gave you the right to randomly test him at any time."

"You *gave* me the right? I demanded it! And you fought me on it every step of the way."

"We shared the risk," Myron said. "I made his salary contingent on his staying clean. I let you put in a strict morals clause."

She smiled, crossed her arms. "You know who you sound like? Those hypocritical car commercials where General Motors or Ford tout all the pollution-saving devices they've put on their cars. As though they did it on their own. As though they woke up one day more concerned with the environment than the bottom line. They leave out the fact that the government forced them to put on those devices, that they fought the government tooth and nail the whole way."

"He was my client," Myron said again.

"And you think that's an all-purpose excuse?"

"It's my job to get him the best deal."

"Keep telling yourself that, Myron."

"I can't stop a man from returning to an addiction. You knew that."

"But you said you'd watch him. You said you'd work on keeping him straight."

Myron swallowed and shifted in his chair again. "Yes."

"But you didn't watch him, Myron, did you?"

Silence.

"You took a vacation and didn't tell anyone. You left Clu alone. You acted irresponsibly, and so I blame you in part for his falling off the wagon."

Myron opened his mouth, closed it. She was right, of course, but he didn't have the luxury of wallowing in that right now. Later. He'd think about his role in this later. The pain from last night's beating was angrily stirring from its snooze. He reached into his pocket and shook out a couple of extra-strength Tylenols.

Satisfied—or maybe satiated—Sophie Mayor sat down. Seeing the pills, she asked, "Would you like some water?"

"Please."

She nodded at Jared. Jared poured Myron a glass of water and handed it to him. Myron thanked him and swallowed the tablets. The placebo effect jumped in, and he immediately felt better.

Before Sophie Mayor could strike again, Myron tried to shift gears. "Tell me about Clu's failed drug test," he said.

Sophie Mayor looked puzzled. "What's to tell?"

"Clu claimed he was clean."

"And you believe that?"

"I want to look into it."

"Why?"

"Because when Clu was caught in the past, he begged forgiveness and promised to get help. He never pretended a test result was wrong."

She crossed her arms. "And that's evidence of what exactly?"

"Nothing. I'd just like to ask a few questions."

"Ask away then."

"How often did you test him?"

Sophie looked over at her son. His cue. Jared spoke for the first time since greeting Myron at the door. "At least once a week," he said.

"Urine tests?" Myron asked.

"Yes," Jared said.

"And he passed them all? I mean, except for the last one."

"Yes."

Myron shook his head. "Every week? And no other positives? Just that one?"

"That's right."

He looked back at Sophie. "Didn't you find that odd?"

"Why?" she countered. "He'd been trying to stay clean, and he fell off the wagon. It happens every day, doesn't it?"

It did, Myron guessed, and still something about it didn't sit right with him. "But Clu knew you were testing him?"

"I assume so, yes. We'd been testing him at least once a week."

"And how were the tests conducted?"

Sophie again looked over at Jared. Jared asked, "What do you mean?"

"Step by step," Myron said. "What did he do?"

Sophie took that one. "He peed in the cup, Myron. It's pretty simple."

It was never pretty simple. "Did someone watch him urinate?"

"What?"

"Did someone actually witness Clu peeing or did he step into a stall?" Myron said. "Was he naked when he did it or did he have on shorts—"

"What difference does any of that make?"

"Plenty. Clu had spent his lifetime beating these tests. If he knew they were coming, he'd be prepared."

"Prepared how?" Sophie asked.

"Lots of ways, depending on the sophistication of the test," Myron said. "If the testing was more primitive, you can put motor oil on your fingers and let the urine hit them while urinating. The phosphates throw the results out of whack. Some testers know this, so they check for phosphates. If the tester lets the guy urinate in a stall, he can strap clean urine onto his inner thigh and use that. Or the testee keeps the clean urine hidden in a condom or small balloon. He stores it in the lining of his boxer shorts maybe. Or between his toes. Under his armpit. In his mouth even."

"Are you serious?"

"It gets worse. If the testee gets tipped off a strict test is coming up—one where the administrators are watching every move he makes—he'll drain his bladder and use a catheter to pump in clean urine."

Sophie Mayor looked horror-stricken. "He pumps someone else's urine into his bladder?"

"Yes," Myron said.

"Jesus." Then she pinned him down with her eyes. "You seem to know quite a bit about this, Myron."

"So did Clu."

"What are you saying?"

"It raises some questions, that's all."

"He probably got caught by surprise."

"Maybe," Myron said. "But if you were testing him every week, how surprised could he have been?"

"He might have just messed up," Sophie went on. "Drug addicts have a way of doing that."

"Could be. But I'd like to speak with the person who administered the test."

"Dr. Stilwell," Jared said. "He's the team doctor. He handled it. Sawyer Wells assisted him."

"Sawyer Wells, as in the self-help guru?"

"He's a psychologist specializing in human behavior and an excellent motivational therapist," Jared corrected.

Motivational therapist. Uh-huh. "Are either of them around now?"

"No, I don't think so. But they'll be here later. We have a home game tonight."

"Who on the team was especially friendly with Clu? A coach, a player?"

"I really wouldn't know," Jared said.

"Who did he room with on the road?"

Sophie almost smiled. "You really were out of touch, weren't you?"

"Cabral," Jared said. "Enos Cabral. He's a Cuban pitcher."

Myron knew him. He nodded, glancing about, and that was when he saw it. His heart lurched, and it took all his willpower not to scream.

He had just been sweeping the room with his eyes, taking the room in but not really seeing anything, just the normal thing everyone does, when an object snagged his gaze as though on a rusted hook. Myron froze. On the credenza. On the right side of the credenza, mixed in with the other framed photos and the trophies and those latex cubes that encased civic awards and the first issue of Mayor Software stock and the like. Right there. A framed photograph.

A framed photograph of the girl on the computer diskette.

Myron tried to maintain a calm facade. Deep breath in, deep breath out. But he could feel his pulse quicken. His mind fought through the haze, searching for a temporary clearing. He scanned his internal memory banks. *Okay, slow down. Breathe. Keep breathing.*

No wonder the girl had looked familiar to him.

But what was her deal? More memory bank scanning. She was Sophie Mayor's daughter, of course. Jared Mayor's sister. What was her name again? His recollections were vague. What had happened to her? A runaway, right? Ten, fifteen years ago. There had been an estrangement or something. Foul play was not suspected. Or was it? He didn't remember.

"Myron?"

He needed to think. Calmly. He needed space, time. He couldn't just blurt out, "Oh, I got this weird diskette with an image of your daughter melting in blood on it." He had to get out of here. Do some research. Think it through. He stood, clumsily looking at his watch.

"I have to go," he said.

"What?"

"I'd like to speak with Dr. Stilwell as soon as possible," he said.

Sophie's eyes stayed on him. "I don't see the relevance."

"I just explained—"

"What difference would it make? Clu is dead now. The drug test isn't relevant."

"There might be a connection."

"Between his death and a drug test?"

"Yes."

"I'm not sure I agree."

"I'd still like to check it out. I have that right."

"What right?"

"If the drug test was inconclusive, it changes things."

"Changes what—" Then Sophie stopped, smiled a bit, and nodded to herself. "I think I see now."

Myron said nothing.

"You mean in terms of his contract, don't you?"

"I have to go," he repeated.

She leaned back and recrossed her arms. "Well, Myron, I have to hand it to you. You are definitely an agent. Trying to squeeze one more commission out of a corpse, eh?"

Myron let the insult roll off. "If Clu was clean, his contract would still be valid. You'd owe the family at least three million dollars."

"So this is a shakedown? You're here for money?"

He glanced at the picture of the young girl again. He remembered the diskette, the laugh, the blood. "Right now," he said, "I'd just like to talk with the team doctor."

Sophie Mayor looked at him like he was a turd on the carpet. "Get out of my office, Myron."

"Will you let me speak to the doctor?"

"You don't have any legal standing here."

"I think I do."

"You don't, believe me. The blood money has run dry here. Get out, Myron. Now."

He took one more look at the photograph. Now was not the time to argue the point. He hurried out the door.

18

Myron was starting to hurt. The Tylenol alone wasn't doing the trick. He had Tylenol with codeine in his back pocket, but he did not dare. He needed to stay sharp, and that stuff put him to sleep faster than, er, sex. He quickly cataloged the sore spots. His sliced-up shin hurt most, followed closely by his bruised ribs. The rest of the aches were an almost welcome distraction. But the pain made him conscious of every movement.

When he got back to his office, Big Cyndi handed him a huge pile of message slips.

"How many reporters have called?" he asked.

"I stopped counting, Mr. Bolitar."

"Any messages from Bruce Taylor?"

"Yes."

Bruce covered the Mets, not the Yankees. But every reporter wanted in on this story. Bruce was also something of a friend. He would know about Sophie Mayor's daughter. The question was, of course, how to raise the subject without getting him overly curious.

Myron closed his office door, sat down, dialed a number. A voice answered on the first ring.

"Taylor."

"Hey, Brucie."

"Myron? Jesus Christ. Hey, I appreciate you calling me back."

"Sure, Bruce. I love to cooperate with my favorite reporter."

Pause. Then: "Uh-oh."

"What?" Myron said.

"This is too easy."

"Pardon."

"Okay, Myron, let's skip the part where you break down my defenses with your supernatural charisma. Cut to it."

"I want to make a deal."

"I'm listening."

"I'm not willing to make a statement yet. But when I do, you get first crack. An exclusive."

"An exclusive? Sheesh, Myron, you really do know your media lingo, don't you?"

"I could have said scoop. It's one of my favorite words."

"Okay, Myron, great. So in return for your *not* telling me anything, you get what?"

"Just some information. But you don't read into anything that I ask and you don't report on it. You're just my source."

"More like your bitch," Bruce said.

"If that's what you're into."

"Not today, dear, I have a headache. So let me get this straight. You tell me nothing. I report nothing. In return I get to tell you everything. Sorry, big guy, no deal."

"Bye-bye, Brucie."

"Whoa, whoa, Myron, hold up. Christ, I'm not a general manager. Don't pull that negotiating crap on me. Look, let's stop tugging each other's chains here. This is what we do: You give me something. A statement, anything. It can be as innocuous as you want to make it. But I want to be the first with a statement from Myron Bolitar. Then I tell you what you want, I keep quiet, you give me the exclusive scoop or whatever before everyone else. Deal?"

"Deal," Myron said. "Here's your statement: Esperanza Diaz did not kill Clu Haid. I stand behind her one hundred percent."

"Was she having an affair with Clu?"

"That's my statement, Bruce. Period."

"Okay, fine, but what's this about your being out of the country at the time of the murder?"

"A statement, Bruce. As in, 'no further comment.' As in, 'I'll be answering no questions today.' "

"Hey, it's already public knowledge. I just want a confirmation. You were in the Caribbean, right?"

"Right."

"Where in the Caribbean?"

"No comment."

"Why not? Were you really in the Cayman Islands?"

"No, I was not in the Caymans."

"Then where?"

See how reporters work? "No comment."

"I called you immediately following Clu's positive drug test. Esperanza said you were in town but would not comment."

"And I still won't," Myron said. "Now it's your turn, Bruce."

"Come on, Myron, you're giving me nothing here."

"We had a deal."

"Yeah, all right, sure, I want to be fair," he said in a tone that made it clear he would start up again later. "Ask away."

Casual, casual. He couldn't just ask about Sophie Mayor's daughter. Subtlety. That was the key. Myron's office door opened, and Win swept into the room. Myron signaled with one finger. Win nodded and opened a closet door. There was a full-length mirror on the inside back. Win stared at his reflection and smiled. A nice way of passing the time.

"What were the rumors about Clu?" Myron asked.

"You mean before the positive test results?"

"Yes."

"Time bomb," Bruce said.

"Explain."

"He was pitching great, no question. And he looked good. Thinned down, seemed focused. But then a week or so before the drug test, he started looking like hell. Christ, you must have seen it, right? Or were you out of the country then too?"

"Just go on, Bruce."

"What else can I tell you? With Clu you've seen it a hundred times before. The guy breaks your heart. His arm was touched by God. The rest of him was, well, just touched, if you follow my meaning."

"So there were signs before the positive test?"

"Yeah, I guess. In hindsight, sure there were lots of signs. I hear his wife threw him out. He was unshaven, red-eyed, that kind of thing."

"It didn't have to be drugs," Myron said.

"True. It could have been booze."

"Or maybe it was just the strain of marital discord."

"Look, Myron, maybe some guys like Orel Hershiser get the benefit of the doubt. But when it comes to Clu Haid or Steve Howe or some other perennial screwup, you figure it's substance abuse, and eleven times out of ten you're right."

Myron looked over at Win. Win had finished patting the blond locks and was now using the mirror to practice his different smiles. Right now he was working on roguish.

Subtle, Myron reminded himself, subtle. . . . "Bruce?"

"Yeah?"

"What can you tell me about Sophie Mayor?"

"What about her?"

"Nothing specific."

"Just curious, huh?"

"Right, curious."

"Sure you are," Bruce said.

"How much damage did Clu's drug test do to her?"

"Tremendous damage. But you know this. Sophie Mayor stuck her neck out, and for a while she was a genius. Then Clu fails the drug test, and presto, she's an idiotic bimbo who should let the men run things."

"So tell me about her background."

"Background?"

"Yes. I want to get a feel for her."

"Why?" Bruce asked. Then: "Ah, what the hell. She's from Kansas, I think, or Iowa or Indiana or Montana. Someplace like that. An aged Ivory Girl type. Loves fishing, hunting, all that nature stuff. She was also something of a math prodigy. Came East to go to MIT. That's where she met Gary Mayor. They got married and lived most of their lives as science professors. He taught at Brandeis; she taught at Tufts. They developed a software program for personal finance in the early eighties and suddenly went from middle-class professors to millionaires. They took the company public in '94 and changed the *m* to a *b*."

"The *m* to a *b*?"

"Millionaire to billionaire."

"Oh."

"So the Mayors did what lots of superwealthy people do: They bought a sports franchise. In this case, the Yankees. Gary Mayor grew up loving them. It was going to be a nice toy for him, but of course he never got to enjoy it."

Myron cleared his throat. "And they, uh, have children?" Señor Subtle-o.

"They had two. You know Jared. He's actually a pretty good kid, smart, went to your alma mater, Duke. But everyone hates him because he got the job through nepotism. His main responsibility is to keep an eye on Mommy's investment. My understanding is that he's actually pretty good at that and that he leaves the baseball to the baseball guys."

"Uh-huh."

"They also have a daughter. Or had a daughter."

With great effort, Win sighed, closed the closet door. So difficult to pull himself away from a mirror. He sat across from Myron looking, as always, completely at ease. Myron cleared his throat and said into the phone, "What do you mean, *had* a daughter?"

"The daughter's very estranged. Don't you remember the story?"

"Vaguely. She ran away, right?"

"Right. Her name was Lucy. She took off with a boyfriend, some grunge musician, a few weeks before her eighteenth birthday. This was, I don't know, ten, fifteen years ago. Before the Mayors had any money."

"So where does she live now?"

"Well, that's the thing. No one knows."

"I don't understand."

"She ran away, that much is known for sure. She left them a note, I think. She was going to hit the road with her boyfriend and seek her fortune, the usual teenage stuff. Sophie and Gary Mayor were typical East Coast college professors who read too much Dr. Spock, so they gave their daughter 'space,' figuring of course that she'd come back."

"But she didn't."

"Duh."

"And they never heard from her?"

"Duh again."

"But I remember reading about this a few years ago. Didn't they start a search for her or something?"

"Yeah. First off, the boyfriend came back after a few months. They'd broken up and gone their separate ways. Big shock, right? Anyway, he didn't know where she went. So the Mayors called the police, but they treated it like no big deal. Lucy was eighteen by this time, and she had clearly run away on her own. There was no evidence of foul play or anything and remember that this was before the Mayors had beaucoup bucks."

"And after they became rich?"

"Sophie and Gary tried to find her again. They made it like a search for the missing heiress. The tabloids loved it for a while. There were some wild reports but nothing concrete. Some say Lucy moved overseas. Some say she's living in a commune somewhere. Some say she's dead. Whatever. They never found her, and there was still no sign of foul play, so the story eventually petered out."

Silence. Win looked at Myron and arched an eyebrow. Myron shook his head.

"So why the interest?" Bruce asked.

"I just want to get a feel for the Mayors."

"Uh-huh."

"No big deal."

"Okay, I buy that. Not."

"It's the truth," Myron lied. "And how about using a more up-to-date reference? No one says *not* anymore."

"They don't?" Pause: "Guess I gotta watch more MTV. But Vanilla Ice is still hip, right?"

"Ice, ice, baby."

"Fine, okay, we'll play it your way for now, Myron. But I don't know anything else about Lucy Mayor. You can try a search on Lexis. The papers might have more detail."

"Good idea, thanks. Listen, Bruce, I got another call coming in."

"What? You're just going to cut me loose?"

"That was our deal."

"So why all the questions about the Mayors?"

"Like I said, I want to get a feel for them."

"Does the phrase *what a crock* mean anything to you?"

"Good-bye, Bruce."

"Wait." Pause. Then Bruce said, "Something serious is going down here, right?"

"Clu Haid has been murdered. Esperanza's been arrested for the crime. I'd say that's pretty serious."

"There's more to it. Tell me that much. I won't print it, I promise."

"Truth, Bruce? I don't know yet."

"And when you do?"

"You'll be the first to know."

"You really think Esperanza's innocent? Even with all that evidence?"

"Yes."

"Call me, Myron. If you need anything else. I like Esperanza. I want to help if I can."

Myron hung up. He looked over at Win. Win seemed in deep thought. He was tapping his chin with his index finger. They sat in silence for several seconds.

Win stopped tapping and asked, "Whatever happened to the King Family?"

"You mean the ones with the Christmas specials?"

Win nodded. "Every year you were supposed to watch the King Family Christmas Special. There must have been a hundred of the buggers—big Kings with beards, little Kings in knickers, Mommy Kings, Daddy Kings, Uncle and Aunt and Cousin Kings. Then one year—poof—they're gone. All of them. What happened?"

"I don't know."

"Strange, isn't it?"

"I guess."

"And what did the King clan do the rest of the year?"

"Prepared for the next Christmas special?"

"What a life, no?" Win said. "Christmas passes, and you start thinking about next Christmas. You live in a snow globe of Christmas."

"I guess."

"I wonder where they are now, all those suddenly unemployed Kings. Do they sell cars? Insurance? Are they drug dealers? Do they get sad every Christmas?"

"Yeah, poignant point, Win. By the way, did you come down here for a reason?"

"Discussing the King Family isn't reason enough? Weren't you the one who came up to my office because you didn't understand the meaning of a Sheena Easton song?"

"You're comparing the King Family to Sheena Easton?"

"Yes, well, in truth, I came up here to inform you that I quashed the subpoenas against Lock-Horne."

Myron shouldn't have been surprised. "The power of payoffs," he said with a shake of his head. "It never fails to amaze me."

"*Payoff* is such an offensive term," Win said. "I prefer the more politically correct *assisting the contribution-challenged.*" He sat back, crossed his legs in that way of his, folded his hands on his lap. He gestured at the phone and said, "Explain."

So Myron did. He filled him in on everything, especially on the Lucy Mayor incident. When Myron was finished, Win said, "Puzzling."

"Agreed."

"But I am not sure I see a connection."

"Someone mails me a diskette with Lucy Mayor's image on it and a little while later Clu is murdered. You think that's just a coincidence?"

Win mulled that over. "Too early to tell," he concluded. "Let's do a little recap, shall we?"

"Go ahead."

"Let's start with a straight time line: Clu gets traded to New York, he pitches well, he gets thrown out by Bonnie, he starts collapsing, he fails a drug test, he desperately searches for you, he comes to me and withdraws two hundred thousand dollars, he strikes Esperanza, he gets murdered." Win stopped. "That sound fair?"

"Yes."

"Now let's explore some possible tangents from this line."

"Let's."

"One, our old fraternity chum Billy Lee Palms appears to be missing. Clu purportedly contacted him shortly before the murder. Aside from that, is there any reason to tie Billy Lee into all this?"

"Not really. And according to his mother, Billy Lee isn't the most dependable tool in the shed."

"So maybe his disappearance has nothing to do with this."

"Maybe."

"But that would be yet another bizarre coincidence," Win said.

"It would at that."

"Fine, let's move on for the moment. Tangent two, this Take A Guess nightspot."

"All we know is that Clu called them."

Win shook his head. "We know a great deal more."

"For example?"

"They overreacted to your visit. Tossing you out would have been one thing. Roughing you up a bit would have been one thing. But this sort of interrogation complete with knife slashes and electrocution—that's overkill."

"Meaning?"

"Meaning that you struck a nerve, poked the hive, stirred the nest, choose your favorite cliché."

"So they're connected into all this."

"Logical," Win said, again doing his best Spock.

"How?"

"Heavens, I haven't a clue."

Myron chewed it over a bit. "I had thought maybe Clu and Esperanza hooked up there."

"And now?"

"Let's say they did hook up there. What would be the big deal about that? Why the overkill?"

"So it's something else."

Myron nodded. "Any more tangents?"

"The big one," Win said. "The disappearance of Lucy Mayor."

"Which happened more than ten years ago."

"And we must confess that her connection is tenuous at best."

"So confessed," Myron said.

Win steepled his fingers and raised the pointers. "But the diskette was addressed to you."

"Yes."

"Ergo we cannot be sure that Lucy Mayor is connected to Clu Haid at all—"

"Right."

"—but we can be sure that Lucy Mayor is somehow connected to you."

"Me?" Myron made a face. "I can't imagine how."

"Think hard. Perhaps you met her once."

Myron shook his head. "Never."

"You might not have known. The woman has been living in some sort of clandestine state for a very long time. Perhaps she was someone you met in a bar, a one-night stand."

"I don't one-night stand."

"That's right," Win said. Then with flat eyes: "God, I wish I were you."

Myron waved him off. "But suppose you're right. Suppose I did meet her but didn't know it. So what? She decides to repay me by sending me a diskette of her face melting into a puddle of blood?"

Win nodded. "Puzzling."

"So where does that leave us?"

"Puzzled."

The speaker buzzed. Myron said, "Yes?"

Big Cyndi said, "Your father is on line one, Mr. Bolitar."

"Thank you." Myron picked up the receiver. "Hi, Dad."

"Hey, Myron. How are you?"

"Good."

"You readjusting to being home?"

"Yeah, I am."

"Happy to be back?"

Dad was stalling. "Yeah, Dad, I'm great."

"All this stuff with Esperanza. It must be keeping you hopping, huh?"

"I guess so, yeah."

"Soooo," Dad said, stretching out the word, "think you have time for lunch with your old man?"

There was a strain in the voice.

"Sure, Dad."

"How about tomorrow? At the club?"

Myron bit back a groan. Not the club. "Sure. Noon, okay?"

"Good, son, that'll be fine."

Dad didn't call him son very often. More like never. Myron switched hands. "Anything wrong, Dad?"

"No, no," he said too quickly. "Everything's fine. I just want to talk to you about something."

"About what?"

"It'll keep, no biggie. See you tomorrow."

Click.

Myron looked at Win. "That was my father."

"Yes, I picked up on that when Big Cyndi said your father was on the line. It was further reemphasized when you said 'Dad' four times during the conversation. I'm gifted that way."

"He wants to have lunch tomorrow."

Win nodded. "And I care because—?"

"Just telling you."

"I'll write about it in my diary tonight," Win said. "In the meantime, I had another thought, vis-à-vis Lucy Mayor."

"I'm listening."

"If you recall, we were trying to figure out who was being injured in all this."

"I recall."

"Clu obviously. Esperanza. You. I."

"Yes."

"Well, we must add a new person: Sophie Mayor."

Myron thought about it. Then he started nodding. "That could very well be the connection. If you wanted to destroy Sophie Mayor, what would you do? First, you'd do something to undermine any support she had with the Yankee fans and management."

"Clu Haid," Win said.

"Right. Then you might hit her in what has to be a vulnerable spot— her missing daughter. I mean, if someone sent her a similar diskette, can you imagine the horror?"

"Which raises an interesting question," Win said.

"What?"

"Are you going to tell her?"

"About the diskette?"

"No, about recent troop movements in Bosnia. Yes, the diskette."

Myron thought about it but not for very long. "I don't see where I have any choice. I have to tell her."

"Perhaps that too is part of the theoretical plan to wear her down," Win said. "Perhaps someone sent you the diskette knowing it would get back to her."

"Maybe. But she still has the right to know. It's not my place to decide what Sophie Mayor is strong enough to handle."

"Too true." Win rose. "I have some contacts trying to locate the official reports on Clu's murder—autopsy, crime scene, witness statements, labs, what have you. But everyone is tight-lipped."

"I got a possible source," Myron said.

"Oh?"

"The Bergen County medical examiner is Sally Li. I know her."

"Through Jessica's father?"

"Yes."

"Go for it," Win said.

Myron watched him head for the door. "Win?"

"Yes?"

"You have any thoughts on how I should break the news to Sophie Mayor?"

"None whatsoever."

Win left then. Myron stared at the phone. He picked it up and dialed Sophie Mayor's phone number. It took some time, but a secretary finally patched him through to her. Sophie sounded less than thrilled to hear his voice.

She opened sharply. "What?"

"We need to talk," Myron said. There was distortion on the line. A cell or car phone probably.

"We already talked."

"This is different."

Silence. Then: "I'm in the car right now, about a mile from my house out on the Island. How important is this?"

Myron picked up a pen. "Give me your address," he said. "I'll be right over."

19

On the street the man was still reading a newspaper.

Myron's elevator trip down to the lobby featured mucho stops. Not atypical. No one spoke, of course, everyone busying themselves by staring up at the descending flashing numbers as though awaiting a UFO landing. In the lobby he joined the stream of suits and flowed out onto Park Avenue, salmons fighting upstream against the tide until, well, they died. Many of the suits walked with heads high, their expressions kick-ass-runway-model; others walked with backs bent, flesh versions of the statue on Fifth Avenue of Atlas carrying the world on his shoulders, but for them the world was simply too heavy.

Whoa, again with the deep.

Perfectly situated on the corner of Forty-sixth and Park, standing reading a newspaper but positioned in such way as to watch all entering or leaving the Lock-Horne building, was the same man Myron had noticed standing there when he entered.

Hmm.

Myron took out his cell phone and hit the programmed button.

"Articulate," Win said.

"I think I got a tail."

"Hold please." Maybe ten seconds passed. Then: "The newspaper on the corner."

Win keeps a variety of telescopes and binoculars in his office. Don't ask.

"Yep."

"Good Lord," Win said. "Could he be any more obvious?"

"Doubt it."

"Where's the pride in his work? Where's the professionalism?"

"Sad."

"That, my friend, is the whole problem with this country."

"Bad tails?"

"It's an example. Look at him. Does anybody really stand on a street corner and read a newspaper like that? He might as well cut out two eye-holes."

"Uh-huh," Myron said. "You got some free time?"

"But of course. How would you like to play it?"

"Back me up," Myron said.

"Give me five."

Myron waited five minutes. He stood there and studiously avoided looking at the tail. He checked his watch and huffed a bit as though he expected someone and was getting impatient. When the five minutes passed, Myron walked straight over to the tail.

The tail spotted his approach and ducked into the newspaper.

Myron kept walking until he stood directly next to the tail. The tail kept his face in the newspaper. Myron gave him Smile 8. Big and toothy. A televangelist being handed a hefty check. Early Wink Martindale. The tail kept his eyes on the newspaper. Myron kept smiling, his eyes wide as a clown's. The tail ignored him. Myron inched closer, leaned his *über*-wattage smile within inches of the tail's face, wriggled his eyebrows.

The tail snapped closed the newspaper and sighed. "Fine, hotshot, you made me. Congratulations."

Still with the Wink Martindale smile: "And thank you for playing our game! But don't worry, we won't let you go home empty-handed! You get the home version of Incompetent Tail and a year's subscription to *Modern Doofus*."

"Yeah, right, see you around."

"Wait! Final *Jeopardy!* round. Answer: He or she hired you to follow me."

"Bite me."

"Ooo, sorry, you needed to put that in the form of a question."

The tail started walking away. When he looked back, Myron gave him the smile and a big wave. "This has been a Mark Goodsón-Bill Todman production. Good-bye, everybody!" More waving.

The tail shook his head and continued down the street, joining another stream of people. Lots of people in this stream; Win happened to be one of them. The tail would probably find a clearing and then call his boss. Win would listen in and learn all. What a plan.

Myron headed to his rented car. He circled the block once. No more tails. At least none as obvious as the last. No matter. He was driving out to the Mayor estate on Long Island. It didn't much matter if anyone knew.

He spent his time in the car working on the cell phone. He had two arena football players—indoor football on a smaller field, for those who don't know—both of whom were hoping to scratch a bench spot on an NFL roster before the waiver wire closed down. Myron called teams, but nobody was interested. Lots of people asked him about the murder. He brushed them off. He knew his efforts were fairly futile, but he stuck to it. Big of him. He tried concentrating on his work, tried to lose himself in the numb bliss of what he did for a living. But the world kept creeping in. He thought about Esperanza in jail. He thought about Jessica in California. He thought about Bonnie Haid and her fatherless boys at home. He thought about Clu in formaldehyde. He thought about his father's phone call. And strangely, he kept thinking about Terese alone on that island.

He blocked out the rest.

When he reached Muttontown, a section of Long Island that had somehow escaped him in the past, he turned right onto a heavily wooded road. He drove about two miles, passing maybe three driveways. He finally reached a simple iron gate with a small sign that read THE MAYORS. There were several security cameras and an intercom. He pressed the button. A woman's voice came on and said, "May I help you?"

"Myron Bolitar to see Sophie Mayor."

"Please drive up. Park in front of the house."

The gate opened. Myron drove up a rather steep hill. Tall hedges lined both sides of the driveway, giving the aura of being a rat in amaze. He spotted a few more security cameras. No sign of the house yet. When he reached the top of the hill, he hit upon a clearing. There was a slightly overgrown grass tennis court and croquet field. Very Norma Desmond. He made another turn. The house was dead straight ahead. It was a mansion, of course, though not as huge as some Myron had seen. Vines clung to pale yellow stucco. The windows looked leaded. The whole scene screamed Roaring Twenties. Myron half expected Scott and Zelda to pull up behind him in a slick roadster.

This part of the driveway was made up of small loose pebbles rather than pavement. His tires crunched them as it drew closer. There was a fountain in the middle of the circular drive, about fifteen feet in front of the door. Neptune stood naked with a triton in his hand. The fountain, Myron realized, was a smaller version of the one in the Piazza della Signoria in Florence. Water spouted up but not very high or with much enthusiasm, as if someone had set the water pressure on "light urination."

Myron parked the car. There was a perfectly square swimming pool on his right, complete with lily pads floating on the top. A poor man's

Giverny. There were statues in the gardens, again something from old Italy or Greece or the like. Venus de Milo–like except with all the limbs.

He got out of the car and stopped. He thought about what he was about to unearth, and for a brief moment he considered turning back. *How,* he wondered again, *do I tell this woman about her missing daughter melting on a computer diskette?*

No answer came to him.

The door opened. A woman in casual clothes led him through a corridor and into a large room with high tin ceilings and lots of windows and a semidisappointing view of more white statues and woods. The interior was art deco, but it didn't try too hard. Nice. Except, of course, for the hunting trophies. Taxidermy birds of some sort sat on the shelves. The birds looked upset. Probably were. Who could blame them?

Myron turned and stared at a mounted deer. He waited for Sophie Mayor. The deer waited too. The deer seemed very patient.

"Go ahead," a voice said.

Myron turned around. It was Sophie Mayor. She was wearing dirt-smeared jeans and a plaid shirt, the very essence of the weekend botanist.

Never short of a witty opening gambit, Myron countered, "Go ahead and what?"

"Make the snide remark about hunting."

"I didn't say anything."

"Come, come, Myron. Don't you think hunting is barbaric?"

Myron shrugged. "I never really thought about it." Not true, but what the hey.

"But you don't approve, do you?"

"Not my place to approve."

"How tolerant." She smiled. "But you of course would never do it, am I right?"

"Hunt? No, it's not for me."

"You think it's inhumane." She gestured with her chin to the mounted deer. "Killing Bambi's mother and all."

"It's just not for me."

"I see. Are you a vegetarian?"

"I don't eat much red meat," Myron said.

"I'm not talking about your health. Do you ever eat any dead animals?"

"Yes."

"So do you think it's more humane to kill, say, a chicken or a cow than it is to kill a deer?"

"No."

"Do you know what kind of awful torture that cow goes through before it's slaughtered?"

"For food," Myron said.

"Pardon?"

"Slaughtered for food."

"I eat what I kill, Myron. Your friend up there"—she nodded to the patient deer—"she was gutted and eaten. Feel better?"

Myron thought about that. "Uh, we're not having lunch, are we?"

That got a small chuckle. "I won't go into the whole food chain argument," Sophie Mayor said. "But God created a world where the only way to survive is to kill. Period. We all kill. Even the strict vegetarians have to plow fields. You don't think plowing kills small animals and insects?"

"I never really thought about it."

"Hunting is just more hands-on, more honest. When you sit down and eat an animal, you have no appreciation for the process, for the sacrifice made so that you could survive. You let someone else do the killing. You're above even thinking about it. When I eat an animal, I have a fuller understanding. I don't do it casually. I don't depersonalize it."

"Okay," Myron said, "while we're on the subject, what about those hunters who don't kill for food?"

"Most do eat what they kill."

"But what about those who kill for sport? I mean, isn't that part of it?"

"Yes."

"So what about that? What about killing merely for sport?"

"As opposed to what, Myron? Killing for a pair of shoes? Or a nice coat? Is spending a full day outdoors, coming to understand how nature works and appreciating her bountiful glory, is that worth any less than a leather pocketbook? If it's worth killing an animal because you prefer your belt made of animal skin instead of something man-made, is it not worth killing one because you simply enjoy the thrill of it?"

He said nothing.

"I'm sorry to ride you about this. But the hypocrisy of it all drives me somewhat batty. Everyone wants to save the whale, but what about the thousands of fish and shrimp a whale eats each day? Are their lives worthless because they aren't as cute? Ever notice how no one ever wants to save ugly animals? And the same people who think hunting is barbaric put up special fences so the deer can't eat their precious gardens. So the deers overpopulate and die of starvation. Is that better? And don't even get me started on those so-called ecofeminists. Men hunt, they say, but women are too genteel. Of all the sexist nonsense. They want to be environmentalists? They want to stay as close to a state of nature as possible?

Then understand the one universal truth about nature: You either kill or
you die."

They both turned and stared at the deer for a moment. Proof positive.

"You didn't come here for a lecture," she said.

Myron had welcomed this delay. But the time had come. "No, ma'am."

"Ma'am?" Sophie Mayor chuckled without a hint of humor. "That
sounds grim, Myron."

Myron turned and looked at her. She met his gaze and held it.

"Call me Sophie," she said.

He nodded. "Can I ask you a very personal, maybe hurtful question,
Sophie?"

"You can try."

"Have you heard anything from your daughter since she ran away?"

"No."

The answer came fast. Her gaze remained steady, her voice strong. But
her face was losing color.

"Then you have no idea where she is?"

"No idea."

"Or even if she's . . ."

"Alive or dead," she finished for him. "None."

Her voice was so monotone it seemed on the verge of a scream. There
was a quaking near her mouth now, a fault line starting to give way. Sophie Mayor stood and waited for his explanation, afraid perhaps to say
any more.

"I got a diskette in the mail," he began.

She frowned. "What?"

"A computer diskette. It came in the mail. I put it in my A drive, and
it just started up. I didn't have to hit any keys."

"Self-starting program," she said, suddenly the computer expert.
"That's not complicated technology."

Myron cleared his throat. "A graphic came on. It started out as a photograph of your daughter."

Sophie Mayor took a step back.

"It was the same photograph that's in your office. On the right side of
the credenza."

"That was Lucy's junior year of high school," she said. "The school
portrait."

Myron nodded, though he didn't know why. "After a few seconds her
image started melting on the screen."

"Melting?"

"Yes. It sort of dissolved into a puddle of, uh, blood. Then a sound
came on. A teenage girl laughing, I think."

Sophie Mayor's eyes were glistening now. "I don't understand."

"Neither do I."

"This came in the mail?"

"Yes."

"On a floppy disk?"

"Yes," Myron said. Then he added for no reason: "A three-and-a-half-inch floppy."

"When?"

"It arrived in my office about two weeks ago."

"Why did you wait so long to tell me?" She put a hand up. "Oh, wait. You were out of the country."

"Yes."

"So when did you first see it?"

"Yesterday."

"But you saw me this morning. Why didn't you tell me then?"

"I didn't know who the girl was. Not at first anyway. Then when I was in your office, I saw the photograph on the credenza. I got confused. I wasn't sure what to say."

She nodded slowly. "So that explains your abrupt departure."

"Yes. I'm sorry."

"Do you have the diskette? My people will analyze it."

He reached into his pocket and withdrew it. "I don't think it'll be any help."

"Why not?"

"I took it to a police lab. They said it automatically reformatted itself."

"So the diskette is blank?"

"Yes."

It was as though her muscles had suddenly decided to flee the district. Sophie Mayor's legs gave way. She dropped to a chair. Her head lolled into her hands. Myron waited. There were no sounds. She just sat there, head in hands. When she looked up again, the gray eyes were tinged with red.

"You said something about a police lab."

He nodded.

"You used to work in law enforcement."

"Not really."

"I remember Clip Arnstein saying something about it."

Myron said nothing. Clip Arnstein was the man who had drafted Myron in the first round for the Boston Celtics. He also had a big mouth.

"You helped Clip when Greg Downing vanished," she continued.

"Yes."

"I've been hiring private investigators to search for Lucy for years.

Supposedly the best in the world. Sometimes we seem to get close but . . ." Her voice drifted off, her eyes far away. She looked at the diskette in her hand as if it had suddenly materialized there. "Why would someone send this to you?"

"I don't know."

"Did you know my daughter?"

"No."

Sophie took a couple of careful breaths. "I want to show you something. Wait here a minute." It took maybe half that time. Myron had just begun to stare into the eyes of some dead bird, noting with some dismay how closely they resembled the eyes of some human beings he knew, and Sophie was back. She handed him a sheet of paper.

Myron looked at it. It was an artist's rendering of a woman nearing thirty years of age.

"It's from MIT," she explained. "My alma mater. A scientist there has developed a software package that helps with age progression. For missing people. So you can see what they might look like today. He made this up for me a few months ago."

Myron looked at the image of what the teenage Lucy might look like as a woman heading toward thirty. The effect was nothing short of startling. Oh, it looked like her, he guessed, but talk about ghosts, talk about life being a series of what-ifs, talk about the years slipping away and then smacking you in the face. Myron stared at the image, at the more conservative haircut, the small frown lines. How painful must it be for Sophie Mayor to look at this?

"Does she look familiar at all?" Sophie asked.

Myron shook his head. "No, I'm sorry."

"You're sure?"

"As sure as you can be in these situations."

"Will you help me find her?"

He wasn't sure how to answer. "I can't see how I can help."

"Clip said you're good at these things."

"I'm not. But even if I were, I can't see what I can do. You've hired experts already. You have the cops—"

"The police have been useless. They view Lucy as a runaway, period."

Myron said nothing.

"Do you think it's hopeless?" she asked.

"I don't know enough about it."

"She was a good girl, you know." Sophie Mayor smiled at him, her eyes misty with time travel. "Headstrong, sure. Too adventurous for her own good. But then again I raised Lucy to be independent. The police. They think she was simply a troubled kid. She wasn't. Just confused.

Who isn't at that age? And it wasn't as if she ran off in the middle of the night without telling anyone."

Against his better judgment Myron asked, "Then what happened?"

"Lucy was a teenager, Myron. She was sullen and unhappy, and she didn't fit in. Her parents were college math professors and computer geeks. Her younger brother was considered a genius. She hated school. She wanted to see the world and live on the road. She had the whole rock 'n' roll fantasy. One day she told us she was going off with Owen."

"Owen was her boyfriend?"

She nodded. "An average musician who fronted a garage band, certain that his immense talent was being held back by them." She made a lemon-sucking face. "They wanted to run off and get a record deal and become famous. So Gary and I said okay. Lucy was like a wild bird trapped in a small cage. She wouldn't stop flapping her wings no matter what we did. Gary and I felt we had no choice in the matter. We even thought it might be good for her. Lots of her classmates were backpacking through Europe. What was the difference?"

She stopped and looked up at him. Myron waited. When she didn't say anything, he said, "And?"

"And we never heard from her again."

Silence.

She turned back to the mounted deer. The deer looked back at her with something akin, it seemed, to pity.

Myron said, "But Owen came back, right?"

"Yes." She was still staring at the deer. "He's a car salesman in New Jersey. He plays in a wedding band on weekends. Can you imagine? He dresses up in a cheap tuxedo and belts out 'Tie a Yellow Ribbon' and 'Celebration' and introduces the bridal party." She shook her head at the irony. "When Owen came back, the police questioned him, but he didn't know anything. Their story was so typical: They went out to Los Angeles, failed miserably, started fighting, and broke up after six months. Owen stayed out there another three months, certain this time it had been Lucy who was holding back his immense talent. When he failed again, he came back home with his tail between his legs. He said he hadn't seen Lucy since their breakup."

"The police checked it out?"

"So they said. But it was a dead end."

"Do you suspect Owen?"

"No," she said bitterly. "He's too big a nothing."

"Have there been any solid leads at all?"

"Solid?" She thought about it. "Not really. Several of the investigators we've hired think she joined a cult."

Myron made a face. "A cult?"

"Her personality fit the profile, they said. Despite my attempts to make her independent, they claim she was just the opposite—someone needing guidance, alone, suggestible, alienated from friends and family."

"I don't agree," Myron said.

She looked at him. "You said you never met Lucy."

"The psychological profile may be right, but I doubt she's with a cult."

"What makes you say that?"

"Cults like money. Lucy Mayor is the daughter of an extraordinarily wealthy family. Maybe you didn't have money when she first would have joined, but believe me, they'd know about you by now. And they would have been in touch, if for no other reason than to extort vast sums."

She started blinking again. Her eyes closed, and she turned her back to him. Myron took a step forward and then stopped, not sure what to do. He chose discretion, kept his distance, waited.

"The not knowing," Sophie Mayor said after some time had passed. "It gnaws at you. All day, all night, for twelve years. It never stops. It never goes away. When my husband's heart gave out, everyone was so shocked. Such a healthy man, they said. So young. Even now I don't know how I'll get through the day without him. But we rarely spoke about Lucy after she disappeared. We just lay in bed at night and pretended that the other one was asleep and stared at the ceiling and imagined all the horrors only parents with missing children can conjure up."

More silence.

Myron had no idea what to say. But the silence was growing so thick he could barely breathe. "I'm sorry," he said.

She didn't look up.

"I'll go to the police," he said. "Tell them about the diskette."

"What good will that do?"

"They'll investigate."

"They already have. I told you. They think she's a runaway."

"But now we have this new evidence. They'll take the case more seriously. I can even go to the media. It'll jump-start their coverage."

She shook her head. Myron waited. She stood and wiped her palms on the thighs of her jeans. "The diskette," she said, "was sent to you."

"Yes."

"Addressed to you."

"Yes."

"So," she said, "someone is reaching out to you."

Win had said something similar. "You don't know that," Myron said. "I don't want to douse your hopes, but it could be nothing more than a prank."

"It's not a prank."

"You can't be sure."

"If it was a prank, it would have been sent to me. Or Jared. Or someone who knew her. It wasn't. It was sent to you. Someone is reaching out to you specifically. It might even be Lucy."

He took a deep breath. "Again I don't want to douse your—"

"Don't patronize me, Myron. Just say what you want to say."

"Okay . . . if it were Lucy, why would she send an image of herself melting into a puddle of blood?"

Sophie Mayor did not wince, but she came close. "I don't know. Maybe you're right. Maybe it's not her. Maybe it's her killer. Either way, they're seeking *you* out. It's the first solid lead in years. And if we make it loud and public, I fear that whoever sent this will go back into hiding. I can't risk that."

"I don't know what I can do," Myron said.

"I'll pay you whatever you want. Name a price. A hundred thousand? A million?"

"It's not the money. I just don't see where I can help."

"You can investigate."

He shook his head. "My best friend and business partner is in jail for murder. My client was shot in his own home. I have other clients who rely on me for their job security."

"I see," she said. "So you don't have time, is that it?"

"It's not a question of time. I really have nothing to go on. No clue, no connection, no source. There's nothing to start with here."

Her eyes pinned him down. "You can start with you. You're my clue, my connection, my source." She reached out and took his hand. Her flesh was cold and hard. "All I'm asking is that you look closer."

"At what?"

"Maybe," she said, "at yourself."

Silence. They stood there, she holding his hand.

"That sounds good, Sophie, but I'm not sure what it means."

"You don't have children, do you?"

"No," Myron said. "But that doesn't mean I don't sympathize."

"So let me ask you, Myron: What would you do if you were me? What would you do if the first real clue in ten years just walked in your door?"

"The same thing you're doing."

So under the mounted deer, he told her he would keep his eyes open. He told her he would think about it. He told her he would try to figure out the connection.

20

Back at the office Myron strapped on the Ultra Slim phone headset and started making phone calls. Very Jerry Maguire. Not just in appearance but in the fact that clients were abandoning him left and right. And he hadn't even written a mission statement.

Win called. "Newspaper Tail's name is Wayne Tunis. He lives in Staten Island and works in construction. He placed one call to a John McClain, telling him that he had been spotted. That's it. They're pretty careful."

"So we don't yet know who hired him?"

"That would be correct."

"When in doubt," Myron said, "we should go with the obvious choice."

"Young FJ?"

"Who else? He's been following me for months."

"Course of action?"

"I'd like to get him off my back."

"May I recommend a well-placed bullet through the back of the skull?"

"We've got enough problems without adding one more."

"Fine. Course of action?"

"We confront him."

"He usually hangs out at a Starbucks on Forty-ninth Street," Win said. "Starbucks?"

"The old mob espresso bars have gone the way of leisure suits and disco music."

"Both of them are coming back."

"No," Win said, "bizarre mutations of them are coming back."

"Like coffee bars in place of espresso bars?"

"Then you understand."

"So let's pay FJ a visit."

"Give me twenty minutes," Win said before hanging up.

As soon as Myron hit the disconnect, Big Cyndi buzzed his line.

"Mr. Bolitar?"

"Yes?"

"A Miss or Mr. Thrill is on the phone," Big Cyndi said.

Myron closed his eyes. "You mean from last night?"

"Unless you know someone else named Thrill, Mr. Bolitar."

"Take a message."

"Both her words and tone suggest urgency, Mr. Bolitar."

Suggest urgency? "Fine. Patch her—or him—through."

"Yes, Mr. Bolitar."

There was a click.

"Myron?"

"Uh, yeah, hi, Thrill."

"That was some exit you made last night, big fella," Thrill said. "You really know how to impress a girl."

"Yeah, I usually don't jump through a plate glass window until the second date."

"So how come you haven't called me?"

"I've been really busy."

"I'm downstairs," Thrill said. "Tell the guard to let me up."

"It's not a good time. Like I said before—"

"Men rarely say no to Thrill. I must be losing my touch."

"It's not that," he said. "It's just that the timing is all wrong."

"Myron, my name isn't really Thrill."

"I hate to burst your bubble, but I kinda suspected it read something else on your birth certificate."

"No, that's not what I mean. Look, let me up. We need to talk about last night. About something that happened after you left."

So he shrugged and called down to the guard at the front desk and told him to let up anyone identifying themselves as Thrill. The guard was puzzled but said okay. The headset was still strapped on so Myron speed-dialed a sports apparel company. Before dashing to the Caribbean, Myron had been on the verge of landing a sneaker deal for a track and field client with said company. But now he was being put on hold. An assistant to an assistant finally came on the line. Myron asked him about the deal. It had fallen through, he was told. Why? he asked.

"Ask your client," the assistant said. "Oh, and ask his new agent too."

Click.

Myron closed his eyes and pulled off his headset. Damn.

There was a knock on his office door. The alien sound caused a ripple of pain. Esperanza had never knocked. Never. She prided herself on interrupting him. She would sooner give up a limb than knock.

"Come in."

The door opened. Someone stepped inside and said, "Surprise."

Myron tried not to stare. He took off the headset. "You're . . . ?"

"Thrill, yup."

Nothing was the same. Gone was the Cat Woman costume, the blond wig, the high heels, the, uh, prodigious bosom. Thrill was still female, thank heavens. Still quite attractive in her conservative navy suit with matching blouse, her hair done in a pixie style, her eyes less luminous behind round tortoiseshell glasses, her makeup now applied with a far lighter hand. Her figure was thinner, more toned, less, uh, shapely. Nothing to complain about, mind you. Just different.

"To answer your first question," she said, "when I dress like Thrill, I wear the aptly named Raquel Wonder Breast Enhancements."

Myron nodded. "That the stuff that looks like flattened Silly Putty?"

"The very. You jam them in your bra. Guess you've seen the infomercial on TV."

"Seen it? I bought the video."

Thrill laughed. Last night her laugh—not to mention her walk, her movements, her tone of voice, her choice of words—had been a double entendre. In the light of day the sound was melodic and almost childlike.

"I also strap on the aptly named Miracle Bra," she continued. "To lift it all up high."

"Any higher," Myron said, "and they could have doubled as earrings."

"Too true," she said. "The legs and ass, however, are mine. And for the record, I do not have a penis."

"So noted."

"Can I sit down?"

Myron looked at his watch. "I hate to be a pest—"

"You'll want to hear this, believe me." She sat in the chair in front of his desk. Myron folded his arms and leaned his butt on the desk's lip. "My real name is Nancy Sinclair. I don't dress like Thrill for kicks. I'm a journalist, and I'm doing a story on Take A Guess. An insider's look at what goes on, what kind of people go there, what makes them tick. In order to get people to open up, I go undercover as Thrill."

"So you do all this for a story?"

"I do all what?"

"Dress up and, uh . . ." His gestures were unintelligible.

"Not that I see where it's even vaguely any of your concern, but the answer is no. I dress a part. I strike up conversations. I flirt. Period. I like to watch people's reaction to me."

"Oh." Then Myron cleared his throat and said, "Just, uh, out of curiosity, I'm not going to be in your story, am I? I mean, I've really never been there before and I was—"

"Relax. I recognized you as soon as you came in the door."

"You did?"

"I follow basketball. I got season tickets to the Dragons."

"I see." The Dragons were New Jersey's pro basketball team. Myron had tried a comeback with them not long ago.

"That's why I approached you."

"To see if I was into, uh, gender ambiguity?"

"Everyone else there is. Why not you?"

"But I explained to you that I was there to ask about someone."

"Clu Haid, right. Still, your reaction to me was interesting."

"I found you to be a witty conversationalist," Myron said.

"Uh-huh."

"And I also have a Julie-Newmar-as-Cat-Woman fetish."

"You'd be surprised how many people have that same fetish."

"No, I don't think I would be," Myron said. "So why are you here, Nancy?"

"Pat saw us talking last night."

"The bartender?"

"He's also one of the owners. He has shares in a couple of places in the city."

"And?"

"And after the smoke cleared from your exit, Pat pulled me aside."

"Because he saw us talking?"

"Because he saw me giving you my phone number."

"So?"

"So I'd never done that before."

"I'm flattered."

"Don't be. I'm just making a point. I come on to a ton of girls and guys and whatever in there. But I never give out a phone number."

"So why did you give it to me?"

"Because I was curious to see if you'd call. You rebuffed Thrill, so you clearly weren't there for sex. I wondered what you were up to."

Myron frowned. "That was the only reason?"

"Yes."

"Nothing about my rugged good looks and brawny body?"

"Oh, yeah. I almost forgot."

"So what did Pat want?"

"He wants me to bring you to another club tonight."

"Tonight?"

"Yes."

"How did he know I'd call?"

Again the smile. "Nancy Sinclair might not guarantee an immediate phone call . . ."

"But Thrill does?"

"Bosoms are empowerment. And if you didn't, he told me I could look up your business number in the phone book."

"Which is what you did."

"Yes. He also promised me you wouldn't be hurt."

"How comforting. And your interest in all this?"

"Isn't it obvious? A story. The Clu Haid murder is huge news. Now you're tying this week's murder-of-the-century to a kinky New York nightclub."

"I don't think I can help you."

"Cow dooky."

"Cow dooky?"

She shrugged.

"What else did Pat say to you?" Myron asked.

"Nothing much. He just said that he wanted to talk."

"If he wanted to talk, he could have looked up my phone number too."

"Thrill, not the brightest bulb on the tree, didn't pick up on that."

"But Nancy Sinclair did."

She smiled again. It was a damn nice smile. "Pat was also huddled up with Zorra."

"Who?"

"That's their psycho bouncer. A cross-dresser with a blond wig."

"Like Veronica Lake?"

She nodded. "He's absolutely nuts. Lift up your shirt."

"Pardon?"

"He can do anything with that razor heel. His favorite is a Z slash on the right side. You were in the back room with him."

Made sense. Myron hadn't made him miss. Zorra—*Zorra?*—just wanted to brand him. "I have one."

"He's seriously whacked out. Did some sort of stuff in the Persian Gulf War. Undercover. Worked for the Israelis too. There are all kinds of rumors about him, but if five percent of the stories I've heard are true, he's killed dozens."

Just what he needed—Cross-Dressing Mossad. "Did they talk about Clu at all?"

"No. But Pat said something about your trying to kill somebody."

"Me?"

"Yes."

"They think I killed Clu?"

"I don't think so. It sounded more like they thought you were at the club to find someone and kill him."

"Who?"

"No idea. They just said you were out to kill him."

"They didn't say who?"

"If they did, I didn't hear them." She smiled. "So do we have a date?"

"Guess so."

"You're not scared?"

"I'll have backup."

"Someone good?"

Myron nodded. "Oh, yeah."

"Then I better go home and strap up my breasts."

"Need any help?"

"My hero. But no, Myron, I think I can handle it myself."

"And if you can't?"

"I have your phone number," she said. "See you tonight."

21

Win frowned. "Nonsurgical breast enhancements?"

"Yes. They're an accessory of some sort."

"An accessory? Like a matching pocketbook?"

"In a way." Then thinking about it, Myron added, "But they're probably more noticeable."

Win showed him the flat eyes. Myron shrugged.

"False advertising," Win said.

"Pardon?"

"Breast enhancements. It's false advertising. There should be a law."

"Right, Win. But the politicians in Washington—where are they when it comes to the real issues?"

"Then you understand."

"I understand that you're a snorting pig."

"A thousand pardons, O Enlightened One." Win put a hand to his ear and tilted his head to the side. "Tell me again, Myron: What first attracted you to this Thrill?"

"The catsuit," Myron said.

"I see. So if, say, Big Cyndi came into the office in the catsuit—"

"Hey, c'mon, I just ate a muffin."

"Exactly."

"Fine, I'm a pig too. Happy?"

"Yes, ecstatic. And perhaps you misread me. Perhaps I wish to outlaw such accessories because of what they do to a woman's self-esteem. Perhaps I tire of a society that forces unobtainable beauty on a woman—size four dresses with D cups."

"The key word here being *perhaps*."

Win smiled. "Love me for all my faults."

"What else is there?"

Win adjusted his tie. "FJ and the two oversized hormonal glands that guard him are at Starbucks. Shall we?"

"Let's. Then I want to head over to Yankee Stadium. I need to question a couple of folks."

"Sounds almost like a plan," Win said.

They strolled up Park Avenue. The light changed, and they waited at the corner. Myron stood next to a man in a business suit talking on a cell phone. Nothing unusual about that, except the man was having phone sex. He was actually rubbing his, uh, nether parts and saying into the phone, "Yeah, baby, like that," and other stuff not worth repeating. The light changed. The man crossed, still rubbing and talking. Talk about I Love New York.

"About tonight," Win said.

"Yes."

"You trust this Thrill?"

"She checks out."

"There is of course a chance that they'll just shoot you when you show up."

"I doubt it. This Pat is part owner. He wouldn't want the trouble in his own place."

"So you think they're extending this invitation to buy you a drink?"

"Could be," Myron said. "With my preference-crossing animal magnetism, I'm considered something of a tasty morsel to the swinger set."

Win chose not to argue.

They headed east on Forty-ninth Street. The Starbucks was four blocks up on the right. When they arrived, Win signaled for Myron to wait. He leaned in and took a quick peek through the glass before backing away. "Young FJ is at a table with someone," Win reported. "Hans and Franz are two tables over. Only one other table is occupied."

Myron nodded. "Shall we?"

"You first," Win said. "Let me trail."

Myron had stopped questioning Win's methods a long time ago. He immediately stepped inside and headed toward FJ's table. Hans and Franz, the Mr. Universe Bookends, were still wearing the tank tops and the semipajama pants smeared with a pattern that resembled melted paisley. They bolted upright when Myron entered, fingers tightened into fists, necks in midcrack.

FJ was decked out in a light herringbone sports coat, collared shirt buttoned all the way to the top, cuffed pants, and Cole-Haan tasseled loafers.

Too natty for words. He spotted Myron and raised his hand in the bruisers' direction. Hans and Franz froze.

"Hi, FJ," Myron said.

FJ was sipping something foamy; it kinda looked like shaving cream. "Ah, Myron," he said with what he must have been sure was *savoir faire*. He gestured at his table companion. His companion got up without a word and scooted toward the exit like a scared gerbil. "Please, Myron, join me. This is such a strange coincidence."

"Oh?"

"You saved me a trip. I was just going to pay you a visit." FJ tossed Myron the snake smile. Myron let it land on the floor and watched it slither away. "I guess it's kismet, huh, Myron? Your coming here. Pure kismet."

FJ cracked up at that. Hans and Franz laughed too.

"Kismet," Myron repeated. "Good one."

FJ waved a modest hand as if to say, *I got a million like that.* "Please sit, Myron."

Myron pulled out a chair.

"Care for a drink?"

"An iced latte would be fine. Grande, skim, with a dash of vanilla."

FJ motioned to the guy working behind the coffee bar. "He's new," FJ confided.

"Who?"

"The guy working the espresso machine. The last guy who worked here made a wonderful latte. But he quit for moral reasons."

"Moral reasons?"

"They started selling Kenny G CDs," FJ said. "Suddenly he couldn't sleep at night. It was tearing him apart. Suppose an impressionable kid bought one? How could he live with himself? Pushing caffeine was okay. But Kenny G . . . the man had scruples."

Myron said, "Commendable."

Win chose that moment to enter. FJ spotted him and looked over at Hans and Franz. Win did not hesitate. He beelined straight toward FJ's table. Hans and Franz went to work. They stepped in Win's path and expanded their chests to dimensions large enough to apply for a parking permit. Win kept walking. Both men wore turtlenecks so high and loose they looked like something awaiting circumcision.

Hans managed a smirk. "You Win?"

"Yes," Win said, "me Win."

"You don't look so tough." Hans looked at Franz. "He look tough to you, Keith?"

Keith said, "Not so tough."

Win did not break stride. Almost casually and without the slightest warning, he struck Hans with the knife-edge of his hand behind the ear. Hans's whole body stiffened and then collapsed as though someone had ripped the skeleton out of him. Franz gaped at the sight. But not for long. In the same motion Win pirouetted and struck Franz in the oft vulnerable throat. An awful gurgling noise shot out of Franz's lips, as though he were choking on a slew of small bones. Win reached for the carotid artery, found it, and squeezed with his pointer and thumb. Franz's eyes closed, and he too slid into Nighty-Night Land.

The couple at the other table exited quickly. Win smiled down at the unconscious bruisers. Then he glanced at Myron. Myron shook his head. Win shrugged and turned to the guy manning the coffee bar.

"Barista," Win said. "One caffe mocha."

"What size?"

"Grande, please."

"Skim or whole milk?"

"Skim. I'm watching my figure."

"Right away."

Win joined Myron and FJ. He sat and crossed his legs. "Nice sports coat, FJ."

"Glad you like it, Win."

"It really brings out the demonic red in your eyes."

"Thank you."

"So where were we?"

Myron played along. "I was just about to tell FJ that I'm getting a little tired of the tail."

"And I was just about to tell Myron that I'm getting tired of him meddling in my affairs," FJ said.

Myron looked at Win. "Meddling? Does anybody really use that word anymore?"

Win thought about it. "The old man at the end of every *Scooby Doo.*"

"Right. You meddling kids, stuff like that."

"You will never guess who does the voice for Shaggy," Win said.

"Who?"

"Casey Kasem."

"Get out," Myron said. "The top-forty radio guy?"

"The very same."

"Live and learn."

On the floor Hans and Franz started to stir. Win showed FJ the gun he had semihidden in his one hand. "For the safety of all concerned," Win said, "please ask your employees to refrain from moving."

FJ told them. He was not scared. His father was Frank Ache. That was protection enough. The muscles here were for show.

"You've been following me for weeks now," Myron said. "I want it to end."

"Then I suggest that you stop interfering with my company."

Myron sighed. "Fine, FJ, I'll bite. How am I interfering with your company?"

"Did you or did you not visit Sophie and Jared Mayor this morning?" FJ asked.

"You know I did."

"For what purpose?"

"It had nothing to do with you, FJ."

"Wrong answer."

"Wrong answer?"

"You visited the owner of the New York Yankees even though you currently represent no one who plays for the team."

"So?"

"So why were you there?"

Myron looked at Win. Win shrugged. "Not that I need to explain myself to you, FJ, but just to assuage your paranoid delusions, I was there about Clu Haid."

"What about him?"

"I was asking about his drug tests."

FJ's eyes narrowed. "That's interesting."

"Glad you think so, FJ."

"You see, I'm just a new guy trying to learn this confusing business."

"Uh-huh."

"I'm young and inexperienced."

Win said, "Ah, how often I've heard that line."

Myron just shook his head.

FJ leaned forward, his scaly features coming closer. Myron feared his tongue would dart out and sniff him. "I want to learn, Myron. So please tell me: What possible significance could Clu's drug test results have now?"

Myron quickly debated answering and decided, What's the harm? "If I can show the drug test was faulty, his contract would still be active."

FJ nodded, seeing the thought trail now. "You'd be able to get his contract paid out."

"Right."

"Do you have reason to believe that the test was faulty?"

"I'm afraid that's confidential, FJ. Agent-client privilege or whatever you want to call it. I'm sure you understand."

"I do," FJ said.

"Good."

"But you, Myron, are not his agent."

"I am still responsible for his estate's financial well-being. Clu's death doesn't alter my obligation."

"Wrong answer."

Myron looked at Win. "Again with the wrong answer?"

"You are not responsible." FJ reached to the floor and pulled a briefcase into view. He snapped it open with as much flair as possible. His finger danced through a stack of papers before withdrawing the one he sought. He handed it to Myron and smiled. Myron looked into FJ's eyes, and again he was reminded of the eyes of that mounted deer.

Myron skimmed it over. He read the first line, felt a thump, checked the signature. "What the hell is this?"

FJ's smile was like a dripping candle now. "Exactly what it looks like. Clu Haid changed representation. He fired MB SportsReps and hired TruPro."

He remembered what Sophie Mayor had said in her office, about his having no legal standing. "He never told us."

"Never told *us,* Myron, or never told *you*?"

"What the hell does that mean?"

"You weren't around. Perhaps he tried to tell you. Perhaps he told your associate."

"So he just happened by you, FJ?"

"How I recruit is none of your business. If you kept your clients happy, the best recruitment efforts wouldn't work."

Myron checked the date. "This is quite a coincidence, FJ."

"What's that?"

"He dies two days after he signs with you."

"Yes, Myron, I agree. I don't think it was a coincidence. Fortunately for me, it means that I had no motive to kill him. Unfortunately for the sizzling Esperanza, the opposite is true."

Myron glanced over at Win. Win was staring down at Hans and Franz. They were both awake now, face to the floor, hands behind their heads. Customers occasionally came into the coffee bar. Some saw the two men on the floor and exited right away. Others were unfazed, walking past as though Hans and Franz were just two more Manhattan panhandlers.

"Very convenient," Myron said.

"What's that?"

"Clu signing with you so close to his death. On the surface it eliminates you as a serious suspect."

"On the surface?"

"It draws attention away from you, makes it look like his death hurts your interests."

"It does hurt my interests."

Myron shook his head. "He had failed a drug test. His contract was null and void. He's thirty-five years old with several suspensions. As a monetary commodity Clu was fairly worthless."

"Clu had overcome adversity before," FJ said.

"Not like this. He was through."

"If he stayed with MB, yes, that's probably true. But TruPro has influence. We would have found a way to relaunch his career."

Doubtful. But all this raised some interesting questions. The signature looked real, the contract legit. So maybe Clu had left him. Why? Well, lots of reasons. His life was being flushed down the toilet while Myron lollygagged in the sands of the Caribbean. Okay, but why TruPro? Clu knew their reputation. He knew what the Aches were all about. Why would he choose them?

Unless he had to.

Unless Clu was in debt to them. Myron remembered the missing two hundred thousand dollars. Could Clu have been in debt to FJ? Had he gotten in too deep—so deep he had to sign with TruPro? But if that was the case, why not take out more money? He still had more in the account.

No, maybe this was far simpler. Maybe Clu got himself in big trouble. He looked to Myron for help. Myron wasn't there. Clu felt abandoned. He had no one. In desperation he turned to his old friend Billy Lee Palms. But Billy Lee was too messed up to help anyone. He looked again for Myron. But Myron was still gone, possibly avoiding him. Clu was weak and alone, and FJ was there with promises and power.

So maybe Clu didn't have an affair with Esperanza after all. Maybe Clu told her he was leaving the agency and she got upset and then he got upset. Maybe Clu gave her a good-bye smack in that garage.

Hmm.

But there were problems with that scenario too. If there was no affair, how do you explain Esperanza's hairs at the crime scene? How do you explain the blood in the car, the gun in the office, and Esperanza's continued silence?

FJ was still smiling.

"Let's cut to it," Myron said. "How do I get you off my back?"

"Stay away from my clients."

"The same way you stayed away from mine?"

"Tell you what, Myron." FJ sipped more shaving cream. "If I desert my clients for six weeks, I give you carte blanche to pursue them with as much gusto as you can muster."

Myron looked at Win. No solace. Scary as it might sound, FJ had a point.

"Esperanza has been indicted for Clu's murder," Myron said. "I'm involved until she's cleared. Outside of that, I'll stay out of your business. And you stay out of mine."

"Suppose she's not cleared," FJ said.

"What?"

"Have you considered the possibility that Esperanza did indeed kill him?"

"You know something I don't, FJ?"

FJ put his hand to his chest. "Me?" The most innocent lamb ever to lie next to a lion. "What would I know?" He finished his coffee whatever and stood. He looked down at his goons, then at Win. Win nodded. FJ told Hans and Franz to get up. They did. FJ ordered them out the door. They went out, heads high, chests out, eyes up, but still looking like a pair of whipped dogs.

"If you find anything that might help me get Clu's contract reinstated, you'll let me know?"

"Yeah," Myron said. "I'll let you know."

"Great. Then let's stay in touch, Myron."

"Oh," Myron said. "Let's."

22

They took the subway to Yankee Stadium. The 4 train was fairly empty this time of the day. After they found seats, Myron asked, "Why did you beat up those two muscleheads?"

"You know why," Win said.

"Because they challenged you?"

"I hardly call what they mustered a challenge."

"So why did you beat them up?"

"Because it was simple."

"What?"

Win hated repeating himself.

"You overreacted," Myron said. "As usual."

"No, Myron, I reacted perfectly."

"Meaning?"

"I have a reputation, do I not?"

"As a violent psycho, yes."

"Exactly—a reputation that I've culled and created through what you call overreacting. You trade off that reputation sometimes, do you not?"

"I guess I do."

"It helps us?"

"I guess so."

"Guess nothing," Win said. "Friends and foes believe I snap too easily—overreact, as you put it. That I'm unstable, out of control. But that's nonsense, of course. I'm never out of control. Just the opposite. Every attack has been well thought out. The pros and cons have been weighed."

"And in this case, the pros won?"

"Yes."

"So you knew you were going to beat up those two before we entered?"

"I considered it. Once I realized that they were unarmed and that taking them out would be easy, I made the final decision."

"Just to enhance your reputation?"

"In a word, yes. My reputation keeps us safe. Why do you think FJ was ordered by his father not to kill you?"

"Because I'm a ray of sunshine? Because I make the world a better place for all?"

Win smiled. "Then you understand."

"Does it bother you at all, Win?"

"Does what?"

"Attacking someone like that."

"They're goons, Myron, not nuns."

"Still. You just walloped them without provocation."

"Oh, I see. You don't like the fact that I sucker-punched them. You would have preferred a fairer fight?"

"I guess not. But suppose you miscalculated?"

"Highly unlikely."

"Suppose one of them was better than you thought and didn't go down so easily. Suppose you had to maim or kill one."

"They're goons, Myron, not nuns."

"So you would have done it?"

"You know the answer to that."

"I guess I do."

"Who would have mourned their passing?" Win asked. "Two scums in the night who freely chose a profession that bullies and maims."

Myron did not answer. The train stopped. Passengers exited. Myron and Win stayed in their seats.

"But you enjoy it," Myron said.

Win said nothing.

"You have other reasons, sure, but you enjoy violence."

"And you don't, Myron?"

"Not like you."

"No, not like me. But you feel the rush."

"And I usually feel sick after it's all over."

"Well, Myron, that's probably because you're such a fine humanitarian."

They exited the subway at 161st Street and walked in silence to Yankee Stadium. Four hours to game time, but there were already several hundred fans lining up to watch the warm-ups. A giant Louisville Slugger bat cast a long shadow. Cops aplenty stood near clusters of unfazed ticket scalpers. Classic détente. There were hot dog carts, some with— gasp!—Yoo-Hoo umbrellas. Yum. At the press entrance Myron flashed his business card, the guard made a call, they were let in.

They traveled down the stairs on the right, reached the stadium tunnel, and emerged into bright sunshine and green grass. Myron and Win had just been discussing the nature of violence, and now Myron thought again about his dad's phone call. Myron had seen his father, the most gentle man he had ever known, grow violent only once. And it was here at Yankee Stadium.

When Myron was ten years old, his father had taken him and his younger brother, Brad, to a game. Brad was five at the time. Dad had secured four seats in the upper tier, but at the last minute a business associate had given him two more seats three rows behind the Red Sox bench. Brad was a huge fan of the Red Sox. So Dad suggested that Brad and Myron sit by the dugout for a few innings. Dad would stay in the upper tier. Myron held Brad's hand, and they walked down to the box seats. The seats were, in a word, awesome.

Brad started cheering his five-year-old lungs out. Cheering like mad. He spotted Carl Yastrzemski in the batter's box and started calling out, "Yaz! Yaz!" The guy sitting in front of them turned around. He was maybe twenty-five and bearded and looked a bit like a church image of Jesus. "That's enough," the bearded guy snapped at Brad. "Quiet down."

Brad looked hurt.

"Don't listen to him," Myron said. "You're allowed to yell."

The bearded man's hands moved fast. He grabbed the ten-year-old Myron by his shirt, bunching the Yankee emblem in his seemingly giant fist, and pulled Myron closer to him. There was beer on his breath. "He's giving my girlfriend a headache. He shuts up now."

Fear engulfed Myron. Tears filled his eyes, but he wouldn't let them escape. He remembered being shocked, scared, and mostly, for some unknown reason, ashamed. The bearded man glared at Myron another few seconds and then pushed him back. Myron grabbed Brad's hand and rushed back to the upper tier. He tried to pretend everything was all right, but ten-year-olds are not great actors, and Dad could read his son as if he lived inside his skull.

"What's wrong?" Dad asked.

Myron hesitated. Dad asked again. Myron finally told him what happened. And something happened to Myron's father, something Myron had never seen before or since. There was an explosion in his eyes. His face turned red; his eyes went black.

"I'll be right back," he said.

Myron watched the rest through binoculars. Dad moved down to the seat behind the Red Sox dugout. His father's face was still red. Myron saw Dad cup his hands around his mouth, lean forward, and start screaming for all he was worth. The red in his face turned to crimson. Dad kept screaming. The bearded man tried to ignore him. Dad leaned into his ear à la Mike Tyson and screamed some more. When the bearded man finally turned around, Dad did something that shocked Myron to the core. He pushed the man. He pushed the man twice and then gestured toward the exit, the international sign inviting another man to step outside. The guy with the beard refused. Dad pushed him again.

Two security guards raced down the steps and broke it up. No one was tossed. Dad came back to the upper tier. "Go back down," Dad said. "He won't bother you again."

But Myron and Brad shook their heads. They liked the seats up here better.

Win said, "Time traveling again, are we?"

Myron nodded.

"You realize, of course, that you are far too young for so many reflective spells."

"Yeah, I know."

A group of Yankee players were sitting on the outfield grass, legs sprawled, hands back, still kids under the collars waiting for their Little League game to start. A man in a too-nicely-fitted suit was talking to them. The man gestured wildly, smiling and enthusiastic and as enraptured with life as the new born-again on the block. Myron recognized him. Sawyer Wells, the motivational speaker né con man of the moment. Two years ago Wells was an unknown charlatan, spouting the standard reworded dogma about finding yourself, unlocking your potential, doing something for yourself—as though people weren't self-centered enough. His big break came when the Mayors hired him to do talks for their workforce. The speeches were, if not original, successful, and Sawyer Wells caught on. He got a book deal—cleverly monikered *The Wells Guide to Wellness*—along with an infomercial, audiotapes, video, a planner, the full self-help schematic. Fortune 500 companies started hiring him. When the Mayors took over the Yankees, they brought him on board as a consulting motivational psychologist or some such drivel.

When Sawyer Wells spotted Win, he almost started panting.

"He smells a new client," Myron said.

"Or perhaps he's never seen anyone quite this handsome before."

"Oh, yeah," Myron said. "That's probably it."

Wells turned back to the players, shouted out a bit more enthusiasm, spasmed with gestures, clapped once, and then bade them good-bye. He looked back over at Win. He waved. He waved hard. Then he started bounding over like a puppy chasing a new squeaky toy or a politician chasing a potential contributor.

Win frowned. "In a word, decaf."

Myron nodded.

"You want me to befriend him?" Win asked.

"He was supposedly present for the drug tests. And he's also the team psychologist. He probably hears a lot of rumors."

"Fine," Win said. "You take the roommate. I'll take Sawyer."

Enos Cabral was a good-looking wiry Cuban with a flame-throwing fastball and breaking pitches that still needed work. He was twenty-four, but he had the kind of looks that probably got him carded at any liquor store. He stood watching batting practice, his body slack except for his mouth. Like most relief pitchers, he chewed gum or tobacco with the ferocity of a lion gnawing on a recently downed gazelle.

Myron introduced himself.

Enos shook his hand and said, "I know who you are."

"Oh?"

"Clu talked about you a lot. He thought I should sign with you."

A pang. "Clu said that?"

"I wanted a change," Enos continued. "My agent. He treats me well, no? And he made me a rich man."

"I don't mean to knock the importance of good representation, Enos, but you made you a rich man. An agent facilitates. He doesn't create."

Enos nodded. "You know my story?"

The thumbnail sketch. The boat trip had been rough. Very rough. For a week everyone had assumed they had been lost at sea. When they finally did pop up, only two of the eight Cubans were still alive. One of the dead was Enos's brother Hector, considered the best player to come out of Cuba in the past decade. Enos, considered the lesser talent, was nearly dead of dehydration.

"Just what I've read in the papers," Myron said.

"My agent. He was there when I arrived. I had family in Miami. When he heard about the Cabral brothers, he loaned them money. He paid for my hospital stay. He gave me money and jewelry and a car. He promised me more money. And I have it."

"So what's the problem?"

"He has no soul."

"You want an agent with a soul?"

Enos shrugged. "I'm Catholic," he said. "We believe in miracles."

They both laughed.

Enos seemed to be studying Myron. "Clu was always suspicious of people. Even me. He had something of a hard shell."

"I know," Myron said.

"But he believed in you. He said you were a good man. He said that he had trusted you with his life and would gladly do so again."

Another pang. "Clu was also a lousy judge of character."

"I don't think so."

"Enos, I wanted to talk to you about Clu's last few weeks."

He raised an eyebrow. "I thought you came here to recruit me."

"No," Myron said. Then: "But have you heard the expression *killing two birds with one stone?*"

Enos laughed. "What do you want to know?"

"Were you surprised when Clu failed the drug test?"

He picked up a bat. He gripped and regripped it in his hands. Finding the right groove. Funny. He was an American League pitcher. He would probably never have the opportunity to bat. "I have trouble understanding addictions," he said. "Where I come from, yes, a man may try to drink away his world, if he can afford it. You live in such stink, why not leave, no? But here, when you have as much as Clu had . . ."

He didn't finish the thought. No point in stating the obvious.

"One time Clu tried to explain it to me," Enos continued." 'Sometimes,' he said, 'you don't want to escape the world; sometimes you want to escape yourself.' " He cocked his head. "Do you believe that?"

"Not really," Myron said. "Like a lot of cute phrases, it sounds good. But it also sounds like a load of self-rationalization."

Enos smiled. "You're mad at him."

"I guess I am."

"Don't be. He was a very unhappy man, Myron. A man who needs so much excess . . . there is something broken inside him, no?"

Myron said nothing.

"Clu tried. He fought hard, you have no idea. He wouldn't go out at night. If our room had a minibar, he'd make them take it out. He didn't hang out with old friends because he was afraid of what he might do. He was scared all the time. He fought long and hard."

"And he lost," Myron added.

"I never saw him take drugs. I never saw him drink."

"But you noticed changes."

Enos nodded. "His life began to fall apart. So many bad things happened."

"What bad things?"

The organ music revved immediately into high gear, the legendary Eddie Layton opening up with his rendition of that ballpark classic "The Girl from Ipanema." Enos lifted the bat to his shoulder, then lowered it again. "I feel uncomfortable talking about this."

"I'm not prying for the fun of it. I'm trying to find out who killed him."

"The papers said your secretary did it."

"They're wrong."

Enos stared at the bat as though there were a message hidden beneath the word *Louisville*. Myron tried to prompt him.

"Clu withdrew two hundred thousand dollars not long before he died," Myron said. "Was he having financial problems?"

"If he did, I didn't see it."

"Did he gamble?"

"I didn't see him him gamble, no."

"Do you know that he changed agents?"

Enos looked surprised. "He fired you?"

"Apparently he was going to."

"I didn't know," he said. "I know he was looking for you. But no, I didn't know that."

"So what was it then, Enos? What made him cave?"

He lifted his eyes and blinked into the sun. The perfect weather for a night game. Soon fans would arrive, and memories would be made. Happened every night in stadiums around the world. It was always some kid's first game.

"His marriage," Enos said. "That was the big thing, I think. You know Bonnie?"

"Yes."

"Clu loved her very much."

"He had an odd way of showing it."

Enos smiled. "Sleeping with all those women. I think he did it more to hurt himself than anyone else."

"That sounds like another one of those big, fat rationalizations, Enos. Clu may have made self-destruction an art form. But that's not an excuse for what he put her through."

"I think he'd agree with that. But Clu hurt himself most of all."

"Don't kid yourself. He hurt Bonnie too."

"Yes, you're right, of course. But he still loved her. When she threw him out, it hurt him so much. You have no idea."

"What can you tell me about their breakup?"

Another hesitation. "Not much to tell. Clu felt betrayed, angry."

"You know that Clu had fooled around before."

"Yes."

"So what made it different this time? Bonnie was used to his straying. What made her finally snap? Who was his girlfriend?"

Enos looked puzzled. "You think Bonnie threw him out over a girl?"

"She didn't?"

Enos shook his head.

"You're sure."

"It was never about girls with Clu. They were just part of the drugs and alcohol. They were easy for him to give up."

Myron was confused. "So he wasn't having an affair?"

"No," Enos said. "*She* was."

That was when it clicked. Myron felt a cold wave roll through him, squeezing the pit of his stomach. He barely said good-bye before he hurried away.

23

He knew Bonnie would be home.

The car had barely come to a full stop when he shot out the driver's door. There were perhaps a dozen other vehicles parked on the street. Mourners. The front door was opened. Myron headed inside without knocking. He wanted to find Bonnie and confront her and end this. But she wasn't in the living room. Just mourners. Some approached him, slowing him down. He offered his condolences to Clu's mother, her face ravaged with grief. He shook other hands, trying to swim through the thick sea of grief-stricken and glad-handers and find Bonnie. He finally spotted her outside in the backyard. She sat alone on the deck, her knees tucked under her chin, watching her children play. He steeled himself and pushed open the sliding glass doors.

The porch was cedarwood and overlooked a large swing set. Clu's boys were on it, both dressed in red ties and untucked short-sleeve shirts. They ran and laughed. Miniature versions of their dead father, their smiles so like his, their features eternal echoes of Clu's. Bonnie watched them. Her back was to Myron, a cigarette in her hand. She did not turn around as he approached.

"Clu didn't have the affair," Myron said. "You did."

Bonnie inhaled deeply and let it out. "Great timing, Myron."

"That can't be helped."

"Can't we talk about this later?"

Myron waited a beat. Then: "I know who you were sleeping with."

She stiffened. Myron looked down at her. She finally turned and met his gaze.

"Let's take a walk," Bonnie said.

She reached out a hand, and Myron helped her to her feet.

They walked down the backyard to a wooded area. The din of traffic filtered through a sound barrier up the hill. The house was spanking new, large and innately nouveau-riche. Airy, lots of windows, cathedral ceilings, small living room, huge kitchen flowing into huge California room, huge master bedroom, closets large enough to double as Gap outlets. Probably went for about eight hundred thou. Beautiful and sterile and soulless. Needing to be lived in a bit. Properly aged like a fine Merlot.

"I didn't know you smoked," he said.

"You don't know a lot of things about me, Myron."

Touché. He looked at her profile, and again he saw that young coed heading into the fraternity basement. He flashed back to that very moment, to the sound of Clu's sharp intake of air when he first laid eyes on her. Suppose she'd come down a little later, after Clu had passed out or hooked up with another woman. Suppose she had gone to another frat party that night. Dumb thoughts—life's arbitrary forks in the road, the series of what ifs—but there you go.

"So what makes you think I was the one having an affair?" she said.

"Clu told Enos."

"Clu lied."

"No," Myron said.

They kept walking. Bonnie took a last drag and tossed the cigarette on the ground. "My property," she said. "I'm allowed."

Myron said nothing.

"Did Clu tell Enos who he thought I was sleeping with?"

"No."

"But you think you know who this mystery lover is."

"Yes," Myron said. "It's Esperanza."

Silence.

"Would you believe me if I insisted you were wrong?" she said.

"You'd have a lot of explaining to do."

"How's that?"

"Let's start with you coming to my office after Esperanza was arrested."

"Okay."

"You wanted to know what they had on her—that was the real reason. I wondered why you warned me away from finding the truth. You told me to clear my friend but not dig too hard."

She nodded. "And you think I said that because I didn't want you to know about this affair?"

"Yes. But there's more. Like Esperanza's silence, for one thing. Win and I theorized that she didn't want us to know about her affair with Clu.

It would look bad on several levels to be having an affair with a client. But to be having an affair with a client's wife? What could be dumber than that?"

"That's hardly evidence, Myron."

"I'm not finished. You see, all the evidence that points to an affair between Esperanza and Clu actually points to an affair between you two. The physical evidence, for example. The pubic hairs and DNA found at the Fort Lee apartment. I started thinking about that. You and Clu lived there for a short time. Then you moved into this house. But you still had the lease on the apartment. So before you threw him out, it was empty, right?"

"Right."

"What better place to meet for a tryst? It wasn't Clu and Esperanza meeting there. It was you two."

Bonnie said nothing.

"The E-Z Pass records—most of the bridge crossings were on days when the Yankees were out of town. So Esperanza wasn't coming out to see Clu. She was coming out to see you. I checked the office phone records. She never called the apartment after you threw Clu out—only this house. Why? Clu wasn't living here. You were."

She took out another cigarette and struck a match.

"And lastly, the fight in the garage when Clu struck Esperanza. That bothered the hell out of me. Why would he hit her? Because she broke off an affair? That didn't make sense. Because he wanted to find me or was crazed from taking drugs? Again, no. I couldn't figure it out. But now the answer is obvious. Esperanza was having an affair with his wife. He blamed her for breaking up the marriage. Enos said the breakup shook him to the core. What could be worse for a psyche as fragile as Clu's than his wife having an affair with a woman?"

Her voice was sharp. "Are you blaming me for his death?"

"Depends. Did you kill him?"

"Would it help if I said no?"

"It would be a start."

She smiled, but there was no joy in it. Like the house, it was beautiful and sterile and almost soulless. "Do you want to hear something funny?" she said. "Clu's beating the drugs and the drinking didn't help our marriage—it ended it. For so long Clu was . . . I don't know . . . a work in progress. I blamed his shortcomings on the drugs and drinking and all that. But once he finally exorcised his demons, what was left was just"—she lifted her palms and shrugged—"just him. I saw Clu clearly for the first time, Myron, and you know what I realized? I didn't love him."

Myron said nothing.

"And don't blame Esperanza. It wasn't her fault. I held on purely for the sake of my kids, and when Esperanza came along—" Bonnie stopped, and this time her smile seemed more genuine. "You want to hear something else funny? I'm not a lesbian. I'm not even a bisexual. It's just . . . she treated me tenderly. We had sex, sure, but it was never about sex. I know that sounds weird, but her gender was irrelevant. Esperanza is just a beautiful person, and I fell in love with that. Does that make sense?"

"You know how this looks," Myron said.

"Of course I know how it looks. Two dykes got together and offed the husband. Why do you think we're trying so hard to keep it secret? The weakness in their case right now is motive. But if they find out we were lovers—"

"Did you kill him?"

"What do you expect me to say to that, Myron?"

"I'd like to hear it."

"No, we didn't kill him. I was leaving him. Why would I throw him out and start filing papers if I planned on killing him?"

"To prevent a scandal that would surely hurt your kids."

She made a face. "Come on, Myron."

"So how do you explain the gun in the office and the blood in the car?"

"I can't."

Myron thought about it. His head hurt—from the physical altercation or this latest revelation, he couldn't say. He tried to concentrate through the haze. "Who else knows about the affair?"

"Just Esperanza's lawyer, Hester Crimstein."

"No one else?"

"No one. We were very discreet."

"You're sure?"

"Yes. Why?"

"Because," Myron said, "if I were going to murder Clu and I wanted to frame someone for it, his wife's lover would be my first choice."

Bonnie saw where he was heading. "So you think the killer knew about us?"

"It might explain a lot."

"I didn't tell anyone. And Esperanza said she didn't either."

Pow. Right between the eyes. "You couldn't have been too careful," Myron said.

"What makes you say that?"

"Clu found out, didn't he?"

She thought about it, nodded.

"Did you tell him?" he asked.

"No."

"What did you say when you threw him out?"

She shrugged. "That there was no one else. That was true in a sense. It wasn't about Esperanza."

"So how did he find out?"

"I don't know. I assumed he became obsessed. That he followed me."

"And he found out the truth?"

"Yes."

"And then he went after Esperanza and attacked her?"

"Yes."

"And before he has a chance to tell anyone else about this, before it has a chance of getting out and hurting either of you, he ends up dead. And the murder weapon ends up with Esperanza. And Clu's blood ends up in the car she's been driving. And the E-Z Pass records show Esperanza came back to New York an hour after the murder."

"Again, yes."

Myron shook his head. "It doesn't look good, Bonnie."

"That's what I've been trying to tell you," she said. "If even you won't believe us, how do you think a jury is going to react?"

There was no need to answer. They headed back to the house then. The two young boys were still at play, oblivious of what was going on around them. Myron watched for a moment. *Fatherless,* he thought, shuddering at the word. With one last look he turned and walked away.

24

Thrill, not Nancy Sinclair, met him outside a bar called the Biker Wannabee. Honesty in advertising. Nice to see.

"Howdy," Myron said. Tex Bolitar.

Her smile was full of pornographic promise. Totally into Thrill mode now. "Howdy yourself, pardner," she cooed. With some women, every syllable is cooed. "How do I look?"

"Mighty tasty, ma'am. But I think I prefer you as Nancy."

"Liar."

Myron shrugged, not sure if he was telling the truth or not. This whole thing reminded him of when Barbara Eden would play her evil sister on *I Dream of Jeannie.* He was often torn back then too, not sure if Larry Hagman should stay with Jeannie or run off with the enticingly evil sister. But hey, talk about your great dilemmas.

"I thought you were bringing backup," Thrill said.

"I am."

"Where is he?"

"If things go well, you won't see him."

"How mysterious."

"Isn't it?"

They headed inside and grabbed a corner booth in the back. Yep, biker wanna-be. Lots of guys aiming for that hairy, Vietnam vet–cum–hit-the-road look. The jukebox played "God Only Knows (What I'd Be Without You)"—the Beach Boys, but unlike anything else the Beach Boys did. The song was a plaintive wail, and despite its pop misgivings, it always struck Myron to the bone, the trepidation of what the future might hold so naked in Brian's voice, the words so hauntingly simple. Especially now.

Thrill was studying his face. "You okay?" she asked.

"Fine. So what happens next?"

"We order a drink, I guess."

Five minutes passed. "Lonely Boy" came on the jukebox. Andrew Gold. Serious seventies AM bubble gum. Chorus: "Oh, oh, oh . . . oh what a lonely boy . . . oh what a lonely boy . . . oh what a lonely boy." By the time the chorus was repeated for the eighth time, Myron had it down pat so he sang along. Megamemory. Maybe he should do an infomercial.

Men at nearby tables checked out Thrill, some surreptitiously, most not. Thrill's smile was practically a leer now, sinking deeper into the role.

"You get into this," Myron said.

"It's a part, Myron. We're all actors on a stage and all that."

"But you enjoy the attention."

"So?"

"So I was just saying."

She shrugged. "I find it fascinating."

"What's that?"

"What a large bosom does to a man. They get so obsessed."

"You just reached the conclusion that men are mammary-obsessed? I hate to break this to you, Nancy, but the research has been done."

"But it's weird when you think about it."

"I try not to."

"Bosoms do weird things to men, no doubt," she said, "but I don't like what they do to women either."

"How's that?"

Thrill put her palms on the table. "Okay, everyone knows that we women put too much of our self-worth into our bodies. Old news, right?"

"Right."

"I know it, you know it, everyone knows it. And unlike my more feminist sisters, I don't blame men for this."

"You don't?"

"*Mademoiselle, Vogue, Bazaar, Glamour*—those are run by women and have a totally female clientele. They want to change the image, start there. Why ask the men to change a perception that women themselves won't change?"

"Refreshing viewpoint," Myron noted.

"But bosoms do funny things to people. Men, okay, that's obvious. They become brain-dead. It's as if the nipples shoot out like two grapefruit spoons, dig into their frontal lobe, and scrape away all cognitive thought."

Myron looked up, the imagery giving him pause.

"But for women, well, it starts when you're young. A girl develops early. Adolescent boys start lusting after her. How do her girlfriends react? They take it out on her. They're jealous of the attention or feeling inadequate or whatever. But they take it out on the young girl who can't help what her body is going through. With me?"

"Yes."

"Even now. Look at the glances the women in here give me. Pure hatred. You get a group of women together and a chesty counterpart walks by and they all sigh, 'Oh, please.' Professional women, for example, feel the urge to dress down—not just because of leering men but because of women. Because of how women treat them. A businesswoman sees a big-chested businesswoman with a better title—well, she got the job because of her tits. Plain and simple. Might be true, might not be. Is this animosity spawned again from dormant jealousy or a misplaced feeling of inadequacy or because they unfairly equate bosoms with stupidity? Any way you look at it, it's an ugly thing."

"I never really thought about it," Myron said.

"And finally I don't like what it does to me."

"Your reaction to seeing a big chest or having one?"

"The latter."

"Why?"

"Because the big-breasted woman gets used to it. She takes it for granted. She uses them to her advantage."

"So?"

"What do you mean, so?"

"All attractive people do that," Myron said. "It's not just bosoms. If a woman is beautiful, she knows it and uses it. Nothing wrong with that. Men use it too, if they can. Sometimes—I'm ashamed to admit this—even I shake my little tush to get my way."

"Shocking."

"Well, not really. Because it never works."

"I think you're being modest. But either way, don't you see anything wrong with that?"

"With what?"

"With using a physical attribute to get your way."

"I didn't say there was nothing wrong with it. I'm simply noting that what you're talking about is not merely a mammarial phenomenon."

She made a face. "Mammarial phenomenon?"

Myron shrugged, and mercifully the waitress came over. Myron made a point of not looking anywhere near her chest, which was tantamount to telling yourself not to scratch that irksome itch. The waitress had a pen behind her ear. Her overtreated hair aimed for on-the-farm strawberry blond but landed far closer to fell-at-the-4H-fair cotton candy.

"Get you?" she said. Skipping the preliminaries like "Hello" and "What can I . . . ?"

"Rob Roy," Thrill said.

The pen came out of the ear holster, jotted it down, back in the holster. Wyatt Earp. "You?" she said to Myron.

Myron doubted that they had any Yoo-Hoo. "A diet soda, please."

She looked at him as if he'd ordered a bedpan.

"Maybe a beer," Myron said.

She clacked her gum. "Bud, Michelob, or some pansy brew?"

"Pansy would be fine, thank you," Myron said. "And do you have any of those little cocktail umbrellas?"

The waitress rolled her eyes and walked away.

They chatted for a while. Myron had just started relaxing and yes, even enjoying himself when Thrill said, "Behind you. By the door."

He was not much in the mood for clandestine games. They wanted him here for a reason. No sense beating around the bush. He turned without an iota of subtlety and spotted Pat the bartender and Veronica Lake aka Zorra dressed again in a cashmere sweater—peach-toned, for those keeping score—long skirt, and a strand of pearls. Zorra, the Steroid Debutante. Myron shook his head. Bonnie Franklin and Mall Girl were nowhere to be seen.

Myron gave a big wave. "Over here, fellas!"

Pat scowled, feigning surprise. He looked toward Zorra, She-Man of the Saber Heel. Zorra showed nothing. The great ones never do. Myron always wondered if their blaséness was an act or if, in truth, nothing really surprised them. Probably a bit of both.

Pat strode toward their table, acting as though he were shocked— shocked!—that Myron was in his bar. Zorra followed, more gliding than walking, the eyes soaking in everything. Like Win, Zorra moved economically—albeit in stylish red pumps—no motion wasted. Pat was still scowling when he reached the table.

"What the hell are you doing here, Bolitar?" Pat asked.

Myron nodded. "Not bad, but it could use work. Do me a favor. Try it again. But add a little gasp first. Gasp, what the hell are you doing here, Bolitar? Like that. Better yet, why not give a wry shake of your head and say something like 'All the gin joints in all the world, you have to walk into mine—two nights in a row.' "

Zorra was smiling now.

"You're crazy," Pat said.

"Pat." It was Zorra. He looked at Pat and shook his head just once. The shake said, Stop with the games.

Pat turned to Thrill. "Do me a favor, hon."

Thrill offered up breathless. "Sure, Pat."

"Go powder your nose or something, okay?"

Myron made a face. "Go powder your nose?" He looked pleadingly at Zorra. Zorra's small shrug was semiapologetic. "What next, Pat? You going to threaten to make me sleep with the fishes? Make me an offer I can't refuse. I mean, go powder your nose?"

Pat was fuming. He looked over at Thrill. "Please, hon."

"No problem, Pat." She slid out of the booth. Pat and Zorra immediately took her place. Myron frowned at the change in scenery.

"We need some information," Pat said.

"Yeah, I picked up on that last night," Myron said.

"That got out of control. I'm sorry."

"I bet."

"Hey, we let you go, right?"

"As soon as I was electrocuted with a cattle prod, slashed twice with a heel blade, kicked in the ribs, and then jumped through a glass mirror. Yeah, you let me go."

Pat smiled. "If Zorra here didn't want you to escape, you wouldn't have escaped. Get my meaning?"

Myron looked at Zorra. Zorra looked at Myron. Myron said, "A peach sweater with red pumps?"

Zorra smiled, shrugged.

"Zorra here could have killed you easy as pie," Pat continued.

"Right, fine, Zorra is a tough guy, you're super-generous to me. Get to it."

"Why were you asking about Clu Haid?"

"Sorry to disappoint you, but I was telling you the truth last night. I'm trying to find his killer."

"So what does my club have to do with that?"

"Before I got dragged into the back room, I would have said, 'Nothing.' But now, well, that's what I'd like to know."

Pat looked at Zorra. Zorra did not move. Pat said, "We want to take you for a ride."

"Damn."

"What?"

"You'd gone nearly three minutes without a mob cliché. Then you come up with the take a ride bit. It's sad really. Can I powder my nose first?"

"You want to crack wise or you want to come with us?"

"I can do both," Myron said. "I'm rather multitalented."

Pat shook his head. "Let's go." Myron started to slide out the booth.

"No," Zorra said.

Everyone stopped. "What's wrong?" Pat said.

Zorra looked at Myron. "We are not interested in hurting you," Zorra said.

More reassurances.

"But we can't let you know where you're going, dreamboat. You'll have to be blindfolded."

"You're kidding, right?"

"No."

"Fine, blindfold me. Let's go."

"No," Zorra said again.

"What now?"

"Your friend Win. Zorra assumes he's close by."

"Who?"

Zorra smiled. He-she wasn't pretty. Lots of transvestites are. Lots of times you can't even tell. But Zorra had a five o'clock shadow (a look Myron found to be less than alluring in a woman), big hands with hairy knuckles (ditto), a skewered wig (call him picky), a rather masculine, whispery voice (*comme ci, comme ça*) and despite the outer trappings, Zorra looked like, well, a guy wearing a dress. "Don't insult Zorra's intelligence, dreamboat."

"You see him?"

"If Zorra could," Zorra said, "then someone has grossly overexaggerated his reputation."

"So what makes you so sure Win's here?"

"You're doing it again," Zorra said.

"Doing what?"

"Insulting Zorra's intelligence."

Nothing like a psycho who refers to himself in the third person.

"Please ask him to come forward," Zorra said. "We have no interest in hurting anyone. But Zorra knows that your colleague will follow wherever you go. Then Zorra will have to follow him. It will lead to conflict. None of us wants that."

Win's voice came from Myron's cell phone. Must have taken off the mute. "What guarantee do we have that Myron will return?"

Myron lifted the cell phone into view.

"You and Zorra will sit and enjoy a drink, dreamboat," Zorra said into the phone. "Myron will travel with Pat."

"Travel where?" Myron asked.

"We can't tell you."

Myron frowned. "Is this cloak-and-dagger stuff really necessary?"

Pat leaned back now, letting Zorra handle it. "You have questions, we have questions," Zorra said. "This meeting is the only way to satisfy both."

"So why can't we talk here?"

"Impossible."

"Why?"

"You have to go with Pat."

"Where?"

"Zorra cannot tell you."

"Who are you taking me to see?"

"Zorra cannot tell you that either."

Myron said, "Does the fate of the free world rest in Zorra's maintaining silence?"

Zorra adjusted his lips, forming what he probably read someplace was known as a smile. "You mock Zorra. But Zorra has kept silent before. Zorra has seen horrors you cannot imagine. Zorra has been tortured. For weeks on end. Zorra has felt pain that makes what you felt with that cattle prod seem like a lover's kiss."

Myron nodded solemnly. "Wow," he said.

Zorra spread his hands. Hairy knuckles and pink nail polish. Hold me back. "We can always choose to part ways, dreamboat."

From the cell phone Win said, "Good idea."

Myron lifted the receiver. "What?"

"If we agree to their terms," Win said, "I cannot guarantee they won't kill you."

"Zorra guarantees it," Zorra said. "With her life."

Myron said, "Excuse me?"

"Zorra stays here with Win," Zorra went on, the glint in the overmascaraed eye sparkling anew. Something was there, and it was not lucidity. "Zorra will be unarmed. If you don't return in perfect health, Win kills Zorra."

"Heck of a guarantee," Myron said. "Ever thought about becoming a car mechanic?"

Win entered the bar now. He walked straight toward the table, sat down, hands under it. "If you'd be so kind," Win said to Zorra and Pat, "please put all hands on the table."

They did.

"And, Ms. Zorra, if you wouldn't mind kicking off your heels?"

"Sure, dreamboat." Win kept his eyes on Zorra. Zorra kept his on Win. There would be no blinking here. Win said, "I still cannot guarantee his safety. Yes, I have the option of killing you if he does not return. But for all I know, Pat the Bunny here doesn't give a rodent's buttocks about you."

"Hey," Pat said, "you have my word."

Win just looked at him for a moment. Then he turned back to Zorra. "Myron goes armed. Pat drives. Myron keeps the gun on him."

Zorra shook his head. "Impossible."

"Then we have no deal."

Zorra shrugged. "Then Zorra and Pat must bid you adieu."

They rose to leave. Myron knew that Win wouldn't call them back. He whispered to Win, "I need to know what's going on here."

Win shrugged. "It's a mistake," he said, "but it's your call."

Myron looked up. "We agree," he said.

Zorra sat back down. Under the table Win kept the gun on him.

"Myron keeps his cell phone on," Win said. "I listen to every word."

Zorra nodded. "Fair enough."

Pat and Myron started to leave.

"Oh, Pat?" Win said.

Pat stopped.

Win's voice was how's-the-weather casual. "If Myron isn't returned, I may or may not kill Zorra. I will decide at the appropriate time. Either way, I will use all my considerable influence and money and time and effort to find you. I will offer rewards. I will search. I will not sleep. I will find you. And when I do, I *won't* kill you. Do you understand?"

Pat swallowed, nodded.

"Go," Win said.

25

When they reached the car, Pat frisked him. Nothing. Then he handed Myron a black hood. "Put this on."

Myron made a face. "Tell me you're joking."

"Put it on. Then lie down in the backseat. Don't look up."

Myron rolled his eyes, but he did as he was asked. His six-four frame wasn't all that comfortable, but he made do. Big of him. Pat got in the front seat and started the car.

"Quick suggestion," Myron said.

"What did you say?"

"Next time you do this, try vacuuming out the car first. It's disgusting back here."

Pat drove. Myron tried to concentrate, listening for sounds that would give him a clue where they were going. That always worked on TV. The guy would hear, say, a boat horn and know he'd gone to Pier 12 or something, and they'd all rush in and find him. But all Myron heard were, not surprisingly, traffic noises: the occasional horn, cars passing or being passed, loud radios, that kind of thing. He tried to keep track of turns and distances but quickly realized the futility. What did he think he was, a human compass?

The drive lasted maybe ten minutes. Not enough time to leave the city. Clue: He was still in Manhattan. Gee, that was helpful. Pat turned off the engine.

"You can sit up," he said. "But keep the hood on."

"You sure the hood goes with this ensemble? I want to look my best for Mr. Big."

"Someone once tell you you were funny, Bolitar?"

"You're right. Black goes with everything."

Pat sighed. When nervous, some people run. Some hide. Some grow silent. Some get chatty. And some make dumb jokes.

Pat helped Myron out of the car and led him by the elbow. Myron again tried to pick up sounds. The cooing of a seagull maybe. That too always seemed to happen on TV. But in New York seagulls didn't coo as much as phlegm cough. And if you heard a seagull in New York, it was more likely you were near a trash canister than a pier. Myron tried to think of the last time he had seen a seagull in New York. There was a picture of one on a sign for his favorite bagel store. Caption: "If a bird flying over the sea is a seagull, what do you call a bird flying over the bay?" Clever when you think about it.

The two men walked—where to, Myron had no idea. He stumbled on uneven pavement, but Pat kept him upright. Another clue. Find the spot in Manhattan with uneven pavement. Christ, he practically had the guy cornered.

They walked up what felt like a stoop and entered a room with heat and humidity slightly more stifling than a Burmese forest fire. Myron was still blindfolded, but light from what might be a bare bulb filtered through the cloth. The room reeked of mildew and steam and dried sweat—like the most popular sauna at Jack La Lanne's gone to seed. It was hard to breathe through the hood. Pat put a hand on Myron's shoulder.

"Sit," Pat said before pushing down slightly.

Myron sat. He heard Pat's footsteps, then low voices. Whispers actually. Mostly from Pat. An argument of some sort. Footsteps again. Coming closer to Myron. A body suddenly cut off the bare lightbulb, bathing Myron in total darkness. One more step. Someone stopped directly over him.

"Hello, Myron," the voice said.

There was a tremor there, an almost manic twang in the tone. But there was no doubt. Myron was not great with names and faces, but voices were imprints. Memories flooded in. After all these years his recall was instantaneous.

"Hello, Billy Lee."

The missing Billy Lee Palms, to be exact. Former frat brother and Duke baseball star. Former best bud of Clu Haid. Son of Mrs. My-Life-Is-but-a-Wallpaper-Tapestry.

"Mind if I take the hood off now?" Myron asked.

"Not at all."

Myron reached up and grabbed the top of the hood. He pulled it off. Billy Lee was standing over him. Or at least he assumed it was Billy Lee. It was as if the former pretty boy had been kidnapped and replaced with this fleshier counterpart. Billy Lee's formerly prominent cheekbones looked malleable, tallow skin in mid-shed clung to sagging features, his eyes sunken deeper than any pirate treasure, his complexion the gray of a city street after a rainfall. His hair was greasy and jutting all over the place, as unwashed as any MTV video jockey's.

Billy Lee was also holding what looked liked a sawed-off shotgun about six inches from Myron's face.

"He's holding what looks like a sawed-off shotgun about six inches from my face," Myron said for the benefit of the cell phone.

Billy Lee giggled. That sound too was familiar.

"Bonnie Franklin," Myron said.

"What?"

"Last night. You were the one who hit me with the cattle prod."

Billy Lee spread his hands impossibly wide. "Bingo, baby!"

Myron shook his head. "You definitely look better with the makeup, Billy Lee."

Billy Lee giggled again and retrained the shotgun on Myron. Then he held out his free hand. "Give me the phone."

Myron hesitated but not for long. The sunken eyes, once Myron could see them, were wet and unfocused and tinged with a dull red. Billy Lee's body was one tremor. Myron checked out the short sleeves and saw the needle tracks. Billy Lee looked like the wildest and most unpredictable of animals: a cornered junkie. Myron handed him the phone. Billy Lee put it to his ear.

"Win?"

Win's voice was clear. "Yes, Billy Lee."

"Go to hell."

Billy Lee giggled again. Then he clicked off the phone, untethering them from the outside world, and Myron felt the dread rise in his chest.

Billy Lee stuck the phone in Myron's pocket and looked over at Pat. "Tie him to the chair."

Pat said, "What?"

"Tie him to the chair. There's rope right behind it."

"Tie him how? I look like a goddamn Boy Scout?"

"Just wrap it around him and tie a knot. I want to slow him down in case he gets dumb before I kill him."

Pat moved toward Myron. Billy Lee kept an eye on Myron.

Myron said, "It's not really a good idea to upset Win."

"Win doesn't scare me."

Myron shook his head.

"What?"

"I knew you were strung out," Myron said. "But I didn't realize how badly."

Pat started winding the rope around Myron's chest. "Maybe you should call him back," Pat said. If the San Andreas quaked like his voice, they'd be calling for an evacuation. "We don't need him searching for us too, you know what I'm saying?"

"Don't worry about it," Billy Lee said.

"And Zorra's still there—"

"Don't worry about it!" Screaming this time. A shrill, awful scream. The shotgun bounced closer to Myron's face. Myron tensed his body, preparing to make a move before the rope was knotted. But Billy Lee jumped back suddenly, as if realizing for the first time that Myron was in the room.

Nobody spoke. Pat tightened the rope and tied it in a knot. Not well done, but it'd serve its stated purpose—i.e., slow him down so that Billy Lee would have plenty of time to blow Myron's head off.

"You trying to kill me, Myron?"

Strange question. "No," Myron said.

Billy Lee's fist slammed into the lower part of Myron's belly. Myron doubled over, the air gone, his lungs spasming in the pure, naked need for oxygen. He felt tears push into his eyes.

"Don't lie to me, asshole."

Myron fought for breath.

Billy Lee sniffed, wiped his face with his sleeve. "Why are you trying to kill me?"

Myron tried to respond, but it took too long. Billy Lee hit him hard with the butt of the shotgun, exactly on the Z spot Zorra had sliced into him the night before. The stitches split apart, and blood mushroomed onto Myron's shirt. His head began to swim. Billy Lee giggled some more. Then he raised the butt of the shotgun over his head and started it in an arc toward Myron's head.

"Billy Lee!" Pat shouted.

Myron saw it coming, but there was no escape. He managed to tilt the chair with his toes and roll back. The blow glanced the top of his head, scraping his scalp. The chair teetered over, and Myron's head banged against the wooden floor. His skull tingled.

Oh Christ . . .

He looked up. Billy Lee was raising the butt of the shotgun again. A straight blow would crush his skull. Myron tried to roll, but he was hopelessly tangled up. Billy Lee smiled down at him. He held the shotgun high above his head, letting the moment drag out, watching Myron struggle the way some people watch an injured ant before stomping it with their foot.

Billy Lee suddenly frowned. He lowered the weapon, studying it for a moment. "Hmm," he said. "Might break my gun that way."

Myron felt Billy Lee grab his shoulders and lift him and the chair back up. The shotgun was at eye level now.

"Fuck it," Billy Lee said. "Might as well just shoot your sorry ass, am I right?"

Myron barely heard the giggling now. When a gun is pointed so directly in your face, it has a tendency to block out everything else. The double barrel's opening grows, moves closer, surrounds you until everything you are and see and hear is consumed in its black mouth.

Pat tried again. "Billy Lee . . ."

Myron felt the sweat under his arms begin to gush. Calm. Keep the tone calm. Don't excite him. "Tell me what's going on, Billy Lee. I want to help."

Billy Lee snickered, the shotgun still shaking in his hand. "You want to help me?"

"Yes."

That made him laugh. "Bullshit, Myron. Total bullshit."

Myron kept still.

"We were never even friends, were we, Myron? I mean, we were frat brothers, and we hung out and stuff. But we were never really friends."

Myron tried to keep his eyes on Billy Lee's. "This is a heck of a time to go tiptoeing through the past, Billy Lee."

"I'm trying to make a point here, asshole. You're peddling this crap about wanting to help me. Like we're friends. But that's a load of bullshit. We're not friends. You never really liked me."

Never really liked me. Like they were third graders during recess. "I still helped pull your ass out of a few fires, Billy Lee."

The smile. "Not my ass, Myron. Clu's. It was always about Clu, wasn't it? The drunk driving thing when we were living in Massachusetts. You didn't drive up to save my ass. You drove up because of Clu. And that brawl at that bar in the city. That was also because of Clu."

Billy Lee suddenly tilted his head like a dog hearing a new sound. "Why weren't we friends, Myron?"

"Because you didn't invite me to your birthday party at the roller rink?"

"Don't fuck with me, asshole."

"I liked you just fine, Billy Lee. You were a fun guy."

"But it got tired after a while, didn't it? My whole act, I mean. While I was a college star, it was pretty cool, right? But when I failed in the pros, I wasn't so cute and funny anymore. I was suddenly pathetic. That sound about right, Myron?"

"You say so."

"So what about Clu?"

"What about him?"

"You were friends with him."

"Yes."

"Why? Clu partied the same way. Maybe even harder. He was always getting his ass in trouble. Why were you his friend?"

"This is stupid, Billy Lee."

"Is it?"

"Put the gun down already."

Billy Lee's smile was wide and knowing and somewhere just south of sane. "I'll tell you why you stayed friendly with Clu. Because he was a better baseball player than me. He was going to the bigs. And you knew that. That's the only difference between Clu Haid and Billy Lee Palms. He got drunk and took drugs and screwed tons of women, but it was all so funny because he was a pro."

"So what are you trying to say, Billy Lee?" Myron countered. "That pro athletes are treated differently from the rest of us? Hell of a revelation."

But the revelation sat uneasily on Myron. Probably because Billy Lee's words, while wholly irrelevant, were at least in part true. Clu was charming and quirky simply because he was a pro athlete. But if the velocity of his fastball had dropped a few miles per hour, if the rotation of his arm had been just a little askew or if his finger position had not allowed for good ball movement on his pitches, Clu would have ended up like Billy Lee. Alternate worlds—totally different lives and fates—are right there, separated by a curtain no thicker than membrane. But with athletes, you can see your alternate life a little too clearly. You have the ability to throw the ball just a little faster than the next guy, you end up a god rather than the most pitiful of mortals. You get the girls, the fame, the big house, the money instead of the rats, the dull anonymity, the crummy apartment, the menial job. You get to go on TV and offer life insights. People want to be near you and hear you speak and touch the hem of your cloak. Just because you can hurl the rawhide with great velocity or put an orange ball in a metallic circle or swing a stick with a slightly more pure arc. You are special.

Nuts when you think about it.

"Did you kill him, Billy Lee?" Myron said.

Billy Lee looked like he'd been slapped. "What?"

"You were jealous of Clu. He had everything. He left you behind."

"He was my best friend!"

"A long time ago, Billy Lee."

Myron again debated making a move. He could try to slip the ropes—they were not on very tightly—but it would take time and he was still too far away. He wondered how Win was reacting to being cut off from all this and shuddered. Not worth dwelling upon.

A funny, tranquil flat line crossed Billy Lee's face. He stopped shaking, looked straight at Myron without jerking or twitching. His voice was suddenly soft.

"Enough," he said.

Silence.

"I have to kill you, Myron. It's self-defense."

"What are you talking about?"

"You killed Clu. And now you want to kill me."

"That's crazy."

"Maybe you had your secretary do it. And she got caught. Or maybe Win did it. That guy's always been your lapdog. Or maybe you did it yourself, Myron. The gun was found in your office, right? The blood in your car?"

"Why would I kill Clu?"

"You use people, Myron. You used him to start up your business. But after he failed his last drug test, Clu was finished. So you figured, why not cut your losses?"

"That makes no sense," Myron said. "And even if it did, why would I want to kill you?"

"Because I can talk too."

"Talk about what?"

"About how helpful you are."

Tears started rolling down Billy Lee's face. His voice tailed off. And Myron knew he was in huge trouble.

The moment of calm was over. The barrel of the gun was shaking. Myron tested the ropes. Nope. Despite the heat, something icy flooded his veins. He was trapped. No chance of making a move.

Billy Lee tried to giggle again, but something inside him was too weary now. "Bye."

Panic squeezed Myron's insides. Billy Lee was only seconds away from killing him. Period. There was no chance of talking him out of it. The combo of drugs and paranoia had scooped out all his ability to reason. Myron accessed his options and liked none of them.

"Win," Myron said.

"I already told you. I ain't afraid of him."

"I'm not talking to you." Myron glanced over at Pat. The bartender was breathing hard, and his shoulders were drooping as though someone had packed them with wet sand. "Once he pulls that trigger," Myron said to him, "I'm better off than you are."

Pat started toward Billy Lee. "Let's just calm down a second, Billy Lee. Think this through, okay?"

"I'm going to kill him."

"Billy Lee, this Win guy. I've heard stories—"

"You don't understand, Pat. You just don't get it."

"Then tell me, man. I'm here to help."

"After I kill him."

Billy Lee stepped toward Myron. He put the barrel of the gun against Myron's temple. Myron went rigid.

"Don't!"

Pat was close enough now. Or at least that was what he thought. He made his move, diving for Billy Lee's legs. But beneath the diminished drug addict lurked some of the athlete's old reflexes. Enough of them anyway. Billy Lee spun and fired. The bullet hit Pat's chest. For the briefest moment Pat looked surprised. Then he went down.

Billy Lee screamed, "Pat!" He dropped onto his knees and crawled toward the still body.

Myron's heart was flapping like a caged condor. He did not wait. He struggled with the ropes. No go. He slid down in a frenzied slither. The rope was tighter than he thought, but he made some headway.

"Pat!" Billy Lee screamed again.

Myron's knees were on the floor now, his body contorted, his spine bow-bending in a way it was never supposed to. Billy Lee was wailing over a too-silent Pat. The rope got caught under Myron's chin, pushing his head back and temporarily strangling him. How long did he have? How long before Billy Lee regained his senses? Impossible to say. Myron tilted his chin even higher, and the rope began to pass over him. He was almost out.

Billy Lee startled and turned around.

Myron was still caught in the rope. The two men locked eyes. It was over. Billy Lee lifted the shotgun. Maybe eight feet separated them. Myron saw the barrel, saw Billy Lee's eyes, saw the distance.

No chance. Too late.

The gun fired.

The first bullet hit Billy Lee's hand. He screamed in pain and dropped the shotgun. The second bullet hit Billy Lee's knee. Another scream. Blood spurted. The third bullet came so fast Billy Lee didn't have time to hit the floor. His head flew back from the impact, his legs splaying in midair. Billy Lee dropped out of sight like something at a shooting gallery.

The room was still.

Myron pulled the rope the rest of the way off and rolled into a corner. "Win?" he shouted.

No answer.

"Win?"

Nothing.

Pat and Billy Lee did not so much as twitch. Myron stood, the only sound his own breath. Blood. Everywhere blood. They had to be dead. Myron pressed back into the corner. Someone was watching him. He knew that now. He crossed the room and looked out a window. He looked left. Nothing. He looked right.

Someone stood in the shadows. A silhouette. Fear engulfed Myron. The silhouette seemed to hover and then vanished into the darkness. Myron spun around and found the doorknob. He threw the door open and began to run.

26

He vomited three blocks away. He pulled up, leaned against a building, and puked his guts out. Several homeless men stopped and applauded. Myron gave a wave, acknowledging his fans. Welcome to New York.

Myron tried his cell phone, but it'd been crushed in the melee. He found a street sign and saw that he was only ten blocks south of the Biker Wannabee bar, in the meat-packing district near the West Side Highway. He jogged, holding his side, trying to stop the blood flow. He located a working pay phone, a feat that in this section of Manhattan normally involved a burning bush, and dialed Win's cellular.

Win picked up on the first ring. "Articulate."

"They're dead," Myron said. "Both of them."

"Explain."

Myron did.

When he finished, Win said, "I'll be there in three minutes."

"I have to call the cops."

"Unwise."

"Why?"

"They will not believe your tale of woe," Win said, "especially the part about a mystery savior."

"Meaning they'll think you killed them?"

"Precisely."

Win had a point.

"But we'd be able to clear it up," Myron said.

"Yes perhaps, eventually. But it would take serious time."

"Time we don't have."

"Then you understand."

Myron thought about it. "But witnesses saw me leave the bar with Pat."

"So?"

"So the police will question people. They'll learn about that. They'll be able to place me at the scene."

"No more."

"What?"

"On the phone. No more discussion. I'll be there in three minutes."

"What about Zorra? What did you do to him?"

But Win was already off the line. Myron hung up the phone. A new set of homeless guys eyed him like he was a dropped sandwich. Myron met their gaze and did not look away until they did. He was not in the mood to be afraid anymore tonight.

A car pulled up in the promised three minutes. A Chevy Nova. Win had a collection of them—all old, all very used, all untraceable. Disposable cars, he called them. Win liked to use them for certain night activities. Don't ask.

The front passenger door opened. Myron glanced inside and saw Win behind the wheel. Myron slid in next to him.

"The die is cast," Win said.

"What?"

"The police are already at the scene. It was on the scanner."

Bad news. "I can still come forward."

"Yes, of course. And why, Mr. Bolitar, did you not call the police? Why, in fact, did you call your friend before the proper authorities? Are you or are you not suspected of aiding Ms. Esperanza Diaz in the murder of Billy Lee Palms's oldest friend? What exactly were you doing in that bar in the first place? Why would Mr. Palms want to kill you?"

"It can all be explained."

Win shrugged. "Your call."

"Just as it was my call to go alone with Pat."

"Yes."

"Which I called wrong."

"Yes. You were too vulnerable going in like that. There were other ways."

"What other ways?"

"We could have grabbed Pat at another time and made him tell us."

"Made him?"

"Yes."

"You mean, rough him up? Or torture him?"

"Yes."

"I don't do that."

"Grow up," Win said. "It is a simple cost-benefit analysis: By causing temporary discomfort to a malfeasant, you greatly lower the risk of being killed. It's a no-brainer." Win glanced at him. "By the way, you look like hell."

"You should see the other guy," he said. Then: "Did you kill Zorra?"

Win smiled. "You know me better than that."

"No, Win, I don't. Did you kill him?"

Win pulled up to the Biker Wannabee bar. He put the car in park. "Take a look inside."

"Why are we back here?"

"Two reasons. One, you never left."

"I didn't?"

"That's what I'll swear to. You were here all night. You just walked Pat out for a moment. Thrill will back me on it." He smiled. "So will Zorra."

"You didn't kill him?"

"Her. Zorra prefers to be called a her."

"Her. You didn't kill her?"

"Of course not."

They got out of the car.

"I'm surprised," Myron said.

"Why?"

"Usually when you threaten—"

"I never threatened Zorra. I threatened Pat. I said I *may* kill Zorra. But what would have been the point? Should Zorra suffer because a drugged-out psychotic like Billy Lee Palms hangs up a phone? Methinks not."

Myron shook his head. "You're a constant surprise."

Win stopped. "And lately you're a constant screwup. You got lucky. Zorra said she'd be willing to use her life to guarantee your safety. I recognized that she couldn't do it. It's why I told you not to go."

"I didn't think I had a choice."

"Now you know better."

"Maybe."

Win put a stilling hand on Myron's arm. "You're not over her yet. Esperanza has a point when she tells you that."

Myron nodded. Win dropped his arm.

"Take this," Win said, handing him a small bottle. "Please."

Trial-size mouthwash. Count on Win. They made their way inside the Biker Wannabee. Myron stopped in the bathroom, rinsed out his mouth, splashed water on his face, checked the wound. It hurt. He looked in the mirror. His face was still tan from his three weeks with Terese, but Win was right: He looked like hell.

He met up with Win outside the bathroom door. "You said two reasons before, that there were two reasons you wanted me to come back here."

"Reason two," Win said. "Nancy—or Thrill, if you prefer. She was worried about you. I thought it best if you saw her."

When they reached the corner booth, Zorra and Thrill were busy chatting like, well, two single women at a bar.

Zorra smiled at Myron. "Zorra is sorry, dreamboat."

"Not your fault," Myron said.

"Zorra means that they're dead," Zorra said. "Zorra would have liked a few hours alone with them first."

"Yeah," Myron said. "Pity."

"Zorra already told Win all Zorra knows, which is very little. Zorra is just a beautiful hired gun. She likes to know as little as possible."

"But you worked for Pat?"

He-she nodded, but the wig did not. "Zorra was a bouncer and body-guard. Do you believe that? Zorra Avrahaim having to settle for work as a common bouncer?"

"Yeah, times are tough. So what was Pat into?"

"A little of everything. Mostly drugs."

"And how were Billy Lee and Pat connected?"

"Billy Lee claimed to be his uncle." Zorra shrugged. "But that could have been a lie."

"Did you ever meet Clu Haid?"

"No."

"Do you know why Billy Lee was hiding?"

"He was terrified. He thought someone was trying to kill him."

"That someone being me?"

"So it seemed."

Myron couldn't figure that one out. He asked a few more questions, but there was nothing else to learn. Win offered his hand. Zorra took it and stepped out of the booth. She handled the high heels well. Not everyone does.

Zorra kissed Win on the cheek. "Thanks for not killing Zorra, dreamboat."

Win bowed slightly. "A pleasure, madame." Win the charmer. "I'll walk you out."

Myron slid into the booth next to Thrill. Without saying a word, she grabbed his face with both hands and kissed him hard. He kissed her back. Win and his mouthwash. What a guy.

When they came up for air, Thrill said, "You do know how to show a girl a good time."

"Ditto."

"You also scared the hell out of me."

"I didn't mean to."

She searched his face. "Are you okay?"

"I will be."

"Part of me wants to invite you back to my place."

He said nothing, lowering his eyes. She kept her eyes on his face. "This is it, isn't it?" she said. "You won't call, will you?"

Myron said, "You're beautiful, intelligent, fun—"

"And about to get the big kiss-off."

"It's not you."

"Oh, that's original. Don't tell me. It's you, right?"

He tried a smile. "You know me so well."

"I'd like to."

"I'm damaged goods, Nancy."

"Who isn't?"

"I'm just over a long-term relationship—"

"Who said anything about a relationship? We could just go out, right?"

"No."

"What?"

"I don't work that way," he said. "I can't help it. I go out with someone, I start picturing kids and a backyard barbecue and a rusted hoop in the driveway. I try to size up all that stuff right away."

She looked at him. "Christ, you're strange."

Hard to argue.

She started fiddling with a mixing straw. "And you can't imagine me in any of those domestic settings?"

"Just the opposite," Myron said. "That's the problem."

"I see. At least I think I see." She shifted in her seat. "I better go."

"I'll take you home."

"No, I'll get a taxi."

"That's not necessary."

"I think it is. Good night, Myron."

She walked away. Myron stood. Win moved up next to him. They watched her disappear out the door.

"You'll make sure she gets home safely?" Myron asked.

Win nodded. "I already called a car service for her."

"Thanks."

Silence. Then Win put his hand on Myron's shoulder.

"May I make one observation at this juncture?" Win asked.

"Shoot."

"You're a total moron."

*   *   *

They stopped at the doctor's apartment on the Upper West Side. He restitched the wound, making a tsk-tsk noise as he sewed. When they reached Win's apartment at the Dakota building, the two friends settled into the Louis the Someteenth decor with their favorite beverages. Myron chugged on a Yoo-Hoo; Win sipped an amber liquor.

Win flipped channels with a remote control. He stopped on CNN. Myron looked at the screen and thought of Terese on that island by herself. He checked the time. This was normally Terese's anchor slot. A bad dye job filled in. Myron wondered when or if Terese would be back on the air. And he wondered why he kept thinking about her.

Win turned the TV off. "Need a refill?"

Myron shook his head. "So what did Sawyer Wells tell you?"

"Not very much, I'm afraid. Clu was a drug addict. He tried to help him. Blah, blah, blah. Sawyer is leaving the Yankees, you know."

"I didn't."

"He credits them with raising him out of obscurity. But alas, now it's time for dear Sawyer to take hold of his reins and motivate more minions. He's going to start touring soon."

"Like a rock star?"

Win nodded. "Complete with overpriced T-shirts."

"Are they black?"

"I don't know. But at the end of each performance he encores after frenzied fans flick their Bics and shout, 'Freebird!' "

"That's so 1977."

"Isn't it? But I did a little checking. Guess who's sponsoring the tour."

"Budweiser, the undisputed King of Beer?"

"Close," Win said. "His new publisher. Riverton Press."

"As in Vincent Riverton, former owner of the New York Yankees?"

"The very."

Myron whistled, processed it, came up with nothing. "With all the buyouts in publishing, Riverton owns half the books in town. Probably means nothing."

"Probably," Win agreed. "If you have more questions, Sawyer is giving a seminar tomorrow at the Cagemore Auditorium at Reston University. He invited me to attend. I'm allowed to bring a date."

"I don't put out on the first date."

"And you're proud of that?"

Myron took a deep chug. Maybe he was getting older, but Yoo-Hoo didn't have the same kick anymore. He craved a venti-size skim iced latte with a splash of vanilla, though he hated ordering it in front of other men. "I'm going to try to find out about Clu's autopsy tomorrow."

"Through this Sally Li?"

Myron nodded. "She's been in court, but she's supposed to be back at the morgue tomorrow morning."

"Think she'll tell you anything?"

"I don't know."

"You may have to turn on the charm again," Win said. "Is this Sally Li of the heterosexual persuasion?"

"She is now," Myron said. "But once I turn on the charm—"

"All bets are off, yes."

"Charm so potent," Myron said, "he can turn a woman against men."

"You should print that on your business card." Win did that snifter circle, palm up and under the glass. "Before our old chum Billy Lee perished, did he reveal anything of import?"

"Not really," Myron said. "Just that he thought I was the one who killed Clu and now wanted to kill him."

"Hmm."

"Hmm what?"

"Once again, your name rears its ugly head."

"He was a strung-out addict."

"I see," Win said. "So he was just ranting?"

Silence.

"Somehow," Myron said, "I keep ending up in the middle of this."

"So it seems."

"But I can't imagine why."

"Life's little mysteries."

"I also can't figure out how Billy Lee fits into any of this: into Clu's murder, into Esperanza's affair with Bonnie, into Clu getting thrown off the team, into Clu signing with FJ, into any of it."

Win put down his snifter and stood. "I suggest we sleep on it."

Good advice. Myron crawled under the covers and plunged immediately into slumber land. It was several hours later—after the REM and alpha sleep cycles, when he started rising to consciousness and his brain activity started going haywire—that it came to him. He thought again about FJ and about his having tailed Myron. He thought about what FJ had said, about how he had even seen Myron at the cemetery before Myron disappeared with Terese in the Caribbean.

And a big click sounded in his head.

27

He called FJ at nine in the morning. FJ's secretary said that Mr. Ache could not be disturbed. Myron told her it was urgent. Sorry, Mr. Ache was out of the office. But, Myron reminded her, you just said he could not be disturbed. He cannot be disturbed, the secretary countered, because he is not in the office. Ah.

"Tell him I want to meet with him," Myron said. "And it has to be today."

"I can't promise you—"

"Just tell him."

He looked at his watch. He was meeting Dad at "the Club" at noon. It gave him time to try to rendezvous with Sally Li, chief medical examiner for Bergen County. He called her office and told her he wanted to talk.

"Not here," Sally said. "You know the Fashion Center?"

"It's one of the malls on Route Seventeen, right?"

"On the Ridgewood Avenue intersection, yeah. There's a sub shop outside the Bed, Bath and Beyond. Meet me there in an hour."

"Bed, Bath and Beyond is part of the Fashion Center?"

"Must have something to do with the Beyond part."

She hung up. He got in the rental car and started out to Paramus, New Jersey. Motto: There's No Such Thing as Too Much Commerce. The town of Paramus was like a muggy, jam-packed elevator with some jerk holding the door-open button and shouting, "Come on, we can squeeze in one more strip mall."

Nothing about the Fashion Center was particularly fashionable; the mall was in fact so unhip that teenagers didn't even hang out there. Sally Li sat on a bench, an unlit cigarette dangling from her lips. She wore green hospital scrubs and rubber sports sandals with no socks—footwear sported by many a coroner because it made cleaning off blood and guts and other human debris easy with a simple garden hose.

Okay, a little background here: For the past decade or so, Myron had been involved in an on-again, off-again romance with Jessica Culver. More recently they'd been in love. They'd moved in together. And now it was over. Or so he thought. He was not sure what exactly had happened. Objective observers might point to Brenda. She came along and changed a lot of things. But Myron was not sure.

So what's that have to do with Sally Li?

Jessica's father, Adam Culver, had been the Bergen County chief medical examiner until he was murdered several years ago. Sally Li, his assistant and close friend, had taken his place. That was how Myron knew her.

He approached. "Another no-smoking mall?"

"No one uses the word *no* anymore," Sally said. "They say *free* instead. This isn't a no-smoking mall; it's a smoke-free zone. Next they'll call underwater an air-free zone. Or the Senate a brain-free zone."

"So why did you want to meet here?"

Sally sighed, sat up. "Because you want to know about Clu Haid's autopsy, right?"

Myron hesitated, nodded.

"Well, my superiors—and I use that term knowing I don't even have equals—would frown upon seeing us together. In fact, they'd probably try to fire my ass."

"So why take the risk?" he asked.

"First off, I'm going to change jobs. I'm going back West, probably UCLA. Second, I'm cute, female, and what they now call Asian-American. It makes it harder to fire me. I might make a stink and the politically ambitious hate to look like they're beating up a minority. Third, you're a good guy. You figured out the truth when Adam was killed. I figure I owe you." She took the cigarette out of her mouth, put it back in the package, took out another one, put it in her mouth. "So what do you want to know?"

"Just like that?"

"Just like that."

Myron said, "I thought I'd have to turn on my charm."

"Only if you want to get me naked." She waved a hand. "Ah, who am I kidding? Go ahead, Myron, fire away."

"Injuries?" Myron asked.

"Four bullet wounds."

"I thought there were three."

"So did we at first. Two to the head, both at close range, either one of which would have been fatal. The cops thought there was only one. There was another in the right calf, and another in the back between the shoulder blades."

"Longer range?"

"Yeah, I'd say at least five feet. Looked liked thirty-eights, but I don't do ballistics."

"You were at the scene, right?"

"Yup."

"Could you tell if there was forced entry?"

"The cops said no."

Myron sat back and nodded to himself. "Let me see if I got the DA's theory right. Correct me if I'm wrong."

"I look forward to it."

"They figure Clu knew the killer. He let him or her in voluntarily, they talked or whatever, and something went wrong. The killer draws a gun, Clu runs, the killer fires two shots. One hits his calf, the other his back. Could you tell which came first?"

"Which what?"

"The calf shot or the back shot."

"No," Sally said.

"Okay, so Clu goes down. He's hurt but not dead. The killer puts the gun to Clu's head. Bang, bang."

Sally arched an eyebrow. "I'm impressed."

"Thanks."

"As far as it goes."

"Pardon?"

She sighed and shifted on the bench. "There are problems."

"Such as?"

"The body was moved."

Myron felt his pulse pick up. "Clu was killed someplace else?"

"No. But his body was moved. After he was killed."

"I don't understand."

"The lividity wasn't affected, so the blood didn't have time to settle. But he was dragged around on the floor, probably immediately after death, though it could be up to an hour later. And the room was tossed."

"The killer was searching for something," Myron said. "Probably the two hundred thousand dollars."

"Don't know about that. But there were blood smears all over the place."

"What do you mean, smears?"

"Look, I'm an ME. I don't interpret crime scenes. But the place was a mess. Overturned furniture and bookshelves, drawers emptied out, and blood everywhere. On the walls. And on the floor. Like he'd been dragged like a rag doll."

"Maybe he was dragging himself around. After he was shot in the leg and back."

"Could be, I guess. Of course it's hard to drag yourself across walls unless you're Spider-Man."

Myron's blood chilled a few degrees. He tried to sort and sift and process. How did all this fit? The killer was on a rampage to find the cash. Okay, that makes sense. But why drag around the body? Why smear the walls with blood?

"We're not finished," Sally said.

Myron blinked as though coming out of a trance.

"I also ran a full tox screen on the deceased. Know what I found?"

"Heroin?"

She shook her head. "El Zippo."

"What?"

"*Nada,* nothing, the big zero."

"Clu was clean?"

"Not even a Tums."

Myron made a face. "But that could have been temporary, right? I mean, the drugs might have just been out of his system."

"Nope."

"What do you mean, nope?"

"Let's keep the science simple here, shall we? If a guy abuses drugs or alcohol, it shows up somewhere. Enlarged heart, liver damage, lung modules, whatever. And it did. There was no question that Clu Haid had liked some pretty potent chemicals. *Had,* Myron. Had. There are other tests—hair tests, for example—that give you a more recent snapshot. And those were clean. Which means he'd been off the stuff for a while."

"But he failed a drug test two weeks ago."

She shrugged.

"Are you telling me that test was fixed?"

Sally held up both hands. "Not me. I'm telling you that my data disputes that data. I never said anything about a fix. It could have been an innocent error. There are such things as false positives."

Myron's head swam. Clu had been clean. His body had been dragged around after being shot four times. Why? None of this made any sense.

They chatted a few more minutes, mostly about the past, and headed for the exit ten minutes later. Myron started back to his car. Time to see Dad. He tried the new cellular—count on Win to have "extras" lying about his apartment—and called Win.

"Articulate," Win answered.

"Clu was right. The drug test was fixed."

Win said, "My, my."

"Sawyer Wells witnessed the drug test."

"More my, my."

"What time is he doing the motivational talk at Reston?"

"Two o'clock," Win said.

"In the mood to get motivated?"

"You have no idea."

28

The Club.

Brooklake Country Club, to be more exact, though there was no brook, no lake, and they were not in the country. It was, however, most definitely a club. As Myron's car made its way up the steep drive, the clubhouse's white Greco-Roman pillars rising through the clouds, childhood memories popped up in fluorescent flashes. It was how he always saw the place. In flashes. Not always pleasant ones.

The Club was the epitome of nouveau-riche, Myron's wealthy brethren proving that they could be just as tacky and exclusive as their goyish counterparts. Older women with perpetual tans on large, freckled chests sat by the pool, their hair shellacked into place by fake French hairdressers to the point where the strands resembled frozen fiber optics, never allowing it, God forbid, to touch the water, sleeping, he imagined, without putting their heads down lest they shatter the dos like so much Venetian glass; there were nose jobs and liposuction and face-lifts so extreme that the ears almost touched in the back, the overall effect bizarrely sexy in the same way you might find Yvonne De Carlo on *The Munsters* sexy; women fighting off old age and on the surface winning, but Myron wondered if they doth protest too much, their fear just a little too bare in the scar-revealing, harsh overhead lights of the dining room.

Men and women were separated at the Club, the women animatedly playing mah-jongg, the men silently chewing on cigars over a hand of cards; women still had special tee times so as not to interfere with the breadwinners'—i.e., their husbands'—precious leisure moments; there was tennis too, but that was more for fashion than exercise, giving everyone an excuse to wear sweatsuits that rarely encountered sweat, couples sometimes sporting matching ones; a men's grill, a women's lounge, the oak boards memorializing golf champions in gold leaf, the same man winning seven years in a row, now dead, the large locker rooms with masseur's tables, the bathrooms with combs sitting in blue alcohol, the pickle-and-coleslaw bar, cleat marks on the rug, the Founders Board with his grandparents' names still on it, immigrant dining room help, all referred to by their first names, always smiling too hard and at the ready.

What shocked Myron now was that people *his* age were members. The same young girls who had sneered at their mothers'idleness now abandoned their own foundering careers to "raise" the kids—read: hire nannies—came here to lunch and bore each other silly with a continuous game of one-upmanship. The men Myron's age had manicures and long hair and were well fed and too well dressed, kicking back with their cellular phones and casually swearing to a colleague. Their kids were there too, dark-eyed youngsters walking through the clubhouse with hand-held video games and Walkmans and too regal a bearing.

All conversations were inane and depressed the hell out of Myron. The grandpas in Myron's day had the good sense not to talk much to one another, just discarding and picking up what was dealt, occasionally grumbling about a local sports team; the grandmothers interrogated one another, measuring their own children and grandchildren against the competition, seeking an opponent's weakness and any conversational opening to jab forward with tales of offspring heroics, no one really listening, just preparing for the next frontal assault, familial pride getting confused with self-worth and desperation.

The main clubhouse dining room was as expected: waaaay too overstated. The green carpeting, the curtains that resembled corduroy leisure suits, the gold tablecloths on huge round mahogany, the floral centerpieces piled too high and with no sense of proportion, not unlike the plates traipsing down the buffet line. Myron remembered attending a sports-themed bar mitzvah here as a child: jukeboxes, posters, pennants, a Wiffle ball batting cage, a basket for foul shots, an artist wanna-be stuck sketching sports-related caricatures of thirteen-year-old boys—thirteen-year-old boys being God's most obnoxious creation short of television lawyers—and a wedding band complete with an overweight lead singer who handed the kids silver dollars shrouded in leather pouches that were emblazoned with the band's phone number.

But this view—these flashes—were too quick and thus simplistic. Myron knew that. His remembrances were all screwed up about this place—the derision blending with the nostalgia—but he also remembered coming here as a child for family dinners, his clip-on tie slightly askew, sent by Mom into the inner sanctum of the men's card room to find his grandfather, the undisputed family patriarch, the room reeking of cigar smoke, his pop-pop greeting him with a ferocious embrace, his gruff compatriots who wore golf shirts that were too loud and too tight, barely acknowledging the interloper because their own grandkids would do the same soon, the card game trickling down, participant by participant.

These same people he so easily picked apart were the first generation fully out of Russia or Poland or Ukraine or some other shtetl-laced combat zone. They'd hit the New World running—running away from the past, the poverty, the fear—and they just ran a bit too far. But under the hair and the jewelry and the gold lamé, no mother bear would ever be so quick to kill for her cubs, the women's hard eyes still seeking out the pogrom in the distance, suspicious, always expecting the worst, bracing themselves to take the blow for their children.

Myron's dad sat in a yellow, pseudo-leather swivel chair in the brunch room, fitting in with this crowd about as well as a camel-riding mufti. Dad did not belong here. Never had. He didn't play golf or tennis or cards. He didn't swim and he didn't brag and he didn't brunch and he didn't talk stock tips. He wore his work clothes of all things: charcoal gray slacks, loafers, and a white dress shirt over a sleeveless white undershirt. His eyes were dark, his skin pale olive, his nose jutting forward like a hand waiting to be shook.

Interestingly enough, Dad was not a member of Brooklake. Dad's parents, on the other hand, had been founding members, or in the case of Pop-pop, a ninety-two-year-old quasi vegetable whose rich life had been dissolved into useless fragments by Alzheimer's, still was. Dad hated the place, but he kept up the membership for the sake of his father. That meant showing up every once in a while. Dad looked at it as a small price to pay.

When Dad spotted Myron, he rose, more slowly than usual, and suddenly the obvious hit Myron: The cycle was beginning anew. Dad was the age Pop-pop had been back then, the age of the people they'd made fun of, his ink-black hair wispy, static gray now. The thought was far from comforting.

"Over here!" Dad called, though Myron had seen him. Myron threaded his way through the brunchers, mostly overkept women who constantly pendulumed between chewing and chatting, bits of coleslaw caught in the corners of their glossy mouths, water glasses stained with pink lipstick. They eyed Myron as he walked by for three reasons: under forty, male, no marriage band. Measuring his son-in-law potential. Always on the lookout, though not necessarily for their own daughters, the yenta from the shtetl never too far away.

Myron hugged his father and as always kissed his cheek. The cheek still felt wonderfully rough, but the skin was loosening. The scent of Old Spice wafted gently in the air, as comforting as any hot chocolate on the coldest of days. Dad hugged him back, released, then hugged him again. No one noticed the display of affection. Such acts were not uncommon here.

The two men sat. The paper place mats had an overhead diagram of the golf course's eighteen holes and an ornate letter *B* in the middle. The club's logo. Dad picked up a stubby green pencil, a golf pencil, to scribble down their order. That was how it worked. The menu had not changed in thirty years. As a kid Myron always ordered either the Monte Cristo or Reuben sandwich. Today he asked for a bagel with lox and cream cheese. Dad wrote it down.

"So," Dad began. "Getting acclimated to being back?"

"Yeah, I think so."

"Hell of a thing with Esperanza."

"She didn't do it."

Dad nodded. "Your mother tells me that you've been subpoenaed."

"Yep. But I don't know anything."

"You listen to your aunt Clara. She's a smart lady. Always has been. Even in school, Clara was the smartest girl in the class."

"I will."

The waitress came by. Dad handed her the order. He turned back to Myron and shrugged. "It's getting near the end of the month," Dad said. "I have to use your pop-pop's minimum before the thirtieth. I didn't want the money to go to waste."

"This place is fine."

Dad made a face signaling disagreement. He grabbed some bread, buttered it, then pushed it away. He shifted in his chair. Myron watched him. Dad was working up to something.

"So you and Jessica broke up?"

In all the years Myron had been dating Jessica, Dad had never inquired about their relationship past the polite questions. It just wasn't his way. He'd ask how Jessica was, what she was up to, when her next book was coming out. He was polite and friendly and greeted her warmly, but he'd never given a true indication of how he really felt about her. Mom had made her own feelings on the subject crystal clear: Jessica was not good enough for her son, but then again, who was? Dad was like a great newscaster, the kind of guy who asks questions without giving the viewer any hint of how he was really leaning on the issue.

"I think it's over," Myron said.

"Because"—Dad stopped, looked away, looked back—"of Brenda?"

"I'm not sure."

"I'm not big on giving advice. You know that. Maybe I should have been. I read those life instruction books fathers write for their children. You ever see those?"

"Yes."

"All kinds of wisdom in there. Like: Watch a sunrise once a year. Why? Suppose you want to sleep in? Another one: Overtip a breakfast waitress. But suppose she's grumpy? Suppose she's really bad? Maybe that's why I never dealt with it. I always see the other side."

Myron smiled.

"So I was never big on advice. But I have learned one thing for sure. One thing. So listen to me because this is important."

"Okay."

"The most important decision you'll ever make is who you marry," Dad said. "You can take every other decision you'll ever make, add them together, and it still won't be as important as that one. Suppose you choose the wrong job, for example. With the right wife, that's not a problem. She'll encourage you to make a change, cheer you on no matter what. You understand?"

"Yes."

"Remember that, okay?"

"Okay."

"You have to love her more than anything in the world. But she has to love you just as much. Your priority should be her happiness, and her priority should be yours. That's a funny thing—caring about someone more than yourself. It's not easy. So don't look at her as just a sexual object or as just a friend to talk to. Picture everyday with the person. Picture paying bills with that person, raising children with that person, being stuck in a hot room with no air-conditioning and a screaming baby with that person. Am I making sense?"

"Yes." Myron smiled and folded his hands on the table. "Is that how it is with you and Mom? Is she all those things to you?"

"All those things," Dad agreed, "plus a pain in the *tuchus*."

Myron laughed.

"If you promise not to tell your mother, I'll let you in on a little secret."

"What?"

He leaned in and whispered conspiratorially. "When your mother walks in the room—even now, even after all these years, if she were to, say, stroll by us right now—my heart still does a little two-step. You understand what I'm saying?"

"I think so, yeah. That used to happen with Jess."

Dad spread his hands. "Enough then."

"Are you saying Jessica is that person?"

"Not my place to say one way or the other."

"Do you think I'm making a mistake?"

Dad shrugged. "You'll figure that out, Myron. I have tremendous confidence in you. Maybe that's why I never gave you much advice. Maybe I always thought you were smart enough without me."

"Bull."

"Or maybe it was easier parenting, I don't know."

"Or maybe you led by example," Myron said. "Maybe you led gently. Maybe you showed rather than told."

"Yeah, well, whatever."

They fell into silence. The women around them chatted up their white noise.

Dad said, "I turn sixty-eight this year."

"I know."

"Not a young man anymore."

Myron shook his head. "Not old either."

"True enough."

More silence.

"I'm selling the business," Dad said.

Myron froze. He saw the warehouse in Newark, the place Dad had worked for as long as Myron could remember. The *schmata* business—in Dad's case, undergarments. He could picture Dad with his ink-black hair in his glass-walled warehouse office, barking out orders, sleeves rolled up, Eloise, his long-time secretary, fetching him whatever he needed before he knew he needed it.

"I'm too old for it now," Dad went on. "So I'm getting out. I spoke to Artie Bernstein. You remember Artie?"

Myron managed a nod.

"The man's a rat bastard, but he's been dying to buy me out for years. Right now his offer is garbage, but I still might take it."

Myron blinked. "You're selling?"

"Yes. And your mother is going to cut back at the law firm."

"I don't understand."

Dad put a hand on Myron's arm. "We're tired, Myron."

Myron felt two giant hands press down on his chest.

"We're also buying a place in Florida."

"Florida?"

"Yes."

"You're moving to Florida?" Myron's Theory on East Coast Jewish Life: You grow up, you get married, you have kids, you go to Florida, you die.

"No, maybe part of the year, I don't know. Your mother and I are going to start traveling a little more." Dad paused. "So we'll probably sell the house."

They'd owned that house Myron's entire life. Myron looked down at the table. He grabbed a wrapped Saltine cracker from the breadbasket and tore open the cellophane.

"Are you okay?" Dad asked.

"I'm fine," he said. But he wasn't fine. And he couldn't articulate why, even to himself.

The waitress served them. Dad was having a salad with cottage cheese. Dad hated cottage cheese. They ate in silence. Myron kept feeling tears sting his eyes. Silly.

"There's one other thing," Dad said.

Myron looked up. "What?"

"It's not a big deal really. I didn't even want to tell you, but your mother thought I should. And you know how it is with your mother. When she has something in her mind, God himself—"

"What is it, Dad?"

Dad fixed his eyes on Myron's. "I want you to know this has nothing to do with you or your going to the Caribbean."

"Dad, what?"

"While you were gone"—Dad shrugged and started blinking; he put down his fork, and there was the faintest quiver in his lower lip—"I had some chest pains."

Myron felt his own heart sputter. He saw Dad with the ink-black hair at Yankee Stadium. He saw Dad's face turning red when he told him about the bearded man. He saw Dad rise and storm off to avenge his sons.

When Myron spoke, his voice sounded tinny and far away. "Chest pains?"

"Don't make a thing of it."

"You had a heart attack?"

"Let's not blow it out of proportion. The doctors weren't sure what it was. It was just some chest pains, that's all. I was out of the hospital in two days."

"The hospital?" More images: Dad waking up with the pains, Mom starting to cry, calling an ambulance, rushing to the hospital, the oxygen mask on his face, Mom holding his hand, both their faces devoid of any color. . . .

And then something broke open. Myron couldn't stop himself. He got up and half sprinted to the bathroom. Someone said hello to him, called out his name, but he kept moving. He pushed open the bathroom door, opened a stall, locked himself in, and nearly collapsed.

Myron started to cry.

Deep, bone-crushing cries, full-body sobs. Just when he thought he couldn't cry anymore. Something inside him had finally given way, and now he sobbed without pause or letup.

Myron heard the bathroom door open. Someone leaned against the stall door. Dad's voice, when he finally spoke, was barely a whisper. "I'm fine, Myron."

But Myron again saw Dad at Yankee Stadium. The ink-black hair was gone, replaced with the gray, fly-away wisps. Myron saw Dad challenge the bearded man. He saw the bearded man rise, and then he saw Dad clutch his chest and fall to the ground.

29

Myron tried to shake it off. No choice really. But he couldn't stop thinking about it. And he couldn't stop worrying. Worrying had never been his style in the past, even when a crisis loomed. All of a sudden he had the worry-queasies in his stomach. It was true what they said: The older you become, the more you are like your parents. Soon he'd be telling a kid not to stick his elbow out the car window or he'd lose it.

Win met him in front of the auditorium. He was in classic Win pose, eyes level, arms crossed, totally relaxed. He wore designer sunglasses and looked ultrasleek. *GQ* casual.

"Problem?" Win said.

"No."

Win shrugged.

"I thought we were going to meet inside," Myron said.

"That would mean I'd have to listen to more of Sawyer Wells."

"That bad?"

"Imagine, if you will, a Mariah Carey–Michael Bolton duet," Win said.

"Eeuw."

Win checked his watch. "He should be finishing up now. We must be brave."

They headed inside. The Cagemore Center was a sprawling facility that featured oodles of concert and lecture halls that could be cut to any size by sliding walls back and forth. There was a summer camp for young children in one room. Win and Myron stopped and listened to the children sing "Farmer in the Dell." The sound made Myron smile.

". . . the farmer in the dell, the farmer in the dell, hi-ho-the-dairy-o, the farmer in the dell . . ."

Win turned to Myron. "What's a dell?" Win asked.

"No idea."

Win shrugged and moved on to the main auditorium. There was a table out front selling Sawyer Wells paraphernalia. Cassettes, videos, books, magazines, posters, pennants (though what one does with a Sawyer Wells pennant went beyond Myron's capacity to imagine) and yep, T-shirts. Groovy titles too: *The Wells Guide to Wellness, The Wells Rules for Wellness, Key to Wellness: It's All About You.* Myron shook his head.

The auditorium was packed, the crowd so silent they'd put the Vatican to shame. Up on the stage, jittering to and fro like Robin Williams in his stand-up comic days, was the self-help guru himself. Sawyer Wells was resplendent in a business suit with the jacket off, shirt cuffs turned once, fancy suspenders cutting into his shoulders. A good look for a self-help guru: The expensive suit makes you reek of success while the jacket off and rolled-up sleeves give you the air of a regular guy. A perfectly balanced ensemble.

"It's all about you," Sawyer Wells told the enraptured audience. "If you remember nothing else today, remember that. It's all about you. Make everything about you. Every decision is about you. Everything you see, everything you touch is a reflection of you. No . . . more than that— it *is* you. You are everything. And everything is you."

Win leaned toward Myron. "Isn't that a song?"

"The Stylistics, I think. Circa early seventies."

"I want you to remember that," Sawyer continued. "Visualize. Visualize everything as you. Your family is you. Your job is you. When you're walking down the street, that beautiful tree is you. That blooming rose is you."

Win said, "That dirty commode at the bus terminal."

Myron nodded. "You."

"You see the boss, the leader, the breadwinner, the successful, fulfilled person. That person is you. No one can lead you because the leader is you. You stand in front of your opponent, and you know you can win because you are your opponent. And you know how to beat you. Remember you are your opponent. Your opponent is you."

Win frowned. "But don't you know how to beat you too?"

"It's a paradox," Myron agreed.

"You fear the unknown," Sawyer Wells ranted. "You fear success. You fear taking chances. But now you know that the unknown is you. Success is you. Taking chances is you. You don't fear you, do you?"

Win frowned.

"Listen to Mozart. Take long walks. Ask yourself what you did today. Do that every night. Before you go to sleep, ask yourself if the world is better because of you. After all, it's your world. You are the world."

Win said, "If he breaks into a rendition of 'We Are the World,' I'm using my gun."

"But you are your gun," Myron countered.

"And he is my gun too."

"Right."

Win considered that. "So if he is my gun and my gun kills him, it's a suicide."

"Take responsibility for your actions," Wells said. "That's one of the Wells Rules for Wellness. Take responsibility. Cher once said, 'Excuses won't lift your butt, 'kay?' Listen to that. Believe that with all your heart."

The man was quoting Cher. The crowd was nodding. There is no God.

"Confess something about yourself to a friend—something awful, something you'd never want anyone to know. You'll feel better. You'll still see that you're worthy of love. And since your friend is you, you are really just telling yourself. Have an interest in everything. Thirst for knowledge. That's another rule. Remember that it's all about you. When you learn about other things, you are actually learning about yourself. Get to know you better."

Win looked at Myron, his face pained.

"Let's wait outside," Myron said.

But luck was with them. Two sentences later Sawyer Wells was done. The crowd went ballistic. They stood, they applauded, they hooted like an old Arsenio Hall audience.

Win shook his head. "Four hundred dollars a pop."

"That what this thing costs?"

"He is your money."

People approached the stage, stretching their hands toward the heavens in the vain hope that Sawyer Wells might reach out and touch them. Myron and Win watched. The table with the Wells paraphernalia was swarmed now like rotting fruit with buzzing flies.

"The citified version of a tent revival," Win noted.

Myron nodded.

Eventually Sawyer Wells waved and ran offstage. The crowd continued to cheer and purchase. Myron half expected a voice-over to announce that Elvis had left the building. Win and Myron swam through the crowd.

"Come," Win said. "I have backstage passes."

"Please tell me you're joking."

He wasn't. They actually said "Backstage Pass" on them. A plainclothes security guard scowled at them and scrutinized the passes as if they were the Zapruder film. Satisfied, he let them past the velvet rope. Yep, velvet rope. Sawyer Wells spotted Win and bounced toward them.

"So glad you could come, Win!" He turned to Myron and stuck out his hand. "Hi, I'm Sawyer Wells."

Myron shook it. "Myron Bolitar."

Sawyer's smile flickered but stayed on. "Nice to meet you, Myron."

Myron decided to try a frontal assault. "Why did you fix Clu Haid's drug test so it would appear he was taking heroin?"

The smile was still there, but it wasn't sitting right. "Pardon?"

"Clu Haid. The name ring a bell?"

"Of course. As I told Win yesterday, I worked very hard with him."

"Worked how?"

"To keep him off drugs. I have an extensive background as a drug counselor. That's how I was trained. To help addicts."

"Not so different from what you're doing now," Myron said.

"Pardon?"

"People with addictive personalities need an addiction. If it's not booze or drugs, maybe it's religion or self-help mumbo jumbo. They're simply swapping addictions; we hope to one less damaging."

Sawyer Wells overnodded. "That's a really interesting viewpoint, Myron."

"Gee, thanks, Sawyer."

"I learned much about human frailty, about our lack of self-esteem, from addicts like Clu Haid. As I said, I worked very hard with him. His failure hurt me greatly."

Win said, "Because it was your failure."

"Pardon?"

"You are everything, and everything is you," Win said. "You are Clu Haid. He failed, ergo you failed."

Sawyer Wells maintained the smile. But it was different when he looked at Win. His gestures were tighter too, more controlled. He was one of those guys who tried to imitate the person with whom he was conversing. Myron hated that. "I see you came in at the end of my seminar, Win."

"Did I misunderstand your message?"

"No, it's not that. But a man creates his own world. That's my point. You are what you create, what you perceive. Take responsibility. That's the most important component of the Wells Guide to Wellness. You take responsibility for your own actions. And you admit fault. You know what the two most beautiful sentences in the world are?"

Win opened his mouth, stopped, looked at Myron, shook his head. "Too easy," he said.

" 'I am responsible,' " Sawyer continued. " 'It's my fault.' " He turned toward Myron. "Say it, Myron."

"What?"

"Come on. It's exhilarating. Say, 'I am responsible. It's my fault.' Stop passing the buck in your life. Say it. Come on, I'll say it with you. Win, you too."

Myron and Sawyer said, "I am responsible. It's my fault." Win remained silent.

"Feel better?" Sawyer said.

"It was almost like sex," Myron said.

"It can be powerful, yes."

"Yeah, uh-huh. Look, Sawyer, I'm not here to critique your seminar. I want to know about Clu's drug test. It was fixed. We have evidence that proves that fact. You helped administer that test. I want to know why you made it look like Clu was on drugs."

"I don't know what you're talking about."

"The autopsy shows conclusively that Clu hadn't taken drugs for at least two months before his death. Yet you tested him positive two weeks ago."

"Maybe the test was faulty," Sawyer said.

Win tsk-tsked. "Say, 'I am responsible. It's my fault.' "

"Stop passing the buck in your life," Myron added.

"Come on, Sawyer. It's exhilarating."

"That's not funny," Sawyer said.

"Wait," Win said. "You are everything, thus you are the drug test."

"And you are a positive guy," Myron added.

"Ergo the test result was positive."

Sawyer said, "I think I've had just about enough."

"You're finished, Wells," Myron said. "I'll blab to the papers."

"I don't know what you're talking about. I don't know anything about a fixed test."

"Want to hear my theory?" Myron said.

"No."

"You're leaving the Yankees and going to work for Vincent Riverton, right?"

"I'm not working exclusively for anyone. His conglomerate publishes my book."

"He's also Sophie Mayor's archenemy."

"You don't know that," Sawyer said.

"He lived for owning the team. When she took over, he was pissed.

She ends up being everything New York wants in an owner because she minds her own business. She makes only one move, acquiring Clu Haid, and it's a beauty. Clu pitches better than anyone dared hope. The Yankees start heading for greatness. Then you step in. Clu fails a drug test. Sophie Mayor looks incompetent. The Yankees tumble."

Sawyer seemed to recoup a bit. Something in what Myron had just said had given him a new lease. Odd. "That makes no sense whatsoever."

"What part?"

"All of it," Sawyer said, chest back out. "Sophie Mayor has been good to me. I was working as a drug counselor at the Sloan State and Rockwell rehab centers when she gave me my chance to move up. Why would I want to hurt her?"

"You tell me."

"I have no idea. I firmly believed that Clu was on drugs. If he wasn't, then the test was faulty."

"You know the results are double-tested. There was no mistake. Someone had to fix it."

"It wasn't me. Maybe you should speak to Dr. Stilwell."

"But you were there? You admit that?"

"Yes, I was there. And I will no longer dignify your questions with answers." With that Sawyer Wells abruptly spun and stormed off.

"I don't think he liked us," Myron said.

"But if it's all about you, then we are he."

"So he doesn't like himself?"

"Sad, isn't it?"

"Not to mention confusing," Myron said.

They headed for the exit.

"So where to, O Motivated One?" Win asked.

"Starbucks."

"Latte time?"

Myron shook his head. "Confront FJ time."

30

FJ was not there. Myron called his office again. The same secretary told him that FJ was still unavailable. Myron repeated that it was imperative that he speak to Francis Ache Junior as soon as humanly possible. The secretary remained unimpressed.

Myron returned to his office.

Big Cyndi wore a bright green spandex bodysuit with a slogan across the chest—this on a woman who could barely squeeze into a caftan. The fabric screamed in pain, the letters in the slogan so elongated that Myron couldn't read them, kinda like what happens to Silly Putty after you press it against a newspaper headline and stretch it out.

"Lots of clients have been calling, Mr. Bolitar," Big Cyndi said. "They are not pleased by your absence."

"I'll take care of it," he said.

She gave him the messages. "Oh, and Jared Mayor called," she said. "He seemed very anxious to talk to you."

"Okay, thanks."

He called Jared Mayor first. He was in his mother's office at Yankee Stadium. Sophie switched on the speakerphone.

"You called?" Myron said.

"I was hoping you could give us an update," Jared said.

"I think someone is setting up your mother."

Sophie said, "Setting me up how?"

"Clu's drug test was a fix. He was clean."

"I know you want to believe that—"

"I have proof," Myron said.

Silence.

"What kind of proof?" Jared asked.

"There's no time for that now. But trust me on this. Clu was clean."

"Who would have fixed the test?" Sophie asked.

"That's what I want to know. The logical suspects are Dr. Stilwell and Sawyer Wells."

"But why would they want to hurt Clu?"

"Not Clu, Sophie. You. It fits in with everything else we have. Raising the specter of your missing daughter, taking your big baseball trade and turning it against you—I think someone's out to hurt you."

"You're jumping to conclusions," Sophie said.

"Could be."

"Who would want to hurt me?"

"I'm sure you've made your share of enemies. How about Vincent Riverton, for one?"

"Riverton? No. Our whole takeover was far more amicable than the press portrayed it."

"Still, I wouldn't rule him out."

"Listen, Myron, I don't really care about any of this. I just want you to find my daughter."

"They're probably connected."

"How?"

Myron changed ears. "You want me to be blunt, right?"

"Absolutely."

"Then I have to remind you what the odds are that your daughter is still alive."

"Slim," she said.

"Very slim."

"No, I'll stay with slim. In fact, I think it's better than slim."

"Do you really believe Lucy is alive someplace?"

"Yes."

"She's out there somewhere, waiting to be found?"

"Yes."

"Then the big question," Myron said, "is why."

"What do you mean?"

"Why isn't she home?" he asked. "Do you think someone's been holding her hostage all these years?"

"I don't know."

"Well, what other choices are there? If Lucy is still alive, why hasn't she come home? Or phoned home? What is she hiding from?"

Silence.

Sophie broke it. "You think someone has resurrected my daughter's memory as part of some vendetta against me?"

Myron was not sure how to answer. "I think it's a possibility we have to consider."

"I appreciate your bluntness, Myron. I want you to remain honest with me. Don't hold back. But I'll also keep my hope. When your child disappears into thin air, it creates a huge void. I need something to fill that void, Myron. So until I find out otherwise, I'll fill it with hope."

Myron said, "I understand."

"Then you'll keep looking."

There was a knock on the door. Myron put his hand over the phone and said to come in. Big Cyndi opened the door. Myron gestured to a chair. She took it. In the bright green she looked a bit like a planet.

"I'm not sure what I can do, Sophie."

"Jared will investigate Clu's drug test," she said. "If there was anything amiss, he'll find out about it. You keep your eyes open for my daughter. You may be right about Lucy's fate. Then again you may be wrong. Don't give up."

Before he could reply, the line was disconnected. Myron put the phone back in the cradle.

"Well?" Big Cyndi asked.

"She still has hope."

Big Cyndi scrunched up her face. "There's a fine line between hope and delusion, Mr. Bolitar," she said. "I think Ms. Mayor may have crossed it."

Myron nodded. He shifted in his chair. "Something I can do for you?" he asked.

She shook her head. Her head was a nearly perfect cube and reminded Myron of the old game of Rock'Em Sock'Em Robots. Not sure what else to do, Myron folded his hands and put them on his desk. He wondered how many times he had been alone with Big Cyndi like this. Less than a handful for sure. Wrong to say, but she made him uncomfortable.

After some time had passed, Big Cyndi said, "My mother was a big, ugly woman."

Myron had no comeback for that one.

"And like most big, ugly women, she was a shrinking violet. That's how it is with big, ugly women, Mr. Bolitar. They get used to standing alone in the corner. They hide. They become angry and defensive. They keep their heads down, and they let themselves be treated with disdain and disgust and—"

She stopped suddenly, waved a meaty paw. Myron sat still.

"I hated my mother," she said. "I swore that I would never be like that."

Myron risked a small nod.

"That's why you have to save Esperanza."

"I'm not sure I see the connection."

"She's the only one who sees past this."

"Past what?"

She thought about that one for a moment. "What's the first thing you think when you see me, Mr. Bolitar?"

"I don't know."

"People like to stare," she said.

"Hard to blame them, don't you think?" Myron said. "I mean, the way you dress and stuff."

She smiled. "I'd rather see shock on their faces than pity," she said. "And I'd rather they see brazen or outrageous than shrinking or scared or sad. Do you understand?"

"I think so."

"I'm not standing alone in the corner anymore. I've done enough of that."

Myron, unsure what to say, settled for a nod.

"When I was nineteen, I started wrestling professionally. And of course I was cast as a villain. I sneered. I made faces. I cheated. I hit opponents when they weren't looking. It was all an act, of course. But that was my job."

Myron sat back and listened.

"One night I was scheduled to fight Esperanza—Little Pocahontas, I should say. It was the first time we'd met. She was already the most beloved wrestler on the circuit. Cute and pretty and small and all the things . . . all the things that I'm not. Anyway, we were performing in some high school gym outside Scranton. The script was the usual. A back-and-forth match. Esperanza winning with her skill. Me cheating. Twice I was supposed to nearly have her pinned when the crowd would go wild and she'd start stamping her foot, like the cheers were giving her strength, and then everyone would start clapping in unison with her stomps. You know how it works, right?"

Myron nodded.

"She was supposed to pin me with a backflip at the fifteen-minute mark. We executed it perfectly. Then as she was raising her hands in victory, I was supposed to sneak up on her and whack her in the back with a metal chair. Again it went perfectly. She collapsed to the canvas. The crowd gasped. I, the Human Volcano—that's what I was called then— raised my hands in victory. They started booing and throwing things. I sneered. The announcers acted all concerned for poor Little Pocahontas. They brought out the stretcher. Again you've seen the same act a million times on cable."

He nodded again.

"So there was another match or two, and then the crowd was ushered out. I decided not to change until I got back to the motel. I left for the bus a few minutes before the other girls. It was dark, of course. Nearly midnight. But some of the spectators were still out there. They confronted me. There must have been twenty of them. They started shouting at me. I decided to play back. I did my ring sneer and flexed"—her voice caught—"and that was when a rock hit me square in the mouth."

Myron kept perfectly still.

"I started bleeding. Then another rock hit me in the shoulder. I couldn't believe what was happening. I tried to head back inside, but they circled around me. I didn't know what to do. They started moving in closer. I ducked down. Someone hit me over the head with a beer bottle. My knees hit the pavement. Then someone kicked me in the stomach and someone else pulled my hair."

She stopped. Her eyes blinked a few times and she looked up and away. Myron thought about reaching out to her, but he didn't. Later he'd wonder why.

"And that's when Esperanza stepped in," Big Cyndi said after a few moments had passed. "She jumped over someone in the crowd and landed right on me. The morons thought she was there to help beat me up. But she just wanted to put herself between me and the blows. She told them to stop. But they wouldn't listen. One of them pulled her away so they could keep beating me. I felt another kick. Someone yanked my hair so hard my neck snapped back. I really thought they were going to kill me."

Big Cyndi stopped again and took a deep breath. Myron stayed where he was and waited.

"You know what Esperanza did then?" she asked.

He shook his head.

"She announced that we were going to be tag team partners. Just like that. She shouted that after she'd been taken off on the stretcher, I'd visited her and we realized that we were actually long-lost sisters. The Human Volcano was now going to be called Big Chief Mama and we were going to be partners and friends. Some of the spectators backed off then. Others looked wary. 'It's a trap!' they warned her. 'The Human Volcano is setting you up!' But Esperanza insisted. She helped me to my feet and by then the police showed up and the moment was over. The crowd dispersed pretty easily."

Big Cyndi threw up her thick arms and smiled. "The end."

Myron smiled back. "So that's how you two became tag team partners?"

"That's how. When the president of FLOW heard about the incident, he decided to capitalize on it. The rest, as they say, is history."

They both sat back in silence, still smiling. After some time had passed, Myron said, "I had my heart broken six years ago."

Big Cyndi nodded. "By Jessica, right?"

"Right. I walked in on her with another man. A guy named Doug." He paused. He could not believe he was telling her this. And it still hurt. After all this time it still hurt. "Jessica left me then. Isn't that weird? I didn't throw her out. She just left. We didn't speak for four years—until she came back and we started up again. But you know about that."

Big Cyndi made a face. "Esperanza hates Jessica."

"Yeah, I know. She doesn't exactly go to pains to hide that fact."

"She calls her Queen Bitch."

"When she's in a good mood," Myron said. "But that's why. Up until we broke up that first time, she was more or less indifferent. But after that—"

"Esperanza doesn't forgive easily," Big Cyndi said. "Not when it comes to her friends."

"Right. Anyway, I was devastated. Win was no help. When it comes to matters of the heart, well, it's like explaining Mozart to a deaf man. So about a week after Jess left me, I moped into the office. Esperanza had two airplane tickets in her hand. 'We're going away,' she said. 'Where?' I asked. 'Don't worry about it,' she said. 'I already called your folks. I told them we'd be gone for a week.' " Myron smiled. "My parents love Esperanza."

"That should tell you something," Big Cyndi said.

"I told her I didn't have any clothes. She pointed to two suitcases on the floor. 'I bought you all you'll need.' I protested, but I didn't have much left, and you know Esperanza."

"Stubborn," Big Cyndi said.

"To put it mildly. You know where she took me?"

Big Cyndi smiled. "On a cruise. Esperanza told me about it."

"Right. One of those big new ships with four hundred meals a day. And she made me go to every dumb activity. I even made a wallet. We drank. We danced. We played friggin' bingo. We slept in the same bed and she held me and we never so much as kissed."

They sat for another long moment, both smiling again.

"We never asked her for help," Big Cyndi said. "Esperanza just knows and does the right thing."

"And now it's our turn," Myron said.

"Yes."

"She's still hiding something from me."

Big Cyndi nodded. "I know."

"Do you know what it is?"

"No," she said.

Myron leaned back. "We'll save her anyway," he said.

At eight o'clock Win called down to Myron's office. "Meet me at the apartment in an hour. I have a surprise for you."

"I'm not much in the mood for surprises, Win."

Click.

Great. He tried FJ's office again. No answer. He didn't much like waiting. FJ was a key in all this, he was sure of it now. But what choice did he have? It was getting late anyway. Better to go home and be surprised by whatever Win had in store and then get some rest.

The subway was still crowded at eight-thirty; the so-called Manhattan rush hour had grown to more like five or six. People worked too hard, Myron decided. He got off and walked to the Dakota. The same doorman was there. He had been given instructions to let Myron in at any time, that indeed Myron was now officially a resident of the Dakota, but the doorman still made a face like there was a bad odor whenever he passed.

Myron took the elevator up, fumbled for his key, and opened the door. "Win?"

"He's not here."

Myron turned. Terese Collins gave him a small smile.

"Surprise," she said.

He gaped. "You left the island?"

Terese glanced in a nearby mirror, then back at him. "Apparently."

"But—"

"Not now."

She stepped toward him and they embraced. He kissed her. They fumbled with buttons and zippers and snaps. Neither one spoke. They made it into the bedroom, and then they made love.

When it was over, they clung to each other, the sheets tangled and binding them close together. Myron rested his cheek against her soft breast, hearing her heartbeat. Her chest was hitching a bit, and he knew that she was quietly crying.

"Tell me," he said.

"No." Terese's hand stroked his hair. "Why did you leave?"

"A friend is in trouble."

"That sounds so noble."

Again with that word. "I thought we agreed we wouldn't do this," he said.

"You complaining?"

"Hardly," he said. "Just curious why you changed your mind."

"Does it matter?"

"I don't think so."

She stroked his hair some more. He closed his eyes, not moving, wanting only to enjoy the wonderful suppleness of her skin against his cheek and ride the rise and fall of her chest.

"Your friend in trouble," she said. "It's Esperanza Diaz."

"Win told you?"

"I read it in the papers."

He kept his eyes closed.

"Tell me about it," she said.

"We were never great at talking on the island."

"Yeah, but that was then, this is now."

"Meaning?"

"Meaning you look a little worse for wear," she said. "I think you'll need the recovery time."

Myron smiled. "Oysters. The island had oysters."

"So tell me."

So he did. Everything. She stroked his hair. She interrupted a lot with follow-up questions, relaxing in the more familiar role of interviewer. It took him almost an hour.

"Some story," she said.

"Yes."

"Does it hurt? I mean, where you got beaten up?"

"Yes. But I'm a tough guy."

She kissed the top of his head. "No," she said. "You're not."

They sat in comfortable silence.

"I remember the Lucy Mayor disappearance," Terese said. "At least the second round."

"The second round?"

"When the Mayors had the money to run the big campaign to find her. Before that there really wasn't much of a story. An eighteen-year-old runaway. No big deal."

"You remember anything that might help me?"

"No. I hate covering stories like that. And not just for the obvious reason that lives are being shattered."

"Then what?"

"There's just too much denial," she said.

"Denial?"

"Yes."

"You mean with the family?"

"No, with the public. People block when it comes to their children. They deny because it's too painful to accept. They tell themselves it can't happen to them. God is not that fickle. There has to be a reason. Do you remember the Louise Woodward case a couple of years ago?"

"The nanny who killed the baby in Massachusetts?"

"Reduced to manslaughter by the judge, but yes. The public kept denying, even those who thought she was guilty. The mother shouldn't have been working, they said. Never mind the fact that the mother worked only part-time and came home at lunch every day to breast-feed the baby. It was her fault. And the father. He should have checked out the nanny's background better. The parents should have been more careful."

"I remember," Myron said.

"In the Mayors' case it was the same kind of thing. If Lucy Mayor had been raised right, she would have never run away in the first place. That's what I mean by denial. It's too painful to think about, so you block and convince yourself it can't happen to you."

"Do you think there's any merit to that argument in this case?"

"What do you mean?"

"Were Lucy Mayor's parents part of the problem?"

Terese's voice was soft. "It's not important."

"What makes you say that?"

She was silent, her breathing a little more hitched again.

"Terese?"

"Sometimes," she said, "a parent is to blame. But that doesn't change anything. Because either way—your fault or not—your child is gone and that's all that matters."

More silence.

Myron broke it. "You okay?" he asked.

"Fine."

"Sophie Mayor told me that the worst part was the not knowing."

"She's wrong," Terese said.

Myron wanted to ask her more, but she got out of bed then. When she came back, they made love again—languid and bittersweet, as the song says—both feeling loss, both searching for something in the moment or at least settling for the numb.

They were still snarled in the sheets when the phone woke Myron early in the morning. He reached over her head and picked up the receiver.

"Hello?"

"What's so important?"

It was FJ. Myron quickly sat up.

"We need to chat," Myron said.

"Again?"
"Yes."
"When?"
"Now."
"Starbucks," FJ said. "And Myron?"
"What?"
"Tell Win to stay outside."

31

FJ sat alone at the same table. He had his legs crossed at the knee and sipped as if maybe there were something in the bottom of the cup he wanted no part of. A bit of foam clung to his upper lip. His face was clean and wax-treatment smooth. Myron checked for Hans and Franz or some new goons, but nobody was there. FJ smiled and as always, something cold scrambled down Myron's back.

"Where's Win?" FJ asked.

"Outside," Myron said.

"Good. Have a seat."

"I know why Clu signed with you, FJ."

"Care for an iced latte? You take it skim, correct?"

"It was bugging the hell out of me," Myron said. "Why would Clu sign with you? Don't get me wrong. He had every reason to leave MB. But he knew about TruPro's reputation. Why would he go there?"

"Because we offer a valuable service."

"At first I figured it was a gambling or drug debt. It's how your dad always worked. He gets his hooks into someone, and then he gnaws on the carcass. But Clu was clean. And he had plenty of cash. So that wasn't it."

FJ put his elbow on the table and leaned his chin against his palm. "This is so fascinating, Myron."

"It gets better. When I ran off to the Caribbean, you were keeping tabs on me. Because of the whole Brenda Slaughter situation. You even admitted it when I first got back, remember? You knew I'd been visiting the cemetery."

"A very poignant moment for us all," FJ agreed.

"When I vanished, you still wanted to keep tabs on me. If anything, my disappearance probably piqued your curiosity. You also saw an opening for TruPro, but that's not here or there. You wanted to know where I was. But I wasn't around. So you did the next best thing: You followed Esperanza, my partner and closest friend."

FJ made a clucking noise. "And here I thought Win was your closest friend."

"They both are. But that's not the point. Following Win would be too difficult. He'd spot the tail before you even had him in place. So you followed Esperanza instead."

"I still don't see what any of this has to do with Clu's decision to improve his representation."

"I was missing. You knew that. You took advantage. You called my clients, telling them that I'd abandoned them."

"Was I wrong?"

"I don't care about that now. You saw a weakness and you exploited it. You couldn't help yourself. It's how you were raised."

"Ouch."

"But the important thing here is that you were following Esperanza, hoping she'd lead you to me or at least give you a clue to how long I'd be gone. You followed her out to New Jersey. And you stumbled upon something you were never supposed to learn."

His smile was positively wet. "And what would that be?"

"Wipe that smile off your face, FJ. You're no better than a peeping Tom. Even your father wouldn't stoop that low."

"Oh, you'd be surprised how low my father would stoop."

"You're a pervert, and worse, you used what you learned as leverage against a client. Clu went nuts when Bonnie threw him out. He had no idea why. But now you knew. So you made a deal with him. He signs with TruPro, he learns the truth about his wife."

FJ leaned back, recrossed the legs, folded his hands, and placed them on his lap. "Quite a spin, Myron."

"It's true, isn't it?"

FJ tilted his head in a maybe-yes, maybe-no fashion. "Let me tell you how I see it," he began. "Clu Haid's old agency, MB SportsReps, was clearly screwing him. In every way. His agent—that would be you, Myron—abandoned him when he needed him most. Your partner—that would be the lovely and rather lithe Esperanza—was engaging in a lick fest with his wife. True?"

Myron said nothing.

FJ unfolded the hands, took a sip of foam, refolded the hands. "What I did," he continued, "was take Clu Haid out of this awful situation. I brought him to an agency that would not abuse his trust. An agency that would look out for his interests. One of the ways we do that is through information. Valuable information. So the client understands what is happening to him. That's part of an agent's job, Myron. One of our agencies engaged in questionable ethics here. And it wasn't TruPro."

It was a reverse spin, but it was also true. One day, when Myron had the time to dwell upon them, the words would undoubtedly wound. But not now.

"So you admit it?"

FJ shrugged.

"But if you were following Esperanza, you know she didn't do it."

Again the head tilt. "Do I?"

"Stop playing games with me, FJ."

"Please hold a moment." FJ took out his cell phone and dialed a number. He stood, walked toward the corner, chatted. He put the phone between his shoulder and ear, took out a pen and paper, jotted something down. He hung up and returned to the table.

"You were saying?"

"Did Esperanza do it?"

He smiled. "You want the truth?"

"Yes."

"I don't know. Honest. Yes, I followed her. But as I am sure you know, even lesbian scenes get repetitive. So after a while we'd stop watching her once she crossed the Washington Bridge. There was no point."

"So you really don't know who killed Clu?"

"Afraid not."

"Are you still following me, FJ?"

"No."

"Last night. You didn't have a man on me?"

"No. And truth be told, I didn't have a man on you when you came in here yesterday."

"The guy I spotted outside my office wasn't yours?"

"Sorry, no."

Myron was missing something here.

FJ leaned forward again. His smile was so creepy that his teeth seemed to wiggle. "How far are you willing to go to save Esperanza?" he whispered.

"You know how far."

"The ends of the earth?"

"What are you getting at, FJ?"

"You're right, of course. I did learn about Esperanza and Bonnie. And I saw an opening. So I called Clu at the apartment in Fort Lee. But he wasn't there. I left a rather intriguing message on his machine. Something to the effect of 'I know who your wife is sleeping with.' He called me back on my private line within the hour."

"When was this?"

"What . . . three days before his death?"

"What did he say?"

"His reaction was the obvious. But the *what* is not nearly as important as the *where*."

"The where?"

"I have caller ID on my private line." FJ sat back. "Clu was out of town when he returned my call."

"Where?"

FJ took his time. He picked up the coffee, took a long sip, made an aaah noise as if he were filming a 7-Up commercial, put the cup back down. He looked at Myron. Then he shook his head. "Not so fast."

Myron waited.

"My specialty, as you've now seen, is gathering information. Information is power. It's currency. It's cash. I just don't give away cash."

"How much, FJ?"

"Not money, Myron. I don't want your money. I could buy you ten times over; we both know that."

"So what do you want?"

He took another long sip. Myron wanted so very much to reach across the table and throttle him. "Sure you don't want anything to drink?"

"Cut the crap, FJ."

"Temper, temper."

Myron made two fists and hid them under the table. He willed himself to stay calm. "What do you want, FJ?"

"You are familiar, are you not, with Dean Pashaian and Larry Vitale."

"They're two of my clients."

"Correction. They are seriously considering leaving MB Sports-Reps and joining TruPro. They are on the fence as we speak. So here is my deal. You stop pursuing them. You don't call them and hand them crap about TruPro being run by gangsters. You promise to do that"—he showed Myron the piece of paper he'd been writing on in the corner—"I give you the number Clu called from."

"Your agency will destroy their careers. It always does."

FJ smiled again. "I can guarantee you, Myron, that no one on my staff will have a lesbian affair with their wives."

"No deal."

"Good-bye then." FJ stood.

"Wait."

"Your promise or I walk."

"Let's talk about this," Myron said. "We can come up with something."

"Good-bye."

FJ started for the door.

"Okay," Myron said.

FJ put a hand to his ear. "I missed that."

Selling out two clients. What would he stoop to next, running political campaigns? "You have a deal. I won't talk to them."

FJ spread his hands. "You really are a master negotiator, Myron. I'm in awe of your skills."

"Where did he call from, FJ?"

"Here's the phone number." He handed Myron the piece of paper. Myron read it and sprinted back to the car.

32

Myron was on the cell phone before he reached Win. He pressed in the number and heard three rings.

"Hamlet Motel," a man said.

"Where are you located?"

"In Wilston. On Route Nine off Ninety-one."

Myron thanked the man and hung up. Win looked at him. Myron dialed Bonnie's number. Bonnie's mother answered. Myron identified himself and asked to speak with Bonnie.

"She was very upset after you left yesterday," Bonnie's mother said.

"I'm sorry about that."

"Why do you want to talk to her?"

"Please. It's very important."

"She's in mourning. You realize that. Their marriage may have been in trouble—"

"I understand that, Mrs. Cohen. Please let me speak to her."

A deep sigh, but two minutes later Bonnie came on. "What is it, Myron?"

"What does the Hamlet Motel in Wilston, Massachusetts, mean to you?"

Myron thought he heard a short intake of air. "Nothing."

"You and Clu lived there, didn't you?"

"Not at the motel."

"I mean, in Wilston. When Clu was playing for the Bisons in the minor leagues."

"You know we did."

"And Billy Lee Palms. He lived there too. At the same time."

"Not Wilston. I think he was in Deerfield. It's the neighboring town."

"So what was Clu doing staying at the Hamlet Motel three days before he died?"

Silence.

"Bonnie?"

"I don't have the slightest idea."

"Think. Why would Clu need to go up there?"

"I don't know. Maybe he was visiting an old friend."

"What old friend?"

"Myron, you're not listening. I don't know. I haven't been up there in almost ten years. But we lived there for eight months. Maybe he made a friend. Maybe he went up there to fish or take a vacation or get away from it all. I don't know."

Myron gripped the phone. "You're lying to me, Bonnie."

Silence.

"Please," he said. "I'm just trying to help Esperanza."

"Let me ask you something, Myron."

"What?"

"You keep digging and digging, right? I asked you not to. Esperanza asked you not to. Hester Crimstein asked you not to. But you keep digging."

"Is there a question in there?"

"It's coming now: Has all your digging helped? Has all your digging made Esperanza look more guilty or less?"

Myron hesitated. But it didn't matter. Bonnie hung up before he had the chance to answer. Myron put the phone back in his lap. He looked at Win.

"I'll take Awful Songs for two hundred, Alex," Win said.

"What?"

"Answer: Barry Manilow and Eastern Standard."

Myron almost smiled. "What is 'Time in New England,' Alex?"

"Correct answer." Win shook his head. "Sometimes when our minds are that in tune—"

"Yeah," Myron said. "It's scary."

"Shall we?"

Myron thought about it. "I don't think we have a choice."

"Call Terese first."

Myron nodded, started dialing. "You know how to get there?"

"Yes."

"It'll probably take three hours."

Win hit the accelerator. No easy trick in midtown Manhattan. "Try two."

33

Wilston is in western Massachusetts, about an hour shy of the New Hampshire and Vermont borders. You could still see remnants of the old days, the oft artistically rendered New England town with V-shaped brick walks, colonial clapboard homes, the historical society bronze signs welded onto the front of every other building, the white-steepled chapel in the center of the town—the whole scene screaming for the lush leaves of autumn or a major snowstorm. But like everywhere else in the US of A, the superstore boom was playing havoc with the historical. The roads between these postcard villages had widened over the years, as though guilty of gluttony, feeding off the warehouse-size stores that now lined them. The stores sucked out the character and the quaintness and left in their wake a universal blandness that plagued the byroads and highways of America. Maine to Minnesota, North Carolina to Nevada—there was little texture and individuality left. It was about Home Depot and Office Max and the price clubs.

On the other hand, whining about the changes progress imposes upon us and longing for the good ol' days make for easy pickings. Harder to answer the question of why, if these changes are so bad, do every place and everybody so quickly and warmly welcome them.

Wilston had the classic New England Christmas card–conservative facade, but it was a college town, the college in question being Wilston College, and was thus liberal—liberal in the way only a college town can be, liberal in the way only the young can be, liberal in the way only the isolated and protected and rose-tinted can be. But that was okay. In fact, that was how it should be.

But even Wilston was changing. Yes, the old signs of liberalism were there: the tofu sweet shop, the migrant-friendly coffeehouse, the lesbian bookstore, the shop with the black lightbulbs and the pot paraphernalia, the clothing store that sold only ponchos. But the franchises were sneaking in quietly, slowly eating away at the gray stone corners: Dunkin' Donuts, Angelo's Sub Shop, Baskin-Robbins, Seattle Coffee.

Myron started softly singing "Time in New England."

Win looked at him. "You realize, of course, that I'm well armed."

"Hey, you're the one who got the song stuck in my head."

They sped through town—with Win driving, you only sped—and arrived at the Hamlet Motel, a quasi-dump on Route 9 hovering on the town's edge. A sign advertised FREE HBO! and the ice machine was so large you could see it from your average space station. Myron checked his watch. Less than two hours to get here. Win parked the Jag.

"I don't get it," Myron said. "Why would Clu stay here?"

"Free HBO?"

"More likely because he could pay in cash. That's why we didn't see anything about this on his credit cards. But why wouldn't he want anyone to know he was here?"

"Such good questions," Win said. "Perhaps you should go inside and see if you can find some of the answers."

They both stepped out of the car. Win noticed a restaurant next door. "I'll try there," he said. "You take the desk clerk."

Myron nodded. The desk clerk, definitely a college kid on break, sat behind the counter and stared straight ahead at nothing. He could have looked more bored, but only if a qualified physician induced a coma. Myron took a glance around and spotted the computer terminal. This was a good thing.

"Hello?"

The kid's eyes slid toward Myron. "Yeah?"

"This computer. It keeps track of outgoing calls, right? Even local ones."

The kid's eyes narrowed. "Who wants to know?"

"I need to see records for all outgoing guest calls from the tenth and eleventh of this month."

That got the kid to his feet. "You a cop? Let me see your badge."

"I'm not a cop."

"Then—"

"I'll pay you five hundred dollars for the information." No sense in playing around here, Myron thought. "No one will ever know."

The kid hesitated but not for long. "Hell, even if I get canned, that's more money than I clear in a month. What dates did you need?"

Myron told him. The kid punched a few buttons. The printer started cranking. It all fitted on one sheet. Myron handed the kid the money. The kid handed him the sheet. Myron quickly scanned the list.

Instant bingo.

He spotted the long-distance call to FJ's office. It had come from room 117. Myron looked for other calls made from the same room. Clu had called his answering machine at home twice. Okay, good, fine. Now how about something more local? No reason to come up here just to make long-distance calls.

Bingo again.

Room 117. The first call on the list. A local number. Myron's heart started pumping, his breath growing shallow. He was close now. So close. He walked outside. The driveway was gravel. He kicked it around a bit. He took out his phone and was about to dial the number. No. That might be a mistake. He should learn all he could first. If he called, he might tip someone off. Of course, he didn't know whom he'd tip off or how they'd be tipped off or what they'd be tipped off about. But he didn't want to screw up now. He had the phone number. Big Cyndi at the office would have a reverse directory. These were easy to come by now. Any software store sold CD-ROMs that had the entire country's phone books on them or you could visit www.infospace.com on the Web. You plug in a number, it tells you who the number belongs to and where they live. More progress.

He called Big Cyndi.

"I was just about to call you, Mr. Bolitar."

"Oh?"

"I have Hester Crimstein on the line. She says that she urgently needs to talk to you."

"Okay, put her through in a sec. Big Cyndi?"

"Yes."

"About what you said yesterday. About people staring. I'm sorry if—"

"No pity, Mr. Bolitar. Remember?"

"Yes."

"Please don't change a thing, okay?"

"Okay."

"I mean it."

"Put Hester Crimstein through," he said. "And while I'm on the line, do you know where Esperanza keeps the reverse phone directory CDs?"

"Yes."

"I want you to look up a number for me." He read it off to her. She repeated it. Then she put Hester Crimstein through.

"Where are you?" the attorney barked at him.

"Why do you care?"

Hester was not pleased. "God damn it, Myron, stop acting like a child. Where are you?"

"None of your business."

"You're not helping."

"What do you want, Hester?"

"You're on a cell phone, right?"

"Right."

"Then we don't know if the line is safe," she said. "We have to meet right away. I'll be in my office."

"No can do."

"Look, do you want to help Esperanza or not?"

"You know the answer to that."

"Then get your ass in here, pronto," Hester said. "We got a problem, and I think you can help."

"What kind of problem?"

"Not on the phone. I'll be waiting for you."

"It'll take me some time," Myron said.

Silence.

"Why will it take some time, Myron?"

"It just will."

"It's almost noon," she said. "When can I expect you?"

"Not until at least six."

"That's too late."

"Sorry."

She sighed. "Myron, get here now. Esperanza wants to see you."

Myron's heart did a little flip. "I thought she was in jail."

"I just got her released. It's hush-hush. Get your ass over here, Myron. Get over here now."

Myron and Win stood in the Hamlet Motel parking lot.

"What do you make of it?" Win asked.

"I don't like it," Myron said.

"How so?"

"Why is Hester Crimstein so desperate to see me all of a sudden? She's been trying to get rid of me from the moment I returned. Now I'm the answer to a problem?"

"It is bizarre," Win agreed.

"And not only that, I don't like this whole hush-hush release for Esperanza."

"It happens."

"Sure, it happens. But if it did, why hasn't Esperanza called me? Why is Hester making the call for her?"

"Why indeed?"

Myron thought about it. "Do you think she's involved in all this?"

"I cannot imagine how," Win said. Then: "Except that she may have spoken to Bonnie Haid."

"So?"

"So then she may have deduced that we are in Wilston."

"And now she urgently wants us to return," Myron said.

"Yes."

"So she's trying to get us out of Wilston."

"It is a possibility," Win said.

"So what is she afraid we'll find?"

Win shrugged. "She's Esperanza's advocate."

"So something detrimental to Esperanza."

"Logical," Win said.

A couple in their eighties stumbled out of one of the motel rooms. The old man had his arm around the woman's shoulder. They both looked postsex. At noon. Nice to see. Myron and Win watched them in silence.

"I pushed too hard last time," Myron said.

Win did not reply.

"You warned me. You told me I didn't keep my eye on the prize. But I didn't listen."

Win still said nothing.

"Am I doing the same now?"

"You are not good at letting things go," Win said.

"That's not an answer."

Win frowned. "I'm not some holy wise man on the mount," he said. "I don't have all the answers."

"I want to know what you think."

Win squinted, though the sun was pretty much gone by now. "Last time, you lost sight of your goal," he said. "Do you know what your goal is this time?"

Myron thought about it. "Freeing Esperanza," he said. "And finding the truth."

Win smiled. "And if those two are mutually contradictory?"

"Then I bury the truth."

Win nodded. "You seem to have a good handle on the goal."

"Should I let it go anyway?" Myron asked.

Win looked at him. "There's one other complication."

"What's that?"

"Lucy Mayor."

"I'm not actively looking for her. I'd love to find her, but I don't expect to."

"Still," Win said, "she is your personal connection into all this."

Myron shook his head.

"The diskette came to you, Myron. You can't run away from that. You're not built that way. Somehow you and this missing girl are linked."

Silence.

Myron checked the address and name Big Cyndi had given him. The phone was listed to a Barbara Cromwell at 12 Claremont Road. The name meant nothing to him. "There's a rental car place down the street," Myron said. "You go back. Talk to Hester Crimstein. See what you can learn."

"And you?"

"I'm going to check out Barbara Cromwell of Twelve Claremont Road."

"Sounds like a plan," Win said.

"A good one?"

"I didn't say that."

34

Massachusetts, like Myron's home state of New Jersey, can quickly turn from big city to full-fledged town to hicksville. That was the case here. Twelve Claremont Road—why the numbers reached twelve when the whole road had only three buildings on it Myron could not say—was an old farmhouse. At least it looked old. The color, probably once a deep red, had faded to a barely visible, watery pastel. The top of the structure curled forward as though suffering from osteoporosis. The front roof overhang had split down the middle, the right lip dipping forward like the mouth of a stroke victim. There were loose boards and major cracks and the grass was tall enough to go on the adult rides at a Six Flags.

He stopped in front of Barbara Cromwell's house and debated his approach. He hit the redial button and Big Cyndi answered.

"Got anything yet?"

"Not very much, Mr. Bolitar. Barbara Cromwell is thirty-one years old. She was divorced four years ago from a Lawrence Cromwell."

"Children?"

"That's all I have right now, Mr. Bolitar. I'm terribly sorry."

He thanked her and said to keep trying. He looked back at the house. There was a dull, steady thudding in his chest. Thirty-one years old. He reached into his pocket and took out the computer rendering of the aged Lucy Mayor. He stared at it. How old would Lucy be if she were still alive? Twenty-nine, maybe thirty. Close in age, but who cares? He shook the thought away, but it didn't go easy.

Now what?

He turned off the engine. A curtain jumped in an upstairs window.

Spotted. No choice now. He opened the door and walked up the drive. It had been paved at one time, but the grass now laid claim to all but a few patches of tar. The side yard had one of those plastic Fisher-Price tree houses with a slide and rope ladder; the loud yellow, blue, and red of the play set shone through the brown grass like gems against black velvet. He reached the door. No bell, so he knocked and waited.

He could hear house sounds, someone running, someone whispering. A child called out, "Mom!" Someone hushed him.

Myron heard footsteps, and then a woman said, "Yes?"

"Ms. Cromwell?"

"What do you want?"

"Ms. Cromwell, my name is Myron Bolitar. I'd like to talk to you a moment."

"I don't want to buy anything."

"No, ma'am, I'm not selling—"

"And I don't accept door-to-door solicitations. You want a donation, you ask by mail."

"I'm not here for any of that."

Brief silence.

"Then what do you want?" she said.

"Ms. Cromwell"—he'd clipped on his most reassuring voice now—"would you mind opening your door?"

"I'm calling the police."

"No, no, please, just wait a second."

"What do you want?"

"I want to ask you about Clu Haid."

There was a long pause. The little boy started talking again. The woman hushed him. "I don't know anybody by that name."

"Please open the door, Ms. Cromwell. We need to talk."

"Look, mister, I'm friendly with all the cops around here. I say the word, they'll lock you up for trespassing."

"I understand your concerns," Myron said. "How about if we talk by phone?"

"Just go away."

The little boy started crying.

"Go away," she repeated. "Or I'll call the police."

More crying.

"Okay," Myron said. "I'm leaving." Then, figuring what the hey, he shouted, "Does the name Lucy Mayor mean anything to you?"

The child's crying was the only reply.

Myron let loose a sigh and started back to the car. Now what? He hadn't even been able to see her. Maybe he could poke around the house, try to peek in a window. Oh, that was a great idea. Get arrested for peeping. Or worse, scare a little kid. And she'd call the cops for sure—

Hold the phone.

Barbara Cromwell said that she was friendly with the police in town. But so was Myron. In a way. Wilston was the town where Clu had been nabbed on that first drunk driving charge when he was in the minors. Myron had gotten him off with the help of two cops. He scanned the memory banks for names. It didn't take him long. The arresting officer was named Kobler. Myron didn't remember his first name. The sheriff was a guy named Ron Lemmon. Lemmon was in his fifties then. He might have retired. But odds were pretty good one of them would still be on the force. They might know something about the mysterious Barbara Cromwell.

Worth a shot anyway.

35

One might expect the Wilston police station to be in a dinky little building. Not so. It was in the basement of a tall, fortresslike structure of dark, old brick. The steps down had one of those old bomb shelter signs, the black and yellow triangles still bright in the ominous circle. The image brought back memories of Burnet Hill Elementary School and the old bombing drills, a somewhat intense activity in which children were taught that crouching in a corridor was a suitable defense against a Soviet nuclear blitzkrieg.

Myron had never been to the station house before. After Clu's accident he'd met with the two cops in the back booth of a diner on Route 9. The whole episode took less than ten minutes. No one wanted to hurt the up-and-coming superstar. No one wanted to ruin Clu's promising young career. Dollars changed hands—some for the arresting officer, some for the sheriff in charge. Donations, they'd called it with a chuckle. Everyone smiled.

The desk sergeant looked up at Myron when he came in. He was around thirty and, like so many cops nowadays, built as if he spent more time in the weight room than the doughnut shop. His nametag read "Hobert." "May I help you?"

"Does Sheriff Lemmon still work here?"

"No, sorry to say. Ron died, oh, gotta be a year now. Retired about two years before that."

"I'm sorry to hear that."

"Yeah, cancer. Ate through him like a hungry rat." Hobert shrugged as if to say, What can you do?

"How about a guy named Kobler? I think he was a deputy about ten years ago."

Hobert's voice was suddenly tight. "Eddie's not on the force anymore."

"Does he still live in the area?"

"No. I think he lives in Wyoming. May I ask your name, sir?"

"Myron Bolitar."

"Your name sounds familiar."

"I used to play basketball."

"Nah, that's not it. I hate basketball." He thought a moment, then shook his head. "So why are you asking about two former cops?"

"They're sort of old friends."

Hobert looked doubtful.

"I wanted to ask them about someone a client of mine has become involved with."

"A client?"

Myron put on his helpless-puppy-dog smile. He usually used it on old ladies, but hey, waste not, want not. "I'm a sports agent. My job is to look after athletes and, well, make sure they're not being taken advantage of. So this client of mine has an interest in a lady who lives in town. I just wanted to make sure she's not a gold digger or anything."

Two words: *truly lame.*

Hobert said, "What's her name?"

"Barbara Cromwell."

The officer blinked. "This a joke?"

"No."

"One of your athletes is interested in dating Barbara Cromwell?"

Myron tried a little backpedal. "I might have gotten the name wrong," he said.

"I think maybe you have."

"Why's that?"

"You mentioned Ron Lemmon before. The old sheriff."

"Right."

"Barbara Cromwell is his daughter."

For a moment Myron just stood there. A fan whirred. A phone rang. Hobert said, "Excuse me a second," and picked it up. Myron heard none of it. Someone had frozen the moment. Someone had suspended him above a dark hole, giving Myron plenty of time to stare down at the nothingness, until suddenly the same someone let go. Myron plunged down into the black, his hands wheeling, his body turning, waiting, almost hoping, to smash against the bottom.

36

Myron stumbled back outside. He walked the town square. He grabbed something to eat at a Mexican place, wolfing it down without even tasting the food. Win called.

"We were correct," Win said. "Hester Crimstein was trying to divert our attention."

"She admitted it?"

"No. She offers no explanation, She claims that she will speak with you and only you and only in person. She then pushed me for details on your whereabouts."

No surprise.

"Would you like me to"—Win paused—"interrogate her?"

"Please no," Myron said. "Ethics aside, I don't think there's much need anymore."

"Oh?"

"Sawyer Wells said he was a drug counselor at Rockwell."

"I remember."

"Billy Lee Palms was treated at Rockwell. His mother mentioned it when I visited her house."

"Hmm," Win said. "Wonderful coincidence."

"Not a coincidence," Myron said. "It explains everything."

When he finished talking to Win, he strolled the main street of Wilston seven or eight times over. The shopkeepers, light on business, smiled at him. He smiled back. He nodded hello to the large assortment of people passing by. The town was so stuck in the sixties, the kind of place where people still wore unkempt beards and black caps and looked like Seals and Crofts at an outdoor concert. He liked it here. He liked it a lot.

He thought about his mother and his father. He thought about them getting old and wondered why he could not accept it. He thought about how his father's "chest pains" were partially his fault, how the strain of his running away had at least tangentially contributed to what happened. He thought about what it would have been like for his parents if they had suffered the same fate as Sophie and Gary Mayor, if he had disappeared at seventeen without a trace and were never found. He thought about Jessica and how she claimed she would fight for him. He thought about Brenda and what he had done. He thought about Terese and last night and what, if anything, it meant. He thought about Win and Esperanza and the sacrifices that friends make.

For a long time he did not think about Clu's murder or Billy Lee's death. He did not think about Lucy Mayor and her disappearance and his connection to it. But that lasted only so long. Eventually he made a few phone calls, did some digging, confirmed what he already suspected.

The answers never come with cries of "Eureka!" You stumble toward them, often in total darkness. You stagger through an unlit room at night, tripping over the unseen, lumbering forward, bruising your shins, toppling over and righting yourself, feeling your way across the walls and hoping your hand happens upon the light switch. And then—to keep within this piss-poor but sadly accurate analogy—when you find the switch, when you flick it on and bathe the room in light, sometimes the room is just as you pictured it. And then sometimes, like now, you wonder if you'd have been better off staying forever stumbling in the dark.

Win of course would say that Myron was limiting the analogy. He would point out that there were other options. You could simply leave the room. You could let your eyes get accustomed to the dark, and while you would never see everything clearly, that was okay. You could even flick the switch back off once you turned it on. In the case of Horace and Brenda Slaughter, Win would be right. In the case of Clu Haid, Myron was not so sure.

He had found the light switch. He had flicked it on. But the analogy did not hold—and not just because it was a dumb one from the start. Everything in the room was still murky, as though he were looking through a shower curtain. He could see lights and shadows. He could make out shapes. But to know exactly what had happened, he would have to push aside the curtain.

He could still back off, let the curtain rest or even flick the light back off. But that was the problem with darkness and Win's options. In the dark you cannot see the rot fester. The rot is free to continue to eat away, undisturbed, until it consumes everything, even the man huddled in the corner, trying like hell to stay away from that damned light switch.

So Myron got in his car. He drove back out to the farmhouse on Claremont Road. He knocked on the door, and again Barbara Cromwell told him to go away. "I know why Clu Haid came here," he told her. He kept talking. And eventually she let him in.

When he left, Myron called Win again. They talked a long time. First about Clu Haid's murder. Then about Myron's dad. It helped. But not a lot. He called Terese and told her what he knew. She said that she'd tried to check some of the facts with her sources.

"So Win was right," Terese said. "You are personally connected."

"Yes."

"I blame myself every day," Terese said. "You get used to it."

Again he wanted to ask more. Again he knew that it wasn't time.

Myron made two more calls on the cell phone. The first was to the law office of Hester Crimstein.

"Where are you?" Hester snapped.

"I assume you're in contact with Bonnie Haid," he said.

Pause. Then: "Oh Christ, Myron, what did you do?"

"They aren't telling you everything, Hester. In fact, I bet Esperanza barely told you anything."

"Where are you, dammit?"

"I'll be in your office in three hours. Have Bonnie there."

His final call was to Sophie Mayor. When she answered, he said three words: "I found Lucy."

37

Myron tried to drive like Win, but that was beyond his capabilities. He sped, but he still hit construction on Route 95. You always hit construction on Route 95. It was a Connecticut state law. He listened to the radio. He made phone calls. He felt frightened.

Hester Crimstein was a senior partner in a high-rise, higher-bill, mega New York law firm. The attractive receptionist had clearly been expecting him. She led him down a hallway lined with what looked like mahogany wallpaper and into a conference room. There was a rectangular table big enough to seat twenty, pens and legal pads in front of each chair, billable no doubt to some unsuspecting client at wildly inflated prices. Hester Crimstein sat next to Bonnie Haid, their backs to the window. They started to rise when he entered.

"Don't bother," he said.

Both women stopped.

"What's this all about?" Hester asked.

Myron ignored her and looked at Bonnie. "You almost told me, didn't you, Bonnie? When I first came back. You said you wondered if we did Clu a disservice by helping him. You wondered if our sheltering him and protecting him had eventually led to his death. I said you were wrong. The only person to blame is the person who shot him. But I didn't know everything, did I?"

"What the hell are you talking about?" Hester said.

"I want to tell you a story," he said.

"What?"

"Just listen, Hester. You might find out what you've gotten yourself involved in."

Hester closed her mouth. Bonnie kept silent.

"Twelve years ago," Myron said, "Clu Haid and Billy Lee Palms were minor-league players for a team called the New England Bisons. They were both young and reckless in the way athletes tend to be. The world was their oyster, they thought they were the cat's pajamas, you know the fairy tale. I won't insult you by going into details."

Both women slid back into their seats. Myron sat across from them and continued.

"One day Clu Haid drove drunk—well, he probably drove drunk more than once, but on this occasion he wrapped his car around a tree. Bonnie"—he gestured to her with his chin—"was injured in the accident. She suffered a bad concussion and spent several days in the hospital. Clu was unhurt. Billy Lee broke a finger. When it happened, Clu panicked. A drunk driving charge could ruin a young athlete, even as little as twelve years ago. I had just signed him to several profitable endorsement deals. He was going to move up to the majors in a matter of months. So he did what a lot of athletes did. He found someone who'd get him out of trouble. His agent. Me. I drove up to the scene like a madman. I met with the arresting officer, a guy named Eddie Kobler, and the town sheriff, Ron Lemmon."

Hester Crimstein said, "I don't understand any of this."

"Give me time, you will," Myron said. "The officers and I came to an understanding. It happens all the time with big-time athletes. Matters like this are swept under the rug. Clu was a good kid, we all agreed. No reason to destroy his life over this little incident. It was a somewhat victimless crime—the only person hurt was Clu's own wife. So money changed hands, and an agreement was reached. Clu wasn't drunk. He swerved to avoid another car. That's what caused the accident. Billy Lee Palms and Bonnie would swear to it. Incident over and forgotten."

Hester wore her annoyed-but-curious scowl. Bonnie's face was losing color fast.

"It's twelve years later now," Myron said. "And the incident is almost like one of those mummy curses. The drunk driver, Clu, is murdered. His best friend and passenger, Billy Lee Palms, is shot to death—I won't call that murder because the shooter saved my life. The sheriff I bought off—he died of prostate cancer. Nothing too strange about that or perhaps God got to him before the mummy. And as for Eddie Kobler, the other officer, he was caught last year taking bribes in a big drug string. He was arrested and plea-bargained down. His wife left him. His kids won't talk to him. He lives alone in a bottle in Wyoming."

"How do you know about this Kobler guy?" Hester Crimstein asked.

"A local cop named Hobert told me what happened. A reporter friend confirmed it."

"I still don't see the relevance," Hester said.

"That's because Esperanza kept you in the dark," Myron said. "I was wondering how much she told you. Apparently not much. Probably just insisted that I be kept totally out of this, right?"

Hester gave him the courtroom eyes. "Are you saying Esperanza has something to do with all this?"

"No."

"You're the one who committed a crime here, Myron. You bribed two police officers."

"And there's the rub," Myron said.

"What are you talking about?"

"Even that night something struck me as odd about the whole incident. The three of them in the car together. Why? Bonnie didn't much care for Billy Lee Palms. Sure, she'd go out with Clu and Clu would go out with Billy Lee and maybe they'd even double-date or something. But why were the three of them in that car so late at night?"

Hester Crimstein stayed the lawyer. "Are you saying one of them wasn't in the car?"

"No. I'm saying that there were four people in the car, not three."

"What?"

They both looked at Bonnie. Bonnie lowered her head.

"Who were the four?" Hester asked.

"Bonnie and Clu were one couple." Myron tried to meet Bonnie's eyes, but she wouldn't look up. "Billy Lee Palms and Lucy Mayor were the other."

Hester Crimstein looked as if she'd been hit with a two-by-four. "Lucy Mayor?" she repeated. "As in the missing Mayor girl?"

"Yes."

"Jesus Christ."

Myron kept his eyes on Bonnie. Eventually she raised her head. "It's true, isn't it?"

Hester Crimstein said, "She's not talking."

"Yes," Bonnie said. "It's true."

"But you never knew what happened to her, did you?"

Bonnie hesitated. "Not then, no."

"What did Clu tell you?"

"That you bought her off too," Bonnie said. "Like with the police. He said you paid her to keep silent."

Myron nodded. It made sense. "There's one thing I don't get. There was a ton of publicity about Lucy Mayor a few years back. You must have seen her picture in the paper."

"I did."

"Didn't it ring a bell?"

"No. You have to remember. I only saw her that one time. You know Billy Lee. A different girl every night. And Clu and I sat in the front. Her hair was a different color too. She was a blonde then. So I didn't know."

"And neither did Clu."

"That's right."

"But eventually you learned the truth."

"Eventually," she said.

"Whoa," Hester Crimstein said. "I'm not following any of this. What does an old traffic accident have to do with Clu's murder?"

"Everything," Myron said.

"You better explain, Myron. And while you're at it, why did Esperanza get framed for it?"

"That was a mistake."

"What?"

"Esperanza wasn't the one they intended to frame," Myron said. "I was."

38

Yankee Stadium hunched over in the night, crouching shoulders low as though trying to escape the glow from its own lights. Myron parked in Lot 14, where the executives and players parked. There were only three other cars there. The night guard at the press entrance said he was expected, that the Mayors would meet him on the field. Myron moved down the lower tier and hopped the wall near the batter's box. The stadium lights were on, but nobody was there. He stood alone on the field and took a deep breath. Even in the Bronx nothing smelled like a baseball diamond. He turned toward the visitor's dugout, scanning the lower boxes and finding the exact seats he and his brother had sat in all those years ago. Funny what you remember. He walked toward the pitcher's mound, the grass making a gentle whooshing sound, and sat down on the rubber and waited. Clu's home. The one place he'd always felt at peace.

Should have buried him here, Myron thought. *Under a pitcher's mound.*

He stared up into the thousands of seats, empty like the shattered eyes of the dead, the vacant stadium merely a body now without a soul. The whites of the foul lines were muddied, nearly dirt-toned now. They'd be put down anew tomorrow before game time.

People say that baseball is a metaphor for life. Myron did not know about that, but staring down the foul line, he wondered. The line between good and evil is not so different from the foul line on a baseball field. It's often made of stuff as flimsy as lime. It tends to fade over time. It needs to be constantly redrawn. And if enough players trample on it, the line becomes smeared and blurred to the point where fair is foul and foul is fair, where good and evil become indistinguishable from each other.

Jared Mayor's voice broke the stillness. "You said you found my sister."

Myron squinted toward the dugout. "I lied," he said.

Jared stepped up the cement stairs. Sophie followed. Myron rose to his feet. Jared started to say something more, but his mother put her hand on his arm. They kept walking as though they were coaches coming out to talk to the relief pitcher.

"Your sister is dead," Myron said. "But you both know that."

They kept walking.

"She was killed in a drunk driving accident," he went on. "She died on impact."

"Maybe," Sophie said.

Myron looked confused. "Maybe?"

"Maybe she died on impact, maybe she didn't," Sophie continued. "Clu Haid and Billy Lee Palms weren't doctors. They were dumb, drunk jocks. Lucy might have just been injured. She may have been alive. A doctor might have been able to save her."

Myron nodded. "I guess that's possible."

"Go on," Sophie said. "I want to hear what you have to say."

"Whatever your daughter's condition actually was, Clu and Billy Lee believed that she was dead. Clu was terrified. Drunk driving charges would be serious enough, but this was vehicular homicide. You don't walk away from that, no matter how far your curveball breaks. He and Billy Lee panicked. I don't know the details here. Sawyer Wells can tell us. My guess is that they hid the body. It was a quiet road, but there still wouldn't be enough time to bury Lucy before the police and ambulance arrived. So they probably stashed her in the brush. And when it all calmed down, they came back and buried her. Like I said, I don't know the details. I don't think they're particularly relevant. What is relevant is that Clu and Billy Lee got rid of the body."

Jared stepped into Myron's face. "You can't prove any of this."

Myron ignored him, keeping his eyes on Jared's mother. "The years pass. Lucy is gone. But not in the minds of Clu Haid and Billy Lee Palms. Maybe I'm overanalyzing. Maybe I'm being too easy on them. But I think what they did that night defined the rest of their lives. Their self-destructive tendencies. The drugs—"

"You're being too easy," Sophie said.

Myron waited.

"Don't give them credit for having consciences," she continued. "They were worthless scum."

"Maybe you're right. I shouldn't analyze. And I guess it doesn't matter. Clu and Billy Lee may have created their own hell, but it wasn't close to the agony your family experienced. You told me about the awful torment of not knowing the truth, how it lives with you every day. With Lucy dead and buried like that, the torment just went on."

Sophie's head was still high. There was no flinch in her. "Do you know how we finally learned our daughter's fate?"

"From Sawyer Wells," Myron said. "The Wells Rules of Wellness, Rule Eight: 'Confess something about yourself to a friend—something awful, something you'd never want anyone to know. You'll feel better. You'll still see that you're worthy of love.' Sawyer was a drug counselor at Rockwell. Billy Lee was a patient there. My guess is that he caught him during a withdrawal episode. When he was delirious probably. He did what his therapist asked. Rule eight. He confessed the worst thing he could imagine, the one moment in his life that shaped all others. Sawyer suddenly saw his ticket out of Rockwell and into the spotlight. Through the wealthy Mayor family, owners of Mayor Software. So he went to you and your husband. And he told you what he'd heard."

Again Jared said, "You have no proof of any of this!"

And again Sophie silenced him with her hand. "Go on, Myron," she said. "What happened then?"

"With this new information, you found your daughter's body. I don't know if your private investigators did it or if you just used your money and influence to keep the authorities quiet. It wouldn't have been difficult for someone in your position."

"I see," Sophie said. "But if all that's true, why would I want to keep it quiet? Why not prosecute Clu and Billy Lee—and even you?"

"Because you couldn't," Myron said.

"Why not?"

"The corpse had been buried for twelve years. There was no evidence there. The car was long gone—no evidence there either. The police report listed a Breathalyzer test that showed Clu was not drunk. So what did you have: the ranting of a drug addict going through withdrawal? Billy Lee's confession to Sawyer Wells would probably be suppressed, and even if it wasn't, so what? His testimony about the police payoffs was complete hearsay since he wasn't even there when it happened. You realized all that, didn't you?"

She said nothing.

"And that meant justice was up to you, Sophie. You and Gary would have to avenge your daughter." He stopped, looked at Jared, then back at Sophie. "You told me about a void. You said that you preferred to fill that void with hope."

Sophie nodded. "I did."

"And when the hope was gone—when the discovery of your daughter's body sucked it all away—you and your husband still needed to fill that void."

"Yes."

"So you filled it with revenge."

She fixed her gaze on his. "Do you blame us, Myron?"

He said nothing.

"The crooked sheriff was dying of cancer," Sophie said. "There was nothing to be done about him. The other officer, well, as your friend Win could tell you, money is influence. The Federal Bureau of Investigation set him up at our behest. He took the bait. And yes, I shattered his life. Gladly."

"But Clu was the one you wanted to hurt most," Myron said.

"Hurt nothing. I wanted to crush him."

"But he too was fairly broken down," Myron said. "In order to really crush him, you had to give him hope. Just like you and Gary had all these years. Give him hope, then snatch it away. Hope hurts like nothing else. You knew that. So you and your husband bought the Yankees. You overpaid, but so what? You had the money. You didn't care. Gary died soon after the transaction."

"From heartache," Sophie interrupted. She raised her head, and for the first time he saw a tear. "From years of heartache."

"But you carried on without him."

"Yes."

"You concentrated on one thing and one thing only: getting Clu in your grasp. It was a silly trade—everyone thought so—and it was strange coming from an owner who kept out of every other baseball decision. But it was all about getting Clu on the team. That's the only reason you bought the Yankees. To give Clu a last chance. And even better, Clu cooperated. He started straightening out his life. He was clean and sober. He was pitching well. He was as happy as Clu Haid was ever going to get. You had him in the palm of your hand.

"And then you closed your fist."

Jared put his arm around her shoulders and pressed her close.

"I don't know the order," Myron went on. "You sent Clu a computer diskette like you sent me. Bonnie told me that. She also told me that you blackmailed him. Anonymously. That explains the missing two hundred thousand dollars. You made him live in terror. And Bonnie even inadvertently helped you by filing for divorce. Now Clu was in the perfect position for your coup de grace: the drug test. You fixed it so he would fail. Sawyer helped. Who better, since he already knew what was going on? It worked beautifully. Not only did it destroy Clu, but it also diverted any attention from you. Who would ever suspect you, especially since the test seemingly hurt you too? But you didn't care about any of that. The Yankees meant nothing to you except as a vehicle to destroy Clu Haid."

"So true," Sophie said.

"Don't," Jared said.

She shook her head and patted her son's arm. "It's okay."

"Clu had no idea the girl he buried in the woods was your daughter. But after you bombarded him with the calls and the diskette and especially after he failed the drug test, he put it together. But what could he do about it? He certainly couldn't say the drug test was fixed because he'd killed Lucy Mayor. He was trapped. He tried to figure out how you'd learned the truth. He thought maybe it was Barbara Cromwell."

"Who?"

"Barbara Cromwell. She's Sheriff Lemmon's daughter."

"How did she know?"

"Because as quiet as you tried to keep the investigation, Wilston is a small town. The sheriff was tipped off about the discovery. He was dying. He had no money. His family was poor. So he told his daughter about what had really happened that night. She could never get in trouble for it—it was his crime, not hers. And they could use the information to blackmail Clu Haid. Which they did. On several occasions. Clu figured Barbara had been the one who opened her mouth. When he called her to find out if she'd told anyone, Barbara played coy. She demanded more money. So Clu drove up to Wilston a few days later. He refused to pay her. He said it was over."

Sophie nodded. "So that's how you put it together."

"It was the final piece, yes," Myron said. "When I realized that Clu had visited Lemmon's daughter, it all fell into place. But I'm still surprised, Sophie."

"Surprised about what?"

"That you killed him. That you let Clu out of his misery."

Jared's arm dropped off his mother. "What are you talking about?" he said.

"Let him speak," Sophie said. "Go on, Myron."

"What more is there?"

"For starters," she said, "how about your part in all this?"

A lead block formed in his chest. He said nothing.

"You're not going to claim that you were blameless in all this, are you, Myron?"

His voice was soft. "No."

In the distance, out beyond center field, a janitor started cleaning off the memorials to the Yankees' greats. He sprayed and wiped, working, Myron knew from past stadium visits, on Lou Gehrig's stone. The Iron Horse. Such bravery in the face of so awful a death.

"You've done this too, haven't you?" Sophie said.

Myron kept his eyes on the janitor. "Done what?" But he knew.

"I've looked into your past," she said. "You and your business associate often take the law into your own hands, am I right? You play judge and jury."

Myron said nothing.

"That's all I did. For the sake of my daughter's memory."

The blurry line between fair and foul again. "So you decided to frame me for Clu's murder."

"Yes."

"The perfect way to wreak vengeance on me for bribing the officers."

"I thought so at the time."

"But you messed up, Sophie. You ended up framing the wrong person."

"That was an accident."

Myron shook his head. "I should have seen it," he said. "Even Billy Lee Palms said it, but I didn't pay attention. And Hester Crimstein said it to me the first time I met her."

"Said what?"

"They both pointed out that the blood was found in *my* car, the gun in *my* office. Maybe I killed Clu, they said. A logical deduction except for one thing. I was out of the country. You didn't know that, Sophie. You didn't know that Esperanza and Big Cyndi were playing a shell game with everybody, pretending I was still around. That's why you were so upset with me when you found out I'd been away. I messed up your plan. You also didn't know that Clu had an altercation with Esperanza. So all the evidence that was supposed to point to me—"

"Pointed instead to your associate, Miss Diaz," Sophie said.

"Exactly," Myron said. "But there's one other thing I want to clear up."

"More than one thing," Sophie corrected.

"What?"

"There's more than one thing you'll want to clear up," Sophie said. "But please go ahead. What would you like to know?"

"You were the one who had me followed," he said. "The guy I spotted outside the Lock-Horne building. He was yours."

"Yes. I knew Clu had tried to hook up with you. I hoped the same might happen with Billy Lee Palms."

"Which it did. Billy Lee thought that maybe I killed Clu to keep my part in the crime buried. He thought I wanted to kill him too."

"It makes sense," she agreed. "You had a lot to lose."

"So you were following me then? At the bar?"

"Yes."

"Personally?"

She smiled. "I grew up a hunter and a tracker, Myron. The city or the woods, it makes little difference."

"You saved my life," he said.

She did not reply.

"Why?"

"You know why. I didn't come there to kill Billy Lee Palms. But there are degrees of guilt. Simply put, he was more guilty than you. When it came down to a question of you or him, I chose to kill him. You deserve to be punished, Myron. But you didn't deserve to be killed by scum like Billy Lee Palms."

"Judge and jury again?"

"Luckily for you, Myron, yes."

He sat down hard on the pitcher's mound, his whole body suddenly drained. "I can't just let you get away with this," he said. "I may sympathize. But you killed Clu Haid in cold blood."

"No."

"What?"

"I didn't kill Clu Haid."

"I don't expect you to confess."

"Expect or don't expect. I didn't kill him."

Myron frowned. "You had to. It all adds up."

Her eyes remained placid pools. Myron's head started spinning. He turned and looked up at Jared.

"He didn't kill him either," Sophie said.

"One of you did," Myron said.

"No."

Myron looked at Jared. Jared said nothing. Myron opened his mouth, closed it, tried to come up with something.

"Think, Myron." Sophie crossed her arms and smiled at him. "I told you my philosophy when you were last here. I'm a hunter. I don't hate what I kill. Just the opposite. I respect what I kill. I honor my kill. I consider the animal brave and noble. Killing, in fact, can be merciful. That's why I kill with one shot. Not Billy Lee Palms, of course. I wanted him to have at least a few moments of agony and fear. And of course, I would never show Clu Haid mercy."

Myron tried to sort through it. "But—"

And then he heard yet another click. His conversation with Sally Li started uncoiling in his head.

The crime scene . . .

Christ, the crime scene. It was in such a state of disarray. Blood on the walls. Blood on the floor. Because blood splatters would show the truth. So splatter some more. Destroy the evidence. Fire more shots into the corpse. To the calf, to the back, even to the head. Take the gun with you. Mess things up. Cover up what really happened.

"Oh God . . ."

Sophie nodded at him.

Myron's mouth felt dry as a sandstorm. "Clu committed suicide?"

Sophie tried a smile, but she just couldn't quite make it.

Myron started to stand, his bad knee audibly creaking as he rose. "The end of his marriage, the failed drug test, but mostly the past coming back at him—it was all too much. He shot himself in the head. The other shots were just to throw the police off. The crime scene was messed up so no one would be able to analyze the blood splatters and see it was a suicide. It was all a diversion."

"A coward to the end," Sophie said.

"But how did you know he killed himself? Did you have his place bugged or under surveillance?"

"Nothing so technical, Myron. He wanted us to find him—me specifically."

Myron just stared at her.

"We were supposed to have our big confrontation that night. Yes, Clu had hit rock bottom, Myron. But I was not through with him. Not by a long shot. An animal deserved a quick kill. Not Clu Haid. But when Jared and I arrived, he'd already taken the gutless way out."

"And the money?"

"It was there. As you noted, the anonymous stranger who sent him the diskette and made all those phone calls was blackmailing him. But he knew it was us. I took the money that night and donated it to the Child Welfare Institute."

"You caused him to kill himself."

She shook her head, her posture still ramrod. "Nobody causes someone to kill himself. Clu Haid chose his fate. It was not what I intended but—"

"Intended? He's dead, Sophie."

"Yes, but it was not what I *intended*. Just as you, Myron, did not *intend* to cover up my daughter's murder."

Silence.

"You took advantage of his death," Myron said. "You planted the blood and gun in my car and office. Or you hired someone to do it."

"Yes."

He shook his head. "The truth has to come out," he said.
"No."
"I'm not letting Esperanza rot in jail—"
"It's done," Sophie Mayor said.
"What?"
"My attorney is meeting with the DA as we speak. Anonymously, of
course. They won't know whom he represents."
"I don't understand."
"I kept evidence that night," she said. "I took pictures of the body.
They'll test Clu's hand for powder residue. I even have a suicide note, if
need be. The charges against Esperanza will be dropped. She'll be re-
leased in the morning. It's over."
"The DA isn't going to settle for that. He's going to want to know the
whole story."
"Life is full of wants, Myron. But the DA won't get it in this case.
He'll just have to live with that reality. And in the end it's just a suicide
anyway. High profile or not, it won't be a priority." She reached into her
pocket and took out a piece of paper. "Here," she said. "It's Clu's suicide
note."
Myron hesitated. He took the note, immediately recognizing Clu's
handwriting. He started reading:

Dear Mrs. Mayor,
*   The torment has gone on long enough. I know you won't accept my*
apology and I can't say that I blame you. But I also don't have the
strength to face you. I've been running away from that night all my life.
I hurt my family and my friends, but I hurt nobody so much as I hurt
you. I hope my death gives you some measure of comfort.
*   I am the one to blame for what happened. Billy Lee Palms just did*
what I told him to. The same goes for Myron Bolitar. I paid off the po-
lice. Myron just delivered the money. He never knew the truth. My wife
was knocked out in the accident. She also never knew the truth and she
still doesn't.
*   The money is all here. Do with it what you will. Tell Bonnie that I'm*
sorry and that I understand everything. And let my children know that
their father always loved them. They were the only thing pure and good
in my life. You, of all people, should understand that.

*   Clu Haid*

Myron read the note again. He pictured Clu writing it, then putting it
aside, then picking up the gun and pressing it against his head. Did he

close his eyes then? Did he think of his children, the two boys with his smile, before he pulled the trigger? Did he hesitate at all?

His eyes stayed on the note. "You didn't believe him," he said.

"About the culpability of the others? No. I knew he was lying. You, for example. You were more than a delivery boy. You bribed those officers."

"Clu lied to protect us," Myron said. "In the end he sacrificed himself for those he loved."

Sophie frowned. "Don't make him out to be a martyr."

"I'm not. But you just can't walk away from what you did."

"I did nothing."

"You made a man—the father of two boys—kill himself."

"He made a choice, that's all."

"He didn't deserve that."

"And my daughter didn't deserve to be murdered and buried in an anonymous pit," she said.

Myron looked up into the stadium lights, letting them blind him a bit. "Clu was off drugs," he said. "You'll pay the rest of his salary."

"No."

"You'll also let the world know—and his children—that in the end Clu wasn't on drugs."

"No," Sophie said again. "The world won't know that. And they also won't know Clu was a murderer. I'd say that's a pretty good bargain, wouldn't you?"

He read the note again, tears stinging his eyes.

"One heroic moment in the end doesn't redeem him," Sophie said.

"But it says something."

"Go home, Myron. And be glad it's over. If the truth were ever to come out, there is only one guilty party left to take the fall."

Myron nodded. "Me."

"Yes."

They stared at each other.

"I didn't know about your daughter," he said.

"I know that now."

"You thought I helped Clu cover it up."

"No, I *know* you helped Clu cover it up. What I wasn't sure about is if you knew what you were doing. It was why I asked you to look for Lucy—so I could see how deep your involvement was."

"The void," Myron said.

"What about it?"

"Did this help fill it?"

Sophie thought about it. "Strangely enough, the answer is yes, I think.

It doesn't bring Lucy back. But I feel as though she's been properly buried now. I think we can begin to heal."

"So we all just go on?"

Sophie smiled. "What else can we do?"

She nodded to Jared. Jared took his mother's hand, and they started back for the dugout.

"I am very sorry," Myron said.

Sophie stopped. She dropped her son's hand and studied Myron for a moment, her eyes moving over his face. "You committed a felony by bribing those police officers. You put my family and me through years of agony. You probably contributed to my husband's premature death. You had a hand in the deaths of Clu Haid and Billy Lee Palms. And in the end you made me commit horrible acts I always thought I was incapable of committing." She stepped back toward her son, her gaze more tired now than accusatory. "I won't hurt you any further. But if you don't mind, I'll let you keep your apology."

She gave Myron a moment for rebuttal. He didn't use it. They strode down the steps and disappeared, leaving Myron alone with the grass and the dirt and the bright stadium lights.

39

In the lot Win frowned and holstered his .44. "No one even pulled a gun."

Myron said nothing. He got into his car. Win got into his. Myron's cellular phone rang before he had driven five minutes. It was Hester Crimstein.

"They're dropping the charges," she said to him. "Esperanza will be out tomorrow morning. They're offering up a full exoneration and apology if we promise not to sue."

"Will you accept that?"

"It's up to Esperanza. But I think she'll agree."

Myron drove to Bonnie's house. Her mother opened the door and looked angry. Myron pushed past her and found Bonnie alone. He showed her the note. She cried. He held her. He looked in on the two sleeping boys and stayed in the doorway until Bonnie's mother tapped him on the shoulder and asked him to leave. He did.

He headed back to Win's apartment. When he opened the door, Terese's suitcase was by the entrance. She stepped into the foyer.

"You're packed," Myron said.

She smiled. "I love a man who misses nothing."

He waited.

"I'm leaving in an hour for Atlanta," she said.

"Oh."

"I spoke to my boss at CNN. Ratings have been down. He wants me back on the air tomorrow."

"Oh," Myron said again.

Terese pulled at a ring on her finger. "You ever try a long-distance relationship?" she asked.

"No."

"Might be worth a try."

"Might be," he said.

"I hear the sex is great."

"That's never been our trouble, Terese."

"No," she said. "It hasn't."

He checked his watch. "Only an hour, you said?"

She smiled. "Actually, an hour and ten minutes."

"Whew," he said, moving closer.

At midnight Myron and Win were in the living room watching television.

"You'll miss her," Win said.

"I'm flying down to Atlanta this weekend."

Win nodded. "Best-case scenario."

"Meaning?"

"Meaning you are the pitiful, needy type who feels incomplete without a steady girlfriend. Who better than a career woman who lives a thousand miles away?"

More silence. They watched a repeat of *Frasier* on Channel 11. The show was starting to grow on them both.

"An agent represents his clients," Win said during a commercial. "You're his advocate. You can't worry about the repercussions."

"You really believe that?"

"Sure, why not?"

Myron shrugged. "Yeah, why not?" He watched another commercial. "Esperanza said I'm starting to get too comfortable with breaking the rules."

Win said nothing.

"Truth is," Myron said, "I've been doing it for a while. I paid off police officers to cover up a crime."

"You didn't know the severity."

"Does that matter?"

"Of course it does."

Myron shook his head. "We trample on that damned foul line until we can't see it anymore," he said softly.

"What are you talking about?"

"I'm talking about us. Sophie Mayor said that you and I do the same thing she did. We take the law into our own hands. We break the rules."

"So?"

"So it's not right."

Win frowned. "Oh, please."

"The innocent get hurt."

"The police hurt the innocent too."

"Not like this. Esperanza suffered when she had nothing to do with any of this. Clu deserved to be punished, but what happened to Lucy Mayor was still an accident."

Win drummed his chin with two fingers. "If we put aside an argument on the relative severity of drunk driving," he said, "in the end it was not merely an accident. Clu chose to bury the body. The fact that he couldn't live with it doesn't excuse it."

"We can't keep doing this, Win."

"Keep doing what?"

"Breaking the rules."

"Let me pose a question to you, Myron." Win continued his chin drumming. "Suppose you were Sophie Mayor and Lucy Mayor were your daughter. What would you have done?"

"Maybe the same thing," Myron said. "Does that make it right?"

"Depends," Win said.

"On?"

"On the Clu Haid factor: Can you live with yourself?"

"That's it?"

"That's it. Can you live with yourself? I know that I could."

"And you're comfortable with that?"

"With what?"

"With a world where people take the law into their own hands," Myron said.

"Good lord, no. I'm not prescribing this remedy for others."

"Just you."

Win shrugged. "I trust my judgment. I'd trust yours too. But now you want to go back in time and take an alternate route. Life is not like that. You made a decision. It was a good one based on what you knew. A tough call, but aren't they all? It could have worked out the other way. Clu might have smartened up from the experience, become a better person. My point is, you can't concern yourself with distant, impossible-to-see consequences."

"Just worry about the here and now."

"Precisely."

"And what you can live with."

"Yes."

"So maybe next time," Myron said, "I should opt for doing the right thing."

Win shook his head. "You're confusing the right thing with the legal or seemingly moral thing. But that's not the real world. Sometimes the good guys break the rules because they know better."

Myron smiled. "They cross the foul line. Just for a second. Just to do good. Then they scramble back into fair territory. But when you do that too often, you start smearing the line."

"Perhaps the line is supposed to be smeared," Win said.

"Perhaps."

"On balance, you and I do good."

"That balance might be better if we didn't stray across the line so much—even if that meant letting a few more injustices remain injustices."

Win shrugged. "Your call."

Myron sat back. "You know what's bothering me the most about this conversation?"

"What's that?"

"That I don't think it'll change anything. That I think you're probably right."

"But you're not sure," Win said.

"No, I'm not sure."

"And you still don't like it."

"I definitely don't like it," Myron said.

Win nodded. "That's all I wanted to hear."

40

Big Cyndi was totally in orange. An orange sweatshirt. Orange parachute pants like something stolen from MC Hammer's 1989 closet. Dyed orange hair. Orange fingernail polish. Orange—don't ask how—skin. She looked like a mutant teenage carrot.

"Orange is Esperanza's favorite color," she told Myron.

"No, it's not."

"It's not?"

Myron shook his head. "Blue is." For a moment, he pictured a giant Smurf.

Big Cyndi mulled that one over. "Orange is her second favorite color?"

"Sure, I guess."

Satisfied, Big Cyndi smiled and strung up a sign across the reception area that read WELCOME BACK, ESPERANZA!

Myron moved into his inner office. He made some calls, managed to do a little work, kept listening for the elevator.

Finally, the elevator dinged at 10:00 A.M. The doors slid open. Myron stayed put. He heard Big Cyndi's squeal of delight; the floors below them almost evacuated at the sound. He felt the vibrations of Big Cyndi leaping to her feet. Myron stood now and still waited. He heard cries and sighs and reassurances.

Two minutes later Esperanza entered Myron's office. She didn't knock. As always.

Their hug was a little awkward. Myron backed off, shoved his hands in his pockets. "Welcome back."

Esperanza tried a smile. "Thanks."

Silence.

"You knew about my personal involvement the whole time, didn't you?"

Esperanza said nothing.

"That's the part I could never resolve," Myron said.

"Myron, don't—"

"You're my best friend," he continued. "You know I'd do anything for you. So I couldn't for the life of me figure out why you wouldn't talk to me. It made no sense. At first I thought you were angry at me for disappearing. But that isn't like you. Then I thought you had an affair with Clu and you didn't want me to know. But that was wrong. Then I thought it was because you had an affair with Bonnie—"

"Showing very poor judgment," Esperanza added.

"Yes. But I'm hardly in a position to lecture you. And you wouldn't be afraid to tell me about it. Especially with the stakes so high. So I kept wondering, What could be so bad that you wouldn't talk to me? Win thought that the only explanation was that you did indeed kill Clu."

"That Win," Esperanza said. "Always the sunny side."

"But even that wouldn't do it. I'd still stick by you. You knew that. There is only one reason you wouldn't tell me the truth—"

Esperanza sighed. "I need a shower."

"You were protecting me."

She looked at him. "Don't get all mushy on me, okay? I hate when you do that."

"Bonnie told you about the car accident. About my bribing the cops."

"Pillow talk," Esperanza said with a shrug.

"And once you were arrested, you made her swear to keep her mouth shut. Not for your sake or hers. But for mine. You knew that if the bribes ever became public, I'd be ruined. I'd committed a serious felony. I'd be disbarred or worse. And you knew that if I ever found out, you wouldn't be able to stop me from telling the DA because it would've been enough to get you off."

Esperanza put her hands on her hips. "Is there a point to this, Myron?"

"Thank you," he said.

"Nothing to thank me for. You were too weak coming off Brenda. I was afraid you'd do something stupid. You have that habit."

He hugged her again. She hugged him back. Nothing felt awkward this time. When they broke the embrace, he stepped back. "Thank you."

"Stop saying that."

"You are my best friend."

"And I did it for my sake too, Myron. For the business. My business."

"I know."

"So do we still have any clients left?" she asked.

"A few."

"Maybe we better get on the horn then."

"Maybe," he said. "I love you, Esperanza."

"Shut up before I puke my guts out."

"And you love me."

"If you start singing 'Barney,' I'll kill you. I've already done prison time. I'm not afraid to do more."

Big Cyndi stuck her head in. She was smiling. With the orange skin, she looked like the most frightening jack-o'-lantern imaginable. "Marty Towey on line two."

"I'll take it," Esperanza said.

"And I have Enos Cabral on line three."

"Mine," said Myron.

At the end of a wonderfully long workday Win came into the office. "I spoke to Esperanza," he said. "We're all doing pizza and old CBS Sunday at my place."

"I can't."

Win arched an eyebrow. *"All in the Family, M*A*S*H, Mary Tyler Moore, Bob Newhart, Carol Burnett?"*

"Sorry."

"The Sammy Davis episode of *All in the Family?*"

"Not tonight, Win."

Win looked concerned. "I know you want to punish yourself," he said, "but this is taking self-flagellation too far."

Myron smiled. "It's not that."

"Don't tell me you want to be alone. You never want to be alone."

"Sorry, I got other plans," Myron said.

Win arched the eyebrow, turned, left without another word.

Myron picked up the phone. He dialed the familiar number. "I'm on my way," he said.

"Good," Mom said. "I already called Fong's. I got two orders of shrimp with lobster sauce."

"Mom?"

"What?"

"I really don't like their shrimp in lobster sauce anymore."

"What? You've always loved it. It's your favorite."

"Not since I was fourteen."

"So how come you never told me?"

"I have. Several times."

"And what, you expect me to remember every little thing? So what are you trying to tell me, Myron, your taste buds are too mature for Fong's shrimp with lobster sauce now? Who do you think you are, the Galloping Gourmet or something?"

Myron heard his father yell in the background. "Stop bothering the boy."

"Who's bothering him? Myron, am I bothering you?"

"And tell him to hurry," Dad shouted. "The game's almost on."

"Big deal, Al. He doesn't care."

Myron said, "Tell Dad I'm on my way."

"Drive slowly, Myron. There's no rush. The game will wait."

"Okay, Mom."

"Wear a seat belt."

"Sure thing."

"And your father has a surprise for you."

"Ellen!" It was Dad again.

"What's the big deal, Al?"

"I wanted to tell him—"

"Oh stop being silly, Al. Myron?"

"Yeah, Mom?"

"Your father bought tickets to a Mets game. For Sunday. Just the two of you."

Myron swallowed, said nothing.

"They're playing the Tunas," Mom said.

"The Marlins!" Dad shouted.

"Tunas, marlins—what's the difference? You going to be a marine biologist now, Al? Is that what you're going to do with your leisure time, study fish?"

Myron smiled.

"Myron, you there?"

"I'm on my way, Mom."

He hung up. He slapped his thighs and stood. He said good night to Esperanza and Big Cyndi. He stepped into the elevator and managed a smile. Friends and lovers were great, he thought, but sometimes a boy just wanted his mom and dad.

DARKEST FEAR

When a father gives to his son, they both laugh.
When a son gives to his father, they both cry.

—Yiddish proverb

This one is for your father. And mine.

1

An hour before his world exploded like a ripe tomato under a stiletto heel, Myron bit into a fresh pastry that tasted suspiciously like a urinal cake.

"Well?" Mom prompted.

Myron battled his throat, won a costly victory, swallowed. "Not bad."

Mom shook her head, disappointed.

"What?"

"I'm a lawyer," Mom said. "You'd think I'd have raised a better liar."

"You did the best you could," Myron said.

She shrugged and waved a hand at the, uh, pastry. "It's my first time baking, *bubbe*. It's okay to tell me the truth."

"It's like biting into a urinal cake," Myron said.

"A what?"

"In men's public bathrooms. In the urinals. They put them there for the smell or something."

"And you eat them?"

"No—"

"Is that why your father takes so long in there? He's having a little Tastykake? And here I thought his prostate was acting up."

"I'm joking, Mom."

She smiled through blue eyes tinged with a red that Visine could never hope to get out, the red you can only get through slow, steady tears. Normally Mom was heavily into histrionics. Slow, steady tears were not her style. "So am I, Mr. Smarty Pants. You think you're the only one in this family with a sense of humor?"

Myron said nothing. He looked down at the, uh, pastry, fearing or perhaps hoping it might crawl away. In the thirty-plus years his mother had lived in this house, she had never baked—not from a recipe, not from scratch, not even from one of those Pillsbury morning croissant thingies that came in small mailing tubes. She could barely boil water without strict instructions and pretty much never cooked, though she could whip up a mean Celeste frozen pizza in the microwave, her agile fingers dancing across the numerical keypad in the vein of Nureyev at Lincoln Center. No, in the Bolitar household, the kitchen was more a gathering place—a Family Room Lite, if you will—than anything related to even the basest of the culinary arts. The round table held magazines and catalogs and congealing white boxes of Chinese takeout. The stovetop saw less action than a Merchant-Ivory production. The oven was a prop, strictly for show, like a politician's Bible.

Something was definitely amiss.

They were sitting in the living room with the dated pseudo-leather white modular couch and aqua-tinged rug whose shagginess reminded Myron of a toilet-seat cover. Grown-up Greg Brady. Myron kept stealing glances out the picture window at the For Sale sign in the front yard as though it were a spaceship that had just landed and something sinister was about to step out.

"Where's Dad?"

Mom gave a weary wave toward the door. "He's in the basement."

"In my room?"

"Your *old* room, yes. You moved out, remember?"

He did—at the tender age of thirty-four no less. Childcare experts would salivate and tsk-tsk over that one—the prodigal son choosing to remain in his split-level cocoon long after the deemed appropriate deadline for the butterfly to break free. But Myron might argue the opposite. He might bring up the fact that for generations and in most cultures, offspring lived in the familial home until a ripe old age, that adopting such a philosophy could indeed be a societal boom, helping people stay rooted to something tangible in this era of the disintegrating nuclear family. Or, if that rationale didn't float your boat, Myron could try another. He had a million.

But the truth of the matter was far simpler: He liked hanging out in the burbs with Mom and Dad—even if confessing such a sentiment was about as hip as an Air Supply eight track.

"So what's going on?" he asked.

"Your father doesn't know you're here yet," she said. "He thinks you're not coming for another hour."

Myron nodded, puzzled. "What's he doing in the basement?"

"He bought a computer. Your father plays with it down there."

"Dad?"

"My point exactly. The man can't change a lightbulb without a manual—all of a sudden he's Bill Gates. Always on the nest."

"The Net," Myron corrected.

"The what?"

"It's called the Net, Mom."

"I thought it was nest. The bird's nest or something."

"No, it's Net."

"Are you sure? I know there's a bird in there somewhere."

"The Web maybe," Myron tried. "Like with a spider."

She snapped her fingers. "That's it. Anyway your father is on there all the time, weaving the Web or whatever. He chats with people, Myron. That's what he tells me. He chats with complete strangers. Like he used to do with the CB radio, remember?"

Myron remembered. Circa 1976. Jewish Dads in the suburbs checking for "smokeys" on the way to the delicatessen. Mighty convoy of Cadillac Sevilles. Ten-four, good buddy.

"And that's not all," she went on. "He's typing his memoirs. A man who can't scribble down a grocery list without consulting Strunk and White suddenly thinks he's an ex-president."

They were selling the house. Myron still could not believe it. His eyes wandered about the overly familiar surroundings, his gaze getting snagged on the photographs running up the stairwell. He saw his family mature via fashion—the skirts and sideburns lengthening and shortening, the quasi-hippie fringes and suede and tie-dyes, the leisure suits and bell-bottoms, the frilly tuxedos that would be too tacky for a Vegas casino—the years flying by frame by frame like one of those depressing life insurance commercials. He spotted the poses from his basketball days—a sixth-grade suburban-league foul shot, an eighth-grade drive to the hoop, a high school slam dunk—the row ending with *Sports Illustrated* cover shots, two from his days at Duke and one with his leg in a cast and a large-fonted IS HE FINISHED? emblazoned across his knee-cast image (the answer in the mind's eye being an equally large-fonted YES!).

"So what's wrong?" he asked.

"I didn't say anything was wrong."

Myron shook his head, disappointed. "And you a lawyer."

"Setting a bad example?"

"It's no wonder I never ran for higher office."

She folded her hands on her lap. "We need to chat."

Myron didn't like the tone.

"But not here," she added. "Let's take a walk around the block."

Myron nodded and they rose. Before they reached the door, his cell phone rang. Myron snatched it up with a speed that would have made Wyatt Earp step back. He put the phone to his ear and cleared his throat.

"MB SportsReps," he said, silky-smooth, professional-like. "This is Myron Bolitar speaking."

"Nice phone voice," Esperanza said. "You sound like Billy Dee ordering two Colt 45s."

Esperanza Diaz was his longtime assistant and now sports-agent partner at MB SportsReps (M for Myron, the B for Bolitar—for those keeping score).

"I was hoping you were Lamar," he said.

"He hasn't called yet?"

"Nope."

He could almost see Esperanza frown. "We're in deep doo-doo here," she said.

"We're not in deep doo-doo. We're just sucking a little wind, that's all."

"Sucking a little wind," Esperanza repeated. "Like Pavarotti running the Boston Marathon."

"Good one," Myron said.

"Thanks."

Lamar Richardson was a power-hitting Golden Glove shortstop who'd just become a free agent—"free agent" being a phrase agents whisper in the same way a mufti might whisper "Praise Allah." Lamar was shopping for new representation and had whittled his final list down to three agencies: two supersized conglomerates with enough office space to house a Price Club and the aforementioned pimple-on-the-buttocks but oh-so-personal MB SportsReps. Go, pimple-butt!

Myron watched his mother standing by the door. He switched ears and said, "Anything else?"

"You'll never guess who called," Esperanza said.

"Elle and Claudia demanding another ménage à trois?"

"Oooo, close."

She would never just tell him. With his friends, everything was a TV game show. "How about a hint?" he said.

"One of your ex-lovers."

He felt a jolt. "Jessica."

Esperanza made a buzzing noise. "Sorry, wrong bitch."

Myron was puzzled. He'd only had two long-term relationships in his life: Jessica on and off for the past thirteen years (now very off). And before that, well, you'd have to go back to . . .

"Emily Downing?"

Esperanza made a *ding-ding* noise.

A sudden image pierced his heart like a straight-blade. He saw Emily sitting on that threadbare couch in the frat basement, smiling that smile at him, her legs bent and tucked under her, wearing his high school varsity jacket that was several sizes too big, her gesturing hands slipping down and disappearing into the sleeves.

His mouth went dry. "What did she want?"

"Don't know. But she said that she simply *had* to talk to you. She's very breathy, you know. Like everything she says is a double entendre."

With Emily, everything was.

"She good in the sack?" Esperanza asked.

Being an overly attractive bisexual, Esperanza viewed everyone as a potential sex partner. Myron wondered what that must be like, to have and thus weigh so many options, and then he decided to leave that road untraveled. Wise man.

"What did Emily say exactly?" Myron said.

"Nothing specific. She just spewed out a colorful assortment of breathy teasers: urgent, life-and-death, grave matters, etceteras, etceteras."

"I don't want to talk to her."

"I didn't think so. If she calls back, you want me to give her the runaround?"

"Please."

"*Más tarde* then."

He hung up as a second image whacked him like a surprise wave at the beach. Senior year at Duke. Emily so composed as she dumped the varsity jacket onto his bed and walked out. Not long after that, she married the man who'd ruin Myron's life.

Deep breaths, he told himself. In and out. That's it.

"Everything okay?" Mom asked.

"Fine."

Mom shook her head again, disappointed.

"I'm not lying," he said.

"Fine, right, sure, you always breathe like an obscene phone call. Listen, if you don't want to tell your mother—"

"I don't want to tell my mother."

"Who raised you and . . ."

Myron tuned her out, as was his custom. She was digressing again, taking on a past life or something. It was something she did a lot. One minute she was thoroughly modern, an early feminist who marched alongside Gloria Steinem and became proof that—to quote her old T-shirt—A Woman's Place Is in the House . . . and Senate. But at the sight of her son, her progressive attire slid to the floor and revealed the babushka-clad yenta beneath the burned bra. It made for an interesting childhood.

They headed out the front door. Myron kept his eyes on the For Sale sign as though it might suddenly brandish a gun. His mind flashed onto something he had never actually seen—the sunny day when Mom and Dad had arrived here for the first time, hand in hand, Mom's belly swelling with child, both of them scared and exhilarated realizing that this cookie-cut three-bedroom split-level would be their life vessel, their SS *American Dream*. Now, like it or not, that journey was coming to an end. Forget that "close one door, open another" crap. That For Sale sign marked the end—the end of youth, of middle age, of a family, the universe of two people who'd started here and fought here and raised kids here and worked and carpooled and lived their lives here.

They walked up the street. Leaves were piled along the curb, the surest sign of suburban autumn, while leaf blowers shattered the still air like helicopters over Saigon. Myron took the inside track so his path would skim the piles' edges. The dead leaves crackled under his sneakers and he liked that. He wasn't sure why.

"Your father spoke to you," Mom said, half-question. "About what happened to him."

Myron felt his stomach tense up. He veered deeper into the leaves, lifting his legs high and crunching louder. "Yes."

"What did he say exactly?" Mom asked.

"That he'd had chest pains while I was in the Caribbean."

The Kaufman house had always been yellow, but the new family had painted it white. It looked wrong with the new color, out of place. Some homes had gone the aluminum-siding route, while others had built on additions, bumping out the kitchens and master bedrooms. The young family who'd moved into the Miller home had gotten rid of the Millers' trademark overflowing flower boxes. The new owners of the Davis place had ripped out those wonderful shrubs Bob Davis had worked on every weekend. It all reminded Myron of an invading army ripping down the flags of the conquered.

"He didn't want to tell you," Mom said. "You know your father. He still feels he has to protect you."

Myron nodded, stayed in the leaves.

Then she said, "It was more than chest pains."

Myron stopped.

"It was a full-blown coronary," she went on, not meeting his eyes. "He was in intensive care for three days." She started blinking. "The artery was almost entirely blocked."

Myron felt his throat close.

"It's changed him. I know how much you love him, but you have to accept that."

"Accept what?"

Her voice was gentle and firm. "That your father is getting older. That I'm getting older."

He thought about it. "I'm trying," he said.

"But?"

"But I see that For Sale sign—"

"Wood and bricks and nails, Myron."

"What?"

She waded through the leaves and took hold of his elbow. "Listen to me. You mope around here like we're sitting shiva, but that house is not your childhood. It isn't a part of your family. It doesn't breathe or think or care. It's just wood and bricks and nails."

"You've lived there for almost thirty-five years."

"So?"

He turned away, kept walking.

"Your father wants to be honest with you," she said, "but you're not making it any easier."

"Why? What did I do?"

She shook her head, looked up into the sky as though willing divine inspiration, continued walking. Myron stayed by her side. She snaked her arm under his elbow and leaned against him.

"You were always a terrific athlete," she said. "Not like your father. Truth be told, your father was a spaz."

"I know this," Myron said.

"Right. You know this because your father never pretended to be something he wasn't. He let you see him as human—vulnerable even. And it had a strange effect on you. You worshipped him all the more. You turned him into something almost mythical."

Myron thought about it, didn't argue. He shrugged and said, "I love him."

"I know, sweetheart. But he's just a man. A good man. But now he's getting old and he's scared. Your father always wanted you to see him as human. But he doesn't want you to see him scared."

Myron kept his head down. There are certain things you cannot picture your parents doing—having sex being the classic example. Most people cannot—probably should not even try to—picture their parents in flagrante delicto. But right now Myron was trying to conjure up another taboo image, one of his father sitting alone in the dark, hand on his chest, scared, and the sight, while achievable, was aching, unbearable. When he spoke again, his voice was thick. "So what should I do?"

"Accept the changes. Your father is retiring. He's worked his whole life and like most moronically macho men of his era, his self-worth is wrapped up in his job. So he's having a tough time. He's not the same. You're not the same. Your relationship is shifting and neither one of you likes change."

Myron stayed silent, waiting for more.

"Reach out to him a little," Mom said. "He's carried you your whole life. He won't ask, but now it's his turn."

When they turned the final corner, Myron saw the Mercedes parked in front of the For Sale sign. He wondered for a moment if it was a Realtor showing the house. His father stood in the front yard chatting with a woman. Dad was gesturing wildly and smiling. Looking at his father's face—the rough skin that always seemed in need of a shave, the prominent nose Dad used to "nose punch" him during their giggling fun-fights, the heavy-lidded eyes à la Victor Mature and Dean Martin, the wispy hairs of gray that held on stubbornly after the thick black had fled—Myron felt a hand reach in and tweak his heart.

Dad caught his eye and waved. "Look who stopped by!" he shouted.

Emily Downing turned around and gave him a tight smile. Myron looked back at her and said nothing. Fifty minutes had passed. Ten more until the heel crushed the tomato.

2

Too much history.

His parents made themselves scarce. For all their almost legendary butting in, they both had the uncanny ability to trample full tilt through the Isle of Nosiness without tripping any gone-too-far mines. They quietly disappeared into the house.

Emily tried a smile, but it just wasn't happening. "Well, well, well," she said when they were alone. "If it isn't the good one I let get away."

"You used that line last time I saw you."

"Did I?"

They had met in the library freshman year at Duke. Emily had been bigger then, a bit fleshier, though not in a bad way, and the years had definitely slimmed her down and toned her up, though again not in a bad way. But the visual whammy was still there. Emily wasn't so much pretty as, to quote *SuperFly*, foxy. Hot. Sizzlingly so. As a young coed, she'd had long, kinky hair that always had that just-did-the-nasty muss to it, a crooked smile that could knock a movie up a rating, and a subconsciously undulating body that continuously flickered out the word *sex* like an old movie projector. It didn't matter that she wasn't beautiful; beauty had little to do with it, in fact. This was an innate thing; Emily couldn't turn it off if she donned a muumuu and put roadkill on her head.

The weird thing was, they were both virgins when they met, somehow missing the perhaps overblown sexual revolution of the seventies and early eighties. Myron always believed that the revolution was mostly hype or, at the very least, that it didn't seep past the brick façades of suburban high schools. But then again, he was pretty good at self-rationalization. More likely, it was his fault—if you could consider not being promiscuous a fault. He'd always been attracted to the "nice" girls, even in high school. Casual affairs never interested him. Every girl he met was gauged as a potential life partner, a soul mate, an undying love, as though every relationship should be a Carpenters song.

But with Emily it had been complete sexual exploration and discovery. They learned from each other in stuttering, though achingly blissful, steps. Even now, as much as he detested her very being, he could still feel the tightening, could still recall the way his nerve endings would sing and surge when they were in bed. Or the back of a car. Or a movie theater or a library or once even during a poly sci lecture on Hobbes's *Leviathan*. While he may have yearned to be a Carpenters man, his first long-term relationship had ended up more like something off Meat Loaf's *Bat Out of Hell* album—hot, heavy, sweaty, fast, the whole "Paradise by the Dashboard Light."

Still, there had to have been more to it. He and Emily had lasted three years. He had loved her, and she'd been the first to break his heart.

"There a coffee bar near here?" she asked.

"A Starbucks," Myron said.

"I'll drive."

"I don't want to go with you, Emily."

She gave him the smile. "Lost my charms, have I?"

"They lost their effect on me a long time ago." Half lie.

She shifted her hips. Myron watched, thinking about what Esperanza had said. It wasn't just her voice or her words—even her movements ended up a double entendre. "It's important, Myron."

"Not to me."

"You don't even know—"

"It doesn't matter, Emily. You're the past. So is your husband—"

"My *ex*-husband. I divorced him, remember? And I never knew what he did to you."

"Right," Myron said. "You were just the cause."

She looked at him. "It's not that simple. You know that."

He nodded. She was right, of course. "I always knew why I did it," Myron said. "I was being a competitive dumbass who wanted to get one up on Greg. But why you?"

Emily shook her head. The old hair would have flown side to side, ending up half covering her face. Her new coif was shorter and more stylized, but his mind's eye still saw the kinky flow. "It doesn't matter anymore," she said.

"Guess not," he said, "but I've always been curious."

"We both had too much to drink."

"Simple as that?"

"Yes."

Myron made a face. "Lame," he said.

"Maybe it was just about sex," she said.

"A purely physical act?"

"Maybe."

"The night before you married someone else?"

She looked at him. "It was dumb, okay?"

"You say so."

"And maybe I was scared," she said.

"Of getting married?"

"Of marrying the wrong man."

Myron shook his head. "Jesus, you're shameless."

Emily was about to say more, but she stopped as though her last reserves had suddenly been zapped away. He wanted her gone, but with ex-loves there is also a pulling sadness. There before you stands the true road untraveled, the lifetime what-if, the embodiment of a totally alternate life if things had gone a little different. He had absolutely no interest in her anymore, yet her words still drew out his old self, wounds and all.

"It was fourteen years ago," she said softly. "Don't you think it's time we moved on?"

He thought about what that "purely physical" night had cost him. Everything, maybe. His lifelong dream, for sure. "You're right," he said, turning away. "Please leave."

"I need your help."

He shook his head. "As you said, time to move on."

"Just have coffee with me. With an old friend."

He wanted to say no, but the past had too strong a pull. He nodded, afraid to speak. They drove in silence to Starbucks and ordered their complicated coffees from an artist-wannabe *barista* with more attitude than the guy who works at the local record store. They added whatever condiments at the little stand, playing a game of Twister by reaching across one another for the nonfat milk or Equal. They sat down in metal chairs with too-low backs. The sound system was playing reggae music, a CD entitled *Jamaican Me Crazy*.

Emily crossed her legs and took a sip. "Have you ever heard of Fanconi anemia?"

Interesting opening gambit. "No."

"It's an inherited anemia that leads to bone marrow failure. It weakens your chromosomes."

Myron waited.

"Are you familiar with bone marrow transplants?"

Strange line of questioning, but he decided to play it straight. "A little.

A friend of mine had leukemia and needed a transplant. They had a marrow drive at the temple. We all went down and got tested."

"When you say 'we all'—"

"Mom, Dad, my whole family. I think Win went too."

She tilted her head. "How is Win?"

"The same."

"Sorry to hear that," she said. "When we were at Duke, he used to listen to us making love, didn't he?"

"Only when we pulled down the shade so he couldn't watch."

She laughed. "He never liked me."

"You were his favorite."

"Really?"

"That's not saying much," Myron said.

"He hates women, doesn't he?"

Myron thought about it. "As sex objects, they're fine. But in terms of relationships . . ."

"An odd duck."

She should only know.

Emily took a sip. "I'm stalling," she said.

"I sorta figured that."

"What happened to your friend with leukemia?"

"He died."

Her face went white. "I'm sorry. How old was he?"

"Thirty-four."

Emily took another sip, cradling the mug with both hands. "So you're listed with the bone marrow national registry?"

"I guess. I gave blood and they gave me a donor card."

She closed her eyes.

"What?" he asked.

"Fanconi anemia is fatal. You can treat it for a while with blood transfusions and hormones, but the only cure is a bone marrow transplant."

"I don't understand, Emily. Do you have this disease?"

"It doesn't hit adults." She put down her coffee and looked up. He was not big on reading eyes, but the pain was neon-obvious. "It hits children."

As though on cue, the Starbucks soundtrack changed to something instrumental and somber. Myron waited. It didn't take her long.

"My son has it," she said.

Myron remembered visiting the house in Franklin Lakes when Greg disappeared, the boy playing in the backyard with his sister. Must have been, what, two, three years ago. The boy was about ten, his sister maybe eight. Greg and Emily were in the midst of a bloody take-no-prisoners custody battle, the two children pinned down in the crossfire, the kind no one walks away from without a serious hit.

"I'm sorry," he said.

"We need to find a bone marrow match."

"I thought siblings were an almost automatic match."

Her eyes flicked around the room. "One-in-four chance," she said, stopping abruptly.

"Oh."

"The national registry found only three potential donors. By potential I mean that the initial HLA tests showed them as possibilities. The A and B match, but then they have to do a full blood and tissue workup to see—" She stopped again. "I'm getting technical. I don't mean to. But when your kid is sick like this, it's like you live in a snow globe of medical jargon."

"I understand."

"Anyway, getting past the initial screening is like winning a second-tier lottery ticket. The chance of a match is still slim. The blood center calls in the potential donors and runs a battery of tests, but the odds they'll be a close enough match to go through with the transplant are pretty low, especially with only three potential donors."

Myron nodded, still having no idea why she was telling him any of this.

"We got lucky," she said. "One of the three was a match with Jeremy."

"Great."

"There's a problem," she said. Again the crooked smile. "The donor is missing."

"What do you mean, missing?"

"I don't have the details. The registry is confidential. No one will tell me what's going on. We seemed to be on the right track, and then all of a sudden, the donor just pulled out. My doctor can't say anything—like I said, it's protected."

"Maybe the donor just changed his mind."

"Then we better change it back," she said, "or Jeremy dies."

The statement was plain enough.

"So what do you think happened?" Myron asked. "You think he's missing or something?"

"He or she," Emily said. "Yes."

"He or she?"

"I don't know anything about the donor—age, sex, where they live, nothing. But Jeremy isn't getting any better and the odds of finding another donor in time are, well, almost nonexistent." She kept the face tight, but Myron could see the foundation starting to crack a bit. "We have to find this donor."

"And that's why you've come to me? To find him?"

"You and Win found Greg when no one else could. When he disappeared, Clip went to you first. Why?"

"That's a long story."

"Not so long, Myron. You and Win are trained in this sort of thing. You're good at it."

"Not in a case like this," Myron said. "Greg is a high-profile athlete. He can take to the airwaves, offer rewards. He can buy private detectives."

"We're already doing that. Greg has a press conference set up for tomorrow."

"So?"

"So it won't work. I told Jeremy's doctor we would pay anything to the donor, even though it's illegal. But something else is wrong here. I'm afraid all the publicity might even backfire—that it may send the donor deeper into hiding or something, I don't know."

"What does Greg say to that?"

"We don't talk much, Myron. And when we do, it's usually not very pretty."

"Does Greg know you're talking to me now?"

She looked at him. "He hates you as much as you hate him. Maybe more so."

Myron decided to take that as a no. Emily kept her eyes on him, searching his face as though there were an answer there.

"I can't help you, Emily."

She looked like she'd just been slapped.

"I sympathize," he went on, "but I'm just getting over some major problems of my own."

"Are you saying you don't have time?"

"It's not that. A private detective would have a better chance—"

"Greg's hired four already. They can't even find out the donor's name."

"I doubt I can do any better."

"This is my son's life, Myron."

"I understand, Emily."

"Can't you put aside your animosity for me and Greg?"

He wasn't sure that he could. "That's not the issue. I'm a sports agent, not a detective."

"That didn't stop you before."

"And look how things ended up. Every time I meddle, it leads to disaster."

"My son is thirteen years old, Myron."

"I'm sorry—"

"I don't want your sympathy, dammit." Her eyes were smaller now, black. She leaned toward him until her face was scant inches from his. "I want you to do the math."

He looked puzzled. "What?"

"You're an agent. You know all about numbers, right? So do the math."

Myron tilted back, giving himself a little distance. "What the hell are you talking about?"

"Jeremy's birthday is July eighteenth," she said. "Do the math."

"What math?"

"One more time: He's thirteen years old. He was born July the eighteenth. I was married October tenth."

Nothing. For several seconds, he heard the mothers chatting over one another, one baby cry, one *barista* call out an order to another, and then it happened. A cold gust blew across Myron's heart. Steel bands wrapped around his chest, making it almost impossible to breathe. He opened his mouth but nothing came out. It was like someone had whacked his solar plexus with a baseball bat. Emily watched him and nodded.

"That's right," she said. "He's your son."

3

You can't know that for sure," Myron said.

Emily's whole persona screamed exhaustion. "I do."

"You were sleeping with Greg too, right?"

"Yes."

"And we only had that one night during that time. You probably had a whole bunch with Greg."

"True."

"So how can you possibly know—?"

"Denial," she interjected with a sigh. "The first step."

He pointed a finger at her. "Don't hand me that psychology-major crap, Emily."

"Moving quickly to anger," she continued.

"You can't know—"

"I've always known," she interrupted.

Myron sat back. He stayed composed but underneath he could almost feel the fissure widening, his foundation starting to shift.

"When I first got pregnant, I figured like you: I'd slept with Greg more, so it was probably his baby. At least, that's what I told myself." She closed her eyes. Myron stayed very still, the knot in his stomach tightening. "And when Jeremy was born, he favored me, so who was to say? But—and this is going to sound so goddamn stupid—a mother knows. I can't tell you how. But I knew. I tried to deny it too. I told myself I was just feeling guilty over what we'd done, and that this was God's way of punishing me."

"How Old Testament of you," Myron said.

"Sarcasm," she said with almost a smile. "Your favorite defense."

"Your maternal intuition hardly counts as evidence, Emily."

"You asked before about Sara."

"Sara?"

"Jeremy's sister. You wondered about her matching as a donor. She didn't."

"Right, but you said there was only a one-in-four chance with siblings."

"For *full* siblings, yes. But the match wasn't even close. Because she's only Jeremy's half sister."

"The doctor told you this?"

"Yes."

Myron felt the stone footing beneath his feet give way. "So . . . Greg knows?"

Emily shook her head. "The doctor pulled me aside. Because of the divorce, I'm Jeremy's primary custodian. Greg has custody too, but the children live with me. I'm in charge of the medical decisions."

"So Greg still believes . . . ?"

"That Jeremy is his, yes."

Myron was floundering in deep water with no land in sight. "But you said you've always known."

"Yes."

"Why didn't you tell me?"

"Are you kidding? I was married to Greg. I loved him. We were starting our life together."

"You still should have told me."

"When, Myron? When should I have told you?"

"As soon as the baby was born."

"Aren't you listening? I just told you I wasn't sure."

"A mother knows, you said."

"Come on, Myron. I was in love with Greg, not you. You with your corny sense of morality—you would have insisted I divorce Greg and marry you and live some suburban fairy tale."

"So instead you chose to live a lie?"

"It was the right decision based on what I knew then. With hindsight"—she stopped, took a deep sip—"I probably would have done a lot of things differently."

He tried to let some of it sink in, but it was a no-go. Another group of stroller-laced soccer moms entered the coffee shop. They took a corner table and started jabbering about little Brittany and Kyle and Morgan.

"How long have you and Greg been separated?" Myron's voice sounded sharper than he intended. Or maybe not.

"Four years now."

"And you were no longer in love with him, right? Four years ago?"

"Right."

"Earlier even," he went on. "I mean, you probably fell out of love with him a long time ago, right?"

She looked confused. "Right."

"So you could have told me then. At least four years ago. Why didn't you?"

"Stop cross-examining me."

"You're the one who dropped this bombshell," he said. "How do you expect me to react?"

"Like a man."

"What the hell does that mean?"

"I need your help. Jeremy needs your help. That's what we should be concentrating on."

"I want some answers first. I'm entitled to that much."

She hesitated, looked like she might argue, then nodded wearily. "If it'll help you get past this—"

"Get past this? Like it's a kidney stone or something?"

"I'm too tired to fight with you," she said. "Just go on. Ask your questions."

"Why didn't you tell me before now?"

Her eyes drifted over his shoulder. "I almost did," she said. "Once."

"When?"

"Do you remember when you came to the house? When Greg first vanished?"

He nodded. He had just been thinking about that day.

"You were looking out the window at him. He was in the yard with his sister."

"I remember," Myron said.

"Greg and I were going through that nasty custody battle."

"You accused him of abusing the children."

"It wasn't true. You realized that right away. It was just a legal ploy."

"Some ploy," Myron said. "Next time accuse him of war atrocities."

"Who are you to judge me?"

"Actually," Myron said, "I think I'm just the person."

Emily pinned him with her eyes. "Custody battles are war without the Geneva Accords," she said. "Greg got nasty. I got nasty back. You do whatever you have to in order to win."

"And that includes revealing that Greg wasn't Jeremy's father?"

"No."

"Why not?"

"Because I won custody anyway."

"That's not an answer. You hated Greg."

"Yes."

"Still do?" he asked.

"Yes." No hesitation.

"So why didn't you tell him?"

"Because as much as I loathe Greg," she said, "I love Jeremy more. I could hurt Greg. I'd probably enjoy it. But I couldn't do that to my son—take away his father like that."

"I thought you'd do anything to win."

"I'd do anything to Greg," she said, "not Jeremy."

It made sense, he guessed, but he suspected she was holding something back. "So you kept this secret for thirteen years."

"Yes."

"Do your parents know?"

"No."

"You never told anyone?"

"Never."

"So why are you telling me now?"

Emily shook her head. "Are you being purposely dense, Myron?"

He put his hands on the table. They weren't shaking. Somehow he understood that these questions came from more than mere curiosity; they were part of the defense mechanism, the internal barbed wire and moat he'd lavishly built to keep Emily's revelation from reaching him. He knew that what she was telling him was life altering in a way nothing he'd ever heard before was. The words *my son* kept floating through his subconscious. But they were just words right now. They'd get through eventually, he guessed, but for now the barbed wire and moat were holding.

"You think I wanted to tell you? I practically begged you to help, but you wouldn't listen. I'm desperate here."

"Desperate enough to lie?"

"Yes," she said, again with no hesitation. "But I'm not, Myron. You have to believe that."

He shrugged. "Maybe someone else is Jeremy's father."

"Excuse me?"

"A third party," he said. "You slept with me the night before your wedding. I doubt I was the only one. Could be one of a dozen guys."

She looked at him. "You want your pound of flesh, Myron? Go ahead, I can take it. But this isn't like you."

"You know me that well, huh?"

"Even when you got angry—even when you had every right to hate me—you've never been cruel. It's not your way."

"We're in uncharted waters here, Emily."

"Doesn't matter," she said.

He felt something well up, making it hard to breathe. He grabbed his mug, looked into it as though it might have an answer on the bottom, put it back down. He couldn't look at her. "How could you do this to me?"

Emily reached across the table and put her hand on his forearm. "I'm sorry," she said.

He pulled away.

"I don't know what else to say. You asked before why I never told you. My main concern was always Jeremy's welfare, but you were a consideration too."

"Bull."

"I know how you are, Myron. I know you can't just shrug this off. But for now you have to. You have to find the donor and save Jeremy's life. We can worry about the rest after that."

"How long has"—he almost said *my son*—"Jeremy been ill?"

"We learned about it six months ago. When he was playing basketball. He started getting bruised too easily. Then he was short of breath for no reason. He started falling down . . ." Her voice tailed off.

"Is he in the hospital?"

"No. He lives at home and goes to school and he looks fine, just a little pale. But he can't play competitive sports or anything like that. He seems to be doing well, but . . . it's just a matter of time. He's so anemic and his marrow cells are so weak that something will get him. Either he'll contract a life-threatening infection or if he manages to get past that, malignancies will eventually develop. We treat him with hormones. That helps, but it's a temporary treatment, not a cure."

"And a bone marrow transplant would be a cure?"

"Yes." Her face brightened with an almost religious fervor. "If the transplant takes, he can be completely cured. I've seen it happen with other kids."

Myron nodded, sat back, crossed his legs, uncrossed them. "Can I meet him?"

She looked down. The sound of the blender, probably making a frappuccino, exploded while the espresso maker shrieked its familiar mating call to the various lattes. Emily waited for the noise to die down. "I can't stop you. But I'm hoping you'll do the right thing here."

"That being?"

"It's hard enough being thirteen years old and almost terminally ill. Do you really want to take away his father too?"

Myron said nothing.

"I know you're in shock right now. And I know you have a million more questions. But you have to forget that for now. You have to work through your confusion, your anger, everything. The life of a thirteen-year-old boy—our son—is at stake. Concentrate on that, Myron. Find the donor, okay?"

He looked back toward the soccer moms, still cooing about their children. Listening to them, he felt an overwhelming pang.

"Where can I find Jeremy's doctor?" he asked.

4

When the elevator doors opened into the reception area of MB SportsReps, Big Cyndi reached out to Myron with two arms the approximate circumference of the marble columns at the Acropolis. Myron almost leaped out of the way—involuntary survival reflex and all—but he stayed still and closed his eyes. Big Cyndi embraced him, which was like being wrapped in wet attic insulation, and lifted him into the air.

"Oh, Mr. Bolitar!" she cried.

He grimaced and rode it out. Eventually she put him back down as though he were a porcelain doll she was returning to a shelf. Big Cyndi is six-six and on the planetoid side of three hundred pounds, the former intercontinental tag-team wrestling champion with Esperanza, aka Big Chief Mama to Esperanza's Little Pocahontas. Her head was cube shaped and topped with hair spiked to look like the Statue of Liberty on a bad acid trip. She wore more makeup than the cast of *Cats*, her clothing form-fitted like sausage casing, her scowl the stuff of sumos.

"Uh, everything okay?" Myron ventured.

"Oh, Mr. Bolitar!"

Big Cyndi looked like she was about to hug him again, but something stopped her, perhaps the stark terror in Myron's eyes. She picked up luggage that in her manhole-paw resembled a Close'N Play phonograph from the early seventies. She was that kind of big, the kind of big where the world around her always looked like a bad B-monster movie set and she was walking through a miniature Tokyo, knocking over power lines and swatting at buzzing fighter planes.

Esperanza appeared in her office doorway. She folded her arms and rested against the frame. Even after her recent ordeal, Esperanza still looked immensely beautiful, the shiny black ringlets still falling over her forehead just so, the dark olive skin still radiant—the whole image a sort of gypsy, peasant-blouse fantasy. But he could see some new lines around the eyes and a slight slouch in the perfect posture. He'd wanted her to take time off after her release, but he knew she wouldn't. Esperanza loved MB SportsReps. She wanted to save it.

"What's going on?" Myron asked.

"It's all in the letter, Mr. Bolitar," Big Cyndi said.

"What letter?"

"Oh, Mr. Bolitar!" she cried again.

"What?"

But she didn't respond, hiding her face in her hands and ducking into the elevator as though entering a tepee. The elevator doors slid closed, and she was gone.

Myron waited a beat and then turned to Esperanza. "Explanation?"

"She's taking a leave of absence," Esperanza said.

"Why?"

"Big Cyndi isn't stupid, Myron."

"I didn't say she was."

"She sees what's going on here."

"It's only temporary," Myron said. "We'll snap back."

"And when we do, Big Cyndi will come back. In the meantime she got a good job offer."

"With Leather-N-Lust?" Big Cyndi worked nights as a bouncer at an S&M bar called Leather-N-Lust. Motto: Hurt the ones you love. Sometimes—or so he had heard—Big Cyndi was part of the stage show. What part she played Myron had no idea nor had he worked up the courage to ask—another taboo abyss his mind did its best to circumvent.

"No," Esperanza said. "She's returning to FLOW."

For the wrestling uninitiated, FLOW is the acronym for the Fabulous Ladies of Wrestling.

"Big Cyndi is going to wrestle again?"

Esperanza nodded. "On the senior circuit."

"Excuse me?"

"FLOW wanted to expand its product. They did some research, saw how well the PGA is doing with the senior golf tour and . . ." She shrugged.

"A senior ladies' wrestling tour?"

"More like retired," Esperanza said. "I mean, Big Cyndi is only thirty-eight. They're bringing back a lot of the old favorites: Queen Qaddafi, Cold War Connie, Brezhnev Babe, Cellblock Celia, Black Widow—"

"I don't remember the Black Widow."

"Before our time. Hell, before our parents' time. She must be in her seventies."

Myron tried not to make a face. "And people are going to pay money to see a seventy-year-old woman wrestle?"

"You shouldn't discriminate on the basis of age."

"Right, sorry." Myron rubbed his eyes.

"And professional women's wrestling is struggling right now, what with the competition from Jerry Springer and Ricki Lake. They need to do something."

"And grappling old ladies is the answer?"

"I think they're aiming more for nostalgia."

"A chance to cheer on the wrestler of your youth?"

"Didn't you go see Steely Dan in concert a couple of years ago?"

"That's different, don't you think?"

She shrugged. "Both past their prime. Both mining more on what you remember than what you see or hear."

It made sense. Scary sense maybe. But sense. "How about you?" Myron asked.

"What about me?"

"Didn't they want Little Pocahontas to return?"

"Yep."

"Were you tempted?"

"To what? Return to the ring?"

"Yes."

"Oh, sure," Esperanza said. "I busted my shapely ass working full-time while getting my law degree, so I could once again don a suede bikini and grope aging nymphs in front of drooling trailer trash." She paused. "Still, it is a step above being a sports agent."

"Ha-ha." Myron walked over to Big Cyndi's desk. There was an envelope with his name scrawled across the top in glow-in-the-dark orange.

"She wrote it in crayon?" Myron said.

"Eye shadow."

"I see."

"So are you going to tell me what's wrong?" she asked.

"Nothing," Myron said.

"Bullshit," she said. "You look like you just heard Wham split up."

"Don't bring that up," Myron said. "Sometimes, late at night, I still suffer flashbacks."

Esperanza studied his face a few more seconds. "This have something to do with your college sweetheart?"

"Sort of."

"Oh Christ."

"What?"

"How do I say this nicely, Myron? You are beyond moronic in the ways of women. Exhibits A and B are Jessica and Emily."

"You don't even know Emily."

"I know enough," she said. "I thought you didn't want to talk to her."

"I didn't. She found me at my parents' place."

"She just showed up there?"

"Yep."

"What did she want?"

He shook his head. He still wasn't ready to talk about it yet. "Any messages?"

"Not as many as we'd like."

"Win upstairs?"

"I think he went home already." She picked up her coat. "I think I'll do likewise."

"Good night."

"If you hear anything from Lamar—"

"I'll call you."

Esperanza put on her coat, flipping the glistening black flow out of the collar. Myron headed into his office and made a few phone calls, mostly of a recruiting nature. It was not going well.

Several months ago, a friend's death had sent Myron into a tail-spin, causing him to—and we're using complex psychiatric jargon here—wig out. Nothing overly drastic, no nervous breakdown or institutional commitment. He had instead fled to a deserted Caribbean island with Terese Collins, a beautiful TV anchorwoman he didn't know. He had told no one—not Win, not Esperanza, not even Mom and Dad—where he was going or when he'd be back.

As Win put it, when he wigged out, he wigged out in style.

By the time Myron was forced to return, their clients were scattering into the night like kitchen help during an immigration bust. Now Myron and Esperanza were back, attempting to revive the comatose and perhaps dying MB SportsReps. This was no easy task. The competition in this business was a dozen starving lions, and Myron was one heavily limping Christian.

The MB SportsReps office was nicely situated on Park Avenue and Forty-sixth Street in the Lock-Horne Building, owned by the family of Myron's college-and-current roommate, Win. The building was in primo midtown location and offered up some semi-dazzling views of the Manhattan skyline. Myron soaked it in for a moment and then looked down at the suits speeding below. The sight of the working ants always depressed him, a chorus of "Is That All There Is?" playing in his head.

He turned now toward his Client Wall, the one with action shots of all the athletes represented by MB SportsReps, which now looked as spotty and sparse as a bad hair transplant. He wanted to care, but unfair as it was to Esperanza, his heart wasn't really in it. He wanted to go back, to love MB and have that old hunger, but no matter how much he tried to stoke the old fire, it wouldn't flame up.

Emily called about an hour later.

"Dr. Singh doesn't have office hours tomorrow," Emily said. "But you can hook up during rounds tomorrow morning."

"Where?"

"Babies and Children's Hospital. It's part of Columbia Presbyterian on 167th Street. Tenth floor, south."

"What time?"

"Rounds start at eight," Emily said.

"Okay."

Brief silence.

"You okay, Myron?"

"I want to see him."

It took her a few seconds. "Like I said before, I can't stop you. But sleep on it, okay?"

"I just want to see him," Myron said. "I won't say anything. Not yet, at least."

"Can we talk about this tomorrow?" Emily asked.

"Yeah, sure."

She hesitated again. "Do you have Web access, Myron?"

"Yes."

"We have a private URL."

"What?"

"A private Web address. I take photos with the digital camera and post them there. For my parents. They moved to Miami last year. They check it out every week. Get to see new pictures of the grandkids. So if you want to see what Jeremy looks like . . ."

"What's the address?"

She gave it to him and Myron typed it in. He hung up before hitting the return button. The images came up slowly. He drummed his fingers on the desk. On top of the screen was a banner saying HI, NANA AND POP-POP. Myron thought about his parents and shook it off.

There were four photographs of Jeremy and Sara. Myron swallowed. He placed the arrow on Jeremy's image and clicked the mouse, zooming in closer, enlarging the boy's face. He tried to keep his breathing steady.

He stared at the boy's face for a long time without really registering anything. Eventually his vision blurred, his own face reflecting on the monitor over the boy's, blending the images together, creating a visual echo of he knew not what.

5

Myron heard the cries of ecstasy through the door.

Win—real name: Windsor Horne Lockwood III—was letting Myron temporarily crash at his apartment in the Dakota on Seventy-second Street and Central Park West. The Dakota was an old New York landmark whose rich and lush history had been totally eclipsed by the murder of John Lennon twenty-some-odd years ago. Entering meant crossing over the spot where Lennon had bled to death, the feeling not unlike trampling over a grave. Myron was finally getting used to it.

From the outside, the Dakota was beautiful and dark and resembled a haunted house on steroids. Most apartments, including Win's, had more square footage than a European principality. Last year, after a lifetime of living in Mom and Dad's suburban sprawl, Myron had finally moved out of the basement and into a SoHo loft with his ladylove, Jessica. It was a huge step, the first sign that after more than a decade, Jessica was ready to—gasp!—commit. So the two lovers clasped hands and took the live-together plunge. And like so many plunges in life, it ended in an ugly splat.

More cries of ecstasy.

Myron pressed his ear against the door. Cries, yes, and a soundtrack. Not live action, he decided. He used his key and pushed open the door. The cries were coming from the TV room. Win never used that room for, uh, filming. Myron sighed and stepped through the portal.

Win wore his casual WASP uniform: khakis, shirt with a color so loud you couldn't look at it straight on except through a pinhole, loafers, no socks. His blond locks had been parted with the precision of old ladies dividing up a lunch check; his skin was the color of white china with dabs of golf-ruddy red on both cheeks. He sat yoga-lotus-style, his legs pretzeled to a point man was never supposed to achieve. His index fingers and thumbs formed two circles, the hands resting against the knees. Yuppie Zen. Old World European clashing heads with Ancient Oriental. The sweet smell of Main Line mixed with the heavy Asian incense.

Win breathed in for a twenty count, held it, breathed out for a twenty count. He was meditating, of course, but with a Win-like twist. He did not, for example, listen to soothing nature sounds or chimes; no, he preferred meditating to the sound tracks of, uh, skin flicks from the seventies, which basically sounded like a bad Jimi Hendrix impersonator making wah-wah-wah noises on an electric kazoo. Just listening to it was enough to make you rush out for a shot of antibiotics.

Win did not close his eyes either. He did not visualize a deer sipping water by a lapping stream or a gentle waterfall against green foliage or any of that. His gaze remained fixed on the television screen; more specifically, on homemade videotapes of himself and a potpourri of females in the throes of passion.

Myron stepped fully into the room. Win turned one of his finger-Os into a flat-palm stop sign, then lifted the index finger up to indicate he wanted another moment. Myron risked a glance at the screen, saw the writhing flesh, turned away.

A few seconds later, Win said, "Hello."

"I'd like my disgust noted for the record," Myron said.

"So noted."

Win moved fluidly from the lotus position to a full stand. He popped out the tape and put it in a box. The box was labeled *Anon 11*. *Anon*, Myron knew, stood for *Anonymous*. It meant Win had either forgotten her name or never learned it.

"I can't believe you still do this," Myron said.

"Are we moralizing again?" Win asked with a smile. "How nice for us."

"Let me ask you something."

"Oh, please do."

"Something I always wanted to know."

"My ears are all atwitter."

"Putting aside my repugnancy for a moment—"

"Not on my account," Win said. "I so enjoy when you're superior."

"You claim this"—Myron motioned vaguely at the videotape and then the TV screen—"relaxes you."

"Yes."

"But doesn't it also . . . I mean, sick as it is . . . doesn't it also arouse you?"

"Not at all," Win replied.

"That's the part I don't understand."

"Viewing the act does not arouse me," Win explained. "Thinking about the act does not arouse me. Videos, dirty magazines, *Penthouse Forum*, cyberporn—none of them arouse me. For me, there is no substitute for the real thing. A partner must be present. The rest has the same effect as tickling myself. It's why I never masturbate."

Myron said nothing.

"Problem?" Win asked.

"I'm just wondering what possessed me to ask," Myron said.

Win opened a Ming dynasty cabinet that had been converted into a small fridge and tossed Myron a Yoo-Hoo. He poured himself a snifter of cognac. The room was lush antiques and rich tapestries and Oriental carpets and busts of men with long, curly hair. If not for the state-of-the-art home entertainment system, the room could have been something you'd stumble across on a tour of a Medici palace.

They grabbed their usual seats.

Win said, "You look troubled."

"I have a case for us."

"Ah."

"I know I said we weren't going to do this anymore. But this is sort of a special circumstance."

"I see," Win said.

"Do you remember Emily?"

Win did that swirl thing with his snifter. "College girlfriend. Used to make monkey noises during sex. Dumped you in the beginning of our senior year. Married your archenemy Greg Downing. Dumped him too. Probably still makes monkey noises."

"She has a son," Myron said. "He's sick." He quickly explained the situation, leaving out the part about possibly being the kid's father. If he couldn't talk about it with Esperanza, there was no way he could raise the subject with Win.

When he finished, Win said, "It shouldn't be too difficult. You're going to talk to the doctor tomorrow?"

"Yes."

"Find out what you can about who handles the records."

Win picked up the remote and flicked on the television. He flipped the channels because there were a lot of commercials on and because he was male. He stopped at CNN. Terese Collins was anchoring the news.

"Is the lovely Ms. Collins visiting us tomorrow?" Win asked.

Myron nodded. "Her flight comes in at ten."

"She's been visiting quite a bit."

"Yep."

"Are you two"—Win crinkled his face as if someone had just flashed him a particularly nasty case of jock rot— "getting serious?"

Myron looked at Terese on the screen. "Still too new," he said.

There was an *All in the Family* marathon on cable, so Win flipped to it. They ordered in some Chinese food and watched two episodes. Myron tried to get lost in the bliss of Archie and Edith, but it wasn't happening. His thoughts naturally kept returning to Jeremy. He managed to deflect the paternity issue, concentrating, as Emily had asked, on the disease and task at hand. Fanconi anemia. That was what she said the boy had. Myron wondered if they had anything about it on the Web.

"I'll be back in a little while," Myron said.

Win looked at him. "The Stretch Cunningham funeral episode is up next."

"I want to check something on the Web."

"The episode where Archie gives the eulogy."

"I know."

"Where he comments that he never thought Stretch Cunningham was Jewish because of the 'ham' in his last name."

"I know the episode, Win."

"And you're willing to miss it for the sake of the Web?"

"You have it on tape."

"That's not the point."

The two men looked at each other, comfortable in the silence. After some time passed, Win said, "Tell me."

He barely hesitated. "Emily said I'm the boy's father."

Win nodded and said, "Ah."

"You don't sound surprised."

Win used the chopsticks to grab another shrimp. "You believe her?"

"Yes."

"Why?"

"For one thing, it's a hell of a thing to lie about it."

"But Emily is good at lying, Myron. She's always lied to you. She lied to you in college. She lied to you when Greg disappeared. She lied in court about Greg's behavior with the children. She betrayed Greg the night before their wedding by sleeping with you. And, if you will, if she is telling the truth now, she lied to you for the better part of thirteen years."

Myron thought about it. "I think she's telling the truth about this."

"You *think*, Myron."

"I'm going to take a blood test."

Win shrugged. "If you must."

"What does that mean?"

"I'll let the statement speak for itself."

Myron made a face. "Didn't you just say I should find out for sure?"

"Not at all," Win said. "I was merely pointing out the obvious. I didn't say it made a difference."

Myron thought about it. "You're confusing me."

"Simply put," Win said, "so what if you are the boy's biological father? What difference does it make?"

"Come on, Win. Not even you can be that cold."

"Quite the opposite. As strange as this might sound, I am using my heart on this one."

"How do you figure?"

Win swirled the liquid again, studied the amber, took a sip. It colored his cheeks a bit. "Again I'll put it simply: No matter what a blood test might indicate, you are not Jeremy Downing's father. Greg is. You may be a sperm donor. You may be an accident of lust and biology. You may have provided a simple microscopic cell structure that combined with one slightly more complex. But you are not this boy's father."

"It's not that simple, Win."

"It is that simple, my friend. The fact that you insipidly choose to confuse the issue does not change the fact. I'll demonstrate, if you'd like."

"I'm listening."

"You love your father, correct?"

"You know the answer to that."

"I do," Win said. "But what makes him your father? The fact that he once grunted on top of Mommy after a few drinks—or the way he has cared for you and loved you for the past thirty-five years?"

Myron looked down at the can of Yoo-Hoo.

"You owe this boy nothing," Win continued, "and equally important, he owes you nothing. We will try to save his life, if that is what you wish, but that should be where it ends."

Myron thought about it. The only thing scarier than Win irrational was when Win made sense. "Maybe you're right."

"But you still don't think it's that simple."

"I don't know."

On the television, Archie approached the pulpit, a yarmulke on his head. "It's a start," Win said.

6

Myron mixed childlike Froot Loops and very adult All-Bran into a bowl and poured on skim milk. For those not reading the Cliffs Notes, this act denotes that there is still a great deal of boy in the man. Heavy symbolism. How poignant.

The Number 1 train took Myron to a platform on 168th Street so far below ground that commuters had to take a urine-encapsulated elevator to reach the surface. The elevator was big and dark and shaky and brought on images of a PBS documentary on coal mining.

Located in Washington Heights, a quick stone's toss from Harlem and directly across Broadway from the Audubon Ballroom where Malcolm X was gunned down, Columbia Presbyterian Medical Center's famed pediatric building was called Babies and Children's Hospital. It used to be called just Babies Hospital, but a committee of learned medical experts was formed and after hours of intense study, they decided to change the name from Babies Hospital to Babies and Children's Hospital. Moral of the story: Committees are really, really important.

But the name, while not exactly Madison Avenue, does adequately reflect the reality of the situation—the hospital is strictly pediatric and deliveries, a well-worn twelve-floor edifice with eleven of them devoted to sick children. There was something very wrong with that, but probably nothing beyond the theologically obvious.

Myron stopped before the entranceway and looked up at the pollution-brown brick. Lots of misery in the city and much of it ended up here. He ducked inside and checked in at the security desk. He gave his name to a guard. The guard tossed him a pass, almost glancing up from his *TV Guide* in the process. Myron waited a long time for the elevator, reading the Patient's Bill of Rights, which was printed in both English and Spanish. There was a sign for the Sol Goldman Heart Center right next to a sign for the hospital's Burger King. Mixed messages or assuring future business—Myron wasn't sure which.

The elevator opened on the tenth floor. Directly in front of him, there was a rainbow-hued "Save the Rain Forest" mural, painted, according to the sign, by the "pediatric patients" of the hospital. Save the Rain Forest. Oh, like these kids didn't have enough on their plate, right?

Myron asked a nurse where he might find Dr. Singh. The nurse pointed to a woman leading a dozen interns through the corridor. Myron was a little surprised to see that Dr. Singh was of the female persuasion, mostly because he had somehow imagined her being a man. Terribly sexist, but there you go.

Dr. Singh was, as her name strongly implied, Indian, from-India Indian as opposed to Native American Indian. Mid-thirties, he figured, her hair a lighter brown than what he was used to seeing on India Indians. She wore a white doctor coat, of course. So did all the interns, most of them appearing to be about fourteen years of age, their white coats more like smocks, like they were about to finger-paint or maybe dissect a frog in a junior high biology class. Some wore grave expressions that were almost laughable on their cherubic faces, but most emanated that medical-intern exhaustion from too many nights on call.

Only two of the interns were men—boys really—both sporting blue jeans, colorful ties, and white sneakers like waiters at Bennigan's. The women—to call them girls would use up Myron's anti-PC quota for the week—favored hospital scrubs. So young. Babies taking care of babies.

Myron followed the group at a semi-discreet distance. Every once in a while he glanced in a room and immediately regretted it. The corridor walls were festive and brightly painted, jammed with Disney/Nick Junior/PBS kiddie images and collages and mobiles, but Myron only saw black. A floor filled with dying children. Bald little boys and girls in pain, their veins blackened by toxins and poisons. Most of the children looked so calm and unafraid and unnaturally brave. If you wanted to see the stark terror, you had to look in the eyes of the parents, as though Mom and Dad were sucking the horror toward them, taking it on so that their child wouldn't have to.

"Mr. Bolitar?"

Dr. Singh met his eye and held out her hand. "I'm Karen Singh."

Myron almost asked her how she did this, how she stayed on this floor day in and day out, watching children die. But he didn't. They exchanged the usual pleasantries. Myron had expected an Indian accent, but the only thing he picked up was a little Bronx.

"We can talk in here," she said.

She pushed open one of the superheavy, superwide doors endemic to hospitals and nursing homes, and they stepped into an empty room with stripped beds. The barrenness ignited Myron's imagination. He could almost see a loved one rushing into the hospital, repeatedly pushing the elevator call button, diving inside, pushing more buttons, sprinting down the corridor into this silent room, the bed being stripped by a nurse, then the sudden cry of anguish. . . .

Myron shook his head. He watched too much TV.

Karen Singh sat on the corner of the mattress, and Myron studied her face for a moment. She had long sharp features. Everything pointed down—her nose, her chin, her eyebrows. Sort of harsh.

"You're staring," she said.

"I don't mean to."

She pointed to her forehead. "You were maybe expecting a dot?"

"Er, no."

"Very good, then let's get to it, shall we?"

"Okay."

"Mrs. Downing wants me to tell you whatever you want to know."

"I appreciate your taking the time."

"Are you a private investigator?" she asked.

"More like a family friend."

"Did you play basketball with Greg Downing?"

Myron was always surprised by the memory of the public. After all these years, people could still recall his big games, his big shots, sometimes with more clarity than Myron could. "You're a fan?"

"Nope," she said. "Can't stand sports actually."

"So how did you—"

"Just a deduction. You're tall and about the right age and you said you were a family friend. So . . ." She shrugged.

"Nice deduction."

"It's what we do here when you think about it. Deduce. Some diagnoses are easy. Others must be deduced from the evidence. You ever read Sherlock Holmes?"

"Sure."

"Sherlock said that you should never theorize before you have facts—because then you twist facts to suit theories rather than twisting theories to suit facts. If you see a misdiagnosis, nine times out of ten they ignored Sherlock's axiom."

"Did that happen with Jeremy Downing?"

"As a matter of fact," she said, "it did."

Somewhere down the hall, a machine started beeping. The sound hit the nerves like a police taser.

"So his first doctor screwed up?"

"I won't get into that. But Fanconi anemia isn't common. And because it looks like other things, it's often misdiagnosed."

"So tell me about Jeremy."

"What's to tell? He has it. Fanconi anemia, that is. In simple terms, his bone marrow is corrupted."

"Corrupted?"

"In layman's term, it's shit. It makes him susceptible to a host of infections and even cancers. It commonly turns into AML." She saw the puzzled look on his face and added, "That's acute myelogenous leukemia."

"But you can cure him?"

" 'Cure' is an optimistic word," she said. "But with a bone marrow transplant and treatments with a new fludarabine compound, yes, I believe his prognosis is excellent."

"Fluda-what?"

"Not important. We need a bone marrow donor that matches Jeremy. That's what counts here."

"And you don't have one."

Dr. Singh shifted on the mattress. "That's correct."

Myron felt the resistance. He decided to back off, test another flank. "Could you take me through the transplant process?"

"Step by step?"

"If it's not too much trouble."

She shrugged. "First step: find a donor."

"How do you go about that?"

"You try family members, of course. Siblings have the best chance of matching. Then parents. Then people of similar background."

"When you say people of similar background—"

"Blacks with blacks, Jews with Jews, Latino descent with Latino descent. You'll see that quite often in marrow drives. If the patient is, for example, a Hasidic Jew, the donation drives will take place within their shuls. Mixed blood is usually the hardest to match."

"And Jeremy's blood or whatever you need to match—it's fairly rare?"

"Yes."

Emily and Greg were both of Irish descent. Myron's family came from the usual potpourri of old Russia and Poland and even a little Palestine thrown in. Mixed blood. He thought about the paternity implications.

"So after you exhausted the family, how do you search for the match?"

"You go to the national registry."

"Where are they located?"

"In Washington. You listed?"

Myron nodded.

"They keep computer records there. We search for a preliminary match in their banks."

"Okay, now assuming you find a match in the computer—"

"A *preliminary* match," she corrected. "The local center calls the potential donor and asks them to come in. They run a battery of tests. But the odds of matching are still fairly slim."

Myron could see that Karen Singh was relaxing, comfortable with the familiar subject matter, which was exactly what he wanted. Interrogations are a funny thing. Sometimes you go for the full frontal attack, and sometimes you sidle up, friendly-like, and sneak in the back. Win put it simpler: Sometimes you get more ants with honey, but you should always pack a can of Raid.

"Let's suppose you find a full-fledged donor," Myron said. "What then?"

"The center acquires the donor's permission."

"When you say 'center,' do you mean the national registry in Washington?"

"No, I mean the local center. Do you have your donor card in your wallet?"

"Yes."

"Let me see it."

Myron took out his wallet, flipped through about a dozen supermarket discount cards, three video club memberships, a couple of those buy-a-hundred-coffees-get-ten-cents-off-the-hundredth coupon, that sort of thing. He found the donor card and handed it to her.

"See here," she said, pointing to the back. "Your local center is in East Orange, New Jersey."

"So if I was a preliminary match, the East Orange center would call me?"

"Yes."

"And if I ended up being a full match?"

"You'd sign some papers and donate marrow."

"Is that like donating blood?"

Karen Singh handed the card back to him and shifted again. "Harvesting bone marrow is a more invasive procedure."

Invasive. Every profession has its own buzzwords. "How so?"

"For one thing, you have to be put under."

"Anesthesia?"

"Yes."

"And then what do they do?"

"A doctor sticks a needle through the bone and sucks the marrow out with a syringe."

Myron said, "Eeuw."

"As I just explained, you're not awake during the procedure."

"Still," Myron said, "it sounds much more complicated than giving blood."

"It is," she said. "But the procedure is safe and relatively painless."

"But people must balk. I mean, most probably signed up the same way I did: They had a friend who was sick and ran a drive. For someone you know and care about, sure, you're willing to make a sacrifice. But for a stranger?"

Karen Singh's eyes found his and settled in hard. "You are saving a life, Mr. Bolitar. Think about that. How many opportunities do you get to save a fellow human being's life?"

He had hit a nerve. Good. "Are you saying people don't balk?"

"I'm not saying it never happens," she said, "but most people do the right thing."

"Does the donor get to meet the person he or she is saving?"

"No. It's totally anonymous. Confidentiality is very important here. Everything is held in the utmost secrecy."

They were getting to it now, and Myron could sense that her defenses were starting to slide back up like a car window. He decided to pull back again, let her resettle on comfy ground. "What's the patient going through during all this?" he asked.

"At what point?"

"While the marrow is being harvested. How do you prep the patient?" Prep. Myron had said "prep." Like a real doctor. Who said watching *St. Elsewhere* was a waste of time?

"It depends on what you're treating," Dr. Singh said. "But for most diseases, the recipient goes through about a week's worth of chemotherapy."

Chemotherapy. One of those words that hush a room like a nun's scowl. "They get chemo before the transplant?"

"Yes."

"I would think that would weaken them," Myron said.

"To some degree, yes."

"Why would you do it, then?"

"You have to. You're giving the recipient new bone marrow. Before you do that, you have to kill the old marrow. With leukemia, for example, the amount of chemo is high because you have to kill off all the living marrow. In the case of Fanconi anemia, you can be less aggressive because the marrow is already very weak."

"So you kill off all the bone marrow?"

"Yes."

"Isn't that dangerous?"

Dr. Singh gave him the steady eyes again. "This is a dangerous procedure, Mr. Bolitar. You are in effect replacing a person's bone marrow."

"And then?"

"And then the patient is infused with new marrow through an IV. He or she is kept isolated in a sterile environment for the first two weeks."

"Quarantined?"

"In effect. Do you remember the old TV movie *The Boy in the Plastic Bubble*?"

"Who doesn't?"

Dr. Singh smiled.

"Is that what the patient lives in?" Myron asked.

"A bubble chamber of sorts, yes."

"I had no idea," Myron said. "And this works?"

"Rejection is always a possibility, of course. But our success rate is quite high. In the case of Jeremy Downing, he can live a normal, active life with the transplant."

"And without it?"

"We can keep treating him with male hormones and growth factors, but his premature death is inevitable."

Silence. Except for that steady mechanical beep coming from down the hall.

Myron cleared his throat. "When you said that everything involving the donor is confidential—"

"I meant totally."

Enough wading. "How does that sit with you, Dr. Singh?"

"What do you mean?"

"The national registry located a donor who matched Jeremy, didn't they?"

"I believe so, yes."

"So what happened?"

She tapped her chin with her index finger. "May I speak candidly?"

"Please."

"I believe in the need for secrecy and confidentiality. Most people don't understand how easy, painless, and important it is to put their name in the registry. All they have to do is give a little blood. Just a little tube of the stuff, less than you would for any blood donation. Do that simple act—and you can save a life. Do you understand the significance of that?"

"I think so."

"We in the medical community must do all we can to encourage people to join the bone marrow registry. Education, of course, is important. So, too, is confidentiality. It has to be honored. The donors have to trust us."

She stopped, crossed her legs, leaned back on her hands. "But in this case, something of a quandary has developed. The importance of confidentiality is bumping up against the welfare of my patient. For me, the quandary is easy to resolve. The Hippocratic oath trumps all. I'm not a lawyer or a priest. My priority must be to save the life, not protect confidences. My guess is that I'm not the only doctor that feels that way. Perhaps that's why we have no contact with the donors. The blood center—in your case, the one in East Orange—does everything. They harvest the marrow and ship it to us."

"Are you saying that you don't know who the donor is?"

"That's right."

"Or if it's a he or she or where they live or anything?"

Karen Singh nodded. "I can only tell you that the national registry found a match. They called and told me so. I later received a call telling me that the donor was no longer available."

"What does that mean?"

"My question exactly."

"Did they give you an answer?"

"No," she said. "And while I see things on the micro level, the national registry has to remain macro. I respect that."

"You just gave up?"

She stiffened at his words. Her eyes went small and black. "No, Mr. Bolitar, I did not give up. I raged against the machine. But the people at the national registry are not ogres. They understand that this is a life-or-death situation. If a donor backs out, they try their best to bring them back into the fold. They do everything I would do to convince the donor to go through with it."

"But nothing worked here?"

"That seems to be the case."

"The donor would be told that he's sentencing a thirteen-year-old boy to death?"

She didn't hesitate. "Yes."

Myron threw up his hands. "So what do we conclude here, Doctor? That the donor is a selfish monster?"

Karen Singh chewed on that one for a moment. "Perhaps," she said. "Or perhaps the answer is simpler."

"For example?"

"For example," she said, "maybe the center can't find the donor."

Hello. Myron sat up a bit. "What do you mean, 'can't find'?"

"I don't know what happened here. The center won't tell me, and that's probably how it should be. I'm the patient's advocate. It's their job to deal with the donors. But I believe they were"—she stopped, searching for the right word—"perplexed."

"What makes you say that?"

"Nothing concrete. Just a feeling that this might be more than a donor with cold feet."

"How do we find out?"

"I don't know."

"How do we find the donor's name?"

"We can't."

"There has to be a way," Myron said. "Play pretend with me. How could I do it?"

She shrugged. "Break into the computer system. That's the only way I know."

"The computer in Washington?"

"They network with the local centers. But you'd have to know codes and passwords. Maybe a good hacker could get through, I don't know."

Hackers, Myron knew, worked better in the movies than in real life. A few years ago, maybe—but most computer systems nowadays were secure against such invasions.

"How long do we have here, Doctor?"

"There's no way of telling. Jeremy is reacting well to the hormones and growth factors. But it's only a question of time."

"So we have to find a donor."

"Yes." Karen Singh stopped, looked at Myron, looked away.

"Is there something else?" Myron asked.

She did not face him. "There is one other remote possibility," she said.

"What?" Myron asked.

"Keep in mind what I said before. I'm the patient's advocate. It's my job to explore every possible avenue to save him."

Her voice was funny now.

"I'm listening," Myron said.

Karen Singh rubbed her palms on her pant legs. "If Jeremy's biological parents were to conceive again, there is a twenty-five percent chance that the offspring would be a match."

She looked at Myron.

"I don't think that's a possibility," he said.

"Even if it's the only way to save Jeremy's life?"

Myron had no reply. An orderly walked by, looked in the room, mumbled an apology, left. Myron stood and thanked her.

"I'll show you to the elevator," Dr. Singh said.

"Thank you."

"There's a lab on the first floor in the Harkness Pavilion." She handed him a slip of paper. Myron looked at it. It was an order form. "I understand you might want to take a certain confidential blood test."

Neither of them said anything else as they walked toward the elevators. There were several children being wheeled through the corridor. Dr. Singh smiled at them, the pointed features softening into something almost celestial. Again the children looked unafraid. Myron wondered if the calmness spawned from ignorance or acceptance. He wondered if the children did not understand the gravity of what was happening to them or if they possessed a quiet clarity their parents would never know. Such philosophical queries, Myron knew, were best left to those more learned. But maybe the answer was simpler than he imagined: The children's suffering would be relatively short; their parents' would be eternal.

When they reached the elevator, Myron said, "How do you do it?"

She knew what he meant. "I could say something fancy about finding solace in helping, but the truth is, I block and I compartmentalize. It's the only way."

The elevator door opened, but before Myron could move he heard a familiar voice say, "What the hell are you doing here?"

Greg Downing stepped toward him.

7

Too much history. Again.

The last time the two men had been in the same room, Myron was straddled over Greg's chest, trying to kill him, punching him repeatedly in the face until Win—Win of all people—pulled him off. Three years ago. Myron hadn't seen him since, except on highlight films during the evening news.

Greg Downing glared at Myron, then at Karen Singh, then back at Myron as though he expected him to have evaporated by then.

"What the hell are you doing here?" he asked again.

Greg was clad in a flannel shirt over some waffle knit you'd buy at Baby Gap, faded jeans, and preternaturally scuffed work boots. The Suburban Lumberjack.

Something sparked hot in Myron's chest, ignited, took flight.

From the day they first battled for a rebound in the sixth grade, Greg and Myron were the pure definition of cross-town rivals. In high school, where their competitive cup truly runneth over, Greg and Myron met up eight times, splitting the games evenly. Rumor had it that there was bad blood between the budding superstars, but that was just standard sports hyperbole. The truth was, Myron barely knew Greg off the court. They were killer competitors, sure, willing to do just about anything to win, but once the final buzzer sounded, the two boys shook hands and the rivalry hibernated until the next opening tap.

Or so Myron had always thought.

When he accepted a scholarship at Duke and Greg chose the University of North Carolina, basketball fans rejoiced. Their seemingly innocent rivalry was ready for ACC prime time. Myron and Greg did not disappoint.

The Duke-UNC matchups drew fantastic television ratings, no game decided by more than three points. Both had spectacular college careers. Both were named first-team All-Americans. Both were on covers of *Sports Illustrated*, once even sharing it. But the rivalry stayed on the court. They would do battle until bloody, but the competition never overlapped into their personal arenas.

Until Emily.

Before the start of senior year, Myron broached the subject of marriage with Emily. The next day she came to him, held his hands, looked into his eyes, and said, "I'm not sure I love you." Bam, like that. He still wondered what happened. Too much too soon, he guessed. A need to spread the proverbial wings a bit, play the proverbial field, what have you. Time passed. Three months, by Myron's count. Then Emily took up with Greg. Myron publicly shrugged it off—even when Greg and Emily got engaged just before graduation. The NBA draft took place right about then too. Both went in the first round, though Greg was surprisingly picked before Myron.

That was when it all unraveled.

The end result?

Almost a decade and a half later, Greg Downing was winding down an All-Star pro basketball career. People cheered him. He made millions and was famous. He played the game he loved. For Myron, his lifelong dream had ended before it had begun. During his first preseason game with the Celtics, Big Burt Wesson had slammed into him, sandwiching Myron's knee between himself and another player. There was a snap, crackle, pop—and then a hot, ripping pain, as though metal talons were shredding his kneecap into thin strips.

His knee never recovered.

A freak accident. Or so everyone thought. Including Myron. For more than ten years, he'd believed that the injury was merely a fluke, the fickle work of the Fates. But now he knew better. Now he knew the man who stood in front of him had been the cause. Now he knew that their seemingly innocent childhood rivalry had grown monstrous, had feasted upon his dream, had slaughtered Greg and Emily's marriage, and had in all probability led to the birth of Jeremy Downing.

He felt his hands tighten into fists. "I was just leaving."

Greg put a hand on Myron's chest. "I asked you a question."

Myron stared at the hand. "One good thing," he said.

"What?"

"No transportation time," Myron said. "We're already at the hospital."

Greg sneered. "You sucker-punched me last time."

"You want to go again?"

"Pardon me," Karen Singh said. "But are you guys for real?"

Greg kept glaring at Myron.

"Stop it," Myron said, "or I'll wet myself."

"You're a son of a bitch."

"And you're not on my Christmas card list either, Greggy-poo." Greggy-poo. Very mature.

Greg leaned closer. "You know what I'd like to do to you, Bolitar?"

"Kiss me on the lips? Buy me flowers?"

"Flowers for your grave maybe."

Myron nodded. "Good one, Greg. I mean, ouch, I'm wounded."

Karen Singh said, "Just because this is a children's floor doesn't mean you two have to act like ones."

Greg took a step back, his eyes never leaving Myron. "Emily," he spat suddenly. "She called you, right?"

"I have nothing to say to you, Greg."

"She asked you to find the donor. Like you found me."

"You always were a bright boy."

"I'm calling a press conference today. I'm going to make a direct appeal to the donor. Offer a reward."

"Good."

"So we don't need you, Bolitar."

Myron looked at Greg, and for a moment they were back on the court, faces drenched with sweat, the crowd cheering, the clock ticking down, the ball bouncing. Nirvana. Gone forever. Snatched away by Greg. And by Emily. And maybe most of all, when he looked at it honestly, by Myron's own stupidity.

"I've got to go," Myron said.

Greg took a step back. Myron moved past him and pressed the elevator button.

"Hey, Bolitar."

He faced Greg.

"I came here to talk to the doc about my son," Greg said, "not rehash our past."

Myron said nothing. He turned back to the elevator.

"You think you can help save my boy?" Greg asked.

Myron's mouth went dry. "I don't know."

The elevator dinged and opened. There were no good-byes, no nods, no further communication of any sort. Myron stepped inside and let the doors close. When he reached the first level, he went to the lab. He rolled up his sleeve. A woman drew his blood, untied the tourniquet, and said, "Your doctor will be in touch with you about the results."

8

Win was bored, so he drove Myron to the airport to pick up Terese. His foot pushed down on the gas pedal as though it had offended him. The Jag flew. As was his custom when driving with Win, Myron kept his eyes averted.

"It would appear," Win began, "that our best option would be to locate a satellite marrow clinic in a somewhat remote area. Upstate maybe or in western Jersey. We would then break in at night with a computer expert."

"Won't work," Myron said.

"Por qua?"

"The Washington center shuts down the computer network at six o'clock. Even if we were to break in, we couldn't bring up the mainframe."

Win said, "Hmm."

"Don't fret," Myron said. "I have a plan."

"When you talk like that," Win said, "my nipples harden."

"I thought only the real thing aroused you."

"This isn't the real thing?"

They parked in JFK Airport's short-term parking and reached the Continental Airlines gate ten minutes before the flight touched down. When the passengers began to appear, Win said, "I'll stand over in the corner."

"Why?"

"I wouldn't want to cast a shadow on your greeting," he said. "And standing over there affords me a better view of Ms. Collins's derriere."

Ah, Win.

Two minutes later, Terese Collins—to use a purely transportational term—disembarked. She was casually decked out in a white blouse and green slacks. Her brown hair was up in a ponytail. People lightly elbowed one another, whispering and subtly gesturing, giving her that surreptitious glance, the one that says "I recognize you but don't want to appear fawning."

Terese approached Myron and offered up her breaking-to-commercial smile. It was small and tight, trying to be friendly but reminding viewers that she was telling them about war and pestilence and tragedy and that maybe a big happy smile would be somewhat obscene. They hugged a little too tightly, and Myron felt the familiar sadness overwhelm him. It happened to him every time they hugged—a sense that something inside of him was crumbling anew. He sensed that the same thing happened to her.

Win came over.

"Hello, Win," she said.

"Hello, Terese."

"Checking out my ass again?"

"I prefer the term 'derriere.' And yes."

"Still choice?"

"Grade A."

"Ahem," Myron said. "Please wait for the meat inspector."

Win and Terese looked at each other and rolled their eyes.

Myron had been wrong before. Emily was not Win's favorite. Terese was—though it was strictly because she lived far away. "You are the pitiful, needy type who feels incomplete without a steady girlfriend," Win had told him. "Who better than a career woman who lives a thousand miles away?"

Win headed for his Jag while they waited for her luggage. Terese watched Win walk away.

Myron said, "Is his ass better than mine?"

"No ass is better than yours," she said.

"I know that. I was just testing you."

Terese kept looking. "Win is an interesting fellow," she said.

"Oh yeah," Myron agreed.

"On the outside, he's all cold and detached," she said. "But underneath that—way down deep inside—he's all cold and detached."

"You read people well, Terese."

Win dropped them off at the Dakota and returned to the office. When Myron and Terese got inside the apartment, she kissed him hard. Always an urgency with Terese. A desperation in their love-making. Pleasant, sure. Awesome even. But there was still the aura of sadness. The sadness didn't go away when they made love, but for a little while it lifted like cloud cover, hovering above instead of weighing them down.

They had hooked up at a charity function a few months back, both dragged there by well-meaning friends. It was their mutual misery that drew them, as though it were one of those psychic crowns only they could spot on each other. They met and ran away that very night to the Caribbean on a let's-just-flee dare. For the usually predictable Myron, the spontaneous act felt surprisingly right. They spent a numbingly blissful three weeks alone on a private island, trying to stave off the flow of pain. When Myron was finally forced to return home, they'd both assumed it was over. They'd assumed wrong. At least, it appeared that way.

Myron recognized that his own healing was finally under way. He wasn't back to full strength or normal or any of that. He doubted he ever would be. Or even wanted to be. Giant hands had twisted him and then let go, and while his world was slowly untwisting, he knew that it would never fully return to its original position.

Again with the poignant.

But whatever had happened to Terese—whatever had brought on the sadness and twisted her world, if you will—still held firm, refusing to let go.

Terese's head lay on his chest, her arms wrapped around him. He could not see her face. She never showed him her face when they finished.

"You want to talk about it?" he asked.

She still hadn't told him, and Myron rarely asked. Doing so, he knew, was breaking an unspoken though cardinal rule.

"No."

"I'm not pushing," he said. "I just wanted you to know that if you're ever ready, I'm here."

"I know," she said.

He wanted to say something more, but she was still at a place where words were either superfluous or they stung. He stayed quiet and stroked her hair.

"This relationship," Terese said. "It's bizarre."

"I guess."

"Someone told me you're dating Jessica Culver, the writer."

"We broke up," he said.

"Oh." She did not move, still holding him a little too tightly. "Can I ask when?"

"A month before we met."

"And how long were you two together?"

"Thirteen years, on and off."

"I see," she said. "Am I the recovery?"

"Am I yours?"

"Maybe," she said.

"Same answer."

She thought about that a little. "But Jessica Culver is not the reason you ran away with me."

He remembered the cemetery overlooking the school yard. "No," he said, "she's not the reason."

Terese finally turned to him. "We have no chance. You know that, right?"

Myron said nothing.

"That's not unusual," she went on. "Plenty of relationships have no chance. But people stay in them because it's fun. This isn't fun either."

"Speak for yourself."

"Don't get me wrong, Myron. You're a hell of a lay."

"Could you put that in a sworn affidavit?"

She smiled but there was still no joy. "So what do we have here?"

"Truth?"

"Preferably."

"I always overanalyze," Myron said. "It's my nature. I meet a woman, and I immediately picture the house in the burbs and the white picket fence and the two-point-five kids. But for once I'm not doing that. I'm just letting it happen. So, to answer your question, I don't know. And I'm not sure I care."

She lowered her head. "You realize that I'm pretty damaged."

"I guess."

"I have more baggage than most."

"We all have baggage," Myron said. "The question is, does your baggage go with mine?"

"Who said that?"

"I'm paraphrasing from a Broadway musical."

"Which one?"

"*Rent.*"

She frowned. "I don't like musicals."

"Sorry to hear that," Myron said.

"You do?"

"Oh yeah."

"You're in your mid-thirties, single, sensitive, and you like show tunes," she said. "If you were a better dresser, I'd say you were gay."

She pressed a hard, quick kiss to his lips, and then they held each other a little more. Once again he wanted to ask her what had happened to her, but he wouldn't. She would tell him one day. Or she wouldn't. He decided to change subjects.

"I need your help with something," Myron said.

She looked at him.

"I need to break into a bone marrow center's computer system," he said. "And I think you can help."

"Me?"

"Yup."

"You got the wrong technophobe," she said.

"I don't need a technophobe. I need a famous anchorwoman."

"I see. And you're asking for this favor postcoital?"

"Part of my plan," Myron said. "I've weakened your will. You cannot refuse me."

"Diabolical."

"Indeed."

"And if I refuse?"

Myron wiggled his eyebrows. "I'll once again use my brawny body and patented lovemaking technique to make you succumb."

" 'Succumb,' " she repeated, pulling him closer. "Is that one word or two?"

9

t took a shockingly short time to set up.

Myron told Terese his plan. She listened without interruption. When he finished, she started placing calls. She never asked why he was looking for the donor or how he and the donor were connected. The unspoken rule again, he guessed.

Within the hour a news van complete with a handheld television camera was delivered to the Dakota. The director of the Bergen County Blood Center—a nearby New Jersey bone marrow center—had agreed to drop everything for an immediate interview with Terese Collins, anchorwoman extraordinaire. The power of the idiot box.

They took the Harlem River Drive up to the George Washington Bridge, crossing the Hudson and exiting onto Jones Road in Englewood, New Jersey. After they parked, Myron hoisted up the camera. Heavier than he thought. Terese showed him how to hold it, how to lean it against his shoulder and aim. There was something bazooka-like about the whole thing.

"Do you think I should wear a disguise?" Myron asked.

"Why?"

"People still recognize me from my playing days."

She made a face.

"I'm rather famous in certain circles."

"Get real, Myron. You're an ex-jock. If someone by some miracle recognizes you, they'll think you got lucky and didn't end up in a gutter like most ex-jocks."

He thought about it. "Fair enough."

"One other thing," she said. "And this will be nearly impossible for you."

"What?"

"You have to keep your big mouth shut," Terese said.

"Egads."

"You're just the cameraman here."

"We prefer to be called 'photographic artists.' "

"Just play your part. Trust me to handle him."

"Can I at least use a pseudonym?" He put the camera to his eye. "You can call me Lens. Or Scoop."

"How about Bozo? No, wait, that would be a synonym."

Everyone's a wise guy.

When they entered the clinic's lobby, people turned toward Terese and did that surreptitious stare again. Myron realized that today was the first time he had been with her in public. He had never quite thought about how famous she was.

"You get these stares wherever you go?" he whispered.

"Pretty much."

"Does it bother you?"

She shook her head. "That's horseshit."

"What is?"

"Celebrities who complain about people staring at them. Want to really piss off a celebrity? Let him go someplace and not be recognized."

Myron smiled. "You're so self-realized."

"That a new way of saying cynical?"

The receptionist said, "Mr. Englehardt will see you now."

She led them down a corridor with thin plaster walls and a bad paint job. Englehardt sat behind a plastic-wood desk. He was probably late twenties with a slight build and a chin weaker than machine-dispensed coffee.

Myron quickly noted the computer setup. Two of them. One on his desk. One on the credenza. Hmm.

Englehardt jumped up as though he'd just been passed a note that his chair had cooties. His eyes were wide and fixed on Terese. Myron was ignored and felt like, well, the cameraman. Terese smiled brightly at Englehardt, and he was lost.

"I'm Terese Collins," she said, extending her hand. Englehardt did everything but take a knee and kiss it. "This is my cameraman, Malachy Throne."

Myron sort of smiled. After the Broadway-musical debacle, he had worried. But Malachy Throne? Genius. Pure genius.

They all exchanged quick pleasantries. Englehardt kept touching his hair, trying very hard to look subtle about it and not like he was prepping for the camera. Not happening, bub. Finally Terese signaled that they were ready to begin.

"Where would you like me to sit?" Englehardt asked.

"Behind the desk would be nice," she said. "Don't you agree, Malachy?"

"Behind the desk," Myron said. "Yeah, that's the ticket."

The interview began. Terese kept her gaze on her subject; Englehardt, trapped in the beam, could look nowhere else. Myron put his eye to the camera. The consummate professional. Very Richard Avedon.

Terese asked Englehardt how he'd gotten started in this business, his background, general crap, relaxing him, putting him on that comfy ground, not all that different from the technique Myron had used with Dr. Singh. She was in on-air mode now. Her voice was different, her eyes steadier.

"So the national registry in Washington keeps track of all donors?" Terese asked.

"That's correct."

"But you can access the records?"

Englehardt tapped the computer on his desk. The screen faced him, the back of the monitor toward them. Okay, Myron thought, so it was the one on his desk. That would make it more difficult, but not impossible.

Terese looked at Myron. "Why don't you get a back shot, Malachy?" Then turning to Englehardt, "If that's okay with you."

"No problem at all," Englehardt said.

Myron started moving into position. The monitor was off. No surprise.

Terese continued to hold Englehardt's gaze. "Does everyone in the office have access to the national registry's computer?"

Englehardt shook his head firmly. "I'm the only one."

"Why's that?"

"The information is confidential. We don't breach the secrecy under any circumstance."

"I see," she said. Myron was in place now. "But what's to stop someone from coming in here when you're not around?"

"I always lock my office door," Englehardt said, up on his haunches and eager to please. "And you can only access the network with a password."

"You're the only one who knows the password?"

Englehardt tried not to preen, but he didn't try too hard. "That's correct."

Ever see those hidden-camera stories on *Dateline* or *20/20*? They always shoot from some strange angle and in black-and-white. Truth is, it's easy for any layperson to buy one and it's even easy to get one that films in color. There are stores that sell them right in Manhattan, or you can go online and search under "spy stores." You'll see hidden cameras in clocks, pens, briefcases and, most common of all, smoke detectors—available to anyone with the proper buckage. Myron had one that looked like a film case. He dropped it now on the window ledge with the lens pointing toward the computer monitor.

When it was in place, Myron tapped his nose with his finger, à la Redford in *The Sting*. Their signal. *Bolitar. Myron Bolitar. A Yoo-Hoo. Shaken not stirred*. Terese picked up her cue. The smile dropped off her face like an anvil.

Englehardt looked startled. "Ms. Collins? Are you okay?"

For a moment she could not bear to face him. Then: "Mr. Englehardt," Terese said, her voice Gulf War-grave, "I must confess something."

"I'm sorry?"

"I am here under somewhat false pretenses."

Englehardt looked confused. Terese was so good, Myron almost looked confused.

"I sincerely believe you are doing important work here," she continued. "But others are not so sure."

Englehardt's eyes were widening. "I don't understand."

"I need your help, Mr. Englehardt."

"Billy," he corrected.

Myron made a face. Billy?

Terese didn't miss a beat. "Someone is trying to disrupt your work, Billy."

"My work?"

"The national registry's work."

"I'm still not sure what you—"

"Are you familiar with the case of Jeremy Downing?"

Englehardt shook his head. "I never know the names of patients."

"He's the son of Greg Downing, the basketball star."

"Oh, wait, yes, I heard about this. His son has Fanconi anemia."

Terese nodded. "That's correct."

"Isn't Mr. Downing supposed to hold a press conference today? To track down a donor?"

"Exactly, Billy. And that's the problem."

"What is?"

"Mr. Downing has found the donor."

Still confused. "That's a problem?"

"No, of course not. If the person is the donor. And if the person is telling the truth."

Englehardt looked at Myron. Myron shrugged and moved back to the front of the desk. He left the film case on the windowsill.

"I'm not following you, Ms. Collins."

"Terese," she said. "A man has come forward. He claims that he is the matching donor."

"And you think he's lying?"

"Let me finish. He not only claims he's the donor, but he says that the reason he refused to donate his marrow was because of the terrible treatment he received from this center."

Englehardt nearly tipped back. "What?"

"He claims he was treated shabbily, that your staff was rude, and that he's even debating leveling a lawsuit."

"That's ridiculous."

"Probably."

"He's lying."

"Probably," she said again.

"And he'll be found out," Englehardt continued. "They'll test his blood and see he's a phony."

"But when, Billy?"

"What?"

"When will they do that? A day from now? A week from now? A month? But by then the damage is done. He's going to appear at the press conference today with Greg Downing. The media will be there in force. Even if it ends up being false, no one remembers the retraction. They just remember the allegation."

Englehardt sat back. "Jesus."

"Let me be frank, Billy. A number of my colleagues believe him. I don't. I smell a publicity hound. I'm having some of my best investigators dig into this man's past. So far they've come up with nothing, and time is running short."

"So what can I do?"

"I need to *know* it's not true. I can't stop it merely because I *believe* it's not true. I have to know for certain."

"How?"

Terese chewed on her lower lip. Deep thought. "Your computer network."

Englehardt shook his head. "The information in here is confidential. I explained that before. I can't tell you—"

"I don't need to know the name of the donor." She leaned forward. Myron moved as far away from the action as possible, trying to be no threat whatsoever. "I need to know what's *not* the name."

Englehardt looked hesistant.

"I'm sitting over here," she said. "I can't see the monitor. Malachy is by the door." She turned to Myron. "Your camera is off, Malachy?"

"Yes, Terese," Myron said. He put it down for emphasis.

"So here is what I suggest," Terese said. "You look up Jeremy Downing in your computer. It will list a donor. I give you a name. You tell me if the name matches. Simple?"

Englehardt still looked hesitant.

"You wouldn't be violating anyone's confidentiality," she said. "We can't see your screen. We can even leave the room while you look it up, if you'd like."

Englehardt said nothing. Terese said nothing either. Waiting him out. The perfect interviewer. She finally turned to Myron. "Grab your stuff," she said to him.

"Wait." Englehardt's eyes slid left, then right, up then down. "Jeremy Downing, you say?"

"Yes."

He did another quick series of eye-slides. When he saw that the coast was clear, he hunched over the keyboard and typed quickly. A few seconds later, he asked, "What's the name of this supposed donor?"

"Victor Johnson."

Englehardt looked at the monitor and smiled. "That's not him."

"You're sure?"

"Absolutely."

Terese matched the smile. "That's all we needed to know."

"You'll stop him?"

"He won't even get to the press conference."

Myron grabbed the film case and camera, and they hurried down the corridor. Once outside he turned to her and said, "Malachy Throne?"

"You know who he is?"

"He played False Face on *Batman*."

Terese smiled and nodded. "Very good."

"Can I tell you something?"

"What?"

"It turns me on when you talk *Batman*," he said.

"And even when I don't."

"Are you trying to make a point?"

Five minutes later they were watching the tape in the van.

10

Mr. Davis Taylor
221 North End Ave.
Waterbury, Connecticut

The social security and phone numbers were there too. Myron took out his cell phone and dialed. After two rings, a machine picked up and a robotic voice, the default greeting, asked him to leave a message at the tone. He left his name and mobile number and asked Mr. Taylor to return his call.

"So what are you going to do?" Terese asked.

"I guess I'll drive up and try to talk to Mr. Davis Taylor."

"Hasn't the clinic already tried that?"

"Probably."

"But you're more persuasive?"

"Questionable."

"I have to cover the Waldorf tonight," she said.

"I know. I'll go alone. Or maybe I'll bring Win."

She still would not face him. "This boy who needs the transplant," she said. "He's not a stranger, is he?"

Myron was not sure how to answer that. "I guess not."

Terese nodded in a way that told him not to say any more. He didn't. He picked up the phone and called Emily. She answered halfway through the first ring.

"Hello?"

"When is Greg doing the news conference?" he asked.

"In two hours," Emily said.

"I need to reach him."

He heard a hopeful gasp. "Did you find the donor for Jeremy?"

"Not yet."

"But you have something."

"We'll see."

"Don't patronize me, Myron."

"I'm not patronizing you."

"This is my son's life we're talking about here."

And mine? "I have a lead, Emily. That's all."

She gave him the number. "Myron, please call me if—"

"The moment I know something."

He hung up and called Greg.

"I need you to put off the press conference," Myron said.

"Why?" Greg asked.

"Just give me till tomorrow."

"You have something?"

"Maybe," Myron said.

"Maybe nothing," Greg said. "Do you have something or not?"

"I have a name and address. It might be our man. I want to check it out before you make a public plea."

"Where does he live?" Greg asked.

"Connecticut."

"You driving up?"

"Yes."

"Right now?"

"Pretty much."

"I want to go with you," Greg said.

"That's not a good idea."

"He's my kid, dammit."

Myron closed his eyes. "I understand that."

"So then you'll understand this: I'm not asking your permission. I'm going. So stop dicking around and tell me where you want me to pick you up."

Greg drove. He had one of those fancy SUV four-by-fours that are all the rage with New Jersey suburbanites whose idea of "off-road" is a speed bump at the mall. Très truck chic. For a long while neither man spoke. The tension in the air was more than the cut-with-a-knife variety; it pressed against the car windows, weighed Myron down, made him tired and gloomy.

"How did you get this name?" Greg asked.

"It's not important."

Greg left it alone. They drove some more. On the radio, Jewel earnestly insisted that her hands were small, she knew, but they were hers and not someone else's. Myron frowned. Not exactly "Blowing in the Wind," was it?

"You broke my nose, you know," Greg said.

Myron kept quiet.

"And my vision hasn't been the same. I'm having trouble focusing on the basket."

Myron could not believe what he was hearing. "You blaming me for your crappy season, Greg?"

"I'm just saying—"

"You're getting old, Greg. You've played fourteen seasons, and sitting out the strike didn't help you."

Greg waved a hand. "You wouldn't understand."

"You're right." Myron's knob turned from Simmer to Boil. "I never got to play pro ball."

"Right, and I never fucked my friend's wife."

"She wasn't your wife," Myron said. "And we weren't friends."

They both stopped then. Greg kept his eyes on the road. Myron turned away and stared out the passenger window.

Waterbury is one of those cities you bypass to reach another city. Myron had probably taken this stretch of 84 a hundred times, always remarking that at a distance Waterbury was a butt-ugly city. But now that he had the opportunity to see the city up close, he realized that he had underestimated the city's offensiveness to the eyes, that indeed the city had a butt-ugly quality to it that you just couldn't appreciate from afar. He shook his head. And people make fun of New Jersey?

Myron had gotten directions from the MapQuest Web site. He read them off to Greg in a voice he barely recognized as his own. Greg followed them in silence. Five minutes later, they pulled up to a dilapidated clapboard house in the middle of a street of dilapidated clapboards. The houses were uneven and crammed so close together, they looked like a set of teeth needing extensive orthodontic work.

They got out of the car. Myron wanted to tell Greg to stay back, but that would be pointless. He knocked on the door and almost immediately a gruff voice said, "Daniel? That you, Daniel?"

Myron said, "I'm looking for Davis Taylor."

"Daniel?"

"No," Myron said, yelling through the door. "Davis Taylor. But maybe he calls himself Daniel."

"What are you talking about?" An old man opened the door, already in full-suspicious squint. He wore glasses too small for his face, so that the metal earpieces were embedded into the folds of skin beneath both temples, and a bad yellow wig, like something Carol Channing wore once too often, adorned his crown. He had on one slipper and one shoe, and his bathrobe looked as if it'd been trampled over during the Boer War.

"I thought you was Daniel," the old man said. He tried to readjust the glasses, but they wouldn't move. He squinted again. "You look like Daniel."

"Must be the clouds in your eyes," Myron said.

"What?"

"Never mind. Are you Davis Taylor?"

"What do you want?"

"We're looking for Davis Taylor."

"Don't know no Davis Taylor."

"This is 221 North End Drive?"

"That's right."

"And there's no Davis Taylor living here?"

"Just me and my boy Daniel. But he's been away. Overseas."

"Spain?" Myron asked. He pronounced it Spahhheeeen. Elton would have been proud.

"What?"

"Never mind." The old man turned to Greg, tried again to readjust the glasses, gave another squint. "I know you. You play basketball, right?"

Greg gave the old man a gentle if not superior smile—Moses gazing down at a skeptic after the Red Sea parted. "That's right."

"You're Dolph Schayes."

"No."

"You look like Dolph. Helluva shooter. Saw him play in St. Louis last year. What a touch."

Myron and Greg exchanged a glance. Dolph Schayes had retired in 1964.

"I'm sorry," Myron said. "We didn't catch your name."

"You're not wearing uniforms," the old man said.

"No, sir, he only wears it on the court."

"Not that kind of uniform."

"Oh," Myron said, though he had no idea why.

"So you can't be here about Daniel. That's what I mean. I was afraid you were with the army and . . ." His voice drifted off then.

Myron saw where this was going. "Your son is stationed overseas?"

The old man nodded. "Nam."

Myron nodded, feeling bad now about the Elton John teasing. "We still didn't catch your name."

"Nathan. Nathan Mostoni."

"Mr. Mostoni, we're looking for someone named Davis Taylor. It's very important we find him."

"Don't know no Davis Taylor. He a friend of Daniel's?"

"Might be."

The old man thought about it. "Nope, don't know him."

"Who else lives here?"

"Just me and my boy."

"And it's just the two of you?"

"Yep. But my boy is overseas."

"So right now you live here alone?"

"How many different ways you gonna ask that question, boy?"

"It's just that it's a pretty big house," Myron said.

"So?"

"Ever take in any boarders?"

"Sure. Had a college girl just moved out of here."

"What was her name?"

"Stacy something. I don't remember."

"How long did she live here?"

"About six months."

"And before that?"

That one took some thought. Nathan Mostoni scratched his face like a dog going after his own belly. "A guy named Ken."

"Did you ever have a tenant named Davis Taylor?" Myron asked. "Or something like that?"

"Nope. Never."

"Did this Stacy have a boyfriend?"

"I don't think so."

"Do you know her last name?"

"My memory ain't so good. But she's at the college."

"Which college?"

"Waterbury State."

Myron turned to Greg and another thought hit him. "Mr. Mostoni, have you heard the name Davis Taylor before today?"

Another squint. "What do you mean?"

"Has anybody else visited you or called you and asked about Davis Taylor?"

"No, sir. Never heard the name before."

Myron looked at Greg again, then turned back to the old man. "So no one from the bone marrow center has been in touch with you?"

The old man cocked his head and put a hand to his ear. "The bone what?"

Myron asked a few more questions, but Nathan Mostoni started time-traveling again. There was nothing more to get here. Myron and Greg thanked him and headed back down the cracked pathway.

When they were back in the car, Greg asked, "Why didn't the bone marrow center contact this guy?"

"Maybe they did," Myron said. "Maybe he just forgot."

Greg didn't like it. Neither did Myron. "So what's next?" Greg asked.

"We run a background check on Davis Taylor. Find out everything we can about him."

"How?"

"It's easy nowadays. Just a few keystrokes and my partner will know it all."

"Your partner? You mean that violent wacko you used to room with in college?"

"A, it is unhealthy to refer to Win as a violent wacko, even when he appears not to be in the vicinity. B, no, I mean my partner at MB Sports-Reps, Esperanza Diaz."

Greg looked back at the house. "What do I do?"

"Go home," Myron said.

"And?"

"And be with your son."

Greg shook his head. "I don't get to see him until the weekend."

"I'm sure Emily wouldn't mind."

"Yeah, right." Greg smirked, shook his head. "You don't know her too well anymore, do you, Myron?"

"I guess not, no."

"If she had her way, I'd never get to see Jeremy again."

"That's a bit harsh, Greg."

"No, Myron. If anything, it's being generous."

"Emily told me that you're a good father."

"Did she also tell you what she charged in our custody battle?"

Myron nodded. "That you abused the kids."

"Not just abused them, Myron. *Sexually* abused them."

"She wanted to win."

"And that's an excuse?"

"No," Myron said. "It's deplorable."

"More than that," Greg said. "It's sick. You have no idea what Emily's capable of doing to get her way."

"For example?"

But Greg just shook his head and started up the car. "I'll ask you again: What can I do to help?"

"Nothing, Greg."

"No good. I'm not sitting around while my kid is dying, you understand?"

"I do."

"You have anything besides this name and address?"

"Nope."

"Fine," Greg said. "I'll drop you off at the train station. I'm staying up here and watching the house."

"You think the old man is lying?"

Greg shrugged. "Maybe he's just confused and forgot. Or maybe I'm wasting my time. But I got to do something."

Myron said nothing. Greg continued to drive.

"You'll call me if you hear something?" Greg asked.

"Sure."

During the train ride back to Manhattan, Myron thought about what Greg had said. About Emily. And about what she'd done—and what she'd do—to save her son.

11

Myron and Terese started out the next morning showering together. Myron controlled the temperature and kept the water hot. Prevents, er, shrinkage.

When they stepped out of the steamy stall, he helped Terese towel off.

"Thorough," she said.

"We're a full-service operation, ma'am." He toweled her off some more.

"One thing I notice when I shower with a man," Terese said.

"What's that?"

"My breasts always end up squeaky clean."

Win had left several hours ago. Lately he liked to get to the office by six. Overseas markets or something. Terese toasted a bagel while Myron fixed himself a bowl of cereal. Quisp cereal. They didn't have it in New York anymore, but Win had it shipped in from a place called Woodsman's in Wisconsin. Myron downed an industrial-size spoonful; the sugar rush came at him so fast he nearly ducked.

Terese said, "I have to go back tomorrow morning."

"I know."

He took another spoonful, feeling her eyes on him.

"Run away with me again," Terese said.

He glanced up at her. She looked smaller, farther away.

"I can get us the same house on the island. We can just hop on a plane and—"

"I can't," he interrupted.

"Oh," she said. Then: "You need to find this Davis Taylor?"

"Yes."

"I see. And after that . . . ?"

Myron shook his head. They ate some more in silence.

"I'm sorry," Myron said.

She nodded.

"Running away isn't always the answer, Terese."

"Myron?"

"What?"

"Do I look in the mood for platitudes?"

"I'm sorry."

"Yeah, you said that already."

"I'm just trying to help."

"Sometimes you can't help," she said. "Sometimes all that's left is running away."

"Not for me," he said.

"No," she agreed. "Not for you."

She wasn't angry or upset, just flat and resigned, and that scared him all the more.

An hour later Esperanza came into Myron's office without knocking.

"Okay," she began, grabbing a seat, "here's what we've got on Davis Taylor."

Myron leaned back and put his hands behind his head.

"One, he's never filed a tax return with the IRS."

"Never?"

"Glad you're paying attention," Esperanza said.

"Are you saying he's never shown any income?"

"Will you let me finish?"

"Sorry."

"Two, he has virtually no paperwork. No driver's license. One credit card, a Visa recently issued by his bank. It has very little activity. Only one bank account, with a current balance of under two hundred dollars."

"Suspicious," Myron said.

"Yes."

"When did he open the account?"

"Three months ago."

"And before that?"

"Nada. At least nada that I've been able to come up with so far."

Myron stroked his chin. "No one flies that far below the radar screen," he said. "It has to be an alias."

"I thought the same thing," Esperanza said.

"And?"

"The answer is yes and no." Myron waited for the explanation. Esperanza tucked some loose tresses behind both ears. "It appears to be a name change."

Myron frowned. "But we got his social security number, right?"

"Right."

"And most records are kept by social security number, not name, right?"

"Another right."

"So I don't get it," Myron said. "You can't change your social security number. A name change might make you harder to find, but it wouldn't wipe out your past. You'd still have tax returns and stuff like that."

Esperanza turned both palms upward. "That's what I mean by yes and no."

"There's no paperwork under the social security number either?"

"That's correct," Esperanza said.

Myron tried to digest this. "So what's Davis Taylor's real name?"

"I don't have it yet."

"I would have thought it'd be easy to locate."

"It would," she said, "if he had any records at all. But he doesn't. The social security number has no hits. It's as though this person hasn't done a thing in his whole life."

Myron thought about it. "Only one explanation," he said.

"That being?"

"A fake ID."

Esperanza shook her head. "The social security number exists."

"I don't doubt that. But I think someone pulled the classic tombstone-fake-ID trick."

"That being?"

"You go to a graveyard and find the tombstone of a dead child," Myron said. "Someone who would be about your age if he'd lived. Then you write and request his birth certificate and paperwork and *voilà*, you've set up the perfect fake ID. Oldest trick in the book."

Esperanza gave him the look she saved for his most idiotic moments. "No," she said.

"No?"

"You think the police don't watch TV, Myron? That doesn't work anymore. Hasn't worked in years, except maybe on cop shows. But just to make sure, I double-checked."

"How?"

"Death records," she said. "There's a Web site that has the social security numbers of all the deceased."

"And the number isn't there."

"Ding, ding, ding," Esperanza said.

Myron leaned forward. "This makes absolutely no sense," he said. "Our phony Davis Taylor has gone to a great deal of trouble to create this phony ID—or at least to fly below the radar, right?"

"Right."

"He wants no records, no paperwork, nothing."

"Right again."

"Even changes his name."

"You go, boy."

Myron put his arms out. "Then why would he sign up to be a bone marrow donor?"

"Myron?"

"Yeah."

"I don't know what you're talking about," Esperanza said.

True enough. He'd called last night and asked her to check out Davis Taylor. He had not yet told her why.

"I guess I owe you an explanation," he said.

She shrugged.

"I sort of promised you I wouldn't be doing this anymore," he said.

"Investigating," she said.

"Right. And I meant it. I wanted this to be a straight agency from now on."

She didn't respond. Myron glanced at the wall behind her. The sparse Client Wall again reminded him of a hair transplant that hadn't taken. Maybe he should paint on a couple of coats of Rogaine.

"You remember Emily's call?" he said.

"It was yesterday, Myron. My memory can sometimes go back a whole week."

He explained it all. Some men—men Myron grudgingly admired— keep it all inside, bury their secrets, hide the pain, the whole cliché. Myron rarely did. He was not one to walk down the mean streets alone—he liked Win to be his backup. He didn't grab a bottle of whiskey and drown his sorrows—he discussed them with Esperanza. Not very macho, but there you have it.

Esperanza stayed silent as he spoke. When he got to the part about being Jeremy's father, she let out a small groan and closed her eyes and kept them shut for a very long time. When she finally opened them, she asked, "So what are you going to do?"

"I'm going to find the donor."

"That's not what I meant."

He knew that. "I don't know," he said.

She thought about it, shook her head in disbelief. "You have a son."

"Seems so."

"And you don't know what you're going to do about it?"

"That's right."

"But you're leaning," she said.

"Win made a pretty good case for not saying anything."

She made a sound. "Win would."

"Actually he claims to be using his heart."

"If only he had one."

"You don't agree?"

"No," she said. "I don't agree."

"You think I should tell Jeremy?"

"I think first and foremost you should put aside your Batman complex," she said.

"What the hell does that mean?"

"It means you always try a little too hard to be heroic."

"And that's bad?"

"Sometimes it clouds your thinking," she said. "The heroic thing is not always the right thing."

"Jeremy already has a family. He has a mother and a father—"

"He has," Esperanza interrupted, "a lie."

They sat there and stared at each other. The phone, usually so active, was silent, as it had been for too long now. Myron wondered how he could explain it so that she would understand. She stayed still, waiting.

"We were both lucky when it came to parents," Myron said.

"Mine are dead, Myron."

"That's not what I mean," he said. He took a deep breath. "How many days pass that you don't still miss them?"

"None," she said without hesitation.

He nodded. "We were both loved unconditionally and we both loved our parents the same way."

Esperanza's eyes started misting. "So?"

"So—and this was what Win said—isn't that what makes a mother or father? Isn't it about who raised us and loved us and not simply an accident of biology?"

Esperanza leaned back. "Win said that?"

Myron smiled. "He has his moments."

"That he does," she said.

"And think about your father—the one who raised and loved you. What happens to him?"

Her eyes were still misty. "My love for him is strong enough to survive the truth. Isn't yours?"

He tilted back as though the words were jabs at his chin. "Sure," he said. "But it would still hurt him."

"Your father would be hurt?"

"Of course."

"I see," Esperanza said. "So now you're worried about poor Greg Downing?"

"Hardly. You want to hear something awful?"

"Love to."

"When Greg constantly refers to Jeremy as 'my son,' I want to yell out the truth. Right in his smug face. Just to see his reaction. Just to watch his world crumble."

"So much for your Batman complex," Esperanza said.

Myron held out his hands. "I have my moments too," he said.

Esperanza stood and headed for the door.

"Where you going?"

"I don't want to talk about this anymore," she said.

He sat back.

"You're blocking," she said. "You know that?"

He nodded slowly.

"When you move past it—and you will—we'll talk about it again. Otherwise, we're wasting our time here, okay?"

"Okay."

"Just don't be stupid."

" 'Don't be stupid,' " he repeated. "Check."

Her departing smile was brief.

12

Myron spent the rest of the day working the phones. He strapped on his Ultra Slim headset and paced the office. He talked up college coaches, mining for potential free agents. He touched base with his clients and listened to their problems, both real and imagined, therapist-style, which was a large part of his job. He sifted through his Rolodex of companies, trying to conjure up a few endorsement deals.

One serious lead came a-knocking on its own:

"Mr. Bolitar? I'm Ronny Angle from Rack Enterprises. Are you familiar with us?"

"You run a bunch of topless bars, right?"

"We prefer they be called upscale exotic nightclubs."

"And I prefer to be called a well-endowed stallion," Myron said. "What can I do for you, Mr. Angle?"

"Ronny please. Can I call you Myron?"

"Myron please."

"Great, Myron. Rack Enterprises is entering a new venture."

"Uh-huh."

"You've probably read about it. A chain of coffeehouses called La, La, Latte."

"For real?"

"Pardon?"

"Well, I think I did see something about this, but I figured it was a joke."

"It's no joke, Mr. Bolitar."

"So you guys are really going to open up topless coffee bars?"

"We prefer they be called upscale erotic coffee experiences."

"I see. But your, uh, *baristas* will be topless, correct?"

"Correct."

Myron thought about it. "Makes asking for milk something of a double entendre, don't you think?"

"That's very funny, Myron."

"Thanks, Ronny."

"We're going to open with a big splash."

"That another milk joke, Ronny?"

"No, Myron, but you're a pretty funny guy."

"Thanks, Ronny."

"Let me cut right to it, okay? We like Suzze T." Suzze T was Suzze Tamirino, a journeyman (or is it journeywoman?) on the pro tennis circuit. "We saw her picture in the *Sports Illustrated* swimsuit issue, and, well, we were very impressed. We'd like her to do a cameo for our grand opening."

Myron rubbed the bridge of his nose with his thumb and forefinger. "When you say cameo—"

"A brief performance."

"How brief?"

"No more than five minutes."

"I don't mean brief in terms of time. I mean in terms of clothing."

"We'd require full frontal nudity."

"Well, thanks for thinking of us, Ronny, but I don't think Suzze will be interested."

"We're offering two hundred thousand dollars."

Myron sat up. Easy to hang up, but with this kind of dough, he had a responsibility to follow up. "How about if she wears a small top?"

"No."

"A bikini?"

"No."

"An itsy-bitsy, teeny-weeny bikini?"

"Like in the song?"

"Exactly," Myron said. "Like in the song."

"I'm going to state this as plainly as I can," Ronny said. "There must be nipple visibility."

"Nipple visibility?"

"This point is nonnegotiable."

"So to speak."

Myron promised to call him back later in the week. The two men hung up. Negotiating nipple visibility. What a business.

Esperanza came in without knocking. Her eyes were wide and bright. "Lamar Richardson is on line one," she said.

"Lamar himself?"

She nodded.

"No relative or personal manager or favorite astrologer?"

"Lamar himself," Esperanza repeated.

They both nodded. This was a good thing.

Myron picked up the phone. "Hello."

"Let's meet," Lamar said.

"Sure," Myron said.

"When?"

"You name it."

"When are you free?"

"You name it," Myron said.

"I'm in Detroit right now."

"I'll catch the next plane out."

"Just like that?" Lamar said.

"Yup."

"Shouldn't you pretend you're really busy?"

"We going to date, Lamar?"

Lamar chuckled. "No, I don't think so."

"Then I'll skip the playing-hard-to-get stage. Esperanza and I want you to sign up with MB SportsReps. We'll do a good job. We'll make you a priority. And we won't play mind games with you."

Myron smiled at Esperanza. Was he good or what?

Lamar said he was going to be in Manhattan later in the week and would like to meet then. They set up a time. Myron hung up. He and Esperanza sat there and smiled at each other.

"We have a chance," she said.

"Yep."

"So what's our strategy?"

"I thought I'd impress him with my nimble mind," he said.

"Hmm," Esperanza said. "Maybe I should wear something low cut."

"I was kinda counting on that."

"Hit him with brains and beauty."

"Yes," Myron said. "But which one of us is which?"

When Myron got back to the Dakota, Win was heading out with his leather gym bag and Terese was gone.

"She left a note," Win said, handing it to Myron.

Had to go back early. I'll call.
   Terese

Myron read the note again. It didn't change. He folded it up and put it away.

"You going to Master Kwon's?" Myron asked. Master Kwon was their martial arts instructor.

Win nodded. "He's been asking for you."

"What did you tell him?" Myron asked.

"That you wigged out."

"Thanks."

Win gave a slight bow and lifted his gym bag. "May I make a suggestion?"

"Shoot."

"You haven't been to the *dojang* in a long while."

"I know."

"You have a great deal of stress in your life," Win said. "You need an outlet. You need some focus. Some balance. Some structure."

"You're not going to make me snatch a pebble from your hand, are you?"

"Not today, no. But come with me."

Myron shrugged. "I'll grab my stuff."

They were halfway out the door when Esperanza called. He told her they were just on their way out.

"Where?" she asked.

"Master Kwon's."

"I'll meet you there."

"Why? What's up?"

"I got some information on Davis Taylor."

"And?"

"And it's more than a little strange. Is Win going with you?"

"Yes."

"Ask him if he knows anything about Raymond Lex's family."

Silence. "Raymond Lex is dead, Esperanza."

"Duh, Myron. I said *family*."

"This has something to do with Davis Taylor?"

"It'll be easier to explain in person. I'll see you down there in an hour."

She hung up.

One of the doormen had already fetched Win's Jag. It sat waiting for them on Central Park West. The rich. Myron settled into the lush leather. Win hit the accelerator pad. He was big with the accelerator pad; he had a bit more trouble when it came to the brake.

"Do you know Raymond Lex's family?"

"They used to be clients," Win said.

"You're kidding?"

"Oh yes, I'm a regular Red Buttons."

"Were you directly involved in this inheritance squabble?"

"Calling this a squabble would be similar to calling nuclear Armageddon a campfire."

"Hard to divide up billions, huh?"

"Indeed. So why are we discussing the Lex clan?"

"Esperanza is going to meet us down at the *dojang*. She has some information on Davis Taylor. Somehow the Lex family is connected."

Win arched his eyebrow. "The plot doth thicken."

"So tell me a little about them."

"Most of it was in the media. Raymond Lex writes a controversial bestseller called *Midnight Confessions*. Said bestseller becomes an Oscar-winning blockbuster. Suddenly he goes from obscure junior-college instructor to millionaire. Unlike most of his artistic brethren, he understands business. He invests and amasses private holdings with a substantial yet confidential net worth."

"The papers place it in the billions."

"I won't argue."

"That's a lot of money."

"The way you word things," Win said. "It's like Proust."

"He never wrote another book?"

"No."

"Odd."

"Not really," Win said. "Harper Lee and Margaret Mitchell never wrote another book. And at least Lex kept busy. It's hard to build one of the largest privately held corporations and do book signings."

"So now that he's dead, his family is—how to say it?—nuclear Armageddoning?"

"Close enough."

Master Kwon had moved his headquarters and main *dojang* into the second floor of a building on Twenty-third Street near Broadway. Five rooms—studios really—with hardwood floors, mirrored walls, high-tech sound system, sleek and shiny Nautilus equipment—oh, and some of those rice-paper Oriental scroll-posters. Gave the place a real Old World Asia feel.

Myron and Win slipped into their *dobok*, a white uniform, and tied their black belts. Myron had been studying tae kwon do and *hapkido* since Win had first introduced him to them in college, but he hadn't been to a *dojang* more than five times in the past three years. Win, on the other hand, remained devoutly lethal. Don't tug on Superman's cape, don't spit in the wind, don't pull the mask off the ol' Lone Ranger, and you don't mess around with Win. Bah, bah, dee, dee, dee, dee, dee.

Master Kwon was in his mid-seventies but could easily pass for two decades younger. Win had met him during his Asian travels when he was fifteen. As near as Myron could tell, Master Kwon had been a high priest or some such thing at a small Buddhist monastery straight out of a Hong Kong revenge flick. When Master Kwon emigrated to the United States, he spoke very little English. Now, some twenty years later, he spoke almost none. As soon as the wise master hit our shores, he opened up a chain of state-of-the-art tae kwon do schools—with Win's financial backing, of course. Once he saw the *Karate Kid* movies, Master Kwon started playing the old wise man to the hilt. His English disappeared. He started dressing like the Dalai Lama and began every sentence with the words "Confucius say," ignoring the small fact that he was Korean and Confucius was Chinese.

Win and Myron headed to Master Kwon's office. At the entrance, both men bowed deeply.

"Please in," Master Kwon said.

The desk was fine oak, the chair rich leather and orthopedic looking. Master Kwon was standing near a corner. He held a putter in his hands and wore a splendidly tailored suit. His face brightened when he saw Myron, and the two men embraced.

When they broke apart, Master Kwon said, "You better?"

"Better," Myron agreed.

The old man smiled and grabbed his own lapel. "Armani," he said.

"I thought so," Myron said.

"You like?"

"Very nice."

Satisfied, Master Kwon said, "Go."

Win and Myron bowed deeply. Once in the *dojang*, they fell into their customary roles: Win led and Myron followed. They started with meditation. Win loved meditating, as we already graphically witnessed. He sat in the lotus position, palms tilted up, hands resting on knees, back straight, tongue folded against the upper teeth. He breathed in through his nose, forcing the air down, letting his abdomen do all the work. Myron tried to duplicate—had been trying for years—but he had never quite gotten the hang of it. His mind, even during less chaotic times, wandered. His bad knee tightened. He got fidgety.

They cut down the stretching to only ten minutes. Again Win was effortless, executing splits and toe touches and deep bends with ease, his bones and joints as flexible as a politician's voting record. Myron had never been a naturally limber guy. When he was training seriously, he could touch his toes and complete a hurdle stretch with little problem. But just then, that felt like a long time ago.

"I'm already sore," Myron said through a grunt.

Win tilted his head. "Odd."

"What?"

"That's precisely what my date said last night."

"You weren't kidding before," Myron said. "You really are another Red Buttons."

They did a little sparring, and Myron immediately realized how out of shape he was. Sparring is the most tiring activity in the world. Don't believe it? Find a punching bag and pretend-box with it for one three-minute round. Just a bag that can't fight back. Try it, just one round. You'll see.

When Esperanza came in, the sparring mercifully ceased and Myron grabbed his knees, sucking wind. He bowed to Win, threw a towel over his shoulder, grabbed some Evian. Esperanza folded her arms and waited. A group of students walked past the door, saw Esperanza, did a double take.

Esperanza handed Myron a sheet of paper. "The birth certificate of Davis Taylor né Dennis Lex."

"Lex," Myron repeated. "As in . . . ?"

"Yep."

Myron scanned the photocopy. According to the document, Dennis Lex would be thirty-seven years old. His father was listed as one Raymond Lex, his mother as Maureen Lehman Lex. Born in East Hampton, New York.

Myron handed it to Win.

"They had another child?"

"Apparently so," Esperanza said.

Myron looked at Win. Win shrugged.

"He must have died young," Win said.

"If he did," Esperanza said, "I can't find it anywhere. There's no death certificate."

"No one in the family ever mentioned another child?" Myron asked Win.

"No one," Win said.

He turned back to Esperanza. "What else you got?"

"Not much. Dennis Lex changed his name to Davis Taylor eight months ago. I also found this." She handed him a photocopy of a news clipping. A small birth announcement from the *Hampton Gazette* dated thirty-seven years ago:

Raymond and Maureen Lex of Wister Drive in East Hampton are delighted to announce the birth of their son, Dennis, six pounds eight ounces on June 18th. Dennis joins his sister Susan and his brother Bronwyn.

Myron shook his head. "How could no one know about this?"

"It's not all that surprising," Win said.

"How do you figure?"

"None of the Lex family holdings are public. They are fiercely protective of their privacy. Security around them is around-the-clock and the best money can buy. Everyone who works with them must sign confidentiality agreements."

"Even you?"

"I don't do confidentiality agreements," Win said. "No matter how much money is involved."

"So they never asked you to sign one?"

"They asked. I refused. We parted ways."

"You gave them up as clients?"

"Yes."

"Why? I mean, what would have been the big deal? You keep everything confidential anyway."

"Exactly. Clients hire me not only because of my brilliance in the ways of finance but because I am the very model of discretion."

"Don't overlook your startling modesty," Myron added.

"I don't need to sign a contract saying I won't reveal anything. It should be a given. It's the equivalent of signing a document saying that I won't burn down their house."

Myron nodded. "Nice analogy," he said.

"Yes, thank you, but I'm trying to illustrate how far this family will go to maintain their privacy. Until this inheritance feud erupted, the media had no idea how extensive Raymond Lex's holdings were."

"But come on, Win. This is Raymond Lex's son. You'd know about a son."

Win pointed to the top of the clipping. "Notice when the child was born—*before* Raymond Lex's book came out, when Lex was just a typical small-town professor. It wouldn't make news."

"You really buy that?"

"Do you have a better explanation?"

"So where is the kid now? How can the son of one of America's wealthiest families have no paperwork? No credit cards, no driver's license, no IRS filings, no trail at all? Why did he change his name?"

"The last one is easy," Win said.

"Oh?"

"He's hiding."

"From?"

"His siblings perhaps," Win said. "As I said before, this inheritance battle is rather nasty."

"That might make sense—and I stress the word 'might'—if he'd been around before. But how can there be no paperwork on him? What is he hiding from? And why on earth would he put his name in the bone marrow registry?"

"Good questions," Win said.

"Very good," Esperanza added.

Myron reread the article and looked at his two friends. "Nice to have a consensus," he said.

13

The mobile phone blew him out of his sleep like a shotgun blast. Myron's hand reached up blindly, his fingers bouncing along the night table until they located the phone.

"Hello?" he croaked.

"Is this Myron Bolitar?"

The voice was a whisper.

"Who is this?" Myron asked.

"You called me."

Still whispering, the sound like leaves skittering across pavement.

Myron sat upright, his heartbeat picking up a little steam. "Davis Taylor?"

"Sow the seeds. Keep sowing. And open the shades. Let the truth come in. Let the secrets finally wither in the daylight."

Ooookay. "I need your help, Mr. Taylor."

"Sow the seeds."

"Yes, of course, we'll sow away." Myron flicked on the light. 2:17 A.M. He checked the LCD display on the phone. The Caller ID was blocked. Damn. "But we have to meet."

"Sow the seeds. It's the only way."

"I understand, Mr. Taylor. Can we meet?"

"Someone must sow the seeds. And someone must unlock the chains."

"I'll bring a key. Just tell me where you are."

"Why do you wish to see me?"

What to say? "It's a matter of life and death."

"Whenever you sow the seeds, it's a matter of life and death."

"You donated blood for a bone marrow drive. You're a match. A young boy will die if you don't help."

Silence.

"Mr. Taylor?"

"Technology cannot help him. I thought you were one of us." Still whispering but sad now.

"I am. Or at least I want to be—"

"I'm hanging up now."

"No, wait—"

"Good-bye."

"Dennis Lex," Myron said.

Silence, except for the sound of breathing. Myron wasn't sure if the sound was coming from him or the caller.

"Please," Myron said. "I'll do whatever you ask. But we have to meet."

"Will you remember to sow the seeds?"

Small chunks of ice dropped down his back.

"Yes," Myron said, "I'll remember."

"Good. Then you know what you must do."

Myron gripped the receiver. "No," he said. "What must I do?"

"The boy," the voice whispered. "Say one last good-bye to the boy."

14

Sow the seeds?" Esperanza said.

They were in Myron's office. The morning sun striped the floor with Venetian slits, two cutting across Esperanza's face. She didn't seem to mind.

"Right," Myron said. "And something about that phrase keeps gnawing at me."

"It was a Tears for Fears song," Esperanza said.

" 'Sowing the Seeds of Love.' I remember."

"Wasn't that the name of the tour too? We saw them at the Meadowlands in, what, 1988?"

"Eighty-nine."

"What happened to those guys?"

"They broke up," Myron said.

"Why do they all do that?"

"Got me."

"Supertramp, Steely Dan, the Doobie Brothers—"

"Not to mention Wham."

"They break up and then they never make anything decent on their own. They flounder around and end up a segment of VH-1's *Where Are They Now?*"

"We're getting off the subject."

Esperanza handed him a slip of paper. "Here's the office number for Susan Lex, Dennis's older sister."

Myron read the number like it was in code and might mean something. "I had another thought."

"What's that?"

"If Dennis Lex exists, then he had to have gone to school, right?"

"Maybe."

"So let's see if we can find out where the Children Lex schooled—public, private, whatever."

Esperanza frowned. "You mean like college?"

"Start there, yes. Not that siblings go to the same school, but maybe they did. Or maybe they all went to Ivy League schools. Something like that. You might want to start with high school. It's more likely that they all went to the same one."

"And if I don't find any record of him in high school?"

"Go back even further."

She crossed her legs, folded her arms. "How far?"

"As far as you can."

"And what good will this exercise in futility do us?"

"I want to know when Dennis Lex fell off the radar screen. Did people know him in high school? In college? In grad school?"

She did not look impressed. "And assuming I somehow manage to find, say, his elementary school, what exactly is that going to do for us?"

"Damn if I know. I'm grasping at straws here."

"No, you're asking *me* to grasp at straws."

"Then don't do it, Esperanza, okay? It was just a thought."

"Nah," she said with a wave of her hand. "You may be right."

Myron put his palms on his desk, arched his back, looked left, looked right, looked up, looked down.

"What?" she said.

"You said I may be right. I'm waiting for the world as we know it to end."

"Good one," Esperanza said, standing. "I'll see what I can dig up."

She left the room. Myron picked up the telephone and dialed Susan Lex's number. The receptionist transferred the call, and a woman identifying herself as Ms. Lex's secretary picked it up. She had a voice like a steel-wool tire over gravel.

"Ms. Lex does not see people she doesn't know."

"It's a matter of grave importance," Myron said.

"Perhaps you did not hear me the first time." Classic Battle-ax. "Ms. Lex does not see people she doesn't know."

"Tell her it's about Dennis."

"Excuse me?"

"Just tell her that."

Battle-ax put Myron on hold without another word. Myron listened to a Muzak version of Al Stewart's "Time Passages." Myron had thought the original was Muzak-y enough, thank you very much.

The battle-ax came back with a snap. "Ms. Lex does not see people she doesn't know."

"I've been thinking about that, but it doesn't really make sense."

"Excuse me?"

"I mean, at some time she must see people she doesn't know—otherwise she'd never meet anybody new. And if we follow my logic, how did you ever get to see her for the first time? She was willing to see you before she knew you, right?"

"I'm hanging up now, Mr. Bolitar."

"Tell her I know about Dennis."

"I just—"

"Tell her if she doesn't agree to see me, I'll go to the press."

Silence. "Hold." A click and then the Muzak came back on. Time passed. So, mercifully, did "Time Passages," replaced by the Alan Parsons Project's "Time." Myron nearly slipped into a coma.

Battle-ax returned. "Mr. Bolitar?"

"Yes?"

"Ms. Lex will give you five minutes of her time. I have an opening on the fifteenth of next month."

"No good," Myron said. "It has to be today."

"Ms. Lex is a very busy woman."

"Today," Myron said.

"That simply will not be possible."

"At eleven. If I'm not let in, I go immediately to the press."

"You're being terribly rude, Mr. Bolitar."

"To the press," Myron repeated. "Do you understand?"

"Yes."

"Will you be there?"

"What possible difference could that make?"

"All this sexual tension is driving me batty. Maybe afterward we could get together for a nice cool latte."

He heard the phone go click and smiled. The charm, he thought. It's baaaaack.

Esperanza buzzed in. "Topless tennis, anyone?"

"What?"

"I got Suzze T on line one."

He hit a button. "Hey, Suzze."

"Hey, Myron, what's shaking?"

"I got an offer for you to refuse."

"You mean you're going to hit on me?"

The charm suffers a setback. "Where are you going to be this afternoon?"

"Same place as now," she said. "The Morning Mosh. You know it?"
"No."

She gave him the address, and Myron agreed to meet her there in a few hours. He hung up the phone and leaned back.

" 'Sow the seeds,' " he said out loud.

He stared at the wall. An hour to kill before he headed over to the Lex Building on Fifth Avenue. He could sit here and think about life and maybe contemplate his navel. No, too much of that already. He swiveled his seat to the computer, double-clicked the proper icon, connected to the Net. He tried Yahoo first and typed *sow the seeds* into the search field. Only one hit: a Web site for the San Francisco League of Urban Gardeners. They went by the acronym SLUG. Tough guys probably. A gang. Probably wore green bandannas and engaged in drive-by waterings.

He tried Alta Vista's search engine next, but they listed 2,501 Web pages. It was kinda like Goldilocks and the Three Bears. Yahoo's search was toooo small. Alta Vista's was toooo big. They didn't have LEXIS–NEXIS at the office, but Myron tried a less powerful media engine. He typed in the same three words and pressed the return key, and bammo.

http://www.nyherald.com/archives/9800322

Myron hit the link and the article came up:

New York Herald
THE MIND OF TERROR—YOUR DARKEST FEAR
by Stan Gibbs

Whoa, hold the phone. Myron knew the name. Stan Gibbs had been a big-time newspaper columnist, the kind of guy who regularly pontificated (read: pimped) on the cable news talk shows, though he'd been less annoying than most, which is like saying syphilis is less annoying than gonorrhea. But that had all been before the scandal gutted him like Ted Nugent over a fallen moose. Myron read:

The phone call comes out of the blue.
"What is your darkest fear?" the voice whispers. "Close your eyes now and picture it. Can you see it? Do you have it yet? The very worst agony you can imagine?"
After a long pause, I say, "Yes."
"Good. Now imagine something worse, something far, far worse . . ."

Myron took a deep breath. He remembered the series of articles. Stan Gibbs had broken a story about a bizarre kidnapper. He'd told the heart-wrenching tale of three abductions that the police had supposedly wanted to keep quiet, out of, Stan Gibbs claimed, embarrassment. No names were mentioned. He had spoken with the families under the condition of anonymity. And, the coup de grâce, the kidnapper had granted Gibbs access:

> I ask the kidnapper why he does it. Is it for the ransom?
>
> "I never pick up the ransom money," he says. "I usually leave explosives at the spot and burn it. But sometimes money helps me sow the seeds. That is what I'm trying to do. Sow the seeds."

Myron felt his blood stop.

> "You all think you're safe," he continues, "in your technological cocoon. But you're not. Technology has made us expect easy answers and happy endings. But with me, there is no answer and there is no end."
>
> He has kidnapped at least four people: the father of two young children, age 41; a female college student, age 20; and a young couple, newlyweds ages 28 and 27. All were abducted while in the New York City area.
>
> "The idea," he says, "is to keep the terror going. Let it grow, not with gore or obvious bloodletting, but with your own imagination. Technology is trying to destroy our ability to imagine. But when someone you love is taken away, your mind can conjure up horrors darker than any machine—than anything even I can do. Some minds won't go that far. Some minds stop and put up a barrier. My job is to push them through that barrier."
>
> I ask him how he does that.
>
> "Sow the seeds," he repeats. "You sow the seeds over time."
>
> He explains that sowing the seeds means giving hope and taking it away over a sustained period of time. His first call to the victim's family is naturally devastating, but merely the beginning of a long and torturous ordeal.
>
> He begins the call, he claims, with a normal hello and asks the family member to please hold. After a pause, the family member hears their loved one give a blood-curdling shriek. "Just one," he says, "and it's very short. I cut them off in mid-scream.
>
> "This is the last they'll ever hear from their loved one," he continues. "Imagine how that scream echoes."
>
> But for the victim's family, it does not end there. He demands a ransom that he has no intention of claiming. He calls after midnight and asks

the family to imagine their darkest fear. He convinces them that this time, he will really let their loved one go, but he is only extending hope to those who no longer have it, rekindling their agony.

"Time and hope," he says, "sow the seeds of despair."

The father of two has been missing for three years. The young premed college student has been missing for twenty-seven months. The newly-weds were married almost two years ago this weekend. To date, not a trace of any of them has been found. Rarely does a week pass when the families don't get a call from their tormentor.

When I ask him if his victims are alive or dead, he is coy. "Death is closure," he explains, "and closure stops the sowing."

He wants to talk about society, how computers and technology are doing our thinking for us, how what he does lets us see the power of the human brain.

"That is where God exists," he says. "That is where all things valuable exist. True bliss can only be found inside of you. The meaning of life is not in your new home entertainment system or sports car. People must see their limitless potential. How do you make them see? Right now imagine what these families are going through."

His voice soft, he invites me to try.

"Technology could never conjure up the horrors you are now imagining. Sow the seeds. Sowing the seeds shows us the potential."

Myron's heart pounded in big thuds. He sat back, shook his head, started reading again. The crazed kidnapper ranted on, his theories feverishly demented, sort of Symbionese Liberation Army by way of Ted Kaczynski. Stan Gibbs's column continued into the next day's paper. Myron hit the link and read on. During the second day, Gibbs opened with some heartbreaking quotes from the family of the victims. Then he questioned the kidnapper some more:

I ask him how he has managed to keep these kidnappings out of the media.

"By sowing the seeds," he repeats yet again.

I ask for an example.

"I tell his wife to go to the garage and open the red Stanley toolbox on the third shelf. I tell her to pick out the black pliers with the bubble grip. Then I send her to the basement. I tell her to stand in front of the Mission chair they bought the previous summer at that tag sale on the Cape. Imagine, I say, your husband tied naked to that chair. Imagine those pliers in my hand. And finally, imagine what I'll do if I see anything about him in the newspaper."

But he does not stop there.

"I ask her about the children. I mention their names. I mention their schools and their teachers and their favorite breakfast cereal."

I ask him how he knows these things.

His answer is simple. "Daddy tells me."

Myron fell back. "Jesus," he uttered.

Deep breaths, he told himself again. In and out. That's it. Think it through. Slowly now. Carefully. Okay, first off: Horrible as this is, what does it have to do with Davis Taylor né Dennis Lex? Probably nothing. The worst sort of long shot. And again, horrible as this is, Myron knew that there was more to the story. More—and in a sense, less.

The Gibbs columns drew weeks' worth of nationwide attention and criticism—until, Myron remembered, it all blew up in the most public way possible. What had happened exactly? Myron hit some keys and clicked the mouse. He started a search of articles where Stan Gibbs was the subject. They came up in date order:

FEDS DEMAND GIBBS'S SOURCE

The Federal Bureau of Investigation, which in recent weeks has been denying the allegations listed in Stan Gibbs's columns, took a new tack today. They demanded his notes and information.

Dan Conway, a spokesman for the FBI, began by saying, "We know nothing about these crimes," then added, "But if Mr. Gibbs is being truthful, he has important information on a possible serial kidnapper and killer, perhaps even harboring or aiding him. We have a right to that information."

Stan Gibbs, a popular columnist and television journalist, has refused to reveal his sources. "I'm not protecting a killer here," Mr. Gibbs said. "The families of the victims as well as the perpetrator of the crimes spoke to me under the strict condition of confidentiality. It's a cry as old as our country: I will not reveal my sources."

The *New York Herald* and American Civil Liberties Union have already denounced the FBI and plan on backing Mr. Gibbs. The judge has ordered the case sealed from the public.

Myron read on. The arguments on both sides were pretty standard. Gibbs's attorneys naturally wrapped themselves in the First Amendment, while the feds equally naturally countered that the First Amendment was not an absolute, that you can't yell "Fire!" in a crowded theater, and that freedom of expression does not include protecting possible criminals.

The country also argued the issue. It played well on CNBC and MSNBC and CNN and a bunch of other cable letters, lighting up the phone lines like a radio giveaway. The judge was about to render a verdict when the whole story exploded in a way no one expected.

Myron hit the link:

GIBBS FIBS?
Reporter accused of plagiarism

Myron read the endgame shocker: Someone had found a mystery novel published by a tiny press with a minuscule print run in 1978. The novel, *Whisper to a Scream*, by F. K. Armstrong, closely mirrored Gibbs's story. Too closely. Certain snippets of dialogue were pretty much copied verbatim. The crimes in the novel—kidnappings with no resolution—were too similar to what Gibbs had written to be dismissed as coincidence.

The plagiaristic spectres of Mike Barnicle and Patricia Smith and the like rose from the grave and would not disperse. Heads rolled. There were resignations and hand-wringing. For his part, Stan Gibbs refused to comment, which didn't look good. Gibbs ended up "taking a leave of absence," a modern-day euphemism for *getting fired*. The ACLU issued an ambiguous statement and retreated. The *New York Herald* quietly retracted the story, saying that the matter "was under internal review."

After some time passed, Myron reached for the phone and dialed.

"News desk. Bruce Taylor speaking."

"How about meeting me for a drink?"

"I know this is out nowadays, Myron, but I'm strictly hetero."

"I have the ability to change you."

"I don't think so, pal."

"Several women I've dated started out hetero," Myron said. "But one date with me and whammo, they switched teams."

"I love it when you're self-deprecating, Myron. It's just so real."

"So what do you say?"

"I'm on deadline."

"You're always on deadline."

"You buying?"

"To quote my brethren during Passover seders, why should this night be different from any other night?"

"I buy sometimes."

"Do you even own a wallet?"

"Hey, I'm not the one asking for favors," Bruce said. "Four o'clock. The Rusty Umbrella."

15

The Lex Building's wrought-iron gates lined a Fifth Avenue façade with vegetation so dense you wouldn't see light through it if a supernova burst on the other side. The famed edifice was a converted Manhattan mansion with a European courtyard and a regal art deco exterior and enough security to handle a Tyson boxing match. The building had wonderful old lines and detailed Venetian touches, except that for the sake of privacy, the windows had been converted into the smoky-limo variety. It made for a distracting and unnatural mix.

Four blue-blazered, gray-slacked guards stood at the entrance—real guards, Myron noted, with cop eyes and KGB facial tics, not the rent-a-uniforms you saw at department stores or airports. The four of them stood silently, eyeing Myron like he was wearing a tube top in the Vatican.

One of the guards stepped forward. "May I see some ID please?"

Myron took out his wallet and showed him a credit card and driver's license.

"There's no photo on the driver's license," the guard said.

"New Jersey doesn't require them."

"I need a photo ID."

"I have my picture on my health club membership card."

Cop-patient sigh. "That won't do, sir. Do you have a passport?"

"In midtown Manhattan?"

"Yes, sir. For the purposes of ID."

"No," Myron said. "Besides, it's a terrible picture. Doesn't fully capture the radiant blue in my eyes." Myron batted them for emphasis.

"Wait here, sir."

He waited. The other three guards frowned, crossed their arms, studied him as though he might start drinking from a toilet. Myron heard a whirring noise and looked up. A security camera was on him now, focusing in. Myron waved, smiled into the lens, performed a few flexes he had picked up from watching he-man events on ESPN 2. He ended with a pretty dramatic back lat spread and waved to the appreciative crowd. The blue-blazers looked unimpressed.

"All natural," Myron said. "I've never taken steroids."

No replies.

The first guard came back. "Follow me, please."

Stepping into the courtyard was like stepping into C. S. Lewis's wardrobe, another world, the other side of the shrubbery, so to speak. Here in the middle of Manhattan, the street noises were suddenly very far away, muted. The garden was lush, the tile walkways forming a pattern not unlike an Oriental carpet. There was a spouting fountain in the middle with a statue of a horse rearing back its head.

A new set of blue-blazers greeted him by the ornate front door. This place, Myron thought, must rack up a hell of a dry-cleaning bill. They made him empty his pockets, confiscated his cell phone, frisked him by hand, ran a metal wand over his person so thoroughly he almost asked for a condom, walked him through a metal detector twice, again frisked him with a little too much gusto.

"If you touch my wee-wee one more time," Myron said, "I'm telling my mommy."

More no replies. Maybe the Lexes demanded not only confidentiality but a discriminating sense of humor.

"Follow me, sir," the talking blue-blazer said.

The stillness of the place—a building in the middle of Manhattan, for chrissake—was unnerving, the only sound now the steady echo of their footsteps against the cool marble. It was like walking through an old museum at night, the whole experience like something out of *From the Mixed-up Files of Mrs. Basil E. Frankweiler*. The guards formed a poor man's presidential motorcade—the talking blue-blazer and a buddy three paces in front of him, two other blue-blazers three paces back. Just for fun, Myron would slow down or speed up and watch the guards do likewise. Like a really bad line dance, which was something of a redundancy. At one point he almost did a moonwalk, à la Michael Jackson, but these guys were already viewing him as a potential pedophile.

The mahogany staircase was wide and smelled a bit like lemon Pledge. There were enormous tapestries on the wall, the kind with swords and horses and hedonistic feasts of suckling pig. There were two more blue-blazers on the second floor. Now it was their turn to inspect Myron as though they'd never seen a man before. Myron twirled for their benefit. They too seemed unimpressed.

"You should have seen me flex before," Myron said.

The double doors opened and Myron entered a room slightly larger than a sports arena. Two guards followed him and took up positions in the back corners. There was a big man sitting to the right in a wing chair. At least he looked big in the chair. Or maybe the chair was tiny. The man was probably in his mid-forties. His head and neck formed a near-perfect trapezoid, the top buzzed into a military crew cut. He had a flat nose and ham-hock hands and knockwurst fingers. Ex-boxer or ex-marine or probably both. A man of ninety-degree angles and granite blocks.

Granite Man gave Myron more hard eyes, though his were more relaxed, as though Myron amused him in the way a little kitty nipping at his pant leg might. He didn't stand, choosing instead to stare at Myron and crack his knuckles one at a time.

Myron looked at Granite Man. Granite Man cracked another knuckle.

"Shiver," Myron said.

No one asked him to take a seat. Hell, no one spoke. Myron stood there and waited with the three sets of eyes weighing on him.

"Okay," Myron said. "I'm intimidated. Can we get past this, please?"

Granite Man nodded at the two blazers. They both left. Almost simultaneously, a door on the other side of the room opened and two women appeared. They were pretty far away, but Myron guessed that the first one was Susan Lex. Her hair was done up in an impossibly neat, semi-shellacked bun, and her lips were pursed as if she'd just swallowed a live beetle. The other woman—she looked no more than eighteen or nineteen—had to be her daughter, a carbon copy with the same pursed lips and twenty-five years less wear and tear, not to mention better hair.

Myron started to cross the room with his hand extended, but Susan Lex held up her palm in a stop gesture. Granite Man sat forward, nearly leaning into Myron's path. He gave Myron a small shake of the head, which was no easy task when you have no neck. Myron stayed where he was.

"I don't like being threatened," Susan Lex called from across the room.

"I apologize for that. But I had to see you."

"And that makes it right to threaten and blackmail me?"

Myron had no quick answer to that. "I need to talk to you about your brother Dennis."

"So you said on the phone."

"Where is he?"

Susan Lex looked at Granite Man. Granite Man frowned and cracked his knuckles again. "Just like that, Mr. Bolitar?" Susan Lex said. "You call my office. You threaten me. You insist I alter my schedule to accommodate you. And then you come in here and make demands?"

"I don't mean to be abrupt," Myron said. "But this is a matter of life and death."

Whenever he said "a matter of life and death," he expected to hear that melodramatic *dum-dum-duuuummm* music.

"That's hardly an explanation," Susan Lex said.

"Your brother registered with the national bone marrow center," Myron said. "His marrow matched a sick child's." After the creepy say-good-bye-to-the-boy conversation last night, Myron had decided to stop being gender specific. "Without that transplant, the child will die."

Susan Lex arched an eyebrow. The rich are really good at that, at arching eyebrows without altering anything else on their face. Myron wondered if they learned it at rich-people summer camp. Susan Lex looked at Granite Man again. Granite Man was trying to smile now. "You're mistaken, Mr. Bolitar," she said.

Myron waited for her to say more. When she didn't, he said, "Mistaken how?"

"If you're telling the truth, you've made a mistake. I will say no more."

"With all due deference," Myron said, "that's not good enough."

"It will have to be."

"Where is your brother, Ms. Lex?"

"Please leave, Mr. Bolitar."

"I can still go to the press."

Granite Man crossed his legs and started cracking his knuckles again.

Myron turned to him. "Yes, but can you do this?" Myron patted his head with one hand and rubbed his belly with the other.

Granite Man didn't like that one.

"Look," Myron said, "I don't want to cause any trouble here. You're private people. I understand that. But I need to find this donor."

"It's not my brother," Susan Lex said.

"Then where is he?"

"He's not your donor. More than that is none of your concern."

"Does the name Davis Taylor mean anything to you?"

Susan Lex repursed the lips as though a fresh beetle had sneaked through. She turned and walked out. Her daughter did likewise. Again on cue, the door behind Myron opened and the two blue-blazers filled it. More glares. They stepped fully into the room. Granite Man finally stood, which took some time. He was indeed big. Very big.

The men approached Myron.

"Let's go to the judges," Myron said. "Charles Nelson Reilly, your score?"

Granite Man stepped in front of him, shoulders square, eyes calm.

"The not introducing yourself," Myron said, doing his best Charles Nelson Reilly lisp, which was not very good. "I thought that was really very macho. And that whole silent persona combined with the amused glare. Very nicely done, really. Professional. But—and here's where you kinda lost me—the knuckle cracking, well, Gene, that was overkill, don't you think? Overall score: an 8. Comment: stick with the subtle."

Granite Man said, "You finished?"

"Yes."

"Myron Bolitar. Born in Livingston, New Jersey. Mother Ellen, father Al—"

"They like to be called El-Al," Myron interjected. "Like the Israeli airline."

"Basketball All-American at Duke University. Picked eighth in the NBA draft by the Boston Celtics. Blew out your knee in your first preseason game, ending your career. Currently owns MB SportsReps, a sports representation firm. Dated the novelist Jessica Culver since you graduated college, but you two recently parted ways. Should I go on?"

"You left off the part about my being a snazzy dancer. I can demonstrate if you like."

Granite Man smirked. "You want my score on you now?"

"Suit yourself."

"You wisecrack too much," Granite Man said. "I know you do it to look confident, but you're trying too hard. And since you raised the issue of subtlety, your story about a dying kid needing a bone marrow transplant was touching. The only thing missing was the string quartet."

"You don't believe me?"

"No, I don't believe you."

"So why am I here, then?"

Granite Man spread his satellite-dishes excuse for hands. "That's what I'd like to know."

The three men formed a triangle, Granite in front, the two blue-blazers in back. Granite made a small nod. One of the blazers produced a gun and aimed at Myron's head.

This was not good.

There are ways of disarming a man with a gun, but there's an inherent problem: It might not work. If you miscalculate or if your opponent is better than you think—something not unlikely in an opponent who knows how to handle a gun—you could get shot. That's a serious drawback. And in this particular situation there were two other opponents, both of whom looked good and were probably armed. There is a word expert fighters use for a sudden move at this juncture: *suicide*.

"Whoever did your research on me left something out," Myron said.

"What might that be?"

"My relationship with Win."

Granite Man didn't flinch. "You mean Windsor Horne Lockwood the Third? Family owns Lock-Horne Security and Investments on Park Avenue. Your college roommate from Duke. Since moving out of the Spring Street loft you shared with Jessica Culver, you've been living at his apartment in the Dakota. You have close business and personal ties, might even be called best friends. That relationship?"

"That would be the one," Myron said.

"I am aware of it. I am also aware of Mr. Lockwood's"—he paused, searching for the word—"talents."

"Then you know that if that bozo gets itchy"—Myron head-gestured toward the blazer with the gun—"you die."

Granite Man wrestled with his facial muscles and this time he achieved a smile, though not without effort. Heart's song "Barracuda" played in Myron's head. "I am not without my own, uh, talents, Mr. Bolitar."

"If you really believe that," Myron said, "then you don't know enough about Win's, uh, talents."

"I won't debate the point. But I will point out that he doesn't have an army like this at his disposal. Now, are you going to tell me why you're asking about Dennis Lex?"

"I told you," Myron said.

"You're really going to stick with the dying-child story?"

"It's the truth."

"And how did you get Dennis Lex's name?"

"From the bone marrow center."

"They just gave it to you?"

Myron's turn. "I too am not without my own, uh, talents." It somehow didn't sound right when he said it about himself.

"So you're saying that the bone marrow center told you that Dennis Lex was a donor—that about right?"

"I'm not saying anything," Myron said. "Look, this is a two-way street here. I want some information."

"Wrong," Granite Man said. "It's a one-way street. I'm a Mack truck. You're like an egg in the road."

Myron nodded. "Cutting," he said. "But if you're not going to give me anything, I'm not giving you anything."

The guy with the gun stepped closer.

Myron felt a quiver in his legs, but he didn't blink. Maybe he did overplay the wisecracks, but you don't show fear. Ever. "And let's not pretend you're going to shoot me over this. We both know you won't. You're not that stupid."

Granite Man smiled. "I might beat on you a bit."

"You don't want trouble, I don't want trouble. I don't care about this family or its fortune or any of that. I'm just trying to save a kid's life."

Granite Man played air violin for a moment. Then he said, "Dennis Lex is not your salvation."

"And I'm just supposed to believe you?"

"He's not your donor. That much I personally guarantee."

"Is he dead?"

Granite Man folded his arms across his paddleball-court chest. "If you're telling the truth, the bone marrow people either lied to you or made a mistake."

"Or you're lying to me," Myron said. Then added, "Or you're making a mistake."

"The guards will show you out."

"I can still go to the press."

Granite Man walked away then. "We both know you won't," he said. "You're not that stupid either."

16

Bruce Taylor was in print-journalist garb—like he'd gone to his laundry hamper and dug out whatever was on the bottom. He sat at the bar, scooped up the free pretzels, and pushed them into his mouth as though he were trying to swallow his palm.

"Hate these things," he said to Myron.

"Yeah, I can see that."

"I'm at a bar, for crying out loud. I gotta eat something. But nobody serves peanuts anymore. Too fattening or some such crap. Pretzels instead. And not real pretzels. Little tiny buggers." He held one up for Myron to see. "I mean, what's up with that?"

"And the politicians," Myron said. "They spend all that time on gun control."

"So what do you want to drink? And don't ask for that Yoo-Hoo crap here. It's embarrassing."

"What are you having?"

"The same thing I always have when you pay. Twelve-year-old Scotch."

"I'll just have a club soda with lime."

"Wuss." He ordered it. "What do you want?"

"You know Stan Gibbs?"

Bruce said, "Whoa."

"What whoa?"

"I mean, whoa, you get involved in some hairy-ass shit, Myron. But Stan Gibbs? What the hell could you possibly have to do with him?"

"Probably nothing."

"Uh-huh."

"Just tell me about him, okay?"

Bruce shrugged, took a sip of Scotch. "Ambitious s.o.b. who went too far. What else do you need to know?"

"The whole story."

"Starting with?"

"What exactly did he do?"

"He plagiarized a story, the dumbass. That's not unusual. But to be so stupid about it."

"Too stupid?" Myron asked.

"What do you mean?"

"I mean we both agree that stealing from a published novel is not only unethical but idiotic."

"So?"

"So I'm asking if it's *too* idiotic."

"You think he's innocent, Myron?"

"Do you?"

He chucked down a few more pretzels. "Hell no. Stan Gibbs is guilty as sin. And as stupid as he was, I know plenty stupider. How about Mike Barnicle? The guy steals jokes from a George Carlin book. George Carlin, for chrissake."

"Does seem pretty stupid," Myron agreed.

"And he's not the only one. Look, Myron, every profession's got their dirty laundry, right? The stuff they want swept under the rug. Cops got their blue line when one of them pounds a suspect into the earth. Doctors cover each other's asses when they take out the wrong gallbladder or whatever. Lawyers . . . well, don't even get me started on their dirty little secrets."

"And plagiarism is yours?"

"Not just plagiarism," Bruce said. "Wholesale fabrication. I know reporters who make up sources. I know guys who make up dialogue. I know guys who make up whole conversations. They run stories about crack mothers and inner-city gang leaders who never existed. Ever read those columns? Ever wonder why so many drug addicts, say, sound so friggin' poignant when they can't even watch *Teletubbies* without a tutor?"

"And you're saying this happens a lot?"

"Truth?"

"Preferably."

"It's epidemic," Bruce said. "Some guys are lazy. Some are too ambitious. Some are just pathological liars. You know the type. They'll lie to you about what they had for breakfast just because it comes so naturally."

The drinks came. Bruce pointed at the empty pretzel bowl. The bartender replaced it.

"So if it's so epidemic," Myron said, "how come so few get caught?"

"First off, it's hard to catch. People hide behind anonymous sources and claim people moved, stuff like that. Second, it's like I said before. It's our dirty little secret. We keep it buried."

"I'd think you'd want to clean house."

"Oh, right. Like cops want to. Like doctors want to."

"You're not the same thing, Bruce."

"Let me give you a scenario, Myron, okay?" Bruce finished up his drink, and now he pointed to his glass for a refill. "You're an editor with, say, *The New York Times*. A story is written for you. You print it. Now it's brought to your attention that the story was fabricated or plagiarized or maybe just totally inaccurate, whatever. What do you do?"

"Retract it," Myron said.

"But you're the editor. You're the dumbass responsible for its publication. You're probably the dumbass who hired the writer in the first place. Who do you think the higher-ups are going to blame? And do you think the higher-ups are going to be happy to hear that their paper printed something false? You think the *Times* wants to lose business to the *Herald* or the *Post* or whatever? And hell, the other papers don't even want to hear about it. The public already doesn't trust us as an institution, right? If the truth gets out, who gets hurt? Answer: everyone."

"So you quietly fire the guy," Myron said.

"Maybe. But, again, you're this editor for *The New York Times*. You fire, say, a columnist. Don't you think a higher-up is going to want to know why?"

"So you just let it go?"

"We're like the church used to be with pedophiles. We try to control the problem without hurting ourselves. We transfer the guy to another department. We pass the problem to someone else. Maybe we team him up with another writer. Harder to make shit up with someone looking over your shoulder."

Myron took a sip of his club soda. Flat. "Okay, let me ask the obvious question then. How did Stan Gibbs get caught?"

"He was dumb, dumber and dumbest. It was too high profile a piece to plagiarize like that. Not only that, but Stan rubbed the feds' face in a public crapper and flushed. You don't do that if you don't have the facts, especially to the feds. My guess is he thought he was safe because the novel had a negligible print run from some shitass vanity press in Oregon. I don't think they published more than five hundred copies of the thing, and that was more than twenty years ago. And the author was long dead."

"But someone dug it up."

"Yup."

Myron thought about it. "Strange, don't you think?"

"Most of the time I'd say yes, but not when it's this high-profile. And once the truth was uncovered, boom, Stan was done. Every media outlet got an anonymous press release about it. The feds held a press conference. I mean, there was almost a campaign against him. Someone—probably the feds—were out for their pound of flesh. And they got it."

"So maybe the feds were so pissed they set him up."

"How do you figure?" Bruce countered. "The novel exists. The passages Stan copied exist. There is no way around that."

Myron mulled that one over, looking for a way around it. Nothing came to him. "Did Stan Gibbs ever defend himself?"

"He never commented."

"Why not?"

"The guy's a reporter. He knew better. Look, stories like these become the worst kind of brushfire. Only way to get the fire out is to stop feeding the flame. No matter how bad, if there's nothing new to report—nothing new to feed the flame—it dies out. People always make the mistake of thinking they can douse the flame with their words, that they're so smart, their explanations will work like water or something. It's always a mistake to talk to the press. Everything—even wonderfully worded denials—feed the flames and keep it stoked."

"But doesn't silence make you look guilty?"

"He *is* guilty, Myron. Stan could only get himself in more trouble by talking. And if he hung around and tried to defend himself, someone would dig into his past too. Mainly his old columns. All of them. Every fact, every quote, everything. And if you've plagiarized one story, you've plagiarized others. You don't do it for the first time when you're Stan's age."

"So you think he was trying to minimize the damage?"

Bruce smiled, took a sip. "That Duke education," he said. "It wasn't wasted on you." He grabbed more pretzels. "Mind if I order a sandwich?"

"Suit yourself."

"It'll be worth it," Bruce said with a suddenly big smile. "Because I haven't yet mentioned the last little tidbit that convinced him to keep quiet."

"What's that?"

"It's big, Myron." The smile slid off his face. "Very big."

"Fine, order fries too."

"I don't want this to become public knowledge, you understand?"

"Come on, Bruce. What?"

Bruce turned back to the bar. He picked up a cocktail napkin and tore it in half. "You know the feds took Stan to court to find his sources."

"Yes."

"The court documents were kept sealed, but there was a bit of nastiness. See, they wanted Stan to provide some sort of corroboration. Something to show he didn't totally make the story up. He wouldn't offer any. For a while he claimed that only the families could back him and he wouldn't give them up. But the judge pressed. He finally admitted that there was one other person who could back his story."

"Back up his made-up story?"

"Yes."

"Who?"

"His mistress," Bruce said.

"Stan was married?"

"Guess the word 'mistress' gave it away," Bruce said. "Anyway, he was. Still is, technically, but now they're separated. Naturally Stan was hesitant about naming her—he loved his wife, had two kids, the backyard, whatever—but in the end he gave the judge her name under the condition that it stay sealed."

"Did the mistress back him?"

"Yes. This mistress—one Melina Garston—claimed to have been with him when he met the Sow the Seeds psycho."

Myron's brow creased. "Why does that name ring a bell?"

"Because Melina Garston is dead now. Tied and tortured and you don't want to know what."

"When?"

"Three months ago. Right after the shit hit Stan's fan. Worse, the police think Stan did it."

"To keep her from telling the truth?"

"Again that Duke education."

"But that makes no sense. She was killed after the plagiarism was discovered, right?"

"Right after, yeah."

"So it was too late by then. Everyone thinks he's guilty already. He's lost his job. He's disgraced. If his mistress now comes out and says 'Yeah, I lied,' it wouldn't really change a thing. What would Stan have gained by killing her?"

Bruce shrugged. "Maybe her retraction would have removed any doubt."

"But there's not much doubt there anyway."

The bartender came over. Bruce ordered a sandwich. Myron shook him off. "Can you find out where Stan Gibbs is hiding?"

Bruce waved down the bartender again. "I already know."

"How?"

"He was my friend."

"Was or is?"

"Is, I guess."

"You like him?"

"Yeah," Bruce said. "I like him."

"Yet, you still think he did it."

"Murder, probably not. Plagiarize . . ." He shrugged. "I'm a cynical guy. And just because a guy is a friend of mine doesn't mean he can't do dumb things."

"Will you give me his address?"

"Will you tell me why?"

Myron sipped his flat club soda. "Okay, this is the part where you say you want to know what I have. Then I say I have nothing and when I do, you'll be the first to know. Then you get kinda huffy and say I owe you and that's not good enough, but in the end you take the deal. So why don't we skip all that and just give me the address?"

"Will I still get my sandwich?"

"Sure."

"Fine, then," Bruce said. "Doesn't matter. Stan hasn't talked to anyone since he resigned—not even his close friends. What makes you think he'll talk to you?"

"Because I'm a witty dinner companion and natty dresser?"

"Yeah, that." He turned to Myron and looked at him heavily. "Now, this is the part where I tell you that if you find anything, anything, that suggests that Stan Gibbs is being set up, you tell me because I'm his friend and I'm a reporter hungry for a big story."

"Not to mention a sandwich."

No smile. "You got me?"

"Got you."

"Anything you want to tell me now?"

"Bruce, I got less than nothing. It's just a thread I need to snip away."

"You know Cross River in Englewood?"

"A mid-eighties condo development that looks like something out of *Poltergeist*."

"Twenty-four Acre Drive. Stan just came back to the area. He's renting there."

17

The Morning Mosh was not really the establishment's name. Located in a converted warehouse downtown on the West Side, the Mosh had a neon sign that changed as the day went on. The word *Mosh* stayed lit all the time, but in the morning it blinked *Morning Mosh*, then *Mid-Day Mosh* (as it now read) and later on, *Midnight Mosh*. And that's *Mosh*, not *Nosh*. Myron had expected a bagel store. But the letter was *M*, not *N*, and this place was *Mosh*. As in *Mosh Pit*. As in some retro heavy-metal band minus the talent blaring sounds that could strip paint while kids danced—and we're using that term in its loosest form here—in a pit, careening off one another like a thousand pinballs released into the machine at the same time.

A sign by the front door read FOUR BODY PIERCE MINIMUM TO ENTER (EARS DON'T COUNT).

Myron stayed on the sidewalk and used his cell phone. He called the Mosh's number. A voice answered, "Go for it, dude."

"Suzze T please."

"Dig."

Dig?

Suzze came on two minutes later. "Hello?"

"It's Myron. I'm out on the curb."

"Come in. No one bites. Well, except for that guy who bit the legs off a live frog last night. Man, that was so cool."

"Suzze, please meet me out here, okay?"

"What-ev-er."

Myron hung up, feeling old. Suzze came out less than a minute later. She wore bell-bottom jeans with a gravity-defying waist that stayed up south of her hips. Her top was pink and much too small, revealing not only a flat stomach but a bottom-side hint of what interested the fine folks at Rack Enterprises. Suzze sported only one tattoo (a tennis racket with a snake's head grip) and no piercings, not even her ears.

Myron pointed to the sign. "You don't meet the minimum piercing requirement."

"Yeah, Myron, I do."

Silence. Then Myron said, "Oh."

They started walking down the street. Another strange Manhattan neighborhood. Kids and the homeless hung out together. There were bars and nightclubs alongside daycare centers. The modern city. Myron passed a storefront with a sign: TATTOOS WHILE U WAIT. He reread the sign and frowned. Like how else would you do it?

"We got a weird endorsement offer," Myron said. "You know the Rack Bars?"

Suzze said, "Like, upscale topless, right?"

"Well, topless anyway."

"What about them?"

"They're opening up a chain of topless coffee bars."

Suzze nodded. "Cool," she said. "I mean, taking the popularity of Starbucks and mixing it with Scores and Goldfingers, well, it's totally wise."

"Uh, right. Anyway, they're having this big grand opening and they're trying to generate excitement and media attention and all that. So they want you to make a, uh, guest appearance."

"Topless?"

"Like I said on the phone, I had an offer I wanted you to refuse."

"Totally topless?"

Myron nodded. "They insist on nipple visibility."

"How much they willing to pay?"

"Two hundred thousand dollars."

She stopped. "Are you shitting me?"

"I shit you not."

She whistled. "Lots of cha-ching."

"Yes, but I still think—"

"This was, like, their first offer?"

"Yes."

"Do you think you could get them up?"

"No, that would be your job."

She stopped and looked at him. Myron shrugged his apology.

"Tell them yes," she said.

"Suzze . . ."

"Two hundred grand for flashing a bit of booby? Christ, last night I think I did it in there for free."

"That isn't the same thing."

"Did you see what I wore in *Sports Illustrated?* I might as well have been naked."

"That isn't the same thing either."

"This is Rack, Myron, not some sleazoid place like Buddy's. It's upscale topless."

"Saying 'upscale topless' is like saying 'good toupee,' " Myron said.

"Huh?"

"It might be good," he said, "but it's still a toupee."

She cocked her head. "Myron, I'm twenty-four years old."

"I know that."

"That's like 107 in women-tennis years. I'm ranked thirty-one in the world right now. I haven't made two hundred grand over the past two years on tour. This is a big score, Myron. And man, will it change my image."

"Exactly my point."

"No, listen up, tennis is looking for draws. I'll be controversial. I'll get tons of attention. I'll suddenly be a big name. Admit it, my appearance fees will quadruple."

Appearance fees are the money paid to the big names just to show up, win or lose. Most name players make far more in appearance fees than prize money. It's where the potential major *dinero* is, especially for a player ranked thirty-first.

"Probably," Myron said.

She stopped and grabbed his arm. "I love playing tennis."

"I know that," he said softly.

"Doing this will extend my career. That means a lot to me, okay?"

Christ, she looked so young.

"All of what you're saying may be true," Myron said. "But at the end of the day, you're still appearing at a topless bar. And once it's done, it's done. You will always be remembered as the tennis player who appeared topless."

"There are worse things."

"Yes. But I didn't become an agent to get in the stripping business. I'll do what you want. You're my client. I want what's best for you."

"But you don't think this is best for me?"

"I have trouble advising a young woman to appear topless."

"Even if it makes sense?"

"Even if it makes sense."

She smiled at him. "You know something, Myron? You're cute when you're being a prude."

"Yeah, adorable."

"Tell them yes."

"Think about it for a few days, okay?"

"It's a no-brainer, Myron. Just do what you do best."

"What's that?"

"Get the number up. And tell them yes."

18

Cross River Condos was one of those complexes that looked like a movie façade, like whole buildings might topple over if you pushed against any one wall. The development was sprawlingly cramped, with every building looking exactly the same. Walking through it was like something out of *Alice in Wonderland*, all avenues mirroring the others, until you got dizzy. Have too much drink and you're bound to stick your key in the wrong lock.

Myron parked near the complex pool. The place was nice but too close to Route 80, the major artery that ran from, well, here in New Jersey to California. The traffic sounds sloshed over the fence. Myron located the door to 24 Acre Drive and then tried to figure out which windows belonged to it. If he had it right, the lights were on. So was the television. He knocked on the door. Myron saw a face peer through the window next to the door. The face did not speak.

"Mr. Gibbs?"

Through the glass, the face said, "Who are you?"

"My name is Myron Bolitar."

A brief pause. "The basketball player?"

"At one time, yes."

The face looked through the window for a few more seconds before opening the door. The odor of too many cigarettes wafted through the opening and happily nested inside Myron's nostrils. Not surprisingly, Stan Gibbs had a cigarette in his mouth. He had a gray stubble-to-beard going, too far gone for retro *Miami Vice*. He wore a yellow Bart Simpson sweatshirt, dark green sweatpants, socks, sneakers, and a Colorado Rockies baseball cap—the standard fashion fare shared with equal fervor by joggers and couch potatoes. Myron suspected the latter here.

"How did you find me?" Stan Gibbs asked.

"It wasn't difficult."

"That's not an answer."

Myron shrugged.

"It doesn't matter," Stan said. "I have no comment."

"I'm not a reporter."

"So what are you?"

"A sports agent."

Stan took a puff of the cigarette, didn't remove it from his mouth. "Sorry to disappoint you, but I haven't played competitive football since high school."

"May I come in?"

"No, I don't think so. What do you want?"

"I need to find the kidnapper you wrote about in your article," Myron said.

Stan smiled with very white teeth, especially when you considered the smoking. His skin was sort of clumpy and winter-colorless, his hair thin and tired, but he had those bright eyes, superbright eyes, the kind that look like supernatural beacons are shining out from within. "Don't you read the papers?" he asked. "I made the whole thing up."

"Made it up or copied it from a book?"

"I stand corrected."

"Or maybe you were telling the truth. In fact, maybe the subject of your articles called me on the phone last night."

Stan shook his head, the growing ash on the cigarette holding on like a kid on an amusement park ride. "This is not something I want to revisit."

"Did you plagiarize the story?"

"I already said I wouldn't comment—"

"This isn't for public consumption. If you did—if the story was a fake—just tell me now and I'll go away. I don't have time to waste on false leads."

"Nothing personal," Stan said, "but you're not making a whole lot of sense here."

"Does the name Davis Taylor mean anything to you?"

"No comment."

"How about Dennis Lex?"

That threw him. The dangling cigarette started to slip from Stan's lips, but he caught it with his right hand. He dropped it on the walkway and watched it sizzle for a moment.

"Maybe you better come in."

The condo was a duplex centered with that staple of new American contruction, the cathedral ceiling. Plenty of light came in from the big windows, splashing down on a decor straight out of a Sunday circular. A blond-wood entertainment center took up one wall, a matching coffee table not far from it. There was also a white-and-blue-striped couch— Myron would bet his lunch money it was a Serta Sleeper—and matching love seat. The carpeting was the same neutral as the exterior, a sort of in-offensive tan, and the place was clean yet disorderly in a divorcé way, newspapers and magazines and books piled here and there, nothing really put in a specific place.

He had Myron sit on the couch. "Want something to drink?"

"Sure, whatever," Myron said. The coffee table had one photograph on it. A man had his arms around two boys. All three were smiling too hard, like they'd just come in second place and didn't want to appear disappointed. They were standing in a garden of some sort. Behind them loomed a marble statue of a woman with a bow and arrow over her shoulder. Myron picked up the frame and studied it. "This you?"

Gibbs lifted his head while scooping a handful of ice into a glass. "I'm on the right," he said. "With my brother and my father."

"Who's that a statue of?"

"Diana the Huntress. You familiar with her?"

"Didn't she turn into Wonder Woman?"

Stan chuckled. "Sprite okay?"

Myron put the photograph down. "Sure."

Stan Gibbs poured the drink, brought it out to Myron, handed it to him. "What do you know about Dennis Lex?"

"Just that he exists," Myron said.

"So why mention his name to me?"

Myron shrugged. "Why did you react so strongly to hearing it?"

Gibbs took out another cigarette, lit it. "You're the one who came to me."

"True."

"Why?"

No secret. "I'm looking for a man named Davis Taylor. He's a bone marrow donor who matched a kid and then vanished. I traced him to an address in Connecticut, but he's not there. So I dug a little more and found out that Davis Taylor is a name change. His real name is Dennis Lex."

"I still don't see what this has to do with me."

"This might sound a little nutty," Myron said. "But I left a voice mail message for Davis Taylor né Dennis Lex. When he called back, he made little sense. But he kept telling me to 'sow the seeds.' "

A small quake ran through Stan Gibbs. It passed quickly. "What else did he say?"

"That was pretty much it. I should sow the seeds. I should say good-bye to the child. Stuff like that."

"It's probably nothing," Gibbs said. "He probably just read my article and decided to have a little fun at your expense."

"Probably," Myron said. "Except that wouldn't really explain your reaction to Dennis Lex's name."

Stan shrugged, but there wasn't much behind it. "The family is famous."

"If I said Ivana Trump, would you have reacted the same?"

Gibbs stood. "I need some time to think about this."

"Think out loud," Myron said.

Stan just shook his head.

"Did you make up the story, Stan?"

"Another time."

"Not good enough," Myron said. "You owe me something here. Did you plagiarize the story?"

"How do you expect me to answer that?"

"Stan?"

"What?"

"I don't care about your situation. I'm not here to judge you or tell on you. I don't give a rat's ass if you made up the story or not. All I care about is finding the bone marrow donor. Period. End of story. *El Fin.*"

Stan's eyes started to well up. He took another puff of the cigarette. "No," he said. "I never plagiarized. I never saw that book in my life."

It was like the room had been holding its breath and finally let go.

"How do you explain the similarities between your article and that novel?"

He opened his mouth, stopped, shook his head.

"Your silence makes you look guilty."

"I don't have to explain anything to you."

"Yeah, you do. I'm trying to save a kid's life here. You're not that wrapped up in your problems, are you, Stan?"

Stan moved back into the kitchen. Myron stood and followed him. "Talk to me," Myron said. "Maybe I can help."

"No," he said. "You can't."

"How do you explain the similarities, Stan? Just tell me that, okay? You must have thought about it."

"I don't need to think about it."

"Meaning?"

He opened the refrigerator and grabbed another can of Sprite. "Do you think all psychotics are original?"

"I'm not following you."

"You received a call from a guy who told you about sowing the seeds."

"Right."

"There are two possibilities that explain why he did that," Stan said. "One, he is the same killer I wrote about. Or two?" Stan looked at Myron.

"He just repeated what he'd read in the article," Myron said.

Stan snapped and pointed at Myron.

"So you're saying that the kidnapper you interviewed read this novel and it, what, influenced him somehow? That he copied it?"

Stan took a swig from the can. "That's a theory," he said.

And a damn good one, Myron thought. "So why didn't you say that to the press? Why didn't you defend yourself?"

"None of your goddamn business."

"Some people say it's because you were afraid they'd look closer at your work. That they'd find other fabrications."

"And some people are morons," he finished.

"So why didn't you fight?"

"I spent my whole life being a journalist," Stan said. "Do you know what it means for a journalist to be called a plagiarist? It's like a daycare worker being called a child molester. I'm done. No words can change that. I've lost everything to this scandal. My wife, my kids, my job, my reputation—"

"Your mistress?"

He shut his eyes suddenly, tightly, like a child trying to make the bogeyman go away.

"The police think you killed Melina," Myron said.

"I'm well aware of that."

"Tell me what's going on here, Stan."

He opened his eyes and shook his head. "I have to make some calls, check out some leads."

"You can't just cut me loose."

"I have to," he said.

"Let me help."

"I don't need your help."

"But I need yours."

"Not right now," Stan said. "You'll have to trust me on this."

"I'm not big on trust," Myron said.

Stan smiled. "Neither am I," he said. "Neither am I."

19

Myron pulled out. So, too, he noticed, did two men in a black Oldsmobile Ciera. Hmm.

The cell phone rang.

"Have you learned anything?" It was Emily.

"Not really," Myron said.

"Where are you?"

"Englewood."

"Do you have any plans for dinner?" Emily asked.

Myron hesitated. "No."

"I'm a good cook, you know. We dated in college, so I didn't have much chance to demonstrate my culinary skills."

"I remember you cooking for me once," Myron said.

"I did?"

"In my wok."

Emily chuckled. "That's right, you had an electric wok in your dorm, right?"

"Yep."

"I almost forgot about that," Emily said. "Why did you have one, anyway?"

"To impress chicks."

"Really?"

"Sure. I thought I'd invite a girl up to my room, slice up some vegetables, add a little soy sauce—"

"To the vegetables?" she asked.

"For starters."

"So how come you never pulled that one on me?"

"Didn't have to."

"You calling me easy, Myron?"

"How exactly does one answer that," Myron asked, "and maintain possession of both testicles?"

"Come on over," Emily said. "I'll make us some dinner. No soy sauce." Another hesitation.

"Please don't make me ask again," Emily said.

He wanted very much to say no. "Okay."

"Just take Route 4—"

"I know the way, Emily."

He hung up then and checked the rearview mirror. The black Oldsmobile Ciera was still following. Better safe than sorry. Myron hit the preprogrammed number on his cell phone. After one ring, Win answered.

"Articulate," Win said.

"Got a tail, methinks."

"License plate?"

Myron read it off to him.

"Where should we coordinate?"

"Garden State Plaza mall," Myron said.

"On my way, fair maiden."

Myron stayed on Route 4 until he saw a sign for the Garden State Plaza. He took a rather complicated cloverleaf overpass and veered into the mall's lot. The black Olds followed, dropping back a bit. Stall time. Myron circled a few times before finding a parking space. The Olds kept its distance. He turned off the car and headed for the "Northeast Entrance."

The Garden State Plaza had all the artificial elements endemic in malls—the mall ear-pop when you enter, the stale mall air, the mall hollow acoustics, as though all sound were traveling through a high-volume distorter—the audial equivalent of a shower door, voices somehow rendered both loud and incomprehensible. Too much with the high ceilings and faux marble, nothing soft to cushion the sound.

He strolled through the nouveau riche section of the Garden State Plaza, past several barren shoe stores, the kind that display maybe three pairs of shoes on the ends of what look like deer antlers. He reached a store called Aveda, which sold wildly overpriced cosmetics and lotions. The Aveda saleswoman, a starving young thang in tourniquet-tight black, informed Myron that they were having a sale on face moisturizers. Myron refrained from crying out "Yippee!" and went on his way. Victoria's Secret was next, and Myron did that male surreptitious glance at the lingerie window displays. Most of your more sophisticated heterosexual males are well versed in this art, awarding the racily clad supermodels the most casual of once-overs, feigning a lack of interest in the blown-up, blown-clear images of Stephanie and Frederique in Miracle Bras. Myron, of course, did the same thing—and then he thought, why pretend? He stopped short, squared his shoulders, ogled in earnest. Honesty. Shouldn't a woman respect that in a man too?

He checked his watch. Not yet. More stall. The plan, as it were, was fairly simple. Win drives to the Garden State Plaza. When he arrives, he calls Myron on the cell phone. Myron then goes back to his car. Win looks for the black Olds and follows the followee. Super clever, no?

Myron hit Sharper Image, one of the few places in the world where people use the words *shiatsu* and *ionic* and nobody laughs. He tried out a massage chair (setting: Knead) and debated purchasing a $5,500 life-size statue of a *Star Wars* star-trooper that had been reduced to a mere $3,499. Talk about redefining nouveau riche. Here's a little tip for you: If you've purchased a Sharper Image life-size *Star Wars* star-trooper, take out your platinum-est charge card, hand it to the nearest cashier, and buy a life.

The cell phone rang. Myron picked it up.

"They're feds," Win said.

"Yikes."

"Yes."

"No reason to follow them, then."

"No."

Myron spotted two men in suits and sunglasses behind him. They were studying the fruit-flavored shampoos in the Garden Botanica store window a little too closely. Two men in suits and sunglasses. Oh, like that happens. "I think they're following me in here too."

"If they arrest you with lingerie," Win said, "tell them it's for your wife."

"That what you do?"

"Keep the phone on," Win said.

Myron did as he asked. An old trick of theirs. Myron kept his cell phone on, thereby freeing Win to listen in. Okay, fine, now what? He kept strolling. Two more men in business suits were window-shopping up ahead. They turned as Myron approached, both staring him down. Some tail. Myron glanced behind him. The first two feds were right there.

The two feds in front of him stepped directly into his path. The other two came up behind him, boxing him in.

Myron stopped, looked at all four feds. "Did you guys check out the facial moisturizer sale at Aveda?"

"Mr. Bolitar?"

"Yes."

One of them, a short guy with a severe haircut, flashed a badge. "I'm

Special Agent Fleischer with the Federal Bureau of Investigation. We'd like a word with you, sir."

"What about?"

"Would you mind coming with us?"

They had the standard-issue stone expressions; Myron would get nothing out of them. Probably didn't even know anything themselves. Probably just delivery boys. Myron shrugged and followed them out. Two got into a white Olds Ciera. The other two stayed with Myron. One opened the back door of the black Ciera and head-gestured for Myron to get in. He did so. The interior was very clean. Nice, smooth seats. Myron ran his hand over it.

"Corinthian leather?" he asked.

Special Agent Fleischer turned around. "No, sir, that would be the Ford Granada."

Touché.

No one spoke. No radio played. Myron settled back. He debated calling Emily and postponing their soy-sauce-less encounter, but he didn't want the feds to hear him. He sat tight and kept his mouth shut. He didn't do that often. It felt odd and somehow right.

Thirty minutes later, he was in the basement of a modest high-rise in Newark. He sat at a table with his hands on a semi-sticky table. The room had one barred window and cement walls the color and texture of dried oatmeal. The feds excused themselves and left Myron alone. Myron sighed and sat back. He'd figured that this was the old soften-him-up-by-making-him-wait bit, when the door flew open.

The woman was first. She wore a pumpkin-orange blazer, blue jeans, sneakers, and ball-and-chain earrings. The word that came to mind was *husky*. Not big really. Husky. Everything was husky—even her hair, a sort of canned-corn yellow. The guy riding in on her fumes was geeky thin with a pointy head and a small, greased shock of black hair. He looked like an upside-down pencil. He spoke first.

"Good afternoon, Mr. Bolitar," Pencil said.

"Good afternoon."

"I'm Special Agent Rick Peck," he said. "This is Special Agent Kimberly Green."

The orange-blazered Green did a caged-lion pace. Myron nodded at her. She nodded back but grudgingly, like her teacher had just told her to apologize for something she didn't do.

Pencil Peck continued. "Mr. Bolitar, we'd like to ask you a few questions."

"What about?"

Peck kept his eyes on his notes and spoke like he was reading. "Today you visited one Stan Gibbs at 24 Acre Drive. Is that correct?"

"How do you know I didn't visit two Stan Gibbs?"

Peck and Green exchanged a glance. Then Peck said, "Please, Mr. Bolitar, we'd appreciate your cooperation. Did you visit Mr. Gibbs?"

"You know I did," Myron said.

"Fine, thank you." Peck wrote something down slowly. Then he looked up. "We'd very much like to know the nature of your visit."

"Why?"

"You are the first visitor Mr. Gibbs has had since moving to his current residence."

"No, I mean, why do you want to know?"

Green crossed her arms. She and Peck looked at each other again. Peck said, "Mr. Gibbs is part of an ongoing investigation."

Myron waited. No one said anything. "Well, that pretty much clears it up."

"That's all I can say for the moment."

"Same here."

"Pardon?"

"If you can't say any more, I can't say any more."

Kimberly Green put her hands on the table, gave a toothy grimace—husky teeth?—and leaned down like she might take a bite out of him. The canned-corn hair smelled like Pert Plus. She eyeballed him—must have read a memo on intimidating glares—and then spoke for the first time. "Here's how we're going to play it, asshole. We're going to ask you questions. You're going to listen to them and then you're going to answer them. You got it?"

Myron nodded. "I want to make sure I got this straight," he said to her. "You're playing bad cop, right?"

Peck picked up the ball. "Mr. Bolitar, no one is interested in making trouble here. But we'd very much like your cooperation in this matter."

"Am I under arrest?" Myron asked.

"No."

"Bye then."

He started to stand. Kimberly Green gave him a shove mid-rise and he fell back into the chair. "Sit down, asshole." She looked over at Peck. "Maybe he's part of it."

"You think so?"

"Why else would he be so reluctant to answer questions?"

Peck nodded. "Makes sense. An accomplice."

"We can probably arrest him now," Green said. "Lock him up for the night, maybe leak it to the press."

Myron looked up at her. "Gasp," he said. "Now. I. Am. Really. Scared. Second gasp."

She narrowed her eyes. "What did you say?"

"Don't tell me," Myron said. "Maybe I'm guilty of aiding and abetting. That's my personal favorite. Does anyone actually get prosecuted for that?"

"You think we're playing games here?"

"I do. And by the way, how come you're all called 'special' agent? Doesn't that sound like something someone made up one day? Like a kid's game to raise self-esteem. 'We're promoting you from agent to special agent, Barney,' and then what, super-special agent?"

Green grabbed his lapels and leaned his chair back. "You're not funny."

Myron looked at her hands gripping him. "Are you for real?"

"You want to try me?" she said.

Peck said, "Kim."

She ignored him and kept her glare on Myron. "This is serious," she said.

Her tone aimed for angry but came out more like a frightened plea. Two more agents entered. With the four delivery boys, that made eight. This was something big. What, Myron had no idea. The murder of Melina Garston maybe. But that was doubtful. The locals usually handled murders. You don't call in the feds.

The new guys came at Myron in different ways, but there were only so many routes to travel and Myron knew them all. Threatening, friendly, flattering, insulting, building up, belittling, hard, soft, every sell. They denied him the bathroom, they made excuses to keep him longer, all the while they're working him and he's working them and neither one is giving. Sweat started flowing, mostly from them, the stains and stench filling the air, metastasizing into something Myron could swear was genuine fear.

Kimberly Green came in and out and she kept shaking her head at him. Myron wanted to cooperate, but here's the pertinent cliché: Once the genie is out of the bottle, you can't put it back in. He didn't know what they were investigating. He didn't know if it would benefit Jeremy to talk or hurt him. But once he spoke, once his words were in the public domain, he couldn't take them back. Any leverage he might later be able to apply would be gone. So, for now, even if he might want to help, he wouldn't. Not until he learned more. He had the contacts. He could find out quickly enough, make an informed decision.

Sometimes, negotiating meant shutting up.

When things wound down, Myron got up to leave. Kimberly Green blocked his path. "I'm going to make your life hell," she said.

"That your way of asking me out?"

She leaned back as if he'd slapped her. When she recovered, she shook her head slowly. "You have no idea, do you?"

Shutting up, he reminded himself. Myron pushed past her and headed outside.

20

He called Emily from the car.

"I thought I was being stood up," she said.

Myron checked out the rearview mirror and spotted what might be another fed tail. No matter. "Sorry," he said. "Something came up."

"Involving the donor?"

"I don't think so."

"You still in Jersey?" Emily asked.

"Yes."

"Come on over. I'll reheat dinner."

He wanted to say no. "Okay."

Franklin Lakes was about sprawling. Everything sprawled. The houses were mostly new construction, big brick mansions on eternal cul-de-sacs, little gates at the front of the driveways that opened with push-button or intercom, like that would really protect the owners from what lay outside the lush lawns and pedicure-clipped hedges. The interiors were sprawling too, dining rooms big enough to house helicopters, remote-controlled blinds, Sub-Zero/Viking Stove kitchens with marble islands that overlooked family rooms the size of movie theaters, always with complicated state-of-the-art entertainment centers.

Myron rang the bell and the door opened and for the first time in his life, Myron was face-to-face with his son.

Jeremy smiled at him. "Hi."

Strong, totally alien surges ricocheted haphazardly through Myron, his nervous system melting down and in overdrive all at once. His diaphragm contracted and his lungs stopped. So, he was sure, did his heart. His mouth weakly opened and closed like a dying fish on a boat deck. Tears headed up and pushed toward the eyes.

"You're Myron Bolitar, right?" Jeremy said.

An ocean-shell rushing filled Myron's ears. He managed a nod.

"You played ball against my dad," Jeremy said, still with the smile that ripped at the corners of Myron's heart. "In college, right?"

Myron found his voice. "Yes."

The kid nodded back. "Cool."

"Yeah."

A horn honked. Jeremy leaned to the right and looked behind Myron. "That's my ride. Later."

Jeremy leaped past Myron. Myron numbly turned and watched the boy jog down the driveway. Imagination maybe, but that gait was oh-so-familiar. From Myron's old game films. More surges. *Oh Christ . . .*

Myron felt a hand on his shoulder, but he ignored it and watched the boy. The car door opened and swallowed Jeremy into the darkness. The driver's window slid down and a pretty woman called out, "Sorry I'm late, Em."

From behind him, Emily said, "No problem."

"I'll take them to school in the morning."

"Great."

A wave and the pretty woman's window slid back into place. The car started on its way. Myron watched it disappear down the road. He felt Emily's eyes on him. He slowly turned to her.

"Why did you do that?"

"I thought he'd be gone by now," Emily said.

"Do I really look that stupid?"

She stepped back into the house. "I want to show you something."

Trying to get his legs back, his head wobbly and his internal referee still giving him the eight count, Myron followed her silently up the stairway. She led him down a darkened corridor lined with modern lithographs. She stopped, opened a door, and flipped on the lights. The room was teenage-cluttered, as if someone had put all the belongings in the center of the room and dropped a hand grenade on them. The posters on the walls—Michael Jordan, Keith Van Horn, Greg Downing, Austin Powers, the words *YEAH, BABY!* across his middle in pink tie-dye lettering—had been hung askew, all tattered corners and missing pushpins. There was a Nerf basketball hoop on the closet door. There was a computer on the desk and a baseball cap dangling from a desk lamp. The corkboard had a mix of family snapshots and construction-paper crayons signed by Jeremy's sister, all held up by oversized pushpins. There were footballs and autographed baseballs and cheap trophies and a couple of blue ribbons and three basketballs, one with no air in it. There were stacks of computer-game CD-ROMs and a Game Boy on the unmade bed and a surprising amount of books, several opened and facedown. Clothes littered the floor like war wounded; the drawers were half open, shirts and underwear hanging out like they'd been shot mid-escape. The room had the slight, oddly comforting smell of kids' socks.

"He's a slob," she said. Leaving off the obvious "like you."

Myron stayed still.

"He keeps Oxy 10 in his desk drawer," Emily said. "He thinks I don't know. He's at that age where crushes keep him up all night, but he's never even kissed a girl." She walked over to the corkboard and snatched up a photograph of Jeremy. "He's beautiful, don't you think?"

"This isn't helping, Emily."

"I want you to understand."

"Understand what?"

"He's never been kissed. He is going to die and he's never even kissed a girl."

Myron held up his hands. "I don't know what you want me to say here."

"Try to understand, okay?"

"I don't need melodrama. I understand."

"No, Myron, you don't. You look back at the night and see it as some sort of Gothic blunder. We did something sinful and for that we all paid a heavy price. If we could just go back and erase that tragic mistake, well, it's all so *Hamlet* and *Macbeth*, isn't it? Your ruined basketball career, Greg's future, our marriage—all laid to waste in that one moment of lust."

"It wasn't lust."

"Let's not go through that argument again. I don't care what it was. Lust, stupidity, fear, fate. Call it whatever the hell you want to—but I would never want to go back. That 'mistake' was the best thing that ever happened to me. Jeremy, our son, came out of that mess. Do you hear what I'm saying? I'd destroy a million careers and marriages for him."

She looked at him, challenging. He said nothing.

"I'm not religious and I don't believe in fate or destiny or any of that," she went on. "But maybe, just maybe, there had to be a balance. Maybe the only way to produce something so wonderful was to surround the event with so much destruction."

Myron started backing out of the room. "This isn't helping," he said again.

"Yes," she said, "it is."

"You want me to find the donor. I'm trying to do that. But this kind of distraction doesn't help. I need to stay detached."

"No, Myron, you need attachment. You need to get emotional. You have to understand the stakes—your son, that beautiful boy who opened the door—is going to die before he's even kissed a girl." She moved closer to him and looked into his eyes and Myron thought that her eyes had never looked so clear before.

"I watched you play every game at Duke," she said. "I fell in love with you on that court—not because you were the team star or because you were graceful or athletic. You were so open out there, so raw and emotional. And the more emotional you got, the more pressure there was, the better you played. If the game was a blowout, you lost interest. You needed it to matter. You needed to be double-teamed with only a few seconds on the clock. You needed to lose control a little."

"This isn't a game, Emily."

"Right," she said. "The stakes are higher. The emotion should be higher. I want you desperate, Myron. That's when you're at your best."

He looked at the photograph of Jeremy, and he knew that he was feeling something that he had never felt before. He blinked, caught the expression on his face in the closet-door mirror, and for a moment he saw his own father staring back.

Emily hugged him then. She buried her face in his shoulder and started to cry. Myron held on tight. They stood that way for several minutes before making their way downstairs. Over dinner, Emily told him about Jeremy, and he soaked in every story. They moved to the couch and broke out the photo albums. Emily tucked her legs under her, her elbow on the top of the couch, her head leaning on the heel of her hand, and told him more. It was nearly two in the morning when she walked him to the door. They were holding hands.

"I know you spoke to Dr. Singh," she said in the open door.

"Yes."

She let loose a deep breath. "I'm just going to say this, okay?"

"Okay."

"I've been keeping track. I bought one of those home tests. The, uh, optimum conception day will be Thursday."

He opened his mouth but she stopped him with her hand.

"I know all the arguments against this, but it might be Jeremy's only chance. Don't say anything. Just think about it."

She closed the door. Myron stared at it for a few moments. He tried to conjure up the moment Jeremy had opened it, the crooked smile on the boy's face, but already the image was hazy and fading fast.

21

First thing in the morning, Myron called Terese. Still no answer. He frowned at the phone. "Am I getting the big kiss-off?" he asked Win.

"Doubtful," Win said. He was reading the newspaper and wearing silk pajamas with a matching bathrobe and slippers. Give him a pipe and he could have been something Noël Coward created on an off day.

"What makes you say that?"

"Our Ms. Collins appears to be rather direct," Win said. "If you were being tossed into the dung heap, you'd know the smell."

"And then there's the part about my being irresistible to women," Myron said.

Win turned the page.

"So what's she up to?"

Win tapped his chin with his index finger. "What's the term you relationship people use? Oh, yes. Space. Perhaps she needs some space."

" 'Needing space' is usually a code phrase for the big kiss-off."

"Yes, well, whatever." Win crossed his legs. "You want me to look into it?"

"Into what?"

"What Ms. Collins might be up to."

"No."

"Fine," Win said. "Let's move on, shall we? Tell me about your encounter with the Federal Bureau of Investigation."

Myron recapped the interrogation.

"So we don't know what they wanted," Win said.

"Correct."

"Not a clue?"

"Nothing. Except that they were scared."

"Curious."

Myron nodded.

Win took a sip of tea, pinky up. Oh, the horrors that pinky had witnessed, partaken in, even. They sat in Win's formal dining room and used a silver tea set. Victorian mahogany table with lion-paw feet, silver tea set, silver milk pitcher, boxes of Cap'n Crunch and some new cereal called Oreo, which is exactly what you would imagine. "Theorizing at this juncture is a waste of time. I'll make some calls, see what I can find out."

"Thanks."

"I'm still not sure I see a connection between Stan Gibbs and our blood donor."

"It's a long shot," Myron agreed.

"More than that. A newspaper columnist makes up a story about a serial kidnapper and now—what?—we think the fictional character is the donor?"

"Stan Gibbs claims the story is real."

"Does he now?"

"Yes."

Win rubbed his chin. "Pray tell, why does he not defend himself?"

"No clue."

"Presumably because he is guilty," Win said. "Man is, above all, selfish. He's into self-preservation. It's instinctive. He does not martyr himself. He cares about one thing above all else: saving his hide."

"Assuming I agree with your sunny view of human nature, wouldn't you agree that man would lie to save himself?"

"Of course," Win said.

"So armed with this pretty decent defense—the idea that the serial kidnapper copycatted the novel—why wouldn't Stan use it to defend himself, even if he was guilty of plagiarism?"

Win nodded. "I like the way you're thinking."

"Cynically, yes."

The intercom buzzed. Win pressed the button, and the doorman announced Esperanza. A minute later, she swept into the room, grabbed a chair, and poured herself a bowl of Oreo cereal.

"Why do they always say it's 'part of this complete breakfast'?" Esperanza asked. "Every single time, every single cereal. What's all that about?"

Nobody replied.

Esperanza took a spoonful, looked at Win, head-gestured toward Myron. "I hate it when he's right," she said to Win.

"A bad omen," Win agreed.

Myron said, "I was right?"

She turned her gaze to Myron. "I did that school check on Dennis Lex. I tracked down any and all educational institutions any of his siblings or parents had gone to. Nothing. College, high school, middle school—even grammar school. No trace of Dennis Lex."

"But?" Myron said.

"Preschool."

"You're kidding me."

"Nope."

"You found his preschool?"

"I'm more than just a great piece of ass," Esperanza said.

Win said, "Not to me, my dear."

"You're sweet, Win."

Win bowed his head slightly.

"Miss Peggy Joyce," Esperanza said. "She still teaches and runs the Shady Wells Montessori School for Children in East Hampton."

"And she remembers Dennis Lex?" Myron said. "From thirty years ago?"

"Apparently." Esperanza shoved in another spoonful and tossed Myron a sheet of paper. "This is her address. She's expecting you this morning. Drive safely now, ya hear?"

22

The car phone rang.

"The old man is a lying sack of shit." It was Greg Downing.

"What?"

"The geezer is lying."

"You mean Nathan Mostoni?"

"Jesus Christ, what other old man have I been watching?"

Myron switched ears. "What makes you think he's lying, Greg?"

"Lots of things."

"Like?"

"Like starting with Mostoni never hearing from the bone marrow center. Does that sound logical to you?"

He thought of Karen Singh and her dedication and the stakes. "No," Myron said, "but it's like we said before—he might be confused."

"I don't think so."

"Why not?"

"Nathan Mostoni goes out plenty on his own, for one thing. Sometimes he acts loony, but other times, he seems just fine. He shops himself. He talks to people. He dresses like a normal person."

"That doesn't mean anything," Myron said.

"No? An hour ago he went out, right? So I got close to the house, right up against the back window, and I dialed that number, the one you got for the donor."

"And?"

"And I hear a phone inside the house ringing."

That made Myron pause.

"So what do you think we should do?" Greg asked.

"I'm not sure. Have you seen anybody else at the house?"

"Nobody. Mostoni goes out but nobody's been here. And I tell you something else. He looks younger now. I don't know how else to explain it. It's weird. You making any headway on your end?"

"I'm not sure."

"That's some answer, Myron."

"The only one I got."

"So what do you think we should do about Mostoni?"

"I'll have Esperanza do a background check. In the meantime, stay on him."

"Time's a-ticking away here, Myron."

"I know that. I'll be in touch."

He disconnected the call and flipped on the radio. Chaka Khan was singing "Ain't Nobody Love You Better." If you can listen to that one without moving your feet, you got some serious rhythm issues. He took the Long Island Expressway east, which was shockingly clear today. Usually the road was more or less a parking lot that swayed forward every couple of minutes.

People always tell you that the Hamptons, the swanky Long Island summer spot where Manhattanites get away from it all by being with other Manhattanites, is best in the off season. You always hear that about vacation spots. People, mostly vacationers themselves, whine through the high-season months, waiting to reach this apex of a theoretically swarmless nirvana. But—and this was the part Myron never understood—no one is ever in the Hamptons in the off months. No one. Downtown is dead to the point of craving tumbleweeds. Shop owners sigh and discount nothing. The restaurants are less crowded, sure, but they're also closed. And hey, let's be honest here, the weather and beaches and even the people-watching are big draws here. Who goes to a Long Island beach in the winter?

The school was in a residential neighborhood with older, more modest homes—a place where the true Long Island regulars, none of whom hang out with Alec and Kim at Nick and Toni's, resided. Myron parked in a church lot and followed the signs down the steps into the rectory's basement. A young woman, a hall monitor of sorts, greeted Myron at the landing. He gave her his name and said he was here to see Ms. Joyce. The young woman nodded and told him to follow her.

The corridor was silent. Strange when one considered that this was a preschool. *Preschool.* Another new term. In Myron's day, they had called them nursery schools. Myron wondered when the name had changed and what group had considered the term *nursery school* somehow discriminatory. Professional RNs? Breast-feeding mothers? Bottle-fed infants maybe?

Still silent. Perhaps it was vacation or naptime. Myron was about to ask the young hall monitor when she opened a door. He looked in. Wrong-a-mundo. The room was chock full of small children, probably twenty give or take, and they were all working independently and in total silence. The older teacher smiled at Myron. She whispered to the little boy she was working with—he was doing something with blocks and letters—and stood.

"Hello," she said to Myron, speaking softly.

"Hi," Myron whispered back.

She leaned toward the young monitor. "Miss Simmons, will you help Mrs. McLaughlin?"

"Of course."

Peggy Joyce wore an open yellow sweater over a buttoned-at-the-neck blouse. The collar was frilly. She had half-moon glasses dangling from a chain around her neck. "We can chat in my office."

"Okay." He followed her. The place was silent as, well, a place without children. Myron asked, "Do you give those kids Valium?"

She smiled. "Just a little Montessori."

"A little what?"

"You don't have children, do you?"

The question caused a pang, but he answered in the negative.

"It's a teaching philosophy created by Dr. Maria Montessori, Italy's first female physician."

"It seems to work."

"I suppose."

"Do the children act like this at home?"

"Good Lord, no. Truth be told, it doesn't translate into the real world. But few things do."

They moved into the office, which consisted of a wooden desk, three chairs, one file cabinet.

"How long have you taught here?" Myron asked.

"I'm in my forty-third year."

"Wow."

"Yes."

"I guess you've seen lots of changes?"

"In kids? Almost none. Children don't change, Mr. Bolitar. A five-year-old is still a five-year-old."

"Still innocent."

She cocked her head. " 'Innocent' isn't the word I would use. Children are total id. They are perhaps the most naturally vicious creatures on God's green earth."

"Strange outlook for a preschool teacher."

"Just an honest one."

"So what word would you use?"

She thought about it. "If pressed, I'd say 'unformed.' Or maybe 'undeveloped.' Like a picture you've already taken but haven't processed yet."

Myron nodded, though he had no idea what she meant. There was something about Peggy Joyce that was a little, well, scary.

"Do you remember that book *All I Really Need to Know I Learned in Kindergarten?*" she asked him.

"Yes."

"It's true, but not in the way you think. School removes children from their warm parental cocoon. School teaches them to bully or be bullied. School teaches them how to be cruel to one another. School teaches them that Mommy and Daddy lied to them when they told them that they were special and unique."

Myron said nothing.

"You don't agree?"

"I don't teach preschool."

"That's sidestepping, Mr. Bolitar."

Myron shrugged. "They learn socialization. That's a hard lesson. And like every hard lesson, you have to get it wrong before you can get it right."

"They learn boundaries, in other words?"

"Yes."

"Interesting. And perhaps true. But you remember when I was giving the film-processing example earlier?"

"Yes."

"School only processes the picture. It doesn't snap it."

"Okay," Myron said, not wanting to follow her train of thought.

"What I mean is, everything is pretty much decided by the time these children leave here and enter kindergarten. I can tell who will be successful and who will fail, who will end up happy and who will end up in prison, and ninety percent of the time I'm right. Maybe Hollywood and video games have an influence, I don't know. But I can usually tell which kid will be watching too many violent movies or playing too many violent games."

"You can tell all this by the time they're five years old?"

"Pretty much, yes."

"And you feel that's it? That they don't have the ability to change?"

"The ability? Oh, probably. But they're already on a path, and while they may still be able to change it, the majority do not. Staying on the path is easier."

"So let me ask you the eternal question: Is it nature or nurture?"

She smiled. "I get asked that all the time."

"And?"

"I answer nurture. Know why?"

Myron shook his head.

"Believing in nurture is like believing in God. You might be wrong, but you might as well cover your bases." She folded her hands and leaned forward. "Now, what can I do for you, Mr. Bolitar?"

"Do you remember a student named Dennis Lex?"

"I remember all my students. Does that surprise you?"

Myron didn't want her going off on another tangent. "Did you teach the other Lex children?"

"I taught them all. Their father made a lot of changes after his book became a bestseller. But he kept them here."

"So what can you tell me about Dennis Lex?"

She sat back and regarded him as though seeing him for the first time. "I don't want to be rude, but I'm wondering when you're going to tell me what this is all about. I'm talking to you, Mr. Bolitar—and breaching confidences, I suspect—because I think you're here for a very specific reason."

"What reason is that, Ms. Joyce?"

Her eyes had a steely glint. "Don't play games with me, Mr. Bolitar."

She was right. "I'm trying to find Dennis Lex."

Peggy Joyce kept still.

"I know this sounds weird," he went on. "But as far as I can tell, he fell off the earth after preschool."

She stared straight ahead, though Myron had no idea at what. There were no photographs on the walls, no diplomas, no drawings by little hands. Just cold wall. "Not after," she said finally. "During."

There was a knock on the door. Peggy Joyce said, "Come in." The young hall monitor, Miss Simmons, entered with a little boy. His head was down and he'd been crying. "James needs a little time," Miss Simmons said.

Peggy Joyce nodded. "Let him lie on the mat."

James eyed Myron and left with Miss Simmons.

Myron turned to Peggy Joyce. "What happened to Dennis Lex?"

"It's a question I've been waiting for someone to ask for more than thirty years," she said.

"What's the answer?"

"First, tell me why you're looking for him."

"I'm trying to find a bone marrow donor. I think it might be Dennis Lex." He gave her as few details as he could. When he finished, she put a bony hand to her face.

"I don't think I can help you," she said. "It was so long ago."

"Please, Ms. Joyce. A child will die if I don't find him. You're my only lead."

"You spoke to his family?"

"Only his sister Susan."

"What did she tell you?"

"Nothing."

"I'm not sure what I can add."

"You could start by telling me what Dennis was like."

She sighed and neatly arranged her hands on her thighs. "He was like the other Lex children—very bright, thoughtful, contemplative, perhaps a bit too much so for so young a child. With most students, I try to get them to grow up a bit. With the Lex children, that was never an issue."

Myron nodded, trying to encourage.

"Dennis was the youngest. You probably know that. He was here the same time as his brother Bronwyn. Susan was older." She stopped, looked lost.

"What happened to him?"

"One day he and Bronwyn didn't come to school. I got a call from their father saying that he was taking them on an unplanned vacation."

"Where?"

"He didn't say. He wasn't being very specific."

"Okay, go on."

"That's pretty much it, Mr. Bolitar. Two weeks later, Bronwyn came back to school. I never saw Dennis again."

"You called his father?"

"Of course."

"What did he say?"

"He told me that Dennis wouldn't be coming back."

"Did you ask him why?"

"Of course. But . . . did you ever meet Raymond Lex?"

"No."

"You didn't question a man like that. He mentioned something about home schooling. When I pressed, he made it clear it was none of my concern. Over the years, I've tried to keep track of the family, even when they moved out of the area. But like you, I never heard anything about Dennis."

"What did you think happened?"

She looked at him. "I assumed he was dead."

Her words, though not all that surprising, worked like a vacuum, sucking the room dry, forcing out the air.

"Why?" Myron asked.

"I figured that he was ill, and that was why he was pulled out of school."

"Why would Mr. Lex try to hide something like that?"

"I don't know. After his novel became a bestseller, he became private to the point of paranoia. Are you sure this donor you're looking for is Dennis Lex?"

"Not sure, no."

Peggy Joyce snapped her fingers. "Oh, wait, I have something you may find interesting." She stood and opened a file drawer. She sifted through it, pulled something out, studied it for a moment. Her elbow smacked the drawer closed. "This was taken two months before Dennis left us."

She handed him an old class photograph, the color not so much fading as greening from age. Fifteen kids flanked by two teachers, one a far younger Peggy Joyce. The years had not been unkind to her, but they'd passed anyway. A small black sign with the white lettering read SHADY WELLS MONTESSORI SCHOOL and the year.

"Which one is Dennis?"

She pointed to a boy sitting in the front row. He had a Prince Valiant cut and a face-splitting smile that never quite hit his eyes. "Can I have this?"

"If you think it will help."

"It might."

She nodded. "I better get back to my students."

"Thank you."

"Do you remember your preschool, Mr. Bolitar?"

Myron nodded. "Parkview Nursery School in Livingston, New Jersey."

"How about your teachers? Do you remember them at all?"

Myron thought about it. "No."

She nodded as though he'd answered correctly. "Good luck," she said.

23

AgeComp. Or age-progression software, if you prefer.

Myron had learned a bit about it when searching for a missing woman named Lucy Mayor. The key was in the digital imaging. All Myron had to do—or in the case of their office, all Esperanza had to do—was take the class photograph and scan it into the computer. Then, using common software programs like Photoshop or Picture Publisher, you blow up the face of young Dennis Lex. AgeComp, a software program constantly being retooled and perfected by missing-children organizations, does the rest. Using advanced mathematical algorithms, AgeComp stretches, merges, and blends digital photographs of missing children and produces a color image of what they might look like today.

Naturally, a lot is left to chance. Scarring, facial fractures, facial hair, cosmetic surgery, hairstyle or, in the case of some of the older ones, male pattern baldness. Still, the class photo could be a serious lead.

When he was back in Manhattan, the cell phone rang.

"I spoke to the feds," Win said.

"And?"

"Your impression is correct."

"What impression?"

"They are indeed frightened."

"Did you speak to PT?"

"I did. He put me onto the right person. They requested a face-to-face."

"When?"

"Pretty pronto. We are, in fact, waiting in your office."

"The feds are in my office right now?"

"Affirmative."

"Be there in five."

More like ten. When the elevator opened, Esperanza was sitting at Big Cyndi's desk.

"How many?" he asked.

"Three," Esperanza said. "One blond woman, one extra-strength dork, one nice suit."

"Win's with them?"

"Yep."

He handed her the photograph and pointed to Dennis Lex's face. "How long before we could get an age progression on this?"

"Jesus, when was this taken?"

"Thirty years ago."

Esperanza frowned. "You know anything about age progression?"

"Some."

"It's mostly used to find missing kids," she said. "And it's usually used to age them five, maybe ten years."

"But we can get something, right?"

"Something very rough, yeah maybe." She flicked on the scanner and placed the photo facedown. "If they're in the lab, we'll probably have it by the end of the day. I'll crop it and e-mail it over."

"Do it later," he said, gesturing toward the door. "Mustn't keep the feds waiting. Our tax dollars and all that."

"You want me in there?"

"You're a part of everything that goes on here, Esperanza. Of course I want you in there."

"I see," she said. Then: "Is this the part where I blink back tears because you're making me feel oh-so-special?"

Wiseass.

Myron opened his office door. Esperanza followed. Win sat behind Myron's desk, probably so that none of the feds would. Win could be territorial—just one of the ways he was like a Doberman. Kimberly Green and Rick Peck rose with lack-of-sleep-luggage eyes and squared-off smiles. The third fed stayed in his seat, not moving, not even turning to see who'd entered. Myron saw his face and felt a jolt.

Whoa.

Win watched Myron, an amused smile curling the ends of his mouth. Eric Ford, deputy director of the Federal Bureau of Investigation, was the man in the suit. His presence meant one thing: This was serious big-time.

Kimberly Green pointed at Esperanza. "What's she doing in here?"

"She's my partner," Myron said. "And it's not polite to point."

"Your partner? You think this is a business transaction?"

"She stays," Myron said.

"No," Kimberly Green said. She was still wearing the ball-and-chain earrings, still the jeans and black turtleneck, but the jacket now was spearmint green. "We're not exactly thrilled talking to you and Cheekbones boy over there"—she gestured toward Win—"but at least you have some clearance. We don't know her. She goes."

Win's smile spread and his eyebrows did a quick up-and-down. Cheekbones. He liked that.

"She goes," Green said again.

Esperanza shrugged. "No biggie," she said.

Myron was about to say something, but Win shook his head. He was right. Save it for the important battles.

Esperanza left. Win got up and gave Myron the chair. He stood on Myron's right, arms crossed, totally at ease. Green and Peck fidgeted. Myron turned to Eric Ford. "I don't think we've met."

"But you know who I am," Ford said. He had one of those smooth soft-rock-DJ voices.

"Yes."

"And I know who you are," he said. "So what would be the point?"

Oookay. Myron glanced back at Win. Win shrugged.

Ford nodded at Kimberly Green. She cleared her throat. "For the record," she said, "we don't think we should have to go through this."

"Through what?"

"Telling you about our investigation. Debriefing you. As a good citizen, you should be willing to cooperate with our investigation because it's the right thing to do."

Myron looked at Win and said, "Oh boy."

"Some aspects of an investigation need to be contained," she continued. "You and Mr. Lockwood should understand that better than most. You should be anxious to cooperate with any federal investigation. You should respect what we're trying to do here."

"Right, okay, we respect. Can we skip ahead, please? You looked us up. You know we'll keep our mouths shut. Otherwise none of us would be here."

She folded her hands and put them in her lap. Peck kept his head down and scribbled notes, Lord knew on what. Myron's decor maybe. "What we say here cannot leave this room. It is classified to the highest—"

"Skipping," Myron said with an impatient hand roll. "Skipping."

Green slid her eyes toward Ford. He nodded again. She took a deep breath and said, "We have Stan Gibbs under surveillance."

She stopped, settled back. Myron waited a few seconds and then said, "Label me surprised."

"That information is classified," she said.

"Then I'll leave it out of my diary."

"He isn't supposed to know."

"Well, that's usually implied with words like 'classified' and 'surveillance.' "

"But Gibbs does know. He loses us whenever he really wants. Because when he's out in public, we can't get too close."

"Why can't you get too close?"

"He'll see us."

"But he already knows you're there?"

"Yes."

Myron looked up at Win. "Wasn't there an Abbott and Costello skit that went like this?"

"Marx Brothers," Win said.

"If we were out in the open about tailing him," Green said, "the fact that he's a target could become public knowledge."

"And you're trying to contain that?"

"Yes."

"How long has he been under surveillance?"

"Well, it's not that simple. He's been out of range a lot—"

"How long?"

Again Green looked at Ford. Again Ford nodded. She balled her hands into fists. "Since the first article on the kidnappings appeared."

Myron sat back, feeling something akin to a head rush. He shouldn't have been surprised, but damned if he wasn't. The article came flooding back to him—the sudden disappearances, the awful phone calls, the constant, eternal anguish, the picket-fenced lives suddenly bulldozed over by inexplicable evil.

"My God," Myron said. "Stan Gibbs was telling the truth."

"We never said that," Kimberly Green said.

"I see. So you've been tailing him because you don't like his syntax?"

Silence.

"The articles were true," Myron said. "And you've known it all along."

"What we did or did not know is not your concern."

Myron shook his head. "Unbelievable," he said. "So let me see if I got this straight. You have a serial psycho out there who snatches people out of the blue and torments their families. You want to keep a lid on it because if word got out to the public, you'd have a panic situation. Then the psycho goes directly to Stan Gibbs and suddenly the story is in the public domain . . ." Myron's voice died off, seeing that his logic trail had hit a major pothole. He frowned and forged ahead. "I don't know how that old novel or the plagiarism charges tie in. But either way, you decided to ride it. You let Gibbs get fired and disgraced, probably in part because you were pissed off that he upset your investigation. But mostly"—he spotted what he thought was a clearing—"but mostly you did it so you could watch him. If the psycho contacted him once, you figured, he'd probably do it again—especially if the articles had been discredited."

Kimberly Green said, "Wrong."

"But close."

"No."

"The kidnappings Gibbs wrote about took place, right?"

She hesitated, gave Ford an eye check. "We can't verify all of his facts."

"Jesus, I'm not taking a deposition here," Myron said. "Was his column true, yes or no?"

"We've told you enough," she said. "It's your turn."

"You haven't told me squat."

"And you've told us less."

Negotiating. Life is being a sports agent—constant negotiating. He had learned the importance of leverage, of doling out, of being fair. People forget that last one, and it always costs you in the end. The best negotiator isn't the one who gets the whole pie while leaving scant crumbs behind. The best negotiator is the one who gets what he wants while keeping the other side happy. So normally, Myron would dole out a little something here. Classic give-and-take. But not this time. He knew better. Once he told them the reason for his visit to Stan Gibbs, his leverage would be zippo.

The best negotiator, like the best species, also knows how to adapt.

"First answer my question," Myron said. "Yes or no, was the story Stan Gibbs wrote true?"

"There is no yes-or-no answer to that," she said. "Parts were true. Parts were not true."

"For example?"

"The young couple was from Iowa, not Minnesota. The missing father had three children, not two." She stopped, folded her hands.

"But there have been kidnappings?"

"We knew about those two," she said. "We had no information about the missing college student."

"Probably because the psycho got to her parents. They probably never reported it."

"That's our theory," Kimberly Green said. "But we don't know for sure. Still, there are major discrepancies. The families swear they never spoke to him, for example. Many of the phone calls and events don't match what we know to be true."

Myron saw more clearing. "So you asked Gibbs about it? About his sources?"

"Yes."

"And he refused to tell you anything."

"That's right."

"So you destroyed him."

"No."

"The one part I don't get is the plagiarism," Myron said. "I mean, did you guys somehow set that up? I can't see how. Unless you made up a book and . . . no, that's too far-fetched. So what's the deal with that?"

Kimberly Green leaned forward. "Tell us why you went to his apartment."

"Not until—"

"For several months we couldn't find Stan Gibbs," she interrupted. "We think maybe he left the country. But since he's moved into that condo, he's always alone. As I said before, he loses us sometimes. But he never accepts visitors. Several people have tracked him down. Old friends even. They come to his door or they call on the phone. And you know what always happens, Myron?"

Myron didn't like her tone of voice.

"He sends them away. Every single time. Stan Gibbs sees no one. Except you."

Myron looked up at Win. Win nodded very slowly. Myron took a look at Eric Ford before going back to Kimberly Green. "You think I'm the kidnapper?"

She leaned back with a partial shrug, looking satiated. Turning the tables and all that. "You tell us," she said.

Win started for the door. Myron rose and followed.

"Where the hell are you two going?" Green asked.

Win grabbed the knob. Myron headed around the desk and said, "I'm a suspect. I'm not talking until I have an attorney present. If you'll excuse me."

"Hey, we're just talking here," Kimberly Green said. "I never said I thought you were the kidnapper."

"Sounded that way to me," Myron said. "Win?"

"He snatches hearts," Win told her, "not people."

"You got something to hide?" Green said.

"Just his fondness for cyber pornography," Win said. Then: "Oops."

Kimberly Green stood and blocked Myron's path. "We think we know about the missing college student," she said, her eyes locked hard on his. "Do you want to know how we found out about it?"

Myron kept still.

"Through her father. He got a call from the kidnapper. I don't know what was said. He hasn't said a word since. He's catatonic. Whatever that psycho said to that girl's father put him in a padded room."

Myron felt the room shrink, the walls closing in.

"We haven't found any bodies yet, but we're pretty sure he kills them," she went on. "He kidnaps them, does Lord knows what, and makes the families suffer interminably. And you know he won't stop."

Myron kept his eyes steady. "What's your point?"

"This isn't funny."

"No," he said. "It's not. So stop playing stupid games."

She said nothing.

"I want to hear it from your mouth," Myron said. "Do you think I'm involved in this, yes or no?"

Eric Ford took this one. "No."

Kimberly Green slid back into her chair, her eyes never leaving Myron's. Eric Ford made a big hand gesture. "Please sit down."

Myron and Win moved back to their original positions.

Eric Ford said, "The novel exists. So do the passages Stan Gibbs plagiarized. The book was sent to our office anonymously—more specifically, to Special Agent Green here. We admit that we found that issue confusing at first. On the one hand, Gibbs knows about the kidnappings. On the other hand, he doesn't know everything and he clearly copied excerpts from an old, out-of-print mystery novel."

"There's an explanation," Myron said. "The kidnapper might have read the book. He might have identified with the character, become a copycat of sorts."

"We considered that possibility," Eric Ford said, "but we don't believe that's the case here."

"Why not?"

"It's complicated."

"Does it involve trigonometry?"

"You still think this is a joking manner?"

"You still think it's smart to play games?"

Ford closed his eyes. Green looked on edge. Peck continued scribbling notes. When Ford opened his eyes, he said, "We don't believe Stan Gibbs made up the crimes," he said. "We believe he perpetrated them."

Myron felt a pow. He looked up at Win. Nothing.

"You have some background in the criminal mind, do you not?" Ford asked.

Myron might have nodded.

"Well, here we have an old pattern with a new twist. Arsonists love to watch firemen put out the blaze. Ofttimes they're even the ones who report the fire. They play the good Samaritan. Murderers love to attend the funerals of their victims. We videotape funerals. I'm sure you know this."

Myron nodded again.

"Sometimes killers make themselves part of the story." Eric Ford was gesturing a lot now, his knotted hands rising and falling as though this were a press conference in too big a room. "They claim to be witnesses. They become the innocent bystanders who happened to find the body in the brush. You're familiar with this moth-near-the-flame phenomenon, are you not?"

"Yes."

"So what could be more enticing than being the only columnist to report the story? Can you imagine the high? How mind-bogglingly close to the investigation you'd be. The brilliance of your deception—for a psychotic, it's almost too delicious. And if you are perpetrating these crimes to get attention, then here you get a double dose. Attention as the serial kidnapper, one. Attention as the brilliant reporter with the scoop and possible Pulitzer, two. You even get the bonus attention of a man bravely defending the First Amendment."

Myron was holding his breath. "That's a hell of a theory," he said.

"You want more?"

"Yes."

"Why won't he answer any of our questions?"

"You said it yourself. First Amendment."

"He's not a lawyer or psychiatrist."

"But he is a reporter," Myron said.

"What kind of monster would continue to protect his source in this situation?"

"I know plenty."

"We spoke to the victims' families. They swore they never spoke to him."

"They could be lying. Maybe the kidnapper told them to say that."

"Okay, then why hasn't Gibbs done more to defend himself against the charges of plagiarism? He could have fought them. He could have even provided some detail that would have proved he was telling the truth. But no, instead he goes silent. Why?"

"You think it's because he's the kidnapper? The moth flew too close to the flame and is licking his wounds in darkness?"

"Do you have a better explanation?"

Myron said nothing.

"Lastly, there's the murder of his mistress, Melina Garston."

"What about it?"

"Think it through, Myron. We put the screws to him. Maybe he expected that, maybe he didn't. Either way, the courts don't see everything his way. You don't know about the court findings, do you?"

"Not really, no."

"That's because they were sealed. In part, the judge demanded that Gibbs show some proof he had been in contact with the killer. He finally said that Melina Garston would back him."

"And she did, right?"

"Yes. She claimed to have met the subject of his story."

"I still don't understand. If she backed him up, why would he kill her?"

"The day before Melina Garston died, she called her father. She told him that she lied."

Myron sat back, tried to take it all in.

Eric Ford said, "He's back now, Myron. Stan Gibbs has finally surfaced. While he was gone, the Sow the Seeds kidnapper was gone too. But this brand of psycho never stops on his own. He's going to strike again and soon. So before that happens, you better talk to us. Why were you at his condominium?"

Myron thought about it but not for long. "I was looking for someone."

"Who?"

"A missing bone marrow donor. He could save a child's life."

Ford looked at him steadily. "I assume that Jeremy Downing is the child in question."

So much for being vague, but Myron was not surprised. Phone records probably. Or maybe there had indeed been a tail when he visited Emily's. "Yes. And before I go on, I want your word that you will keep me in the loop."

Kimberly Green said, "You're not a part of this investigation."

"I'm not interested in your kidnapper. I'm interested in my donor. You help me find him, I'll tell you what I know."

"We agree," Ford said, waving Kimberly Green silent. "So how does Stan Gibbs fit in with your donor?"

Myron reviewed it for them. He started with Davis Taylor and then moved on to Dennis Lex and then the cryptic phone call. They kept their faces steady, Green and Peck scratching on their pads, but there was a definite jolt when he mentioned the Lex family.

They asked a few follow-up questions, like why he got involved in the first place. He said that Emily was an old friend. He wasn't about to go into the patrimony issue. Myron could see Green getting antsy. He had served his purpose. She was anxious to get out and start tracking things down.

A few minutes later, the feds snapped their pads closed and rose.

"We're on it," Ford said. He looked straight at Myron. "And we'll find your donor. You stay out."

Myron nodded and wondered if he could. After they left, Win took a seat in front of Myron's desk.

"Why do I feel like I was picked up at a bar and now it's the next morning and the guy just handed me the 'I'll call you' line?" Myron asked.

"Because that's precisely what you are," Win said. "Slut."

"Think they're holding something back?"

"Without question."

"Something big?"

"Gargantuan," Win said.

"Not much we can do about it now."

"Nope," Win said. "Nothing at all."

24

Myron's mom met him at the front door.

"I'm picking up the takeout," Mom said.

"You?"

She put her hands on her hips and shot him her best wither. "There a problem with that?"

"No, it's just . . ." He decided to drop it. "Nothing."

Mom kissed his cheek and fished through her purse for the car keys. "I'll be back in a half hour. Your father is in the back." She gave him the imploring eyes. "Alone."

"Okay," he said.

"No one else is here."

"Uh-huh."

"If you catch my drift."

"It's caught."

"You'll be alone."

"Caught, Mom. Caught."

"It'll be an opportunity—"

"Mom."

She put her hands up. "Okay, okay, I'm going."

He walked around the side of the house, past the garbage cans and recycling bins, and found Dad on the deck. The deck was sanded redwood with built-in benches and resin furniture and a Weber 500 barbecue, all brought to being during the famed Kitchen Expansion of 1994. Dad was bent over a railing with a screwdriver in his hand. For a moment, Myron fell back to those "weekend projects" with Dad, some of which lasted almost an entire hour. They would go out with toolbox in tow, Dad bent

over like he was now, muttering obscenities under his breath. Myron's
sole task consisted of handing Dad tools like a scrub nurse in the operat-
ing room, the whole exercise boring as hell, shuffling his feet in the sun,
sighing heavily, finding new angles from which to stand.

"Hey," Myron said.

Dad looked up, smiled, put down the tool. "Screw loose," he said. "But
let's not talk about your mother."

Myron laughed. They found molded-resin chairs around a table im-
paled by a blue umbrella. In front of them lay Bolitar Stadium, a small
patch of green-to-brown grass that had hosted countless, oft-solo football
games, baseball games, soccer games, Wiffle ball games (probably the
most popular sport at Bolitar Stadium), rugby scrums, badminton, kick-
ball, and that favorite pastime for the future sadist, bombardment. Myron
spotted Mom's former vegetable garden—the word *vegetable* here being
used to describe three annual soggy tomatoes and two flaccid zucchinis;
it was now slightly more overgrown than a Cambodian rice paddy. To
their right were the rusted remnants of their old tetherball pole. Tetherball. Now, there was a really dumb game.

Myron cleared his throat and put his hands on the table. "How you
feeling?"

Dad gave a big nod. "Good. You?"

"Good."

The silence floated down, puffy and relaxed. Silence with a father can
be like that. You drift back and you're young and you're safe, safe in that
all-encompassing way only a child can be with his father. You still see
him hovering in your darkened doorway, the silent sentinel to your adolescence, and you sleep the sleep of the naive, the innocent, the unformed. When you get older, you realize that this safety was just an illu-
sion, another child's perception, like the size of your backyard.

Or maybe, if you're lucky, you don't.

Dad looked older today, the flesh on his face more sagged, the once-
knotted biceps spongy under the T-shirt, starting to waste. Myron wondered how to start. Dad closed his eyes for a three count, opened them,
and said, "Don't."

"What?"

"Your mother is about as subtle as a White House press release," Dad
said. "I mean, when was the last time she picked up the takeout instead
of me?"

"Has she ever?"

"Once," Dad said. "When I had a fever of a hundred and four. And
even then she whined about it."

"Where's she going?"

"She has me on a special diet now, you know. Because of the chest pains." *Chest pains.* Euphemism for *heart attack.*

"Yeah, I figured that."

"She's even tried cooking a little. She told you?"

Myron nodded. "She baked something for me yesterday."

Dad's body went stiff. "By God," he said. "Her own son?"

"It was pretty scary."

"The woman has many, many talents, but they could airdrop that stuff into starving African nations and no one would eat it."

"So where's she going?"

"Your mother is high on some crazy Middle Eastern health food place. Just opened in West Orange. Get this, it's called Ayatollah Granola."

Myron gave him flat eyes.

"Hand to God, that's the name. Food is almost as dry as that Thanksgiving turkey your mother made when you were eight. You remember that?"

"At night," Myron said. "It still haunts my sleep."

Dad looked off again. "She left us alone so we could talk, right?"

"Right."

He made a face. "I hate when she does stuff like that. She means well, your mother. We both know that. But let's not do it, okay?"

Myron shrugged. "You say so."

"She thinks I don't like growing old. News flash: No one does. My friend Herschel Diamond—you remember Heshy?"

"Sure."

"Big guy, right? Played semipro football when we were young. So Heshy, he calls me and he says now that I'm retired, I can do tai chi with him. I mean, tai chi? What the hell is that anyway? If I want to move slowly, I have to drive down to the Y to do it with a bunch of old yentas? I mean, what's that about? I tell him no. So then Heshy, this great athlete, Myron, he could hit a softball a country mile, this marvelous big ox, he tells me we can walk together. Walk. At the mall. Speedwalk, he calls it. At the mall, for chrissake. Heshy always hated the place—now he wants us to trot around like a bunch of jackasses in matching sweatsuits and expensive walking shoes. Pump our arms with these little *faigelah* barbells. Walking shoes, he calls them. What the hell is that anyway? I never had a pair of shoes I couldn't walk in, am I right?"

He waited for an answer. Myron said, "As rain."

Dad stood up. He grabbed a screwdriver and feigned working. "So now, because I don't want to move like an old Chinaman or walk around a godforsaken mall in overpriced sneakers, your mother thinks I'm not adjusting. You hear what I'm saying?"

"Yes."

Dad stayed bent, fiddling a little more with the railing. In the distance, Myron heard children playing. A bike bell rang. Someone laughed. A lawn mower purred. Dad's voice, when he finally spoke again, was surprisingly soft. "You know what your mother really wants us to do?" he said.

"What?"

"She wants you and I to reverse roles." Dad finally looked up through his heavy-lidded eyes. "I don't want to reverse roles, Myron. I'm the father. I like being the father. Let me stay that, okay?"

Myron found it hard to speak. "Sure, Dad."

His father put his head back down, the gray wisps upright in the humidity, his breathing tool-work heavy, and Myron again felt something open up his chest and grab hold of his heart. He looked at this man he'd loved for so long, who'd gone without complaint to that damn muggy warehouse in Newark for more than thirty years, and Myron realized that he didn't know him. He didn't know what his father dreamed about, what he wanted to be when he was a kid, what he thought about his own life.

Dad kept working on the screw. Myron watched him.

Promise me you won't die, okay? Just promise me that.

He almost said it out loud.

Dad straightened himself out and studied his handiwork. Satisfied, he sat back down. They started talking about the Knicks and the recent Kevin Costner movie and the new Nelson DeMille book. They put away the toolbox. They had some iced tea. They lounged side by side in matching molded-resin chaises. An hour passed. They fell into a comfortable silence. Myron fingered the condensation on his glass. He could hear his father's breathing, moderately wheezy. Dusk had settled in, bruising the sky purple, the trees going a burnt orange.

Myron closed his eyes and said, "I got a hypothetical for you."

"Oh?"

"What would you do if you found out you weren't my real father?"

Dad's eyebrows went skyward. "You trying to tell me something?"

"Just a hypothetical. Suppose you found out right now that I wasn't your biological son. How would you react?"

"Depends," Dad said.

"On?"

"How you reacted."

"It wouldn't make a difference to me," Myron said.

Dad smiled.

"What?" Myron said.

"Easy for both of us to say it wouldn't matter. But news like that is a bombshell. You can't predict what someone will do when a bomb lands. When I was in Korea—" Dad stopped, Myron sat up. "Well, you never knew how someone would react . . ." His voice tailed off. He coughed into his fist and then started up again. "Guys you were sure would be heroes completely lost it—and vice versa. That's why you can't ask stuff like this as a hypothetical."

Myron looked at his father. His father kept his eyes on the grass, taking another deep sip. "You never talk about Korea," Myron said.

"I do," Dad said.

"Not with me."

"No, not with you."

"Why not?"

"It's what I fought for. So we wouldn't have to talk about it."

It didn't make sense and Myron understood.

"There a reason you raised this particular hypothetical?" Dad asked.

"No."

Dad nodded. He knew it was a lie, but he wouldn't push it. They settled back and watched the familiar surroundings.

"Tai chi isn't so bad," Myron said. "It's a martial art. Like tae kwon do. I've been thinking of taking it up myself."

Dad took another sip. Myron sneaked a glance. Something on his father's face began to quiver. Was Dad indeed getting smaller, more fragile—or was it like the backyard and safety, again the shifting perception of a child turned adult?

"Dad . . . ?"

"Let's go inside," his father said, standing. "We stay out much longer, one of us is going to get misty and say, 'Wanna play catch?' "

Myron bit off a laugh and followed him inside. Mom came home not long after that, lugging two bags of food as though they were stone tablets. "Everybody hungry?" she called out.

"Starving," Dad said. "I'm so hungry I could eat a vegetarian."

"Very funny, Al."

"Or even your cooking . . ."

"Ha-ha," Mom said.

". . . though I'd prefer the vegetarian."

"Stop it, Al, I'm going to phlegm up, you keep making me laugh like this." Mom dropped the bags onto the kitchen counter. "See, Myron? It's a good thing your mother is shallow."

"Shallow?" Myron asked.

"If I judged a man on brains or sense of humor," Mom continued, "you'd have never been born."

"Right-o," Dad said with a hearty smile. "But one look at your old man in a bathing suit and whammo—all mine."

"Oh please," Mom said.

"Yes," Myron said. "Please."

They both looked at him. Mom cleared her throat. "So did you two, uh, have a nice talk?"

"We talked," Dad said. "It was very life-affirming. I see the errors of my ways."

"I'm being serious."

"So am I. I see everything differently now."

She put her arms around his waist and nuzzled him. "So you'll call Heshy?"

"I'll call Heshy," he said.

"Promise."

"Yes, Ellen, I promise."

"You'll go to the Y and do jai alai with him?"

"Tai chi," Dad corrected.

"What?"

"It's called tai chi, not jai alai."

"I thought it was jai alai."

"Tai chi. Jai alai is the game with the curved rackets down in Florida."

"That's shuffleboard, Al."

"Not shuffleboard. The other thing with the sticks. And the gambling."

"Tai chi?" Mom said, testing it for sound. "Are you sure?"

"I think so."

"But you're not positive?"

"No, I'm not positive," Dad said. "Maybe you're right. Maybe it is called jai alai."

The name debate continued for a while. Myron didn't bother correcting them. Never cut in on that strange dance known as marital discourse. They ate the health food. It was indeed nasty. They laughed a lot. His parents must have said "You don't know what you're talking about" to each other fifty times; maybe it was a euphemism for "I love you."

Eventually Myron said good night. Mom kissed his cheek and made herself scarce. Dad walked him to the car. The night was silent save a lone dribbling basketball somewhere on Darby Road or maybe Coddington Terrace. A nice sound. When he hugged his father good-bye, Myron again noticed that his father felt smaller, less substantial. Myron held on a little longer than usual. For the first time he felt like the bigger man, the stronger man, and he suddenly remembered what Dad had said about reversing roles. So he held on in the dark. Time passed. Dad patted his back. Myron kept his eyes closed and held on tighter. Dad stroked his hair and shushed him. Just for a little while. Just until the roles reversed themselves again, returning both of them to where they belonged.

25

Granite Man was waiting outside the Dakota.

Myron spotted him from his car. He picked up the cell phone and called Win. "I have company."

"A rather large gentleman, yes," Win said. "Two cohorts are parked across the street in a corporate vehicle owned by the Lex family."

"I'll leave the cell phone on."

"They confiscated it last time," Win said.

"Yes."

"Likely they'll do the same."

"We'll improvise."

"Your funeral," Win said, and hung up.

Myron parked in the lot and approached Granite Man.

"Mrs. Lex would like to see you," Granite Man said.

"Do you know what she wants?" Myron asked.

Granite Man ignored the question.

"Maybe she saw me flexing on the security tape," Myron said. "Wanted to get to know me better."

Granite Man did not laugh. "You ever think about doing this comedy thing professionally?"

"There have been offers."

"I bet. Get in the car."

"Okay, but I have a curfew, you know. And I never French-kiss on the first date. Just so we understand each other."

Granite Man shook his head. "Man, I'd like to waste you."

They got in the car. Two blue-blazers sat in front. The car ride was silent except for Granite Man and His Magic Cracking Knuckles. The

Lex building emerged grudgingly through the dark. Myron traveled through the security travail again. As Win predicted, they confiscated his phone. Granite Man and the two blazers turned left this time instead of right. They escorted him into an elevator. It opened into what appeared to be living quarters.

Susan Lex's office had been done sort of Renaissance palatial, but the apartment up here—it looked like an apartment anyway—did a one-eighty. Modern and minimalism were the major themes. The walls were painted stark white and had nothing on them. The floors were a pigeon-gray wood. There were black and white bookshelves made of fiberglass, most empty, some with indistinct figurines. The couch was red and shaped like two lips. There was a well-stocked see-through bar constructed out of Lucite. Two metallic swivel stools were painted red on the base, looking about as inviting as rectal thermometers. A fire danced lazily in the fireplace, fake logs casting an unnatural glow over the black mantel. The whole place had a feel and aura about as warm as a cold sore.

Myron strolled, feigning interest. He stopped at a crystal statue with a marble base. Something modern or cubist or what-have-you. Symmetrical Bowel Movement maybe. Myron put his hand on it. Substantial. He looked out the one-way glass. Too low for much of a view beyond the hedges lining the front gate. Hmm.

The two blue-blazers did the Buckingham Palace Guard thing on either side of the door. Granite Man followed Myron, his hands clasped behind his lower back. A door on the other side of the room opened. Myron was not surprised to see Susan Lex enter, again keeping her distance. There was a man with her this time. Myron did not bother approaching.

"And you are?" he called out.

Susan Lex answered this one. "This is my brother Bronwyn."

"Not the brother I'm interested in," Myron said.

"Yes, I know. Please sit down."

Granite Man gestured toward the lips-couch. Myron sat on the lower lip, waiting to be swallowed. Granite Man sat right next to him. Cozy.

"Bronwyn and I would like you to answer some questions, Mr. Bolitar," Susan Lex said.

"Could you move a little closer?"

She smiled. "I think not."

"I showered."

She ignored the remark. "I understand that you occasionally do some investigative work," Susan Lex said.

Myron did not reply.

"Is that correct?"

"Depends on what you mean by investigative work."

"I'll take that as a yes," Susan Lex said.

Myron gave her a suit-yourself shrug.

"Is that why you're searching for our brother?" she asked.

"I already told you why I was searching for him."

"That bit about him being a bone marrow donor?"

"It's not a bit."

"Please, Mr. Bolitar," Susan Lex said with that rich-people air. "We both know that's a lie."

Myron started to rise. Granite Man put a hand on Myron's knee. It felt like a cinder block. Granite Man shook his head. Myron stayed where he was. "It's not a lie," he said.

"We're wasting time," Susan Lex said. She flicked her eyes at Granite Man. "Show him the pictures, Grover."

Myron turned to him. "Grover is the name of my very favorite *Sesame Street* character. I want you to know that."

"We've been following you, *Myron*." Granite Man handed him a pile of photographs. Myron looked at them. They were eight-by-tens of him at the condo with Stan Gibbs. The first one showed him knocking on the door. The second one showed Stan sticking his head out. The third one showed them both heading inside the condo.

"Well?"

Myron frowned. "I have no knack for accessorizing."

"We know that you're working for Stan Gibbs," Susan Lex said.

"Doing what exactly?" Myron asked.

"Investigating. As I stated earlier. So now that we understand your true motive, tell me how much it will cost for you to go away."

"I don't know what you're talking about."

"Simply put, how much will it cost to have you cease and desist?" Susan Lex asked. "Or are you going to force us to destroy you too?"

Too?

Brain click.

Myron turned his attention to the silent brother. "Let me ask you something, Bronwyn," he said. "You and Dennis were both going to nursery school. You both disappeared. Two weeks later, only you came back. How come? What happened to your brother?"

Bronwyn's mouth opened and closed, marionette style. He looked to his sister for help.

"It's like he disappeared off the face of the earth after that," Myron went on. "For thirty years, he's totally off the radar. But now, well, it's like he's come back for some reason. He changed his name, opened a small checking account, donated blood to a bone marrow center. So what gives, Bron? You got a clue?"

Bronwyn said, "That simply cannot be!"

His sister silenced him with a look. But Myron felt something in the air. He mulled the feeling over and another thought hit him: Maybe the Lex siblings didn't know the answer themselves. Maybe they were looking for Dennis too.

It was while he was lost in that thought that Granite Man punched him deep in the stomach. The fist followed through to the point where it seemed the knuckles must have reached the fabric of the couch. Myron snapped closed at the waist. He dropped to the floor, struggled to regain a breath, suffocating from within. He lowered his head to his knees, consumed with one thought: air. He needed air.

Susan Lex's voice boomed in his ears. "Stan Gibbs knows the truth. His father is a disgusting liar. His accusations are totally without merit. But I'll defend my family, Mr. Bolitar. You tell Mr. Gibbs he has not yet begun to suffer. What has happened to him so far is nothing compared to what I will do to him—and you—if he doesn't stop. Do you understand?"

Air. Gulps of air. Myron managed not to throw up. He took his time, looked up, met her eye. "Not even a little," he said.

Susan Lex looked at Grover. "Then make him."

With that, she left the room. Her brother took one last look and followed.

Myron gathered his breath a hitch at a time. "Nice sucker punch, Grover," he said.

Grover shrugged. "I went easy on you."

"Next time, go easy when I'm looking, tough guy."

"Won't change the outcome."

"We'll see." Myron sat up. "So what the hell is she talking about?"

"I thought Ms. Lex made herself very clear," he said. "But because you appear to be a little vacant between the ears, I'll restate her position. She doesn't like people interfering with her affairs. Stan Gibbs, for example, interfered. You can see what happened to him. You interfered. You're about to see what's going to happen to you."

Myron struggled to his feet. The blue-blazers stayed by the door. Granite Man started cracking his knuckles again. "Listen closely, please," he said. "I'm going to break your leg. Then you're going to limp your sorry ass out of here and tell Gibbs that if he sniffs around again, I will exterminate you both. Any questions?"

"Just one," Myron said. "Don't you think leg breaking is a tad cliché?"

Grover smiled. "Not the way I do it."

Myron looked around the room.

"Nowhere to run, my friend."

"Who wants to run?" Myron countered.

Without warning, he grabbed the heavy bowel-movement statue. The blue-blazers drew their guns. Granite Man ducked. But Myron wasn't going for them. He heaved the statue, straightened his arms, spun around like a discus thrower, and hurled it marble-base-forward at the plate-glass window. The window exploded.

And that was when the gunfire began.

"Hit the deck!" Myron shouted.

The blue-blazers obeyed. Myron dove. The bullets continued. Sniper fire. One took out the overhead light. One hit the lamp.

Gotta love that Win.

"You want to live," Myron shouted, "stay down."

The bullets stopped. One of the blue-blazers started rising. A bullet sang out, nearly parting the man's hair. The blazer dropped back down, flattening himself into a bearskin rug.

"I'm getting up now," Myron said. "And I'm leaving. I'd advise you guys to stay down. And, Grover?"

"What?"

"Radio downstairs. Tell them not to stop me. I can't be certain but I'm pretty sure my friend will lob in grenades if I'm unduly delayed."

Granite Man made the call. No one moved. Myron stood up. He almost whistled as he walked out.

26

I t was midnight when Myron knocked on the door of Stan Gibbs's condo.

"Let's take a walk," Myron said to him.

Stan threw down his cigarette, smothered it with his toe. "A drive might be better," he countered. "The feds use long-range amplifiers."

They got into Myron's Ford Taurus, aka the Chick Trawler. Stan Gibbs flicked on the radio and started playing with the stations. Commercial for Heineken. Does anyone really care that it's imported by Van Munchin and Company?

"Are you wearing a wire, Myron?"

"No."

"But the FBI spoke to you," Stan said. "After you left."

"How did you know?"

"They're watching me," he said with a shrug. "It would only be logical to assume they questioned you."

"Tell me about your connection with Dennis Lex," Myron said.

"I already told you. I don't have one."

"A big guy named Grover picked me up tonight. He and Susan Lex gave me a very stern warning not to play with you anymore. Bronwyn was there too."

Stan Gibbs closed his eyes and rubbed them. "They knew about your visit here."

"Had eight-by-ten glossies."

"And they concluded that you're working for me."

"Bingo."

Stan shook his head. "Get out of this, Myron. You don't want to mess with these people."

"Is that advice you wished someone had given you earlier?"

His smile had nothing behind it. Exhaustion came off him like heat squiggles on a hot sidewalk. "You have no idea," he said.

"Tell me about it."

"No."

"I can help," Myron said.

"Against the Lexes? They're too powerful."

"And being powerful, you wanted to do a story on them, right?"

He said nothing.

"And they didn't like that. In fact, they took exception."

More nothing.

"You started digging where they didn't want you to. You learned that there was another brother named Dennis."

"Yes."

"And that really pissed them off."

Stan started biting a hangnail.

"Come on, Stan. Don't make me drag this out of you."

"You've pretty much got it."

"Then tell me."

"I wanted to do a story on them. An exposé, really. I even had a publisher all lined up for a book deal. But then the Lexes got wind of it. They warned me to stay away. A big man came to my apartment. I didn't catch his name. Looked like Sergeant Rock."

"That would be Grover."

"He told me that I could stop or I could be destroyed."

"And that only made you more curious."

"I guess."

"So you found out about Dennis Lex."

"Just that he existed. And that he vanished into thin air when he was a young child." Stan turned to him. Myron slowed the car and felt something creep along the top of his scalp.

"Like the Sow the Seeds victims," Myron finished.

"No."

"Why not?"

"It's different."

"How?" Myron asked.

"This is going to sound silly," Stan said, "but the family doesn't have that same sense of terror that the other families have."

"The rich are good with façades."

"It's more than that," Stan said. "I can't put my finger on it exactly. But I'm sure Susan and Bronwyn Lex know what happened to their brother."

"But they want to keep it a secret."

"Yes."

"Do you have a guess why?"

"No," Stan said.

Myron glanced back. The feds were following at a discreet enough distance.

"Do you think Susan Lex is responsible for that novel surfacing?"

"The thought has crossed my mind."

"But you never looked into it?"

"I started to. After the scandal hit. But I got a call from the big guy. He told me that it was just the beginning. That he was just flicking his finger and next time he would crush me between both palms."

"He can be a poetic fellow," Myron said.

"Yes."

"But I still don't get something."

"What?"

"You don't scare easily. When they warned you away the first time, you ignored it. After what they did to you, I'd have thought you'd fight back even harder."

"You're forgetting something," Stan said.

"What?"

"Melina Garston."

Silence.

"Think about it," Stan said. "My mistress, the only person who can back up my meeting with the Sow the Seeds kidnapper, ends up dead."

"Her father claims she retracted that."

"Oh, right. In some bizarre before-death confession."

"You think the Lexes arranged that too?"

"Why not? Look at what happened here. Who's the lead suspect in Melina's murder? I am, right? That's what the feds told you. They think I killed her. We know that the Lexes have enough juice to dig up this novel I supposedly plagiarized. Who knows what else they can do?"

"You think they could frame you for the murder?"

"At the very least."

"Are you saying they killed Melina Garston?"

"Maybe. Or it could have been the Sow the Seeds kidnapper. I don't know."

"But you think Melina was a warning."

"She was definitely a warning," Stan Gibbs said. "I just don't know who sent it."

On the radio, Stevie sang out about a landslide coming down. Oh yeah.

"You're leaving something out, Stan."

Stan kept his eyes forward. "What's that?"

"There's a personal connection here," Myron said.

"What do you mean?"

"Susan Lex mentioned your father. She said he was a liar."

Stan shrugged. "She might be right."

"What does he have to do with this?"

"Take me back."

"Don't hold back on me now."

"What do you really want here, Myron?"

"Excuse me?"

"What's your interest here?"

"I told you."

"That boy who needs a bone marrow transplant?"

"He's thirteen years old, Stan. He'll die without it."

"And what if I don't believe you? I did a little research of my own. You used to do government work."

"A long time ago."

"And maybe now you're helping the FBI. Or even the Lex family."

"No."

"I can't take that chance."

"Why not? You're telling me the truth, right? The truth can't hurt you."

He snorted. "You really believe that?"

"Why did Susan Lex mention your father?"

Nothing.

"Where is your father?" Myron said.

"That's just it."

"What?"

Stan looked at him. "He vanished. Eight years ago."

Vanished. That word again.

"I know what you're thinking and you're wrong. My father wasn't a well man. He had been in and out of institutions all his life. We've always assumed he ran off."

"But you never heard from him."

"That's right."

"Dennis Lex vanishes. Your father vanishes—"

"More than twenty years apart," Stan interjected. "It's not connected."

"So I still don't get it," Myron said. "What does your father or his disappearance have to do with the Lexes?"

"They think he's the reason I wanted to do the story. But they're wrong."

"Why would they think that?"

"My father was a student of Raymond Lex's. Before *Midnight Confessions* came out."

"So?"

"So my father claimed the novel was his. He said that Raymond Lex stole it from him."

"Jesus Christ."

"No one believed him," Stan added quickly. "Like I said, he wasn't right in the head."

"Yet you suddenly decided to investigate the family?"

"Yes."

"And you're telling me that's just a coincidence? That your own investigation had nothing to do with your father's accusations?"

Stan leaned his head against the car window like a little kid longing for home. "No one believed my father. That includes me. He was a sick man. Delusional even."

"So?"

"So at the end of the day, he was still my father," Stan said. "Maybe I owed it to him to at least give him the benefit of the doubt."

"Do you think Raymond Lex plagiarized your father?"

"No."

"Do you think your father is still alive?"

"I don't know."

"There has to be a connection here," Myron said. "Your story, the Lex family, your father's accusations—"

Stan closed his eyes. "No more."

Myron switched tracks. "How did the Sow the Seeds kidnapper get in touch with you?"

"I never reveal sources."

"Come on, Stan."

"No," he said firmly. "I may have lost a lot. But not that part of me. You know I can't say anything about my sources."

"You know who it is, don't you?"

"Take me home, Myron."

"Is it Dennis Lex—or did the same kidnapper take Dennis Lex?"

Stan crossed his arms. "Home," he said.

His face closed down. Myron saw it. There would be no more give tonight. He took a right and started heading back. Neither man spoke again until Myron stopped the car in the front of the condominium.

"Are you telling the truth, Myron? About the bone marrow donor?"

"Yes."

"This boy is someone close to you?"

Myron kept both hands on the wheel. "Yes."

"So there's no way you'll walk away from this?"

"None."

Stan nodded, mostly to himself. "I'll do what I can. But you have to trust me."

"What do you mean?"

"Give me a few days."

"To do what?"

"You won't hear from me for a little while. Don't let that shake your faith."

"What are you talking about?"

"You do what you have to," he said. "I'll do the same."

Stan Gibbs stepped out of the car and disappeared into the night.

27

Greg Downing woke Myron early the next morning with a phone call. "Nathan Mostoni left town," he said. "So I came back to New York. I get to pick up my son this afternoon."

Goody-goody for you, Myron thought. But he kept his tongue still.

"I'm going to the Ninety-second Street Y to shoot around," Greg said. "You want to come?"

"No," Myron said.

"Come anyway. Ten o'clock."

"I'll be late." Myron hung up and rolled out of bed. He checked his e-mail and found a JPEG image from Esperanza's contact at AgeComp. He clicked the file and an image slowly appeared on the screen. The possible face of Dennis Lex as a man in his mid to late thirties. Weird. Myron looked at the picture. Not familiar. Not familiar at all. Remarkable work, these age-enhanced images. So lifelike. Except in the eyes. The eyes always looked like the eyes of the dead.

He clicked on the print icon and heard his Hewlett-Packard go to work. Myron checked the clock on the bottom right-hand corner of the screen. Still early in the morning, but he didn't want to wait.

He called Melina Garston's father.

George Garston agreed to meet Myron at his penthouse at Fifth Avenue and Seventy-eighth Street, overlooking Central Park. A dark-haired woman answered the door. She introduced herself as Sandra and led him silently down the corridor. Myron looked out a window. He could see the Gothic outline of the Dakota all the way across the park. He remembered reading somewhere how Woody and Mia would wave towels from their respective apartments on either side of Central Park. Happier days, no doubt.

"I don't understand what you have to do with my daughter," George Garston said to him. Garston wore a collared blue shirt nicely offset by a shock of white neck-to-chest hairs sprouting out like a troll doll's. His bald head was an almost perfect sphere jammed between two boulder-excuses for shoulders. He had the proud, burly build of a successful immigrant, but you could see that he'd taken a hit. There was a slump there now, the stoop of the eternally grieving. Myron had seen it before. Grief like his breaks your back. You go on, but you always stoop. You smile, but it never really reaches the eyes.

"Probably nothing," Myron said. "I'm trying to find someone. He may be connected to your daughter's murder. I don't know."

The study was too-dark cherry-wood with drawn curtains and one lamp giving off a faint yellow glow. George Garston turned to the side, staring at the rich paisley wallpaper, showing Myron his profile. "We've worked together once," he said. "Not us personally. Our companies. Did you know that?"

"Yes," Myron said.

George Garston had made his fortune with a chain of Greek quasi-restaurants, the kind that work best as mall stands in crowded food courts. The chain was called Achilles Meals. For real. Myron had a Greek hockey player who endorsed the chain regionally, in the upper Midwest.

"So a sports agent is interested in my daughter's murder," Garston said.

"It's a long story."

"The police aren't talking. But they think it's her boyfriend. This reporter. Do you agree?"

"I don't know. What do you think?"

He made a scoffing noise. Myron could barely see his face anymore. "What do I think?" he said. "You sound like one of those grief counselors."

"Didn't mean to."

"Spewing all that sensitivity garbage. They're just trying to distract you from reality. They say they want you to face it. But really, it's the opposite. They want you to dig so far into yourself you won't be able to see how terrible your life is now." He grunted and shifted in his chair. "I don't have an opinion on Stan Gibbs. I never met him."

"Did you know he and your daughter were dating?"

In the dark, Myron saw the big head silently go back and forth. "She told me she had a boyfriend," he said. "She didn't tell me his name. Or that he was married."

"You wouldn't have approved?"

"Of course I wouldn't have approved," he said, trying to sound snappish, but he was beyond petty indignation. "Would you approve if it was your daughter?"

"I guess not. So you knew nothing about her relationship with Stan Gibbs?"

"Nothing."

"I understand that you spoke to her not long before she died."

"Four days before."

"Can you tell me about the conversation?"

"Melina had been drinking," he said in that pure monotone you get when the words have been ricocheting around your brain too long. "A lot. She drank too much, my daughter. Got that from her papa—who got it from his papa. The Garston family legacy." He made a chuckling sound that sounded far closer to a sob than anything in the neighborhood of a laugh.

"Melina talked to you about her testimony?"

"Yes."

"Could you tell me what she said exactly?"

" 'I made a mistake, Papa.' That's what she said. She said that she lied."

"What did you say?"

"I didn't even know what she was talking about. It's as I told you before—I didn't know about this boyfriend."

"Did you ask her to explain?"

"Yes."

"And?"

"And she didn't. She said to forget about it. She said she'd take care of it. Then she told me she loved me and hung up."

Silence.

"I had two children, Mr. Bolitar. Did you know that?"

Myron shook his head.

"A plane crash killed my Michael three years ago. Now an animal has tortured and killed my girl. My wife, her name was Melina too, passed away fifteen years ago. There is no one. Forty-eight years ago, I thought I came to this country with nothing. I made a lot of money. And now I truly have nothing. You understand?"

"Yes," Myron said.

"Is that all, then?"

"Your daughter had an apartment on Broadway."

"Yes."

"Are her personal belongings still there?"

"Sandra—that's my daughter-in-law—she's been packing her things. But it's all still there. Why?"

"I'd like to go through them, if it's okay with you."

"The police already did that."

"I know."

"You think you might find something they didn't?"

"I'm almost positive I won't."

"But?"

"But I'm attacking this thing from a different perspective. It gives me a fresh set of eyes."

George Garston flicked on his desk lamp. The yellow from the bulb painted his face a dark jaundice. Myron could see that his eyes were too dry, brittle like fallen acorns in the sun. "If you find whoever killed my Melina, you will tell me first."

"No," Myron said.

"Do you know what he did to her?"

"Yes. And I know what you want to do. But it won't make you feel any better."

"You say this like you know it for a fact."

Myron kept silent.

George Garston flicked off the light and turned away. "Sandra will take you over now."

"He sits in that study all day," Sandra Garston told him, pressing the elevator button. "He won't go out anymore."

"It's still new," Myron said.

She shook her head. Her blue-black hair fell in big, loose curls, like thermal fax paper fresh out of the machine. But despite the hair color, her overall effect was almost Icelandic, the face and build of a world-class speed skater. Her features were sharp and ended rather abruptly. Her skin had the red of raw cold.

"He thinks he has no one," she said.

"He has you."

"I'm a daughter-in-law. He sees me and it's like a tether to Michael. I don't have the heart to tell him I finally started dating."

When they reached the street, Myron asked, "Were you and Melina close?"

"I think so, yes."

"Did you know about her relationship with Stan Gibbs?"

"Yes."

"But she never told her father."

"Oh, she would never. Papa didn't approve of most men. A married one would have sent him off the ledge."

They crossed the street and into the mid-city wonder known as Central Park. The park was packed on this rather spectacular day. Asian sketch artists hustled business. Men jogged by in those shorts that look suspiciously like diapers. Sunbathers lazed around on the grass, crowded together yet totally alone. New York City is like that. E. B. White once said that New York bestows the gift of loneliness and the gift of privacy. Damn straight. It was like everyone was plugged into their own internal Walkman, each playing a different tune, bopping obliviously to his or her own beat.

A yah-dude with a bandanna around his head tossed a Frisbee and yelled "Fetch," but he had no dog. Hard-bodied women skated by in black jogging bras. Lots of men with various builds had their shirts off. Examples: A guy thick with flab that looked like wet Play-Doh jiggled past him. Behind him, a well-built guy skidded to a stop and arrogantly flexed a bicep. Actually flexed. In public. Myron frowned. He didn't know which was worse: guys who shouldn't take their shirts off and do, or guys who should take their shirts off and do.

When they reached Central Park West, Myron asked, "Did you have a problem with her dating a married man?"

Sandra shrugged. "I worried, of course. But he told Melina he would leave his wife."

"Don't they all?"

"Melina believed it. She seemed happy."

"Did you ever meet Stan Gibbs?"

"No. Their relationship was supposed to be a secret."

"Did she ever tell you about lying in court?"

"No," she said. "Never."

Sandra used her key and swung the door open. Myron stepped inside. Colors. Lots of them. Happy colors. The apartment looked like the Magical Mystery Tour meets the Teletubbies, all bright hues, especially greens, with hazy psychedelic splashes. The walls were covered with vivid watercolors of distant lands and ocean voyages. Some surreal stuff too. The effect was like an Enya video.

"I started throwing her stuff in boxes," Sandra said. "But it's hard to pack up a life."

Myron nodded. He started walking around the small apartment, hoping for a psychic revelation or something. None came. He ran his eyes over the artwork.

"She was supposed to have her first show in the Village next month," Sandra said.

Myron studied a painting with white domes and crystal blue water. He recognized the spot in Mykonos. It was wonderfully done. Myron could almost smell the salt of the Mediterranean, taste the grilled fish along the beach, feel the night sand clinging to a lover's skin. No clue here, but he stared another minute or two before turning away.

He started going through the boxes. He found a high school yearbook, class of 1986, and flipped through it until he found Melina's picture. She'd like to paint, it said. He glanced again at the walls. So bright and optimistic, her work. Death, Myron knew, was always ironic. Young death most ironic of all.

He turned his attention back to her photograph. Melina was looking off to the side with the hesitant, unsure smile of high school. Myron knew it well. Don't we all. He closed the book and headed to her closets. Her clothes were neatly arranged, lots of sweaters folded on the top shelf, shoes lined up like tiny soldiers. He moved back to the boxes and found her photographs in a shoebox. A shoebox of all things. Myron shook his head and started going through them. Sandra sat on the floor next to him. "That's her mother," she said.

Myron looked at the photograph of two women, clearly mother and daughter, embracing. There was no sign of the unsure smile this time. This smile—the smile in her mother's arms—soared like an angel's song. Myron stared at the angel-song smile and imagined that celestial mouth crying out in hopeless agony. He thought about George Garston alone in that jaundice-lit study. And he understood.

Myron checked his watch. Time to pick up the pace. He thumbed through pictures of her father, her brother, Sandra, family outings, the norm. No pictures of Stan Gibbs. Nothing helpful.

He found makeup and perfume in another box. In another, he stumbled across a diary, but Melina hadn't written anything in it for two years. He paged through it, but it felt like too much of an unnecessary violation. He found a love letter from an old boyfriend. He found some receipts.

He found copies of Stan's columns.

Hmm.

In her address book. All the columns. There were no markings on them. Just the clippings themselves, held together by a paper clip. So what did that mean? He checked them again. Just clippings. He put them aside and did some more flipping. Something fell out near the back. Myron picked up a piece of cream-colored or aged-white paper torn along the left edge, more a card really, folded in half. The outside was totally blank. He opened it. On the upper half, the words *With Love, Dad* had been written in script. Myron thought again about George Garston sitting alone in that room and felt a deep burn flush his skin.

He sat on the couch now and tried again to conjure up something. That might sound weird—sitting in this too empty room, the sweet smell of a dead woman still hovering, feeling not unlike that tiny old lady in the *Poltergeist* movies—but you never knew. The victims didn't speak to him or anything like that. But sometimes he could imagine what they'd been thinking and feeling and some spark would hit the edges and start to flame. So he tried it again.

Nothing.

He let his eyes wander across the canvases and the burn under his skin started up again. He scanned the bright colors, let them assault him. The brightness should have protected her. Nonsense, but there you have it. She'd had a life. Melina worked and she painted and she loved bright colors and had too many sweaters and stored her precious memories in a shoebox and someone had snuffed that life away because none of that meant anything to him. None of that was important. It made Myron mad.

He closed his eyes and tried to turn the anger down a notch. Anger wasn't good. It clouded reason. He'd let that side of him out before—his Batman complex, as Esperanza had called it—but being a hero seeking justice or vengeance (if they weren't the same thing) was unwise, unhealthy. Eventually you saw things you didn't want to. You learned truths you never should have. It stings and then it deadens. Better to stay away.

But the heat in his blood would not leave him. So he stopped fighting it, let the heat soothe him, relax his muscles, settle gently over him. Maybe the heat wasn't such a bad thing. Maybe the horrors he'd seen and the truths he'd learned hadn't changed him, hadn't deadened him, after all.

Myron closed the boxes, took one last, lingering look at the sunkissed isle of Mykonos, and made a silent vow.

28

Greg and Myron met up on the court. Myron strapped on his knee brace. Greg averted his eyes. The two men shot for half an hour, barely speaking, lost in the pure strokes. People ducked in and pointed at Greg. Several kids came up to him and asked him for autographs. Greg acquiesced, glancing at Myron as he took pen in hand, clearly uncomfortable getting all this attention in front of the man whose career he had ended.

Myron stared back at him, offering no solace.

After some time, Myron said, "There a reason you wanted me here, Greg?"

Greg kept shooting.

"Because I have to get back to the office," Myron said.

Greg grabbed the ball, dribbled twice, took a turn-around jumper. "I saw you and Emily that night. You know that?"

"I know that," Myron said.

Greg grabbed the rebound, took a lazy hook, let the ball hit the floor and slowly bounce toward Myron. "We were getting married the next day. You know that?"

"Know that too."

"And there you were," Greg said, "her old boyfriend, screwing her brains out."

Myron picked up the ball.

"I'm trying to explain here," Greg said.

"I slept with Emily," Myron said. "You saw us. You wanted revenge. You told Big Burt Wesson to hurt me during a preseason game. He did. End of story."

"I wanted him to hurt you, yes. I didn't mean for him to end your career."

"You say tomato, I say tomahto."

"It wasn't intentional."

"Don't take this the wrong way," Myron said in a voice that sounded awfully calm in his own ears, "but I don't give two shits about your intentions. You fired a weapon at me. You might have aimed for a flesh wound, but that didn't happen. You think that makes you blameless?"

"You fucked my fiancée."

"And she fucked me. I didn't owe you anything. She did."

"Are you telling me you don't understand?"

"I understand. It just doesn't absolve you."

"I'm not looking for absolution."

"Then what do you want, Greg? You want us to clasp hands and sing 'Kumbaya'? Do you know what you did to me? Do you know what the one moment cost me?"

"I think maybe I do," Greg said. He swallowed, put out a pleading hand as though he wanted to explain more, and then he let the hand drop to the side. "I'm so sorry."

Myron started shooting but he felt his throat swell.

"You don't know how sorry I am."

Myron said nothing. Greg tried to wait him out. It didn't work.

"What else do you want me to say here, Myron?"

Myron kept shooting.

"How do I tell you I'm sorry?"

"You've already done it," Myron said.

"But you won't accept it."

"No, Greg. I won't. I live without playing pro ball. You live without my accepting your apology. Pretty good deal for you, you ask me."

Myron's cell phone rang. He ran over, picked it up, said hello.

A whisper asked, "Did you do as I instructed?"

His bones turned to solid ice. He swallowed away something thick and said, "As you instructed?"

"The boy," the voice whispered.

The stale air pressed against him, weighed down his lungs. "What about him?"

"Did you say one last good-bye?"

Something inside of Myron withered up and blew away. His knees buckled as the realization seeped into his chest. And the voice came on again:

"Did you say one last good-bye to the boy?"

Myron snapped his head toward Greg. "Where's Jeremy?"
"What?"
"Where is he?"
Greg saw whatever it was on Myron's face and dropped the basketball. "He's with Emily, I guess. I don't get him until noon."
"Got a cell phone?"
"Yes."
"Call her."
Greg was already heading toward his gym bag, the athlete with the wonderful reflexes. "What's going on?"
"Probably nothing."
Myron explained about the call. Greg did not slow down to listen. He dialed. Myron started running toward his car. Greg followed, the phone pressed against his ear.
"No answer," Greg said. He left a message on the machine.
"Does she have a cell phone?"
"If she does, I don't have the number."
Myron hit a stored number as they walked. Esperanza picked up.
"I need Emily's cell phone number."
"Give me five," Esperanza said.
Myron hit another stored number. Win answered and said, "Articulate."
"Possible trouble."
"I'm here."
They reached the car. Greg was calm. That surprised Myron. On the court, when the pressure mounted, Greg's modus operandi was to get

freaky, start screaming, psych himself into a frenzy. But of course, this was not a game. As his father had recently told him, when real bombs drop, you never know how someone will react.

Myron's phone rang. Esperanza gave him Emily's cell phone number. Myron dialed it. After six rings, Emily's voice mail picked up. Damn. Myron left a message. He turned to Greg.

"Any clue where Jeremy might be?" Myron asked.

"No," Greg said.

"How about a neighbor we can call? Or a friend?"

"When Emily and I were married, we lived in Ridgewood. I don't know the neighbors in Franklin Lakes."

Myron gripped the steering wheel. He hit the accelerator. "Jeremy's probably safe," Myron said, trying to believe it. "I don't even know how this guy would know his name. It's probably a bluff."

Greg started shaking.

"He'll be all right."

"Jesus, Myron, I read those articles. If that guy has my kid . . ."

"We should call the FBI," Myron said. "Just in case."

"You think that's the way to go?" Greg asked.

Myron looked at him. "Why? You don't?"

"I just want to pay the ransom and get my boy back. I don't want any-body screwing it up."

"I think we should call," Myron said. "But it's your decision."

"There's something else we have to consider," Greg said.

"What?"

"There's a good chance this wacko is our donor, right?"

"Yes."

"If the FBI kills him, it's over for Jeremy."

"First things first," Myron said. "We have to find Jeremy. And we have to find this kidnapper."

Greg kept shaking.

"What do you want to do, Greg?"

"You think we should call?"

"Yes."

Greg nodded slowly. "Call," he said.

Myron dialed Kimberly Green's number. He felt waves pounding in his head, the blood flowing to his ears. He tried not to think about Jeremy's face, what his smile had looked like when he opened that door.

Did you say one last good-bye to the boy?

A voice said, "Federal Bureau of Investigation."

"Myron Bolitar calling Kimberly Green."

"Special Agent Green is unavailable."

"The Sow the Seeds kidnapper may have taken somebody else. Put her on."

The hold was longer than Myron expected.

Kimberly Green started with a bark. "What the hell are you ranting about?"

"He just called me." Myron filled her in.

"We're on our way," she said.

They hit a patch of traffic where Route 4 met Route 17, but Myron went up on the grass and knocked over several orange construction buckets. He broke off at Route 208 and exited near the synagogue. Two miles later, they made the final turn onto Emily's street. Myron could see two FBI cars making the turn at the same time.

Greg, who had gone into something of a trance, woke up and pointed. "There she is."

Emily was putting her key in the front door. Myron started honking madly. She looked back confused. He turned the car and skidded. The FBI car followed. Myron and Greg were both out the door almost before the car had stopped.

"Where's Jeremy?" they both said in unison.

Emily had her head tilted to the side. "What?" she called back. "What's going on here?"

Greg took it. "Where is he, Emily?"

"He's with a friend—"

From inside the house, the phone started ringing. Everyone froze. Emily snapped out of it first. She ran inside and picked up the phone. She put the phone to her ear, cleared her throat, and said, "Hello."

Through the receiver, they could all hear Jeremy's scream.

30

There were six federal agents in all. Kimberly Green was the task force leader. They set up with quiet efficiency. Myron sat on one couch, Greg the other. Emily paced between them. There was probably something symbolic in that, but Myron was not sure what. He tried to push himself past the numb so he could get to a place where he could do some good.

The phone call had been brief. After the scream, the whispery voice had said, "We'll call back." That was it. No warnings not to contact the authorities. No telling them to prepare funds. No setting up another time to call. Nothing.

They all sat there, the boy's scream still echoing, mauling, shredding, conjuring up images of what could have made a thirteen-year-old boy scream like that. Myron shut his eyes and pushed hard. That was what the bastard wanted. Unwise to play into that.

Greg had contacted his bank. He was not a risky investor, and so most of his assets were liquid. If ransom money was needed, he'd be ready. The various feds, all male except for Kimberly Green, put traces on all the possible phones, including Myron's. She and her men were doing a lot of sotto voce. Myron hadn't pressed them yet. But that wasn't going to last.

Kimberly caught his eyes and waved him over. He stood and excused himself. Greg and Emily paid no attention, still lost in the vortex of that scream.

"We need to talk," she said.

"Okay," Myron said. "Start by telling me what happened when you checked out Dennis Lex."

"You're not family," she said. "I could throw you out."

"This isn't your house," he said. "What happened with Dennis Lex?"

She put her hands on her hips. "It's a dead end."

"How so?"

"We traced it down. He's not involved in any of this."

"How do you know that?"

"Myron, come on. We're not stupid."

"So where is Dennis Lex?"

"It's not relevant," she said.

"The hell it's not. Even if he's not the kidnapper, we still have him as the bone marrow donor."

"No," she said. "Your donor is Davis Taylor."

"Who changed his name from Dennis Lex."

"We don't know that."

Myron made a face. "What are you talking about?"

"Davis Taylor was an employee in the Lex conglomerate."

"What?"

"You heard me."

"So why did he donate blood for a bone marrow drive?"

"It was a work thing," she said. "The plant boss had a sick nephew. Everyone at the plant gave."

Myron nodded. Something finally made sense. "So if he didn't give a blood sample," he said, "it would have been conspicuous."

"Right."

"You got a description on him?"

"He worked on his own, kept to himself. All anyone remembers is a man with a full beard, glasses, and long blond hair."

"A disguise," Myron said. "And we know Davis Taylor's original name was Dennis Lex. What else?"

Kimberly Green raised her hand. "Enough." She sort of hitched herself up, trying to alter momentum. "Stan Gibbs is still our top suspect here. What did you talk about last night?"

"Dennis Lex," Myron said. "Don't you get it?"

"Get what?"

"Dennis Lex is connected into all this. He's either the kidnapper, or maybe he was the first victim."

"Neither," she said.

"Then where is he?"

She shook it off. "What else did you two talk about?"

"Stan's father."

"Edwin Gibbs?" That got her attention. "What about him?"

"That he vanished eight years ago. But you already know about that, don't you?"

She nodded a little too firmly. "We do," she said.

"So what do you think happened to him?" Myron asked.

She hesitated. "You believe that Dennis Lex may be Sow the Seeds' first victim, correct?"

"I think it's something to look into, yes."

"Our theory," she went on, "is that the first victim may have been Edwin Gibbs."

Myron made a face. "You think Stan kidnapped his own father?"

"Killed him. And the others. We don't believe any of them are still alive."

Myron tried not to let that sink in. "You have any evidence or motive?"

"Sometimes the apple doesn't fall far from the tree."

"Oh, that'll go over big with a jury. Ladies and gentlemen, the apple doesn't fall far from the tree. And you should never put the cart before the horse. Plus every dog has his day." He shook his head. "Are you listening to yourself?"

"On its own, I admit it doesn't make sense. But put it all together. Eight years ago, Stan was starting out on his own. He was twenty-four, his father forty-six. By all accounts, the two men did not get along. Suddenly Edwin Gibbs vanishes. Stan never reports it."

"This is silly."

"Maybe. But then add back everything else we already know. The only columnist to get this scoop. The plagiarism. Melina Garston. Everything that Eric Ford discussed with you yesterday."

"It still doesn't add up."

"Then tell me where Stan Gibbs is."

Myron looked at her. "Isn't he at the condo?"

"Last night, after you two talked, Stan Gibbs slipped surveillance. He's done that before. We usually pick him up a few hours later. But that hasn't happened this time. He's suddenly out of sight—and by coincidence, Jeremy Downing has been snatched by the Sow the Seeds kidnapper. You want to explain that one to me?"

Myron's mouth felt dry. "You're searching for him?"

"We got an APB. But we know he's good at hiding. You got any clue where he went?"

"None."

"He said nothing to you about it?"

"He mentioned that he might go away for a few days. But that I should trust him."

"Bad advice," she said. "Anything else?"

Myron shook his head. "Where is Dennis Lex?" he tried again. "Did you see him?"

"I didn't have to," she said. But her voice had a funny monotone to it. "He's not involved in this."

"You keep saying that," Myron said. "But how do you know?"

She slowed down. "The family."

"You mean Susan and Bronwyn Lex?"

"Yes."

"What about them?"

"They gave us reassurances."

Myron almost stepped back. "You just took their word for it?"

"I didn't say that." She glanced around, let loose a sigh. "And it's not my call."

"What?"

She looked straight through him. "Eric Ford handled it personally."

Myron could not believe what he was hearing.

"He told me to stay away," she said, "that he had it covered."

"Or covered up," Myron said.

"Nothing I can do about it." She looked at him. She had stressed the word *I*. Then she walked away without another word. Myron dialed his cell phone.

"Articulate," Win said.

"We're going to need help," Myron said. "Is Zorra still working free-lance?"

"I'll call her."

"Maybe Big Cyndi too."

"Do you have a plan?"

"No time for a plan," Myron said.

"Ooo," Win said. "Then we're going to get nasty."

"Yes."

"And here I thought you weren't going to break the rules anymore."

"Just this once," Myron said.

"Ah," Win countered. "That's what they all say."

31

Win, Esperanza, Big Cyndi, and Zorra were all in his office. Zorra wore a yellow monogrammed sweater (the monogram being one letter: Z), large white pearls à la Wilma Flintstone, a plaid skirt, and white bobby socks. Her—or if you want to be anatomically correct, his—wig looked like early Bette Midler or maybe Little Orphan Annie on methadone. Shiny red high-heel shoes like something stolen from a trampy Dorothy in Oz adorned the men's-size-twelve feet.

Zorra smiled at Myron. "Zorra is happy to see you."

"Yeah," Myron said. "And Myron is happy to see you too."

"This time, we're on the same side, yes?"

"Yes."

"Zorra pleased."

Zorra's real name was Shlomo Avrahaim, and she was a former Israeli Mossad agent. The two had had a nasty run-in not long ago. Myron still carried the wound near his rib cage—a scar-shaped Z made by a blade Zorra hid in her heel.

Win said, "The Lex Building is too well guarded."

"So we go with Plan B," Myron said.

"Already in motion," Win said.

Myron looked at Zorra. "You armed?"

Zorra pulled a weapon out from under her skirt. "The Uzi," Zorra said. "Zorra likes the Uzi."

Myron nodded. "Patriotic."

"Question," Esperanza said.

"What?"

Esperanza settled her eyes on his. "What if this guy doesn't cooperate?"

"We don't have time to worry about it," Myron said.

"Meaning?"

"This psycho has Jeremy," Myron said. "You understand that? Jeremy has to be the priority here."

Esperanza shook her head.

"Then stay behind," he said.

"You need me," she said.

"Right. And Jeremy needs *me*." He stood. "Okay, let's go."

Esperanza shook her head again, but she went along. The group—a sort of cut-rate Dirty (One-Third of a) Dozen—broke off when they reached the street. Esperanza and Zorra would walk. Win, Myron, and Big Cyndi headed into a garage three blocks away. Win had a car there. Chevy Nova. Totally untraceable. Win had a bunch of them. He referred to them as disposable vehicles. Like paper cups or something. The rich. You don't want to know what he does with them.

Win drove, Myron took the front passenger seat, and Big Cyndi squeezed into the back, which was a little like watching a film of childbirth on rewind. Then they were off.

The Stokes, Layton and Grace law firm was one of the most prestigious in New York. Big Cyndi stayed in reception. The receptionist, a skinny skirt-suit of gray, tried not to stare. So Big Cyndi stared at her, daring her not to look. Sometimes Big Cyndi would growl. Like a lion. No reason. She just liked to do it.

Myron and Win were ushered into a conference room that looked like a million other big Manhattan law firm conference rooms. Myron doodled on a yellow legal pad that looked like a million other big Manhattan law firm legal pads, watched through the window the smug, pink, fresh-scrubbed Harvard grads stroll by, again all looking exactly the same as the ones at a million other big Manhattan law firms. Reverse discrimination maybe, but all young white male lawyers looked the same to him.

Then again, Myron was a white Harvard law school graduate. Hmm.

Chase Layton trollied in with his rolly build and well-fed face and chubby hands and gray comb-over, looking like, well, a name partner at a big Manhattan law firm. He wore a gold wedding band on one hand and a Harvard ring on the other. He greeted Win warmly—most wealthy people do—and then gave a firm, I'm-your-guy hand-shake to Myron.

"We're in a rush," Win said.

Chase Layton shoved the big smile out of the room and strapped on his best battle-ready face. Everyone sat. Chase Layton folded his hands in front of him. He leaned forward, putting a bit of a belly push on the vest buttons. "What can I do for you, Windsor?"

Rich people always called him Windsor.

"You've been after my business for a long time," Win said.

"Well, I wouldn't say—"

"I'm here to give it to you. In exchange for a favor."

Chase Layton was too smart to snap-bite at that. He looked at Myron. An underling. Maybe there'd be a clue how to play on this plebeian's face. Myron kept up the neutral. He was getting better at it. Must be from hanging around Win so much.

"We need to see Susan Lex," Win said. "You are her attorney. We'd like you to get her to come here immediately."

"Here?"

"Yes," Win said. "At your office. Immediately."

Chase opened his mouth, closed it, checked on the underling again. Still no clue. "Are you serious, Windsor?"

"You do that, you get the Lock-Horne business. You know how much income that would generate?"

"A great deal," Chase Layton said. "And yet not even a third of what we receive from the Lex family."

Win smiled. "Talk about having your cake and eating it too."

"I don't understand this," Chase said.

"It's pretty straightfoward, Chase."

"Why do you want to see Ms. Lex?"

"We can't divulge that."

"I see." Chase Layton scratched a ham-red cheek with a manicured finger. "Ms. Lex is a very private person."

"Yes, we know."

"She and I are friends."

"I'm sure," Win said.

"Perhaps I can set up an introduction."

"No good. It has to be now."

"Well, she and I usually conduct business at her office—"

"Again no good. It has to be here."

Chase rolled his neck a bit, stalling for time, trying to sort through this, find an angle to play. "She's a very busy woman. I wouldn't even know what to say to get her here."

"You're a good attorney, Chase," Win said, steepling his fingers. "I'm sure you'll come up with something."

Chase nodded, looked down, studied his manicure. "No," he said. He looked back up slowly. "I don't sell out clients, Windsor."

"Even if it meant landing a client as big as Lock-Horne?"

"Even then."

"And you're not doing this just to impress me with your discretion?"

Chase smiled, relieved, as though he finally got the joke. "No," he said. "But wouldn't that be having my cake and eating it too?" He tried to laugh it off. Win didn't join him.

"This isn't a test, Chase. I need you to get her here. I guarantee that she won't find out you helped me."

"Do you think that's all that concerns me here—how it would look?"

Win said nothing.

"If that's the case, you've misread me. The answer is still no, I'm afraid."

"Thank about it," Win said.

"Nothing to think about," Chase said. He leaned back, crossing one leg over the other, making sure the crease sat right. "You didn't really think I'd go along with this, did you, Windsor?"

"I hoped."

Chase again looked at Myron, then back at Win. "I'm afraid I can't help you, gentlemen."

"Oh, you'll help us," Win said.

"Pardon me?"

"It's just a matter of what we need to do to get your cooperation."

Chase frowned. "Are you trying to bribe me?"

"No," Win said. "I already did that. By offering you our business."

"Then I don't understand—"

Myron spoke for the first time. "I'm going to make you," he said.

Chase Layton looked at Myron and smiled. Again he said, "Pardon me?"

Myron rose. He kept his expression flat, remembering what he'd learned from Win about intimidation. "I don't want to hurt you," Myron said. "But you will call Susan Lex and get her to come here. And you'll do it now."

Chase folded his arms and sat them atop his belly. "If you wish to discuss this further—"

"I don't," Myron said.

Myron walked around the table. Chase did not back away. "I will not call her," he said firmly. "Windsor, would you tell your friend to sit down?"

Win feigned a helpless shrug.

Myron stood directly over Chase. He looked back at Win. Win said, "Let me handle it."

Myron shook his head. He loomed over Chase and let his gaze fall. "One last chance."

Chase Layton's face was calm, almost amused. He probably saw this as a bizarre put-on—or perhaps he was just certain that Myron would back down. That was how it was with men like Chase Layton. Physical violence was not a part of the Layton equation. Oh, sure, those uneducated animals on the street might engage in it. They might knock him on the head for his wallet. Other people—lesser people, really—yes, they solved problems with physical violence. But that was another planet—one filled with a more primitive species. In Chase Layton's world, a world of status and position and lofty manners, you were untouchable. Men threatened. Men sued. Men cursed. Men schemed behind one another's backs. Men never engaged in face-to-face violence.

That was why Myron knew that no bluff would work here. Men like Chase Layton believed that anything remotely physical was a bluff. Myron could probably point a gun at him, and he wouldn't budge. And in that scenario, Chase Layton would be right.

But not this one.

Myron boxed Chase Layton's ears hard with his palms.

Chase's eyes widened in a way they probably never had before. Myron put his hand over the lawyer's mouth, muffling the scream. He cupped the back of the man's skull and pulled him back, knocking him off his chair and onto the floor.

Chase lay on his back. Myron looked him straight in the eye and saw a tear roll down the man's cheek. Myron felt ill. He thought about Jeremy and that helped keep his face neutral. Myron said, "Call her."

He slowly released his hand.

Chase's breathing was labored. Myron glanced at Win. Win shook his head.

"You," Chase said, spitting out the word, "are going to jail."

Myron closed his eyes, made a fist, and punched the lawyer up and under the ribs, toward the liver. The lawyer's face fell into itself. Myron held the man's mouth again, but this time there was no scream to smother.

Win eased back in his chair. "For the record, I am the sole witness to this event. I'll swear under oath that it was self-defense."

Chase looked lost.

"Call her," Myron said. He tried to keep the pleading out of his voice. He looked down at Chase Layton. Chase's shirttail was out of his pants, his tie askew, his comb-over unraveling, and Myron realized that nothing would ever be the same for this man. Chase Layton had been physically assaulted. He would always walk a little more warily now. He would sleep a little less deeply. He would always be a little different inside.

Maybe so too would Myron.

Myron punched him again. Chase made an *oof* noise. Win stood by the door. Keep your face even, Myron told himself. A man at work. A man who won't stop no matter what. Myron cocked his fist again.

Five minutes later, Chase Layton called Susan Lex.

32

Would have been better," Win said, "if you let me hurt him." Myron kept walking. "It would have been the same," he said.

Win shrugged. They had an hour to set up. Big Cyndi was now in the conference room with Chase Layton, supposedly going over her new professional-wrestling contract. When she entered the room, all six-six, three hundred pounds of her wearing her Big Chief Mama costume, Chase Layton barely looked up. The pain from the punches, Myron was sure, was ebbing. He had not struck the man in any place that would do lasting damage, except maybe to the obvious.

Esperanza was set up in the lobby. Myron and Win met Zorra two levels down, on the seventh floor. Zorra had staked out the lower floors and decided that this would be the quietest and easiest to contain. The office suites on the northern side were empty, Zorra noted. Anyone entering or leaving had to do so from the west. Zorra was stationed there with one cell phone. Esperanza had the other one downstairs. Win held the third. They were on a three-way line with one another. Myron and Win were in position. In the last twenty minutes, the elevator had stopped at their floor only twice. Good. Both times the door opened, Myron and Win feigned conversation, just two guys waiting for an elevator heading in the opposite direction. Real undercover commandos.

Myron hoped like hell no one happened upon the scene when it all went down. Zorra would warn them, of course, but once the operation was under way, it couldn't be stopped. They'd have to come up with some excuse, say it was a drill maybe, but Myron was not sure he could stomach hurting any more innocents today. He closed his eyes. Can't back down now. Too far gone.

Win smiled at him. "Wondering yet again if the ends justify the means?"

"Not wondering," Myron said.

"Oh?"

"I know they don't."

"And yet?"

"I'm not in the mood for introspection right now."

"But you're so good at it," Win said.

"Thanks."

"And knowing you as well as I do, you'll save it for later—for when you have more time. You'll gnash your teeth over what you just did. You'll feel ashamed, remorseful, guilty—though you'll also be oddly proud that you didn't have *moi* do your dirty work. You'll end up making a clear declaration that it will never happen again. And perhaps it won't— not, at least, until the stakes are this high."

"So I'm a hypocrite," Myron said. "Happy?"

"But that is my point," Win said.

"What?"

"You're not a hypocrite. You aim toward lofty heights. The fact that your arrow cannot always reach them does not make you a hypocrite."

"So in conclusion," Myron said, "the ends do not justify the means. Except sometimes."

Win spread his hands. "See? I just saved you hours of soul-searching. Perhaps I should consider penning one of those how-to-manage-your-time manuals."

Esperanza broke in through the phone. "They're here," she said.

Win put the phone to his ear. "How many?"

"Three coming in. Susan Lex. That granite guy Myron keeps talking about. Another bodyguard. Two more staying parked outside."

"Zorra," Win said into the phone. "Please keep an eye on the two gentlemen outside."

Zorra said, "And if they move?"

"Detain them."

"With pleasure." Zorra giggled. Win smiled. Welcome to the Psycho Hotline. Only $3.99 per minute. First call is free.

Myron and Win waited now. Two minutes past. Esperanza said, "Middle elevator. All three are inside."

"Anyone else with them?"

"No . . . wait. Damn, two businessmen are going in."

Myron closed his eyes and cursed.

Win looked at him. "Your call."

Panic squeezed Myron's chest. Innocent people in the elevator. There was sure to be violence. Witnesses now.

"Well?"

"Hold the phone." It was Esperanza. "The granite guy blocked their path. Looks like he told them to wait for another elevator."

"Top-notch security," Win said. "Good to see we're not dealing with amateurs."

"Okay," Esperanza said. "Just the three of them are inside now."

The relief in Myron's face was palpable.

Esperanza said, "Elevator closing . . . now."

Myron pressed the Up button. Win took out his forty-four. Myron pulled out a Glock. They waited. Myron kept the gun by his thigh. It felt heavy in a terrible, comforting way. Myron kept glancing down the corridor. No one. He hoped their luck would hold. He felt his pulse start to race. His mouth was dry. The room suddenly felt warmer.

A minute later, the light above the middle elevator dinged.

Win's face was in the zone, semi-euphoric. He wriggled his eyebrows and said, "Showtime."

Myron tensed his muscles, leaned in a bit. The elevator's whirring noise stopped. There was a delay and then the doors started sliding open. Win didn't wait. He was inside before the opening had reached a foot. He found Grover and stuck the gun in the big man's ear. Myron did the same with the other guard.

"Waxy ear buildup a problem, Grover?" Win said in his best voice-over. "Smith and Wesson has the solution!"

Susan Lex started to open her mouth. Win cut her off with a finger against her lip and a gentle "Shh."

Win frisked and disarmed Grover. Myron followed his lead with the second guard. Grover glared daggers at Win. Win took them on and said, "Please—no, pretty please—make a sudden move."

Grover didn't budge.

Win stepped back. The elevator door started closing. Myron stopped it with his foot. He pointed the weapon at Susan Lex. "You're coming with me," Myron said.

"Don't you want revenge first?" Grover said.

Myron looked at him.

"Go ahead." Grover spread his hands. "Hit me in the gut. Go ahead, give it your best shot."

"Pardon *moi*," Win said. "But does that offer apply to me too?"

Grover looked at the smaller man like a tasty leftover. "I heard you're not bad," he said.

Win looked back at Myron. " 'Not bad,' " he repeated. "Monsieur Grover heard I was 'not bad.' "

"Win," Myron said.

Win snapped his knee deep into Grover's groin. He followed through, driving the man's testicles all the way into his stomach. Grover did not make a sound. He simply folded like a bad hand of poker.

"Oh, wait, you said 'gut,' didn't you?" Win looked down at him, frowned. "Must work on my aim. Perhaps you're right. Perhaps I am merely 'not bad.' "

Grover was on his knees, his hands between his legs. Win kicked him in the head with his instep. Grover toppled over like a bowling pin. Win looked over at the other guard, who was putting his hands up and backing quickly into a corner.

"Will you tell your friends I was 'not bad?' " Win asked him.

The guard shook his head.

"Enough," Myron said.

Win picked up the cell phone. "Zorra, report."

"They are not moving, handsome."

"Come back up then. You can help me clean up."

"Clean up? Ooo, Zorra will hurry."

Win laughed.

"No more," Myron said. Win did not reply, but Myron hadn't really expected him to. Myron grabbed Susan Lex's arm. "Let's go."

He pulled her into the stairwell. Zorra bounded into view—on high heels no less. Leaving two unarmed men alone with Win and Zorra. Talk about scary. But he had no choice here. Myron turned to Susan Lex, keeping tight hold of her elbow.

"I need your help," he said to her.

Susan Lex looked at him, head high, not backing off.

"I promise not to say anything," he went on. "I have no interest in hurting you or your family. But you're going to take me to see Dennis."

"And if I say no?"

Myron just looked at her.

"You'd hurt me?" she said.

"I just beat up an innocent man," Myron said.

"And you'd do the same to a woman?"

"I wouldn't want to be accused of sexism."

Her expression remained defiant, but unlike Chase Layton, she seemed to understand how the real world worked. "You know what sort of power I have."

"I do."

"Then you know what I'll do to you when this is all over?"

"I don't much care. A thirteen-year-old boy has been kidnapped."

She almost smiled. "I thought you said he needed a bone marrow transplant."

"I don't have time to explain."

"My brother isn't involved in this."

"I keep hearing that."

"Because it's true."

"Then prove it to me."

Something in her face shifted then, changing her features, relaxing them into something strangely approaching tranquility. "Come," she said. "Let's go."

33

Susan Lex directed him north on the FDR to the Harlem River Drive and then north again to 684. Once they were in Connecticut, the roads grew quieter. Woods thickened. Buildings grew scarce. Traffic was pretty much nonexistent.

"We're almost there," Susan Lex said. "I'd like the truth now."

"I'm telling you the truth."

"Fine," she said. Then: "How do you plan on getting away with this?"

"With what?"

"Are you going to kill me when this is all over?"

"No."

"Then I'll come back after you. I'll press charges, if nothing else."

"I told you before. I don't much care. But I've thought of something."

"Oh?"

"Dennis will save me."

"How?"

"If he is the Sow the Seeds kidnapper—"

"He's not."

"—or somehow involved with him, then what I'm doing here will be small potatoes by comparison."

"And if he's not?"

Myron shrugged. "Either way, I'm going to learn whatever it is you want to hide. We make a deal. I never tell what I saw. In exchange, you leave me alone."

"Or I can simply kill you."

"I don't believe you'd do that."

"No?"

"You're not a killer. And even if you were, it would be too complicated. I'd leave evidence behind. I have Win covering my back. It would be too messy."

"We'll see," she said, but there was no starch there. She pointed up ahead. "Turn off up here."

She pointed to a dirt road that seemed to materialize from nowhere. There was a guardhouse fifty yards down and to the left. Myron pulled up. Susan Lex leaned over and smiled. The guard waved her through. There were no signs, no identification marks, nothing. The whole setup looked like some sort of militia compound.

After the gatehouse, the dirt road stopped and a paved one began. New pavement from the looks of it colored the dark black-gray of heavy rain. Trees crowded the sides like parade watchers. Up ahead, the road narrowed. The trees closed in too. Myron veered the car to the left and passed through wrought-iron gates guarded by two stone falcons.

"What is this?" Myron asked.

Susan Lex did not reply.

A mansion seemed to push out of the green, elbowing its way forward. The exterior was classic off-white Georgian but on an oversized scale. Palladian windows, pilasters, fancy pediments, curved balconies, brick cornering and what looked like real stone masonry were all garnished with hints of green ivy. A set of oversized double doors were dead center, the entire edifice perfectly symmetrical.

"Park in the lot over there," Susan Lex said.

Myron followed her finger. There was indeed a paved lot. Myron figured it contained close to twenty cars. Various makes. A BMW, a couple of Honda Accords, three Mercedes of different lineage, Fords, SUVs, one station wagon. Your basic American melting pot. Myron glanced back at the oversized manor. He noticed ramps now. Lots of them. He checked the cars. Several had MD license plates.

"A hospital," he said.

Susan Lex smiled. "Come along."

They headed up the brick path. Gloved gardeners were on their knees, working on the flower beds. A woman walked by in the opposite direction. She smiled politely but said nothing. They passed through an arched entranceway and into a two-story foyer. A woman seated behind the desk stood, slightly startled.

"We weren't expecting you, ma'am," she said.

"That's fine."

"I don't have security set up."

"That's fine too."

"Yes, ma'am."

Susan Lex barely broke stride. She took the sweeping staircase on her left, staying in the middle, not touching a handrail. Myron followed.

"What did she mean about security?" Myron asked.

"When I visit, they make sure the hallways are kept clear and that no one else is present."

"To keep your secret?"

"Yes," she said. She did not stop moving. "Perhaps you noticed that she called me 'ma'am.' That's part of the discretion here. They never use names."

When they reached the top level, Susan turned to the left. The corridor had raised wallpaper in a classic floral design and nothing else. No small tables, no chairs, no pictures in frames, no Oriental runners. They passed by maybe a dozen rooms, only two with doors open. Myron noticed that the doors were extra wide and he remembered his visit to Babies and Children's Hospital. Extra wide doors there too. For wheelchairs and stretchers and the like.

When they reached the end of the corridor, Susan stopped, took a deep breath, looked back at Myron. "Are you ready?"

He nodded.

She opened the door and stepped inside. Myron followed. A four-poster antique bed, like something you'd see on a tour of Jefferson's Monticello, overwhelmed the room. The walls were warm green with woodwork trim. There was a small crystal chandelier, a burgundy Victorian couch, a Persian rug with deep scarlets. A Mozart violin concerto was playing a bit too loudly on the stereo. A woman sat in the corner reading a book. She too started upright when she saw who it was.

"It's okay," Susan Lex said. "Would you mind leaving us for a few moments?"

"Yes, ma'am," the woman said. "If you need anything—"

"I'll ring, thank you."

The woman did a semi-curtsy/semi-bow and hurried out. Myron looked at the man in the bed. The resemblance to the computer rendering was uncanny, almost perfect. Even, strangely enough, the dead eyes. Myron moved closer. Dennis Lex followed him with the dead eyes, unfocused, empty, like windows over a vacant lot.

"Mr. Lex?"

Dennis Lex just stared at him.

"He can't talk," she said.

Myron turned to her. "I don't understand," he said.

"You were right before. It's a hospital. Of sorts. In another era, I suppose one would have called it a private sanitarium."

"How long has your brother been here?"

"Thirty years," she said. She moved toward the bed, and for the first time, she looked down at her brother. "You see, Mr. Bolitar, this is where the wealthy store unpleasantness." She reached down and stroked her brother's cheek. Dennis Lex did not respond. "We're too cultured not to give our loved ones the best. All very humane and practical, don't you know."

Myron waited for her to say more. She kept stroking her brother's cheek. He tried to see her face, but she kept it lowered and away from him.

"Why is he here?" Myron asked.

"I shot him," she said.

Myron opened his mouth, closed it, did the math. "But you were only a child when he disappeared."

"Fourteen years old," she said. "Bronwyn was six." She stopped stroking the cheek. "It's an old story, Mr. Bolitar. You've probably heard it a thousand times. We were playing with a loaded gun. Bronwyn wanted to hold it, I said no, he reached for it, it went off." She said it all in one breath, staring down at her brother, still stroking the cheek. "This is the end result."

Myron looked at the still eyes in the bed. "He's been here since?"

She nodded. "For a while I kept waiting for him to die. So I could officially be a murderer."

"You were a child," Myron said. "It was an accident."

She looked at him and smiled. "My, that means so much coming from you, thank you."

Myron said nothing.

"No matter," she said. "Daddy took care of it. He arranged for my brother to have the best care. He was a very private person, my father. It was his gun. He'd left it where his children could play with it. His business and reputation were both growing. He had political aspirations at the time. He just wanted it all to go away."

"And it did."

She tilted her head back and forth. "Yes."

"What about your mother?"

"What about her?"

"What did she say?"

"My mother hated unpleasantness, Mr. Bolitar. After the incident, she never saw her son again."

Dennis Lex made a sound, a guttural scrape, nothing remotely human. Susan gently shushed him.

"Did you and Bronwyn ever get help?" Myron asked.

She cocked an eyebrow. "Help?"

"Counseling. To help you through it."

She made a face. "Oh please," she said.

Myron stood there, his mind circling nowhere over nothing.

"So now you know the truth, Mr. Bolitar."

"I guess," he said.

"Meaning?"

"I wonder why you told me all this. You could have just shown Dennis to me."

"Because you won't talk."

"How can you be so sure?"

She smiled. "After you shoot your own brother, shooting strangers becomes so easy."

"You don't really believe that."

"No, I suppose not." Susan Lex turned and faced him. "The fact is, you really don't have much to tell. As you said earlier, we both have reasons to keep our mouths shut. You'll be arrested for kidnapping and Lord knows what. The evidence of my crime—if indeed it was a crime—is nonexistent. You'd be worse off than I."

Myron nodded, but his mind still whirred. Her story might be true or just something she told him to gain sympathy, to contain the damage. Still, there was the ring of truth in her words. Maybe her reason for talking was simpler. Maybe, after all this time, she just needed someone who'd listen to her confession. Didn't matter. None of it mattered. There was nothing here. Dennis Lex was truly a dead end.

Myron looked out the window. The sun was starting to dip away. He checked his watch. Jeremy had been missing five hours now—five hours alone with a madman—and Myron's best lead, his *only* lead, was lying brain-damaged in a hospital room.

The sun was still strong, bathing the expansive garden in white. Myron saw what looked like a maze made of shrubbery. He spotted several patients in wheelchairs, legs covered with blankets, sitting by a fountain. Serene. The rays reflected off a pool of water and a statue in the middle of—

He stopped. The statue.

Myron felt the blood in his veins turn to crystal. He shaded his eyes with his hand and squinted again.

"Oh Christ," he said.

Then he sprinted toward the stairs.

34

Susan Lex's helicopter was starting to descend toward the sanitarium's landing pad when Kimberly Green called him on the cell phone.

"We've caught Stan Gibbs," she said. "But the boy wasn't with him."

"That's because he isn't the kidnapper."

"You know something I don't?"

Myron ignored the question. "Has Stan told you anything?"

"Nope. He lawyered up already. Says he won't talk to anyone but you. You, Myron. Why don't I find that particularly surprising?"

Had Myron responded, the helicopter's propeller would have drowned it out. He backed off a few steps. The copter touched down. The pilot stuck his head out and waved to him.

"I'm on my way," Myron shouted into the phone. He switched it off and turned to Susan Lex. "Thank you."

She nodded.

He ducked and ran toward the helicopter. As they rose, Myron looked back down. Susan Lex's chin was tilted up, her eyes still on him. He waved. And she waved back.

Stan was not in a holding cell because they had nothing to hold him on. He sat in a waiting room with his eyes on the table and let his attorney, Clara Steinberg, do the talking. Myron had known Clara—he called her Aunt Clara though there was no familial relationship—since he was too young to remember. Aunt Clara and Uncle Sidney were Mom and Dad's closest friends. Dad had gone to elementary school with Clara. Mom had roomed with her in law school. Aunt Clara, in fact, had set up Mom and Dad on their first date. She liked to remind Myron with a wink that "you wouldn't be here if it weren't for your aunt Clara." Then she'd wink again. Subtle, that Clara. During the holidays, she always pinched Myron's cheeks in admiration of his *punim*.

"Let me set up the ground rules, *bubbe*," she said to him. Clara had gray hair and a pair of oversized glasses that magnified her eyes to Ant-Man size. She looked up at him and the giant eyes seemed to reel in everything all at once. She wore a white blouse with a gray vest, matching skirt, a kerchief around her neck, and teardrop pearl earrings. Think Shtetl Barbara Bush.

"One," she said, "I am Mr. Gibbs's attorney of record. I have requested that this conversation not be overheard. I have changed rooms four times to make sure the authorities don't listen in. But I don't trust them. They think your aunt Clara is an old dodo bird. They think we're going to chat right here."

"We're not?" Myron said.

"We're not," she repeated. There was little hint of the cheek pincher here; if she were an athlete, you'd say that she'd strapped on her game face. "What we're going to do first is stand up. Got me?"

"Stand up," Myron repeated.

"Right. Then I'm going to lead you and Stan outside, across the street. I'm going to remain on the other side of the street with all those friendly agents. We do this right now, quickly, so they won't have a chance to set up surveillance. Understood?"

Myron nodded. Stan kept his eyes on the Formica.

"Good, just so we're all on the same page here." She knocked on the door. Kimberly Green opened it. Clara walked past her without speaking. Myron and Stan followed. Kimberly rushed up behind them.

"Where do you think you're going?"

"Change of plans, doll."

"You can't do that."

"Sure I can. I'm a sweet little old lady."

"I don't care if you're the Queen Mother," Kimberly said. "You're not going anywhere."

"You married, hon?"

"What?"

"Never mind," Clara said. "Try this on for size. See how it fits. My client demands privacy."

"We already promised—"

"Shh, you're talking when you should be listening. My client demands privacy. So he and Mr. Bolitar are going to take a little walk somewhere. You and I will watch from a distance. We will not listen in."

"I already told you—"

"Shh, you're giving me a headache." Aunt Clara rolled her eyes and kept walking. Myron and Stan followed. They reached the doorway. Clara pointed to a bus depot across the street. "Sit over there," she said to them. "On the bench."

Myron said okay. Clara put a hand on his elbow.

"Cross at the corner," she said. "And wait for the light."

The two men walked to the corner and waited for the light before crossing the street. Kimberly Green and her fellow agents fumed. Clara took them by the hand and led them back toward the building's entrance. Stan and Myron sat on the bench. Stan watched a New Jersey Transit bus go by like it carried the secret to life.

"We don't have time to enjoy the scenery, Stan."

Stan leaned forward, put his elbows on his knees. "This is difficult for me."

"If it makes it any easier," Myron said, "I know that the Sow the Seeds kidnapper is your father."

Stan's head fell into his hands.

"Stan?"

"How did you find out?"

"Through Dennis Lex. I found him in a private sanitarium in Connecticut. He's been there for thirty years. But you already knew that, didn't you?"

Gibbs said nothing.

"At the sanitarium, there's a big garden in the back. With this statue of Diana the Huntress. There's a picture in your condo of you and your father standing in front of that same statue. He was a patient there. You don't have to confirm or deny it. I was just there. Susan Lex has pull. An administrator told us Edwin Gibbs had been in and out of there for fifteen years. The rest is fairly obvious. Your father was there a long time. It'd be easy to learn who else was there, no matter how strict the so-called security. So he knew about Dennis Lex. And he stole his identity. It's a hell of a twist, I'll give him that. Fake IDs used to be somewhat pretty easy to come by. You'd visit a graveyard, find a child who died, request his social security card, bingo. But that doesn't work anymore. Computers closed down that loophole. Nowadays when you die, your social security number dies with you. So your father took the identity of someone still alive, someone who has no use for it, someone committed permanently. In other words, he used the ID of a living person who has no life. And to go deeper undercover, he changed the person's name. Dennis Lex became Davis Taylor. Untraceable."

"Except you traced it."

"I got lucky."

"Go on," Stan said. "Tell me what else you know."

"We don't have time for this, Stan."

"You don't understand," he said.

"What?"

"If you're the one who says it—if you figure it out on your own—it's not as much a betrayal. You see?"

No time to argue. And maybe Myron did see. "Let's start with the question every reporter wanted to know: why you? Why did the Sow the Seeds kidnapper choose you? The answer: because the kidnapper was your father. He knew you wouldn't turn him in. Maybe part of you hoped someone would figure it out. I don't know. I also don't know if you found him or he found you."

"He found me," Stan said. "He came to me as a reporter. Not as a son. He made that clear."

"Sure," Myron said, "double protection. He gets you with the fact that you'd be turning in your own father—plus he gives you an ethical foundation for remaining silent. The beloved First Amendment. You couldn't name a source. It gave you a very neat out—you could be both moralistic and the good son."

Stan looked up. "So you see that I had no choice."

"Oh, I wouldn't be so easy on myself," Myron said. "You weren't being totally altruistic. Everyone says you were ambitious. That played a part here. You got fame out of this. You were handed a monster story—the kind that propels careers into the stratosphere. You were on TV and got your own cable show. You got a big raise and invited to fancy parties. You want to tell me that wasn't a part of it?"

"It was a by-product," Stan said. "It wasn't a factor."

"You say so."

"It's like you said—I couldn't turn him in, even if I wanted to. There was a constitutional principle here. Even if he wasn't my father, I had an obligation—"

"Save it for your minister," Myron said. "Where is he?"

Stan did not reply. Myron looked across the street. Lots of traffic. The cars started blurring and through them, standing on the other side of the street with Kimberly Green, he saw Greg Downing.

"That man over there," Myron said, pointing with his chin. "That's the boy's father."

Stan looked, but his face didn't change.

"There's a kid in danger," Myron said. "That trumps your constitutional cover."

"He's still my father."

"And he's kidnapped a thirteen-year-old boy," Myron said.

Stan looked up. "What would *you* do?"

"What?"

"Would you give up your father? Just like that?"

"If he was kidnapping children? Yeah, I would."

"Do you really think it's that easy?"

"Who said anything about easy?" Myron said.

Stan put his head back in his hands. "He's sick and he needs help."

"And there's also an innocent boy out there."

"So?"

Myron looked at him.

"I don't mean to sound callous, but I don't know this boy. He has no connection to me. My father does. That's what matters here. You hear about a plane crash, right? You hear about how two hundred people die and you sigh and you go on with your life and you thank God it wasn't your loved one in the plane. Don't you do that?"

"What's your point?"

"You do that because the people on the plane are strangers. Like this boy. We don't care about strangers. They don't count."

"Speak for yourself," Myron said.

"Are you close to your father, Myron?"

"Yes."

"And in your heart of hearts, in your deepest, most honest moments, if you could sacrifice his life to save those two hundred people on the airplane, would you do it? Think about it. If God came down to you and said, 'Okay, that plane never crashed. Those people all arrive safely. In exchange, your father will die.' Would you make that trade?"

"I'm not into playing God."

"But you're asking me to," Stan said. "I turn my father in, they'll kill him. He'll get the lethal injection. If that's not playing God, I don't know what is. So I'm asking you. Would you trade those two hundred lives for your father's?"

"We don't have time—"

"Would you?"

"Okay, if it was my father shooting down the plane," Myron said, "yes, Stan, I would make that trade."

"And suppose your father wasn't culpable? If he was sick or deranged?"

"Stan, we don't have time for this."

Something in Stan's face dropped. He closed his eyes.

"There's a boy out there," Myron said. "We can't let him die."

"And if he's already dead?"

"I don't know."

"You'll want my father dead."

"Not by my hand," Myron said.

Stan took a deep breath and looked over at Greg Downing. Greg stared back, stared right through him. "Okay," he said at last. "But we go alone."

"Alone?"

"Just you and me."

Kimberly Green had a major conniption. "Are you insane?"

They were back inside, sitting around the Formica table. Kimberly Green, Rick Peck, and two other faceless feds were hunched together as one. Clara Steinberg sat with her client. Greg sat next to Myron. Jeremy's kidnapping had siphoned all the blood from Greg's face. His hands looked sucked dry, his skin almost crisp, his eyes too solid and unblinking. Myron put a hand on his shoulder. Greg didn't seem to notice.

"You want my client to cooperate or not?" Clara asked.

"I'm supposed to let my number one suspect go?"

"I'm not running away," Stan said.

"How am I supposed to know that?" Kimberly countered.

"It's the only way," Stan said, his voice a plea. "You'll go in with guns blazing. Someone is going to get hurt."

"We're professionals," Green countered. "We don't go in with guns blazing."

"My father is unstable. If he sees a lot of cops, I can guarantee there will be bloodshed."

"Doesn't have to be that way," she said. "It's up to him."

"Exactly," Stan said. "I'm not taking that chance with my father's life. You let us go. You don't follow us. I'll have him surrender to you. Myron will be with me the whole time. He's armed and he has a cell phone."

"Come on," Myron said. "We're wasting time here."

Kimberly Green chewed on her lower lip. "I don't have the authorization—"

"Forget it," Clara Steinberg said.

"Excuse me?"

Clara pointed a meaty finger at Kimberly Green. "Listen up, missy, you haven't arrested Mr. Gibbs, correct?"

Green hesitated. "That's correct."

Clara turned to Stan and Myron and waved the backs of both hands at them. "So shoo, go, good-bye. We're talking nonsense here. Hurry along. Shoo."

Stan and Myron slowly rose.

"Shoo."

Stan looked down at Kimberly. "If I spot a tail, I'm calling this off. You got me?"

She stewed in silence.

"You've been trailing me for three weeks now. I know what one of your tails looks like."

"She won't tail you."

It was Greg Downing. He and Stan locked eyes again. Greg stood. "I want to go with you too," Greg said. "And I probably have the strongest interest in keeping your father alive."

"How do you figure?"

"Your father's bone marrow can save my son's life. If he dies, so does my son. And if Jeremy has been hurt . . . well, I'd like to be there for him."

Stan didn't waste a lot of time thinking about it. "Let's hurry."

35

Stan drove. Greg sat in the front passenger seat, Myron in the back.

"Where are we going?" Myron asked.

"Bernardsville," Stan said. "It's in Morris County."

Myron knew the town.

"My grandmother died three years ago," Stan said. "We haven't sold the house yet. My father sometimes stays there."

"Where else does he stay?"

"Waterbury, Connecticut."

Greg looked back at Myron. The old man, the blond wig. It clicked for both of them at the same time.

"He's Nathan Mostoni?"

Stan nodded. "That's his main alias. The real Nathan Mostoni is another patient at Pine Hills—that's what we call that fancy loony bin, Pine Hills. Mostoni was the one who came up with the idea of using the identification of the committed, mostly for scams. He and my father became close friends. When Nathan slipped into total delirium, my father took his identity."

Greg shook his head, made two fists. "You should have turned the crazy bastard in."

"You love your son, don't you, Mr. Downing?"

Greg gave Stan a look that could have bored holes through titanium. "What the hell does that have to do with anything?"

"Would you want your son to turn you in one day?"

"Don't hand me that. If I'm a raving psychopathic maniac, yeah, my son can turn me in. Or better, he can put a bullet in my head. You knew your old man was sick, right? The least you could have done was get him help."

"We tried," Stan said. "He was in institutions most of his adult life. It didn't do any good. Then he ran off. When he finally called me, I hadn't seen him in eight years. Imagine that. Eight years. He calls me and tells me he needs to talk to me as a reporter. He made that clear. As a reporter. No matter what he told me, I couldn't reveal the source. He made me promise. I was confused as all hell. But I agreed. And then he told me his story. What he'd been doing. I could barely breathe. I wanted to die. I wanted to just dry up and die."

Greg put his fingers to his mouth. Stan concentrated on the road. Myron stared out the window. He thought about the father of three young children, age forty-one; the female college student, age twenty; and the young newlyweds, ages twenty-eight and twenty-seven. He thought about Jeremy's scream over the phone. He thought about Emily waiting at the house, her mind sowing the seeds, sick and blackening.

They got off Route 78 and took 287 north. They exited onto winding streets with no straightaways. Bernardsville was about old money and rustic wealth, a town of converted mills and stone houses and water-wheels. There were fields of long brown grass swaying in death, every-thing a little too old and too neatly overgrown.

"It's on this road," Stan said.

Myron looked out. His mouth was dry. He felt a tingle deep in his belly. The car traveled down another corkscrew of a street, the loose gravel crunching under the tires. There were deeply wooded lots com-mingling with your standard suburban front lawns. Plenty of center-hall colonials and those mid-seventies ranches that aged like milk left out on the counter. A yellow sign warned about children at play, but Myron saw none.

They pulled into a cake-dried driveway with weeds poking up through the cracks. Myron lowered his window. There was plenty of burnt-out grass, but the sweet summer smell of lilies still loomed and even cloyed. Crickets droned. Wildflowers blossomed. Not a hint of menace.

Up ahead Myron spotted what looked like a farmhouse. Black shutters stood out against the white clapboards. There were lights coming from inside, giving the house a glow that was big and soft and oddly welcom-ing. The front porch was the type that craved a swinging settee and a pitcher of lemonade.

When the car reached the front of the house, Stan shifted into park and turned off the ignition. The crickets eased up. Myron almost waited for someone to note that it was "Quiet" and for someone else to add, "Yeah, too quiet."

Stan turned to them. "I think I should go in first," he said.

Neither man argued. Greg stared out the window at the house, probably conjuring up unspeakable horrors. Myron's left leg started jackhammering. It often did when he was tense. Stan reached for the door handle.

That was when the first bullet smashed through the front passenger-side window.

The glass exploded, and Myron saw Greg's head fly back at a rate it was never supposed to achieve. A thick gob of crimson smacked Myron in the cheek.

"Greg!"

No time. Instincts took over. Myron grabbed Greg, pushed him down, trying to keep his own head down too. Blood. Lots of it. From Greg. He was bleeding, bleeding heavily, but Myron couldn't tell from where. Another bullet rang out. Another window shattered, raining shards of glass down on Myron's head. He kept his hand on top of Greg, tried to cover him, protect him. Greg's own hand fumbled absently on his chest and face, calmly searching for the bullet hole. Blood kept flowing. From the neck. Greg's neck. Or collarbone. Whatever. He couldn't see through the blood. Myron tried to stop the flow with his bare hand, pushing the sticky liquid away, finding the wound with his finger, applying pressure with his palm. But the blood slipped through the cracks between his fingers. Greg looked up at him with big eyes.

Stan Gibbs put his hands over his head and ducked into a quasi-emergency-landing position. "Stop!" he yelled, almost childlike. "Dad!"

Another bullet. More glass shards. Myron reached into his pocket and pulled out his gun. Greg grabbed his hand and pulled it down. Myron looked at him.

"Can't kill him," Greg said to Myron. There was blood in his mouth now. "If he dies . . . Jeremy's only hope."

Myron nodded, but he didn't put the gun away. He looked over at Stan. In the distance, they heard a helicopter. Then sirens. The feds were on their way. No surprise. There was no way they weren't going to follow. By air, at the very least.

Greg's breathing was short spurts. His eyes were going hazy-gray.

"We got to do something here, Stan," Myron said.

"Just stay down," Stan said. Then he opened the car door and shouted, "Dad!"

No reply.

Stan got out of the car. He raised his hands and stood. "Please," he shouted. "They'll be here soon. They'll kill you."

Nothing. The air was so motionless that Myron thought he could still hear the echoes from the gun blasts.

"Dad?"

Myron lifted his head a little and risked a glance. A man stepped out from behind the side of the house. Edwin Gibbs wore full army fatigues with combat boots. He had an ammunition belt hanging off his shoulder. His rifle was pointed toward the ground. Myron could see it was Nathan Mostoni, though he looked twenty years younger. His head was high, chin up. His back was straight.

Greg made a gurgling sound. Myron ripped off his shirt and pushed it against the wound. But Greg's eyes were closing. "Stay with me," Myron urged. "Come on, Greg. Stay here."

Greg did not reply. His eyes fluttered and closed. Myron felt his heart slam into his throat. "Greg?"

He felt for a pulse. It was there. Myron was no doctor, but it didn't feel strong. Oh damn. Oh come on.

Outside the car, Stan moved closer to his father. "Please," Stan said. "Put down the rifle, Dad."

The fed cars poured into the driveway. Brakes squealed. Feds jumped out of their vehicles, took position using the open doors as shields, aimed their weapons. Edwin Gibbs looked confused, panicked, Frankenstein's monster suddenly surrounded by angry villagers. Stan hurried toward him.

The air seemed to thicken, molasses-like. It was hard to move, hard to breathe. Myron could almost feel the officers tense up, fingers itchy, tips touching the cold metal of the trigger. He let go of Greg for a moment and shouted, "You can't shoot him!"

A fed had a megaphone. "Put down the rifle! Now!"

"Don't shoot!" Myron shouted.

For a moment nothing happened. Time did that in-and-out motion where everything rushes and freezes all at one time. Another fed car skidded up the driveway. A news van followed, screeching when it hit the brakes. Stan kept walking toward his father.

"You are surrounded," the megaphone said. "Drop the rifle and put your hands behind your head. Drop to your knees."

Edwin Gibbs looked left, looked right. Then he smiled. Myron felt the dread rise up in his chest. Gibbs lifted his rifle.

Myron rolled out of the car. "No!"

Stan Gibbs broke into a sprint. His father spotted him, his face calm. He aimed the rifle at his approaching son. Stan kept running. Time did stop this time, waiting for the blast of gunfire. But it didn't come. Stan had gained on him too fast. Edwin Gibbs closed his eyes and let his son tackle him. The two men fell to the ground. Stan stayed on top of his father, blanketing him, leaving no space open.

"Don't shoot him," Stan yelled. His voice sounded hurt, again so child-like. "Please don't shoot him."

Edwin Gibbs lay on his back. He let go of the rifle. It dropped into the grass. Stan pushed it away, still on top of his father, still shielding him from harm. They stayed there until the officers took over. They gently removed Stan and then rolled Edwin Gibbs onto his stomach, cuffing his hands behind his back. The news camera caught it all.

Myron turned back to the car. Greg's eyes were still closed. He wasn't moving. Two of the officers ran toward the car, calling into their radios for an ambulance. Nothing Myron could do for Greg now. He looked back at the farmhouse, his heart still lodged in his throat. He ran toward the house and grabbed the knob. The door was locked. He used his shoulder. The door came down. Myron stepped into the foyer.

"Jeremy?" he called out.

But there was no reply.

36

They didn't find Jeremy Downing.

Myron checked every room, every closet, the basement, the garage. Nothing. The feds streamed in with him. They started knocking down walls. They used a heat sensor to check for underground caves or hidden places. Nothing. In the garage, they found a white van. In the back of it, they found one of Jeremy's red sneakers.

But that was it.

News vans, lots of them, gathered at the end of the driveway. What with the kidnapped boy, his famous father shot and in critical condition, a potential serial killer in custody, the connection to Stan Gibbs and the famed plagiarism charges—the story was getting the full, round-the-clock, give-it-a-banner-and-theme-music, death-of-Diana coverage. Stiffly coiffed correspondents flashed their best grim-news teeth and led with phrases like "the vigil continues" or "the search is reaching its *x*th hour" or "behind me lurks the lair" or "we'll be here until."

A recent photograph of Jeremy, the one Emily had on the Web, ran continuously on all the stations. Brokaw, Jennings and Rather interrupted their programming. Viewers called in tips, but so far none amounted to anything.

And the hours passed.

Emily drove to the scene. It played on all the usual outlets, her head lowered, hurrying toward a waiting car like an arrested felon, the flashbulbs creating a grotesque strobe effect. Cameramen elbowed each other out of the way to capture a glimpse of the stricken mother collapsing in the back of the car. They even got a shot of her through the passenger seat crying. Great TV.

Nightfall brought out searchlights. Volunteers and law officials scoured the nearby grounds for signs of recent graves or digging. Nothing. They brought in dogs. Nothing. They spoke to neighbors, some of whom "never trusted that family" but most gave the standard "seemed like nice folk, real quiet neighbors" spiel.

Edwin Gibbs had been taken into custody. They tried to question him at the Bernardsville Police Station, but he wasn't talking. Clara Steinberg became his attorney. She stayed with him. So did Stan. They pleaded with Edwin, Myron guessed, but so far, he hadn't talked.

Back at the farmhouse, the wind picked up. Myron's bad knee ached, each step giving him a fresh jolt of pain. The pain was unpredictable, arriving whenever it damn well pleased, staying on like the most unwelcome houseguest. There was no side benefit to the knee pain, no weather forecasting or anything like that. Some days it just ached. Nothing he could do about it. He approached Emily and put his arm around her.

"He's still out there," Emily said to the dark.

Myron said nothing.

"He's all alone. And it's night. And he's probably scared."

"We'll find him, Em."

"Myron?"

"Hmm."

"Is this more payback for that night?"

Another search party returned, their shoulders slumped in resignation, if not defeat. Odd thing, these search parties. You wanted to find something, yet you didn't want to find something.

"No," Myron said. "I think you were right. I think our mistake was the best thing that could have happened. And maybe there's a price to pay to have something so good."

She closed her eyes, but she did not cry. Myron stayed next to her. The wind howled, scattering the surrounding voices like dead leaves, whipping branches, and whispering in your ear like the most frightening lover.

37

Myron and Win looked through the one-way glass at Clara Steinberg's back and the faces of Stan and Edwin Gibbs. Kimberly Green stood with them. So did Eric Ford. Emily had gone to the hospital to sit vigil while Greg was in surgery. No one seemed to know if he'd make it.

"Why aren't you listening in?" Myron asked.

"Can't," Ford replied. "Attorney-client."

"How long they been at it?"

"On and off since we took him into custody."

Myron checked the clock behind his head. Nearly three in the morning. Evidence collection teams had leveled the house, but still no clue where Jeremy was. Fatigue lined everyone's face, except maybe Win's. Fatigue never registered on his face. Win must internalize it. Or maybe it had something to do with having little to no conscience.

"We don't have time for this," Myron said.

"I know," Eric Ford said. "It's been a long night for all of us."

"Do something."

"Like what?" Ford snapped. "What exactly would you like me to do?"

Win picked up that one. "Perhaps you could speak to Ms. Steinberg in private."

That hooked Ford's attention. "What?"

"Take her into another room," Win said, "and leave me alone with your suspect."

Eric Ford looked at him. "You shouldn't even be here. He"—a gesture toward Myron—"represents the Downing family, as much as I don't like it. But you got no reason to be here."

"Make a reason," Win said.

Eric Ford waved his hand as if this wasn't worth his time.

Win kept the voice at a low, soothing level. "You don't have to be a part of it," he said. "Simply talk to his attorney. Leave Gibbs alone in the room. That's all. Nothing unethical about that."

Ford shook his head. "You're crazy."

"We need answers," Win said.

"And you want to beat them out of him."

"Beating leaves marks," Win said. "I never leave marks."

"That's not how it works, pal. Ever heard of the U.S. Constitution?"

"It's a document," Win said, "not a trump card. You have a choice. The obscure rights of that subhuman"—Win gestured through the glass—"or a young boy's right to live."

Ford leaned his forehead against the glass.

"If the boy dies while we're standing here," Win said, "how will you feel then?"

Ford shut his eyes. In the holding room, Clara Steinberg rose from her chair. She turned, and for the first time, Myron saw her face. He knew that she had represented bad people before—very, very bad people—but whatever horrors she was now hearing had washed away her skin tone and etched in something that would probably never leave. She approached the one-way mirror and knocked. Ford hit the sound switch.

"We need to talk," she said. "Let me out."

Eric Ford met Clara and Stan by the door. "Let's head down this way," he said.

"No," Clara said.

"Pardon me?"

"We'll talk in here," she said, "where I can watch my client. Wouldn't want an accident, now, would we?"

There were no chairs so they all stood by the one-way window—Kimberly Green, Eric Ford, Clara Steinberg, Stan Gibbs, Myron and Win. Stan kept his head down and plucked at his lower lip with his fingers. Myron tried to meet his eyes. Stan never gave him the chance.

"Okay," Clara said. "First off, we need a D.A."

"What for?" Eric Ford asked.

"Because we want a deal."

Ford tried to snicker. "Are you out of your mind?"

"No. My client is the only one who can tell you where Jeremy Downing is. He'll only do so under specific conditions."

"What conditions?"

"That's why we need a D.A."

"A D.A. will back whatever I agree to," Eric Ford said.

"I'll still want it in writing."

"And I want to hear what you're looking for here."

"Okay," Clara said, "here's the deal. We help you find Jeremy Downing. In exchange, you guarantee not to seek the death penalty for Edwin Gibbs. You also agree to psychiatric tests. You then recommend he be placed in a proper mental health facility, not a prison."

"You have to be kidding me."

"There's more," Clara said.

"More?"

"Mr. Edwin Gibbs will also agree to donate bone marrow to Jeremy Downing if the need arises. I understand that Mr. Bolitar is representing the family here. For the record, we should note that he is present as a witness to this agreement."

No one said anything.

"So we clear?" Clara said.

"No," Ford said, "we're not."

Clara adjusted her eyeglasses. "This deal is nonnegotiable." She turned to leave, her gaze snagging on Myron's. Myron just shook his head.

"I'm his attorney," she said to him.

"And you'll let a boy die for him?" Myron said.

"Don't start," Clara said, but her voice was soft.

Myron studied her face again, saw no give. He turned to Ford. "Agree," he said.

"Are you nuts?"

"The family cares about retribution. But they care more about finding their son. Agree to her terms."

"You think I'm taking orders from you?"

Myron's voice was soft. "Come on, Eric."

Ford frowned. He rubbed his face with his hands and then dropped them back to his side. "This agreement assumes, of course, that the boy is still alive."

"No," Clara Steinberg said.

"What?"

"Alive or dead does not change the state of Edwin Gibb's mental health."

"So you don't know if he's alive or—"

"If we did, it would be an attorney-client communication and thus confidential."

Myron looked at her in stark horror. She met his eyes and would not blink. Myron tried Stan, but his head was still lowered. Even Win's face, usually the model of neutrality, was on edge. Win wanted to hurt somebody. He wanted to hurt somebody badly.

"We can't agree to that," Ford said.

"Then there's no deal," Clara said.

"You have to be reasonable—"

"Do we have a deal or not?"

Eric Ford shook his head. "No."

"See you in court, then."

Myron moved into her path.

"Step aside, Myron," Clara said.

He just looked down at her. She raised her eyes.

"You think your mother wouldn't be doing the same thing?" Clara said.

"Leave my mother out of this."

"Step aside," she said again. Aunt Clara was sixty-six. For the first time since he'd known her, she looked older than her age.

Myron turned back to Eric Ford. "Agree," he said.

He shook his head. "The boy is probably dead."

"Probably," Myron repeated. "Not definitely."

Win spoke up this time. "Agree," he said.

Ford looked at him.

"He won't get off easily," Win said.

Stan's head finally rose at that one. "What the hell is that supposed to mean?"

Win gave him flat eyes. "Absolutely nothing."

"I want this man kept away from my father."

Win smiled at him.

"You don't get it, do you?" Stan said. "None of you get it. My father is sick. He's not responsible. We're not making this up. Any competent psychiatrist in the world will agree. He needs help."

"He should die," Win said.

"He's a sick man."

"Sick men die all the time," Win said.

"That's not what I mean. He's like someone who has a heart condition. Or cancer. He needs help."

"He kidnaps and probably kills people," Win said.

"And it doesn't matter why he does it?"

"Of course it doesn't matter," Win said. "He does it. That's enough. He should not be put in a comfortable mental hospital. He should not be allowed to enjoy a wonderful film or read a great book or laugh again. He should not be able to see a beautiful woman or listen to Beethoven or know kindness or love—because his victims never will. What part of that don't you understand, Mr. Gibbs?"

Stan was shaking. "You agree," he said to Ford. "Or we don't help."

"If the boy dies because of this negotiation," Win said to Stan, "you will die."

Clara stepped into Win's face. "You threatening my client?" she shouted.

Win smiled at her. "I never threaten."

"There are witnesses."

"Worried about collecting your fee, Counselor?" Win asked.

"That's enough." It was Eric Ford. He looked at Myron. Myron nodded. "Okay," Ford said slowly. "We agree. Now, where is he?"

"I'll have to take you," Stan said.

"Again?"

"I wouldn't be able to give you directions. I'm not even sure I can find it after all these years."

"But we come along," Kimberly Green said.

"Yes."

There was an empty space, a sudden stillness that Myron didn't like.

"Is Jeremy alive or dead?" Myron asked.

"Truth?" Stan said. "I don't know."

38

Eric Ford drove with Kimberly Green riding shotgun and Myron and Stan in the backseat. Several cars' worth of agents followed them. So too did the press. Nothing they could do about that.

"My mother died in 1977," Stan said. "Cancer. My father was already unwell. The one thing in his life that mattered to him—the one good thing—was my mother. He loved her very much."

The time on the car clock read nearly 4:03 A.M. Stan told them where to turn off Route 15. A sign read DINGSMAN BRIDGE. They were heading into Pennsylvania.

"Whatever sanity was still there, my mother's death stripped away. He watched her suffer. Doctors tried everything—used all their technological advances—but it only made her suffer more. That's when my father started with the strength of the mind. If only my mother hadn't relied on technology, he thought. If only she used her mind instead. If only she'd seen its limitless potential. Technology killed her, he said. It gave her false hope. It stopped her from using the one thing that could save her—the limitless human brain."

No one had a comment.

"We had a summerhouse out here. It was beautiful. Fifteen acres of land, walking distance to a lake. My father used to take me hunting and fishing. But I haven't been out here in years. Haven't even thought about the place. He took my mother out here to die. Then he buried her in the woods. See, it's where her suffering finally ended."

The obvious question hung in the air, unasked: *And who else's?*

Myron would later remember nothing about the drive. No buildings, no landmarks, no trees. Outside his window was total night, the black folding over black, eyes squeezed shut in the darkest of rooms. He sat back and waited.

Stan told them to stop at the foot of a wooded area. More crickets sounded. The other cars pulled up alongside them. Feds got out and started combing the area. Beams from powerful flashlights revealed uneven earth. Myron ignored them. He swallowed and ran. Stan ran with him.

Before morning broke, the federal officers would find graves. They'd find the father of three children, the female college student, and the young newlyweds.

But for now, Myron and Stan kept running. Branches whipped Myron's face. He tripped over a root, curled into a roll, stood back up, kept running. They spotted the small house, barely visible in the faint moonlight. There were no lights on inside, no hint of life. Myron did not bother trying the knob this time. He took it full on, crashing the door down. More darkness. He heard a cry, turned, fumbled for the light switch, flipped it up.

Jeremy was there.

He was chained to a wall—dirty and terrified and still very much alive.

Myron felt his knees buckle, but he fought them and stayed upright. He ran to the boy. The boy stretched out his arms. Myron embraced him and felt his heart fall and shatter. Jeremy was crying. Myron lifted his hand and stroked the boy's hair and shushed him. Like his father. Like his father had done to him countless times. A sudden, beautiful warmth streamed through his veins, tingling his fingers and toes, and for a moment, Myron thought that maybe he understood what his father felt. Myron had always cherished being on the son side of the hug, but now, for just the most fleeting of moments, he experienced something so much stronger—the intensity and overwhelming depth of being on the other side—that it shook every part of him.

"You're okay," Myron said to him, cupping the boy's head. "It's over now."

But it wasn't.

An ambulance came. Jeremy was put inside. Myron called Dr. Karen Singh. She didn't mind being woken at five in the morning. He told her everything.

"Wow," Karen Singh said when he finished.

"Yes."

"We'll get someone to harvest the marrow right away. I'll start prepping Jeremy in the afternoon."

"You mean with chemo."

"Yes," she said. "You done good, Myron. Either way, you should be proud."

"Either way?"

"Come by my office tomorrow afternoon."

Myron felt a thumping in his chest. "What's up?"

"The paternity test," she said. "The results should be in by then."

Jeremy was on his way to the hospital. Myron wandered back outside. The feds were digging. The news vans were there. Stan Gibbs watched the mounds of earth grow, his face now beyond emotion. No sound, not even the crickets now, except for shovel hitting dirt. Myron's knee was acting up. He felt bone-weary. He wanted to find Emily. He wanted to go to the hospital. He wanted to know the results of that test and then he wanted to know what he was going to do with them.

He climbed back up the hill toward the car. More media. Someone called out to him. He ignored them. There were more federal officers working in silence. Myron walked past them. He didn't have the heart to hear what they'd found. Not just yet.

When he reached the top of the landing—when he saw Kimberly Green and the lifeless expression on her face—his heart took one more plummet.

He took another step. "Greg?" he said.

She shook her head, her eyes hazy and unfocused. "They shouldn't have left him alone," she said. "They should have watched him. Even after a careful search. You can never search too carefully."

"Search who?"

"Edwin Gibbs."

Myron was sure he'd heard wrong. "What about him?"

"They just found him," she said, having trouble with the words. "He committed suicide in his cell."

39

Karen Singh summed it up for them: You can't get bone marrow from a dead man.

Emily did not collapse when she heard the news. She took the blow without blinking and immediately segued to the next step. She was on a calmer plane now, somewhere just outside panic.

"We have incredible access to the media right now," Emily said. They were sitting in Karen Singh's hospital office. "We'll make pleas. We'll set up bone marrow drives. The NBA will help. We'll get players to make appearances."

Myron nodded, but the enthusiasm wasn't there. Dr. Singh mimicked his motion.

"When will you have the paternity results?" Emily asked.

"I was just about to call for them," Dr. Singh said.

"I'll leave you two alone, then," Emily said. "I have a press conference downstairs."

Myron looked at her. "You don't want to wait for the results?"

"I already know the results."

Emily left without a backward glance. Karen Singh looked at Myron. Myron folded his hands and put them in his lap.

"You ready?" she asked.

He nodded.

Karen Singh picked up the phone and dialed. Someone on the other end answered. Karen read off a reference number. She waited, tapping a pencil on the desk. Someone on the other end said something. Karen said, "Thank you," hung up, focused her eyes on Myron.

"You're the father."

*   *   *

Myron found Emily in the hospital lobby, giving the press conference. The hospital had set up a podium with their logo perfectly positioned behind it, sure to be picked up by any and all television cameras. Hospital logo. Like they were McDonald's or Toyota, trying to sleaze some free advertising. Emily's statement was direct and heartfelt. Her son was dying. He needed new bone marrow. Everyone who wanted to help should give blood and get registered. She plucked the strings of societal grieving, making sure it rang personal in the same way that Princess Diana's and John Kennedy Jr.'s deaths rang personal, wanting the public to mourn as if they actually knew him. The power of celebrity.

When she finished her statement, Emily hurried off without answering questions. Myron caught up to her in the closed-off area near the elevators. She glanced at him. He nodded, and she smiled.

"So now what are you going to do?" she asked him.

"We have to save him," Myron said.

"Yes."

Behind them the press were still yelling out questions. The sound trickled and then faded into the background. Someone ran by with an empty gurney.

"You said Thursday was the optimum day," Myron said.

Hope lit her eyes. "Yes."

"Okay, then," he said. "We try it on Thursday."

The bullet that had struck Greg had entered in the lower part of his neck and traversed toward his chest. It had stopped short of the heart. But it had done plenty of damage anyway. He survived surgery but remained unconscious in "critical" and "guarded" condition. Myron looked in on him. Greg had tubes in his nose and a frightening assortment of machinery Myron hoped never to understand. He looked like a corpse, waxen and gray-white and sucked dry. Myron sat with him for a few minutes. But not very long.

He returned to the offices of MB SportsReps the next day.

"Lamar Richardson is coming in this afternoon," Esperanza said.

"I know."

"You okay?"

"Dandy."

"Life goes on, huh?"

"Guess so."

Special Agent Kimberly Green came semi-bouncing by a few minutes later. "It's all wrapping up," she told him, and for the first time he saw her smile.

Myron sat back. "I'm listening."

"Edwin Gibbs, under his Dennis Lex/Davis Taylor identity, still had a locker at work. We found the wallets of two of his victims, Robert and Patricia Wilson, in there."

"They were the honeymoon couple?"

"Yes."

They both took a moment, out of respect for the dead, Myron guessed. He pictured a healthy young couple beginning their life, coming to the Big Apple to see some shows and do a little shopping, walking the bustling streets hand in hand, a little scared about the future but ready to give it a go. *El fin.*

Kimberly cleared her throat. "Gibbs also rented a white Ford Windstar using the Davis Taylor credit card. It was one of those automatic reservations. You just make a call, walk straight to the rental, and drive off. No one sees you."

"Where did he pick up the van?"

"Newark Airport."

"I assume that's the van we found in Bernardsville," Myron said.

"The very."

"Tidy," he said, using a Win word. "What else?"

"Preliminary autopsies reveal that all the victims were killed with a thirty-eight. Two shots to the head. No other signs of trauma. We don't think he tortured them or any of that. His modus operandus seemed to involve the early scream and then he just killed them."

"He ends the seed sowing for them," Myron said, "but not the families."

"Right."

"Because for his victims, the terror would be real. He wanted it all in the mind." Myron shook his head. "What did Jeremy tell you about his ordeal?"

"You didn't talk to him about it?"

Myron shifted in his chair. "No."

"Edwin Gibbs wore the same disguise he used at work—the blond wig and beard and glasses. He blindfolded Jeremy as soon as he had him in the van and drove straight to that cabin. Edwin told him to scream into the phone—even made him practice first to make sure he had it right. After the call, Edwin chained him up and left him alone. You know the rest."

Myron nodded. He did.

"What about the plagiarism charge and the novel?"

She shrugged. "It was like you and Stan said. Edwin read it, probably right after his wife was dying of cancer. It influenced him."

Myron stared at her for a moment.

"What?" she said.

"You guys figured that part out when you first got the novel," Myron said. "That Stan hadn't plagiarized. That the book influenced the killer."

She shook her head. "No."

"Come on. You knew that the kidnappings had taken place. You just wanted to put pressure on Stan so he'd talk. And maybe you wanted to embarrass him a little."

"That's not true," Kimberly Green said. "I'm not saying some of our agents didn't take it personally, but we believed that he was the Sow the Seeds kidnapper. I already told you some of the reasons why. Now we know that a lot of the same evidence pointed to his father."

"What same evidence?"

She shook her head. "It's not important anymore. We knew Stan was more here than just a reporter. And we were right. We even thought he was getting stuff wrong on purpose—that he was using the book rather than what he'd really done just to throw us off."

Her words didn't resonate the way the truth does, but Myron didn't argue the point. He scanned his Client Wall and tried to bring his focus around to Lamar Richardson's visit. "So the case is closed."

She smiled. "Like legs in a nunnery."

"You make that one up?"

"Yup."

"Good thing you carry a gun," Myron said. "So are you going to get a big promotion?"

She rose. "I think I get to be a super-secret-special agent now."

Myron smiled. They shook hands. Kimberly left then. Myron sat alone for a while. He rubbed his eyes and thought about what she'd said and what she hadn't said and realized that something was still very wrong.

Lamar Richardson, shortstop extraordinaire, showed up on time and by himself. Positively shocking. The meeting went well. Myron gave his standard spiel, but the standard spiel was pretty good. Damn good, actually. All businesspeople need a spiel. Spiel is good. Esperanza spoke up too. She had started developing her own spiel. Well honed. The perfect complement to Myron's. Quite the partnership, this was becoming.

Win stopped by briefly as planned. If recruitment was a baseball game, Win was the big closer. People knew his name. They checked out his reputation—er, his business reputation, that is. When prospective clients learned that Windsor Horne Lockwood III himself would handle their finances, that Win and Myron further insisted that clients meet with Win at least five times a year, they started smiling. Score one for the small agency.

Lamar Richardson played it close to the vest. He nodded a lot. He asked questions but not too many. Two hours after arriving, he shook their hands and said he'd be in touch. Myron and Esperanza walked him to the elevator and bade him good-bye.

Esperanza turned to Myron. "Well?"

"Got him."

"How can you be so sure?"

"I'm all-seeing," Myron said. "All-knowing."

They moved back into Myron's office and sat down. "If Lamar chooses us over IMG and TruPro"—she stopped, smiled—"we're baaaaack."

"Pretty much."

"And that means Big Cyndi will come back."

"That's supposed to be a good thing, right?"

"You're starting to love her, you know."

"Yeah, don't rub it in."

Esperanza studied his face. She did that a lot. Myron didn't much believe in reading faces. Esperanza did. Especially his. "What happened in that law office?" she asked. "With Chase Layton?"

"I boxed his ears once and punched him seven times."

Her eyes stayed on his face.

"You're supposed to say, 'But you saved Jeremy's life,' " Myron added.

"No, that's Win's line." She adjusted herself and faced him full. She wore an aquamarine business suit, cut low with no blouse, and it was a wonder Lamar had been able to concentrate on anything. Myron was used to her, but the effect was still there, still dazzling. He just saw the dazzle from a different angle.

"Speaking of Jeremy," she said.

"Yes."

"You still blocking?"

Myron thought about it, remembered the embrace in that cabin, stopped. "More than ever," he said.

"So what now?"

"The blood test came back. I'm the father."

Something popped onto her face—regret maybe—but it didn't stay long. "You should tell him the truth."

"Right now I just want to save his life."

She kept studying the face. "Maybe soon," she said.

"Maybe soon what?"

"You'll stop blocking," Esperanza said.

"Yeah, maybe."

"We'll chat then. In the meantime . . ."

"Don't be stupid," he finished for her.

The health club was located in a chi-chi hotel in midtown. The walls were fully mirrored. The ceiling and the trim and the front desk were whole-milk white. Same with the clothes worn by the personal trainers. The weights and exercise machines were sleek and chrome and so beautiful you didn't want to touch them. Everything about the place gleamed; you were almost tempted to work out in sunglasses.

Myron found him on a bench press, struggling without a spotter. Myron waited, watching him wage war on gravity and the barbell. Chase Layton's face was pure red, his teeth gritted, veins in his forehead doing their pop-up video. It took some time, but the attorney achieved victory. He dropped the weight onto the stand. His arms fell to his sides like he'd missed a brain synapse.

"You shouldn't hold your breath," Myron said.

Chase looked over at him. He didn't seem surprised or upset. He sat up, breathing heavily. He wiped his face with a towel.

"I won't take up much of your time," Myron said.

Chase put the towel down and looked at him.

"I just wanted to say that if you want to press charges, Win and I won't get in your way."

Chase did not reply.

"And I'm very sorry for what I did," Myron said.

"I watched the news," Chase said. "You did it to save that boy's life."

"Doesn't excuse it."

"Maybe not." He stood and added a plate to both sides of the bar. "Frankly, Mr. Bolitar, I'm not sure what to think."

"If you want to press charges—"

"I don't."

Myron was not sure what to say, so he settled for "Thank you."

Chase Layton nodded and sat back on the bench. Then he looked at Myron. "Do you want to know what the worst part of it is?"

No, Myron thought. "If you want to tell me."

"The shame," Chase said.

Myron started to open his mouth, but Chase waved him quiet.

"It's not the beating or the pain. It's the feeling of total helplessness. We were primitive, We were man to man. And there was nothing I could do but take it. You made me feel like"—he looked up, found the words, looked straight at Myron—"like I wasn't a real man."

The words made Myron cringe.

"I went to these great schools and joined all the right clubs and made a fortune in my chosen profession. I fathered three kids and raised them and loved them the best I could. Then one day you punch me—and I realize that I'm not a real man."

"You're wrong," Myron said.

"You're going to say that violence is no measure of a man. On some level you're right. But on some level, the base level that makes us men, we both know you're wrong. Don't pretend you don't know what I'm talking about. It'd just be a further insult."

Myron swallowed down the clichés. Chase took deep breaths and reached for the bar.

"Need a spotter?" Myron said.

Chase Layton gripped it and jerked it off the stand. "I don't need anybody," he said.

Thursday came. Karen Singh introduced him to a fertility expert named Dr. Barbara Dittrick. Dr. Dittrick handed Myron a small cup and told him to masturbate into it. There were more surreal and embarrassing experiences in life, Myron guessed, but being led to a small room to masturbate into a cup while everyone waited for you in the next room had to be right up there with the best of them.

"Step in here, please," Dr. Dittrick said.

Myron frowned at the cup. "I usually insist on flowers and a movie."

"Well, at least you got the movie," she said, pointing at the television. "The TV has X-rated videos." She left the room and closed the door behind her.

Myron checked the titles. *On Golden Blonde. Father Knows Breast* (starring Robert Hung). *Field of Wet Dreams* ("If you watch it, they will come"). He frowned and passed. So to speak. He stared at the swivel leather chair, one of those lean-back kind, where probably hundreds of other men had sat and . . . He covered it with paper towels and did his bit, though it took some time. His imagination was spinning in the wrong direction, generating an aura about as erotic as mole hair on an old man's buttock. When he was, uh, finished, he opened the door and handed the cup to Dr. Dittrick and tried to smile. He felt like the world's biggest doofus. She wore rubber gloves, even though the, uh, specimen was in a cup. Like it might scald her. She brought it to a lab where they "washed" (their expression, not his) the semen. The semen was declared "serviceable but slow." Like it was falling behind in algebra.

"Funny," Emily said. "I usually found Myron to be serviceable but quick."

"Ha-ha," Myron said.

A few hours later Emily was in a hospital bed. Barbara Dittrick smiled while inserting what looked suspiciously like a turkey baster into her and pressed the plunger. Myron took her hand. Emily smiled.

"Romantic," she said.

Myron made a face.

"What?"

"Serviceable?" he said.

She laughed. "But quick."

Dr. Dittrick finished her part. Emily stayed prone for another hour. Myron sat with her. They were doing this to save Jeremy's life. That was all. He didn't let the future enter the equation. He didn't consider the long-term effects or what this might one day mean. Irresponsible, sure. But first things first.

They had to save Jeremy. The hell with the rest.

Terese Collins called him from Atlanta that afternoon. "Can I come up and visit?" she asked.

"The station will give you more time off?"

"Actually, my producer encouraged me."

"Oh?"

"You, my studly friend, are part of a huge story," Terese said.

"You used the words 'studly' and 'huge' in the same sentence."

"That turn you on?"

"Well, it might a lesser man."

"And you are that lesser man."

"I thank you," he said.

"You're also the only one in this story who won't talk to the press."

"So you just want me for my mind," Myron said. "I feel so used."

"Dream on, hot buns. I want your bod. It's my producer who wants your brain."

"Your producer cute?"

"No."

"Terese?"

"Yes."

"I don't want to talk about what happened."

"Good," she said. "Because I don't want to hear it."

There was a brief silence.

"Yeah," Myron said. "I'd like it very much if you came up."

Ten days later, Karen Singh called him at home.

"The pregnancy didn't take."

Myron closed his eyes.

"We can try again next month," she said.

"Thanks for calling, Karen."

"Sure."

There was empty space. "Anything else?" Myron asked.

"There's been a lot of marrow drives," she said.

"I know."

"One donor looks like a match for an AML patient in Maryland. A young mother. She would have probably died if it weren't for these drives."

"Good news," Myron said.

"But no matches for Jeremy."

"Yeah."

"Myron?"

"What?"

"I don't think we have much time here."

Terese returned to Atlanta later that day. Win invited Esperanza to his place for a night of mindless television. The three of them sat in their customary spots. Fritos and Indian takeout were on the night's menu. Myron had the remote. He paused when he saw a familiar image on CNN. A basketball superstar simply known as "TC," one of the NBA's most controversial players and a teammate of Greg's, was on *Larry King Live*. His hair was razor-carved to spell out *Jeremy*, and both gold earrings had Jeremy's name on them. He wore a ripped T-shirt that simply read HELP OR JEREMY DIES. Myron smiled. TC was something else, but he'd get the people out in droves.

More flipping. Stan Gibbs was on some talking-head show on MSNBC. Nothing new. The only thing the press loves as much as tearing somebody down is a story of redemption. Bruce Taylor had gotten the exclusive, as promised, and he'd set the tone. The public was mixed on what Stan had done, but for the most part, they sympathized with him. In the end, Stan had risked his own life to catch a killer, saved Jeremy Downing from certain death, and been wrongly accused by a too-eager-to-convict

media. The fact that Stan had been confused about turning in his own father played for him, especially since the media was anxious to wipe away
the awful mar of plagiarism they'd so quickly tattooed on him. Stan got
his column back. Rumor had it his show was coming back too but in a
better time slot. Myron wasn't sure what to think. Stan was no hero to
him. But so few people were.

Stan, too, was pounding the bone-marrow-drive drum. "This boy
needs our help," he said directly into the camera. "Please come down.
We'll be here all night."

A blond talking head asked Stan about his own part in this drama,
about tackling his father, about racing to the cabin. Stan played the modesty card. Wise. The man knew the media.

"Boring," Esperanza said.

"Agreed," Win said.

"Isn't there a *Partridge Family* marathon on TV Land?"

Myron suddenly stopped.

"Myron?" Win said.

He did not reply.

"Hello, world." Esperanza snapped her fingers in Myron's face.
"There's a song that we're singing. Come on, get happy."

Myron switched off the television. He looked at Win, then at Esperanza.
"Say one last good-bye to the boy."

Esperanza and Win exchanged a glance.

"You were right, Win."

"About what?"

"Human nature," Myron said.

40

Myron called Kimberly Green at her office. She answered the line and said, "Green."

"I need a favor," Myron said.

"Shit, I thought you were out of my life."

"But never your fantasies. You want to help me or not?"

"Not."

"I need two things."

"Not. I said 'not.' "

"Eric Ford said that the supposedly plagiarized novel was sent directly to you."

"So?"

"Who sent it?"

"You heard him, Myron. It was sent anonymously."

"You have no idea."

"None."

"Where is it now?"

"The book?"

"Yes."

"In an evidence locker."

"Ever do anything with it?"

"Like what?"

Myron waited.

"Myron?"

"I knew you guys were holding something back," he said.

"Listen to me a second—"

"The author of that novel. It was Edwin Gibbs. He wrote it under a pseudonym after his wife died. It makes perfect sense now. You were searching for him right from the get-go. You knew, dammit. You knew the whole time."

"We suspected," she said. "We didn't know."

"All that crap about thinking he was Stan's first victim—"

"It wasn't total crap. We knew it was one of them. We just didn't know which one. We couldn't find Edwin Gibbs until you told us about the Waterbury address. By the time we got there, he was already on his way to kidnap Jeremy Downing. Maybe if you had been more forthcoming—"

"You guys lied to me."

"We didn't lie. We just didn't tell you everything."

"Jesus, you ever listen to yourself?"

"We owed you nothing here, Myron. You weren't a federal agent on this. You were just a pain in the ass."

"A pain in the ass who helped you solve the case."

"And for that I thank you."

Myron's thoughts entered the maze, turned left, turned right, circled back.

"Why doesn't the press know about Gibbs being the author?" Myron asked.

"They will. Ford wants all his ducks in a row first. Then he'll hold yet another big press conference and present it as something new."

"He could do that today," Myron said.

"He could."

"But then the story dies down. Right now the rumors keep it going. Ford gets more time in the limelight."

"He's a politician at heart," she said. "So what?"

Myron took another few turns, hit a few more walls, kept feeling for the way out. "Forget it," he said.

"Good. Can I go now?"

"First I need you to call the national bone marrow registry."

"Why?"

"I need to find out about a donor."

"This case is closed, Myron."

"I know," he said. "But I think a new one might be opening."

Stan Gibbs was at the anchor chair when Myron and Win arrived. His new cable show, *Glib with Gibbs*, was filming in Fort Lee, New Jersey, and the studio, like every television studio Myron had ever seen, looked like a room with the roof ripped off. Wires and lights hung in no discernible pattern. Studios, especially newsrooms, were always much smaller in person than on television. The desks, the chairs, the world map in the background. All smaller. The power of television. A room on a nineteen-inch screen somehow looks smaller in real life.

Stan wore a blue blazer, white shirt, red tie, jeans and sneakers. The jeans would stay under the desk and never get camera time. Classic anchorman-wear. Stan waved to them when they entered. Myron waved back. Win did not.

"We need to talk," Myron said to him.

Stan nodded. He sent away the producers and motioned Myron and Win to the guest chairs. "Sit."

Stan stayed in the anchor chair. Win and Myron sat in guest chairs, which felt pretty strange, as though a home audience were watching. Win checked his reflection in a camera glass and smiled. He liked what he saw.

"Any word on a donor?" Stan asked.

"None."

"Something will come through."

"Yeah," Myron said. "Look, Stan, I need your help."

Stan intertwined his fingers and rested both hands on the anchor desk. "Whatever you need."

"There's a lot of things that don't add up with Jeremy's kidnapping."

"For example?"

"Why do you think your father took a child this time? He never did that before, right? Always adults. Why this time a child?"

Stan mulled it over, chose his words one at a time. "I don't know. I'm not sure taking adults was a pattern or anything. His victims seemed pretty random."

"But this wasn't random," Myron said. "His choosing Jeremy Downing couldn't have been just a coincidence."

Stan thought about that one too. "I agree with you there."

"So he picked him because he was somehow connected with my investigation."

"Seems logical."

"But how would your father have known about Jeremy?"

"I don't know," Stan said. "He might have followed you."

"I don't think so. You see, Greg Downing stayed up in Waterbury after our visit. He kept his eye on Nathan Mostoni. We know he didn't travel out of town until the day before the kidnapping."

Win looked into the camera again. He smiled and waved. Just in case it was on.

"It's strange," Stan said.

"And there's more," Myron said. "Like the call where Jeremy screamed. With the others, your father told the family not to contact the cops. But he didn't this time. Why? And are you aware that he wore a disguise when he kidnapped Jeremy?"

"I heard that, yes."

"Why? If he planned on killing him, why go to the trouble of donning a disguise?"

"He kidnapped Jeremy off the streets," Stan said. "Someone might have been able to identify him."

"Yeah, okay, that makes sense. But then why blindfold Jeremy once he was in the van? He killed all the others. He would have killed Jeremy. So why worry about him seeing his face?"

"I'm not sure," Stan said. "He might have always done it that way, for all we know."

"I guess," Myron said. "But something about it all just rings wrong, don't you think?"

Stan thought about it. "It rings funny," he said slowly. "I'm not sure it rings wrong."

"That's why I came to you. All these questions have been swirling in my head. And then I remembered Win's credo."

Stan Gibbs looked over at Win. Win blinked his eyes and lowered them modestly. "What credo is that?"

"Man is into self-preservation," Myron said. "He is, above all, selfish." He paused a moment. "You agree with that, Stan?"

"To some degree, of course. We're all selfish."

Myron nodded. "You even."

"Yes, of course. And you too, I'm sure."

"The media is making you out to be this noble guy," Myron said. "Torn between family and duty and ultimately doing the right thing. But maybe you're not."

"Not what?"

"Noble."

"I'm not," Stan said. "I did wrong. I never claimed to be a saint."

Myron looked at Win. "He's good."

"Damn good," Win agreed.

Stan Gibbs frowned. "What are you talking about, Myron?"

"Follow me here, Stan. And remember Win's credo. Let's start at the beginning. When your father first contacted you. You talked to him and you decided to write the Sow the Seeds story. What was your motive at first? Were you trying to find an outlet for your fear and guilt? Was it simply to be a good reporter? Or—and here's where we're using the Win credo—did you write it because you knew it would make you a big star?"

Myron looked at him and waited.

"Am I supposed to answer that?"

"Please."

Stan looked in the air and rubbed his fingertips with his thumb. "All of the above, I guess. Yes, I was excited by the story. I thought it could very well be a big deal. If that's selfishness, okay, I'm guilty."

Myron glanced at Win again. "Good."

"Damn good."

"Let's keep following this track, Stan, okay? The story did indeed become a big deal. So did you. You became a celebrity—"

"We covered this already, Myron."

"Right. You're absolutely right. Let's skip to the part where the feds sued you. They demanded to know your source. You refused. Now again there might be several reasons for this. The First Amendment, of course. That could be it. Protecting your father would be another. The combination of the two. But—and again Win's credo—what would be the selfish choice?"

"What do you mean?"

"Think selfishly and you really have only one option."

"That being?"

"If you caved in to the feds—if you said, Okay, now that I'm in legal trouble, my source is my father—well, how would that have looked?"

"Bad," Win said.

"Damn bad. I doubt you'd have been much of a hero if you sold out your father—not to mention the First Amendment—just to save your hide from vague legal threats." Myron smiled. "See what I mean about Win's credo?"

"So you think I acted selfishly by not telling the feds," Stan said.

"It's possible."

"It's also possible that the selfish thing was also the right thing."

"Possible too," Myron agreed.

"I never claimed to be a hero in all this."

"Never denied it either."

Stan smiled this time. "Maybe I didn't deny it because I'm using Win's credo."

"How's that?"

"Denying it would harm me," Stan said. "As would boasting about it."

Myron didn't have a chance to look before he heard Win say, "Damn good."

"I still don't see the relevance of any of this," Stan said.

"Stick with me, I think you will."

Stan shrugged.

"Where were we?" Myron asked.

"The feds take him to court," Win said.

"Right, thanks, the feds take you to court. You battle back. Then something happens you totally didn't foresee. The plagiarism charges. For the sake of discussion, we'll assume the Lex family sent the book to the feds. They wanted to get you off their back—what better way to do that than to ruin your reputation? So what did you do? How did you react to the charges of plagiarism?"

Stan kept quiet. Win said, "He disappeared."

"Correct answer," Myron said.

Win smiled and nodded a thank-you into the camera.

"You took off," Myron said to Stan. "Now the question again is why. Several things come to mind. It could have been because you were trying to protect your father. Or it might have been that you were afraid of the Lex family."

"Which would certainly fit Win's credo," Stan said. "Self-preservation."

"Right. You were afraid they'd harm you."

"Yes."

Myron treaded gently. "But don't you see, Stan? We have to think selfishly too. You're presented with this serious plagiarism charge. What choices did you have? Two really. You could either run off—or you could tell the truth."

Stan said, "I still don't see your point."

"Stay with me. If you told the truth, you would again look like a louse. Here you've been defending the First Amendment and your father and whoops, you get in trouble and you sell them out. No good. You'd still be ruined."

"Damned if you do," Win said. "Damned if you don't."

"Right," Myron said. "So the wise move—the selfish move—was to vanish for a while."

"But I lost everything by vanishing."

"No, Stan, you didn't."

"How can you say that?"

Myron lifted his palms to the skies and grinned. "Look around you."

For the first time, something dark flicked across Stan's face. Myron saw it. So did Win.

"Let's continue, shall we?"

Stan said nothing.

"You go into hiding and start counting your problems. One, your father is a murderer. You're selfish, Stan, but you're not inhumane. You want him off the streets, yet you can't tell on him. Maybe because you love him. Or maybe there's Win's credo."

"Not this time," Stan said.

"Pardon?"

"Win's credo doesn't apply. I kept quiet because I loved my father and because I believe in protecting sources. And I can offer proof."

"I'm listening," Myron said.

"If I wanted to turn my father in—if that would have been in my best interest—I could have done it anonymously." Stan leaned back and folded his arms.

"That's your proof?"

"Sure. I didn't do the selfish thing."

Myron shook his head. "You got to go deeper."

"Deeper how?"

"Turning your father in anonymously wouldn't help you, Stan. Not really. Yes, you needed to put your father behind bars. But more than that, you needed to be redeemed."

Silence.

"So what would answer both those needs? What would put your father away and put you back on top—maybe even more on top than before? First, you had to be patient. That meant staying hidden. Second, you couldn't be the one who turned him in. You had to set him up."

"Set up my father?"

"Yes. You had to leave a trail for the feds to follow. Something subtle, something that would lead to your father, and something you could manipulate at any time. So you took a fake ID, Stan—the same way your father had. You even took a job where people would spot the disguise your father used and hey, maybe you could also tie in your dad's old nemesis the Lex family in the process."

"What the hell are you talking about?"

"You know what bugged me? Your father had been so careful in the past. Now all of a sudden he's leaving incriminating evidence in a locker. He rents the kidnap van on a credit card and leaves a red sneaker in it. It didn't make any sense. Unless someone was setting him up."

Stan's look of disbelief was almost genuine. "You think I killed these people?"

"No," Myron said. "Your father did."

"Then what—?"

"You're the one who used the Dennis Lex identity," Myron said, "not your father."

Stan tried to look stunned, but it wasn't happening.

"You kidnapped Jeremy Downing. And you called me and pretended to be the Sow the Seeds killer."

"And why did I do that?"

"To have this heroic ending. To have your father arrested. To have yourself redeemed."

"How the hell does calling you—"

"To get me interested. You probably learned about my background. You knew I'd investigate. You needed a dupe and a witness. Someone outside the police. I was that dupe."

"The dupe du jour," Win added.

Myron shot him a look. Win shrugged.

"That's ridiculous."

"No, Stan, it adds up. It answers all my earlier questions. How did the kidnapper happen to choose Jeremy? Because you followed me after I left your condo. You saw the feds pick me up. That's how you knew I'd spoken to them. You followed me to Emily's house. From there, any old newsman worth a damn could have figured out her son was the sick kid I told you about. His illness wasn't a secret. So Jeremy's being taken is no longer a coincidence, see?"

Stan folded his arms across his chest. "I see nothing."

"Other questions get answered too now. Like why did the kidnapper wear a disguise and make Jeremy wear a blindfold? Because you couldn't let Jeremy identify you. Why didn't the kidnapper kill Jeremy right away, like he had the others? Same reason you wore the disguise. You had no intention of killing him. Jeremy had to survive the ordeal unharmed. Otherwise you're no hero. Why didn't the kidnapper make his usual demand not to contact the authorities? Because you wanted the feds in. You needed them to witness your heroics. It wouldn't work without their involvement. I wondered how the media was always in the right spot—in Bernardsville, at the cabin. But you set that part up too. Anonymous leaks probably. So the cameras could witness and replay your heroics—your tackling your father, the dramatic rescue of Jeremy Downing. Good television. You knew the power of capturing those moments for all the world to see."

Stan waited. "You finished?"

"Not yet. You see, I think you went too far in spots. Leaving that sneaker in the van, for example. That was overkill. Too obvious. It made me wonder how neatly it all came together in the end. And then I start realizing that I was your main sucker, Stan. You played me like a Stradivarius. But even if I hadn't shown up, you just would have kidnapped someone else. Your main dupes were the feds. For crying out loud, that photograph of your father by the statue was the only picture in the whole condo. It even faced the window. You knew the feds were spying on you. You threw the truth about Dennis Lex right in their faces. Surely they'd go to the sanitarium and put it together. And if not, you could somehow get it out in the end, when they had you in custody. You were all set to cave in and tell on your father when I came through in the clutch. Me, the dupe du jour, saw the truth up at the sanitarium. You must have been so pleased."

"This is crazy."

"It answers all the questions."

"That doesn't mean it's the truth."

"The Davis Taylor address you used at work. It was the same address as your father's in Waterbury. So we would trace it back to him, to Nathan Mostoni. Who else would have done that?"

"My father!"

"Why? Why would your father change identities at all? And if your father needed a new identity, wouldn't he shed the old one? Or hell, at least change addresses? Only you could have pulled it off, Stan. You could have hooked up the extra phone line with no problem. Your father was pretty far gone. He was demented, at the very least. You kidnapped Jeremy. Then you probably told your father to meet you at the house in Bernardsville. He did what you said—for love or because of dementia, I don't know which. Did you know he'd arm himself like that? I doubt it. If Greg had died, you'd probably look worse. But I don't know for sure. Maybe the fact that he fired shots just made you look more heroic in the end. Think selfishly, Stan. That's the key."

Stan shook his head.

" 'Say one last good-bye to the boy,' " Myron said.

"What?"

"That's what the Sow the Seeds killer said to me on the phone. The boy. I made a mistake when he called me. I told him a boy needed help. After that, I only used the word 'child.' When I spoke to Susan Lex. When I spoke to you. I said a thirteen-year-old child needs a transplant."

"So?"

"So when we talked in the car that night, you asked what I was really after, what my real interest in all this was. Remember?"

"Yes."

"And I said I already told you."

"Right."

"And you said, 'That boy who needs a bone marrow transplant?' You said, 'That boy.' How did you know he was a boy, Stan?"

Win turned toward Stan. Stan looked at Win's face.

"Is that your proof?" Stan countered. "I mean, is this supposed to be a Perry Mason moment or something? Maybe you slipped up, Myron. Or maybe I just assumed it was a boy. Or I heard wrong. That's not evidence."

"You're right. It's not. It just got me thinking, that's all."

"Thoughts aren't proof."

"Wow," Win said. "Thoughts aren't proof. I'll have to remember that one."

"But there is proof," Myron said. "Definitive proof."

"Impossible," Stan said, but his voice warbled now. "What?"

"I'll get to that in a moment. First let me back off on my indignation a little."

"I don't understand."

"At the end of the day, what you did was scummy, no question about it. But in its own way, it was almost ethical. Win and I often discuss the ends justifying the means. You could claim that's what happened here. You tried to turn your father in before he struck again. You did all you could to make sure nobody else was harmed. Jeremy was never in any real danger. You couldn't know that Greg would be shot. So in the end, you scared a boy, but so what? Next to the murder and destruction your father would have continued to wreak, it was nothing. So you did some good. The ends perhaps justified the means. Except for one thing."

Stan didn't bite.

"Jeremy's bone marrow transplant. He needs that to live, Stan. You know that. You also know that you're the match, not your father. That was why you slipped him that cyanide pill. Because once we dragged your father to the hospital and realized that he wasn't a match, well, we would have investigated. We would have realized that Edwin Gibbs was not Davis Taylor né Dennis Lex. So you had to have him kill himself and then you pushed for a quick cremation. I don't mean to make it sound as harsh or cold as all that. You didn't murder your father. He took the pill all on his own. He was a sick man. He wanted to die. It's yet another case of the ends justifying the means."

Myron took a moment and just looked into Stan's eyes. Stan did not look away. In a sense, this was more agenting work. Myron was negotiating here—the most important negotiation of his life. He had put his opponent in a corner. Now he needed to reach out. Not help him yet. He had to keep him in the corner. But he had to start reaching out. Just a little.

"You're not a monster," Myron said. "You just didn't count on the complication of being a bone marrow match. You want to do right by Jeremy. It's why you've gone so nuts trying to help the bone marrow drive. If they find another donor, it takes you off the hook. Because you're in this lie too deep now. You couldn't admit the truth—that you are the match. It would ruin you. I understand that."

Stan's eyes were wide and wet, but he was listening.

"Before I told you that I had proof," Myron said. "We checked the bone marrow registry. Know what we found, Stan?"

Stan didn't reply.

"You're not registered," Myron said. "Here you are telling everybody to sign up and you yourself aren't in their computer. The three of us know why. It's because you'd be a match. And if you matched, there would be those questions again."

Stan gave defiance one last shot. "That's not proof."

"Then how will you explain not registering?"

"I don't have to explain anything."

"A blood test will prove it conclusively. The registry still has the blood that Davis Taylor gave during the marrow drive. We can do a DNA test with yours, see if it matches up."

"And if I don't agree to a test?"

Win took that one. "Oh, you'll give blood," he said with just the slightest smile. "One way or another."

Something on Stan's face broke then. He lowered his head. The defiance was over. He was trapped in the corner now. No way to escape. He'd start looking for an ally. It always happened in negotiations. When you're lost, you look for an out. Myron had reached out before. It was time to do it again.

"You don't understand," Stan said.

"Strangely enough, I do." Myron moved a little closer to Stan. He made his voice soft yet unyielding. Total command mode. "Here's what we're going to do, Stan. You and I are going to make a deal."

Stan looked up, confused but also hopeful. "What?"

"You are going to agree to donate bone marrow to save Jeremy's life. You'll do it anonymously. Win and I can set that up. No one will ever know who the donor was. You do that, you save Jeremy, I forget the rest."

"How can I believe you?"

"Two reasons," Myron said. "One, I'm interested in saving Jeremy's life, not ruining yours. Two"—he tilted both palms toward the ceiling— "I'm no better. I bent rules here too. I let the ends justify the means. I assaulted a man. I kidnapped a woman."

Win shook his head. "There's a difference. His reasons were selfish. You, on the other hand, were trying to save a boy's life."

Myron turned to his friend. "Weren't you the one who said that motives are irrelevant? That the act is the act?"

"Sure," Win said. "But I meant that to apply to him, not you."

Myron smiled and faced Stan again. "I'm not your moral superior. We both did wrong. Maybe we can both live with what we've done. But if you let a boy die, Stan, you cross the line. You can't go home again."

Stan closed his eyes. "I would have found a way," he said. "I would have gotten another fake ID, given blood under a pseudonym. I was just hoping—"

"I know," Myron said. "I know all about it."

Myron called Dr. Karen Singh. "I found a matching donor."

"What?"

"I can't explain. But he has to stay anonymous."

"I explained to you that all the bone marrow donors remain anonymous."

"No. The bone marrow registry can't know about this either. We have to find a place that can harvest the marrow without knowing the patient's identity."

"Can't be done."

"Yeah, it can."

"No doctor will agree—"

"We can't play these games, Karen. I have a donor. No one can know who he is. Make it work."

He could hear her breathing.

"He'll have to be retested," she said.

"No problem."

"And pass a physical."

"Done."

"Then okay. Let's get this started."

When Emily heard about the donor, she gave Myron a curious look and waited. He didn't explain. She never asked.

Myron visited the hospital the day before the marrow transplant was to begin. He peeked his head around the doorjamb and saw the boy sleeping. Jeremy was bald from the chemo. His skin had a ghostly glow, like something withering from a lack of sunshine. Myron watched his son sleeping. Then he turned and went home. He didn't come back.

He returned to work at MB SportsReps and lived his life. He visited his father and mother. He hung out with Win and Esperanza. He landed a few new clients and started rebuilding his business. Big Cyndi handed in her wrestling resignation and took over the front desk. His world was wobbly but back on the axis.

Eighty-four days later—Myron kept count—he got a call from Karen Singh. She asked him to visit her office. When he arrived, she wasted no time.

"It worked," she said. "Jeremy went home today."

Myron started to cry. Karen Singh moved around her desk. She sat on the arm of his chair and rubbed his back.

Myron knocked on the half-open door.

"Enter," Greg said.

Myron did so. Greg Downing was sitting up in a chair. He'd grown a beard during his long hospital stretch.

He smiled at Myron. "Nice to see you."

"Same here. I like the beard."

"Gives me that Paul Bunyan touch, don't you think?"

"I was thinking more along the lines of Sebastian Cabot as Mr. French," Myron said.

Greg laughed. "Going home on Friday."

"Great."

Silence.

"You haven't visited much," Greg said.

"Wanted to give you time to heal. And grow that beard in fully."

Greg tried another laugh, but he sort of choked on it. "My basketball career is over, you know."

"You'll get over it."

"That easy?"

Myron smiled. "Who said anything about easy?"

"Yeah."

"But there are more important things in life than basketball," Myron said. "Though sometimes I forget that."

Greg nodded again. Then he looked down and said, "I heard about you finding the donor. I don't know how you did it—"

"It's not important."

He looked up. "Thank you."

Myron was not sure what to say to that. So he kept quiet. And that was when Greg shocked him.

"You know, don't you?"

Myron's heart stopped.

"That was why you helped," Greg said. His voice was pure flat-line. "Emily told you the truth."

The muscles around Myron's throat tightened. There was a whooshing sound in his head.

"Did you take a blood test?" Greg asked.

Myron managed a nod this time. Greg closed his eyes. Myron swallowed and said, "How long . . . ?"

"I'm not sure anymore," Greg said. "I guess right away."

He *knows*. The words fell on Myron, smacking down like raindrops, beading and rolling off, impenetrable. *He's always known. . . .*

"For a while I fooled myself into believing it wasn't so," Greg said. "It's amazing what the mind can do sometimes. But when Jeremy was six, he had his appendix out. I saw his blood type on a chart. It pretty much confirmed what I'd known all along."

Myron didn't know what to say. The realization pushed down on him, swept away the months of blocking like so many children's toys. The mind can indeed do amazing things. He looked at Greg and it was like seeing something in the proper light for the first time and it changed everything. He thought about fathers again. He thought about real sacrifice. He thought about heroes.

"Jeremy's a good boy," Greg said.

"I know," Myron said.

"You remember my father? Screaming on the sidelines like a lunatic?"

"Yes."

"I ended up looking just like him. Spitting image of my old man. He was my blood. And he was the cruelest son of a bitch I ever knew," Greg said. Then he added, "Blood never meant much to me."

A strange echo filled the room. The background noises faded away and there was just the two of them, staring at one another from across the most bizarre chasm.

Greg moved back to the bed. "I'm tired, Myron."

"Don't you think we should talk about this?"

"Yeah," Greg said. He lay back and shut his eyes a little too tightly. "Maybe later. But right now I'm really tired."

At the end of the day, Esperanza stepped into Myron's office, sat down, and said, "I don't know much about family values or what makes a happy family. I don't know the best way to raise a kid or what you have to do to make him happy and well adjusted, whatever the hell 'well adjusted' means. I don't know if it's best to be an only child or have lots of siblings or be raised by two parents or a single parent or a gay couple or a lesbian couple or an overweight albino. But I know one thing."

Myron looked up at her and waited.

"No child could ever be harmed by having you in his life."

Esperanza stood and went home.

Stan Gibbs was playing in the yard with his boys when Myron and Win pulled into the driveway. His wife—at least, Myron guessed it was his wife—sat in a lawn chair and watched. A little boy rode Stan like a horsey. They other boy lay on the ground giggling.

Win frowned. "How very Norman Rockwell."

Myron and Win stepped out of the car. Stan the horsey looked up. The smile stayed on when he saw them, but you could see it starting to lose its grip at the edges. Stan hoisted his son off his back and said something to him Myron couldn't hear. The boy gave an "Aaaw, Dad." Stan jumped to his feet and ruffled the boy's hair. Win frowned again. As Stan jogged toward them, his smile faded away like the end of a song.

"What are you doing here?"

Win said, "Back together with the wife, are we?"

"We're giving it a go."

"Touching," Win said.

Stan turned toward Myron. "What's going on here?"

"Tell the kids to go inside, Stan."

"What?"

Another car pulled in the driveway. Rick Peck was driving. Kimberly Green was in the passenger seat. Stan's face lost color. He snapped a look at Myron.

"We had a deal," he said.

"Remember how I told you that you had two choices when the novel was discovered?"

"I'm not in the mood—"

"I said you could run or you could tell the truth. Remember?"

Stan's façade tottered, and for the first time, Myron saw the rage.

"I left out a third choice. A choice you yourself pointed out to me the first time we met. You could have said that the Sow the Seeds kidnapper was a copycat. That he had read the book. It might have helped you out. Taken some of the heat off."

"I couldn't do that."

"Because it would have led to your father?"

"Yes."

"But you didn't know your father had written the book. Isn't that right, Stan? You said you never knew about the book. I remember that from the first time we talked. I've been watching you say the same thing on TV. You claim you didn't even know your father wrote it."

"All true," Stan said, and the façade slipped back into place. "But—I don't know—maybe subconsciously I suspected something somehow. I can't explain it."

"Good," Myron said.

"Damn good," Win added.

"The problem was," Myron said, "you had to say you hadn't read it.

Because if you had, well, Stan, you'd be a plagiarizer. All this work, all your big plans to regain your reputation—it would be for nothing. You'd be ruined."

"We discussed this already."

"No, Stan, we didn't. At least not this part of it." Myron held up the evidence bag with the sheet of paper inside.

Stan set his jaw.

"Know what this is, Stan?"

He said nothing.

"I found it in Melina Garston's apartment. It says 'With love, Dad.' "

Stan swallowed. "So?"

"Something about it bothered me from the beginning. First off, the word 'Dad.' "

"I don't understand—"

"Sure you do, Stan. Melina's sister-in-law called George Garston 'Papa.' When I spoke to him, he referred to himself as 'Papa.' So why would he sign a note like this 'Dad'?"

"That doesn't mean anything."

"Maybe, maybe not. The second thing that bothered me: Who writes a note like this—on the top inside of a folded card? People use the bottom half, right? But see, Stan, this wasn't a card. It was a sheet of a paper folded in half. That's the key. Then there are those tears along the left edge. See them, Stan? Like someone had ripped it out of something."

Win handed Myron the novel that had been sent to Kimberly Green. Myron opened it and laid the piece of paper inside it.

"Something like a book."

It was a perfect match.

"Your father wrote this inscription," Myron said. "To you. Years ago. You'd known about the book all along."

"You can't prove that."

"Come on, Stan. A handwriting analyst will have no trouble with this. The Lexes weren't the ones who found the book. Melina Garston did. You asked her to lie for you in court. She did. But then she started growing suspicious. So she dug around your house and found this book. She's the one who mailed it to Kimberly Green."

"You have no proof—"

"She sent it in anonymously because she still cared about you. She even tore out the inscription so no one, most especially you, would ever know where the book had come from. You had plenty of enemies. Like Susan Lex. And the feds. She probably hoped you'd think they did it. At least for a little while. But you knew right away it was Melina. She didn't count on that. Or your reaction."

Stan's hands tightened into fists. They started shaking.

"The victims' families wouldn't speak to you, Stan. And you needed that for your article. You ended up following the book more than reality. The feds thought it was to fool them. But that wasn't it. Maybe your father told you he was the killer, but nothing else. Maybe the real story wasn't as interesting, so you needed to embellish. Maybe you weren't that good of a writer and you really felt you needed those family quotes. I don't know. But you plagiarized. And the only one who could tie you to that book was Melina Garston. So you killed her."

"You'll never prove it," Stan said.

"The feds will dig hard now. The Lexes will help. Win and I will help. We'll find enough. If nothing else, the jury—and the world—will hear all you did in this. They'll hate you enough to convict."

"You son of a bitch." Stan cocked his fist and aimed it at Myron. With an almost casual movement, Win swept his leg. Stan fell down in a heap. Win pointed and laughed. Stan's sons watched it all.

Kimberly Green and Rick Peck got out of the car. Myron signaled them to wait, but Kimberly Green shook her head. They cuffed Stan hard and dragged him away. His sons still watched. Myron thought about Melina Garston and his silent vow. Then he and Win headed back to the car.

"You always intended to turn him in," Win said.

"Yes. But first I had to make sure he went along with donating the bone marrow."

"And once you knew Jeremy was okay—"

"Then I told Green, yes."

Win started the car. "The evidence is still marginal. A good attorney will be able to poke holes."

"Not my problem," Myron said.

"You'd be willing to let him walk?"

"Yes," Myron said. "But Melina's father has juice. And he won't."

"I thought you advised him against taking the law into his own hands."

Myron shrugged. "No one ever listens to me."

"That's true," Win said.

Win drove.

"I just wonder," Myron said.

"What?"

"Who was the serial killer here? Did his father really do it? Or was it all Stan?"

"Doubt we'll ever know," Win said.

"Probably not."

"It shan't matter," Win said. "They'll get him for Melina Garston."

"I guess," Myron said. Then he frowned and repeated, " 'Shan't'?"

Win shrugged. "So is it finally over, my friend?"

Myron's leg did that nervous jig again. He stopped it and said, "Jeremy."

"Ah," Win said. "Are you going to tell him?"

Myron looked out the window and saw nothing. "Win's credo about selfishness would say yes."

"And Myron's credo?"

"I don't know that it's much different," Myron said.

Jeremy was playing basketball at the Y. Myron stepped into the bleachers, the rickety kind that shake with each step, and sat. Jeremy was still pale. He was thinner than the last time Myron had seen him, but there'd been a growth spurt over the last few months. Myron realized how fast changes take place for the young and felt a deep, hard thud in his chest.

For a while, he just watched the flow of the scrimmage and tried to judge his son's play objectively. Jeremy had the tools, Myron could see that right away, but there was plenty of rust on them. That wouldn't be a problem though. Again with the young. Rust doesn't stay long on the young.

As Myron watched the practice, his eyes widened. He felt his insides shrivel. He thought again about what he was about to do, and a swelling tide rose inside of him, overwhelming him, pulling him under.

Jeremy smiled when he spotted Myron. The smile cleaved Myron's heart in two even pieces. He felt lost, adrift. He thought about what Win had said, about what a real father was, and he thought about what Esperanza had said. He thought about Greg and Emily. He wondered if he should have spoken to his own father about this, if he should have told him that this wasn't a hypothetical, that the bomb had indeed landed, that he needed his help.

Jeremy continued to play, but Myron could see that the boy was distracted by his presence. Jeremy kept sneaking quick glances toward the stands. He played a little harder, picked up the pace a bit. Myron had been there, done that. The desire to impress. It had driven Myron, maybe as much as wanting to win. Shallow, but there you have it.

The coach had his players run a few more drills and then he lined them up on the baseline. They finished up with the aptly named "suicides," which was basically a series of gut-heaving sprints broken up by bending and touching different lines on the floor. Myron might be nostalgic for many things connected to basketball. Suicides were not one of them.

Ten minutes later, with most of the kids still trying to catch their breath, the coach gathered his troops, gave out schedules for the rest of the week, and dispersed the boys with a big handclap. Most of them headed toward the exit, slinging backpacks over their shoulders. Some went into the locker room. Jeremy walked over to Myron slowly.

"Hi," Jeremy said.

"Hi."

Sweat dripped off Jeremy's hair, his face coated and flushed from exertion. "I'm going to shower," he said. "You want to wait?"

"Sure," Myron said.

"Cool, I'll be right back."

The gymnasium emptied out. Myron stood and picked up an errant basketball. His fingers found the grooves right away. He took a few shots, watching the bottom of the net dance as the ball swished through. He smiled and sat back down, still holding the ball. A janitor came in and swept the floor Zamboni-style. His keys jangled. Someone flipped off the overhead lights. Jeremy came back not long after that. His hair was still wet. He, too, had a backpack over his shoulder.

As Win would say, "Showtime."

Myron gripped the ball a little tighter. "Sit down, Jeremy. We need to talk."

The boy's face was serene and almost too beautiful. He slid the backpack off his shoulder and sat down. Myron had rehearsed this part. He had looked at it from all sides, all the pluses and minuses. He had made up his mind and changed it and made it up again. He had, as Win put it, properly tortured himself.

But in the end, he knew there was one universal truth: Lies fester. You try to put them away. You jam them in a box and bury them in the ground. But eventually they eat their way out of coffins. They dig their way out of graves. They may sleep for years. But they always wake up. When they do, they're rested, stronger, more insidious.

Lies kill.

"This is going to be hard to understand—" He stopped. Suddenly his rehearsed speech sounded so damn canned, filled with "It's nobody's fault" and "Adults make mistakes too" and "It doesn't mean your parents love you any less." It was patronizing and stupid and—

"Mr. Bolitar?"

Myron looked up at the boy.

"My mom and dad told me," Jeremy said. "Two days ago."

His chest shuddered. "What?"

"I know you're my biological father."

Myron was surprised and yet he wasn't. Some might say that Emily and Greg had made a preemptive strike, almost like a lawyer who reveals something bad about his own client because he knows the opposition will do it. Lessen the blow. But maybe Emily and Greg had learned the same lesson he had about lies and how they fester. And maybe, once again, they were trying to do what was best for their boy.

"How do you feel about it?" Myron asked.

"Weird, I guess," Jeremy said. "I mean, Mom and Dad keep expecting me to fall apart or something. But I don't see why it has to be such a big deal."

"You don't?"

"Sure, okay, I see it, but"—he stopped, shrugged—"it's not like the whole world's turned inside out or anything. You know what I mean?"

Myron nodded. "Maybe it's because you've already had your world turned inside out."

"You mean being sick and all?"

"Yes."

"Yeah, maybe," he said, thinking about it. "Must be weird for you too."

"Yeah," Myron said.

"I've been thinking about it," Jeremy said. "You want to hear what I've come up with?"

Myron swallowed. He looked into the boy's eyes—serenity, yes, but not through innocence. "Very much," he said.

"You're not my dad," he said simply. "I mean, you might be my father. But you're not my dad. You know what I mean?"

Myron managed a nod.

"But"—Jeremy stopped, looked up, shrugged the shrug of a thirteen-year-old—"but maybe you can still be around."

"Around?" Myron repeated.

"Yeah," Jeremy said. He smiled again and *pow*, Myron's chest took another blow. "Around. You know."

"Yeah," Myron said, "I know."

"I think I'd like that."

"Me too," Myron said.

Jeremy nodded. "Cool."

"Yeah."

The gym clock grunted and pushed forward. Jeremy looked at it. "Mom's probably outside waiting for me. We usually stop at the supermarket on the way home. Want to come?"

Myron shook his head. "Not today, thanks."

"Cool." Jeremy stood, watching Myron's face. "You okay?"

"Yeah."

Jeremy smiled. "Don't worry. It's going to work out."

Myron tried to smile back. "How did you get to be so smart?"

"Good parenting," he said. "Combined with good genes."

Myron laughed. "You might want to consider a future in politics."

"Yeah," Jeremy said. "Take it easy, Myron."

"You too, Jeremy."

He watched the boy walk out the door, again with the familiar gait. Jeremy didn't look back. There was the sound of the door closing, the echoes, and then Myron was alone. He turned toward the basket and stared at the hoop until it blurred. He saw the boy's first step, heard his first word, smelled the sweet clean of a young child's pajamas. He felt the smack of a ball against a glove, bent over to help with his homework, stayed up all night when he had a virus, all of it, like his own father had, a whirl of taunting, aching images, as irretrievable as the past. He saw himself hovering in the boy's darkened doorway, the silent sentinel to his adolescence, and he felt what remained of his heart burst into flames.

The images scattered when he blinked. His heart started beating again. He stared again at the basket and waited. This time nothing blurred. Nothing happened.